The Light Fantastic

LA Tucker

Yellow Rose Books

Nederland, Texas

ISBN 1-932300-14-7

First Printing 2003

9 8 7 6 5 4 3 2 1

Cover design by Mary D. Brooks
Photography by Julie Spohr

Published by:

Yellow Rose Books
PMB 210, 8691 9th Avenue
Port Arthur, Texas 77642-8025

Find us on the World Wide Web at
http://www.regalcrest.biz

Printed in the United States of America

Acknowledgments

Profuse gratitude to: Sara M., Julie S., Top, Dawn, Maxie, BJ, TK, TLC, Chriss, Jaden, Mary D., Steph, Judith, Meg, Randi, KG, Wendy, Mel, Lor, Patsy Cline, debra, Cate, Tenderware, Kiera, Ado Annie, CathW., Stacia, Barb, Linda, AJ, Carrie, Minerva, Marie F., Canadian Uber Addicts and the always kind folks at Regal Crest. And to the innumerable wonderful people who have corresponded with me throughout. Your continuing encouragement is fun, irreplaceable and at times, anxiety relieving to a proneto panic first time author.

Dedicated to my Dad, who could tell a silly story better than anyone I'll ever know. I miss you, Pop.

Part I:
All the World's a Stooge

Chloe sank low in the red plastic chair and absently reached down to scratch her ankle. She gazed out the school library window at the heavy falling snow outside on this frigid February night. It was going to be a bitch getting home; she hoped that the state had been keeping up with the plowing on the road that led to her small house right outside of town. The town itself had no snowplows, its small number of inhabitants couldn't afford to employ a driver of its own. Luckily, she lived on a road that the state maintained. February was always a harsh time for a town this close to Lake Erie. The constant southeasterly Canadian-driven arctic winds picked up the moisture from the lake, transformed it into snow and dumped inches upon inches of the white stuff down on the tiny Pennsylvania lakefront township from early November right up until late March.

She checked her watch and saw she was early. She had agreed to meet with her friends and colleagues at 8:30 p.m., right after the town library closed. That's where she worked, full-time, as the librarian. Most nights it was open until 8:00 p.m., to benefit any students that might need to access the information there. But those students were coming less and less, because the school library was now outfitted with the latest computers and high speed Internet access, and the small town library that Chloe worked at was saddled with a dinosaur PC with a 14K modem. So, for the most part, the people that Chloe interacted with on a daily basis were the old-fashioned library users, who went in to borrow a few books of the written word. She was fine with that. Chloe got her degree in the library sciences because she loved the smell, the texture and feel of a book. No doubt she loved the contents of them, but the sensory overload of the feel of a volume in her hands, the allure of a book on a shelf, waiting to be discovered by an eager reader, pleased her esthetically. Her least favorite part of the coursework in library sciences had been the increased concentration on the information available on the Internet. Yes, it was practical and, yes, it was the future, but it held no romance for her. She fell asleep, almost nightly, alone in her bed with a book lovingly held in her small hands.

A thirty-something, owlishly handsome brown-haired man appeared in the doorway, saw Chloe sitting at the octagonal table, and grinned at her. He was covered, head to toe, in apparel meant to ward off the harshest of winter weather. He greeted her as he walked toward the table, unwrapping a plaid scarf from around his mouth and nose as he approached.

"Hey, Chloe, think it'll snow?" He brushed snow off his shoulders and pulled his earmuffs off.

Chloe grinned up at him from her chair and stretched. "Nah, Paul, I predict an early spring. Didn't you hear? I went down to Punxsutawney a week ago, and made a hit on that damned groundhog. We should see tulips pushing up any day now."

"Good thing," he replied as he continued to disperse with his coat and gloves, "I was thinking of gunning for him myself."

He piled his coat and scarf on a nearby chair. "I saw Marcy out in the parking lot, she should be in soon." He looked out the window, and shook his head at the thick falling snow. "How the hell can she drive a Miata in this kind of weather? It's gotta get stuck every four feet or so." He sat down in a chair across from her and cracked his cold red knuckles.

"Dunno," Chloe replied, shaking her head. "She likes living on the edge? Maybe she has a death wish? Or maybe she has the hots for the tow truck driver from the Exxon station. What's his name, Ed?"

"It's Fred, and no, I don't have the hots for him," Marcy smartly interjected as she strode into the room toward Paul and Chloe. "Although I could, if he would just..."

"Put in his teeth," finished Chloe, looking into Marcy's sparkling brown eyes. The three friends laughed. All of them were quite aware of Marcy's interest in the male of the species. Proof of that was that Marcy was two months fresh from dumping live-in number four, and she was Chloe's age, a breath away from achieving thirty years on the planet.

"How's the newly single life going, Marse? What's this, number six or so? Going for Julia Roberts status?" teased Chloe as Marcy put her wet coat on top of Paul's things. "You're going to have to rehook one of them soon. This town is running out of single, eligible males for you to ditch at the altar."

Paul cut in before Marcy could reply. "Who ever said they had to be single for her to go after them? There was that one that got away, the married UPS driver from up on Route 20, Dave D'Amico? She never got around to marrying him after his wife found out about their affair. Isn't he still around?"

Marcy shot Paul a dirty look as she plopped down into a chair facing her two grinning buddies. "That was when I was senior in college. I met Stan, Mr. Fiancé number two, before Dave's divorce was finalized. He was already on the way to a divorce. It dragged out for years. Yeah, I've seen him around. I heard he's doing something with that land he has, he's been plowing it for the last two summers. Flattening it out and planting grass for a little nine-hole golf course he's building out there." She paused, then stated, "I know for a fact he never got remarried." She frowned, considering this.

Chloe stared directly at Marcy and gave her a knowing smile. "Well, there ya go, then. Available fresh meat. Divorced, although I think he has a kid, right? Here in school? What, isn't he the quarterback of the football team? Nelson, right?"

Chloe envisioned the tall, sturdily built Nelson D'Amico, with the dark good looks and tousled black hair. The whole town revered the high school quarterback, the one bright light on what was otherwise a mediocre team. He could throw the ball with precision and power. Unfortunately, he never had a competent receiver who could catch it or hold onto it if he did. The fans would religiously attend all the games to alternately thrill to the assuredness of the athletic, spry quarterback, then groan as they watched hapless receivers fumble the ball away. Chloe was sure her grandmother, bad hip and all, could have caught and scored on some of those missiles that Nelson launched.

Paul nodded. "He's a senior here, graduating in May. I heard he's been heavily recruited by Penn State, West Virginia, even some Florida schools. I don't think he's committed himself anywhere yet. Just can't make up his mind. He's in my Honors English class this semester. Nice kid, quiet though." He glanced at Marcy and continued, "Chloe's right, Dave is the one that got away, and hell, Dave's going to be suffering from empty nest syndrome as soon as Nelson heads off to college. Hey, Marcy, Dave's apparently going to be a mini-mogul soon, what with his opening up that golf course. Maybe you could offer to help him—"

"Water his greens?" interrupted Chloe. She just couldn't help herself. Marcy reached across the table and gave Chloe a quick slap on the arm.

"Knock it off there, Chloester, like you have a lot to talk about in the romance department. My apparent overindulgence in the mating department is just nature's way for making up for your total lack of interest in anything relating to...relating, one on one, with anyone, for like, forever, now, right?"

Paul, who had suffered a secret crush on Chloe for years now, leaned forward on his elbows on the brown table, quite interested in Chloe's reply to this.

Chloe squirmed uncomfortably in her seat, now that the conversation was focused on her nonexistent love life. She sighed, and thought a moment before replying with what was decidedly not an answer. "Yeah, well. I like it that way."

Good fortune intervened on Chloe's behalf, as a rustling in the doorway brought forth the form of a very snow-covered, gray-haired school principal, Doris Raeburn. She was pulling on the ties of a plastic rain bonnet, and took it off and shook it to get the snow off. She smiled at the threesome sitting at the library table, and her mind flashed back to when they were all students of hers, some twelve years ago in this very school. She thought it was wonderful that Marcy and Paul had returned to teach here, and that Chloe was the part-time drama teacher as well as director of the senior class plays. The three of them had all been friends then, and it warmed her heart to see that their friendship had continued these many years later.

"Good evening, kids," she greeted them, still seeing them as her students.

The three friends unconsciously replied loudly and in unison, "Good evening, Mrs. Raeburn." They all had a good giggle over that.

Doris walked over to them. "Paul, get your feet off that chair. Marcy, get your curls out of your eyes and—what have you done to your hair? That color was never meant to grace a human head. Chloe, quit slouching."

They did as they were told, and Mrs. Raeburn, who never seemed to get directly to the point, started talking, and talking. The friends knew better than to interrupt her. They were transported back into being sixteen years old, and just listened and marveled at the woman that was Mrs. Raeburn.

"Well, Chloe, it looks like that time again, huh? These two going to help you again this year? Good. We're shooting for, what, the last two weekends in May? Graduation is the first week of June, so that'll work. You're doing a musical this year, right? Much better idea than that idea you had last year. An opera, in high school? What were you thinking?" She looked pointedly at Chloe, expecting no answer, but was satisfied to see Chloe cringing in her chair. "Old musical this year, good idea. Classics are the best. Your art department doing the props and scenery, Marcy? Great. This year, see if you can find someone talented enough to make a tree look like a tree. I'm sure you can find a picture of one somewhere. Show 'em." Doris Raeburn rolled her eyes. "Paul, you're assisting with the acting and working with the stage crew, that's good. Oh, and you need to talk with the band director, get together a decent ensemble for this. I hope you can find six or seven somewhat able musicians out of that school marching band. The halftime shows at the football games sounded like we were slaughtering sheep out on the field. I was told that the song they were playing was "Proud Mary." Yeah, sure it was. It was enough to put Tina Turner into an early grave." She paused and crossed herself.

She took a breath and went on, "Auditions will be held two weeks from now after school? Chloe, can you get away from the library then?" She glanced quickly at the shaggy-haired librarian who was fidgeting in her seat, who nodded at her in agreement. "Yes? Good. I've already had some parents asking what the play was going to be, seems that they want their stars front and center for our little production. And the kids, will they be performing scenes from this on that PBS fundraiser for WQEL over in Erie? I hope it helps this year. Didn't donations actually go down last year, what with that opera? What were you thinking?" Once again, she peered at Chloe, who was now in a full slouch and pouting in her plastic chair. "Anyhoos, I want to remind the three of you that we are dealing with fragile egos here. And I'm not talking the kids in the play, I am talking about their parents. Be nice to them, be patient, be mindful that they have dreams that their little Heather or Justin is going to be the next big thing on the Great White Way." Doris stopped momentarily, just to refill her tapped-out lungs. "That actually happened. We have an alumna that's a star somewhere, don't we?" Doris eyed them all, to see if they knew who she was speaking about.

Paul shrugged and said, "Well, if you count Maria Jacobson, class of '96, doing a stint as a wandering Snow White at Disney World for two years, yeah."

Mrs. Raeburn pursed her lips and nodded slightly. "No, I was thinking more of Sara. Sara D'Amico. She was a few, maybe five years ahead of you three. You never met her, did you? That's who I was thinking of. Although she never showed one bit of interest in acting while she was here in this school. She was too busy smoking in the girls' room, getting detention and just generally raising hell." Doris' lips curled into a smile. "God, I loved that girl. It was hard yelling at her when she got into trouble, which she always was, she just had a way about her. Beautiful. I never saw such eyes, such hair. Such a smile, which she rarely showed. Tall, too." Doris poked the air high over her head in demonstration of how tall Sara was. "I had to stand on a chair to talk eye to eye with her. She was a star on the basketball team, volleyball. She was effortless. Smart. And mean, too, when she wanted to be." Doris paused and looked at Marcy. "Didn't you date her older brother Dave?"

Chloe coughed quietly and answered Doris before Marcy could. "Well, if you call what they did dating," she turned a mischievous eye to Marcy and continued, "yeah, she did." Marcy gave Chloe a warning glare.

Mrs. Raeburn chose to ignore that comment and went on. "Anyway, our star, Sara. Shame about what happened to her, huh? Tragic.

That accident and all, it ruined her career. I've heard so many rumors about her these last few years. Every so often, a reporter shows up here at the school to ask me about her, what was she like, where she is now. As far as I know, she's never shown up for any of our class reunions. I was reading in *People* magazine the other day, about how they still want to make a sequel to that last movie she made, the *Star* whatever. The sci-fi one, from six years ago? And I hear that she refuses to even consider it. They want to throw all kinds of money at her, too. Considering that it was one of the highest-grossing movies ever, you can see why they would want her back to do another one. Just wouldn't be the same without her playing that role. She owns it. Kind of like how they replaced Jodie Foster in that sequel to *Silence of the Lambs*, huh? Dumb move." Doris paused and thoughtfully tapped her lip. "I spend a lot of time wondering what happened to her."

Paul spoke up. "Um, she got pregnant, had the kid, and never said who the father was. There've been rumors about her being a lesbian, although she never confirmed it. She's still acting and directing."

"Um, Paul," Chloe kicked him under the table, "I think Mrs. Raeburn was wondering what happened to Sara D'Amico, not Jodie Foster."

Mrs. Raeburn glared in agreement. Before she could continue on, Marcy quietly spoke.

"She, uh, well, actually, she lives out off Route 20, in a little house on the land that her brother Dave owns. She's been there since last summer. I think she lives near what will soon be the eighth hole."

Three sets of wide eyes stared at the art teacher in stunned disbelief.

"Aunt Sara? What're we listening to? I hate this country stuff," Nelson D'Amico asked in the direction of his aunt's long orange-covered legs. The rest of her was underneath an old tractor, making some adjustments to something he couldn't determine. Nelson didn't have a head for mechanics, but he did know which tool was which, so he was being useful by leaning up against the side of the tractor, in case his aunt needed him to hand her another tool.

"Shut up. It's not country, it's Nanci Griffith. It's more folk," came the muffled reply from under the old John Deere. "Hand me the big monkey wrench."

Nelson placed it in her reaching hand, and it disappeared underneath. He heard some turning, scraping, metallic noises, a clank and an "Ow! Owowow!" which was followed by some fluent cursing.

Nelson grinned and bent to look under the tractor to make sure his aunt was all right. "You okay?" He smiled at her, his head upside down.

Even with the dimness, he could see her blue eyes, so like his own, flashing at him. "Yeah. Damned nut on here is rusted. Wrench slipped."

Nelson was getting dizzy from having his head upside down. He stood back up again. "Aunt Sara? How much longer you going to be under there? I kind of wanted to talk to you about something."

Sara rolled out from under the tractor. It was cold in this barn converted into a garage, and even colder closer to the concrete floor, where she had been for the last hour or so. She was cold and stiff, and now the knuckles she had scraped throbbed. It was time to call it a night with Mr. Deere.

She eyed her tall nephew slouched up against the tractor. They both wore matching thermal coveralls, although his were pristine clean and hers were filthy. *Ah well, at least he's good at handing me the right tools.* She stretched into a sitting position, rolled her shoulders, heard a few vertebrae pop, and then accepted his hand to help her stand up. She leaned against the tractor next to him, and slowly drew a knee up to her chest, pulling on it with both hands to keep it there, so the tight ligaments would stretch. She stood there, a one-legged bird, holding her knee.

"What's up?" she asked, dropping that leg and then grabbing for the other to repeat the stretching process.

Nelson looked down at his booted feet and began quietly, "Well, you know, I have to make a decision about college soon, and well, I just don't know, I don't want to think about it just yet, I'm not sure..."

"You're not sure where you want to go to college?"

"No, that's not it."

"You're not sure if you want to go to college?" Sara sternly inquired, hoping that this wasn't what was troubling Nelson.

Nelson stuffed his hands deeper into his coverall pockets but did not look at her. "No, that's not it either."

Sara grew impatient. "Listen, Nelson, I don't feel like playing twenty questions with you here. Get to the point. Now." She turned and put her hands on her hips, eyeballing the nervous young man.

Nelson was afraid to look up, afraid to say what he hadn't discussed with anyone yet. Up to this point, he had just been thinking about it. For the last couple of years or so.

"I'm not sure about playing football."

Sara, confused, countered, "For Pitt? I know they haven't been the greatest team, but they're getting better every year."

"For anybody, Aunt Sara. I don't know how I feel about playing football anywhere. Dad is going to kill me when he finds out."

Sara let out a frustrated sigh and studied the youth who was obviously afraid to look her in the eye. *Dad? His dad is going to kill him? No,* she thought, *I'm going to kill him. This kid has the greatest arm since Joe Montana, and he doesn't want to play football?* When she was living out in California, years ago, her brother had religiously sent her videotapes of every Peewee, JV and high school game. Sara had even covertly snuck into some of his home games this past fall, just to watch him chuck that football. Since she moved back here early last summer, she and Nelson had slowly formed a bond, a bond woven slowly by late afternoons of him throwing the ball to her. This, of course, was after they had seeded and weeded whatever golf hole they were nurturing for the opening of the little par-three course this spring. Dave was still toiling at UPS, working until after 6:00 on weekdays and then coming home and working long after the sun had gone down. Dave hadn't really been around much, still wasn't, and he wasn't quitting his job until the end of March.

When Sara had moved back, in early June of last summer, Nelson was already off from school and working nonstop getting the course into shape. He didn't have much of a flair for landscaping, so Dave left him with detailed instructions on what needed to get done each day. A couple of Nelson's football buddies would come by and work on the weekends with the three of them, although Sara spent those days apart from them, working solo on different projects. But during the week it was just Sara and Nelson, starting out before dawn each day, working in the sun, riding the rusted tractor from hole to hole, and slowly but surely forging a friendship that they both trusted in and treasured. Neither one of them was a talker by nature; both could get by with an economy of words that was amazing. As the summer progressed Nelson had to spend his mornings at football practice. Sara found that she missed his company, his lanky form riding on the back hitch of the tractor while she drove. Her only company each day until noontime was the soft breeze coming off nearby Lake Erie, and the assorted birds that loved to come take a bath on the greens as she soaked them. Nelson would find her, bringing a sack lunch for both of them. He would tell her about practice that day, the plays the coach had taught them, the injuries they sustained and manfully ignored.

She reflected back now, as she looked at the young man who was miserably standing and staring at an oil spot on the garage floor, that he had never really spoken about football with any joy in his voice, any real thrill in his demeanor. She just remembered him dutifully telling her and Dave about the practices, the upcoming games, the scouting reports on the opposing teams. *Maybe it was for my and Dave's benefit? Because we were so impressed with this young kid's abilities, this is his destiny?*

Sara tapped Nelson on the shoulder, and he finally met her eyes. "Not sure you want to be a football hero, huh, Nels?" She gave him a small grin.

"Nope, not really," he paused for a second, trying to formulate what he wanted to say. "Just because I'm good at it, doesn't mean I want to do it, right?"

In a lopsided kind of way, Sara knew exactly what Nelson was saying.

Chloe watched Marcy pull away out of the school parking lot in her little red Miata. *Kind of like watching a skateboard trying to navigate an ice jam*, she mused. She had a fleeting vision of having to rescue Marcy out of a ditch farther up the main road. *Good thing Marcy lives so close by, she could always hoof it to work if need be. The old brown Subaru I drive is the perfect thing for this kind of climate. Sure, it has 140,000 miles on it. Sure, it's rusted and ugly as hell, and yeah, it costs a fortune to get repaired. If I have any vanity, it isn't centered in the kind of car I drive, that's for sure.*

Her thoughts turned to the surprising revelations about Stonecreek's only claim to movie-stardom, Sara D'Amico. *So Sara D'Amico is back in Stonecreek. How come nobody knew about it? If they did, why did nobody tell me? I mean, I work in a library, for crying out loud, which is a veritable crockpot of gossipy, nebby information. Forget the Internet, the patrons of the library can deliver town gossip faster than any DSL line ever could. The last thing of any glamorous note that happened in this area was that Bob Hope married his wife here on his way to Buffalo. And that Alice from The Brady Bunch was born in Erie.*

She turned on her CD player, while she waited for her old vehicle to warm up. She clicked past the first selection, and the orchestral movement that preceded the next song began with such a sweet familiarity that it brought an ache to her chest. She watched as the defroster warred slowly to remove the frozen condensation that had built up in the short time she had been in the high school for her meeting with Paul, Marcy and Mrs. Raeburn.

Marcy hadn't been forthcoming in any more information about Sara D'Amico's secret return to Stonecreek. She had shrugged off Paul and Mrs. Raeburn's questioning, and she shot Chloe a look that said "Later; I'll tell you later."

So the meeting abruptly ended, with the four of them promising to meet in two weeks to discuss the results of the auditions and to get an update on how everyone was progressing. Mrs. Raeburn, who had never paused long enough in her long-winded dissertations to take her coat off, simply retied her rain bonnet back over her perm and shot straight out the door. She had phone calls to make, no doubt about the return of the mysterious former movie star turned recluse, Sara D'Amico.

Paul tried to get the two remaining women interested in a cup of coffee at the diner, but both had begged off, stating the need to get home safe, out of the weather, and into warm jammies, and other such nonsense. Two more workdays before the weekend, and Chloe had to get notices made up to announce the tryouts for the play so the kids would have ample opportunity to go rent the movie version from Bob's Video Shack or travel to buy the soundtrack at the mall in Erie. Hopefully, there was a student in this senior class whose voice could do some justice to the songs now playing on her CD. Chloe peered out into the near-whiteout conditions, scraped the gear shift into four wheel drive, and steadily crept home in her trusted Subaru.

Sara started again. She was trying mightily to be a patient soul. "If it's not football that you want to do, then, do you even have a clue?"

Instead of being more relaxed, Nelson seemed more pensive. "Well yeah, sort of, but I don't know if I'm any good at it or not. Or would be any good at it."

Sara resisted the urge to grab the needlenose pliers and pull Nelson's teeth out one by one. *God, am I this irritating? I know I don't like to talk a lot, but this kid...*

"Well," started Nelson hesitantly, "there's this girl in my Honors English class, her name's Jeanette, and she told me that the week after..."

Sara leaned over and picked up the monkey wrench from the garage floor, "Go on."

"She said that sometime the week after next, near the end of the week..."

If his toes are as cold as mine are, I can drop this wrench on his foot and he'd never feel it until tomorrow. She nodded, encouraging him to continue.

He took a deep breath, and decided to let his dreams fly free to the ears of his waiting, impatient aunt. It came out in a rush. "There's open tryouts for the senior class play, they're doing *Oklahoma!* and I thought I might try out for it, you know, a lead or something."

Whew. He got it out, and stared expectantly into his aunt's eyes, looking for some kind of reaction. Her face was at first blank, then one eyebrow rose, then fell, then the other did the same, her lips twitched, then pursed, then smoothed into a straight line. She blinked, looked past him for a moment as if lost in thought, then returned her gaze to meet his. Still, he waited. Nothing.

That all happened outwardly. Inwardly, an incredible jumble of thoughts were bouncing around in Sara's mind. *Huh? He wants to act? How deep is that snowdrift outside the garage doors, and if I threw him from here, would he hit it? I love Oklahoma! Oklahoma has a damned fine football team. His father is going to kill him. Oh, hell.*

She put the wrench down, took a small breath and said, "Can you sing?"

He looked at her, relief emanating from every blocked adolescent pore. "A little. Not bad, I think." He blinked and added, "Will you help me?"

She gave the snowdrift outside one last consideration, then dismissed it.

"You bet."

Nelson walked down the long school hall toward the small theater. He could see Jeanette's head, her white-blonde shoulder-length curls bouncing as she chatted with a girlfriend, waiting for him outside the theater's doors. His heart was beating wildly already. It had been for the last two weeks, every time he thought of getting on that stage, speaking his lines out loud, and then singing. He'd never sung anything in front of anyone, and it had taken him two full days to work up the courage to sing in front of his aunt. She had worked with him every night, as she tinkered in the garage with the tractor and the assorted other motorized gadgets needed for tending to the golf course.

Dave was out after work nearly every night, working with different contractors setting up final appointments, applying for licenses, schmoozing the town council and arranging for advertising materials. Tonight he was going to meet again with Nelson's art teacher, Marcy, to discuss the final designs for the golf course sign. Nelson was exceedingly glad that his dad was so busy. Sara had suggested that maybe they should wait until after auditions to break the news to him. No sense in stirring up trouble unnecessarily.

Sara seemed impressed with Nelson's singing, that is, once he got over his shyness and stopped squeaking in his nervousness. She finally got him to let loose by promising to sing along with him. So they started, he shyly and quietly, and thankfully, on tune, and she, well she just stood there and belted it out like the reincarnation of Ethel Merman. He had to sing louder just to hear himself sing, and by the end of "There's No Business Like Show Business" she had slowly lowered her volume to the point where he found himself vocalizing the ending refrain by himself. She was grinning like mad at him, all white teeth, and when he finished with a flourish, she leaned in and gave him an enormous hug that spoke of her enthusiasm and pride. They then sang tune after tune, and not just show tunes, but rock and roll, and she even got him to sing along with some folk music. For two people who were not the most expressive souls in their everyday lives, they sure came alive when the music started. Nelson even jokingly suggested that they go hit karaoke night at Stan's Bar and Grill. He quickly regretted that he even mentioned it when he saw how that idea turned Sara's face from happily beaming to rock hard and impassive. He wanted to take it back, but it was too late. He just nodded and looked contrite.

The acting part came surprisingly naturally to him. He found it quite easy to imagine himself as another person. When he wondered aloud about this trait in himself, Sara merely chuckled and said that many actors were in reality shy, insecure people who found release in being someone other than themselves. The idea was to understand the character, then with that understanding, slip into that persona. Sure, there were brazen, confident actors out there, but that's what they were mostly doing. Acting it. Believing it.

Nelson wanted to ask her more about her acting past, but knew it was a taboo topic with her. She didn't share many, if any, stories from her days as a working actress, she merely shared her knowledge of the craft with him. At times, she would share where her influences and learning came from, and the names that she dropped so casually, big names, made him stare at her in awe. But she never said their names with any reverence, just brought them up as a point of reference. No different than when she told him that Mr. Baughman taught her everything about repairing motors in her high school shop class. Actually, now that Nelson thought about it, Sara did speak of Mr. Baughman with bit of a reverent air.

He arrived wordlessly in front of the excited Jeanette, and she tugged his sleeve and looked in his eyes with a sympathetic smile. "Ready, big guy?"

"Ready."

Chloe ran a hand through her shoulder-length red-blonde hair to get the bangs out of her eyes. She needed a trim. She was feeling rather shaggy. She was sitting near the back of the theater to make sure that the auditioning students' voices carried that far. Every time she leaned a bit forward to check her clipboard, wisps of her bangs trailed down and obscured her view of the sheet in front of her. When she saw a member of Paul's AV crew walking down the aisle past her she yelled, "Hey, buddy, what's your name?"

He stopped in his tracks and said, "Larry, Ms. Donahue."

"Hi, Larry. Larry, give me your hat. You aren't supposed to be wearing hats in the school building. You know that. You can have it back later."

"Aw jeez, okay." He lifted off the hat that was perched on his head in the fashionable backwards way and handed it to her.

"Thank you, Larry, you can get it back after the auditions are over." She grinned and then promptly put the cap on her own head, backwards, too, and tucked her straying bangs into the sides of it.

Larry laughed and went on his way down to the stage area.

Jeanette and Nelson entered the theater and strode down the aisle adjacent to Chloe. Jeanette tugged on Nelson's sleeve to stop him, and she cleared her throat to get Chloe's attention. Jeanette was in Ms. Donahue's drama club that met every Thursday. Chloe looked up to see the young woman beaming at her, and noticed the handsome tall guy with her, who she mentally identified as Nelson D'Amico, the football quarterback. Jeanette was bubbly and vibrant, an apt pupil and a bit of a ditz, truth be told. But she was a nice girl, not hard to take when she was concentrating and kept on subject. Today, Jeanette's dippy enthusiasm made her the poster girl for blonde jokes everywhere.

"Hi, Jeanette," smiled Chloe.

"Hi, Ms. Donahue. You know I'm going to audition for Laurey, right, I think I told you that?"

About a million times. Chloe nodded indulgently.

"Well, this is my friend, well, my boyfriend, well, he doesn't know that yet." Jeanette giggled and slapped Nelson on the chest several times. "Nelson D'Amico."

"Nice to meet you, Nelson. You here to cheer your girlfriend on through her audition, just like she cheers you on in your games?" Chloe asked, knowing Jeanette was also head cheerleader.

Nelson's brain was still spinning about the boyfriend remark. It's not like he didn't have enough on his mind today. "Um, no, I'm actually here to try out. For Curly, the lead," he said stiffly.

Chloe flipped through a few pages on her clipboard and then found his name. "There you are. Well, try and relax and have fun with it, okay? You'd better both get down there, we're starting up shortly."

Jeanette bobbed her head excitedly and grabbed Nelson's sweaty palm. "Thanks, Ms. Donahue, and by the way, nice hat." Jeanette turned and pulled Nelson down the aisle toward the stage.

Paul appeared on the dimly lit stage, and nearly tripped over some wires that were laying across it. "Larry! I thought I told you to move these. Chloe, you out there? Ready to start?" he boomed in a voice that he hoped she could hear back in the cheap seats.

"Ready," shouted Chloe, then toned it down a bit. "Let's start with the girls trying out for Laurey, okay? And I'll need a stand-in for Curly for her to sing to. Get a volunteer."

A rather short, wide, and apparently star-struck thirteen-year-old stagehand came out of the wings and waved his hand in a desperate 'pick me, pick me' kind of gesture.

Paul nodded his head and agreed. "Okay, for today, you're Curly. Just stand there to the side of the girls trying out for Laurey and let them sing to you."

Marcy plopped down in the aisle seat directly behind Chloe. "You ready for this, kiddo? I brought a cane with a long hook on it if you need it." Marcy bit the inside of her cheek, and then said casually, "Nice hat."

Chloe whispered loudly without turning around. "My bangs were falling in my eyes, what do you want from me? Now shush, the first one is coming out."

The lights were dimmed throughout the theater and the spotlight hit center stage. The faux Curly stood on the edge of it.

A rather tall and skinny redheaded girl entered and stood in the spotlight's circle. "Moreen Dean. Trying out for Laurey," she mumbled.

Paul recognized Moreen from his fifth period English class. "Moreen, you're going to have to speak up so they can hear you in the back of the theater. That's where Ms. Donahue is sitting. Okay?"

"Moreen Dean. Trying out for Laurey," she said more forcefully.

Chloe and Marcy were quite sure that she could be heard quite clearly even in the school lunchroom, which was at the other end of the building.

Paul directed her to speak her monologue toward the short, plump Curly. Words of flirtation, which, by the look on the young adolescent's face, he never heard from girls in real life. Moreen boomed out her words with such a southern twang that Paul thought that maybe she was channeling Scarlett O'Hara.

Right in the middle of Moreen's lines, Marcy leaned forward and whispered into Chloe's ear, "Hey, didn't she play Flo on *Alice*? Kiss my grits, Mel!"

Chloe had to chomp down on her pen to keep from laughing out loud.

Moreen had stopped her recitation and waited. Her pimpled, short partner, flushed with silent adoration, motioned to her to lean down so he could whisper in her ear, "That was great, Mo, now knock them dead with the song." She straightened back up, and peered toward the back of the theater, with a newly resolved glint in her eye.

Paul stepped toward her and said, "That was fine, Moreen, now for the singing part. Make sure and emote, move around a bit when you sing to Curly, so we can see how you move, okay?"

Paul moved off to the side of the stage, and then nodded to the pianist, who struck a few opening notes to "People Will Say We're In Love." He positioned Moreen, who was a good head and a half taller than the diminutive Curly, in the center of the spot.

Doris Raeburn slipped into the seat next to Marcy, then leaned forward and said to Chloe, "Who's that?"

Chloe rasped back, irritated with the peanut gallery behind her, "Moreen Dean. Trying out for Laurey."

Marcy said, "Trying is the word for it."

Mrs. Raeburn pointed at Chloe's head and leaned over and said to Marcy, "Nice hat." Marcy bit her lip and nodded in agreement.

The first verse was starting up and Moreen's voice lifted out over the theater like the Starship Enterprise entering warp speed. Chloe, Doris and Marcy all unconsciously leaned back in their seats from the sheer force of it. Doris even gripped her arm rests tighter.

Doris leaned and spoke directly into Marcy's ear, not sure she could be heard above the din. "She's not singing that song, she's beating the hell out of it."

Moreen was standing statue still while in the midst of her singing, and had forgotten Paul's direction to move around during the song.

Paul caught her eye, and made a twirling motion with his hand to jolt her into some movement.

A bell went off in Moreen's head, and she made up for lost time by immediately swinging her arms out, emoting wildly to the lyrics. Her left hand caught the stand-in Curly squarely in the jaw on an upswing with a sucker punch, knocking him senseless and dropping him like an oak to the stage floor. Moreen, lost in the moment, and determined to show off her skills at tripping the light fantastic, succeeded only with the tripping part. She landed in a heap on top of the prone Curly. The pianist stopped cold, and the darkened theater became eerily quiet.

Paul rushed over to them from his spot near the wings and shouted frantically, "Curly! Mo! Larry! Come help me!"

Believing that they had been summoned, Chloe, Doris and Marcy sprinted for the stage.

Sara D'Amico, sporting a ball cap of her own, and largely hidden by the bulk of her big down jacket, had slipped into the theater unnoticed just as Moreen was starting her lines. She had looked around, and was satisfied that no one had noticed her enter. She slid her tall form into a last aisle seat farthest away from the two women sitting on the other side near the back. One was a young, short, strawberry blonde in a backwards ball cap, hands busy with a clipboard. Sara figured she must be the director, Ms. Donahue. The woman behind her was a little taller, and stockier. She looked familiar, but it was hard to tell since the only light was aimed at the stage area. Sara tried to make her body as small as possible, but she didn't fret long about being discovered, for all eyes were directed toward the stage and the tall redhead auditioning for Laurey. The short guy next to her was supposed to be Curly?

Sara saw the older woman come in and join the other two women, just as the sonic boom that was Moreen's singing voice began to erupt. Sara had the odd sensation that her eyebrows were being singed just by the sheer explosiveness of it. She blinked in astonishment. Where was that skinny redhead hiding the lungs that were feeding the power of her vocal cords? Nelson had teased her about her own Ethel Merman-like vocal skills, but they paled in comparison to this red-haired stick of dynamite exploding on the stage. It was too painful to watch and listen at the same time, so Sara closed her eyes until she felt the girl on-stage was nearing either a powerful climax to the song or self-implosion. She opened her eyes again just in time to see the redhead whirling, stage left, and saw the powerful uppercut connect with the small geek standing entranced next to her.

"People will say we're in—" Clonk! "—love!" Crash!

Startled, Sara clamped her legs together in an all-out effort not to pee her pants. She heard the man on stage cryptically call out for the Three Stooges, and at his yell, the ball-capped director and her two female friends went stumbling down the aisle toward the stage. Sara felt herself get up, and she quickly but cautiously approached the stage from the other side, keeping her distance. She saw the redhead in the ball cap somehow vault the not-so-small orchestra pit at a dead run, and saw her land almost directly in front of the fallen students. The other two females prudently went the long way and up the side steps to the stage. The students from the wings had all clambered out to see what was going on. Most of them hadn't heard the commotion when it happened because they had their hands over their ears, protecting their delicate eardrums from the near-AC/DC proportions of Moreen's vocal styling. Sara stopped just short of the stage, near the front row, and looked to see what was going on.

The brown-haired man was helping a dazed Moreen to her feet, and out of the way of Chloe, who was quite worried about the unconscious Curly. She squeezed his hand, and got no response. She tapped his cheek, and rubbed it softly, and he let out a small moan. The stocky woman with the oddly colored hair, who Sara recognized as Dave's friend Marcy, was standing directly behind Curly's head, and hitting numbers into her cell phone. After talking intensely for a few moments, she hung up. All eyes were on the softly moaning Curly.

Everyone was nervously quiet. Paul led Moreen over to a chair on the side of the stage, and went to get her a glass of water, for lack of anything else constructive to do. Curly was becoming more lucid, well, in that his moans were becoming louder; he felt a strong ache at the back of his head, and underneath his jaw. Chloe, in order to get a better idea of his condition, brought her face just inches from his, inspecting him for any signs that he was coming back into touch with the real world. Just as his eyes slid open, and he grasped the fact that a gorgeous, sexy woman was breathing softly on his cheeks, her lips a breath away from his, his vision blurred again and he blissfully passed out. Chloe, in her confusion at the downward turn of events, was slipping her hand under his neck.

"Stop! Don't touch him, don't move him."

Chloe froze her hand and suddenly felt the presence of a blue-jeaned, green-jacketed creature crouching on the other side of Curly. She saw the red of a ball cap, and long raven hair hanging loosely down, obscuring Chloe's view of the stranger's face. She watched as the stranger's long fingers reached up and felt for a pulse at Curly's neck, and she heard the woman's relieved sigh as she felt his pulse throb strongly under her finger tips.

"He could have a neck injury, a head injury or something. It's best not to move him at all," Sara said, never raising her head or taking her eyes from Curly's face. "Did someone call for help?"

Marcy, who was still standing at the head of Curly, quickly said, "Yeah, I called 911. They're already on their way. Thank God they're right across the street."

Chloe, intrigued by this stranger, but feeling suddenly useless and stupid, stuttered, "Oh, God, I'm sorry, I knew that. Not to move him. I just wasn't thinking." She looked up at Marcy with sorrow and embarrassment in her eyes. Chloe sat back on her heels, still crouching. She held onto Curly's right hand, and the stranger held his left. Just then the mass of students parted, and two volunteer firemen made their way to Curly. Both Chloe and Sara stood up, and backed away, and stood side by side, watching the firemen work. They stabilized his neck with a collar, and eased him onto a stretcher. They lifted him up, and started toward the rear exit of the stage. Chloe and Sara watched mutely as Marcy, Paul, Doris and the students followed them out to the ambulance, all of them shouting encouragement along the way. Chloe and Sara were left on the stage, strangely lit by one still spotlight. Chloe still hadn't caught sight of any of the tall woman's face, all she realized was her own wonder at the woman's quiet strength and height.

Sara turned even farther away, and softly said, "I guess I'd better get going. I hope he'll be okay," and started to move away.

Chloe, without thinking, grabbed the woman's elbow and blurted, "Wait, I didn't thank you. Thank you. You stopped me from doing something really stupid there. I could have really hurt him."

Sara, hearing the soft, pleading quality in Chloe's voice, stopped her movement away, but didn't turn around. The hand tugging at her sleeve loosened, but didn't let go.

Chloe, her curiosity peaking, tugged at Sara's elbow again. "I'm Chloe Donahue, the drama teacher here, and the director of this play. Are you a parent of one of the students here?"

Sara had to make a decision, and make it quickly. Either walk away, or talk to this insistent small woman. She took a breath, then decided.

With slow determination, she turned, inch by inch, to face the woman who was still hanging onto her sleeve. She glued a grim smile on her face, and turned to meet the eyes that were searching out her own. Their eyes finally met in the stage's deep shadow and locked. Chloe looked into eyes a shade of blue that only an artist could imagine. Sara saw green irises the same hue that was abundant when the earth was new. They blinked in unison, and never lost their gaze. Small smiles started on the corners of both their mouths, blossoming into larger inexplicable silly grins as they both realized what the other was doing. Neither one was looking away. A softly intent curiosity captured them both. Each realized the other was wearing a ball cap, Sara wearing hers in the proper manner, Chloe looking like a teenage home girl in her backwards cap. Chloe had never let go of the tall woman's elbow, and as they searched each other's eyes, felt the other's smiles, Chloe realized that Sara was now holding Chloe's elbow in a return light grasp. They stood breathless just outside of the harsh circle of the spotlight, faces only lit in profile, both captivated by the other's unique beauty.

"Aunt Sara? What're you doing here?" asked Nelson's bewildered voice. "How did you get here?"

The moment broken, both women quickly turned and faced Nelson as he strode into the spotlight and came to a stop in front of them.

"I have my ways, Nelson. I came to see your audition. I wanted to do it on the sly, you know, so I wouldn't embarrass you."

"Did you meet Ms. Donahue? She's the director. Oh, I guess I told you that." *I can't believe she's here.*

Chloe noticed how uncomfortable both aunt and nephew seemed to be, and jumped in to rescue what seemed to be an awkward moment. She turned toward Sara, eyes searching for and finding Sara's hand in order to give it a proper shake in greeting. She grasped it and pulled Sara into the spotlight and as she was starting her gaze upward past their hands, up past the tall woman's shoulders, she smilingly said, "And this must be your famous aunt, the mysterious Sara D'Amico." Chloe's eyes traveled up Sara's long regal neck and onto Sara's face, where her gaze froze along with her smile.

A bright red scar, starting at the bottom of Sara's chin, traveled with almost ruler-like precision straight up across the very edge of her lips, onward past an incredibly high cheekbone, stopping at the bottom of her eye and then continuing on above it, splitting, like a part, her arched eyebrow, and then disappearing under long straight-cut bangs.

Sara let go of Chloe's hand and said, "Yup. That would be me."

Marcy chose that moment to arrive on stage, making an already uncomfortable moment even more grindingly tense. Chloe, thinking that maybe Marcy could help save her from her own awkwardness, quickly stepped to Marcy's side.

"Marcy, I want you to meet Nelson's aunt, Sara D'Amico. This is my best friend Marcy, she's the art teacher here at the school, and is the art director for the play."

A heartbeat passed then Marcy casually replied, "Sara and I have met. How are you doing, Sara?" *What is she doing here?*

"Fine, Marcy. Just stopped by to see Nelson here make a fool of himself," she tried to make a joke, failed miserably and felt herself edge out of the spotlight that Chloe had dragged her into to make her proper introduction.

Chloe saw the tall woman retreating and all of a sudden felt an outraged clenching rising in her gut. How had her best friend, Marcy, somehow neglected to tell her she had met the infamous Sara D'Amico, not only met her, but seemed comfortable in her presence, and not at all shocked by her appearance? Somewhere, in her rising anger, she realized that this scarred tall woman needed protecting from peering, uncaring eyes, and she felt with a sudden certainty that she wanted to be that protector.

Nelson, being the astute, sensitive young man that all young women fantasize about, but never find, felt that same protective streak when it came to his aunt, and came to her rescue.

"Aunt Sara? Do you think you could go over my lines with me one more time? We could go to the back of the theater. We're going to be starting the auditions again soon, right, Ms. Donahue? That's what Paul—er, Mr. Hoderman said."

Sara softly said, "Sure," although her heart was telling her to flee the theater, right now, just leave, don't ever make the mistake of coming back. But her pride was greater than her fear this day. And she was not going to make a fool out of herself in this young woman's eyes. Sara nodded at both Marcy and Chloe, and both weakly smiled back. Aunt and nephew headed toward the side stairs of the stage.

Once they were safely out of earshot, Chloe leveled her barely contained anger and aimed it directly between Marcy's eyes. "Marcy, I need to talk—"

She was interrupted by the return of the students, and Paul and Doris. Paul saw that Chloe was shooting Marcy daggers and looked like she was ready to blow, so he stepped up between them and folded his arms. They both looked at him.

Paul cleared his throat. "Well, the girls think they're jinxed for today, but they want the show to go on, at least for the guys. I thought that was a good idea, and maybe we could continue the audition for the girls tomorrow right before the secondary part auditions. That okay with you two?"

Both silently nodded their assent. But Chloe, having to stifle her anger, felt jittery and unfulfilled, and she wanted an outlet for it. Her outlet had always been talking, and talking loudly. So these folks, undeserving as they all were, were going to get an earful from a cranky and still-embarrassed Chloe.

"Everyone!" she yelled. The theater quieted. "I want everyone here to place themselves, quickly, in the front three rows. I have something to say, and I'm going to say it now."

Students, teachers and a principal, too, made haste to follow her command. They were never this organized in fire drills. They settled into their seats, and looked expectantly up at the stage, where Chloe, agitated, was pacing back and forth. Even Sara and Nelson, who were in the back corner of the small theater, acquiesced to Chloe's demands and stilled themselves.

God, she looks like a caged tiger up there. Sara watched her, wiping her sweaty hands on her jeans.

Chloe continued to pace as she glanced at the student's faces. She was relieved to see a hesitantly smiling Moreen looking up at her, a little shaky maybe, but no worse for wear. Chloe's anger faded just a tad to see that Moreen was all right.

A cell phone rang. Mortified that Chloe might toss a stage prop at her, Marcy answered it before the second ring, although she almost gave herself a hernia wrestling it out of her front pocket in her panic.

Chloe instead chose to ignore the intrusion and started to speak. Loudly.

"Well, I guess that what happened today could be considered a bad omen for the play, but I choose to believe that the worst has already happened, and things can only get better from here on out, right?" she stopped in mid-pace and squinted meaningfully at them all. "I didn't hear you. Right?"

"Right!" They all roared back. Even Sara.

"Good. Mo here, gave it her all, and I must say, she has bounced back like a trooper. She's displayed remarkable," Chloe searched her mind for the right word here, "energy toward her part, and I expect that same energy from all of you, throughout this whole production. Right?"

"Right!"

"And just because Curly..." She stopped short again. "What is his real name, anyway? Does anyone know?" She glared at the blank faces seated in front of her.

Paul wracked his brain for an answer before he spoke up "I know that when the firemen were loading him into the ambulance, he woke up and told them his name. He's from the junior high, not one of my regular crew."

There were more murmurings from the front three rows as everyone tried to figure out Curly's real identity. Chloe was getting visibly irritated again at the complete ignorance of everyone, well, almost everyone involved in today's unfortunate incident.

"This is just great." Chloe fumed at the group seated nervously in front of her. She resumed her pacing.

From the darkness of the rear of the theater, a deep male voice cleared itself, and said with authority, mostly because his aunt was elbowing him after he quietly told her that he knew who the kid was, "I know his name."

Chloe, happy that something was going better, yelled back into the darkness where she knew that Nelson was seated with his aunt, "Don't keep us in suspense, Nelson! What's his name?"

"Charlie," said Nelson, hoping his voice was carrying to the stage.

"Charlie? Charlie who?" yelled Chloe in impatient frustration.

Nelson responded seriously in his best stage voice, "Charlie Shemp!"

Sara, seeing the incredulous expression on Chloe's face, once again clamped her knees together, prayed her thanks to the gods for a strong bladder and silently voiced her desire for the existence of a nearby ladies' room.

Chloe sunk cross-legged onto the floor into the spotlight. The discovery of the elusive fourth Stooge had left her speechless. She dropped her head in defeat, and took off her hat and laid it aside. She ran her hands across her face, then fluffed her flattened hat-head hair. The front three rows were quiet, waiting for her to speak. She could think of nothing to say. Then she heard it, starting low and slow, a steady chortle that expanded into a chuckle that was trying to restrain itself. It was emanating from the rear of the theater, and she knew who the source had to be. It was Sara. The laugh stopped for a few moments, then exploded forth, louder and louder, this time unfettered and contagious. Chloe felt her shoulders shaking in response, her own helpless giggle rising up inside of her, and it erased all her tensions and anger. She grinned sheepishly in the direction of the back corner of the theater, and grabbed her hat and stood up, still giggling. The students in the front rows were mesmerized by the laughing figure in front of them, standing in the spotlight, and the mystery laughter coming from a woman behind them, bathed in darkness. Chloe trained her flat-out grin in Sara's direction, knowing Sara could see her plainly, but not being able to see Sara at all. She could just hear her, and feel her back there.

Chloe, holding the ball cap by the bill, slapped it back on her head, this time in the proper fashion.

The front three rows burst into hysterical guffaws, and the deep laughs from the rear of the theater started anew.

Chloe, confused at the new eruption of mirth, pulled the bill of the cap lower over her face and placed her hands on her hips and yelled, perplexed, to the crowd howling in front of her, "Now what?"

Chloe was woefully unaware that the insignia on the front of the cap read, in bold embroidered letters: PORN STAR.

Sara, in the back row, could take no more. "Nice hat," she gasped to Nelson, as she bolted in search of a ladies's room.

Part II:
I'm Not Panicking, You're Just Underexcited

For three days now, Chloe had been trying to contact Marcy. She'd left numerous messages, at home and at work, and hadn't gotten a return call. It was now early Sunday afternoon, and Chloe was really getting peeved. Marcy hadn't shown up for the rest of the cast auditions on Friday, though she left a message with Doris to apologize, and to tell Chloe she had an appointment she couldn't miss. Casting choices were Chloe's responsibility, but she liked the friendly input of her three dearest friends when agonizing over who ultimately was chosen. Not like there were that many hard decisions to make. The talent pool that Chloe had to choose from was not the largest to begin with. Fort Lafayette High School, divided into three grades, probably had no more than four hundred students. They could glean juniors and sophomores to play extras, dancers, or work as stage crew, costumers and ushers, but this was the senior class play, so only seniors could be cast in the major roles. From around one hundred and fifty seniors, one could subtract about ninety percent as those students who had no interest in the theater arts, or thought it would be extremely uncool to be involved with anything as lame as wearing chaps or a prairie skirt while singing in front of friends and family.

So, Chloe had twelve girls and eight boys interested in playing the major speaking parts. And as much as Chloe didn't like to admit it, to fill all the roles she needed to accept as a general rule that if they showed up and were able to carry a tune in a bucket, they were in the play. This year, Chloe had to amend that so the 'carry a tune' requisite flew right out the window. After hearing so many tuneless, off key, sometimes bordering-on-caterwauling would-be singers, she had a minor epiphany at one point, and briefly thought of presenting Fort Lafayette High's production of *Oklahoma!* as its first "All Rap Musical Extravaganza." But she really doubted, down deep, that these kids could rap either.

Chloe's phone rang. She picked it up, and heard Marcy singing along with the Backstreet Boys on the radio. On key, even.

"Hey, Marse. You can sing! You wanna be a lead in the musical? I'll let you play all the girls' parts, and the boys' parts. It can be a one woman show." An amused snicker tickled Chloe's ear before she continued, in a much snottier tone, "About time you called me back. I thought you ran off and eloped with number seven or something," leaving no doubt that she was pissed.

"I'm still trying to achieve closure with the latest one. Cut me a break here. What are you doing? I just got out of the grocery store and thought I'd stop out to see you so we can catch up," Marcy was trying to be sweet.

"Get here, now," demanded Chloe.

And so she did.

"When's the last time you spent any quality time under something more interesting than a tractor?"

Sara rolled out from under the John Deere, and looked up into the grinning face of her older brother. "I dunno, Dave, I guess I could ask the same question of you," she shot back with a smirk. "I guess we're in the same club here," she wiped her hands on an old rag that he handed her, and then took the beer he offered her next. She stayed on the floor, and motioned for him to sit down beside her.

He settled in, took a draw off his own beer, and cleared his throat, "I officially resigned from that club last night."

She deliberately and slowly turned her head to give him a wide-eyed unbelieving look, and saw the satisfied smirk on his face. She punched him in the arm. "You slut. How much was she?"

"Nope. Didn't have to pay."

"Been hanging around the senior citizen center again with those rich old widows?"

"Nope. I was banned from there, remember?"

"Yeah. Right after you organized orgy night."

"Yup."

"Cybersex?"

"No thanks, I just had some."

"Finally come to your senses and admitted you're gay?"

"Nope. You have that singular distinction in our little family group."

"Well, brother, I'm running out of choices here. No, wait, you weren't out at the Keller farm, were you?"

Dave was stumped. He rubbed his chin thoughtfully, and said, "Nope. But why?"

She steeled herself for his reaction. "I know they have some mighty hot-looking sheep out there."

He snorted his gulp of beer out his nose and gave her a rough, indignant shove on the shoulder. Since she was still seated on the low dolly, she rolled nearly to the end of the large tractor, laughing all the way. She recovered her bearings, and scooted back to sit next to him, hip to hip. He was picking the label off his beer bottle and staring at it, a soft small smile playing on his lips.

She thought for a moment and then said one word, "Marcy."

Dave looked a little surprised, then nodded, and the soft smile returned to grace his dark features. "How'd you know?"

"Well, Dave, I know very few adult females in this town. It's not like I get out much, is it?" She didn't expect a reply to that and didn't get one. "I know you've mentioned her a few times, and I met her that one time when she came over to drop off the designs for your signs." Sara winced at that memory.

"I apologized about that already. I didn't know she was going to just stop by like that," Dave said, annoyed.

"Hey, don't get all defensive. That's my gig. It's okay. I was just upset at the time. I'll live." She joined him in his label picking.

After a short, uncomfortable silence, Dave nudged her. "Um, I gotta ask you. After last night, and all, she may be around here a lot more often. Would you be all right with that?"

It was Sara's turn to get defensive. "Listen. It's not like I live in your house. I've got my own place up at Chez eighth Hole. I don't have to be around when she's around."

Dave's annoyance turned into aggravation. "But I don't want you to stay up there all by yourself just because I have a new woman in my life. It would be nice if you two could get to know each other. Nelson and I like having you underfoot all the time."

Sara twisted her head from side to side to try and relieve some of the tension that she could feel rising in her neck. She took a deep breath and tried to contain some of her racing thoughts. *Get-a-grip, get-a-grip, get-a-grip. You can do this. He likes her. He loves you. Try and act like a normal human being. Don't be so controlling. You didn't used to be like this. Be happy for him. You've already met her. So what if she thinks you're a loon? She seems nice. Except for that hair color. And, she seems to be a close friend of that adorable Chloe Donahue.*

"Adorable?" Sara said out loud, in consternation that she thought that another human being was adorable. *But she is.*

Dave turned, giving her a strange look. "Well, adorable isn't a word I normally use in my everyday vocabulary, but yeah, I guess she is." He blushed and looked away, knowing he had given away something of the depth of his feelings for Marcy.

She smacked him in the shoulder, "You're a goner. Oh my God. Do I hear wedding bells? Is Nelson gonna have a little brother or sister in his future? Can I pick out the name?" *Curly, Moe, Larry.*

Just a few miles up the road, more beer bottles were suffering
the indignation of losing their coverings. In fact, there was a nice little pyramid in the center of Chloe's coffee table. By the look of it, it
consisted of five or six bottles worth of pickings.

"Um, Chloe, do you mind if I smoke just one little itsy bitsy cigarette in your house? Hmm? Please? It must be ten degrees out there.
Please?" Marcy wrapped a finger around one of her corkscrew curls,
trying to look as pathetic as possible.

Chloe, comfortably reclined against a couple of throw pillows in
one corner of her couch and her bare feet parked on the edge of the
coffee table, had her beer bottle propped on her stomach and was
intently picking away. She had a nice little pile of foil sitting on her
chest and she was feeling too lazy to add to the beautiful pyramid on
the table just yet. She was feeling lovely and woozy and smiley and
giggly, just as she should after imbibing a few on a lazy Sunday afternoon in February, hanging out with her best friend. *Terminator 2* was
turned down low on the TV, and occasionally they would interrupt
each other to point out something fascinating that either Linda
Hamilton or Arnold Schwarzenegger was doing in the name of the
greater good. Normally, she didn't cotton to smoking, or people
smoking in her house, but she decided to be a sport and let Marcy
have her way. But not until after she begged.

"Give me one good reason why I should, besides the weather,
Marcy." *Go ahead and not return my calls, wench. I'll make you
pay.*

"I had sex. I gotta have a cigarette after sex. It's written down in
the rules somewhere." Marcy looked around her for the invisible rule
book she had just conjured up, thanks to her beer-fueled imagination.

Chloe narrowed her eyes and gave her friend a suspicious glare
through her still-shaggy bangs. "That was last night, Marse. Last
night. With someone else. Unless something happened between us
when I nodded off there for my five minute power nap. If that's the
case, it was way too fast, you aren't very memorable, I'm not very
satisfied, and come to think of it, it would be just like the last woman
I slept with."

"There's a twenty-four hour rule about smoking after sex,"
Marcy again looked around for that pesky missing imaginary rule
book. "And it's your fault you aren't sleeping with anyone. You don't
get out much. You live in a town where a wild Saturday night consists of going to the drive-in, drinking beer out of a quart bottle, and
then stopping to pee behind the Dairy Queen before you get home
before midnight," Marcy paused for effect. "And let's see, you hang

around with, oh, an over-sexed love 'em and leave 'em straight woman, an under-sexed and geeky male English teacher who probably should get over himself and go into the seminary, and a geriatric matron school principal who probably gets more sex than the three of us combined."

Chloe couldn't find fault in any of that, so she nodded in agreement.

"So," said Marcy pleadingly, "about that cigarette? Can I?" *You're making me pay, aren'tcha?*

"Only if you give me one too," Chloe grinned and watched for the reaction on her surprised friend's face.

Marcy skeptically handed one over, and lit hers first, then leaned to light Chloe's. "You aren't going to get all green and upchuck all over the place like you did behind the Stefanski's barn that one time, are ya?"

"God, Marcy, we were, what, eleven or so at the time?" She purposely blew her smoke directly into Marcy's face.

Marcy sat back. "So, to what do I owe the honor of you smoking one with me now?"

"Hand me the rule book," Chloe waved impatiently.

Marcy made a show of picking up pillows, moving bottles around, and finally lifted her butt off the couch and pretended to pull something out from under it. She handed it to Chloe, who wiped it off on her green sweat pants before pretending to page through it.

"Aha! Here we go, Chapter Fourteen: Best Friends and The Sexual Experience," Chloe pretended to read, "Rule twenty-one states that if one's best friend has sex when one's own pitiful self isn't getting any, the friend who is going without is allowed to live vicariously through the friend who is getting some."

Marcy nodded solemnly. "That's a mouthful. And that means? Please continue."

Chloe cleared her throat, turned the imaginary page and went on, "This may include some or all of the following: making the best friend who is 'getting some' recount in detail the sexual experience," Chloe frowned and stopped. "Although in my case, you may want to leave out any descriptions of male anatomy. I think that may be covered in Chapter Twenty-Four, Sex and the Single, Desperate Lesbian. Let's see, said best friend is to extend all privileges of the after-sex experience to the best friend who is going without. This includes," she lifted a single finger in the air, "Number one: the twenty-four hour rule applying to cigarettes—been there, doing that." Two fingers now in the air. "Number two: afterglow."

"Afterglow, now how do I share afterglow with you?" remarked

Marcy, glowing, but truly puzzled.

Chloe pointed with a big toe to the row of empty beer bottles sitting on the coffee table, and then leaned and tossed her half finished cigarette into one. "Beer-simulated afterglow effects. We improvised."

"Aha, we're very tricky," said Marcy approvingly.

"Uh-oh. Number three," Chloe said, ominously narrowing her eyes.

Marcy provided the needed fingers this time, and waggled them in the air.

"Thank you. Number three, after-sex guilt." Chloe let out an exaggerated sigh.

Marcy, who really should have stopped after her second beer, but hadn't, tilted her head to the side to show she needed further explanation.

Chloe, who was functioning just fine, at least in her own mind, even after three beers, was quite happy to elaborate on after-sex guilt. "After-sex guilt: am I a slut? Does he/she really care for me? Do I really want to wake up with so and so, or do I kick them out after the after-sex cigarette and afterglow? Were they satisfied? Am I satisfied? What's the point of all of this? Was I too loud, too passionate, a dead fish, too fast, too slow?"

"Oh God," moaned Marcy, "I haven't had my after-sex guilt trip yet. What's the matter with me?"

"Marcy, Marcy, Marcy. Calm down. It hasn't been twenty-four hours yet. You still have time."

"I think I'm starting right this very minute. And we have to share it," whined Marcy.

"Well, start without me, I have to go pee," Chloe grabbed the pile of label pickings off her chest, added them to the pyramid on the table. She slowly stood up, and airplaned her arms through the air to check her balance, found out that it was good enough to get her to the bathroom and back with no problem.

Chloe stopped after a few steps, walked back to the couch, and grabbed the imaginary rule book off the throw pillows.

Marcy looked at her, "Huh?" written plainly all over her face.

Chloe shrugged, "I need something to read in there," and strolled off.

Marcy chuckled to herself. *I should know better. Chloe has an answer for everything.*

Dave, Sara and Nelson were gathered around the kitchen table sharing an old-fashioned Sunday dinner together. Well, it was old in their fashion. Nelson, who had achieved the reputation of being a teenage bottomless pit, was making his sixth piece of peanut butter toast to go along with the salad that Sara had made for all of them. Dave was spooning out the nuked remainders of some take-out Chinese stir fry from Friday, and kept getting up to check on the burgers he was frying on the stove. Sara snitched a piece of toast from a grumbling Nelson, and surreptitiously scouted out the box of Cap'n Crunch that was sitting on top of the fridge.

"Anybody want a Little Debbie while we're waiting on the burgers?" asked Dave, his voice sounding strangely like that guy from *Father Knows Best.*

"Gee, Pop, what kind you got?" piped up a suddenly eight-year-old Sara. *Please be chocolate, please be chocolate.*

"Swiss cake rolls. Want one, Suzy, dear?" intoned Dave.

"That'd be swell, Pop. But are you sure it won't ruin my dinner?"

Nelson finally looked up from the magazine he was reading. "Will you two knock it off? Dinners in this family couldn't possibly get any worse as it is."

Both Dave and Sara looked at Nelson with falsely hurt faces.

Dave looked at Sara and said, "Gee, Suzy, whatever can he mean?"

"I dunno, Pop, gosh, maybe he's having some sort of latent teenage hostility crisis and is going to hack us to pieces while we sleep tonight," blinked Sara.

Nelson, normally a good-humored young man, just grumbled some more and said, as he got up, "Don't think I haven't thought about it." And he left the kitchen.

Dave got up and flipped the burgers. "What do you suppose is up his butt?"

Sara just shrugged, "I blame all bad male behavior on testosterone levels. He either needs more, or needs less. My guess is less right now, with the way he's acting." *I know what's wrong with him. He's fretting about this play. I know he's a shoe-in for the part of Curly. He was great, and he had little, all right, no strong competition for the part. I know, I had to sit through all of those auditions until Nelson could leave and give me a ride home. He's got it. He probably knows it, too. But he's just insecure enough not to get his hopes up about it. And then there's that small problem that if he does have the part, he's going to have to break it to his dad, who can't seem to see him as anything but a jock.* "So, are you going to tell him about you and Marcy? She does teach at his school, after all. And there is that problem of her seeming inability to commit to anyone."

"Like you should talk. She just hasn't met the right guy yet. Maybe she's just not the marrying kind," mused Dave, who secretly had been thinking about the same thing.

Sara watched the hamburger grease skittering from the skillet.

*And she didn't see you as being the married kind all those years back,
big brother, when she was the direct cause of your eventual divorce
from Mary, huh?*

Dave brought a small stack of burnt burgers over to the table.
"Sorry no buns, use bread. Nelson! Burgers!"

Nelson appeared in a flash, slapped a burger on a piece of bread,
squirted some catsup on it, grabbed another piece of bread and disappeared into the living room again.

While Dave was rummaging around in the refrigerator, Sara
assembled their burgers.

Dave sat back down at the table with a can of Cheez Whiz.
"Sorry, no cheese but this. Want some?" Sara shook her head no,
then sat amused as Dave sprayed a ton of it on his burger, then sat
back to watch his face as he took a large bite of it.

He saw her staring, and in mid-chew, he stuck out his tongue
and said, "Twain weck."

Sara laughed and slapped the table top. "We're such fine exam-
ples of adults. Mom and Dad would be horrified if they saw our idea
of a family Sunday dinner."

"Sara, they moved to Orlando twelve years ago just so they
wouldn't have to be subjected to the way we turned out. Smart move,
I'd say."

They ate the rest of their meal and did the dishes in companion-
able silence. Dave went to his office to do some paperwork, and Sara
went out and sat on the couch with Nelson. She reached over and
patted him on the knee.

He half smiled, half grimaced at her, and his eyes flashed onto
her scar for half a moment, then looked back at the TV again. "It's
looking better every day, Aunt Sara. It's healing nicely. Maybe it'll be
like the doctors in Buffalo said, and it'll fade to the point that it'll
hardly be noticeable." *God, please make it so. She doesn't deserve to
live like this, so cut off from everything, so scared.*

Sara ran a finger lightly down the length of the scar. *Nelson's
right, it is healing, and fading more and more every day. Maybe if
they'd done the job right the first time, years ago, I might be on a different path right now. I might be the strong, confident, yeah, even
wild woman I used to be. I might have a life, a career, maybe even a
lover if I wasn't like I am right now. I might I might I might.*

Sara put her head on the couch arm, stretched her long body and
tucked her feet onto Nelson's lap. *He's such a great kid.* "Nelson?"

"Hmm?"

"Tell me everything you know about Chloe Donahue."

Chloe had a weird sensation as she was making a sober-up pot of strong coffee. Her ears were warm. No, they were burning. She shook off the feeling and carried two cups out to the living room, where Marcy was stretched out dozing on the couch. Two hours earlier Chloe had quietly cleaned up the empty beer bottles, the empty pizza box, and turned the lights low so Marcy could get some sleep, but now it was time to have the actual conversation with Marcy that had been nagging at her for days now.

She sat a cup on the coffee table nearest to Marcy's head, and went down to the end of the couch, gently lifted Marcy's feet, sat down, and placed them into her lap. She gently squeezed a big toe.

"Marcy?"

"Hmm?"

"Wake up, hon. There's coffee. Time to wake up."

Marcy slowly opened her eyes, and felt the nice gentle stroking of her feet. She groggily sat up just little, she didn't want to hinder Chloe's tootsie massage. "I should be so lucky to wake up like this all the time. Getting stroked, fresh coffee, warm smile."

"Yeah, whoever lowers their standards and settles for me is going to be one lucky woman," Chloe made a face, and crossed her eyes at her friend, then took a sip of her coffee. "Tell you what, until you get a little more with it, I'll tell you what I've been deciding about the kids in the play. Feel free to interject at any point. Also feel free to keep your opinion to yourself."

Marcy nodded in mute agreement and clutched her coffee cup under her nose.

Chloe wiped a hand through her ever-errant red-blonde locks, doing nothing to their disarray. "Well, I know you know that Nelson is going to be Curly. That's a given. I mean, the kid has talent. He sure was nervous, but he can sing. He seems to be able to act a little. I think with a little work and a little confidence building, he's going to blow everyone away." She leaned over and grabbed her clipboard from the floor by her feet. She flipped it open to the page she needed, and then went back to rubbing Marcy's foot. Marcy sighed, pleased at the continuing attention.

"I've penciled in Justin Makela as Will. And Jason Hellman as Ali Hakim. And last but not least, Justin Swanson as Jud Fry. He's a wrestler, and built like a Land Rover. Perfect for the part." She scratched the tip of her nose with the pencil eraser. "Now, for the girls' principal roles, this was tough. You weren't there on Friday to witness the carnage, I mean, auditions of the other girls. I think you might've been recovering from a two-day migraine right now if you had. I know I am. But I've decided on Jeanette Stavros for Laurey, Heather Hedlund for Aunt Eller, and," she stopped and took a big gulp of her now cooled coffee.

"And?" urged Marcy.

"And Mo Dean as Ado Annie." *I cain't say no!* Chloe closed her eyes, scrunched her shoulders and waited for the negative reaction. And waited. It didn't come.

Marcy took her time and swirled the last sip of coffee around in her mouth before she said, "I think that she's a good choice for that part. She's like you said on Thursday,   energetic. That part needs someone just like her. Now you just have to find a way to have a volume control knob installed on her, and you're all set."

Chloe pinched Marcy's big toe hard.   It was a good thing Marcy's coffee cup was empty, because it would have been all over the both of them by now.

"What was that for?" complained Marcy, pulling her attacked toe away from the grinning librarian.

"Who are you and what have you done with..."

"Yeah, yeah, yeah, I know. I usually argue with you about everything, just for the sake of arguing. I don't feel like it. I agree with you. Mo's a good choice."

"You don't feel like arguing with me? Since when?" Chloe pinched a toe on the other foot for emphasis.

"Hey! I might not feel like arguing with you, but I can still beat the snot out of you if you don't quit grabbing my toes!"

"You and what branch of the armed forces?" challenged Chloe. She flexed a handsome bicep.

"Hey, I've got a new boyfriend now. He has big muscles, big forearms, he's got a really big..." Marcy trailed off, smiling wickedly.

"Wait, you would sic your boyfriend on me? That's great, you big wuss. Have some man do your dirty work for you. Nope, doesn't work that way."

"I argue, I don't fight. Did I mention that he has a really big...sister? Maybe I could get her to come to my rescue." *Marcy, the sly one, that's me.*

Chloe's eyes got wide at the mere thought of Dave's sister. She raised her eyebrows suggestively at Marcy.

Marcy knew exactly what she was doing. "Uh-huh. Now we finally get to the point. You're just dying to know about Sara D'Amico, aren't you, Chloe? What is it? Curiosity? Mystery? You got it bad for her after just one meeting. You've been dying to talk to me about her forever now. Fess up."

"Yes," Chloe said immediately. No sense in trying to fool Marcy. "Tell me everything you know. Right now. This minute."

"I could really use another cup of coffee first, and a cigarette, and I gotta pee," teased Marcy, glad to have the upper hand over her wildly curious friend.

Chloe jumped up from the couch, grabbed Marcy's hand, pulled her up off the couch and pointed emphatically toward the bathroom.

Chloe headed off to the kitchen, empty cups in hand.

When Marcy came back, Chloe handed her a fresh cup of coffee and then an ashtray.

Marcy jutted her jaw out, and squinted distrustfully at Chloe. "I didn't even know you owned an ashtray. Been holdin' out on me?"

"Park it, and get on with it." Chloe wanted answers.

The only other time that Marcy had seen Chloe this impatient was when Marcy was late a few years back and they went out and bought a home pregnancy test and nervously waited for the results together. Thank God it was negative. Marcy snuggled into the crook of the couch and lit a cigarette. "Okay, but first you have to tell me, upfront, before I divulge anything. Are you interested in her?"

Chloe gulped and admitted it out loud, "Yes. Definitely. Well, it would help if I knew if she could be interested in me, too." Chloe mentally crossed her fingers.

"Good. That's good to hear, I mean, I want you to be interested in somebody, you're my best friend and all. I don't like seeing you so alone," Marcy paused, and considered keeping the redhead in suspense just a little longer. When Chloe looked appropriately impatient, she continued. "From what I understand, she is family." Marcy caught the small grin that Chloe made no effort to hide. "But I don't know if she's someone I want you to be interested in."

That cryptic statement wiped out Chloe's grin. "Just tell me what you know and let me make that decision, okay, Marcy?"

"All right. Here goes." She took another sip and a puff and began rattling off facts about Sara D'Amico. "Well, let's see. You know what everyone else does through the media and the tabloids. She graduated from here, did a few years of college, then took off to California, did some modeling for the big magazines for a while. She did small parts on TV shows. She was a regular on that horrible cable cop show for a few years until she got her first movie, and stole it out from under that big actress, Meg Whatshername. They then cast her in *Star Gazers*, she was still up and coming so she got paid very little for it. *Star Gazers* was a huge, huge hit, and it was part of a planned trilogy. Two years after the release of *Star Gazers*, she was a household and grocery tabloid name and supposedly got into trouble doing drugs. The preproduction for *Star Gazers II* kept her from doing very much, so she never really did another movie after that. Now this would bring us up to—"

"Four years ago." Chloe was already aware of everything Marcy had mentioned, she wanted something more illuminating.

"Yeah. The accident. She's on the freeway in L.A., in a convertible, talking on her cell phone, going too fast, not paying attention when..."

Chloe grimaced in preparation for the upcoming description of the accident, and tried to steel herself for what Marcy was going to say.

Marcy sighed and continued, "She slams into the back of a van that had suddenly stopped in her lane. The airbag goes off, saving her from being killed instantly. But the antenna on the front of her car snaps off, and flies backward with such force that it slices her face to the bone from forehead to chin. By some miracle, her eye wasn't damaged."

Chloe looked so troubled that Marcy leaned forward and squeezed her arm. "I'm sorry if I sound so cold-hearted here, Chlo, but I'm just trying to get the background out in the fastest way possible. Hang in there with me, okay?"

"Okay, I've heard most of this before, well, I didn't exactly know the details of the accident, I thought she had broken bones or something. Hearing about this before was one thing, but hearing it now, and actually attaching the events to a real live human being that I've met, that's another thing."

"Now, from what Dave tells me, the ER doctor at the hospital did such a hack job at stitching her face back together that it healed asymmetrically. I have no clue why they didn't call a specialist in right then and there." Marcy saw that Chloe had shifted on the couch and was now hugging her knees tightly to her chin. "This is the tough part, Chloe, hang in there, okay?" She waited for Chloe's response; it came in a quick nod.

Marcy regained her place in her story. "Her face, uh, healed poorly because, oh hell, who knows why, but, I don't know how to say this, other than, well, you saw where the scar was the other day? It's been fixed again, recently, in Buffalo. But Dave says— this is why I was avoiding talking to you about this—that side of her face, just to the right of her nostril, was pulled upward into a little constant smile, her eyebrow up was up too high, and the skin stretched around her eye on that side so tightly that she could hardly blink or close that eye all the way." Marcy's gut clenched at her own words, she wasn't fond of having to recount the details of such a difficult story, even about a woman that she barely knew.

Chloe almost choked at the picture her mind was forming, and swallowed hard.

"But you saw her the other day, right, Chloe? It's all fixed now, except for the scar. Everything's in place. Everything is where it should be. She can smile naturally now, blink her eye, she's so much better now." *I think.*

Chloe pondered the truth of this for a moment, then a thought struck her. "Why'd it take so long for her to get it fixed? I mean, she was living in L.A., home of plastic surgery." Chloe felt like they were talking about some stranger now, not the flesh and blood beautiful woman she'd met the other day.

"From what Dave said, Sara left L.A., soon after it happened. Seems all her movie star pals were fair weather friends, and couldn't handle the way she looked, the way she was behaving afterwards. Dave said she pretty much disappeared for a few years, and no one, including Dave, knew where she was. The only contact he had with her was through some anonymous P. O. Box. He finally used some of the money he borrowed to build the golf course and hired a private detective to find her. He just found her last spring and went and convinced her to come back here, and live on the family land. He told her all about the golf course he was building, that he needed help with it. She had the surgery this past fall, after Thanksgiving. You saw the results. Just a scar now, and it's fading. I noticed the difference, and I've only seen her twice in the space of a month."

Chloe had known of the second meeting, Marcy seeing Sara at the audition but, "Tell me about how and when you first saw her."

Sara awoke on the sofa and noticed from the clock on the VCR that it was after midnight. She felt the old brown afghan either Nelson or Dave had thrown over her. She stretched a little, and considered getting up and going home to sleep in her own bed. *Nah. It's too cold out there.* She listened. The rest of the house was quiet and dark, and the cold wind was whistling outside. There were plenty of nights that she had sacked out here on the big old couch after falling asleep watching a movie or having played cards late into the night with Dave and Nelson. *I like it here. It doesn't feel as lonely as my place, although it's just a hundred yards up the path. I've spent too many nights all alone. I came back here to change that.*

Her stomach growled a little. *Hmm, another advantage to falling asleep on Dave's couch. I can go raid the refrigerator. There's food in there. I have jack squat in mine.* She lightly padded into the kitchen, and her eyes lit upon the box of Cap'n Crunch sitting invitingly on top of the fridge. *Ahoy, Cap'n, we have a date with destiny, little man.*

She poured herself a bowl, and settled in to some satisfying crunching, and took inventory of herself. *I'm feeling pretty relaxed. This feels good. It's nice feeling part of something again. I haven't felt like part of anything for a long time. All my time has been spent avoiding things, people, events and life. And when I haven't been doing that, I've been planning ways to make sure I can continue avoiding things, just so nothing has to change. So I don't have to change. For a few years there, all my avoidance planning just had to do with me. But now that I live with, or around, Dave and Nelson, I end up just expecting them to go along with my little, or big—what's the word I want here? —neuroses. I've been resenting them because they have lives outside of this land, this house. They have friends, they have jobs and school, Dave even has a girlfriend now. I'm really jealous of that.*

She felt her nerves rising, and the small increase in her heartbeat. She pushed her empty bowl away.

I hate this. But it's the only thing I know anymore, the only way I know how to live. Secluded and always on guard. Always protecting myself from the unknown. To do that, I have to control everything around me. And the only thing I can really control is me, so I don't let anyone or anything else come in to perhaps rock my protected little world. Even poor Dave and Nelson have been the victims of my wrath when I feel that they aren't respecting or understanding my need for a surprise-free life. At least that's what Dr. Logan said. She's right. And my angry outbursts, my loss of control when I perceive that my safe little world is threatened, my peace of mind, well, we've seen what happens when the unexpected meets up with my unreasonable demand for nothing but the predictable. I didn't react very well, did I?

Sara pushed herself away from the table, and folded her arms. She began rubbing her elbows absently, remembering the day that Marcy had shown up at the house unexpectedly, and the scene that unfolded.

It had been late in the afternoon and Sara heard a car in the driveway. She was working in the garage, and had the doors propped open to let the fumes out from the engine she was working on.

She heard a car door opening. Good, Nelson's home. He can help me with this, and it won't take half as long, and I can get myself out of this friggin' frigid garage and into the house where it's warm. *She had on her orange coveralls, and a heavy winter coat and a black stocking cap, but was still chilled to the bone. She strolled out to the doorway of the garage, expecting to see Nelson getting out of his old Ford pick-up truck. Instead, she was startled to see a feminine figure emerging from a small red Miata. The curly-headed woman saw Sara standing there, and smiled and waved at her. She then started gingerly walking toward Sara, trying to navigate the large ice and mud puddles that made up the ground separating them.*

Oh, God. *Sara impulsively ducked back into the garage.* What do I do? Who is she? What is she doing here? *An uncontrollable urge to flee, to hide, to avoid this woman in anyway possible, hit her. She looked around the garage. No back exit. No escape. Her heart was hammering.* Something bad is going to happen to me, and there is nothing I can do to stop it. *Her head felt like it was being squeezed, her world was spinning. From behind her, she heard the woman let* out a small curse, and say, *"Damn, I knew I couldn't make it all the way over here without getting a soaker in at least one boot."*

Sara didn't turn around, she was concentrating on the pounding noise in her ears, and willing herself to calm. She was on the beginning edge of a full-fledged panic attack. Here it comes here it comes here it comes.

"Hey there, is Dave around? I'm Marcy, I wanted to drop off some designs for him to look at."

Sara still didn't turn, she just barely heard what the woman had said. She doesn't know. She doesn't know. She can't talk to me right now. Let her just go away so I can breathe again.

Marcy, thinking that the tall woman in the orange coveralls hadn't heard her, stepped up closer, almost directly behind Sara, and tried again.

"Hey, hello there, I'm looking for Dave. I'm Marcy, a friend of his. Is he around?" She reached out and tapped the tall woman on the shoulder.

"Don't touch me! Get away!" Sara whirled around, and Marcy stumbled back a few steps, staring, frightened, at this wild-eyed woman in front of her.

Marcy, stunned by the woman's outburst, immediately recognized who she was. This terror in front of her was Dave's sister Sara, the movie star. With a straight red line running down her face, just to the right of her nose. Oh, no, the accident.

"Are you all right? I won't touch you again. Are you here by yourself? Is there something I can do for you?" She could plainly see Sara was in some sort of trouble, it showed so vividly on her face—her eyes were scrunched tight, her hands were in tight fists, her shoulders were raised and trembling. She looked like she was desperately trying to hold herself together. Marcy vainly hoped that Dave or Nelson was around somewhere. Marcy's natural inclination was to get the hell out of there, away from this troubled woman, but her good sense kicked in, and she knew that the woman needed some help. But what can I do for her? Will she try to hurt me?

Sara slid full blown into her attack, and there was no going back. The world in her head was sheathed in blackness, interrupted with small dots of light flashing in front of her clenched eyelids. I'm dying. This is what it feels like to die. Dying would be a relief. I need to breathe and I can't. I can't get a breath. *Her breaths were coming in rapid, useless spurts. No air was getting to her lungs. Her head felt light.* I need help. I don't know what to ask for. Or if I even can ask.

Marcy saw the woman's distress, and some heretofore-unused maternal instinct kicked in. This looks like it might be, what, a panic attack? I've never seen one, but I've read about them. I hope that's all it is. *She looked around, and saw a low work stool, stepped over and grabbed it. She reminded herself not to touch Sara. She carefully approached Sara, and quickly deposited the stool right behind her stiff form. Sara never moved. The trembling continued. Stool in place, Marcy backed away a few feet in front of Sara, and still unsure that her course of action was correct, started talking in what she hoped was a soothing tone. "You're Sara. Right? Right. Sara, I think you need to sit down. You don't look like you're breathing all that well. I just put a stool behind you. Why don't you try sitting down?"*

Sara's lips lifted into a grimace, although nothing else about her changed. Why doesn't this woman shut up? I can't breathe here. She's not helping. *The blackness, she could feel it, moving throughout her body. Through her arms, settling in her stomach, then lurching, tingling down her legs. It was a black void she was falling into, and all she could do is hold on for the ride.*

Since Sara gave a small reaction, although the snarling grimace that appeared on her face gave Marcy no comfort, she decided to keep talking. Keep it simple, Marse. Keep it simple. *"Sara, there's a stool behind you. Sit down. It'll help. Sara. Sit down. Sara? Honey, sit down." Marcy somehow thought that a term of endearment might be more comforting.*

Sara heard the voice. She took a huge gulp of air, and willed her eyes open a slit, and then closed them again.

Marcy kept on. "Sara, that's good, I'm Marcy. Sit down, hon. Sit down. There's a stool right behind you. I won't touch you unless you want me to."

Sara somehow found the strength to listen to Marcy, and she bent her knees and sat down on the stool. She put her elbows on her knees, pulled off her stocking cap and placed her pounding head into her sweating palms. I still can't breathe. This is hell.

"Aunt Sara? It's Nelson. Breathe. Nice and even." Marcy almost jumped into Sara's lap on the stool at the sound of Nelson's voice behind her. She'd never heard him show up.

Nelson stepped up and stood next to Marcy, and patted Marcy on the shoulder in silent greeting. But he never took his eyes off of Sara, whose head was still cradled in her hands. She was breathing now in a measured cadence.

Nelson had seen this one too many times. "That's right, that's great, Aunt Sara. Think good things. It's almost over now. All you have to do is breathe, slowly, and everything will be over soon. These things don't ever last too long, do they? You're coming back. Just relax. Breathe."

Nelson turned his head to meet Marcy's eyes. He gave her a grim nod of assurance that things were getting better. Marcy let out a long tense breath she didn't even realize she had been holding. Their eyes returned to the woman just in front of them, who was breathing much easier now. Sara's head lifted, she wiped her hands on her knees, and she ran splayed fingers through her long black hair from her cheeks to the very ends. She sat up a little, eyes still closed, and took a long, cleansing breath. A small, exasperated chuckle came from her. She twisted her head from side to side, and then her deep blue eyes slowly slid open, searching out Marcy.

Marcy suddenly felt shy. The big screen didn't do those eyes justice.

Sara gave her a small forced half smile, her lips curling up on one side only. "Well, Marcy, seems you've seen me at my worst. At least I hope so. I'm Sara, and I can't really say I'm glad to have met you." Her voice sounded low and dry, like the crackling of kindling. Sara reached out a long arm toward Marcy, but remained seated.

Marcy stepped forward, leaned and shook her hand, captivated by the embarrassed and still tense blue eyes. After the hell she seems to just have endured, she still can be charming. *"Oh, hell, Sara, I can't think of one person I know that wasn't sorry they met me."*

"Oh, yeah, and just before I left that day, Sara pulled me aside, hugged me around my shoulder and said, 'And Marcy? Next time, call first.'" Marcy chuckled at the recollection. "Can you believe it?"

Chloe just shook her head. *My brain's too full.* Again her mind heard the echoes of Sara's melodious laughter that had floated up and touched her soul from the very recesses of the theater. *Yeah, I can believe it.*

Part III:
So, What's the Plan?

Chloe's Tuesday at the library was progressing swiftly. She would be done at 4:00, so she made plans to head over to the high school to post the results of the audition on the school's bulletin boards outside the theater and main office. That way, the kids would see them first thing on Wednesday morning as they arrived at school. Marcy had said she would be there until around 4:30, and then was heading over to Dave's house to meet him; they were going into Erie for dinner and a movie. Marcy sounded really excited. She and Dave hadn't exactly done the dating thing the last time around.

Chloe stood in front of the library's old ditto machine, an old crank job with heavenly-smelling ink. She was copying off the cast list to be posted, the rehearsal schedule, and contact numbers for everyone involved in the play. *Hell, everyone that showed up for the auditions is on that list. They're all involved in the play.* She had even broken the rules, and had a few juniors signed up to be understudies for the lead roles. *If we have an outbreak of the flu, we're going to have to change the playbills to read "The Fort Lafayette Soon-To-Be-Seniors Proudly Present..."* The pages were rolling off the ditto, and Chloe picked one up and held it under her nose to savor the oddly intoxicating odor. *I think sniffing fresh ditto paper is the closest I've ever come to doing drugs.*

The thought of doing drugs brought the image of Sara D'Amico back to the forefront of Chloe's brain. *That's an awful way to think of her. But I can't help it. There were those rumors that Sara had been in trouble with drugs while she was in Hollywood, all the gossip rags said it, and even Marcy mentioned it the other night. But I don't know if Marcy was just repeating the rumors or if she heard it directly from Dave. Hopefully that's old news now, and doesn't bear being concerned about. I doubt very much that Sara, Dave and Nelson are spending their time snorting cocaine between fertilizings out at that golf course.*

Then there's that other doing drugs. Chloe had spent a good deal of her time the last two days reading about the causes and treatment of panic and anxiety disorders. She had learned the basics, that they were more common than she'd thought, and depending on the severity of the disorder, were quite debilitating and disruptive to the person suffering from them. There were so many variables involved that Chloe hadn't even hazarded a guess as to the reason why Sara was a victim to them. Two things did stick out in her mind. Statistically, women were more likely to suffer from them, and oddly enough, the panic attacks didn't manifest themselves until many of the women had entered their thirties. So it came to happen that perfectly functioning women, maybe outgoing and confident all their lives, were suddenly susceptible to panic attacks so severe, that shook them to their very core, and perhaps became so frequent and overwhelming that they couldn't cope. And they ended up having their whole lives altered. The other thing that stood out about these harrowing disorders was that they were frequently by-products of some traumatic life event. So Chloe felt safe in assuming that first, Sara was in the right age group, gender bracket and had displayed the symptoms, and second, she sure as hell had been experiencing some trauma in her life. The most common treatment for panic disorder was a combination of behavior therapy, counseling and medication. Chloe wondered if Sara was taking any medication. *Oh hell, why torture yourself about this? It's not like you can call her up and just casually take her to the diner for dinner.* Marcy had explained that Dave said Sara rarely left the family land, and when she did, it took her days of planning to psyche herself to do it, and even then, she would end up not going. It must have been quite demanding on her nerves to show up, even in secret, at Nelson's audition last week. *She must really love him.* So Sara D'Amico was apparently very isolated, perhaps even maintaining a self-imposed isolation just for the sake of her own sanity. Even if Chloe wanted to make an effort in Sara's direction, it might not be something Sara would be interested in. *Is this something that's going to get better? Should I even bother? Why did I ever start reading about this stuff? Everything I've read has told me that Sara D'Amico is an impossibility for me. I just can't recall ever being so drawn to anyone like this before. I'm setting myself up for big-time disappointment, even if I could think of a way to get to know her.*

The four o'clock hour drew near, and the twin high school juniors, Byron and Justin Devers, who worked part-time evenings, showed up a couple of minutes late. Chloe gave them a list of some mindless tasks to perform so they wouldn't spend the whole evening making paper airplanes and smacking each other with the small return-date stamp. Chloe threw on her coat, took one last sniff of her ditto sheets before she stuffed them into her canvas briefcase, and headed outside to her car. It was warming a bit, the temperature was above freezing for once, and the snow was beginning to thaw. The skies were darkening already with the swift sunset that comes on a winter's day. *Can spring be far away?* Knowing this area, Chloe knew the answer to that question was a resounding *yes!* It had once snowed here in June, for graduation ceremonies.

Chloe turned the engine over once, twice, three times. She heard a weird buzzing sound each time. She tried holding the pedal to the floor, as her dad had taught her so long ago, and then let up again. She turned the key. Bzzzz. *Maybe I flooded it. I'll wait a minute and try again.*

The Final Jeopardy theme music played in her head. *Okay, here goes.* Click. Bzzzz. Click. Bzzzz.

Chloe stomped back into the library, and noticed that "March 2 2001" was already prominently stamped on Byron's forehead.

Byron looked sufficiently guilty, and mumbled, "Sorry, Ms. Donahue."

"Uh-huh. I gotta use the phone."

She dialed Marcy's cell phone number. Two rings, and Marcy answered.

"H'llo?"

"Marcy, is that you? It's Chloe."

"I had a paintbrush in my mouth, sorry."

"What're you doing? Can you come get me from the library? The Subaru has gone belly up and I don't feel like dealing with it right now."

"My Miata always starts right up. You ever think about getting a car from the new century? Even one from the last decade would be a step up."

"Yeah, well, can you come get me? What are you doing?" Chloe hated repeating herself.

"Yeah, I can come get you. I'm supposed to meet Dave at 5:00, the movie starts at 5:40 p.m. and then we were going for dinner."

"Tell me about it when you get here. I guess the kids can wait until tomorrow afternoon to find out who's in the play."

"On my way, cranky butt."

Ten minutes later, the little red Miata slushed its way into a parking space in front of the library, and Chloe opened the passenger door and got in. Marcy was securing her ever-present cell phone in her shoulder bag.

"Using your floor as an ashtray again?" Chloe sniped as she settled in.

"This one in the dash fills up after three butts, and they bounce out when I hit a goddamned pothole, so shoot me," Marcy helped Chloe snap her seatbelt, and thunked her on the shoulder for being bitchy.

"Don't tempt me. If I weren't the non-violent type—"

"Yeah, yeah, yeah, tell it to your parole officer," Marcy pulled out of the parking space and headed out into traffic.

"Um, Marcy, I hate to be a back seat driver. Wait, this car has no back seat, but you're going the wrong direction to my house."

"Huh. Whaddya know. Too many paint fumes, I guess. Hey, did I tell you that you're coming out to Dave's house with me?" Marcy innocently queried, a nasty smirk threatening to erupt on the corners of her mouth.

Chloe stopped fussing with the radio tuner. "What?"

"I want to stop there first, and leave my car there. We can drop you at your house on the way to the movie theater in his car. He doesn't really fit too well in this car. It's the same direction," Marcy explained, trying to keep her voice light and matter-of-fact.

Chloe shifted a bit in her bucket seat. She didn't like surprises. These kind of surprises. *Sara doesn't like them either.*

Marcy bit the inside of her cheek to keep the grin off her face. "Don't worry, I called first."

"And?" Now Chloe was feeling downright anxious.

"She's there, he's not yet. She knows we're on our way. She sounded fine with it," Marcy chewed on that a moment. "Sorta."

"Sorta?"

This is going to be fine. They're only going to be here a few minutes. I can handle being sociable for a few minutes. I know, well, I've met both of them. And I've been daydreaming, pretty much non-stop, about one of them, and coming up with some pretty lame ideas about how to see her again.

Sara had unzipped out of her usual orange coveralls, and was aimlessly puttering around the garage in a pair of jeans and old barn jacket with a gray hooded sweatshirt underneath. *Now I don't look so much like I'm working on the state road crew patching potholes.* She leaned over, and looked in a greasy old mirror that was propped up on a work table. Her face was clean, and her hair, well, it was there. She had it pulled back in a ponytail today, and when tied back like that, it usually stayed in good shape for the most of the day. Having it pulled back was a little safer, too, considering she worked around engine's moving parts a good bit of her day. She sucked in her cheeks, and raised her brows. *Hey, that's attractive.* That scar wasn't going anywhere, so there wasn't much she could do about that. She flashed her teeth in the mirror, and checked for any remainders of her lunch that might be lodged there. She ran her tongue along the front of them, and then sucked the front ones just for good measure. She checked her hands, and then her nails, grabbed a flat-head screwdriver and ran the edge under a few of them.

I wish Nelson or Dave would show up before they do. That'd take some of the pressure off me. Then I could pretend to myself that I do this every day, that I deal with folks other than my brother and nephew on a regular basis. Sara snorted. *That's a laugh. I hide from the mailman every day.*

She heard a car coming up the drive, and nervously fluffed her dark bangs one more time, and adjusted them to cover the scar that ended halfway up onto her forehead. *I can do this. I have to find out. I have to get through this, and then maybe, if my gaydar is correct, maybe I can get her to come out here for dinner some night. Cap'n Crunch and Little Debbies. Ha. But Marcy probably already told her about how we met. Oh yeah, too good a story not to share that.* She pursed her lips and stuck her tongue out at herself in the mirror. *Loser.* Her heart picked up its rhythm, and she sucked her teeth one more time. *Act. Act like you have confidence. Play a part. Maybe that will work.*

It was dark out, being the middle of February in the Northeast and nearly five o'clock. The lights in the garage were on, as well as the security light shining over the wide snow covered unpaved parking area between the barn and house. Sara stepped out of the building just as Marcy was slowly easing the Miata to a stop in front of it. The engine shut off, and two car doors opened. Marcy had gone all out in honor of date night, and was wearing a dress with high leather boots. Tonight her mop of hair shown a rather odd amber color under the floodlight. She had a satchel hung over her shoulder, and she looked every inch the eccentric art teacher. Chloe, who had been picking between her front teeth with the edge of an old matchbook while fussing with her hair in the vanity mirror, put out a foot to get out. And was unpleasantly surprised to find that her foot never made contact with solid ground until it had passed through about nine inches of dirty slush water. The leg of her khaki pants was soaked up to the knee. *Oh, yeah, way to make a good impression, Chloe. My foot is soaked, my sock, too, and there's enough water still in my boot to keep a goldfish alive. Yup. Hope Dave gets here soon.*

Chloe hauled her canvas bag with her, and she and Marcy tried to walk over to Sara, who stood a good twenty yards away, but it was close to impossible to walk in a straight line to her because of the many slush puddles that marked their path. So they haltingly wove left and right, together then apart, as Sara watched them approach like two college freshman staggering back to the dorm after their first kegger. She couldn't help but see and smile at poor Chloe's soaked leg. Her amusement at the sight helped soothe her rattled nerves, and she called out to them, like an interior designer directing the hanging of a picture over a sofa.

"Marcy, go left. Chloe, a little right, yeah, ooh, watch out, that's a big one coming up. No, Chloe, go right, a little higher, no, that's too high. Marcy, I'd move yourself a little to that end, head for that pile, I think it's safe to step on."

Marcy and Chloe made it, and both grinned, triumphant, at Sara. Marcy looked up at their amused blue-eyed guide. "Thanks for the help. I think we might have lost Chloe in those last few yards if it hadn't been for you directing traffic."

"Yeah, one of those holes might have swallowed her right up, and we wouldn't have found her until May," Sara said quietly, but her voice held a chuckle. "Looks like one of them already tried to get her."

Chloe self-consciously looked down at her soaked pant leg, "Good thing I'm a terrific swimmer." *Dork. Spaz. Geek. Pick one, I'm it.*

"Any fish down there?" Sara couldn't help wanting to tease the poor embarrassed redhead.

"There may be one or two in my boot." Chloe shook it in demonstration.

An awkwardness quickly settled in, and the three women looked around, yet not at each other.

Sara cleared her throat to break the silence. "What say we go into the house until Dave gets here? He should be here any minute. Nelson, too." *Please.*

Chloe was happily anxious to share the good news with Sara's shy nephew. "Nelson? Good, then I can tell him! I was going to have Marcy post the results at school tomorrow, but he can find out tonight, if he gets here in time." *Please.*

Sara turned to her, and looked at her for the first time directly in her expressive green eyes. *Ahh, just like I remember them. But so much better in person.* "Curly?" she said, hopefully.

"Curly," Chloe stated with a shy grin, and watched as Sara's face eased into a delighted smile. *It's nice to see Sara smile like that.*

They all started, haltingly, toward the house. Sara pulled up short and mused, "This might be easier if you two follow me. I know the best way to get there from here. And one wet leg is enough."

Marcy kidded her, "Are you sure we can even get there from here?" Marcy took a long hard look up and down Sara's tall, strong form. "Might be easier if you just piggy backed us both over to the porch."

Sara was suddenly feeling a little more confident. "One, or both of you at the same time?"

Chloe's imaginative and hormonal mind went right into visualization mode. *She could carry me in her arms. I could put my arms around her neck. I don't weigh that much. She could carry me right* up to the front door, over the threshold, right into the kitchen, through the living room, and march us right into the be—

"Earth to Chloe. Ready for the trek?" nudged Marcy. *Oh, it doesn't take much to see where her mind is at!*

They were nearly to the door, playing a funky kind of Twister with right foot mud, then left foot snow pile, when Dave pulled in the drive in his Explorer.

"Hey look, Dave owns a grown-up car. Instead of a Barbie Dream House car, like yours." Chloe pointed at the Miata.

Marcy wasn't about to let her get away with that. "At least mine runs and isn't taking up valuable parking space in front of the dry cleaners right now."

They all stopped on the front porch and stood waiting for Dave.

"I was thinking of bending down and kissing the porch. Dry land, you know," quipped Marcy, eyes glued to her tall honey slopping his way over to them.

"Oh, he's such a manly man," Chloe said, affecting a bass voice, "not even trying to avoid the craters."

"It's winter. Wait 'til summer, and a bumble bee comes around him. Then he acts more like RuPaul. He runs like a girl," Sara grinned, and waved her wrists in the air in her best nancyboy imitation. The three of them laughed, picturing the image of Dave that Sara had described.

Dave hopped onto the porch and gave Marcy a very chaste kiss on the cheek. His cheeks were ruddy and flushed, and Chloe and Marcy, seeing brother and sister together for the first time, both had the same thought: *They look so much alike!*

Sara held open the front door, and with sweeping hand, motioned them all inside. "Hey, Dave," she said loud enough so everyone could hear, "I've seen you give Mom hotter kisses than that."

"Izzat right? Well, I better fix that. Don't want to give Marcy here the wrong idea about me and Mom." With that, he swooped down, took a startled Marcy in his arms and planted a big, fat wet one on her. It took only a moment for her to respond, and she wrapped her arms around his neck and returned the smooch with fervor.

Chloe was a little embarrassed and looked at the ceiling. Sara walked over and leaned against the counter and tried to ignore them. The kissing continued. Sara drummed her fingernails on the counter. Chloe made squishing noises with her soaked foot. Dave and Marcy came up for air, then started in again.

Chloe decided to make some fake conversation. She glanced at Dave and Marcy, who were still sucking air out of each other's lungs, and said airily, "Is it warm in here or is it just me?"

Sara was definitely getting warm, even if it was her own brother involved in this little display. "No, it's not just you. But I know where to find a bucket, and some cold water to put into it," she raised her eyebrows at Chloe, hoping to find a fellow co-conspirator.

"Sounds like a plan." Chloe grinned.

Dave and Marcy, lips all red and smooched soundly, finally broke apart. "I like how you say hello," gasped Marcy, looking a bit winded.

"Wait 'til I have to say goodbye, I'll show you a thing or two then." Dave raised a rakish brow in response.

"Sara, you got that bucket handy? I think I'm gonna hurl here." Chloe looked plaintively at Sara, who just grinned and nodded.

Dave harrumphed and smiled, "Hey there, Chloe, long time no see. Nice that Marcy dragged you over here. I haven't seen you around much since they switched my route. Still Marian the Librarian?" *Still as beautiful as ever.*

"Still wearing those cute brown shorts in the summer, Dave? You have the cutest dimpled knees."

The two old acquaintances laughed, and exchanged a quick hug.

Dave turned to his sister, "So, you've been introduced to Chloe? She's the book pusher down at the local library. I've heard stories about her strong-arming folks for late fees that would turn your hair white."

Sara looked suddenly nervous. "Yeah, we met." She started moving across the kitchen floor and leaned up into the doorway to the living room, just a little behind Dave, obscuring his view of her.

"Yeah, I met your sister there when..." Chloe's eyes fixed on Sara, who was standing behind Dave and frantically making slashing motions across her throat, then she moved her finger to her lips in the international sign of 'stuff a sock in it!'

"Marcy introduced us. She fished me out of the swimming hole that is better known as your driveway." Chloe somehow figured that Dave didn't know about Sara's appearance at the auditions last week. *Maybe I'd better not say anything about the auditions until I get better idea of what's going on.* "My Subaru went kaput in front of Stefanelli's Dry Cleaners, and I'm thinking about calling a priest for last rites."

Dave nodded his head and thought for a moment. His eyes lit up. "Hey, Sara, if Nelson can tow Chloe's rust bucket up here, think you could take a look at it?" He turned to her, knowing that he had put her on the spot, and she didn't like being put in that position. *Maybe, this time, she can handle it?*

Sara, surprised at the idea, unexpectedly found herself immediately and cheerfully agreeing, "Sure. Be happy to." She looked right into Chloe's green eyes to show her that she meant it. "I'm pretty good with cars. Would you mind letting me have a go at it?"

Chloe returned the look and said, "Really? That'd be so great. Usually, I have to get a tow truck to come haul it to a dealership fifteen miles from here."

"She does magic with motors. There's greasepaint and grease in that woman's blood," said Dave proudly. *She looks like she's doing pretty good with these two women being here. She doesn't even look like she's going to jump out of her skin. This is good. And the looks she's sneaking at Chloe! Marcy was right. These two might be a match. And Chloe is looking at Sara like she's a Peanut Buster Parfait on a hot summer day. Now onto Phase II of the plan.*

Marcy was feeling smug about having had the presence of mind to call Dave on her cell phone on the way to picking Chloe up, and discuss some matchmaking between them. *This might be the perfect time to set the plan in motion. I wasn't expecting an opportunity to occur so soon, I was sure that we'd have to do a lot more fancy footwork to get these two together and see if sparks flew. But Chloe needing a ride, and me having to stop at Dave's anyhow, well it seemed to be the fates stepping in. Now onto Phase II of the plan.*

"Um, Marcy?" Dave, who was thinking there was more than one actor in this family, began his previously agreed line readings here on the kitchen stage. "Bad news, hon, we aren't going to be able to make that movie. Mark Benson from the zoning licenses board wants to move up our meeting from next week to tonight. I promised to meet with him at 6:15 at the Embers, down on Route 5. He's bringing his wife, and he suggested I bring you along, too. Would that be all right?" The Embers was in the opposite direction from Chloe's house. Way out of the way.

Marcy feigned disappointment. "Oh, how could I turn down a lovely romantic business dinner with you? Sounds like the perfect evening." Marcy paused, and then pretended to remember something. "Oh, wait, how's Chloe going to get home? By the time we get clear out to her house, and then down to the Embers, it's going to be nearly seven o'clock." Marcy planted a disturbed frown on her face. "Is there some way you can get in touch with Mark to make it later?" *Meryl Streep's got nothing on me.*

"I don't have his home phone number. Damn," sighed Dave, glad that he and Marcy were performing their hastily agreed-upon lines to perfection.

Chloe was standing there, listening, feeling as left out as a piece of patio furniture in January. "Maybe you could give me a ride?" she said, slowly lifting her eyes to meet Sara's.

"I, uh, um, can't drive," mumbled Sara. *Can Chloe see that big flashing 'loser' sign on my forehead?* She turned away, fidgeting with something invisible on the counter.

Dave jumped in to save the rapidly deteriorating situation, "Wait! Nelson should be home any moment. He can give Chloe a ride home, and tow her car back here. That'll kill two birds with one stone." He turned to Chloe, "Would that be all right, Chloe? Would you mind? Nelson should be home any time now." Of course, Nelson was in Erie at the mall and then going to a late movie. He wouldn't be home 'til after 11:00. *I am a bad, bad brother.*

"Well, if Sara doesn't mind me hanging around a bit, I guess that would be okay, " Chloe said, hesitating. *I hope Nelson is late. Fortune is smiling upon me tonight.*

"I guess I could rustle us up something to eat. Nelson will be hungry when he gets home," Sara said, quickly recovered from her bad mood. *Sorry, Nelson, but I hope you get a flat tire. Please get a flat.*

"It's all settled then," Dave cheerfully declared, and then glanced at his watch. "Oops, we'd better get going, Marse, if we're going to get there on time." *Yeah, to the imaginary meeting that isn't going to take place at 6:15, at the Embers. Please let this turn out okay, or Sara is going to drag my body all over my virgin little golf course with that tractor that she loves so much and toss me off a cliff.*

Marcy decided to get going while the going was good. "Okay, Dave. Let's haul butt." She gave her librarian friend a quick questioning smile, just to make sure that she was comfortable with remaining there at the house with the tall actress, and was pleased with the reassuring smile she got in return. She then turned to Dave and sweetly said, "And hon, do you think you could piggy back me over to your Explorer?" *This'd better work, or they're going to find me hanging by my ankles over the stage on opening night.*

With a wave, they were out the door, and Sara and Chloe were alone.

Part IV:
Adventures With Home Appliances

There was a distinct uncomfortable quiet hovering over the kitchen. Not knowing quite what to do, Chloe wandered over to the kitchen table, pulled out a chair and sat down. She looked at Sara, who was leaned up against the kitchen sink, arms folded, seemingly lost in thought. She seemed to be focused on a point somewhere behind Chloe, and Chloe turned in her seat to see what was capturing Sara's attention. There was a microwave, with a pile of cookbooks on it, and some benign painting of a woman standing in a summer rose garden hanging above it. *Okay, that's not it.* She turned back around, folded her hands and placed them on the table.

Sara continued to stare past Chloe, thoughtfully rubbing her chin with her fingers. Chloe took this time to study her, not a flat out stare, she didn't want to be caught doing that, so she just covertly peeked at her, studied something different each time, and then glanced away. Chloe noticed that they still both had their coats on. *I'm getting a bit warm here. I should take off my coat.* But she didn't want to move, afraid any movement would break the trance that Sara seemed to be in. *She looks good in that barn jacket, like a model from an L. L. Bean catalog. I haven't seen her without some sort of coat on since I've met her. She looks thin, but healthy under all that bulk of clothing.* Chloe's eyes just naturally fell to Sara's face, and the long red line that split her dark skin. *How can she be that dark in the middle of February? My legs are so white right now, I'm pretty sure they're glow-in-the-dark.* The scar looked smaller to her somehow, a thinner line, not as bright as even a week ago. *If the redness goes away, there will just be a razor-thin line down her face. And even so, even now, it just looks like it adds to her character, somehow.*

Chloe shifted her eyes and looked at the small cutting board topped cabinet instead. *Don't want to let her catch me staring.* She thought of Sara's face, a picture still fresh in her mind. *I don't ever remember seeing a face that young that held that much character.*

It's the eyes, the set of the face. It looks like she has hundreds of years of memories stored there. Sara had a timeless beauty, high cheekbones, long straight nose, deep-set eyes and lips set in a small, tight horizontal line, the edges not curling up, nor down. *When she smiles, those gloriously white, even teeth help to light up her whole face. I wish she would smile for me now.*

Maybe they were briefly joined by some psychic moment, because Sara finally shook herself out of her small reverie, and blinked at Chloe. *Oh, I went out of town there for a moment and didn't even realize it.* Chloe was sitting at the table, small hands clasped in front of her on the table. She still was wearing her woolen pea coat. *Shit. Get it together, Sara.*

Sara cleared her throat, Chloe shifted in her seat, and their eyes met. Hesitant smiles appeared on their faces.

Sara's low voice cut across the space. "Hey. You'd better get your coat off, you'll catch a chill when you have to go back out there."

"I thought maybe it was required attire around here. You still have yours on," Chloe pointed at Sara's coat, and barely, just barely, held back from a wink.

Sara looked down, and found out that it was true. "Well, let's fix that." She pulled, moved and took her coat off, and threw it over a chair next to Chloe. Chloe stood up, shrugged off her own coat and placed it on top of Sara's. She slid her hands into her back pockets and rocked a little bit on her toes, looking around again, not knowing what to say. She wanted to say something, anything. *Since when am I ever at loss for words?* A small squishing sound emitted as she rocked.

Sara smiled at the sound, and newly determined to be a better hostess, opened her mouth and immediately stuck her foot in it.

"Chloe, do you want to take your pants off for me?"

Chloe's nervous rocking immediately ceased; she removed her hands from her back pockets and placed them firmly on her hips. Her small form, in a blue V-neck sweater, straightened up, military tight. "Excuse me?"

Did I just say that? I couldn't have said that? I said that! Sara's mind scrambled for some kind of quick recovery. She stuttered, nothing comprehensible forming on her lips, and she dumbly pointed at Chloe's very wet pant leg. Her mouth and brain refused to work in tandem. "Your pants. Dryer. Sweat pants. I have. You could. Socks. Laundry room. Over there." Her hand waved desperately in the direction somewhere to the left of Chloe.

Chloe's rigid posture relaxed as the true meaning of Sara's stammered words sunk in. "Oh. I see. Oh." *It sounds like I'm repeating letters from the alphabet.* "I don't want to be any trouble."

Sara, still a bit wide-eyed from her verbal miscue, looked miserable and didn't say anything, for fear of butchering the English language anymore than she already had. *I can't talk, I can't think, and she's just standing over there, smiling at me like she understood everything I just said. I don't even understand what I just said.*

Chloe felt the need to put the flustered woman at ease. "You say that to all the women who get stranded on your property? That's quite a line. Can I use it sometime?" Her green eyes twinkled and her smile expanded to its fullest.

Sara found herself captivated by the glow that seemed to encompass the whole of Chloe's fine features. *This woman sparkles. Not just her eyes, although it seems to start from there, it stretches across those blushing cheeks, that wide pert nose, the openness of her smile, it travels to the point of her chin, and seems even to light up her fine red blonde hair from within. The warmth just spreads from her whole being. It's not just one thing about her, it's the whole of her. Her body carries and just seems to glow with a radiance, and I feel helpless standing in front of such a being.*

Chloe, a little disconcerted that Sara seemed to be in a daze staring at her, tried once again. "Yes."

Sara snapped out of it, well, as best she could. "Um, yes, what?"

"I'll take my pants off for you, you old smoothie, you." *How could I resist?*

She's flirting with me! There is a God! "Um, the bathroom's right through the living room. You can change in there. Hang on." She started to move toward the small laundry room. "And I'll grab you a pair of my sweats and some socks. We can toss your pants in the dryer. Won't take but a few minutes." She reappeared holding the articles of clothing in a wad, and shoved them at Chloe. "Here ya go. Right past the living room. The room with a toilet in it."

"Thanks. Be back in a few minutes," Chloe wandered off in the direction that Sara had pointed.

Sara sighed in relief of her short respite, but couldn't help but take notice of Chloe's shapely backside.

Chloe found the room with a toilet in it and shut the door softly behind her. She untied her boots, and dripped some of the water from the soaked one over the sink, half expecting a fish to fall out. She sat her boots on the floor, pulled off and set her socks on top of them. She wriggled out her khakis and kicked them aside. *That went well. I think. I can't believe she said that about my pants. Almost knocked me over with those words. And I wanted to say yes, before I even knew what her real intentions were. I've got it bad.*

She stood in front of the small vanity in her underwear, and inspected her face. *Same one that still gets me carded in bars.* Sometimes she resented looking so young, although she knew, deep down, that it was a good thing in the long run. In the very infrequent trips she made to the lesbian bar over in Erie, she still had a few college students trying to pick her up. *Not that that's a bad thing, but I don't have much in common with women that age anymore. They still seem to be coming to grips with their sexuality. And they spend a heck of a lot of time acting out little dyke dramas. I already went through that, I don't want to relive that part of my life again.*

She slipped into the seemingly huge sweat pants. *Oh, this is going to be attractive.* She put on the thermal socks that Sara had given her, they were huge, too. They practically were knee socks on her. She tugged the elastic bottoms of the sweat pants over her ankles, and noticed how the legs of the sweats ballooned below her knees. *Oh, yeah, sexy.*

She gathered up her clothing, and padded back into the kitchen, stopping to silently admire Sara's rear end, as she bent peering into the open refrigerator. She apparently was searching for the Holy Grail, and not finding it. "Lose something?" said Chloe, amused when Sara jumped nearly straight up at the unexpected sound of Chloe's voice.

"God, you scared me. You could be a ninja, you walk so quietly." Sara raised an eyebrow in appraisal of Chloe's appearance. "You look like a five year old wearing her dad's pants."

"Excuse me, but this is how I usually dress. The khakis today were an aberration. Not my norm. This is." She twirled, arms loaded with her clothes, for Sara to take in the whole effect. She looked down. "I could carry a lunch and a thermos in these sweats, the crotch is so low on me." It was true, the crotch of the sweats stopped mid-thigh on her. "I tried pulling them up higher, but then the waist was up under my armpits."

"Well, Chloe, somehow, you make it all work," Sara intoned sincerely, and noticed the pleased blush that crept across Chloe's face. "Here. Give me those. I'll take care of them." She placed Chloe's boots near a furnace duct by the stove, and then went into the laundry room with her socks and pants.

Chloe's stomach took that moment to announce its emptiness. Rather loudly.

Sara stuck her head out from the laundry room, "You say something?"

"Uh, no," she shook her head, embarrassed. "It did." And she pointed at her stomach. With perfect comic timing, her belly repeated its loud demands.

Sara chuckled and said, "Wow. You should take that show on the road. 'Chloe and Her Magic Talking Stomach.'" She started the dryer and came back into the kitchen. "I guess we'd better see to that," she pointed at Chloe's belly, "before all hell breaks loose, huh?" *Why am I feeling this relaxed around her? Quit questioning it, Sara, and just go with it. You can't accept things even when they're going good.*

"Whaddya got?"

Sara moved over and opened the fridge door again, and waved Chloe over to look there with her. They stood side by side, Sara much more hunched than Chloe, and peered within. "Let's see, the more identifiable things first. A half of a tuna sandwich with bermuda onions," she held her nose for a moment, "milk, eggs, Cheez Whiz, catsup, beer, apricot jelly, stale bagels, ring bologna, dill pickle slices, marshmallow fluff and mayo. This is not looking good. Now for the mystery items in the Tupperware containers."

They edged closer to the fridge and each other, shoulder to shoulder, the thrill of the unknown drawing their spirits together in expectation of a shared adventure. Sara glanced up at Chloe, her head so close to her own, and whispered, "This could get dangerous. Stay close." Chloe set her jaw and nodded in grim determination. Sara tentatively touched the edge of a pint-sized container. "Here goes," she slowly pried up the edge of it, and they leaned forward to try and ascertain its contents.

"Chicken salad with croutons on top?" said Chloe, uncertainly.

"Nope. Cottage cheese with some kind of blechh on it," they both wrinkled their noses. "You were close, though."

Sara reached for another container, and took an exaggerated deep breath. Chloe instinctively moved even closer to her. Up came the edge of the lid. Numerous purple rubbery oval shaped objects, swimming in a deeper purple fluid, with floating round red purple disks greeted their eyes.

"Ooh. Beet-pickled eggs. I love those!" enthused Chloe.

"We have achieved a first course! Unless we don't have anything better for desert."

A large bowl awaited them on the top shelf. They looked at it, then at each other. Chloe, the flirt in her deciding to emerge, said, "I'm scared. I think you'd better hold my hand for this one." Sara hesitated, then softly took Chloe's hand into her own. *Perfect. This hand feels perfect in mine.* Chloe was experiencing the exact same thought. "It's okay. I gotcha. Here goes nothing," and she gave Chloe's hand a tight squeeze.

Chloe squeezed back. *I think I am going to swoon. If I knew what swooning was, I'd be doing it for sure.*

Sara's hand snuck out, then swiftly ripped the lid up.

They stepped back, staring, still clutching hands.

"I think we have lift-off," said Chloe, pleased with the sight her eyes were taking in.

"Yeah," replied Sara, rather dreamily stroking the hand in hers with her fingertips. "Tuna noodle casserole. And less than three days old."

"Nirvana," said Chloe succinctly.

Both of them suddenly became very aware of their clasped hands, and nervously disengaged.

"Nuke or stovetop?" Sara asked distractedly. She was still feeling the warmth of Chloe's hand, and wondering over the sensations it had invoked in her. *Normally I hate people invading my personal space.*

"Nuked works for me. I don't think my stomach is going to remain calm much longer. And don't forget the pickled eggs."

"I'm glad we found something in there. I didn't even want to think about opening that freezer door. It's like the pits of Hades in there."

Both sets of eyes traveled and settled on the freezer door, and both women shuddered involuntarily at the thought.

The women then moved easily around the kitchen together, in a blossoming of comfortable familiarity that developed into a fluid dance of quiet intimacy. The small work space afforded the women the opportunity to bump elbows, briefly touch fingertips, graze shoulders, and place light hands on the smalls of backs while slowly brushing past each other.

Chloe set out plates, across from each other, and placed utensils around them while Sara spooned up some of the casserole into another bowl to place in the microwave. She silently showed Chloe the amount she had placed in it for her approval. Chloe raised an eyebrow, and gave Sara a frown. Sara spooned two more healthy additions to it. Again, she tipped the bowl for Chloe's inspection. Chloe frowned again. Sara's eyebrows raised high under her bangs. She heaped three more ladles into it, and once more looked to Chloe. There was little to nothing left in the original bowl. Chloe traded the frown for a small grin, and shrugged her shoulders.

Sara whistled, "This I gotta see," covered the nearly overflowing bowl, and set it in the microwave.

Amazing, I thought Nelson could chow down. He's Ally McBeal compared to this woman. Sara resisted the urge to duck her head under the table to see where Chloe was putting it all. It wasn't like she wolfed it down. No, she chewed. She just kept going and going, at a leisurely pace, no hurry, no worry, taking another helping and doing it all again. *I was done fifteen minutes ago and she's still at it. She must have instantaneous metabolism or some such trick of nature. I should tap her leg to see if it's hollow. Her poor mother, I hope she didn't breast feed her, she probably was stuck to her chest 24/7 until it was time for solid foods. She must put restaurants that serve buffets into bankruptcy. I can see her just pulling up a chair to*

*the salad bar now. And she can talk, and eat too, and laugh and listen
to my awkward little jokes. What could a woman like her see in me?
I work as a landscaper and mechanic at a little nine-hole converted
cow pasture barely bigger than a miniature golf course. I don't drive
anymore. I have a red line bisecting my face from north to south. I
barely leave the house, and her best friend probably told her that I'm
a psycho bitch from hell. She's probably only being nice to me
because she's stuck here until Nelson arrives.* She glanced at the
clock on the wall. *It's almost eight o'clock, where is he, anyway? I
hope he eats before he gets here, because I'm pretty sure Chloe's
thinking about having that scary cottage cheese in there for dessert.*

"Got any dessert?" said Chloe, impishly. She was really quite
full, but couldn't resist tweaking the amazed woman seated across
from her. She wasn't embarrassed about her penchant for being a
chow hound, actually, she was quite famous for it. It used to be a big
joke at her college cafeteria, that the students would see her coming,
then all make a mad dash to get in line in front of her before the food
was all gone.

"You have room?"

"Hang on a second." Chloe forced a small burp. "I do now."

"That guy with the ice cream truck that drives up and down the
main road in the summer must love you," Sara jibed, opening her
eyes wide, and shaking her head.

"I told him just to park it at my house. How'd you guess? Saves
him a lot in gas."

Sara laughed, pushed her plate to one side, and folded her arms
and leaned on the table and fixed her gaze on her dinner partner. "So
you live on Route 20, too? Everyone in this town lives on this road.
But you live out on the other side of town, huh?"

Chloe settled back in her chair and let her eyes silently appreciate the view of Sara's long black hair, strong cheekbones and flashing
blue eyes. She had to stop a second to rerun Sara's question through
her mind again before she responded. "Right next to the old '76 station. It was the Murdochs' house. It's tiny, but I like it."

"My house is a couple hundred yards from here, c'mere, you can
see it from the window." Both women stood up, and walked over to
the tiny window over the sink. Sara stood behind Chloe and looked
over her head. A dim light far into the night was the only thing she
could see. "Uh. I'm sure it's out there somewhere, Sara, but I sure
can't see it from here." Chloe was immediately aware of Sara's proximity, and made a quick mental note that yes, physical proximity
with Sara was a very, very good thing.

Sara ducked her head over Chloe's right shoulder to try and see
it from her perspective. Chloe felt the length of Sara's body lean gently into her back. Sara's chin was nearly resting on Chloe's shoulder,

and her mouth was inches from her ear. "There, you see it?" she said softly. She rested her left hand on Chloe's left shoulder and pointed with her right hand. "That light. That's my porch light. Right there."

"Uh." *I should play dumb and pretend not to see it, that way I can keep enjoying this. Does she have any idea what she's doing to me? I think she does.* "Yeah, I see it. Sorta." The small hairs on the back of Chloe's neck were standing at attention, enjoying the warmth of Sara's breath.

They stood like that for a moment, staring into the blackness. Neither one felt any desire to move. Sara took a deep breath, and the sound of it so close to Chloe's ear made her tremble just a little. Chloe turned and tilted her head up to look into Sara's face, Sara looked down and their eyes met. Sara leaned a little more, and Chloe lifted her head just slightly. The clock on the wall seemed to slow. The beating of their hearts took over the measure of the passage of time, until their lips softly met and time stopped completely. Bottom moist lip met an upper, brushing left to right, then stopping in the center. A tongue, running the very edge of a lip, mapped the contours. It was lightness and heat, their heads moving closer then barely away, but never parting the sweet connection that was being forged. A hand moved on a forearm, fingers tickling the fine hairs from wrist to elbow. A warmth that multiplied with the soft meetings of nose to nose, nose to cheek, lips to cheek and tongue to the ridges of teeth.

Sara was the one to break the kiss. She felt overwhelmed, completely stupefied, and totally marvelous. Her blue eyes searched for some answer in Chloe's slowly opening eyes, and found what she was hoping for in the wondrous green orbs before her. Chloe's eyes were smiling even before that impulse hit her mouth. It took but a moment for the smile to appear there, too.

"Oh my," murmured Chloe.

"Yeah," *I was just going to say the same thing.*

They stood at the counter, washing up the dishes and chatting. Neither noticed that each other's voice had taken on new and lustrous tones, and the words they exchanged now held a purpose, a new meaning. Words were spoken with a new intimacy, there were feelings attached to the simplest of phrases. Looks and smiles and stories were being internalized and carefully stored for later retrieval. Mannerisms were being memorized. And the smallest of touches bloomed with the heat of a wildfire on their skin. Everything was new again, and both of them felt ill-prepared for the emotions washing over them. Excitement warred with newly revived nervousness, and nervousness won out. So they did what was natural to them, they searched for a reason not to pursue what they were so evidently feeling.

"I probably should have asked this before," started Sara, a little tentatively. "Are you seeing anyone?"

Chloe, feeling a little giddy because it appeared that the answer was very important to Sara, said, "Why, yes. I am."

Sara, not expecting that answer, got a little irritated. "You are? Who?"

Chloe dried the last dish and put it on the shelf. "I'm seeing you."

"I think that's a terrible idea," blurted Sara, knowing that she meant this.

"I shouldn't be seeing you? Why, did you have someone else in mind for me?" Chloe was still caught up in the near-afterglow effects of that kiss.

"Anyone. Well, almost." *I can't do this.*

"Is Sigourney Weaver married? Did you ever meet her? I'd dump you in a minute if I thought I had a chance with her," Chloe wasn't quite sure if Sara was teasing her or not.

"She's married. Give that one up, it'll never happen." *This shouldn't be happening.*

Sara glanced up at the clock. Nearly 8:30. *Where the hell is Nelson? If he were here, I wouldn't have to deal with this right now.* "I'll be back in a minute." She tossed the dish towel on the counter, and strode quickly into the living room, and disappeared from Chloe's view.

Chloe stared at the dishtowel, and absently went over and folded it several times. *What the heck just happened here? We talk, we eat, we kiss. We do the dishes, and I thought everything was going fine. Now she takes off like there's a fire she needs to put out somewhere. Maybe she's feeling like that kiss was a mistake. Was it? Damn, I am starting to think that it was, and I was feeling so positive about it. Now I'm positive I'm not positive about any of it.* She looked at her watch. *Where the hell is Nelson?*

Sara stepped into the small bathroom and shut the door behind her. She flipped the toilet lid down, and sat down with a sigh. *Here it comes. Don't come. I have to get to my safe place in my head and ward this thing off.* She closed her eyes, and tried to blank her thoughts. She concentrated on taking small even breaths. In, out. In, out. As her breathing took on a measured rhythm, she now turned her mind to conjuring up the vista she had visited so many times before, the place where everything was calm and peaceful. She was lying on a car hood, it was summer and late into the night. Her head and upper back were leaned up against the windshield. The chirping of crickets and the murmurings of other night creatures were the only things breaking the still of the night. In her dream landscape, she opened her eyes to the night sky above, and all of the twinkling stars that it held. She looked for the moon, it was full and had small wisps of clouds passing through its brilliance. She watched the moon for awhile, and the clouds, and then turned her attention to the stars. She looked for familiar formations, she had no idea of the names of the constellations, but she had memorized certain favorite groupings, and she placed them there in her own special version of the night sky. Her breathing became lower, slower. She let herself enjoy the calmed moment, she embraced it, and let it fill her. She could no longer hear the frantic beating of her own heart. She returned her gaze to the moon, and let it settle there.

Chloe wiggled into a corner of the couch in the living room and tucked her feet beneath her. She looked around the warm and apparently well-used room. There were magazines on the coffee table, family pictures on the top of the entertainment center, and a large bookcase that looked like it was a shrine to Nelson and his football skills. Footballs and trophies, certificates and team pictures were on every shelf. Just as Chloe was going to get up and go get a closer look at them, the telephone on the coffee table rang. She started a little and stared at it. *Should I answer it?* Sara was still gone somewhere. The telephone rang a second time. "Sara? You want me to get that?" Chloe called out. No answer. *Nelson's late, maybe it's him.*

Chloe picked it up on the third ring. "Hello, um," Chloe racked her brain for a second, "D'Amico residence. How may I help you?" *Jeez, that's practically how I answer the phone at the library. What a dork I am.*

A short hesitation, and then a young male voice. "Um, this is Nelson. Who's this?"

"Hiya, Nelson. It's Ms. Donahue. I'm just here visiting with your Aunt Sara. I'm not quite sure where she is right this moment."

"Oh, okay, um, I just wanted to ask her something. I called her house and there was no answer, so I figured..." he sounded nervous and disappointed. *Visiting? With Aunt Sara? Since when?*

"Nelson, are you okay? Your dad said you'd be home earlier than this. Is there anything wrong?"

Nelson, standing at a phone booth at the mall, thought this over a second. *I'm pretty sure I told Dad what I was doing tonight.* He shrugged his shoulders. *He must have forgotten.* "Nah, I'm at the mall in Erie, and well, Jeanette and I have enough cash to get into a movie, but I wanted to get something here while I had the chance. I have one of Aunt Sara's credit cards with me, and well, I wanted to call and see if she'd let me get it." *Oh, this conversation is weirding me out.*

"Oh, well, like I said, I don't know where she is at the moment."

He's going to a movie?

"Well, uh, okay then." Silence.

"Nelson, I was going to wait and tell you this in person, but since you aren't going to be home soon, I guess I can tell you now. Get used to being called Curly."

More silence. "Really?" His usually deep voice squeaked in his surprise.

"Really." Chloe smiled. "And since you have Jeanette there with you, you might as well tell her that she's going to be our Laurey, too."

Chloe could hear some muffled pounding sounds. "Nelson?"

"Oh, I'm sorry, I was slapping the side of the phone booth. This is great, really great. Thanks so much. Thank you. Thanks."

"I'm sure you'll be a wonderful Curly, Nelson." *Now if we could just clone you and have you play all the other parts, too.*

"Well, then, maybe I should just go ahead and buy..." Nelson said under his breath.

"What did you want to buy, Nelson?" *Sara's still not back. It's been more than fifteen minutes now. She ditched me.*

"Well, we're at the mall, and we were in this video store, and there are only two copies of *Oklahoma!* left in the store, and I wanted to, kinda..." Nelson felt foolish telling Ms. Donahue that he'd wanted to get the videotape even before he was sure he had the part. "And Bob's Video Shack only has the one copy, and it's always gone."

"So, you wanted to use the credit card and buy one?"

"Yeah." Nelson was glad that Ms. Donahue couldn't see the embarrassed blush on his face.

"Tell you what, Nelson. I'll go out on a limb here and give you the go-ahead. I'll bet Sara won't mind a bit. And tell you what, buy both of them, and give the other one to Jeanette. I'll pay for the second one. That way you'll both have a copy."

"You don't have to do that!" Nelson protested, but grinned at the great idea.

"Well, let's look at it this way, it'll be a payback of sorts."

"Payback?"

"We'll talk about it when you get here. Now go get those tapes before the store closes. And what time do you think you'll be home?" *Soon?*

"Around midnight. I'm not usually out so late on a school night." He apologized, although he didn't know what for.

"Calm down, Nelson, I'm not your parent. Have a good time, and I'll probably be here when you get home." *Unless I start walking now.*

"See you later, Ms. Donahue. And thanks. Thanks again."

"Bye, Nelson."

Nelson hung up and smacked the side of the phone booth wall once again. "Yes!" He scanned the mall hallway, and saw Jeanette walking toward him, shopping bags in both hands. He ran right over to her, put his hands on her waist, lifted the startled girl in the air, and as he set her back down, he leaned over and placed a loud wet kiss on her lips.

"Hell-o, Laurey!" he beamed. "Let's go spend some of my aunt's money!"

"That Nelson?" a contralto voice asked.

Chloe, in the middle of hanging up the phone, nearly knocked the phone off the table when she heard Sara's voice. She looked up to see Sara leaning casually against the hall archway, a tight smile on her face. Chloe studied her a little. *She looks a little calmer now, not so spooked.* She recovered from her surprise, and said, "Yeah, he's in Erie at the mall with Jeanette. They're going to a movie now. They won't be back until midnight or so." Chloe saw the small frown that crossed Sara's features. *Oh, yeah, look at that. She's not pleased with that little bit of information.* Chloe's confusion at Sara's unexplained disappearing act morphed right into defensiveness and she blurted, "Listen, if you want to go home or something, I'm sure I'll be fine until he gets here. I know you didn't expect to have to have to entertain me all evening." *You look like you wish I'd just disappear.*

"Yeah," Sara could see the uncomfortable body language that Chloe was displaying. *I am such an ass.* "I mean, yeah, I didn't expect to have to entertain you. But no, I don't..." *want to go away from you.*

Chloe's mind centered on nothing but the negatives of this little situation. *This evening is just too confusing. This is tiring. I'm tired, this woman disappeared on me, she doesn't want me here. Damned Subaru. Damned Dave and Marcy. Damned Nelson. I could have been home hours ago, and not be dealing with this enigma of a woman.* "Listen, just point me to the remote. I can keep myself company for awhile. And I'll get my clothes out of the laundry room myself," she sounded a little angry, a bit snippy. *Why am I sounding like this?*

"The remote's right beside you. Next to the phone. But..."

"I think I'll get changed now. Those pants should be dry." Chloe stood up from the couch, and hitched the saggy sweats up a little higher. They immediately drooped again. Now frustrated and cranky, Chloe turned and stomped off toward the laundry room.

Sara straightened up in the archway to watch her pass, and folded her arms. *Now what do I do? I just got myself calmed down, and now Chloe is in some kind of a snit. I should just...*

Chloe, still stomping in her socked feet, came out of the kitchen with her pants and socks and blew right by Sara without looking at her. Sara heard the bathroom door behind her close. *Do I stay or do I go? Maybe Chloe is having second thoughts. Maybe she has just come to her senses.* Sara snorted. *Yeah, that's it. I was just about to tell her that she was the one that was entertaining me, and she gets all cranky with me. Well, the hell with that. I've got enough problems.* She walked out and stood in the kitchen, waiting for Chloe to reappear.

Chloe flushed the toilet and washed her hands in the sink. *Why am I acting this way? The poor woman just needed a little space, is all. Neither one of us expected to be spending more than ten minutes in each other's company tonight, and all of a sudden, it turned into date night. I should talk to her instead of just trying to blow her off and out of here. She probably thinks I'm some kind of nut. I need to apologize. Maybe she does. This is so frustrating. Where would we even go from here?* Chloe put on her khakis and socks, and then carefully folded the sweatpants and thermal socks. She stacked the clothes over an arm, and exited the bathroom.

Sara wasn't in the living room, so Chloe went into the kitchen. Sara was standing near the sink, her coat in hand. Chloe stopped, looked at her, then looked away. *She's really going.* "Thanks for the use of the dry clothes. I'll just put these in there."

Sara shuffled her feet a little. "About your car?"

Chloe came back out of the laundry room but didn't make eye contact with Sara when she said, "That's all right. I'll hitch a ride home with Nelson tonight, and have someone from the dealership come tow it tomorrow. Dave shouldn't have imposed on you on my behalf." She paused and looked into Sara's eyes. "I'm sorry." *I mean that not only for the car, but for the way I've been acting, too. Why can't I say that out loud?*

No, I'm the one who's sorry. Sara tried to say it with her eyes, but her mouth finally slipped into gear. "No, uh, I was just thinking that it would be too late for Nelson to tow it tonight. Would it be all right if he brought it here tomorrow, after school?" *Does she really want me to go?* "I'd really like to look at it for you, Chloe, it'd be a nice change of pace from working on the tractor. I probably could have it done by late Thursday. Dave or Nelson could probably bring it out to you." *Because I can't.* She watched as Chloe pondered her answer. *Please say yes.*

Chloe took a step toward Sara, then abruptly changed direction and stooped to grab her boots near the radiator. "Sara, that's nice of you, but I think it would be easier—"

Sara interrupted her, saying, "Look, Chloe, nothing's ever easy.

Nothing worthwhile, anyway." She shut her mouth firmly, and waited.

Chloe stood up, boots in hand, and met Sara's blue eyes boring into her. "Okay." She hesitated, then took a small breath. "But I want it back detailed and waxed, just like they do for me at the dealership." She felt the tight muscles in her cheek relax, and let a grin spring forth.

"Oh, you do, do you?" Sara tossed her coat back onto the chair. "Spit shined?" she inquired, an eyebrow and a corner of her mouth rising in perfect unison.

"I doubt you have that much spit. It's a station wagon. And if you could fix all the rust on it, too," Chloe challenged, the gleam returning to her eyes.

"I have just the thing for that right here in the fridge. Moldy cottage cheese. Takes the rust off of everything."

"Nah, you better save it, Nelson might be hungry when he gets home."

"Why don't we go into the living room and you can tell me what you were talking to Nelson about."

When Nelson came home just after midnight, his face was flushed with all the excitement from the night. He had *Oklahoma!* in hand, he was Curly, and he was feeling a little warm from the goodnight kiss that he had shared with Jeanette. When he pulled up, he saw the living room dark except for the glow from the TV. He took his boots off at the kitchen door, and softly tiptoed into the living room. There he saw two beautiful creatures, asleep on the couch lit in the bluish light being cast from the television. He walked closer, and viewed his Aunt Sara, sitting slouched with her feet on the coffee table, softly snoring. And Ms. Donahue, her reddish hair tinted almost violet from the blue light, was lying on her side with her head just inches from Sara's hip. She had one arm stretched and her hand was lightly resting on Sara's knee. Sara's right hand was softly perched on top of it, gently clasping it. Nelson grinned. *I have to get up really early anyway. I'll leave them be.* He grabbed a couple of afghans and quietly covered them both. He turned off the TV with the remote, and headed off to bed.

Part V:
If I Were Rational, Would I Be Spending My Time Talking to You?

Chloe yawned again. Thank God it's Friday, and I have this weekend off. I think I just want to crawl into bed for two days. I can feel it coming on. I feel all bloated and cranky, and yesterday I literally wanted to bite someone. She looked across to Marcy, who had once again gallantly picked up Chloe and was hauling her to work at the library before she continued on to her day teaching at the high school. Good thing that neither of them were morning people. If Marcy'd been babbling right now, Chloe would have had to drive the car off the road and toss her into a ditch.

It was raining, more of a sleet, and the slow back and forth of the windshield wipers lulled Chloe back to sleep.

"Wake up, Miss Sunshine. Heigh-ho! It's off to work you go."

Chloe slowly opened her eyes, and saw they were parked in front of the library. Marcy, still bleary-eyed, looked like she had made quite the effort just getting that statement out. Chloe blinked a few times, and grabbed her canvas briefcase from the back seat. They looked at each other, thinking they should say something, then both gave up and shrugged.

"Have a good day," Marcy said, with not much hope in her voice.

"Yeah, you too. Thanks for the ride. Call me at lunchtime."

Once Chloe was in the library, she looked around and saw a large stack of returned books on a small cart. She looked at the large clock over the check out desk. *Oh God, I have over an hour before the library opens. Maybe I can catch some more sleep. I'll just stretch out on one of the large tables in the reference section.* She took off her coat and stowed it in the small closet in her office. *On second thought, if I fall asleep, I'll never wake up, and well, it would be bad for one of the patrons to find the town librarian curled up on the table near the encyclopedias. I guess I'll make a pot of coffee and use the extra time before opening to do a little more planning for the play.* She'd heard from all of the kids cast in the play since the list had been posted on Wednesday. They all had called her at home, or stopped in at the library. She could hear excitement in their voices, and see it in their eyes. If enthusiasm alone was going to make this play successful, Chloe was sure that it was going to be a smash hit. Each student had been instructed to pick up their copy of the script from Mrs. Raeburn's office and read it over the weekend. Then, on Tuesday, they would all meet to discuss rehearsal schedules, and have preliminary measurements taken for the costumes they were going to wear. Luckily, most of the boys could just wear blue jeans in the play. It was the girls whose costumes would be the most difficult, it wasn't like anyone had long schoolmarm dresses hanging in their closets. *Okay, well, maybe Paul does.* Chloe snickered to herself. *That guy is so hard to peg.* He still lived with his mom, never had a date that anyone heard of, and although Marcy had insisted for years that Paul had an unrequited crush on Chloe, he had never shown one bit of inclination to follow through on it.

There were boots and Stetson hats yet to be found. She was going to have to call some of the neighboring high schools in the area and see if she could raid their prop rooms. The area schools did this regularly, borrowing costumes and props from each other when ever the need arose. It was much cheaper that way. And something close to the most important prop in this play, the infamous "surrey with the fringe on the top" could probably be found in one of the neighboring barns here around town.

Marcy, who was in charge of costuming as well as the props for the play, had extensively lobbied for a real live horse to pull the surrey. Chloe, being practical before all else, had vehemently argued against this.

"A real horse? Are you going to sweep up after it?" said Chloe, unsure if her friend's brain was hitting on all four cylinders.

"It'll look so much more realistic than a cardboard cutout, or even a couple of kids in a horse suit."

"And where are we going to keep it until it makes its appearances, in your car?" Chloe was once again picking on Marcy's little red Miata.

"Listen, you're the director. You are in charge of these little details. You figure it out. I'm the creative director here, I can't be bothered. I just supply the vision."

"You need your vision checked, then, Marcy."

"Can't you just see Nelson riding in on a big black stallion, next to the gently waving plastic corn stalks, while the beach ball painted yellow is climbing slowly into the sky? What an entrance that will be."

"He can walk next to the damned cornstalks."

"Oh yeah, there ya go. A cowboy walking along. Like he got his license taken away after some drunken horse-driving after a big barn dance?"

"We can work around it," Chloe huffed.

"There are so many scenes that require a horse in this play. He sells the damned horse near the end of it. You think people are going to believe that some cowboy is going to bid good money to buy something that looks like two high school sophomores in a Mr. Ed suit?" Marcy was right. And she knew it, and was being smug about it.

I hate her when she's right. "All right then, we'll both start putting out some feelers about a horse. But if it gets complicated, I'm pulling the plug on this thing." Chloe scratched her chin thoughtfully. "You sure a pony won't do?"

"Oh, yeah, Nelson is what, six foot two? His knees will be dragging on the floor, and someone will call the humane society on us."

So the horse, wherever and if they could find one, seemed now to be part of the play. *If that horse takes even one crap on the stage floor during a performance, I am personally going to make Marcy go out there and shovel it up. Now there's a thought. I hope it does do its business, during every performance and twice during the matinee.*

Chloe remained at the front desk, working, until noon, when Mrs. Cellone, one of the senior volunteers for the library, arrived. Chloe chit-chatted with her a little bit, and then went back into her office to make some phone calls. She found some cowboy hats and boots at one of the larger high schools in Erie, and even some of the longer dresses she needed for the girls. She could go pick them up this weekend and have them for the kids to try on when they came in on Tuesday. Well, she could go pick the stuff up if her car was ready.

She made a decision, opened up her little address book and dialed a number. She felt a little nervous as she heard the phone ringing. A little nervous bloomed right into a lot nervous when she heard the phone answered.

"Hello."

"Hey, Sara. How are you doing today?" *She has such a wonderful voice.*

Sara, who normally hated answering the phone, brightened when she realized it was Chloe. "Hey there. I was just going to call you. Car's all done."

"Really? That's great. I need to get into Erie to pick a few things up for the play this weekend. Cowboy hats and such." Chloe switched the phone from one hand to the other, and wiped her free hand on her pants. Her palms got sweaty just from talking to Sara on the phone.

"When did you want to come get it? This afternoon?" Sara said, not disguising the hopefulness in her voice.

"I probably can get Marcy to run me by after she gets done with school. Would that be all right?"

"That would be more than all right."

"Are you going to be there when we swing by, or—"

"Sure, I'll be here." *Where else would I be?* "See you then."

"'Til then."

It had only taken Sara about half an hour to put the rebuilt starter into the car that morning. She'd ordered the part on Thursday. It hadn't arrived until this morning, so she had used the time in the last day or so to do some maintenance work on the old Subaru. She even patched some of the more troubling rust spots. Chloe and Marcy probably wouldn't be there until after 5:00, so she thought she could do some of that spit-shining Chloe wanted done. *It would be a nice surprise for her. I want to do nice things for her. I don't know when I'll see her again. I suppose I could just ask her, but—*

Sara's mind flashed back to Wednesday morning, when she awoke on the couch next to Chloe. Nelson was gently nudging her shoulder. The living room was dimly lit by the light coming from the kitchen. She opened her eyes to see Nelson grinning at her, and pointing to the couch beside her.

There was Chloe, a fist under her cheek for a pillow, and her other hand resting on Sara's hip in a bit of a vise grip. Sara's hand was touching hers. She looked at the soft red hair, and the peaceful expression Chloe wore in her sleep. Sara sheepishly looked back up at Nelson. Nelson nodded at her, and whispered, "Does she need a ride?" When Sara nodded in the affirmative, Nelson continued in a hushed tone, "I'm going to have to get her out there now, then, because I need to do some stuff around here, and then go pick up Jeanette for school." Sara again nodded, and returned her gaze to the snoozing Chloe.

"Chloe?" Sara softly stroked the hand that was holding onto her leg. "Chloe?"

A small rustle and a "don' wanna." Chloe's hand involuntarily gripped Sara's thigh harder, and ended up goosing her.

"Chloe!" Sara squeaked. "Wake up. Nelson needs to take you home now."

The hand that Chloe had resting under her cheek snaked out and slid under Sara's thigh. Way up high on the inside of Sara's thigh. The hand on top of her thigh reached farther northward and her fingers interlaced. Chloe pulled her head toward her new cushion, and settled in there, her head much more comfortable and her hands so much warmer now. "Inna minute."

Sara was feeling quite warm herself as Chloe's clasped hands twitched gently in her sleep. She would have been enjoying all of it if Nelson hadn't been hovering there with a huge grin on his face, taking in the show. Sara trained an evil eye on Nelson, and lowly growled, "Give me a minute here, Nelson, if you don't mind."

Nelson whispered back, "I don't mind. Not a bit." He sauntered up the hallway and into his bedroom to continue dressing.

With a bit more gentle encouragement from Sara, a half-awake and totally mortified Chloe finally realized where she was and what she'd been doing. To cover, Chloe feigned terminal drowsiness and an inability to form words, which actually wasn't far from the truth. She put on her boots, and allowed Sara to help her into her coat. She nodded a sleepy farewell to Sara, and followed Nelson out to his truck, which thankfully was pulled close to the house, so she didn't have to navigate any pond-size puddles. Sara watched from the darkened porch door, and grinned when she saw Chloe make several unsuccessful attempts to step up onto the high running board to get into the truck. *She really needs to make a running start to make it.* Nelson, ever the gentleman and patiently holding the door open for her, took pity on her and boosted her on her third try.

Sara wistfully watched the truck pull out in the early morning darkness, and waved a small goodbye even though she knew no one could see her.

Sara was singing show tunes at the top of her lungs, and rubbing a smudge off the hood of the Subaru with a chamois. She stepped back and surveyed her work. *Not bad, not bad at all.* She gave a final polish to the windshield, and wiped her hands on her coveralls.

When Nelson towed the car home on Wednesday, it took Sara only two turns of the ignition and a quick peek under the hood to know that the starter was shot, and needed to be replaced. A rather simple job, but probably expensive if Chloe had sent the car to the dealership to be repaired. It was too late in the day to call and order the part she needed, so she waited and called first thing on Thursday morning. The rebuilt part was overnighted to her, and with shipping, came to only just a little more than fifty dollars. She changed the oil and air filter for her, too, and checked the plugs and did some adjustments. Sara figured she saved Chloe a couple of hundred dollars. *So, maybe I can't cook as a way to get to Chloe's heart, maybe I can give her beloved big Subaru some extra TLC as a way of showing...whatever I'm trying to show.* She took one last walk around the car, dragged the rag once more over the "Girls Kick Ass" bumper sticker on the rear bumper, and grinned a satisfied smile. She looked at her watch. *Four o'clock. Probably another hour before she gets here.* Sara figured she could sit and take a load off a few minutes, then go get cleaned up. She took a quick glance of her face in the dirty mirror on the worktable, and smiled again when she saw the streaks of grease and oil across her face. *Yup, gotta get cleaned up.*

She heard Nelson's truck stop in the driveway, and ducked her head out of the garage to wave at him. To her surprise, it looked like he had a smallish passenger with him. *Chloe! I thought she was coming with Marcy later.* Determined to look unfazed, she decided to hold her ground and fight back the desire to duck back into the garage. *Move your feet, Sara.* She strode over to the passenger side of Nelson's truck, and opened the door for her. She lifted a chivalrous hand out to a smiling Chloe, who took hold of her hand, and hopped down.

"Easier for you to get out of Nelson's truck than get into it, huh, Chloe?" said Sara with a tease in her low voice.

When did she see me struggle to get into—oh, no, the other morning. She was watching? Chloe stood next to Sara and playfully gave her a nudge with her elbow. "I really need a pole vault to get into this thing. God, I hate heights."

"Um, you're a tad early, aren't you?" asked Sara, as they watched Nelson come around the truck toward them.

"I stopped at the library to see her, and she mentioned she was coming out here to get her car, so—" Nelson interjected.

"—he gallantly suggested I come with him. I was dying to get out of there today so, naturally, I said 'Hell yeah!'" Chloe nudged Sara again and scanned her face. "You look a little like Daniel Day-Lewis in The Last of the Mohicans."

"I'll take that as a compliment," Sara said as she self-consciously wiped at her face, but only made things worse. She now had large smears across her cheeks. "C'mon into the garage, I've got a rag in there, I can get some of this wiped off."

Nelson waved off Chloe's words of thanks, and headed on into the house. Sara put out her arm for Chloe to hold and said, "Allow me to escort you around the mine field." Chloe put a light hand on Sara's bicep, and Sara consciously made her steps smaller to accommodate Chloe's shorter legs.

"Oh my God! She looks wonderful!" crowed Chloe, when she saw the gleaming automobile in front of her. "She could pass for an '89 or even a '90!" She looked up at Sara, whose blushes were only minimally camouflaged by the grease and dirt on her face. "Thank you so much! I haven't seen her look this good in years!" She looked thoughtfully at the car, and then turned to look up at Sara. "Maybe now would be the time to trade her in, while she's running and has had a bit of a makeover."

Sara, teeth showing in all their glory, answered back, "Nah, she has another 100,000 miles in her, especially if you keep taking care of her." *Especially if you let me take care of her.*

"And you really went through with the spit shine!" Chloe laughed again at the dirt on Sara's face. "And speaking of spit shine, why don't you sit on that stool over there, and let me get that war paint off of your face. You look kind of scary."

Sara grabbed a clean rag, and let Chloe lead her over to the low stool. The low height of the stool put Sara's eyes just about at Chloe's chin level. Chloe took the rag, and gently began dabbing at the spots on Sara's face. Chloe lifted and held Sara's chin in her left hand, and their eyes met.

Chloe, gently caressing Sara's face with the soft rag, murmured, "So how is my baby today?"

Sara, totally on her way to heaven, was unsure if Chloe meant her, or the car. "Um, she's okay, she's glad you're here. I think she was missing you."

"You do, huh?" Chloe was glad that Sara had caught on to her little double meaning. "Well, the feeling is mutual." She daubed one more time at Sara's almost clean face and gently smiled. "I'm afraid that's the best I can do. A hot shower will probably do the rest."

A cold shower is what I need right now. "Uh, yeah. I thought I had time before you showed up."

"Sorry I was the early bird. I just really wanted to get out of there today. I had absolutely no patience today, for some odd reason. And Nelson and I got to talk about the play, and our search for a horse."

"You're looking for a horse? For the play?" Sara shook her head in amusement. "You really like trouble, don't you?" It was her turn for a little double meaning.

"Oh yeah, can't seem to stay away from it." Chloe could give it as good as she could take it, so she decided to give it all she had. "I think I absolutely crave it." She drew out the word "crave" so it nearly had three syllables to it.

Sara grabbed the edges of the stool just to keep herself from falling off of it. *All right, already, anymore of this teasing and I'm going to toss her into the big back seat of that Subaru and...make her refold all my maps.*

Chloe decided that since she had Sara at a bit of a mushed-out, pile-of-quivering-goo disadvantage, she would take a chance and bring up the idea that she had been mulling over in her head most of the afternoon.

"Um, Sara, I have to leave pretty soon," Chloe stepped away from her, not wanting to see the expression on Sara's face when she asked, "I was wondering if you would go with me to Erie tomorrow to pick up the costumes from Tech High?" Chloe kept her back to Sara, not wanting to put any pressure on her.

Sara's autonomic nervous system shouted out an immediate internal "No! I never go anywhere, unless it's with Dave or Nelson. They know me, they know what to do." Sara didn't answer; she just watched Chloe, who still wasn't looking at her, and was walking around her car instead, checking it out.

Chloe stopped and looked at a newly patched rust spot and smiled. *I'm not going to look at her, I'm just going to take her not saying anything as a good sign.* "Listen, Sara. I probably shouldn't be saying this, but," Chloe took a big swallow and continued, "I know you have some difficulties. My guess is that you have a problem with your nerves, and maybe this is simplifying things too much, you let me know, but that problem you might have with anxiety...maybe you don't feel like leaving here very often." Chloe finally looked at Sara, who was sitting stiffly on the stool, and Sara's blank face simply nodded at Chloe. "You can tell me if I'm wrong, or way off base here, Sara. But you have to excuse me, and I have to apologize in advance for Marcy. Marcy told me about the day she met you." Chloe saw a quick stricken look cross Sara's features and then her face returned to its former passive state. "I'm probably making you very uncomfortable right now, just talking about it. But Sara, again, you have to excuse me, well, I tried to guess what you—what your—what you were going through that day that you met Marcy, and well, hell, I work in a library, Sara. I read everything I could about what I thought might be—am I even close here? Give me a sign."

Sara swallowed hard and nodded.

Chloe, unable to gauge how Sara was reacting to this line of conversation, bravely went forward. "Sara, I did the reading because I hoped we could become friends. Not because I was being nosy, but I have to admit, the day I asked Marcy how she met you, well, that day I was being extremely nosy. I guess I'm just as nebby as the next person. I guess I just don't want you to get mad at me now, for the combination of my curiosity, and well, my interest in you. I was just hoping to spend some time with you, Sara. To get to know you better, and if I'm going about it the wrong way, by asking you to go somewhere with me, let me know now, and I won't bring it up again until you do."

Sara looked down at the garage floor and didn't answer Chloe. She felt her heart rate increasing, and a multitude of emotions flowed through her. Her mind formed many thoughts, none of which reached her lips in reply to the waiting Chloe. *No! It's none of your business, I don't want to go anywhere with you, I'm perfectly happy the way I am. I don't want to scare you away. Wait 'til I see that Marcy again. Take your goddamned Subaru and get off the property. And don't come back.* She closed her eyes, and tried to still her thoughts. In, out. In, out.

Chloe just couldn't hold it in any longer. She wasn't the most patient of souls, even though she know this was the time for her to be extra patient. "Sara, what I'm saying here is, whatever you need, whatever you need me to do to make you feel comfortable with me, I'd like to try and do it. Just let me know, Sara. Give me a chance." She tried to lighten what was a very tense time with a very lame joke. "Unless of course, it involves some kind of weird voodoo rituals involving live chickens, that's where I draw the line." She smiled so hopefully at Sara that Sara couldn't help but feel some of her tension dissipate and scatter in the light of Chloe's earnestness. Chloe felt her own anxiety level raising. *Damn, she's just staring at me. Even after that stupid joke. Why did I open my big fat mouth?* Chloe dejectedly stuffed her hands into her coat pockets, hung her head and sighed.

Sara pushed her shoulders back and stretched. She slowly stood up, and chewed on the inside of her cheek. She smiled a little ruefully at Chloe, who looked up, and Sara could see the uncertainty in her eyes. In a voice as rusted as the Subaru's front bumper, Sara said, "You are a brave soul, Chloe." She cleared her throat and continued. "You're right, I do have difficulties, and I would like to trust you with them. I don't want to go into all the details right here, right now, but I'll tell you this: if you can live with a couple of unbreakable ground rules, then, yeah, I think I'd like to go to Erie with you tomorrow." *Although you might have your hands full.*

Chloe, relieved, but not sure as yet if she had done the right thing, said seriously, "Can I ask what those ground rules might be?"

Sara's mind went into automatic, she knew her rules so well. "You have to do what I ask, when I ask, no questions asked. Chloe, when I get an attack, I feel very out of control. So the person that I am with has to be able to just give control over to me. It helps me feel more in control when I feel out of control. It's really pretty simple. If I feel an attack coming on, and I ask you to pull the car over, you don't question me, you just do it. If I tell you not to talk to me, not to touch me, you don't do it. If I ask to leave wherever we are, we do it. Right away. If I feel like walking away or being by myself, you give me my space until I get back. You have to understand, it's not me trying to tell you what to do, I'm not trying to control you, I'm just doing what it takes for me to get through what can be a very lousy time for me." Sara looked carefully into Chloe's eyes, searching for some understanding, some acceptance of what she had said.

She found it there.

"I think I understand. You need to feel safe with me. I want you to feel that way with me, Sara," Chloe vowed, and then tried to bring a smile to an obviously tense woman. "And the live chickens?"

"Nope. None of those." Sara suddenly felt exhausted from the conversation, the honesty it took, and the fear of what might occur tomorrow. *I can do this. Well, at least I want to try. That's got to count for something, doesn't it?* "No more live chickens. The meds I take took all the fun out of that."

Chloe couldn't stop her feet from crossing the garage, nor could she stop her arms from wrapping around Sara in a tight hug. She felt Sara's arms around her, returning the hug.

They stood holding each other for a long time.

Nelson heard Ms. Donahue's Subaru leave the driveway. He tossed on a hooded sweatshirt, and wandered out to the garage. Sara looked a little shell-shocked, like she had just fought a long battle with some unknown enemy. She barely noticed him enter, and gave him a weak smile of acknowledgment.

"I'm going to Erie tomorrow, Nelson. To get a Stetson hat to fit that big fat head of yours so you can make an ass out of yourself in that play."

Nelson wasn't quite cluing in to what Sara was saying. "I'm taking you to Erie tomorrow?" Sara shook her head, no. "Dad's taking you to Erie tomorrow?" Again, no.

"One more strike, Nelson, and you're out."

"Uh," said Nelson. *Huh, not me, not Dad, then who or how?*

Finally, the lights went on in Nelson's icebox. "Ms. Donahue?"

She gave him a sheepish shrug in acknowledgment.

Nelson couldn't quite believe it. "Really?"

Neither could Sara. "Yeah, really."

"Well, well, well." *This is cool. I really like Chlo—um, Ms. Donahue.*

"That's a deep subject there, Nelson. And hey, Nelson, when's the last time you were on a horse?"

"Me? Never. Unless you count the merry-go-round at the county fair about ten years ago."

Sara clapped a hand on Nelson's shoulder. "Well, home boy, it's time for you to saddle up."

"So I've heard. Not only do I have to sing, and dance, I have to try and not fall off a horse."

"I think the falling off the horse part is the least of your problems."

Nelson knew where this was leading. "We still have to tell Dad."

"Yup. You do."

"But I thought you were going to help me tell him? I think he might take it better if you're there." *And I'm in the next county.*

"Since when has your father ever been on his best behavior in front of me? Not gonna happen."

"Yeah, but I may have been a little kid at the time, but I remember his reaction to finding out you were acting. 'My sister the thespian.'"

"Yeah?" Sara snickered.

"And it wasn't pretty, let me tell you." Nelson rolled his eyes in remembrance.

"Probably as pretty as when I told him I was gay. I think it broke his heart."

Nelson was a little baffled by this and replied, "But he seems so good about it now."

"That's now. I think he wanted me to marry his best friend, Stan, so he would have someone to buddy around with all his life. Man, was he pissed."

"Stan, of Stan's Bar and Grill?"

"That's the one. Just think of it, I could be happily grilling kielbasa and emptying the jukebox of quarters every Saturday night."

"Sounds like you're really disappointed."

"Oh, I am. Damned genes that made me this way." She cracked a sarcastic smile. "But you're right, he really gave me an earful when I was doing that little cop show on cable. And I had to wear those little skimpy outfits, remember? They had me playing an undercover whore every week. He was upset that all these men were pawing his little sister on national TV!" She shook her head at the memory.

"I remember. He wouldn't even let me watch that show. Said I shouldn't be seeing my Aunt Sara 'running around half naked.'" Nelson scowled. "See what I mean? He's such a control freak! He's going to go ballistic about this acting thing."

Sara put a consoling arm around his shoulder. "I'll be there for you, Nelson, when you want to tell him. I'll be hiding under a table, but I'll be there for you."

"Aunt Sara?"

"Hmm?"

"I wish I was gay. At least I know he'd take that better."

Sara and Nelson were in the kitchen, tossing containers from the fridge into the garbage can. They were just finishing up when Dave walked in, a bottle of wine in his hand.

"Hello, my dear little family!" Dave practically was oozing happiness from every pore.

"Nelson, go to your room. Your dad has got his 'Love Groove' face on, and you're still too young to witness it. As a matter of fact, I'm too young to have to live through it."

"Got a date tonight, Dad?"

"How'd you guess?" Dave felt like tap dancing.

"It's either that, or you're going to kill off that bottle watching "The Brady Brunch" reruns on cable tonight," Sara quipped.

"Maybe next time. This time, I am going to go spend a lovely evening with Marcy. Dinner, dancing, and then we head back to her place for—"

Sara jumped in, "A marathon Scrabble tournament!"

Dave harrumphed and opened the fridge to put the bottle in to chill. "Hey, the fridge is practically empty. What are we doing for food this weekend?"

"We were just going to ask you the same thing. Nelson and I were just going to throw together a little supper consisting of dill pickles and Cheez Whiz." Sara cocked an eye at him. "Don't look so upset, there's enough for all of us."

"I told you, I'm eating out tonight. Sorry I can't share in the feast. I suppose I can stop on my way back from Marcy's tomorrow and pick a few things up."

Sara leaned up and clapped her hands over Nelson's ears, but not so tightly that he couldn't hear her say, "Tomorrow? You're not planning on coming back until tomorrow? What will your sweet, naïve child think you are doing if you don't come back until tomorrow?" she tsked at him through her teeth.

"He'll think that his dad is having one hell of an all-night Scrabble game," said Nelson, with a sweet, naïve look plastered on his face.

Dave cuffed his son and said, "Watch it there, sonny. You're not so big that I can't still tie you up and sell you off at some roadside stand to some retired couple driving a Winnebago. Like I did that one summer." Dave wore a beatific glow on his face. "Now if you don't mind, the Love Man has got to go shower and shave for his Scrabble tournament." He sauntered past them and headed for the bathroom.

Nelson took another look into the fridge, and then slammed the door. "Pizza tonight?"

"No date tonight?"

"Nope, Jeanette's doing the girl thing tonight. Whatever that is."

I'm not gonna comment on that. I wish I was doing the girl thing tonight.

Nelson was just getting off the kitchen phone after ordering pizzas when he turned and froze. Sara, who was sitting at the kitchen table, sipping some iced tea, saw the look on his face and then she froze, too. They heard a strange sound wafting through the living room, from the bathroom.

Nelson's eyes looked like he'd just taken his fifth ride in a row on the world's biggest roller coaster as he recognized the tune Dave was singing in the shower, a very familiar melody to both Sara and Nelson. Hearing Dave's baritone continue to ring out more of the title song to the musical his son was shortly to star in perplexed both Nelson and Sara. *What? How?* Jumbled thoughts went quickly through both their minds.

They heard the shower stop, but the singing continued on until it progressively got louder.

"What?" Dave was now standing before them, towel wrapped around his middle, and using another towel to rub his hair dry.

"I know my singing is overpowering, jeez, give a guy a break." Both Nelson and Sara were staring at him, open-mouthed.

He grabbed a beer out of the fridge, popped it open, and strolled back out of the room.

Nelson pinched himself, it was the only thing he could think of to do to make sure he wasn't in some sort of a twilight zone. Sara saw him do this, and attuned to what he was thinking, stretched out an arm for him to pinch, too. He did.

"Ouch!"

"Okay, how do you explain this, Aunt Sara?"

"Alternate universe?" queried Sara. When she saw that Nelson wasn't buying that explanation, she tried another. "Marcy?"

"Nah, I think Ms. Donahue told her not to tell. At least I told her to tell her not to tell. It's hard to tell. Do you think Ms. Donahue told her not to tell and she told anyways?"

"Nelson, you are making me dizzy with all these 'tells' and 'tolds.' No, there has to be another explanation."

Both of them crinkled their foreheads in thought. Just when they thought they might be hurting themselves from thinking so hard, Nelson blurted, "I know!"

Sara was relieved, and her face showed it. *Another thirty seconds of that, and the blood would have stopped flowing to my brain permanently.* "So, what is it?"

"I used Dad's truck to tow Chl—Ms. Donahue's car the other day. I left my *Oklahoma!* CD in the player. He's been listening to it for a couple of days now, I bet."

Sara was inordinately relieved not to be living in an alternate universe. *This one is tough enough to deal with.* "Well, Nels, since he seems to have *Oklahoma!* on the brain, what say we go for it before he leaves for his date?" She figured she could hunker down under the kitchen table when the canisters started flying across the room. Nelson's face showed his trepidation. "Don't worry, I won't leave you." *You can duck under the table with me.*

Nelson briefly considered asking if maybe he could just move in with her, and then figured that his dad could just hunt him down there, too. "All right. Enough avoiding this, I guess." He hitched his hands in his belt loops, and straightened up. "Let's do it."

A nattily dressed Dave came back into the kitchen, stinking of aftershave and a self-satisfied grin on his face. He grabbed the bottle of wine out of the refrigerator and noticed that both Nelson and Sara were staring at him intently. "What? Does my hair look funny or something?"

"Well, other than the fact that you overdosed on your stud muffin cologne yet one more time, yeah, there is something your son here wanted to discuss with you." She pointed at Nelson. "Speak now, or forever hold your peace."

Dave looked expectantly at Nelson, who looked like he had lost the power of speech. "Well, what is it?"

"Well, listen, Dad. I need you to listen to what I have to say here. Without interruption. Can you do that?" Nelson wanted this guarantee because he knew he would never get through it otherwise.

Oh great. I'm going to be a grandfather at the ripe old age of forty. "Okay, sure. What?" Dave put on his "Mr. Patient" face.

"All right. Here's the thing. You know you were just singing "Oklahoma" in the shower, right? Anyway, that's what the senior class play is this year. *Oklahoma!* Aunt Sara and I were practicing it, she was helping," Nelson thought it best to spread the blame around, right at the very start, "and I tried out for the lead in it. Chlo—Ms. Donahue is directing. I tried out for the lead, and got the part. I'm going to be Curly, and Jeanette is going to be Laurey. I'm going to act. I have to ride a horse too, if we can find one. Otherwise, I'll just have to stroll along or something." Nelson stopped, because he totally had lost his train of thought. "Or something," he repeated.

Dave looked at him doubtfully. "And you're telling me this because you think getting the lead in a school play is a bad thing?"

Nelson shook his head, and did his best to clarify his jumbled thinking. "Well, it's not just that, Dad, it's this acting thing, and the football thing, too. I mean, I like playing football, I really do, but I think I might like pursuing this acting thing too. In college, I mean. Depending on how well I do in this play. Aunt Sara thinks I'm pretty good," he turned his attention to Sara, who was edging closer to the kitchen table, "and she's been helping me a lot and I've been thinking for quite awhile about this acting and college and football and—"

Dave brusquely interrupted by placing a hand on Nelson's shoulder.

Nelson flinched. *Here it comes.*

"Nelson," Dave began quietly, "Who's to say you can't do both in college? You've got four years there. Quit being such a worrywart.

Try 'em both."

"Huh?" said Nelson. *But that makes such perfect sense.*

Dave straightened his tie, looked at his watch and said, "The lead, huh? Way to go. Can't wait to see you dancing. That should be one for the memory book." He hugged Nelson around the shoulders and then waved his watch at the both of them. "Gotta fly. See you both tomorrow." He winked broadly, and went out the door, whistling.

Sara turned to a dumbstruck Nelson and stuck out her arm. "Pinch me again. I'm still not sure about the alternate universe theory."

Part VI:
That Horny Feeling

They'd been traveling on the lakeside road for some twenty minutes. For the first ten of those, Chloe had nervously babbled about where they were going, and what they needed to pick up. Sometime later, after hearing not a word from Sara in return, Chloe mentally zipped her lip. *Maybe all this yakking is making it worse for her. God knows she looks like I'm hauling her to a funeral as it is.* Chloe leaned forward and fiddled with the buttons on the radio, which was playing so faintly that she couldn't tell if there was music or a call-in talk show on. She snuck a peek at Sara, who was in the same position as when they'd first left. She was just staring out her passenger window. A cold rain was falling, and as it was a dark and dismal day Chloe turned the headlights on. The farmland fell away from view, and the outskirts of Erie appeared, quickly dotted with fast-food restaurants and shopping centers. The traffic increased, and stoplights impeded their progress. The waiting at stoplights made the quiet even more disconcerting, because Chloe couldn't find anything to do during these extended stops except idly drum her fingers on the steering wheel, or pretend to be interested in reading gas station signage. Chloe let a driver, with a large muttly dog in the back seat, pull into traffic in front of her. The dog, quite manic, was pacing back and forth, slobbering on the rear window.

"I think you could have your horse problem solved right there," Sara murmured and she nodded toward the giant canine in the car in front of them.

Chloe snapped her attention to Sara's quietly smiling face. "Well, hello there, stranger."

Sara brushed her palm from Chloe's shoulder down to her elbow. "Thanks for letting me get my bearings. I think I can rejoin the land of the living now."

"And such a lovely land it is, too." Chloe leaned forward, and scanned the scene before her. "Looks like everyone is heading for one of the 'Marts today. K or Wal. When's the last time you were in the big 'burg of Erie?"

Sara thought about it. "Probably right before I left for college. I haven't had a reason to come here since. Still looks exactly the same, nothing but miles of car dealerships, stores, restaurants and bad roads."

"Dreary Erie, the mistake on the lake."

Sara smiled at the familiar moniker. "We used to come out here on the weekends, to the Peninsula, and lie on the beach all day. When I was in high school, we had some pretty awesome parties there, too. You know, I lived in California for a time, pretty near the ocean. It was beautiful, but there's just something different about the ocean smell. It's good, but I prefer freshwater lakes to the ocean. Maybe it's because of growing up so close to Lake Erie. No matter where I've lived, I've always been more comfortable knowing there was a lake or ocean nearby."

"Rivers just don't cut it, huh?"

"A river can be nice, especially for fishing. Do you fish at all?" Sara inquired.

"A few times, when I was little. I remember my dad getting his hook caught in my hair and me screaming bloody murder."

They had made it out of the more congested retail areas, and were heading into the residential part of town. Sara saw a familiar landmark and pointed it out to Chloe. "I dated a girl from that high school when I was a senior. I met her at a basketball tournament. I was guarding her. We beat them pretty badly, but she came and watched the rest of our games." Sara's face took on a melancholy expression. "I wonder what ever became of her."

"You were dating girls in high school? Huh. I didn't officially start dating women until my second year at college." Chloe made a left turn, and they headed south from the lake. "I dated a bazillion boys up until then. I would date them for a month, they would get all antsy, and then I would just toss them away. I never wanted to sleep with them, I just wanted to, I dunno, hang around them, have fun with them. Then all that romantic B.S. would sneak in and ruin all my fun." Chloe laughed at the memory, and then asked, "Whatever happened to the girl from that school?"

"She went off to college, I went off to my college, we wrote, we called, and then it just petered out. Kind of hard being that young and that far away to keep anything going for long."

Chloe nodded in agreement. "The woman I met, Sandy, well, we went our separate ways after college. She was pretty heavily recruited by some companies out west. She was a whiz business major. I'll bet she has a pretty good life right now." Chloe's mind tried to picture her ex-love.

"You didn't want to go with her? Or didn't she ask?"

"Oh, she asked, all right. I think I hurt her pretty badly because

I wanted to stay here, in this area. We talked for over a year about me coming out to live with her. She even came here a couple of times and tried to convince me to change my mind. Finally, she just called me one day and said she had decided to move on with her life. It was tough for me, because although we were apart, I still had it in my head that she was my girlfriend, my lover, you know, and that we would find a way to be together someday. I just never really considered putting an end to it. I guess that wasn't fair to her." Chloe's voice trailed off, and they continued the ride in silence for a while.

The Subaru hit a large pothole and shuddered. "Whoa, I think you ran over a Girl Scout troop there," teased Sara.

They could see a large high school looming in front of them. Chloe shook her head. "I can't get over how large the high schools are here in the city. Their auditorium alone is the size of half of all of Fort Lafayette. By the way, we're going to be met by my friend, John Logan. He's the theater arts director here. It's his full-time job. I can't imagine. I'm just part-time with Lafayette, six hours a week until senior play season. Then, it's just non-stop pandemonium until school lets out."

They pulled up behind the auditorium's back doors. Chloe turned to Sara, and gave her a smile. "Wait here, I'm going to go pound on the door and see if he's here."

Sara nodded, and watched Chloe make a mad dash through the rain over to the doors marked "Auditorium." She pounded a few times, and moments later the door swung open. Sara saw a tall woman with streaked-blonde curly hair, dressed in jeans and a work shirt, hold open her arms, and Chloe jumped into them, giving her an enthusiastic hug. The blonde returned the hug with equal gusto. Sara watched with interest. *The blonde certainly doesn't look like her name would be "John." And it doesn't look like they just met, either.* Chloe stepped into the doorway, and waved at Sara to come in.

Sara arrived inside the building to see the blonde woman hugging Chloe once again. Chloe was giggling, and poked the woman in the ribs. They both turned and saw Sara, and the woman slowly disengaged her arms from around Chloe. Chloe's face was flushed, and she was smiling like a puppy with a new chew toy. "Sara, this is my old friend Audra Simmons. She student-taught at Lafayette the second year I was there as theater director. She helped us out with the play that year. Audra, this is my friend Sara D'Amico."

Audra stuck out her hand, and leaned toward Sara, who gently clasped it and shook it. Audra's eyes fell to Sara's scar, and Sara just smiled and mumbled a "Hello." *It's just natural for her to look. Don't worry about it.*

Audra cocked her head, and said, "Whoa! Now I know where I know you from! *Star Gazers*! Nice to meetcha."

Sara just nodded her acknowledgment and then looked at Chloe. Chloe gave her a small grin, and turned to Audra. "Where's John? I was supposed to meet him here. Am I late or early? I can never remember."

"Two of John's kids came down with the chicken pox earlier this week, and his wife is all run ragged, so he stayed home with them to give her a break. When I heard John say you were coming today, I knew I had to be here, hell or high water, so I volunteered to help him out. Little does he know he's the one who was doing me the favor!" She looked directly into Chloe's eyes, and gave her the brightest smile she could muster. Chloe immediately blushed from her toes to her hair roots.

Sara just stood there, watching the little interaction between Audra and Chloe. *Hmm. What's the story here?*

Chloe, still glowing, turned to Sara. "The storage room is right up this hallway. We can root around and find the stuff we need, get a dolly and haul it out to the Subaru." She watched Sara nod. *Is she uncomfortable around Audra? I need to keep an eye on her.*

"Is there a ladies' room nearby? I need to answer the call," said Sara in a subdued voice.

Audra answered her, "Oh sure, it's two doors up from the storage room. Right this way."

The three women made their way up the short hallway, and then stopped at a door that was propped open. Audra said to Sara, "It's right up there, on your left." Sara continued her walk, saw the entrance and went in.

Once Sara had disappeared from view, Audra grabbed Chloe's hands and said, "Ooh, are you a movie star groupie now?" She gave Chloe the once-over again.

Chloe squeezed Audra's hands and laughed. "Nope, not quite. She's the aunt of one of the leads in the play. I just met her a couple of weeks ago. Nobody in town even knew she was in town. I think she came home for a little quiet R and R."

Audra nodded. "Yeah. I saw the scar." She zinged Chloe with another grin. "And then you met her, and roped her into helping you with the play, huh? Quick thinking, but that's just you, isn't it? You never could get into trouble just by yourself, you had to drag the rest of us down with you, didn't you?"

"It's more fun that way, Audra. And you? How are you and Melanie doing?" Chloe caught the intense frown that passed over Audra's face.

"We are, as they say, no more. We broke up last year. It just wasn't working. You know, the 'we've grown apart' scenario. The whole break-up started out civil, and then quickly deteriorated into a huge fiasco." A smile captured Audra's face again. "But I'm pretty much over it now. I feel pretty good." Audra watched as Chloe took off her coat and threw it onto a table. "How's your love life going, Chloe?"

Chloe began moving back farther into the storage room, reading labels on boxes. She spoke louder, so Audra could hear her. "You know, same old, same old. Spinster librarian." She found a box marked "hats" and tossed it onto the floor. "I'm sorry about you and Melanie." Chloe dragged the box out into the aisle where she could better peruse its contents. "But to be perfectly honest, Audra, I never much cared for her." She looked at Audra's face to see her reaction to her little admission.

Audra responded with a delighted laugh. "Well, Chloe, she never much cared for you, either! She always suspected that I had a crush on you."

Sara really didn't mean to be eavesdropping, but she had approached the doorway just as Audra was querying Chloe about her love life. *Oh, I gotta hear this.* Sara tucked herself just behind the door so neither Chloe or Audra could see her.

Chloe looked at Audra in surprise. Audra searched Chloe's eyes. "And she was right, although at the time I denied it. About the crush." *Why do you think I came here to school on a rainy Saturday? Not to do a favor for that asswipe John.*

Audra saw that her statement had taken Chloe off guard. But it wasn't like she was going to get this opportunity again any time soon. She continued, carefully, "I was glad to have the chance to see you today. I didn't know that you would have someone with you."

Chloe stopped her nervous searching through the boxes. *How do I say this?* "Audra," she began slowly, "I'm not sure yet what Sara is in my life. Right now, right this very instant, we're just on our way to becoming friends." *Although it seems I want so much more.*

Audra nodded at Chloe and said hopefully, "Could I call you then? Maybe we could have dinner?" *C'mon, please say 'yes.'*

Sara stiffened in the hallway. *Tell her no, no thanks. Just say no.*

Chloe smiled shyly. "Sure, that would be nice." *And who knows, maybe it will.*

Sara sighed to herself, and made her way quietly down the hallway to a water fountain, took a long cool drink and tried to regroup. *Why shouldn't Chloe see the woman? Audra is great looking, seems very nice, and very interested in Chloe. Too damned interested, I should just go down there and—*

"Hey Sara, leave some water for the fishes. You gonna come help or what?" Chloe called down to her from the storage room doorway. Sara made her way back to Chloe, who had a devilish look in her eye. She poked Sara. "Ya just can't get good help these days. Six feet of muscle, and all she wants to do is hang out in the hall-

ways." Chloe glared menacingly up into sparkling blue eyes. "You
got a hall pass there, Missy?"

Sara eyed her small friend right back. "I heard that a certain Ms.
Donahue was monitoring detention, so naturally, I wanna get detention." She raised an eyebrow and wiggled it. "Got a cigarette I can
smoke in the ladies' room? Come catch me." Her eyes narrowed and
she lifted her lips into a one-sided grin.

Audra watched the exchange between the two friends. *Oh yeah,
if I'm going to call Chloe and ask her out, it's going to have to be
very, very soon.*

The Subaru was jammed to the limit with boxes and garment
bags. They'd borrowed hats, dresses, boots, a wagon wheel, numerous plastic six-shooters, chaps, and a lariat or two. Sara had argued
against bringing the large stuffed bull's head that Chloe was so sure
would be a perfect prop for the second act. It was huge. It had two
beady glass eyes, the hide had a nasty feel and smell to it, and the
whole thing gave Sara a big case of the willies. She didn't want it in
the same car with her. So using all her mighty powers of persuasion,
and then having to resort to putting her foot down about it, she outright, flat out refused to let that nasty thing go back to Stonecreek
with them.

Chloe was humming, driving along, enjoying the brightening
midafternoon skies. She looked over at a sulking Sara.

"Good thing the horns unscrew, or we'd never gotten that thing
on your lap." Baleful blue eyes were staring into large, glassy bovine
brown.

Sara flipped her hair back over her shoulder, and drolly replied,
"Remind me next time that when you get your mind set about something, that I can't win. No way, no how. I'm sure it'll save a lot of
time and a lot of my energy." Sara then gave a small start, for she
was sure that the bull's head cradled in her lap winked at her. *Even
the bull knows I'm a wuss around her.*

They were passing some fast food joints. On cue, Chloe's stomach rumbled. She blushed and turned to Sara. "Wanna go through
the drive-thru? I'm sorta hungry. My treat."

Sara said innocently, "Oh, that noise was you? I thought it was
Bully here. Sure, I could eat."

Chloe inched the car around the building, stopped, and they
studied the menu board.

"How may I help you today?" crackled the menu board.

Chloe looked at Sara. "You know what you want?"

"Double cheeseburger."

Chloe spoke into the menu board, loudly enunciating, "Double cheeseburger and I want—"

"Tell 'em no onions," whispered Sara.

"No onions on that double cheeseburger and—"

"Extra pickles, I want extra pickles," Sara urgently tugged at Chloe's sleeve.

"And extra pickles. Hold on a sec." Chloe glared at Sara, who was sitting angelically, petting the bull's nose. "Anything else?"

"Large fries. And a large diet."

"That's a value meal."

"Well, that's what I want, then."

Chloe cleared her throat, and started talking at the menu board again. "Um, change that to a double cheeseburger value meal, with large fries, large diet, hold the onions, add extra pickles. And I want—"

Another tug. "No ice. I don't want ice."

Chloe turned to glare at her passenger one more time.

Sara licked her tongue across her front teeth. "I have sensitive teeth."

"And no ice in the diet!" Chloe practically screamed at the menu board. "Tell ya what, just make that two!"

Sara gleefully chuckled and winked back at the bull. *Paybacks are a bitch. That poor woman wearing the headset in there probably had her ears blown out on that one.*

Chloe huffily pulled up to the window to retrieve their order. The teenager in a bright yellow cap was about to hand Chloe their drinks when her eyes fell on the large stuffed head sitting in Sara's lap. She promptly lost her bearings, and dropped the cup onto the ground between the window and the car.

"Oh God, I'm sorry. I'll get you another one." She made no movement, she just kept staring at the bull.

Sara slowly leaned across Chloe, pulling the bull along with her. She gave the wide-eyed girl her best toothy smile and said, "Remember, no ice. He gets cranky if it's too cold."

Sara took her time sliding back into her seat. Chloe just stared at her, chagrined. The drive-thru girl finally snapped out of it, and shut the window to get a replacement soda. Chloe eyed Sara, then the bull, then Sara again. "You're evil." And then broke into a large grin.

Sara gave the bull a tickle under the jaw, and a feral smile crept onto her face. "Yeah." She raised a single eyebrow at an amused Chloe and said, "And don't you forget it."

They were about half through unloading the props at Lafayette High's stage door entrance when Chloe abruptly stopped and sat down on a box. She had a rather uncomfortable look on her face, and she rubbed her stomach a little and let out a small moan.

Sara set down the box she had in her arms and sat down next to Chloe, concerned. "You feeling alright?"

"Well, either I overestimated my abs of steel, or I'm getting cramps." She rubbed her belly a little lower. "Actually, I think it's a little of both."

Sara gave her a sympathetic look and said, "I'll finish up here, you take a load off. I wouldn't want all those extra pickles coming back up to haunt you."

"Normally, I would protest, but I think I'll just concede this one time." Chloe truly looked miserable.

Sara hauled the rest of the boxes into the back stage area and again sat down next to her uncharacteristically quiet friend. She saw the bull's head, horns now screwed back in, perched on top of a nearby box. *Hmm.*

"Hey Chloe," she said slowly, still peering at the bovine head, "You think that Mrs. Raeburn's office door is locked?"

Chloe, who had her eyes closed, opened one and squinted at Sara, who had a definite scheming look about her. She sat up, feeling just a bit better.

"Well, Sara, if it is," Chloe reached in her coat pocket, and then held up her set of school keys, "it's not a problem."

Sara's hand flashed out and grabbed the keys. "Be right back." Sara, accompanied by her stuffed and horny bullheaded buddy, quickly disappeared into the school.

Chloe rubbed her aching belly again and smirked. *Oh yeah, very evil indeed.*

When Chloe pulled into her gravel driveway in front of her house, she frowned for the umpteenth time since she had dropped Sara off at her brother's house. She'd regretfully turned down Sara's invitation to come in for a while, and told her tall friend that she just simply didn't feel well. She could see the disappointment that Sara tried to hide, so she'd slid her hand on top of Sara's and gently said, "Another time, when I feel a little more human." *Damn. I didn't want the night to end this way.* Sara looked down on Chloe's hand on top of hers, and said, "I'm really glad I went with you today. I had a good time."

Awkward. Goodbyes were always awkward, no matter if you were a teenager on a first date or a grown-up town librarian, who felt a bit like a teenager on her first date. Goodbyes given in cars are even worse, what with those inconvenient bucket seats that make it so hard to turn and look at your companion, much less lean across a gear shift to perhaps steal a goodnight kiss. Chloe shyly dropped her eyes to look at her hand covering Sara's. "I want to thank you for coming along with me, helping, maybe we can—"

Chloe stopped because her friend's lips were now lightly grazing her cheek with a soft kiss. Sara leaned back, smiled that smile that was so uniquely hers, and murmured, "Yeah, we can, if you want. Goodnight, Chloe, I hope you feel better." And then she was out of the car, and up the steps before the tingle lingering on Chloe's cheek had time to fade.

When Chloe got home to her small house, she promptly downed some pills for her cramps. She changed into some comfy sweats, and laid down on her couch with a sigh. She noticed that her answering machine was flashing, and she hit the play button and leaned back. Two messages from Marcy, the first cheerful and light, the second a more demanding "I'm your best friend, why don't I know where you are?" rant that made Chloe snicker. Then one from Paul about the play, and then a short, upbeat one from Audra Simmons. *Well, it didn't take her long.* Chloe felt a bit flattered. And the last call, from a voice she didn't recognize, saying something about having a horse for the play. She grabbed a pen and wrote down both Audra's and the unidentified horse person's phone numbers. *I'll call 'em all back tomorrow.* She pulled her afghan tight up around her neck, and in a short time, she fell asleep.

"Early evening, or long afternoon for you?" called Dave, his voice coming from the living room.

Sara crossed into the kitchen archway, and ruefully smiled at her brother, who was leaned back in his recliner, watching a college basketball game.

She took off her coat, and went in and settled into the corner of the couch. She reached down, and started unlacing her boots. "A little of both, I think."

Dave grabbed the remote from his lap and muted the TV. He gave a Sara a thoughtful look up and down. "You don't look any worse for the wear, hon."

"Nope, I actually had a good day. You know that I went into Erie with Chloe? Did Nels tell you?" When Dave nodded, she continued. "Yeah, well, I didn't embarrass myself, or Chloe, at any time. So I guess that's a good day."

Dave snorted. "That's how you gauge whether you had a good day? That's pretty sad, Sis. Most people would say that they had a nice time, a blast, or had fun. Did you have any of those?"

"I had all of those, Dave, and more. I guess it is kind of lame when all I can do is be glad that I made it through the day without any trouble."

"Does Chloe know about your anxiety stuff?"

"Some of it, I just kind of clued her in to what to do if I had one, you know, the rules I have."

"So, did you two end up having to put any of those rules into action?" Dave could see the almost defeated body language his sister was displaying.

"Nope, not today. Actually, I was kind of surprised that nothing happened, since, well, I was pretty worked up when we left here. It was pretty uneventful, I didn't make her pull over, there was nothing that made me feel like an ass." Sara scratched her elbow and out of nowhere, she felt her resentment build. "Not like Marcy did that day, when the poor woman had to wing it with me." Sara didn't try to hide the sarcasm in her voice.

"I had to tell Marse about your problem, Sara, I mean, well, she was concerned. She was there when it happened. It wasn't something I could just gloss over." Dave was getting defensive. Marcy had just been trying to be a friend.

"Well, she was so concerned that she warned Chloe about what happened, and Chloe got all her reference books out at the library, and then Chloe tells me she thinks I have anxiety problems, like I'm some little pet project of hers to help." Sara's anger and frustration was showing in words and in her tone.

Dave picked up on his sister's resentment, and returned it in kind. "Has Chloe treated you like that, like her little psychology project, Sara?" He waited for an answer. When she pursed her lips, and shook her head no, he continued, now outright angry. "Marcy got the idea that Chloe likes you, as in her heart's going pitty-pat for you, and the only thing Marcy had to offer her best friend, Chloe, was what happened the one time she actually met you. And what do you think Marcy took away from that meeting, Sara?" His glare invited no response. "She came away from that thinking you were someone, yes, maybe suffering from some kind of troubles, but all in all, she believes you were very graceful under pressure, and were a worthwhile person for her best friend, Chloe, to get to know better."

"But—" Sara tried to interrupt.

"I'm not done. Why do you always think that everyone wants to think the absolute worst of you? Since when are you all anyone thinks about? I'm tired of walking on pins and needles around you, Sara. I love you, but I think it's about time you started thinking about getting better, not just maintaining your safe little status quo." His voice rose. "Hell, I tell you what! Just print out your rules on some paper, I'll go have copies made, and we can post them around town. That way, you can actually leave the premises once in a while, everyone will know not to bother you, and then you won't think it's such a big hairy deal!"

Dave's voice had risen to the point to where he realized he was yelling at her. He saw that Sara's head had bent low, and she looked like she might start crying. If she would let herself cry. "Damn, I didn't mean it like that, but this gets to be too much sometimes." Dave got out of his chair and sat next to Sara on the couch. Her mixture of sadness and anger kept him at arm's length from her.

"Listen, Sara," he began quietly. "I just hate to see you going through this. I remember how you used to be, before all of this happened. All spit and hellfire, take no prisoners, not scared of anything Sara. You used to mow down everything in your path with just a big dose of attitude and a bitchy look. But now it seems like you're afraid of everything, and I know, I know, you don't know where it went to, or how to get it back. But what you're doing, Sara, is that the way to get it back? Do you even want to get it back?"

He waited. She made a few false starts, trying to put her thoughts together. "Of course I do, Dave. I hate this crap that is my life now. I never had to explain myself to anyone before, they had to take what they got, and if they didn't like it, tough shit. Now I have to explain myself, how I might go all whacko on someone, before I can even feel comfortable around them. That's not me. You know that."

"I know," he sighed, and thought about his next question for a moment before he continued. "But Sara, having panic attacks, that's not harmful to anyone. That's not really even harmful to yourself? Blows your mind for a while? Am I right here? Can't the old you and the panic attacks peacefully coexist? The good and the bad? So what if you have to excuse yourself and go to a quiet place for a bit? If they don't like it, well, the hell with them, Sara. The hell with them." He finally moved closer, and put an arm around her shoulder. She didn't reply, but put her head on his shoulder.

Dave tightened his arm around her. "Trust a few people, Sara. You've got me and Nelson. It looks like you've got Marcy on your side, and it sure looks like Chloe wants to get to know you. I know that these panic attacks aren't going to go away overnight, or maybe even at all, but well, from what you've told me, you've been having them for years now. But shutting yourself away from people, that hasn't helped them go away, right? You lived all by yourself, and you still got the attacks, right? So, try another way, now. I don't know." Dave shook his head. "All I know is that I've got a son, your nephew, who adores you and the ground you walk on, and for some asinine reason or another, he wants to get up on a stage and entertain folks. Can you beat that? But you know what I think would give him the biggest thrill? If he knew you were out there in the audience, throwing rotten tomatoes at him, right along with me."

Sara nodded into his shoulder. "I know, I wish I could. I want to try."

Dave squeezed her one more time, chuckled, and then said in his best Captain Picard voice, "Make it so, Sara, make it so."

Part VII:
Mrs. Cumberland Takes a Holiday

Tuesday came too soon for Nelson. He was wound up, nervous, ready to go, not getting any sleep, unable to concentrate in class. He was dreading the first day of what he was so ardently anticipating. Ever since the cast list had been posted, he'd been getting a lot of good-natured ribbing from his football buddies. This was a small town with a small high school. The reality was that everyone in the school knew, or knew of, Nelson, and had known him since he first dipped his thumb into paste and ate it in kindergarten. And everyone, with the exception of those who had been present at his audition, was doubting that the boy had any kind of acting talent in his body, and were equally convinced that Ms. Donahue had really gone off the deep end casting him as the male lead.

So the young man, already so nervous and unsure of himself, was roundly hooted and teased in every class, in each hallway that he paused to get a drink, and "yee-hawed" and "giddy-uped" by students who weren't even in his circle of friends. He tried to act good natured about the razzing, but by the first day of rehearsals, he had completely psyched himself up to fail, and he was sure doom was inevitable the moment he first stepped out on that stage. It was worse than any nervousness he had ever experienced in his football career. But what he didn't know, and hadn't counted on, was the strength and the support of determined adults and a soon-to-be close-knit family of fellow actors, who were just as determined that he, and everyone around him, was going to succeed.

Nelson strolled into the theater, as casually as he could under the circumstances. He walked down the aisle, and sat in the first row, and saw some of the other cast members wandering about, rolled up scripts in their hands. Some waved at him, and he waved and smiled back. Jeanette was nowhere around.

Chloe Donahue, dressed in jeans and a green sweatshirt, had a Penn State cap on her head and was sitting at a card table at the front of the stage, talking animatedly with Paul and Marcy. Actually, to

Nelson, it looked more like Chloe and Marcy were having a heated discussion. No, it would better be described later as Chloe and Marcy getting close to taking a swing at each other. Paul was prudently keeping his mouth shut. Since Nelson had chosen a seat so close to the stage, with only an empty orchestra pit separating him from the three adults, he was privy to the conversation that was taking place.

Chloe's hands were jabbing the air in full expressive throttle. "Marcy, listen, this was all your idea anyway. I'm so booked up right now, I'm not planning on taking a dump until at least mid-April."

"Yeah, well, I don't know a damned thing about them, so how would I be a good judge? I've never even been near one before."

"Marcy, I just don't have the time. It was your idea, I think you should be the one to follow up on it. I have to work all day, and then come spend my evenings here until God knows when."

"My schedule is the same as yours, toots. I'm going to be doing the same damned thing," Marcy shot back, skilled and experienced in her verbal parries with her obstinate friend.

"Yeah, well, in your capacity as creative director, you can just tell a bunch of your crew to paint a tree, and take off for an hour and go see about this."

"Do you remember what Doris said about me leaving these kids to their own creative devices? You're going to get a tree that looks like a potted palm. And we all know that they're indigenous to Oklahoma. Oh, yeah." Marcy rolled her eyes.

"Well, take Paul, here, with you. He probably knows something about them. Don'tcha, Paul?" Chloe eyed Paul, willing a "yes" out of him.

Paul shook his head no, and edged his chair even farther away from the table.

"See, he doesn't know, either. It's not like he's some farm boy, for God's sake, his mother sells Avon, not Amway," Marcy said sarcastically.

Paul looked left and then right, planning his most likely avenue of escape.

"Well, then, get your boyfriend to take you. You said he thought it was a good idea, so take him and—"

Nelson saw Ms. Donahue's finger point his way, so he just naturally looked behind him. *Hmm, nobody there, wonder who?*

"—our boy Curly there with the two of you. He is the intended victim of all of this. Let him see if he thinks it's a good idea or not."

Three sets of adult eyes settled on Nelson. Three sets of eyes that wanted him to do something that they didn't want to do.

Nelson blinked, and cracked his knuckles. *This doesn't sound good.*

"Hey, Nelson, come up here, would you please?" sweetly called Ms. Donahue, who was giving Marcy a snotty look.

Nelson, being brought up to respect his elders, no matter what their mental state, made his way up to the stage. He stood next to Mr. Hoderman, who could no longer be described as sitting at the table, for he had worked his chair back to almost center stage. Paul took Nelson's arrival as the perfect cover to make his getaway. "Here, Nelson, take my chair. I'll be right back," Paul fibbed, and exited, stage left.

"Pull up your chair, Nelson. Marcy and I were just thinking about how nice it would be—"

"Don't you blame this on me, Chloe, if the poor kid here—"

"Marcy, don't interrupt me. Now, Nelson, as I was saying, Marcy and I agreed—"

"Under duress. I only agree to this under duress. Nelson, do you know what duress is? It's what I am going to plead to when I am charged with Ms. Donahue's murder. I did it because of extreme duress."

The two women glared at each other. Nelson furtively glanced in the direction Paul had gone, and wondered if it would be a smart thing to follow after him.

Chloe nailed him before he could figure out his next move. "Nelson, we were just thinking that if maybe you, and Marcy and perhaps even your dad could, well, go see a man about a horse."

Later, Nelson recounted this conversation to a rapt audience of his closest relatives in the living room.

"So it looks like I've been elected to go check out this horse with you, huh, Nelson?" Dave was pleased. *No one can accuse me of not being supportive of my boy.*

"Well, since neither Marcy or I know anything about them, and you do, I suppose it's a good idea." *Just don't embarrass me, Dad.*

Sara added her opinion. "And it will probably keep your girlfriend out of jail on a murder rap, so, yeah, Dave, why don't you help out your son there."

Nelson didn't give his father an opportunity to refuse. "Ms. Donahue gave me the phone number and address, I think we can go on either Thursday or Friday. Would you call the guy, Dad?"

"Not a problem. I'm not the one who has to ride him while yodeling." Dave chucked Nelson on the shoulder.

"So what's your schedule look like, Nelson?" inquired Sara. *In other words, when does Ms. Donahue have some free time?*

"Let's see, tomorrow, the whole cast sits down and does a read-through. Then we do it again, this time with Ms. Donahue giving us some direction along the way. That will probably take up tomorrow. Then it's pretty much Tuesday through Thursday from 4:00 until 8:00 each day, and Saturday afternoons from 12:00 until 4:00 or so. Saturday is the day we work on the dancing. That's the only day Mrs. Cumberland can make it."

That name brought a smile to Sara's face. "Geez, Dave, wasn't Mrs. Cumberland doing the choreography for these school plays even way back when you were in high school? I remember her." Sara pictured the tiny, wizened woman from her high school years.

"God, yeah, come to think of it. She must be close to 102 by now," Dave said, a bit amazed at the thought.

"That should be some interesting display of dancing. Leaning up against walls and tapping your foot will probably be the extent of it," Sara cracked.

Dave suddenly remembered something. "Hey, Nelson, a buddy of mine is moving on Saturday, and I said I'd help him. I'm going to need to take the Explorer and your truck so we can get more moved at one time. I can give you a ride to rehearsal and pick you up that day, too. And pick up Marcy, too, if she isn't in jail by then." He winked at Nelson. "And maybe, if she isn't dead, we can pick up a little redheaded librarian for your aunt here, too."

Sara felt the color rise in her cheeks, and she gave Dave her best instant-death glare.

Dave grinned, pleased with the embarrassment showing on his sister's face. "Well, on that note, Nels, give me that phone number of the guy with the horse, and I'll go call him and see what I can set up."

Nelson reached in his back pocket, and handed his dad a slip of paper. Dave went off to his office to make the call.

"Oh, Aunt Sara, I forgot to tell you the best part! It was so weird, it was practically surreal." Nelson was grinning wildly. "Ms. Donahue had us all in the front rows of the theater, you know, like at the auditions. And she was giving us all this pep talk, how great we were all going to be, and yadda yadda, and all of a sudden, from the side of the stage, there's the principal, Mrs. Raeburn, coming at Ms. Donahue with a big, I dunno, bull's head in her arms. You know, with great big horns out to here, and she was using the horns to sort of jab at Ms. Donahue, and all the while, Mrs. Raeburn was shouting out something about her having to use adult diapers for the rest of her life, and Ms. Donahue was laughing so hard that her hat was falling off and there were tears rolling down her face. Mrs. Raeburn was just getting madder and madder and chasing Ms. Donahue around the stage," Nelson was slapping his knee now, "and finally, Mrs. Raeburn just threw the bull's head down on the stage and stalked off. I'm telling you, it was the funniest thing I've ever seen. We didn't get much done after that, Ms. Donahue would take one look at that bull, and just start laughing all over again. I wish you could have seen it."

Sara's grin was so wide her face could hardly contain it. "Me too, Nelson. Me too."

"All right, everyone settle down, we're going to read through this thing once." Chloe, Paul and the student cast were in the cafeteria, the only place in the building that had a table large enough to accommodate all of them. "Paul and I will be reading any of the stage directions, such as 'Ado Annie enters and stands next to Ali Hakim.' You folks will be reading your own parts. Take notes if you need to, right on your script. And for this first go 'round, don't try and act the part. Don't try to give any accents to your characters. We'll be giving that a go on the second read-through. Oh, and yes, we will be reading the songs. No singing just yet. Any questions?"

Chloe scanned the group, who mercifully decided that if they did have any questions they could keep until another time. She stood up and moved next to Paul. "Let's begin. Paul?"

Paul began reading the narrative directions of the beginning of the play. It was going along pretty well, with Chloe interjecting corrections along the way. The collected cast quickly found out that Ms. Donahue, who looked like she was all sweetness and light and was imbued with supernatural patience, actually had the heart of a tyrannical, demanding director, and expected to be treated with a mixture of fear and respect.

Chloe began the read-through, making scattershot demands to her cast all the while:

"Justin, excuse me, the word is 'ne'er' pronounced 'nair' like 'never' without the 'v' in it."

"Mo, what is it with you and the word 'the?' Every time you say it, it sounds like you were brought up Quaker. It's 'thuh,' not 'thee.'"

"Jason, did you even open this script before today? I can still put you in as an understudy. For Moreen."

"Jeanette, quit emoting and batting your eyelashes. We're reading this, not flirting it."

"Nelson, I'm pretty sure cowboys didn't chew gum back then. Lose it."

"Why is everyone slipping into accents? This is starting to sound like a bad read-through for *The Dukes of Hazzard*. Knock it off."

The read-through went pretty swiftly, and Chloe, as badly in need of a break as the kids were, gave them ten minutes with the directive to return promptly for the second reading.

Paul sidled up to a silently musing Chloe. "That went pretty

well. Sorta. I think it might have. It could have been worse," he
declared, decisive as ever.

"Uh-huh," agreed Chloe, busily writing notes in her director's
copy of the play.

Paul anxiously twisted his copy of the script in his hands. "Uh,
Chloe, I just found out, just before we started..."

Chloe looked up at Paul, just daring him to screw up her day.

"Uh, Chloe, we have a problem." The fear in Paul's eyes
showed; he didn't want to be the deliverer of bad news. He gulped a
breath and mustered up a bit of bravery. "Mrs. Cumberland called.
She can't do the play this year. Something about all her children,
grandchildren, and great-grandchildren getting together to send her
and her older sister on a six-week cruise."

For some silly reason, the only words that made an impression
on Chloe from that statement were "Mrs. Cumberland" and "older
sister." *That's impossible. No one in the world is older than Mrs.
Cumberland.* Then Chloe's mind fixed on the phrase "can't do the
play" and she yelped, "No way! Mrs. Cumberland has always
directed the dancing parts. I don't know anything about dancing.
What are we gonna do?" She practically wailed. Calming slightly,
she looked Paul up and down. "Do you dance? At all?"

Paul thought a moment about making a smart remark about
being adept at the Hokey Pokey but thought better of it. "Nope, two
left feet."

The kids were milling back into the cafeteria, and finding their
seats.

Chloe blustered on, "But I can't direct the kids and do all I have
to do and teach these kids their dances, too. I just can't. We'll have to
find someone else." *Marcy. Marcy can dance. No, wait, that's after
four margaritas and even then, it's pretty bad. Scary even. Mrs. Raeburn? Nope, can't ask her. I'm currently holding all ten positions on
her top ten shit list after that little stunt that Sara pulled with the
bull's head in her office.*

Chloe's mind whirred and clicked. "Nelson? Can your aunt
dance?"

Everyone's eyes turned to Nelson, nephew of the famous reclu-
sive movie star.

"Like nobody's business. Why?" answered a bewildered Nelson.

"Just curious. Now, let's get started again, and please, everyone,
try to keep your southern accents toned down. We don't want to
have to have closed captioning for this thing."

"Yeah, sure. Marcy probably just looked at you, gave you a
puppy dog look, and said 'Oh, honey, please, for me?' and you fell

for it, didn't you? And then she begs off, and you rope me into coming along." Sara teased, and tried to find a little more room for her long legs in the old Ford pickup. She was squeezed between Nelson, who was driving, and Dave, who was taking up more space than he needed on the passenger side. It was Thursday evening, Nelson had just gotten out of rehearsals, and they were on their way to see a man named Jack Cagney about a horse. The directions he had provided indicated that he lived on Route 20, just as everyone else did from this town. Route 20, the main drag, stretched about two miles east and two miles west of the town center. The houses were widely spaced apart on either side of the road. Some of the land was devoted to growing cherries, and those farms had roadside stands, usually boarded up until late June, when the cherries came to fruition. Others were lined with grape vines, now withered and barren, waiting for spring. A number of these vineyards produced a nice variety of local wines, and some of the larger places even had their own small stores which did a brisk business selling to bus tours of the scenic lakeside area.

They were heading east, having already passed through the town's center, and Sara saw the rusting sign of the old '76 station, and a hundred yards from it, a small yellow house with the porch light on. She wondered if that was Chloe's house. She turned her head to see Chloe's Subaru parked on the side of it. *Yup, that's it. She said it was small. She wasn't kidding. I wonder what she's doing?*

Nelson began to slow the truck. "I think it must be up here, soon. On the left." They scanned the mail box at the end of a long drive. "Cagney. That's it." Nelson turned and carefully drove the truck down a long, rutted drive and then stopped at a large house that had a big barn just behind it. He was just turning off the motor when a small form darted out of the barn and stopped at Nelson's door. Nelson opened his door, immediately recognized the small person, and greeted him with a familiar grin. "Hey, there. We're here about the horse."

The small, round figure nodded eagerly. "Yeah, I know. I made my stepdad call you guys. Wait 'til you see her, she's a beauty."

Sara and Dave were awkwardly trying to get out the other side of the truck, and missed this little conversation. They both stopped to stretch, and then proceeded around the front to the truck. Sara took in the small manic form talking to Nelson. *Oh, good God, it's him. Curly. I mean, Charlie. Charlie Shemp.*

Dave and Sara stopped in front of the chatting pair, and Charlie's eyes surveyed them both, and then looked past them, as if looking for someone else. He looked up at Nelson, and said, rather disappointedly, "Um, I thought Ms. Donahue would be coming. She's not with you?"

Nelson shook his head, and introduced his dad and Aunt Sara to Charlie. "This is my buddy, Charlie Shemp. He's the one who volunteered us the use of his horse. Let's go take a look at her, okay, Charlie?"

Sara and Dave trudged up the path behind Nelson and Charlie, and caught a bit of what Nelson was saying to Charlie.

"She couldn't make it, Charlie, she wanted to, but she is so busy with everything else right now, you know."

Dave nudged Sara, a smirk coloring his voice. "Oh, another one in love with the wonderful Ms. Donahue, huh? Maybe we should start a proper fan club for her, but who would be president? You, Charlie, Paul, or even Nelson?"

Sara's arm shot out and shoved Dave off the path, and nearly onto his keister. Dave, recovering, laughed and said, "All right, all right. You can be president, but I'm holding out for the sergeant in arms position."

Dave and Sara made their way into the brightly lit barn, and over to a stall where Nelson and Charlie were standing.

Nelson looked at the tall horse doubtfully, and the animal turned and made its way over to the four of them.

"You're right, Charlie, she sure is a beauty," Nelson exclaimed.

That's an understatement. Sara's eyes were dazzled by the glow of the tall, golden palomino. She stepped closer to it, and it came to her, and softly nuzzled her outreached hand. The tall dark woman and the horse began a long conversation without words. Sara was so enraptured by the beautiful beast that her mind barely registered the words that were coming, rapid-fire, from Charlie's mouth.

"She's really gentle, and will even listen to whistled commands. Nothing seems to bother her, not even thunderstorms. I don't think all those people in the audience, even if they're clapping or something, will scare her at all. We can put her in the trailer, and bring her out each night right before the play starts. I could stay with her. She listens to me really good. My stepdad won't be able to bring her each time, but I thought if somebody had a hitch on their truck, I could get her all ready and the high school is just a mile or so up the road—"

Dave interrupted the youth, "I have a hitch on my Explorer, and I'm planning on being there for every performance I can, so it won't be a problem getting her there and back." He turned and grinned at his sister, who seemed to be cooing to the large beast. "Charlie, when do you think Nelson could come out and take a trial spin on her? And maybe his aunt here, too. If she wants to?"

Sara, never taking her eyes off the beautiful horse, immediately said, "Oh yeah. You know it. You bet." She then turned to Charlie. "If it's all right with you, Charlie?"

"Sure. How about Sunday? After we get back from church?

Would that be okay, and you could bring Ms. Donahue, if she wants," said Charlie, with desperate hope burning in his eyes.

Charlie, Dave and Nelson settled the final arrangements for Sunday, and then Sara felt a tug at her sleeve. Dave, chuckling, teased her, "I hate to break up this little love fest between you two, but it is a school night, and Charlie here needs to get his beauty rest."

Sara sighed, and gave the tall horse one final scratch behind its ears. "Hey, Charlie," she murmured dreamily, "What's her name?"

"Well," said a still tightly wound Charlie, "Officially, her registration name is Petit Escargot. Something French. But we shortened that up." He turned and patted the big horse on the nose. "We just call her Cargo."

The small inhabitant of the tiny yellow house near the old gas station was busily punching a number into her telephone, unaware that the person she was trying to call was just this second passing her house in a Ford pickup truck. With no answer, or machine to leave a message, Chloe decided to call Dave's house. She dialed the number, and on the fourth ring, the machine picked up. Chloe never knew how long she had to deliver her message, some machines cut her off before she could clear her throat to speak. So, to be on the safe side, she'd have to speak rather rapidly. She never heard the beep after the taped greeting, so there was some dead airtime before she finally began.

"Hello, this is Chloe Donahue, and I'm trying to get in touch with Sara. Please call me back as soon as—" Beep.

Chloe, cut off, but happy that the most important part of her message had gotten across, turned to the next name on her list of calls.

Audra. All right, I told her on Sunday I would call her today, and let her know if I'm free on Saturday night. I haven't really got any plans. But why do I feel like I would be doing something, well, not exactly wrong, but not right, either? She had picked up the phone a few times during the week to call Sara, but always found a shy reason to stop herself. *She sure hasn't attempted to call me, either. Maybe she needs her space. Maybe she isn't as interested as I seem to be. Oh, crap.*

Chloe dialed Audra's number. Audra picked up on the third ring.

"Hey, Audra, it's Chloe," she began pleasantly.

"I recognized your voice, how're you doing?"

"Well, other than rehearsals starting this week, and that I'm already dead tired, and I'm ready to smack the next person who says 'no' or 'can't' to me, I'm perfectly fine. And you?"

"Sounds like my week is going better than yours. So I won't irritate you with the details," Audra paused and then continued, "Well, what do you think about Saturday, think you'll be ready for a break by then?"

"I think that would be," Chloe took a breath, and impetuously decided to take the plunge, "A great idea. As long as you don't try to drag me to a play or anything theatrical. I might start yelling out directions."

"What time are you done on Saturday?"

"Around 4:00 or so, why?"

"Well, I was thinking it would be nice, if you wouldn't mind, if I could come out and see Paul and Marcy for a few minutes, and then we could go up to New York to a little restaurant that I know of near Chautauqua. It's about a forty-five minute drive from where you live, but I'll drive and you could snooze on the way up." Audra was feeling extremely pleased with the way this was turning out.

"That sounds really nice. I haven't been out that way for a long time. And I know that Paul and Marcy will be thrilled to see you. I told them that I ran into you, and they started reminiscing about all the trouble you got into while you were student-teaching at the school."

"All the trouble you got me into, don't deny it," Audra shot back.

Chloe's mouth twitched in amusement. "All right, already. I'm a bad influence. I'll admit it, just not in court. So, how about you come by around 3:00 or so, just come in the back door of the school, you know your way around. Just look around for me, and I'll point you in the direction of the broom closet that I'll have Paul and Marcy tied up in."

Audra chuckled. "Looking forward to it. See you, Chloe."

"Me too. Bye, Audra." Chloe hung up. *Well, this is different. I actually have a real live date. I wonder if—*

Chloe's thought was cut off by the sound of her phone ringing, right in front of her.

"Hello?"

"Chloe? It's Sara. I got your message. We all just got home."

"Family shoplifting night at Walmart again?" Chloe smiled, enjoying the sound of Sara's low voice.

"Pretty much. Got me a nice six-pack of tube socks, and Nelson got a nifty curling iron, and Dave, well, let's just say that he got enough stuff that he'll never have to worry about that pesky jock itch of his," Sara bantered playfully. She pictured the librarian in the yellow house, hopefully she was smiling as she spoke.

"You've got a quick mind, anyone ever tell you that?" Chloe countered.

"Huh?"

"You've got a really qu—oh, I get it now, never mind."

"So, what's up, why are you enjoying the pleasure of me return-ing your call?" *I practically wrestled the phone away from Nelson before he could return Jeanette's call.*

Oh, God. I can't ask her this over the phone. I'm so much more persuasive in person. "I was wondering what you were doing tomor-row night?"

"Friday night. Let's see. Oh, yeah. I have it right here in my date book. 'Librarian brings over Chinese take-out. Much hilarity ensues.'" *God, it's been so long since I flirted with anyone, this feels good.*

"Oh, then you're busy then?" Chloe pumped her free arm in a small victory celebration.

"I suppose I could get out of it."

"No, no. I wouldn't want to impose."

"All righty then. Hey, I didn't write down what time the librar-ian was going to show up. Stupid me," Sara bantered with a smile.

"What time did you think she might show up?"

"I dunno, around six or so?" *Okay, so now was too soon to hope for.*

"I'll bet you're right."

"I always am. But you knew that," Sara declared.

"Well, then, have a good time with the bookworm." Chloe, not wholly satisfied with the previous arm pump, did a bad version of a Snoopy dance next to her coffee table.

"I'm sure I will, she's always good for a laugh, and a funny story. She's going to tell me about Mrs. Raeburn and a bull's head, and I'm going to tell her about a certain little Stooge I met tonight, who has a lovely horse by the name of Cargo."

"Good. Glad to hear you'll be entertained. I guess I'll see you when I see you. And, Sara?" Chloe hesitated, then decided on a plan.

"Yeah, Chloe?"

"Have you ever seen *Fame, Dirty Dancing* or better yet, *Urban Cowboy*?"

"Sure I have, why?" said Sara distractedly. She'd just noticed that her brother and nephew were watching her converse, and they were both having a hell of a good time at her embarrassed expense, watching the gamut of smiles and grins that traveled her face while she was talking with Chloe.

"Just wondering. Take care."

"You too." Sara hung up the phone, sat it down, and immedi-ately started moving menacingly toward Nelson and Dave, who were retreating in different directions in a strategic attempt to evade the thumping that she surely intended to inflict on them.

Chloe got out her own date book and flipped it to Friday. She wrote down "Chinese food, mass quantities" and "Bob's Video

Shack, dancing."

"Not that I mind, but why do you want to eat in the living room?" Sara was tossing the magazines and other clutter off the coffee table.

"Well, I thought it might be a good night for some movies " She rattled a plastic bag that looked like it contained some video tapes.

Sara started placing numerous small cartons of Chinese food onto the coffee table. "Ooh, great! Home movies, or is it porn? Or better yet, home porn movies?"

"Oh, you wish. I lost all those in the flood of '99."

"Haven't made any new since?" Sara was really enjoying the blush on Chloe's face.

"Haven't had the time to edit out the slower parts yet."

"Shame you're so busy. I've got some free time, perhaps I could volunteer to edit," said Sara, a suggestive gleam in her eye.

Perhaps you could volunteer for something, but let's see how this goes first. "I like to do them myself. Relive the memories and all. I'm very sentimental."

Sara brought plates, utensils and a couple of beers to the living room. "You want a beer? I can only have one, doesn't mix well with my meds."

"Sure. Now park it, and let's eat."

Chloe had already put a tape into the VCR. Now all she had to do was get it to the right point in the tape.

They started eating, and chatting about their week. Sara told her that she and Nelson were going over to the infamous Charlie Shemp's on Sunday to let Nelson actually get up on the tall horse and see if he thought he would be able to handle her. Chloe told her pretty much the same story about Mrs. Raeburn and the bull's head, except for the part that Nelson hadn't heard.

"So, every day this week, today included, I have found a—or what I believe is a cow patty on the hood of my car. Right up by the windshield. How they got there, well, I can imagine. But where she gets them, well, that's a mystery."

Sara threw her head back and laughed. "She's one determined woman. I miss her. She was the one thing about that school that I liked." Sara leaned over and poked Chloe softly in the arm. "She's the one woman, I think, that is even able to out-talk you."

Chloe smirked. "Yeah, well, you haven't seen me when I really get going." She spooned some more rice out of a container, and then more sweet and sour chicken.

"Do you do everything with as much enthusiasm as when you talk or eat?" Sara couldn't help herself, she was feeling happy, and very flirtatious.

Chloe coughed some rice out of her mouth. "Sara! Geez oh Pete oh man."

"You really are a nice small-town girl, aren't you?" *So much nicer than those women out in L.A., they had absolutely no qualms about just, well, going for it. Five minutes after they met you. Huh, no challenge there, no build up. Not that I minded. Then.*

Chloe picked some rice off of her lap, and grabbed a napkin and wiped her mouth. She frowned. "I can't help what I am. I've never gotten any complaints before now." She was getting defensive, and didn't know why. *Oh, yeah, she's probably been with some real, I dunno, sophisticated, slutty types out in Lala Land. She probably had her pick every night.* Chloe scowled, and continued eating.

Sara was quiet a moment, and then leaned forward and set her plate on the table. *How do I say this without giving too much away?* "Chloe?" She waited for Chloe to look at her. "I'm not complaining. Not at all." Chloe's green eyes searched hers for sincerity. "Not at all, Chloe. Please believe me."

Chloe felt a bit silly for getting snappish. "Oh, brother. It's okay. I know you didn't mean anything by it. I'm just tired, and I shouldn't be drinking even this one beer. I'll be dozing by the middle of the first movie."

Relieved that Chloe wasn't angry, and had apparently accepted her words as the truth, the smile returned to Sara's face. "So what's on the schedule for tonight? Get anything good? Action, adventure, chopsockey? I love that stuff."

Chloe put her plate on the table, and suddenly scooted to sit right against Sara's hip. Chloe leaned toward her, placing one hand firmly on her upper thigh, and then moved closer across the front of her, brushing softly against her chest, and then reached out her hand to grasp at the remote control. Which was on the other side of Sara. Once Chloe had it safely in hand, she quickly moved back to her original position. And smiled in the direction of the TV, and pressed a button on the remote. The television came to life, and Chloe hit the play button.

Sara wiped her brow. "And I thought I was evil."

Chloe tilted her head at her and said innocently, "What?"

The previews for upcoming releases were playing on the TV. So Chloe hit the fast forward and let the tape run.

"I'll show you what." Sara wanted nothing more at that moment to kiss that smugness off of Chloe's face, so she leaned forward, put a hand under Chloe's chin, and turned her face toward her own. Chloe's smirk turned into an expectant soft smile, and she reveled in the feel of Sara's fingers so gently pulling her chin toward her. Blue met green, and Sara purposefully closed in on those soft red lips and—

The door slammed.

"Man, I just don't get women," came a disgruntled voice from the kitchen. Nelson, looking red-faced and ticked off, came pounding into the living room.

"Hey, Chlo—uh, Ms. Donahue! I didn't know you were going to be here." Nelson pulled off his jacket, and threw it on the recliner. "Hey, Aunt Sara." His eyes traveled to the food cartons on the table. "Wow, is that Chinese? I'm starving."

Chloe and Sara, who were now on opposite ends of the couch, both sitting quite primly, offered indistinct, garbled "hellos."

Chloe found her tongue first. "Grab a plate, Nelson, and help yourself. Your aunt and I were just going to watch a movie."

Nelson went out to the kitchen and the banging of cupboard doors could be heard.

Sara turned quickly to Chloe, and hissed through clenched teeth, "He was supposed to be on a date with Jeanette tonight!"

Chloe barely had time to shrug her shoulders in reply before Nelson came back into the room, and glanced at the TV set. "Are you watching the movie in fast forward?"

Chloe grabbed the remote and hit the play button, and the movie *Urban Cowboy* came on the screen. It had fast-forwarded, luckily for Chloe, right to the part that she wanted to use as an opening for her little discussion with Sara.

Nelson was putting food away like it was his last supper, his eyes glued to the TV screen.

After a few moments, Chloe, using what was happening on the screen as an introduction, casually paused the tape and said to Nelson, "Hey, Nelson, do you know how to line dance? I was thinking we could use it in the play, you know, maybe at the box social scene, or at the train station. I think it'd be easy for everyone to learn."

Nelson chewed a few times, and swallowed. *Why does Aunt Sara look so cranky?* "Nope, I don't much go in for that country stuff, but it looks easy to learn." He looked at his aunt, who was staring at the paused screen, and had her hands folded across her chest. "Aunt Sara can, though. I've seen her doing it out in the garage."

Aunt Sara was counting to one hundred, trying to figure out a way to get rid of Nelson without embarrassing herself and Chloe. *Well, I don't care about embarrassing myself, but she's his advisor in this damned musical. It just wouldn't look right for me to tell him to get lost because I want to neck with his director. I was this close to those lips.*

Chloe's plan was now perfectly set in motion by the unsuspecting Nelson. She turned to Sara. "Do you think you could show him a few steps?"

Sara, who was feeling full-blown snarly now, and didn't care who knew it, humphed, "Sure."

Chloe crossed her arms, and looked at Sara expectantly.

Sara looked back, and then caught on. "You mean now? Right now?"

Chloe smiled her most winning smile. "Why not? I could use a few ideas, and well, we could just use the music from the movie. If Nelson doesn't mind." Chloe turned that winning smile onto Nelson.

Nelson was just cleaning off his plate and let out a contented sigh. "I'm game if Aunt Sara is. We can move the coffee table back and the couch."

Sara was now busily counting back from one hundred, and wondering where she could hide Nelson's body. *Out by the ninth hole, right next to that pond, no, it might flood there.*

Two sets of eyes were now fixed upon Sara, waiting. "Oh, all right!"

Twenty minutes later, with Chloe manning the remote so she could start the music over, and over, and over again, Nelson and his aunt were doing a pretty fair impression of competent line dancers. Chloe was beaming. *She's a natural, so patient teaching him.* She decided to let the whole song play through, and both Nelson and Sara finished with a little bow, and Chloe clapped appreciatively.

"Can you two-step, too, Sara?" Chloe inquired.

Sara, who had forgotten her grumpiness, was actually having a bit of fun. "Sure. Piece of cake. But I only know how to lead."

"Not a problem, hang on." Chloe quickly fast forwarded the tape to a mid-tempo song. Nelson had plopped himself back down into the recliner.

Chloe got up from the couch and said sweetly, "You know how to lead, I know how to follow," and she tossed the remote to Nelson. "Watch and learn, big guy."

Nelson hit the play button, turned the volume up and watched, mesmerized, as his Aunt Sara took Chloe into her arms, grinned her a dazzling smile, and they began to dance around the living room. As the song progressed, Sara began trying more intricate steps, and was pleased to find that Chloe naturally followed along, step for step. Sara whirled Chloe around, and back again, and the two women moved together as if they danced this dance together every night. As the song ended, the women were breathless and quite pleased with themselves and each other, and the room fell away. Nelson was no longer there, they were so close, so heated.

"What's going on? We having a hoedown in the living room?" asked Dave, standing in the kitchen archway. Sara and Chloe, and even Nelson, who was caught up in the moment, were startled to hear his dad's voice.

Two body bags. That's what I need. Two body bags. And the back hoe. "Hey, Dave. No barn dance tonight, we're just showing Nelson here how to two-step," Sara explained.

Chloe, catching her breath, grinned at Dave. "I thought you would be out with Marse tonight. She told me she was seeing you."

Dave hung his head a little, and grumbled to no one in particular, "Yeah, well, we had a little argument, and decided to call it an early evening." He shifted uncomfortably in the doorway, and then looked to Nelson. "Speaking of dates, I thought you had one with Jeanette tonight."

Nelson, uncomfortable in saying it, said it anyway. "Yeah. Me too. But seems she is suffering a bad attack of, you know, female stuff."

Chloe and Sara both broke out in loud laughter. "Well, Nelson, get used to it, about every twenty-eight days or so, you're going to have one unhappy woman on your hands, and there isn't a damned thing you can do about it," Sara teased. "Maybe run. Run far away."

Dave spoke up from the doorway. "Yeah, well, I don't know what Marcy's problem is, female stuff or not, she sure wasn't very agreeable." He looked at Chloe. "Did you find a replacement for Mrs. Cumberland yet? Is that why you have Sara here doing the old Arthur Murray routine? She's the one who taught me how to dance, and I'm hopeless. I can at least waltz without looking like a trained monkey, thanks to her."

Chloe cringed inwardly, and looked a little frazzled. "Uh, no, no replacement yet. Uh, I was kind of hoping that Sara here—"

Sara, not knowing what had transpired concerning Mrs. Cumberland, put her hand on Chloe's shoulder, and tugged her around to face her. Chloe wasn't meeting Sara's eyes. "What happened to Mrs. Cumberland, and what were you hoping about me?" Sara asked, truly puzzled. *Why isn't she looking at me?*

Chloe looked at down at her socked feet. "Mrs. Cumberland, our choreographer, is going on this cruise, and can't do the play." She rubbed the sole of one foot on top of her other foot. "So I was thinking, and I asked Nelson if you could dance and..."

Sara was studying Chloe's newly uncomfortable body language, and she thought about Mrs. Cumberland, the lack of a dance coach, the videos, the way Chloe had charmed Sara into showing Nelson how to line dance. It didn't take the former actress long to form a strong opinion about what had transpired this evening. Her hands, which had been in her jeans pockets, slid out, and formed loose fists. She took a step away from Chloe. "So this is what this is all about. The tapes, the dancing, the 'show Nelson how to line dance.'" Sara took a deep breath and came to a conclusion. She tonelessly asked Chloe, who still had her eyes averted, "What exactly was your little plan, Chloe? What was it that you wanted to happen here?"

"Well, when Nelson told me you could dance, I thought I might ask you if you would be interested..." She stopped, and looked cautiously at Sara's eyes. They seemed to be a blank blue slate. Sara was waiting for her to continue, her hands still working their clench.

Dave, seeing that the situation looked like it was getting a bit tense, motioned to Nelson from the archway, and they both grabbed their jackets, and left out the kitchen door.

Sara continued, her voice a monotone, "Interested in what, exactly?"

Chloe was sure that Sara's voice held no patience for any more hemming and hawing. "I was going to ask you if you would be interested in taking her place. Teaching the kids some dances for the play. Being our choreographer."

Sara hardly heard her; she was expecting that answer. She spoke in hard, even tones. "So, let me get this straight. You lost your choreographer, I'll bet you couldn't find anyone else, so you cook up this little plan to come over here, and in some roundabout way, with what? Chinese food and," she picked up the bag containing the videotapes and pulled the other ones from the bag, "oh, yeah, *Fame* and *Footloose.* I sense a theme here, Chloe." Her voice picked up some of her growing anger. Chloe wasn't saying anything, so she continued. "Butter me up, and then when you dance me around the living room a couple of times, flirt it up with me. How could I possibly say no, right?"

Sara took no pains to hide the bitterness that she was feeling. "You know what, Chloe? You should have been an agent. That's how those people work. They work people, they don't talk to us like we're real, thinking people. We're just things to use." She snorted with derision. "This, tonight, is just another variation on how my old agent got me to take a role I didn't want to do. She wined and dined me, usually straight into bed, and the next morning, she'd just casually talk me into taking some dumb part on some asinine show. I didn't want to let her down, disappoint her by then, so I'd agree. Oh yeah, you missed your calling."

Chloe felt like her feet were nailed to the floor. She was half agreeing with Sara's assessment, and yet knew that the situation was not the same. Her own anger and frustration rose to challenge Sara's. "That's not exactly true. It may look like it, but it's not true. That, this, wasn't my intention. That's not fair for you to think that about me."

"So tell me, Chloe, which part isn't true? You didn't want me to take Mrs. Cumberland's place? No, you already said that you did. So, the videotapes, the dancing with me. What part isn't true?"

"You make it sound like I was manipulating you, that wasn't my intention. I was only trying to..." Chloe darted her eyes away from Sara.

"Oh, what do you call it then, you certainly didn't just call me up last night and ask me then, did you? 'Sara, Mrs. Cumberland, our choreographer, dropped out, and I wondered if you would be interested in taking her place.'" Sara stared Chloe down. "You certainly didn't take the direct route, did you?" Accusation was wrapped around every word that she spoke.

"Well, no, but," Chloe was completely exasperated. *I don't know how to explain this, without it sounding bad to her. She just expects the worst from people, and no matter what, it looks that way to her.*

"Well, then, why didn't you ask me last night, you certainly knew about it then, we talked on the phone and—"

"I wanted to wait and talk to you in person about it. I thought it would be easier." *I wanted to be with you, yes or no.*

"Easier. Oh, I see. That explains everything. You haven't called all week, and then, when you do, it's to set up this." Sara's arms made a wide gesture around the room. She turned away from Chloe, her jaw tight and set.

"Sara, it really wasn't supposed to be like this. Really, I wasn't thinking that." She reached to touch Sara's shoulder, but stopped short. "Let me explain, so you'll understand."

"Chloe, I already understand," Sara's tone was low and controlled, "I'd appreciate it if you'd leave now."

"Sara," pleaded Chloe. "You have to believe me."

Sara whirled and strode down the hallway into Dave's office, and shut the door behind her.

Chloe took a few halting steps toward the hallway to follow, then stopped, and turned around. She slid into her boots, and gathered up her tapes and coat, and left, closing the kitchen door behind her.

Part VIII:
That's Pronounced : Shuh -Tock-Wuh

It was Friday night in Stonecreek, and it seemed that a lot of the residents were in their houses, with nothing better to do besides sit and stew about their lot in life.

Chloe had stopped at Bob's Video Shack, and returned the movies she had rented only hours earlier. The same clerk was working as when she rented them. Chloe just slid them across the counter at the girl, turned, and walked out. She went home, pulled out a book, and tried to read. She kept looking to the telephone, willing it to ring, wanting to dial a number. Neither happened.

Sara, not wanting to face her brother and nephew, who had seemingly disappeared sometime before, during, or after her blow up at Chloe, had walked over to her little bungalow near the eighth hole. She went into each room, turning on the light, looking around, and then turning the light off.

She switched on her TV, and ignored it. She spent a lot of time sparring with her conscience, alternately playing the advocate for her behavior, then berating herself for it.

Marcy, who knew her argument with Dave was silly, and that she had baited him into fighting with her, sat and sketched and smoked cigarettes, one after the other.

Dave, being Dave, talked a bit with Nelson about the argument he had with Marcy, but neither of them could figure it out. He and Nelson had gone to the local diner, and Dave ordered a meatloaf dinner, and Nelson had two pieces of pie and a Coke. When they pulled up to their house an hour later, Chloe's car was gone. They cautiously entered the house, and noticed that the couch and coffee table had been moved back to their proper positions. Nelson idly opened the fridge, found the leftover Chinese food, which he promptly took out, nuked, and ate.

Jeanette, whose parents were out for the evening, took more pain pills and clutched a heating pad to her aching ovaries.

It was eleven o'clock in the morning, Saturday, and Dave was

pacing around the kitchen, waiting for Nelson to get his ass in gear.
They needed to drop off Nelson's truck to Dave's buddy who was
moving today, and then get Nelson to the high school by noon. Dave
had thought about calling Marcy, but decided he would wait and try
to talk with her in person when he went to pick up Nelson at four. He
didn't have a clue as to what to say to her anyway, because for the life
of him, he couldn't figure out what he had done wrong, or how they
had gotten into the argument in the first place. "Nelson! We have to
leave in fifteen minutes!" He could hear the shower running, knew
Nelson couldn't hear him, he just felt like bellowing.

Sara came through the door into the kitchen. Dave looked at
her, she at him. He didn't like the way she looked, a little haggard,
like she hadn't gotten much sleep.

He watched her carefully as she opened the refrigerator door.
She slammed it shut.

"Nelson killed off the leftovers last night," Dave said, reading
her mind.

"I see that."

"You want to talk about it?"

"I knew you were going to say that." Sara sat down tiredly at
the kitchen table. "Oh hell, Dave. I don't know if I was right, or she
was wrong, or what. I don't know if I went overboard in my reaction.
I probably did." She idly played with the salt and pepper shakers.

"How did it end up?"

"I asked her to leave. She did."

Dave carefully picked his words. "Sara, do you think she honestly likes you? I'm not talking romance here. But likes you. Wants
to be your friend."

Sara sighed, and just as carefully thought about her words before
she replied. "Well, yeah, I do. But I don't like my friends playing me.
I've had way too much of that. Everyone skirting around things, not
coming to the point of what they want. It's like they're playing a
chess game, where they're thinking six moves ahead all the time. 'If I
do this, and this, and then that, and that, then I will get her to do
this.'" Sara looked to Dave to see if he understood. "Why didn't she
just come out and ask me if I would do this choreography thing for
her? I don't get it."

"Maybe because she knew you would say 'no.'"

Sara looked up at him in surprise. "Why would she think that?"

Dave shook his head and smiled gently at his sister. "Because
that's what you do, Sara. Everything is a 'no' with you, until someone convinces you otherwise."

Sara didn't understand this, and she looked to Dave for explanation.

"Sara, you live your day to day life as a no—won't do that, can't do that. It's your safe, protected little world. We have to convince you that whatever we want you to be involved in won't rock your world. That the simplest things aren't a threat to you. Nelson and I had to pester and wheedle you to leave here the other night, just to go look at a friggin' horse. And you love horses. And everything turned out all right, right?" She nodded her head, a sheepish yes. "Well, after you reading your hard and fast life rules to Chloe the other day, your controls on 'how to be around you,' do you think she felt secure enough to just approach you honestly and ask you to do this?"

Sara just looked to the shakers again, and clicked them together a few times.

"Sara, we all have to plan on how to approach you about things. Answer me this: do the words 'Chloe' and 'conniving little bitch' go together?"

Sara laughed at the absurdity of that statement. "No, Dave, not at all. Not for a minute."

"So you got mad at her for being creative in her approach to you."

Sara knew he was right, she just hated admitting it. She sighed, and pushed the shakers away from her. "I guess I should talk to her, apologize."

Nelson came into the kitchen, practically shining from his recent shower. "Hey." He opened the fridge, and closed it again.

"Your dad said you killed it all off last night. Short-term memory loss, Nels?"

He looked at her and grinned guiltily. "Yeah. Hey, Dad, can we stop on the way?"

"Yeah sure, we can pick up something." Dave tilted his head at Sara. "How about I pick you up on the way to pick up Nelson, and maybe you can take a few minutes and talk to her? Otherwise, you'll have to call her, and, well, I just think apologies are better in person. I need to talk with Marcy, too."

Sara was about to shake her head no, but caught Dave's eyes and quickly nodded yes. "I gotta quit being so predictable, I guess."

Dave patted her on the shoulder, and he and Nelson headed out.

Dave called Sara, and said he would pick her up a little before 3:30 so they could head out to the school. She hadn't accomplished much with her day; she spent a good deal of it starting things, and then getting distracted, and then not finishing them, and starting something else. She nervously paid careful attention to her appearance today, something she rarely ever did, fussing with her long dark hair, picking out the right clothes, even worrying about her socks. She changed her shirt several times. For every minute that passed,

the clocked seemed to go back two. She was just about to change her
shirt yet another time when she heard Dave's honk from out in her
driveway. She ran a brush through her hair one last time, grabbed her
barn coat, flipped on her porch light, locked the door behind her, and
climbed into the Explorer.

Dave could see the strained look on her face, and knew what the
drill was. He kept quiet on the drive to the school, just glancing over
to gauge any physical clues that Sara might be in the midst of a panic
attack. Her face was still and her breathing was even, although she
kept her eyes closed the whole way there. When Dave pulled into the
parking lot behind the school, he was surprised to see very few cars
parked there. Dave pulled the vehicle into a slot near the doorway,
and put it into park, and turned off the engine.

"Sara? We're here."

Sara opened her eyes, and took in the sight of a nearly empty
parking lot. There were only four or five cars in the lot, but Chloe's
was one of them. She let out a small sigh of relief. *I don't think I
could psych myself up again to do this anytime soon. I just need
some air before I go in there.* She nodded grimly to Dave, and got
out. She breathed in the cool, moist air, and noticed the beginnings
of snow flurries beginning to fall. Dave stood nearby, knowing he
had to be ready to get her out of there quickly if she asked. She took
another cleansing breath, and nodded at him.

"Don't leave without knowing what's happening with me, okay,
Dave?" she reiterated, feeling a comfort in her brother's presence.

"I won't be far, Sara. I'll leave the car unlocked. If it gets to be
too much, just come out here. I won't be long, I promise."

One more cool breath in, and Sara and Dave started toward the
building. They entered the small back hallway that led to the theater.
They made their way to the theater doors, and Dave looked at Sara
once again, once again she nodded her readiness. Dave opened the
door, and peered in. He looked around.

"Nobody in there, it's dark," said Dave. They continued up to
the end of the hallway. Left led to the cafeteria and right led to the
gymnasium. Dave looked at Sara and shrugged.

Dave headed toward the cafeteria, Sara turned right to go to the
gymnasium. She stopped at a water fountain along the way, and got
a quick drink. She looked down the hallway behind her. Dave must
have already gone into the cafeteria. Sara made it to the gymnasium
doors, took another deep breath and tried the door. It was unlocked,
so she pulled on it, and walked in. The lights were on, but she didn't
see anyone. She walked out to the center of the basketball court,
looked around and was turning to leave, when Chloe came out of the
girls' room door to her right. Sara saw her first, and stood still,
hands in her coat pockets. Chloe was paging through her clipboard.

She looks beautiful. Chloe had on a forest green silk shirt, and a pair of dark brown linen pants. Sara thought, not for the first time, how she just seemed to glow. Her shoulder-length reddish hair looked like she'd just combed it. Chloe stopped for a moment, writing something down on her clipboard, and absently tucked some hair behind her ear.

"Hey," said Sara, knowing that there was no way to avoid startling her.

Chloe nearly dropped her clipboard, and looked at Sara with wide, surprised eyes. "Jesus, you scared me. What are you doing here?"

"Dave and I came to pick up Nelson," Sara said in a low voice, and started walking toward Chloe. "And—"

The gymnasium door swung open, and a blonde woman came in, wearing a coat, and carrying another. All three women started, and then nervously laughed. Sara recognized the blonde, Audra Simmons.

"Hey, Chloe, I got your coat for you. You about ready to go? Hi, Sara," said Audra cheerfully. "What are you doing here?"

Sara felt some weird feeling of being caught in a time warp. "Dave and I came to pick up Nelson." She stopped, and looked at Chloe. Chloe wasn't looking at either of them, she seemed to be focused on the basketball hoop at the end of the court.

"Yeah, I'm ready." Chloe turned her attention to Audra, who was smiling at her. She took her coat from Audra, and began to put it on. Sara stood there in silence.

"I didn't know if you wanted to stop at your house before we went, we can if you want," said Audra, oblivious to the tension.

Chloe shrugged her coat on, and started to button it. "Well, I probably could use a sweater, if that would be all right..." her voice trailed off.

"No problem, our reservations aren't until five." Audra looked at Sara. "We're going out for dinner up at Chautauqua," she said in explanation. Sara opened her mouth to say something, but nothing came out. She looked at Audra again, and then at Chloe, who finally met her eyes, but quickly looked away.

Sara said it once more, "Well, Dave and I just came to pick up Nelson." She looked away, and found that her feet were walking her to the gymnasium door. "I'd better go find them before they leave without me." She put her hand on the door, and pushed. "You two have a nice time at dinner." She smiled, merely a show of teeth, and went out the door. Straight down the hallway to the cafeteria, where she saw Dave quietly talking with Marcy. "Dave. Dave. Now!" she said, and when she saw that he had heard her, and understood, she turned and left.

Dave tapped Marcy on the arm and said, "I gotta go. Bring Nelson home for me, okay?" He saw her nod, and he smiled a quick thanks.

Dave hurried out to the hallway, and just as he was going to turn the corner to go down the hallway that led past the theater, he saw Chloe and a taller blonde woman exiting the gymnasium far up the hallway. He kept on going, past the theater and out the doors to the parking lot. Sara was already in the Explorer. He climbed in, and looked at her.

Her eyes were closed, her teeth gritted. "Just get me out of here. Now."

He started the motor, and drove away. The thick falling snowflakes tightly blanketed the vehicle, making Sara's world appear to shrink even smaller.

After dropping Chloe's car off at her house, and procuring a sweater to ward off the increasingly inclement weather, the pair headed in Audra's Civic for just beyond the New York state line, and the small town of Chautauqua. Chautauqua, known worldwide as an artist's haven, is a closed community of carefully cared-for Victorian houses, set along brick roads, and lit by street lamps that imitated the gas lights of the late 1800s.

Chautauqua is also home to a small lake brandishing the same name. The area is marked by cabins with small docks. Tiny candlelit restaurants also line the lakeside, providing customers with both a quiet intimacy and lush view of the water, whether dotted with sailboats in summer, or frozen over and shimmering in the moonlight, as it was this night.

After driving in persistently falling snow showers, the two friends made their way into one of the small restaurants. They were seated in a cozy dining room, so completely lit by hurricane candles that it seemed that the invention of electricity hadn't yet reached this small hamlet. The quiet incandescence of the candles encouraged communication in low tones and discouraged raucous laughter. The glow from the globes surrounding the candles cast a light that would mask any fault, and accentuate the smallest of perfections. The women sat at a table that afforded an unencumbered view of the snow swirling down on the frozen lake. Words said in this atmosphere would be said with an economy; it would be an assault on the senses to clutter the air with wasted, ill-chosen conversation. It was a perfect romantic setting that encouraged long looks and softly spoken phrases. Both women fell easily under the spell of the view, the candles, and the easy camaraderie between them.

After ordering a glass of white wine for Chloe, and some mineral water for Audra, the women simply embraced the atmosphere, and relaxed.

"This is just what I needed," sighed Chloe. She looked at the softly glowing countenance of her dinner partner. "Thank you for thinking of this."

"My pleasure. I love this place."

"I've never been here. The last time I came up here, years ago, I believe I was at that restaurant," and she pointed toward the far side of the lake, "over there. Somewhere."

"It's a little hard to see it. I'll take your word for it." Audra grinned, but made an effort to look where Chloe was pointing.

"I can't believe Chautauqua is so close, and I haven't been here in years," said Chloe, regret in her voice.

"We used to come up here for concerts, Mel and I, in the summers. Symphony, rock and roll, choirs, zither players. We ran the gamut. Have you ever been to a concert in the little open-air amphitheater they have here?"

"Many times. I saw a wonderful presentation of *A Midsummer-Night's Dream* there, too," Chloe reminisced. "Just the perfect way to present it, too, under the stars of a summer sky. I don't think that play should be performed any other way."

Their waitress appeared and took their orders, and just as quickly, disappeared.

Chloe laughed softly after her departure. "I almost forgot there were other people here besides us. She startled me."

"Expecting snow fairies to supply us our repast, are you?" *I think I could believe in them on a night like this.*

"Something like that." Chloe took a small sip of her wine, and twirled the stem of her glass between her fingers. Her mind turned quickly to Sara, and then she just as quickly firmly locked out any further thoughts of her. *I want to have a nice evening.*

The two women relaxed even further, and let small passages of time pass without conversation. They stole small glances at each other, looked out into the night, and felt their aches fall from their shoulders.

The waitress again unobtrusively appeared, deposited their salads, and faded from view.

"I'm thinking not only is she a snow fairy, but she is a ghost, too," remarked Audra.

"I think she drops on strings from the ceiling, and they just pull her back up there again." Chloe giggled. As if to prove her point, the waitress floated in, replaced Chloe's wine glass with a fresh one, and was gone.

"Are you sure this Chautauqua, and not Cueste Verde, the setting for *Poltergeist?*" teased Audra.

"Hey, you were the one driving. I never pay attention to road signs as a passenger. I've put my life entirely into your hands tonight."

"Is that right?" murmured a very pleased Audra.

Chloe raised her wine goblet, and motioned for Audra join her in a toast. As they touched glasses, Chloe noticed the reflection of the candle's glow shining in Audra's eyes. "Absolutely."

Dave looked out his living room window again. "Damn, would you look at it out there? It's practically March, and it just keeps coming and coming. I'm never going to get the course open by the middle of April."

Marcy patted the couch beside her. "Will you calm down already? This is the Northeast, it is doing exactly what it always does this time of year. Come and sit down. Wishing it away doesn't work, I've tried."

Dave, still steaming about what he had no control of, peeked out the window one more time. "I'll tell you this, you are not driving home tonight in that little matchbox car of yours."

Marcy patted the couch one more time, this time with a little more emphasis. Dave settled down beside her. Marcy leaned a little on her side, and put her head on his shoulder. "Well, bub, I'm not staying here, if that's what you're trying to say. No way. I know Nelson's all grown-up, and he probably knows we are more than shaking hands all night when you stay at my place, but I'm still a teacher in his school. I do have some dignity and morals."

Dave snuggled into her, and then stealthily gave her a small tickle to the ribs. "You, dignity? Since when? And don't even get me started about morals."

She laughed, and gave him a quick peck on the cheek. "So how am I getting home, huh, fella? You going to make me walk?"

"I'll drive you. In my grown-up car, like Chloe calls it."

Marcy got up off the couch, and looked out the window, and a small frown came to her face. "Speaking of our dear madam librarian, I'm getting a little concerned about her, too. She and Audra went to Chautauqua tonight for dinner, and they have to drive back in this." She turned and looked at him. "When's the last time you saw a plow go by?"

Dave frowned, and looked at the clock. It was nearly 10:00 p.m. "It's got to be more than an hour now. Do you think they would be headed back by now?"

Marcy looked a little more troubled. "I think Audra said they had reservations for five o'clock. They had to have left by now, the restaurant wouldn't stay open too late in this crap."

"They're big girls, and if it gets too bad, there's plenty of places for them to stay, there and along the way back."

Marcy thought that over, and said cryptically, "That's what I'm afraid of."

Dave raised a puzzled brow at that statement. "Why don't you just call her, and see if she's home yet?"

Marcy didn't answer. She walked to the phone, and dialed the number. After a few moments she said, "Marcy here. Just checking to make sure you two made it home safe. Give me a call at home and let me know you're all right." She hung up the phone, and said needlessly, "Answering machine."

She reached for Dave's hand, and pulled him up off the couch. "Now go tell your son that you're taking me home, and that we have another all-night Scrabble tournament planned."

Not more than a few minutes later, a snow-covered Honda Civic pulled into the driveway behind Chloe's Subaru. Audra turned off the motor, and turned to Chloe.

"Whew, that only took, what, a little over two hours to get here? For what normally takes less than an hour?"

"There's got to be close to seven inches out there, and it had just started snowing when we left for the restaurant. Just look at my car." Chloe nodded to the large white form in front of them.

Audra's headlights, still on, lit the nearly unrecognizable large clump of snow ahead of them. She laughed, and said, "Thank God we got behind the one and only plow running between here and the New York state line, or I think we might still be in New York right now."

"For sure. C'mon, let's get into the house and warmed up. I'm getting colder just looking at it all. And it's still coming down like crazy."

The two women, not properly dressed for the bad weather, trudged up the walk and Chloe unlocked the door to her house. She flipped on the small light near the front door, and they both stamped their feet to get the snow off.

Audra swiped some of the snow off the shoulders of her coat, and looked around. "Still looks the same. Books. Books. And, look! More books!" Audra kidded, knowing that Chloe's passion for books didn't end with her job.

Chloe was already taking off her jacket, and then hung it on the knobbed rack on the wall. "Get your coat off, and stay awhile. I'm going to make us some hot chocolate, or coffee. You have a preference?"

Audra hung her coat next to Chloe's. She rubbed her hands

together. "Hot chocolate sounds perfect. I need to get some circulation into my hands again, I've been gripping that steering wheel for the last two hours."

"Have a seat, I'll be right back."

"I think I'm going to use your bathroom, if you don't mind. I drank entirely too much water tonight."

Chloe's laughter carried from the kitchen. "Thank God for the designated driver rule."

Chloe was getting some cups out from the cupboard when she noticed the blinking light on her answering machine. She touched the play button, and heard Marcy's message. Audra caught the tail end of it as she entered the kitchen.

"Marcy still mother-henning you, huh?"

Chloe smiled and said, "Yeah, always. I guess I'd better call her. It'll just take a sec." Chloe picked up the phone, dialed, and waited, and then said, "Mom? Me and Audra just got back. We're fine. Thanks for caring. Talk to you tomorrow."

Audra came over and stood next to Chloe. "Ooh. You're making it the old fashioned way, you're heating the water in a teakettle, instead of the microwave. I'm impressed."

Chloe tapped out the powder from two envelopes into the cups. "So, I'm not Julia Child. So sue me." She glanced out her kitchen window, the snow was coming down just as thick as before. "And I'm thinking that you shouldn't be trying to drive home to Erie in this stuff either." She turned and found Audra standing directly in front of her.

Audra reached her arms around Chloe's waist, and pulled her close, looking deeply into Chloe's eyes. She touched her nose to Chloe's and said, with a catch in her voice, "I think you're right, I'm not going anywhere tonight." Her lips met Chloe's softly, and she waited but for a moment, and then felt Chloe's arms slide up around her neck. She pulled Chloe in even tighter, and kissed her with all the fervor born of years of hopeless longing, unfulfilled fantasy, and now, finally, wondrous reality.

It was Sunday morning, and Nelson and his aunt were getting ready to head out to Charlie Shemp's house to take a ride on Cargo. "I wasn't sure you were going to come along today. Dad said that," Nelson paused uncomfortably, "that you had a bad day yesterday. That you had an anxiety attack."

Sara leaned back in the kitchen chair, and stirred her coffee. "That's kind of true, Nelson. I spent a lot of time thinking about this last night. To tell you the truth, I spent so much time thinking about it, I didn't even notice all the snow until I woke up this morning.

Look at it, it looks like a foot fell out there."

Nelson smiled, and settled into the chair across from her. "Yeah, Dad drove Marcy home last night. Guess he got stuck."

Sara winked at him, and returned his smile. "I was watching the weather channel, and it's supposed to get up into the fifties today. All of this will be gone by tomorrow morning." She sipped her coffee. "This is such screwy weather."

Nelson stretched his long legs out, and put his bare feet on an empty chair. "So, you had a bad day yesterday?"

Sara got up, and poured herself another cup of coffee. "You're going to make me talk about this, aren't you?"

"Dad said you wouldn't talk to him about it. So, being the second in command, it's my duty to pester you in Dad's stead."

"Nels, for a guy that doesn't talk a lot himself, you sure are asking a lot of me."

"Okay, then, use little sentences. We have an hour and a half before we have to be at Charlie's. I'm all ears."

Sara reached across, and squeezed one of Nelson's toes. "And all feet, too." She stirred some milk into her coffee. "I was anxious about going to the school yesterday. I wanted to talk to Chloe, and tell her I was sorry for last night. I said some pretty unfair things to her. And you know me, I'm not much for apologizing. So I worked myself into a state before Dave and I even left for the school."

Nelson's smile gently urged her to continue.

"Well, I get there, I'm already a mess, because I feel bad about what I said to her. I found her in the gymnasium. I just got out a 'hello' to her, and she really hadn't said anything to me, or me to her, when this woman, an old friend of hers, swoops in and takes off with her. I never got to apologize. I never really got a handle on how Chloe was feeling, if she was mad at me, or just feeling badly, or what."

Nelson scratched his leg. "So, do it again. Try again. Chloe's such a nice person, I'm sure she'll understand."

"Nelson, it's not that simple. I left there so fast, I thought at the time I was simply having one of my panic attacks. But there's more to it. I left there, yeah, because I was anxious, but when I thought about it last night, I realized why I really left."

"Not because of the anxiety attack?" Nelson's brows turned downward.

"I think that was a part of it." Sara pushed her cup away from her and looked out the window and the brightening blue skies beyond. "But I think, no, I know, what really was the biggest part of my having to get out of there. I just had the most overwhelming feeling that I blew it. Blew whatever chances I had with Chloe." She sighed, and continued her staring out the window.

Nelson, not well versed in the matters of the heart, said, "How can you blow it just because of one fight?"

"Timing is everything. One fight, no chance to apologize, and one very interested old friend."

"You mean interested, interested?"

"Yeah. They were leaving on a date," Sara's voice tightened on that word, date.

"Oh." Nelson shrugged his shoulders, and said, "One date. What could happen from one date?"

Sara got up, and watched the icicles dripping from the gutters from over the window. She turned and looked at him.

"Plenty, Nelson. Plenty."

"I absolutely love this bed. It has got to be the greatest bed I've ever been in," crowed Audra, happily hugging a pillow in her arms. "And these quilts, how old are they? They're so soft." She snuggled deeper under the covers.

Chloe came out of her bathroom, dressed in a terry cloth bathrobe, toweling her wet head. She grinned at the blissfully happy Audra, who was rolling around in the bed like a puppy getting its belly scratched.

"Just don't look down from the edge of it. You'll get dizzy. I know I do."

Audra peeked out from under the covers, and moved her head over to the edge of the mattress and looked down. "Ooh, I see what you mean. It's got to be five feet off the floor. A person could get hurt."

"Three feet, four inches. I measured. It was my great-grandmother's bed. And the quilts were my grandmother's." She grabbed her hairbrush off her vanity, and ran it through her hair.

"You should think about padding the floor around it, just in case."

"Oh, just in case, huh? In case something like this should happen?" Chloe grabbed a pillow, and quickly thunked Audra over the head with it. Just as Audra had grabbed the other pillow, and was planning on retaliating, Chloe's phone rang. Chloe threw her pillow down on the bed, and grinned, "Hold that thought, or actually, forget that thought. I'm a sore loser at pillow fights." Chloe answered the phone before the answering machine picked up.

"Hello?"

"Hello yourself. See you made it home safe and sound," Marcy yawned into the phone.

"Yup, we did. We just chained ourselves to a snow plow, and let them pull us along. Where're you at?"

"At home. Dave and I had a late night, we stayed up all night worrying about you."

"I'll just bet you did." Chloe smirked.

"Did Audra make it home okay? That was some nasty storm last night, Dave is sure the golf course won't be opening until July or so."

Chloe had taken the cordless phone into the kitchen with her, and tucked it under her chin while she made a pot of coffee. "Hang on a second, Marse." Audra was standing in the doorway, mouthing "shower" and pointing toward the bathroom. She laughed at Audra's broad expressions. "Geez, you're wonderful at charades. I bet you're a blast at parties. There's clean towels in the cupboard in the bathroom."

Audra stuck her tongue out at her, and went into the bathroom.

"Okay, Marse, I'm back."

A small silence ensued. "I guess Audra didn't get home safely."

"Nope. Listen, Marse, can we talk later? I want to throw some breakfast together for her, and help her get her car cleaned off. She has to get to her parents' house by 1:00, some family gathering." She glanced at the kitchen clock. "And it's nearly 11:00 now."

"Can I stop by later? I have to go get my wind-up car from Dave's driveway. Or maybe I should just let it thaw out for a day or two. The snow's higher than the car."

"Sure. If you see my car out there, that means I'm home."

"All right, I'll probably see you later then."

"Seeya."

Nelson had his new, or borrowed, Stetson on in honor of his first time on a horse. He and Sara were traveling up Route 20, heading east to Charlie Shemp's house.

Nelson adjusted his hat in the rearview mirror. "Well at least the roads are clear. I hope we can make it up that long driveway to Charlie's house." *And I hope I don't fall off that horse.*

Sara was picking snow out of her hair from the snowball fight that she and Nelson had had while cleaning all the snow off of his truck. She felt a cold, small trickle go down her shoulder blades, and she shuddered. "Damn, Nelson, you got snow down my back."

They passed through town, and were coming up on the old '76 station, and now were just a few minutes away from Charlie's.

"Slow down, Nelson, we've got a hat in front of us. They probably just got out of church." *I love that term, hat, meaning old people driving so slow that it made the most patient person erupt into uncontrollable road rage rants.*

Nelson slowed the truck down, and tapped the steering wheel impatiently. "You'd think they would at least go the speed limit. The roads are clear now. Jeez."

Nelson was still grousing when something else caught his attention. "Hey, Aunt Sara, isn't that Chloe?"

Sara didn't answer him right away. She was already taking in the scene that they were slowly passing. It was Chloe, all right. She had a broom in her mittened hands, and was helping clean the snow off of a yellow Honda Civic. Audra playfully brushed snow from the hood onto the small redhead. Already grinning, Chloe smiled even broader after catching sight of Nelson in his truck. She waved at him and Nelson beeped, and waved back.

"I told you, Nelson." Sara turned her head and looked farther up the road. "Timing. Timing is everything."

Part IX:
Angst You Very Much

Marcy was spending yet another Sunday afternoon with her butt parked on Chloe's couch. "So, when are you and Audra going to get together again?"

"That's a tough one. Our schedules aren't exactly compatible right now. She's her school's union representative, and she's been chosen to attend union conferences in Harrisburg most of next week, and then the week after that, she's got a week in Chicago, at the national conference."

Marcy shook her head. "I knew I should have gotten more involved with the union. It would get me out of town for a few weeks in the lousiest part of the winter."

"Oh, yeah, real glamorous. Harrisburg and Chicago in March? That's my idea of a good time."

"Yeah, well, what your idea of a good time and my idea of a good time are two different things."

"Which is why your name and number is on phone booths with 'For a Good Time Call' and mine isn't." Chloe smiled and looked out her front bay window. "Are you going to help me clean my car off or not? I have to check to see if Doris Raeburn made it over here last night, in a raging storm, to deposit yet another cow patty on my windshield."

"I think if we wait two more hours, the snow will just melt off it. That's my plan. My little red zoomer should be all clean and ready to go by then." Marcy brightened. "Hey, maybe one of the D'Amico family took pity on me, and it's all cleaned off now. I mean, one of them had to trip over it to get to Nelson's truck."

Chloe frowned, remembering seeing Nelson earlier this afternoon. "I saw Nelson today, he was passing by, going toward," Chloe's memory clicked in, "Charlie Shemp's! That's right, he and Sara were going over there to ride the horse today." Chloe's face remained in a frown at the mention of Sara's name. "I didn't notice if there was anyone in the truck with him, all I could see was Nelson waving, wearing this ridiculously cute cowboy hat."

"I don't know if she actually went with him or not. Dave hasn't been home, and hadn't talked to anyone before he dropped me off here."

"Doesn't matter. As far as I'm concerned..." Chloe's voice trailed off, and she didn't look like she wanted to complete her thought.

Marcy looked at her skeptically. "So I guess you didn't forgive her, huh?" *Damned hardheaded woman.*

"Forgive her? Just because she practically accused me of trying to seduce her just so I would have a replacement for Mrs. Cumberland?"

"She what?"

"That's right. She apparently thinks I'm the same kind of two bit sleazebags she used to sleep with in L.A."

"I'm sure she didn't mean it that way." *I'm gonna kill that woman.*

"You weren't there. She talked to me like I was just this little schemer, just playing with her so I could have a choreographer for some little stinking high school production of *Oklahoma!*. I mean, get real."

The resentment in Chloe's voice was so thick, Marcy had to sit back a bit before she said anything more. "So did you tell her off yesterday when she apologized?"

"What are you talking about? She showed up yesterday looking for Nelson. To pick him up."

Marcy grabbed Chloe's hand and looked her in the eye. "Chloe, Dave came to pick Nelson up, Sara came to apologize to you."

Chloe sat back, flustered at the new bit of knowledge she had just gained. She searched Marcy's face. "Are you sure? I mean, she didn't say anything, anything at all."

"Maybe because Audra was around? Was she there when you saw Sara?"

"Well, yeah, they both showed up in the gym within seconds of each other. And then Sara just blew out of the door, and then Audra and I left."

"Yeah, well, she must have been upset. She showed up in the cafeteria, and she looked horrible. She just yelled at Dave that she had to leave, now, and he took off after her. I ended up taking Nelson home. I figured she was having some sort of, you know, attack."

Chloe moaned loudly. "Oh lord. I had no idea. Is she okay?"

Marcy shrugged her shoulders. "I don't really know. She was over at her house when Nelson and I got there, and Dave said she didn't say a word to him on the way home. We never saw her again last night."

Chloe got up off the couch, and paced nervously. "I don't know what to do here, Marcy. Should I wait for her to try and apologize again? Should I just leave it be?"

"What do you want from her, Chloe? Maybe you should just leave her be. Let her come to you. She's the one who should be apologizing, it sounds like."

"I think that maybe that was the first and last chance I had to hear an apology from her. I don't know if she thinks it would be worth a second effort."

"Chloe, you must mean something to her. She wouldn't have gone to all that trouble to come out to the school otherwise. I mean, the woman is a hermit, a very contented hermit."

"Damn. She was just starting to get out of her little self-imposed exile, and I ruined all of that."

It was Marcy's turn to get mad. "Oh, no you don't. Don't you dare take that kind of responsibility on your shoulders. She had problems long before you met her, and it looks like she's going to be dealing with them for some time to come. You are not her appointed little savior."

Chloe sighed miserably. "I don't want to save her, I just want..."

"What do you want, Chloe?"

"I don't know. But something is telling me if I don't take some action, now, well, it will just be the end of it. And that just doesn't feel right to me."

Marcy didn't know how to reply to that.

Chloe sat down again, and picked at her fingernail, and frowned in concentration. *Marcy is going to kill me.* "Marse, are you going to help me, or not?"

Marcy just threw her hands up in surrender. "What, pray tell, do you want me to do?"

Marcy and Chloe were standing in the D'Amico family kitchen. Nelson was looking at his feet. *I seem to be doing this a lot lately.*

Chloe said to Nelson. "Did you tell her we were coming?"

"Yeah, I did. I told her you were giving Marcy a ride over to pick up her car."

"And?"

"And she didn't say anything."

Chloe and Marcy looked at each other. *This is not going well,* they mutually thought.

Marcy spoke first. "Chloe, it might be a good idea if you just got out of here." *Why tempt fate?*

Chloe, feeling as determined as she ever had in her life, said, "No. I've got to see her. Nelson, do you know where she is?"

Nelson, who was feeling like he was ten years old again,

answered, "In the garage. Working on some golf carts."

Chloe spun on her heel, and went out of the house, her goal the garage.

Marcy groaned, "Oh, jeez, Nelson. I'm sorry. She twisted my arm and made me make her bring me here. Does that make sense?"

"Yeah, well, there's something Ms. Donahue doesn't know. I didn't know how to tell her." *I mean, you guys are supposed to be the adults here, right?*

"What now? What didn't you want to tell Chloe?"

"I didn't know how to tell her that Aunt Sara knows that Chloe's date spent the night last night. We saw them together on the way over to Charlie Shemp's this afternoon."

Marcy sat down, hard, at the kitchen table. "Nelson? Do you know if there's anything strong to drink in this house?" She put her head in her hands. "Like battery acid, maybe?"

Sara was in the garage, waiting for Chloe to make her entrance. She had heard Chloe's car pull up a few minutes ago, and figured that Chloe would be coming out to the garage to talk to her soon. Sara checked her internal emotional meter again. *Good. I feel fine. Actually, I feel nothing. I've got myself numbed out, just where I wanted to be.*

Sara had been writing and rehearsing her own little script all afternoon. She just didn't expect to have to perform the part she had written for herself so soon. What she was going to say, how she was going to say it, when she saw Chloe again. She knew her part by heart already, although she was a little unnerved by the possibility of Chloe saying something unpredictable, something Sara couldn't foresee. *Well, I'll just have to act my way out of whatever she throws at me. I can get through this little performance, and if I try hard enough, I can make it real.*

Chloe entered the barn, and saw Sara sitting in front of a small, beige electric golf cart with a paintbrush in her hand. She was dabbing over some rust spots, dipping from a small can of paint. Sara looked up at her, and smiled. A big smile. *Good,* thought Sara, *everything is going to go according to plan. She's already reacting like I imagined she would.*

Chloe, surprised to see Sara smiling at her so benignly, was thrown off guard. She had steeled herself to meet a scowling, hostile Sara, and that Sara was not here. Not if that smile meant anything.

Sara smiled wider, and said, "Hey, Chloe. How's it going?"

"Hey, Sara. Pretty good. I just brought Marcy over to get her car. These past few weeks sure have been musical vehicles, huh?" Chloe grimaced at the lameness of her little joke.

Sara squinted at her work, and added another swipe to a stubborn spot. "Sure has. Some weather last night, huh? Ton of snow, and now it's like spring out there," she said genially.

Chloe was feeling completely off-kilter. All worked up, and her emotions had no where to go. Who was this calm woman perched on a low stool, seemingly bent on pleasantly passing the day with her? Chloe tried to regroup. "How'd the horse riding go with Nelson today? Do you think it's going to work out?"

Sara laughed a small laugh and said, "He looked like a regular Roy Rogers up there. He walked her around a bit, got her to stand still for him. She's a wonderfully intelligent horse. I even got to ride her around for a while. I think she and Nelson will go together just fine." Sara returned her attention to her painting.

"That's great. Just great. Uh, Sara?" *At least I think it's Sara. It sure looks like her.*

"Hmm?" Sara was doing some edging work now; she had to pay attention to details.

"About Friday night?"

"Yeah, I wanted to talk to you about that." Sara put down her brush, and fixed on a spot just above Chloe's left eyebrow, and willed her gaze to stay there. From this distance, it would appear to Chloe that Sara was looking her in the eye. "I wanted to apologize about that. I made an ass out of myself, I accused you of some pretty terrible things. I hope you can forgive me for that." Sara was mentally counting the hairs in Chloe's eyebrow. Sara dropped her head and continued, contritely, "Really sorry. And I also wanted to tell you," Sara's eyes came up again and settled on Chloe's right eyebrow. "That the answer is yes, to helping out, taking Mrs. Cumberland's place, if you still want me to. I want to try. I could come by the school on Thursday, and meet with the kids, and then do a real session with them on Saturday." Sara tilted her face, and looked hopeful. *Make it real.* "Would that be all right?"

Chloe was scrambling now, not a thing was going as she had expected. "That's great, Sara, Thursday would be fine, I'll tell the kids." She had expected to have to be in charge of this conversation with Sara, but Sara was throwing her for a loop. *This is too confusing. I have to say it before I lose my nerve.*

"Well, I'm still not sure why you said the things you did, but I realize I may have given you the wrong idea. I really wasn't trying to manipulate you, Sara, I should have told you—I wanted to tell you," Chloe's mind was now on stunned setting, "I wanted to tell you that night." *Say it out loud, Chloe.* "Oh hell, Sara, whether you said yes or no to the whole dancing thing, it really didn't matter." Chloe took a huge breath. "I just wanted to be with you. It didn't matter what the answer was. Don't you know that?" *Let honesty be the best pol-*

icy in this situation. Please.

There popped up that little glitch of unpredictability that Sara wasn't prepared for. *She just wanted to be with me.* Sara needed to ad lib something in reply to that. She wasn't immediately coming up with anything, so she ad libbed silence. It was working. Chloe just stood there, and Sara decided to just go on to her next line.

Sara chuckled. "I mean, there I was, accusing you of something that I've done a million times myself." Dip, wipe, brush stroke. "I can't tell you how many women I've ego-stroked into my bed." Dip, wipe, brush, brush. "Kind of had fun doing it, too." Sara looked up at Chloe, and winked, and returned her eyes to her paint can. *There, I'm a dirt bag. Deal with it.*

Chloe was wildly confused now. *Is she apologizing, bragging, or accusing me of something?*

"I'm not exactly sure how you mean that, Sara, but I'm glad you decided to—"

Sara scooted her stool to begin painting on a different area of the golf cart. Some of the raging jealousy in her heart began to bleed through into her words. *I want to hurt her, like she's hurt me.* She looked at Chloe, and this time, met her eyes for real. "So, Chloe, how did your date with Audra go? Have big fun?" The sarcasm in her voice was plain. Her face was tight and unsmiling. When Chloe didn't immediately respond, she raised her brow and gave her a nasty smirk. "I'll take that as an unequivocal yes, then."

She turned back to the golf cart one more time, determined to get herself under control, and to stay that way, no matter how Chloe responded.

Chloe was totally lost, swimming in the alternately upbeat, friendly, angry, accusatory, then offhand mixture of messages that she was getting from Sara. She reacted the only way she knew how.

She moved the few steps to Sara's side. Chloe dropped to her knees, and put her hands on Sara's face, and turned it to hers.

"Sara. Please. Why are you doing this, why are you being like this?" She searched Sara's eyes for some truth. "Don't you know that I want you?" she asked softly, pleadingly.

Sara closed her eyes, and took Chloe's wrists in her hands, and moved them down, onto her knees. She took a deep breath, and acted her heart out.

"I'm sorry, Chloe. Really I am. But it's not going to work. I'm not a good bet for the long run. I'm just here to get better, then I'm out of here. I don't want to be a grass cutter at a penny-ante golf course. I want to go back, get my career back, get back the life I used to have. I'm almost there now. My face has almost healed, and what won't heal, the makeup people can fix. Just let me have my fun while I'm here. Let me help with this play, see Nelson do his stuff, then I go." Sara finished her little monologue, and saw the pain on Chloe's face. *I have to make this woman go away, so I can go back to being numb again. I won't let her hurt me again. There's only one way to do it.* "Chloe, you're really wonderful. You are. But you just aren't the kind of woman that I want. I'm sorry if I led you to believe something else. I get carried away sometimes, just playing, you know?" Sara could see tears beginning in Chloe's eyes. *There, that should be the fatal blow.*

Behind the tears that were beginning to fall, Chloe's heart and mind gave up. Anger replaced whatever sorrow she was feeling, two-fold. She had offered her heart, her dignity and her trust, and had been told that they were not of any consequence. Her tears mutated from ones of sadness, to ones of raging frustration and hurt. That frustration grew, and she stood up, and began crying in earnest.

Sara's resolve finally broke at the sight of Chloe so completely devastated. *What did I do?* She started to reach out her arms to Chloe, to tell her that she was a liar and a fool. But just as she was about to confess all, Chloe turned and left the barn.

"Chloe, wait." But it was too late, Chloe was in her car, the motor was running, and Chloe wiped her eyes, and floored it, roaring out of the driveway.

Marcy, who had seen Chloe leave from the kitchen window, came tearing out of the house and ran over to Sara.

"What the hell happened out here? Why was Chloe crying like that?" she demanded of Sara. *I don't give a rat's ass about this woman's 'delicate' condition, I want answers, now.*

Sara flinched, and buried her feelings. "I told her I didn't want her. She took it badly," she said as offhandedly as she could.

Incredulous, Marcy blurted, "What, are you nuts? Don't answer that. I know you are. Any damned fool can see that you're in love with her, and have been since the minute you met her." Marcy gulped in air, because she knew she was going to keep yelling. "And she's so in love with you that she can't even see what I can see so clearly about you right now, that you might be the biggest, tallest, dumbest asshole that I've ever met!"

Sara went on the defensive. "Oh yeah, she's so in love with me, we have one fight and she goes and fucks Audra Simmons the very next night." Sara spat the words out, like getting rid of dirt off the tip of her tongue.

Marcy was stunned at Sara's words. Sara stared at her, shaking with anger.

Marcy started slowly, her voice barely containing all the fury she was feeling. "No, I take it back, you are the biggest asshole I will ever meet. Ever. I know that now for a fact." Her eyes bored into Sara's cold blue ones. "She didn't sleep with Audra, you dumbass. She turned her down. She told Audra, for some stupid reason that I can't fathom now, that her heart belongs to you. You, who wouldn't know a good thing if it came up and bit you on the friggin' butt!" *Just one punch. Just one. That's all I want.*

Sara's gut felt the blow as if Marcy had really thrown it. "Oh no. No."

Marcy stared razors across Sara's throat. "Nice going, Miss Movie Friggin' Star. You just screwed over the best thing that will ever happen to you. Congratulations."

"What do I do now?" said Sara weakly, not sure if she had said it aloud.

"You're not asking me how to get her back? She's my best friend, you idiot. I don't care if you are Dave's sister. Why the hell should I help you get her back?"

"You have to help me. Because you're right about two things, Marcy."

Marcy squinted at her, and said, exasperated, "What?"

"I am the biggest asshole you will ever meet, and because," Sara's eyes showed the truth of her soul, "I'm in love with her."

Dave was leaning against the refrigerator. "Still no answer? Is her machine on?"

Marcy glared. "I'll bet she's there, and just doesn't want to talk. I've left two messages now for her to call me on my cell phone."

Nelson was sitting on the kitchen counter, just taking everything in.

Marcy, standing in the kitchen doorway, threw Dave a look. "I swear, Dave, if she wasn't your sister, and for some damned reason I feel like we're all in this together, you'd be dialing 911 right now, and they'd be hauling me off for assault and battery." She kicked Sara's chair for emphasis.

Sara was seated, head hunched in her hands, at the kitchen table. She hadn't said a word, other than a low moan here and there, as Marcy had quite ungracefully filled Dave in on the details of what had happened.

Dave, half sympathizing with his clearly tormented sister, and half wishing he could kick her chair himself, half-heartedly said, "Marse, cut her a break, and take it easy on my furniture, wouldja?"

Sara and Marcy said it simultaneously, "Stay out of it, Dave!"

Marcy ignored Sara's chiming in, and went on to explain, "And your sister here, a total nitwit about love and romance, thinks that Chloe bedded Audra Simmons, so she does everything in her power to hurt Chloe and drive her away. In tears." Marcy kicked Sara's chair one more time.

Sara moaned again.

Nelson, coming to his suffering Aunt's rescue, said, "Well, it sure looked that way. I mean, we passed there on our way to Charlie's this afternoon. And they were outside, cleaning a lot of snow off of that yellow car, so well, we just assumed...I mean, I even saw it that way."

Sara lifted her head, and made an effort to speak. "Yeah, that's right. That's what we—"

Marcy kicked another toe mark onto Sara's chair. "You keep quiet. You got yourself into this mess, and now you want us to help you get out of it. You've already done enough damage."

Sara's head went all the way to the table, and she sprawled her arms out on either side of it.

Marcy was in fourth gear, heading for overdrive. "Audra Simmons would probably be a very good thing for that woman. But no, our dear librarian has to fall for some lunkheaded, self-absorbed, anxiety-stricken former starlet who now tinkers with golf course machinery for a living."

Dave said, "Hey, that's not fair. She also cuts the grass. And stuff."

Sara murmured, "Attaboy Dave, you tell her."

"Well, enough throwing the blame around, I guess. We all know where the blame lies. Right there, crying in her Diet Coke, head on the table. So, now what the hell are we going to do about it?" Marcy looked at Nelson, and then at Dave. Both of them blinked at her and shrugged.

"Oh, great, just great. I forgot, I'm dealing with a family who has a hard time stringing together even one sentence between the three of you."

Dave was offended. "Marcy—"

Nelson frowned. "that's not—"

Sara finished, "—true."

Marcy threw up her hands and spoke, person to person, with God. "Why me?" She kicked Sara's chair again. "God told me to do that." She sat down in the chair closest to Sara, and dropped her head to table level so she could see eye to eye with Sara. "Sara, I see only one solution here. Wait, two."

Sara blinked open a bleary eye and looked hopefully at Marcy.

"Two courses of action. One, Sara has to do entirely by herself. She has to devote herself to it, day and night." Marcy's voice went stern, "Sara, do you think you're up to it? Do you really love Chloe?"

Sara gulped and said, "Yes, to both parts."

Marcy looked her in her one open eye. "Groveling. Twenty-four hours a day until you get her back, and probably the rest of your life after you do. And I know Chloe, she's strong willed. You may think you were a bad ass, cranky bitch in your former life, but I assure you, you were a rank amateur compared with her. As soon as Chloe real- izes you are trying to make nice with her, she's going to go at you with both barrels. It's going to hurt. You have to be tough. I'm not going to commit to this little reunion without a solemn promise from you, Sara. Because there's going to be fallout on all of us, especially me, if she realizes we are all working toward a common goal. Can you promise us this? It's not going to be pretty."

Sara opened both eyes. "I swear."

Marcy growled, "Good. Now, for you two." She cast an eye at father and son. "And me. We have to work together. We have to be devious, not obvious, or it'll throw the whole thing off. She'll string up all of us and hang us from a tree. We'll have to come up with a plan." She scanned Dave and Nelson's blank faces. "Okay, I'll have to come up with a plan. You two just play your parts."

Sara moaned again, "Oh, God, I have to count on them?"

Marcy finally smiled. "Oh, yeah. Aren't you the lucky girl. Now, I have to get out of here, and go check up on Chloe. And if she's really bad off, Sara, I will personally be back to kick your butt just for the fun of it." She grabbed her coat, and gave Dave a scintil- lating kiss goodbye. "Don't worry, big guy, I'm not mad at you. I'll call as soon as I can with a progress report." She kicked Sara's chair leg, once more, in farewell. "And you, pull yourself together. You've got a lot of ass to kiss, you're going to need your strength."

Marcy was a little rattled. Seated on Chloe's couch, she was helpfully holding a box of tissues, and handing them over to Chloe, one by one, when it looked like Chloe was in need of another one. There was a small mountain of snotty, wet tissues on the couch between them. Marcy had only been there for fifteen minutes, but it seemed like hours already. The first five minutes Marcy had spent tapping on Chloe's front door, trying to convince her to let her in. When Chloe finally opened the door, she seemed under control, very red-eyed and face puffy, but under control. As soon as Chloe saw the sympathetic face Marcy was giving her, the crying started anew. Marcy gently guided Chloe over to the couch, and sat her down, and sat down next to her and held her. Chloe was hiccuping her sobs, a sure sign that she had been crying for quite a while.

Marcy patted her, sat back and shoved the dirty Kleenex pile she was sitting on to a space between them. "I'm sorry I didn't get here sooner, kiddo."

Chloe blatted her nose into a tissue and nodded. Her crying stopped, for the time being.

Marcy continued. "When I saw you tear out of there like a bat out of hell, well, I went to the source to find out what happened. We had words, Chloe. Lots of them. Most of them coming from me."

Chloe wadded her Kleenex into a ball and tossed it onto the pile. She felt a zillionth bit better knowing Marcy was out there sticking up for her.

"And then Dave showed up, and wanted to know what was going on, so the whole thing started again. He wasn't real happy with her, either."

Chloe wiped at the end of her red nose, narrowed her eyes, and said the first word she had spoken since Marcy arrived. "Asshole."

Marcy gently smiled. "Yeah, my word exactly. I called her that and quite a few others. And quite loudly, too. Dave and Nelson had to stop me from clocking her."

"You should have."

"I still might."

"Good."

Marcy got up from the couch. "I'm going to get us something to drink from the kitchen, and some pills so you won't get a headache. You're losing entirely too many fluids over that woman." Marcy went off to perform her tasks. When she returned, she handed Chloe a bottle of water, and pills, and sat back down again.

Chloe popped the pills, took a long drink out of the bottle, and sat back. She looked a little more composed now. "Asshole."

Marcy just nodded. "Seems like the perfect word for her. I think they had her in mind when they coined it." Marcy didn't know if it was too soon to do this, but she had to try and get Chloe's mind onto a different track, and soon, before Chloe had her mind fixated on doing nothing but hating Sara. Time to feed Chloe some new information to process.

"Yeah, Chloe, I called her that right after she told me she knew you'd slept with Audra Simmons. You should have seen the look on her face, then, when I told her you hadn't. She looked like she got hit by a piano falling out of a fourth story window. I called her an asshole then, too."

Chloe, who had tissues wadded tightly in both hands, gripped them even tighter, and looked at Marcy with wide, bloodshot eyes. "She what?"

"She looked like, uh, I can't remember what I said. She looked like she'd been hit by—"

"No, Marse, the other part. She thinks I slept with Audra?"

Marcy kept a blank look on her face. *Hook, line and sinker.* "Well, yeah. She said something about you two having a fight, then her making that feeble attempt to apologize at the school, and then you just go and break her heart by sleeping with Audra." Marcy snorted. "I mean, how could she even think such a thing about you, even if she and Nelson saw you and Audra outside this morning. Even Nelson said he figured that was what happened. The whole family are loons, with the exception of Dave so far, and I'm not holding out any hope for him." Marcy took a small sip out of her own bottle of water. "Come to think of it, I came to that conclusion myself, when I called you this morning and found out that Audra was still there." She shrugged. "But that doesn't excuse her behavior, uh-uh, no way. I wasn't about to let her get away with that."

Chloe's mind, rusted with salty tears and backed up snot, tried to engage more gears. "She thinks I slept with Audra? So that's why she was being so mean, blowing me off?"

Marcy was pleased. *Maybe I won't have to enlist the help of the D'Amico men in this. Maybe Chloe will realize on her own that Sara was just reacting to some really bad information and forgive her.*

"That bitch!" spat Chloe.

Nope, no fast forgiveness here. Chloe had leapt the wide gulf from self-pity and landed into righteous indignation in a single bound. "She calls me a casting couch director on Friday night, she does some lame job of trying apologize for it on Saturday, and then I jump Audra on Saturday night? What does she think I am, some kind of femme fatale, for God's sake? Is that what she really thinks of me?"

Marcy just raised her hands in a sign of disbelief. "Sure looks that way. I tried my best to set her straight, though. I don't know if this will make you feel any better, but when I yelled at her, and she realized the truth of the situation, she completely fell apart. She looked like I'd kicked her crutches out from under her."

"You should have kicked her in the ass, too. I can't believe this." Two of Chloe's gears engaged, and clicked. "So she gets all proprietary about me, after just what, one kiss, and that was weeks ago, and she has the nerve to get jealous and do her best to hurt me? I don't think so."

"Sometimes one kiss is all it takes. You know what they say, 'you kiss 'em, you own 'em.' Maybe that's the way she feels, I don't know. That still doesn't excuse her."

Chloe's mood shifted swiftly from righteous indignation to the moral superiority of a televangelist. "I told her how I wanted to be with her, I practically threw myself at her, and begged her. And all the she comes up with is how much fun I must have had with Audra, and how much fun she has had with all the trash she's slept with. She was bragging about her conquests! Well, you know what? I'm tired of being left out of all the damned fun everyone else seems to be having. I should have taken Audra up on her offer, maybe then it would have made all of this a moot point. I'd have had fun, and maybe I would have forgotten that she existed at all. Audra's due back in a few weeks." Chloe narrowed her eyes. "Time for Chloe to have some damned fun. Lots and lots of it."

Marcy saw the look on Chloe's face, and started to panic a little. *This is going from bad to worse. I have to get her back to the here and now.* "Chloe," said Marcy softly, "You don't want to do something like that to Audra if you don't feel that way about her. Not to get back at Sara. No amount of fun is worth hurting somebody."

"All right." Chloe knew Marcy was right. "Forget Audra for the time being. From what you say, Sara feels bad. Well, boo-fucking-hoo. Good. She can just go on feeling bad the rest of her life. Right into her future living as a rock, then the snake under the rock, then the dirt under the snake under the—"

Marcy interrupted her, she saw that Chloe was quite prepared to go on and on with that thought into perpetuity. She decided to cut to the chase. "So, Chloe, what are you going to do?"

"Do? Whaddya mean, do? Nothing. She can rot for all I care. I've got too much going on right now to deal with this. I mean, it was a lot to deal with when things were going good, for Pete's sake!"

"Well, I don't know this for sure, but I know she's hurting, and she's bound to try and I don't know, make it up to you somehow."

Chloe gritted her teeth. "Let her try," she dared.

"And I think she's got it in her stubborn head to still want to be the dance director for the play. I couldn't believe it when she said that." *Oh, yeah, that got her back to where I need her to be.*

"Is she crazy? No way. No way. I don't want her within a mile of me. I don't care if the cowboys end up doing the Macarena at the damned box social scene."

Marcy felt the need to interject a little reality between Chloe's rants. "Now, Chloe, you can't let those kids suffer because of your personal feelings. It's important to the kids, their parents, the school." Marcy had played her trump card, and sat back to see what Chloe was going to do.

She's right, I won't let those kids down because of this. Chloe set her shoulders. "Well, Sara thought I was just using her anyway, so I might as well, huh? They can practice down in the gymnasium. I won't have to have any contact with her at all." Chloe reevaluated that last thought. "Well, very little. I'll keep it professional. I can do that." Chloe said it one more time, this time with a little more conviction. "Yeah. I can do that."

After about an hour more of letting Chloe vent, and vent some more, and realizing Chloe was now just repeating herself, Marcy finally got Chloe tucked into her bed. *I think I have a bigger headache than Chloe does.* Marcy turned off the lights, locked the door behind her and got into her car. She got her cell phone out and dialed Dave's number. "Honey? It's me. Chloe's bad, but she'll be all right."

Marcy started the engine. "Tell Sara to get her ass down to Bob's Video Shack and have her rent every "How To" video there is. She's still the dance guru of this play." Marcy smiled at Dave's expression of surprise. "Oh, yeah. I know. She's got a *lot* of fancy footwork to do."

Part X :
A Doggie is Nothing If He Don't Have a Bone

East of town, west of town, two hearts were unknowingly commiserating over the loss of a love.

Tuesday's rehearsals began smoothly. Ben, the fifteen-year-old pianist extraordinaire, was there, so Chloe took advantage of his availability and had the principals of the play running through their songs. Wednesday was to be a purely acting day, because Ben had other commitments to attend to on that day, that being his standing 4:30 appointment with a local dermatologist. So the students practiced their musical numbers on Tuesdays and Thursdays. Saturdays would now be devoted to dancing, under the direction of That Famous Former Movie Star, Sara D'Amico. Chloe was going to announce Sara's participation to the students today after rehearsals, and since they'd all missed dance time this last Saturday, they'd meet with Sara for the first time on Thursday. She knew it would cause a stir amongst them, and she didn't want them distracted until they were done for the day. Hopefully, by the end of next week, they'd be able to integrate some dance moves into the songs they were now practicing, and the play would start taking shape.

Chloe, feeling a little tired, and not in any mood to be surrounded by people, decided to work one-on-one with the leads. She had the rest of the cast congregate down in the cafeteria, where Paul would work with them backed by a soundtrack recording. Presently on the little theater's stage was Jeanette, in all of her blonde glory. Chloe had turned the spotlight on her, and dimmed all the other lights. She took her normal seat near the back, to make sure that their voices carried. Chloe had met with Marcy for a few minutes. It was the first time since Sunday that they had seen each other, although Marcy had called several times on Monday to check up on Chloe. All they had time for was a supportive hug, a smile, and then they parted, each with their own jobs to perform. The show must go on.

Chloe called out to the blonde on the stage, "Okay, Jeanette, let's start from the top again. And this time, try not to put the cheerleader moves into it." *Jeanette really does possess a pretty passable voice, when she remembers to sing it, instead of cheering the boys on for a touchdown.*

Chloe noticed someone enter the door behind her, so she turned and saw that it was Nelson, who sat in the back row, kitty-corner from her. He nodded a hello at her. Chloe smiled, a bit forced, and again turned her attention to Jeanette on the stage. Chloe sighed. *Poor Nelson, this play has got to be stressful enough, now he's probably feeling strange and awkward around me. I gotta fix that.* Chloe turned again, and motioned for Nelson to come up and sit in the seat next to her. As he settled his long legs in beside her, she gave him her best reassuring smile. *It's not your fault your aunt is a moron.*

Ben, although a wonderful pianist, was not the most graceful of boys, and knocked all of his sheet music onto the floor, in a mess, as he was reaching for his soda. Jeanette saw the papers flying, and graciously left the stage to help the poor boy collect the sheets that seemed to have flown everywhere. Chloe sighed again, and took the small interruption to sneak a peak at Nelson. She felt a bit disconcerted. *I never noticed how much he looks like Sara. Same androgynous features, same deep high cheekbones, and nearly coal-black wavy hair. Even their eyebrows raise in the same, one-sided manner.* Nelson had a dreamy look on his face, his attention glued to the pretty blonde cheerleader helping the pianist. Chloe looked back to see that Jeanette was smiling a coy, shy smile back at Nelson. *That's how love should look.*

Ben finally had all of his music retrieved, and in order. He settled onto his bench, and waited for Jeanette to return on stage.

"Ready, Ben?" the redheaded director inquired.

"Ready!" he replied, cracking his knuckles.

Chloe adjusted her ball cap. "Okay, Jeanette, let's try this again. Remember, this is a love song, it's supposed to be heartfelt and gentle, so try and keep the rah-rahs toned down. You're singing to your one true love, not the home team."

Jeanette giggled a little at that, and then cleared her throat a few times. Ben played the opening bars, and Jeanette began singing. She was center stage, bathed only in a tight spotlight, and as she sang, her slight voice warmed, and she began singing with a purity that Chloe had never heard come from her before. Chloe was amazed over the transformation in Jeanette. Where before she had been merely voicing the lyrics, there was now a lush emotional quality to it.

Chloe studied Jeanette, trying to figure out what had caused the difference. *Of course. She's singing to Nelson.* Jeanette's voice was singing with a new vibrancy. Chloe sat, transfixed, as she felt herself being carried away by the romance embedded in the song. She heard, or rather felt, what Jeanette was singing.

Chloe felt the beginnings of teardrops forming in the corners of her eyes. She was powerless to contain them so she had to forcibly stop listening because the tears were starting to flow profusely now. All of her concentration focused on stemming their flow then she sniffed, and wiped her nose. Suddenly, a hand, Nelson's, was gently nudging her. In his hand was a blue bandana. She glanced at him, knowing he could see her tears, and she gratefully accepted the proffered handkerchief. She dabbed at her eyes, and blew her nose.

The pianist was playing the ending bars of the song. Chloe blew her nose one more time, and cleared her throat. With a shaky voice, she said, "Jeanette, that was awesome. I really mean it. You do that opening night, and you're going to slay them." She cleared her throat several more times. "Jeanette, that's enough today. Would you go down to the cafeteria and get Moreen Dean for me? I need to talk with Nelson for a few minutes. You can work with Paul the rest of the day."

Chloe and Nelson watched the very pleased Jeanette disappear off to the left of the stage. Chloe called down and told Ben to take five.

Nelson, feeling very uncomfortable, slunk farther back into his seat. Chloe quickly glanced at him, and wiped her nose.

"Nelson, I want to thank you. I know this is a very strange situation for everyone involved. I'm going to do my best to keep the personal, personal, and the private, private. I don't want you to think any of this reflects on how I think of you. Are we going to be okay?"

Nelson was relieved. "Oh, yeah, okay, that's good." But then he got a troubled look on his face. "I wanted to tell you, well, let you know, that I can't be here tomorrow, at all. I have to take the whole day off from school."

"Is everything all right?" Chloe asked, concerned.

"Uh, yeah, it just that I have to take Aunt Sara to Buffalo tomorrow, to see her doctor. Dad was going to, but he can't." He saw the frown cross Chloe's face. "It's just a check-up, with her plastic surgeon."

"That's okay, Nelson. Don't worry about it. You're doing great, it'll be okay if you miss a day. We'll work around you."

Nelson put his hands on his knees, as if he was going to get up.

"Uh, Nelson, there's a couple of other things I wanted to talk to you about." She coughed a little, and then said, "Tell your Aunt Sara she is to be here at 4:00 sharp on Thursday. She's going to be working with the cast in the gymnasium that day. Ask her to have something ready for one of the group dance sequences. I may do the same thing as today, work with you guys individually with Ben here in the theater. And we have to do something about blocking out your knife sequence with Jud."

Nelson, who hated to be bringing up his aunt's name once again, said, "Well, I could ask Aunt Sara to give me a few ideas about that. She used to do all those staged fighting moves on that cop show she used to be on."

Chloe bit the inside of her cheek. "Yeah, Nelson. That's a good idea. You do that."

"Aunt Sara? Please? Could we please lose the Patsy Cline? We've listened to her for four solid hours today."

His aunt, who had played "Crazy" for the fourth time in a row, was about to hit the repeat button on Nelson's CD player. She scowled and hit the stop button instead. "I guess a little silence won't kill me," she groused.

Nelson checked his watch. It was nearly 7:30 at night now, and his butt was sore. They were still an hour away from home, and his aunt hadn't said more than a few sentences all day. *Guess Marcy was right about our family being unable to talk.*

"Aunt Sara? I have to pass a few things on to you from Ms. Donahue."

Sara brightened. "Yeah? She wanted you to talk to me?"

"About the play, Aunt Sara, the musical numbers, the dancing."

"Oh." She slunk back down in her seat again and stared out her window. "What about it?"

"Um, she wants you there at four o'clock tomorrow, in the gymnasium. That's where she said you'll be working with us from now on. More room in there, I guess. Anyway, she wants you to have something ready for the big group numbers. And then Saturday, too."

"So we'll all be in the gym, huh? Guess I'd better wear my sneakers then."

"Well, no, Paul works with the acting parts in the cafeteria, and Chlo—uh, Ms. Donahue works with us, in ones and twos, in the theater."

So she won't have to run into me, huh? Probably better that way. I still don't have any idea what to say to her. "All right."

"So, that was great news from the doctor, huh? Everything's going fine. Just a barely noticeable scar, huh?"

"Yup." Sara looked at the rows of bare trees lining the interstate.

Nelson tapped the steering wheel, and checked the gas gauge. "Oh, and Ms. Donahue?"

Sara snapped to again. "Yeah?"

"Well, I told her you had experience working with fight scenes, and we need one blocked out, so I told her maybe you would help out with that. She said okay."

"Uh-huh. okay. No problem."

The miles passed in quiet. Nelson was going a little nuts from it, he was just about to suggest that they listen to "Crazy" again, just to break the monotony, when Sara actually broke the silence.

"Hey, Nelson. I was thinking I should get my Pennsylvania driver's license again. I've got to go down to PENNDOT and apply. You think we can do that next week? It'll take a couple weeks for the application to get processed, and I think I might have to take the test again. I'm not sure. I may have to get my eyes tested. I haven't driven in many years, and my last license was in California, and that one is expired, I know."

Nelson, a bit surprised at the number of words flowing out of Sara's mouth, said, "Sure, we can do it on Monday or Friday, there's no rehearsals those days. Gonna start driving again, huh?"

"Yeah, I'm tired of depending on everyone else to haul my sorry ass around. I have the panic attacks down to a minimum now, the meds seem to have leveled out, and I don't feel as dopey as I used to." She rubbed her chin. "I miss driving. Driving gives you a certain sense of freedom, you know? Like you can just go, and not come back."

Nelson didn't know quite how to take that. *Go and not come back?* "Yeah, I know. I haven't been driving that long myself, so I know what a big difference it can make."

"Yup. Gotta start thinking about making some changes." She hit the play button, and she and Nelson sang along with Patsy the rest of the way home.

"Are you hiding in here, Chloe? Isn't the director of the play supposed to be directing something?" Doris Raeburn's voice called across the theater, and startled Chloe.

Doris shook out her umbrella, and walked down the row to stand behind the director. Chloe was sitting, flipping through some sketches of backdrops that Marcy had given her for her okay, before the crew made the larger versions. Doris, in her ever-present rain bonnet, peered over Chloe's shoulder at the sketches. "Good. Looks like at least Marcy knows what a tree looks like. Now about that barn, looks to me a little like an airplane hangar. Aren't barns supposed to be red?"

Chloe turned her attention back to the sketch in front of her. "Maybe it's an unpainted barn or something. Maybe they don't have red paint in Oklahoma. I don't know," she said, a little peevishly.

Doris always ignored everyone else's moods. But Chloe was a favorite of hers, so she actually took notice this time. "Time of the month, dear? Somebody key your car? Upset I didn't leave a patty present for you last night? Sorry, it was my bridge night. It totally slipped my mind."

That last statement got a little smile out of Chloe, and Doris was pleased to see it. "Well, you didn't answer my question. Are you hiding out in here?" She didn't wait for Chloe to answer, she never did. "It's absolutely pouring out there. I guess I shouldn't complain, it could be snowing. I've had enough of that, haven't you? It's nice and quiet in here. I don't blame you for hiding in here. Although, you work in a library all day, so maybe you need the seclusion for another reason? I hide in the nurse's office, on that nice little bed in there, when I need to get away from all these hormonal teenagers. They make me crazy. And I'm a high school principal, I'm supposed to like kids." She sighed, and took off her raincoat.

Chloe took that opportunity to actually say something. "Well, all the kids are down in the gymnasium, getting together with the, er, new choreographer. They haven't met her yet, and we're a little behind, what with us losing Mrs. Cumberland, so I thought I would give them all a chance to get acquainted without my butting in. Paul, and I think even Marcy, are both down there too. So everything's under control." *Except for me, I feel like I'm going to lose my lunch. Yesterday's lunch.*

Doris Raeburn sat in the chair behind her, and grabbed the sketches from Chloe, and started paging through them. "Shame you lost Mrs. Cumberland for this year's production. I think she invented dancing, she's that old. I feel like a twelve year old around that woman, not that that's a bad thing. What's this? Looks like a trundle bed with bicycle wheels on it. Surely that can't be the creative director's vision of the surrey with a fringe on top." She paged through a few more sketches. "Not bad, all in all, but let's see if her vision actually transfers to the stage. These corn stalks look like yellow feather dusters." She handed the stack of sketches back to Chloe. "So, what poor sap did you rope into being the choreographer for this year's little masterpiece, hmm?"

Chloe cleared her throat, and didn't look at Doris. "Sara," she mumbled.

"What, speak up dear, I don't hear as well as I used to, all that damned feedback from doing morning announcements. Who?"

Chloe sucked her teeth, looked at Doris this time and said, louder, "Sara." When no recognition crossed Doris' face, Chloe continued, "Sara. Sara D'Amico."

Doris grabbed her coat, her umbrella, and then Chloe, by the arm. "C'mon, little girl. This we gotta see." She surged forth, dragging Chloe behind her. "What is that racket?"

Chloe, being half-dragged up the hallway to the gymnasium, heard the din as they approached. A smile split her face when she recognized the song.

"Chloe, quit being so pokey. I want to see what's going on in there. Let's sneak in the side door here, we'll end up under the bleachers and I can do a little spying."

They opened the side door, and were greeted by loud dance music in the brightly lit gym. They stood under the bleachers, and peered through the gaps in the seats in front of them. There in the middle of the basketball court was this year's cast of the senior class play, all dancing their asses off to the deafening music being piped through the PA system. And in the middle of all those seniors, juniors and a few sophomores was Sara D'Amico, dressed in white T-shirt and blue jeans, dancing her heart out to "Who Let the Dogs Out?" All the kids, Sara, Paul and even Marcy, were dancing, hips thrusting, arms waving, and voices providing the barks between beats. It looked like everyone was having a blast. Chloe stood enthralled as Sara danced through the crowd, alternately dancing with Paul, then swirling and dancing with a short junior girl, then spinning over to Marcy, bumping butts and then shoving off to find Nelson, and grinning like a madwoman, she stopped and pumped her arm in the air, barking like a wild wolf.

Chloe almost forgot how to breathe. She had never seen Sara so relaxed, so radiant, or smiling and laughing so much. Chloe never took her eyes off of her, she was easy to find, even as she wove through the crowd of students on the gym floor. She towered over most of them, swaying and playing with all of them. *She looks wonderful. It feels like I'm seeing her for the very first time.* As the song wound down, everyone was breathless, laughing and giddy. The song finished, and Sara, grinning, walked over to the bleachers to the right of them, and turned off the portable CD player that was hooked up to the PA system. Everyone clapped their hands and whistled. Sara waved her hands to settle them all down, and waited for them to quiet. She hopped up onto the first bleacher step, and began speaking.

"All right everyone, now that we've all loosened up and gotten to know each other a little better, we can talk about what we're going to do, dancewise, with this play. I know it's a little intimidating having to dance with your friends, much less in front of a crowd. But if we all look to each other for help, and depend on each other, we can do this, and have a lot of fun, too! Now, if you want to take ten minutes, get a drink and hit the bathroom, well, we can get started with the real stuff when you come back. Okay?"

Most of the students replied with barks. Sara grinned, stepped back down to the gym floor and pulled her damp hair off of her neck, waving some cool air onto it. She was wiping sweat out of her eyes, and that's why she never saw Doris Raeburn, with Chloe in tow, arrive in front of her.

"Still up to your old tricks, huh, Ms. D'Amico?" Doris said through clenched dentures.

Sara opened her eyes, and saw both Doris and Chloe standing in front of her. Chloe was looking everywhere but at Sara. Sara somehow found the wherewithal to greet Doris with some grace. "Mrs. Raeburn! What a great surprise! It's been years!"

Doris eyed her up and down, and tapped her on the knee with her umbrella. "You look exactly the same, a little older, maybe, but not any wiser, that's for sure." A big smile broke across Doris' face, and she reached out and hugged a startled Sara. Sara returned the hug, and said into the older woman's ear, "You were always my favorite thing about this place, you know."

Doris stepped back, and this time, poked the rather stiff Chloe in the thigh with her umbrella. "Well, some of you kids like this place so much, you never leave. Huh, Chloe?" She turned to Sara. "We can't seem to get rid of this one, no matter what I do to her."

Sara smiled her half grin, and stole a glance at Chloe. "Why would anyone want to get rid of her? Although, the cow patties, now that was a nice touch."

"You heard about that, huh? I swear, I still think about wringing her damned neck every time I see her. Have to bodily hold myself back." She squinted at Sara. "You don't look so bad, what are all these stories I keep hearing about you? That thing, you can hardly see it. It looks fine to me, why aren't you out there making any more movies, making the big bucks? I heard you were playing groundskeeper out on that little golf course your brother is building on that old cow pasture out west on Route 20. Hiding from everyone. What the hell for? You should be out, having fun, breaking hearts."

Chloe shifted uncomfortably at those last words, and it helped mute her nervousness, and brought her buried anger to the surface. When Chloe was angry, she felt much stronger. So she let her anger and disdain bubble up, and her whole attitude shifted from uneasy to firm and sure.

She cast a cold eye on Sara, and said, with more than a hint of sarcasm in her voice, "Oh, Doris, give her a little credit. She may not be making movies any more, but she sure can still break a heart when she puts her mind to it. She's famous for it, hell, she's proud of it."

Both Doris and Sara were taken aback at the amount of venom that seemed to be flowing through Chloe's voice. Chloe didn't feel shy about continuing, either. "And I just about had to promise her the moon, stars and my body, just to get her to help me out with our little production here. Didn't I, Sara?" She looked at an astonished Sara, right in her baby blues. "Luckily, for me, it didn't come to that."

Chloe realized she was plainly fuming, so she turned it down a notch, and plastered a cold smile onto her burning cheeks. "I have some work I have to do. Looks like most of the kids are back in here, and ready to begin again. Sara, thank you again."

She walked backwards slowly, still talking. "And oh, Doris? I should have told you this before, but I wasn't the one who put that bull's head in your office and scared the livin' bejesus out of you." She stopped in front of the CD player. "It was Sara."

Chloe waited for the expected reaction to appear on Doris' face, and there it was, a magnificent furious flush. Doris raised her umbrella threateningly and began advancing toward a suddenly befuddled Sara. Chloe hit the play button on the CD player. "Who Let the Dogs Out?" started booming through the gym again. Chloe watched as Sara began nervously retreating from a now clearly livid Mrs. Raeburn, who was waving her umbrella in a thoroughly menacing manner and shouting at her. The kids all started dancing again, and when Chloe saw the surprisingly spry Doris Raeburn begin to chase the wide-eyed Sara around the perimeter of the gym, the suddenly happy redheaded director danced her way toward the exit, barking and pumping her arm with a triumphant "Yip-Yippie-Yi-O!" along with the song on her way out.

Nelson and Sara were driving home from rehearsal. Patsy Cline, now the only thing that Sara would let Nelson play on the CD player in the truck, was singing "I Fall To Pieces" for the third time.

Sara, who should have been feeling good, because the rehearsal went so well, wasn't. "She hates me, Nels. You should have heard her. I couldn't believe it. Chloe hates me." She rubbed a sore spot on her arm where Doris Raeburn had soundly nailed her with her umbrella.

Nelson didn't know what to say to his clearly miserable aunt. "No she doesn't. I don't believe that. Not Ms. Donahue. She doesn't hate anyone. I'll bet she's never hated anyone her whole life."

"Well, there has to be a first time for everything, Nelson. I'm it. I'm Chloe's first hate object. I'm history. I'm mud. I'm dirt under her feet. She hates me, and she should. She looks fine, acts fine, and there I am, a big, quaking doofus, scared to death of her." Sara almost wailed. "We had something beautiful, and I ruined it!"

Nelson had to do something. *Maybe this will help?* "Aunt Sara, I didn't tell you this the other day, but at rehearsals, I was sitting with her, and Jeanette was singing "Out of My Dreams" and Chloe was crying. A lot."

Sara smiled. "I'm a jerk, Nelson. A certifiable bad person."

"Why do you say that?"

"I'm a bad, bad person, because when I hear that Chloe was cry-

ing, it makes me happy, because then I think she might love me after
all."

Marcy stopped at the Quickie Mart, and bought two packs of
cigarettes, enough to last her, she hoped, until tomorrow when she
left for Saturday dance rehearsals. *Why do I have to go? I'm the art
director, for God's sake.* She stopped on her way out of the store,
opened a pack and took one out and lit it. *Dave never says anything
about my smoking, but I can tell he doesn't like it. I try to keep
breath mints handy, but well, they wear out in about five minutes,
and I smoke, what, every seven minutes? This is ridiculous, and
costly. But it's the only thing keeping me sane lately.*

Marcy walked up and down the convenience store sidewalk, and
took in a breath of spring-like air. The skies were blue, it was around
fifty-five degrees, and forecasted to be nice all weekend. She and
Dave should just take off somewhere. But she knew that wasn't a
possibility, his weekends were taken up tending to his fledgling enterprise, his little golf course. He'd told her many times that he felt
guilty leaving so much of the work to Sara and Nelson, and now that
the snow would come less and less, he'd feel the demands even more.
*Thank God he has Sara. I doubt I'd be seeing Dave at all if Sara
hadn't been around fixing this and that, and attending to the more
mundane tasks.*

Dave had one more week with UPS, and then, good lord willing,
decent weather and a working mower, he would be in the golf business. Sunday, he had plans to build a little counter inside the barn,
where golf patrons could sign in, and pick up tees or golf balls. Nelson, Sara and Dave would alternate times and days to work the
counter. Between the golf course, and the demands of the musical,
weekends free for playing were going to be an impossibility for a
good long time. *Why do I keep getting involved with guys whose
busiest times are weekends?* Stan, one of her numerous discards,
owned a bar. He kept suggesting they do things on Mondays and
Tuesdays. *Oh yeah, that's an off time for school teachers.*

Maybe this summer she and Chloe could take off for a week of
"Spin the Car." That was one of their favorite things to do, and they
had done it countless times. The first time was the summer after
their first year of college. They had packed up a two-person tent,
sleeping bags, a cooler, Marcy's mother's gas card, and a bag of
clothes. They'd driven out to a wide deserted intersection east of
town. Chloe, full of excitement, drove Marcy's mom's sedan into the
middle of the intersection, pulled the wheels into a hard left turn,
and told Marcy to close her eyes, and count to nineteen, their ages at
the time. Marcy closed her eyes, and began counting. The car began

turning in a tight circle, and Marcy kept losing count because she was laughing so hard. But when she reached nineteen, the car stopped. Marcy opened her eyes to find Chloe laughing merrily, and saying, "Well, it looks like we're going south!" And they did. Chloe did all the driving, her hair long then, and pulled into a ponytail by her ball cap. They never seemed to have any particular destination in mind, no timetable, no maps, and most of the time, not much money to speak of. A few times, they had even lived without any clocks whatsoever. They put electrical tape over the clock in the car, and left their watches at home. It was odd for the first few days, but after that, they enjoyed trying to figure out what time it was by watching the movement of the sun. They also relied on the precision-like timing of Chloe's digestive system, which announced meal times like clockwork. *Are we too old for "Spin the Car?" No, I'll never get that old.*

She thought of Chloe. *What would I ever do without her? I don't even want to think about it. I've never had to compete with anyone for Chloe's time or affections before. What if Sara and Chloe get back together, and Sara wants to leave this area, and take Chloe with her?* Marcy butted out her cigarette on the ground, and walked to her car. *At least if Chloe were with Audra, I know they would stick around this area. I like Sara, I do, but is she good for Chloe? I've never, ever seen Chloe fall even half this hard for anyone. Even old Whatshername, the old college girlfriend of Chloe's, she couldn't get Chloe to leave here for her.*

Marcy pulled out of the parking lot, and headed west, for Casa D'Amico, and for adventures unknown.

Dave and Sara were in the garage when they heard Marcy pull in. They were putting the final touches on the two used golf carts that Dave had somewhat impulsively bought the week before.

Marcy announced herself by yelling, "Dave! When the hell are you going to fix the potholes in this goddamned driveway? I almost lost the Miata in one of them." She entered the garage, scowling, with her hands on her hips.

"Nice to see you, too, hon. And those aren't potholes, they're underground parking." Dave pulled Marcy into a quick kiss, which at least seemed to alleviate her scowl, if not her foul mood.

"Good, the two D'Amicos I wanted to talk to are here."

"Hello, Miss Congeniality," smirked Sara.

"Shut up, you. I'm still mad at you. I will be for a long time to come. So don't bother playing nice with me. I just talked to Chloe, and she sounds horrid. And don't you take any pleasure from knowing she's still all ripped up about you. If we don't fix this soon, I'm hiring a hit man to put you out of her misery." She wished Sara was sitting in a chair, so she could kick it, hard.

Sara gave her a wide berth. *God, she looks like artsy fartsy granola, but packs the wallop of an M-80.* "I don't take any pleasure in knowing Chloe is miserable. But it gives me hope. You understand that, don't you, Marcy?"

Marcy ignored her and turned to Dave, who was polishing the vinyl seats on one of the two golf carts. "Dave, hon, explain to me why you bought your, uh, fleet of golf carts? All two of them? For a par-three, nine-hole golf course? A toddler could walk this course in less than two hours."

"Well, you know, for practical reasons. They're faster hole to hole than the tractor or lawn mowers. You know, putting the flag poles out in the mornings, checking for damage, golf course stuff," Dave replied, a bit unsure himself.

"In other words, once you get your driveway fixed, you and Sara are going to race around in them like two little kids."

Sara, who didn't feel like minding her own business, said, "Precisely."

Dave looked at Marcy, and then pointed at Sara. "What she said." He walked over to Marcy and put his arm around her. "Just think, sweet pea, one more week with UPS, then I'm on my way to being a tycoon. Stick with me, baby, I'm sugar daddy material."

Marcy finally grinned. "All right, I know when I'm beat. Now before I can relax, we have to take care of some business. Sara, I understand that Chloe did a splice and dice job on you yesterday in front of Mrs. Raeburn. Doris cornered me in the art supply closet today and threatened to pour turpentine down me if I didn't tell her what all the tension between you and Chloe was all about. Don't worry, I didn't tell her a thing. She did say something about 'I swear, I probably should have smacked her harder when I had the chance,' which I can't quite figure out. But I digress. What's your plan for tomorrow?"

"Well, I have something planned," Sara said, rubbing her Mrs. Raeburn-inflicted sore arm again. "Nelson and I have been working on it. I figure I have at least four hours, uninterrupted, with Chloe tomorrow. I mean, Saturday is dance day. The whole day is devoted to it, and hey, I'm the dance monkey for this thing, she has to be around me." *Whether she likes it or not.*

Marcy frowned. "Well, I hope your little plan is good, because if it doesn't make some kind of an impact, you have four long days until you see her again next Thursday. Unless you wanted to suffer the alternative, and use Beavis, Sr. and Butthead, Jr. as your back-up plan for those days."

Dave amiably said, "Hey, I resemble that remark." *Racing*

stripes! They would look great on the golf carts.

Chloe was in the cafeteria. It was 11:30 Saturday morning, and she was giving herself a pep talk before she made the short walk down to the gymnasium where she had to spend a good chunk of her day with Sara D'Amico.

I feel empowered now. Yeah, that's it. I handled her pretty well on Thursday. Who knew I could come up with such nastiness on such short notice? I don't like being nasty, but if that's what it takes, I'll do it. But, oh, it was tough being around Sara. All it takes is a smile, or that cute little way she raises her eyebrow while she stares down at me. I melt like an ice cube in a hot frying pan. I can't think about that. Knock it off. The woman screwed me over. She can bag that eyebrow, for all I care. I can be pretty intimidating. It sure worked on Thursday. She won't catch me off guard. I'll be ready for whatever she comes up with. I always have the option of just walking away. God, this is ridiculous. I'm half excited, half repulsed by the idea of seeing her. I have to act businesslike, professional, and just ignore how long her legs are in those jeans, and how crazy I feel when I see her dance. Maybe she won't dance today. What am I thinking, that's what everyone is here for today!

Chloe pushed some chairs around, just to work off some nervous energy. She knew she had to sit Sara down at some point today, and set up a meeting for the two of them to discuss the ideas for each of the songs, the logistics. Chloe couldn't cut into actual practice time to do that, they were already behind. The kids were tired of standing in one place while they sang their songs. *They want to move around. Oh, well, I'll just have to gauge how to approach it after I see what's actually happening, in real time.*

Chloe pushed open the cafeteria door, took a deep breath, and walked to the gym. Another deep breath and she entered. She saw Sara, in blue jeans again, with a light blue, long sleeved Henley shirt, standing by the CD player on the left side of the bleachers. She wore her hair in a braid, and she looked wonderful. *She looks so fresh and innocent.* Chloe paused her steps, then started again. *But I know she's not innocent.* Sara looked up, and saw Chloe walking toward her. She smiled at Sara, a smile of formality, not familiarity.

Sara waited, hands hitched in pockets, waiting for Chloe to get over to her. *I'll bet she still gets carded in bars. And she should wear green everyday. It's her color. But that look, that smile on her face is so fake. She makes me feel like a puppy who just got caught peeing on the new carpet.*

"Hi."

"Hey, Chloe."

Chloe's face twisted. "Since we seem to have a little time, how about we excuse ourselves so we can talk?"

Sara, uncertain if this was good or bad, said, "Sure, where do you want to go?"

Chloe looked around. Girls' room, no, students in there. Locker room, ditto. "How about the top of the bleachers?" The gym was small, the bleachers only had fourteen rows, so it wouldn't be far to go.

"Lead the way."

Chloe climbed even these small bleachers hesitantly, she hated backless stairsteps, and detested heights of any kind even more. Sara hit the top, using her long legs to ascend two steps at a time. She got there ahead of Chloe and sat down.

Chloe got there, finally, and stopped one bleacher down from Sara, and straddled it, so she could face Sara. "So, I thought it would be a good thing if we talked." Chloe nervously pushed her hair out her collar and composed herself.

"I'm so glad you want to talk, there's so much I want to—" Sara said, a bit too eagerly.

"Not that kind of talking. I'm not interested, now or ever, in having that kind of talk with you." She saw Sara's face flinch. *Good.* Chloe's face was stiff and her voice was stern. "Let's get something straight. Do you plan on staying with this thing, no matter what our relationship is, or isn't? Or are you going to blow out of here when you find out that I don't plan on giving you the time of day? Think about it before you answer." *This is good, I feel very strong.*

Sara had considered that possibility. She had already come to a conclusion about it. "I'll stay. No matter what."

"Fine. Thank you. We have to set some time aside to meet. I don't want to take any of your time with the kids away, we're already behind and they need as much dance time as you can give them. We need to exchange ideas, things I've been thinking about that I'd like to see, things you would like to do. What do you have planned for them today?"

"Well, some stuff, but not completely thought out. I want to concentrate on some fundamentals, and a few different styles. It should take up the whole afternoon." *She has no intention of cutting me a break.*

"Good. Feel free to discuss anything with me. I will avail myself to you, purely as the play's director, as the day goes along. You stay professional, and I will. We can talk at a break and set up a meeting." Chloe stood up and started down the steps. She had gotten down around half way, when she heard Sara call her name.

"Chloe? Wait, one more thing." Sara took two long strides, two steps at a time, and stopped a bleacher step below Chloe. She was almost, but not quite, at eye level with her. She still stood an inch or two above the redheaded librarian.

Chloe folded her arms across her chest. "Yes?"

Sara looked her dead in the eye. "I love you, Chloe. I'm in love with you." Then Sara turned and made her way down to the gym floor in three long strides. "All right, everyone." Sara clapped her hands together. "Let's get started. It's going to be a long day today."

Part XI:
Bleachers, Teachers, and a Preacher's Wife

Chloe was sitting in the center of the middle row of bleachers, halfway from the top, halfway to the gym floor, where Sara D'Amico stood explaining to the cast what the schedule was going to be for the rest of the afternoon. Sara's back was toward Chloe, and for some reason, Chloe's eyes hypnotically traced the movements of the little red tab on the back pocket of Sara's jeans. The tiny piece of cloth bounced to and fro, up and down, side to side, and at some truly wonderful times, it writhed when Sara was speaking with enthusiasm. *I'm just going to sit here, and watch that talented tab move the rest of the day. I've never seen anything so fascinating in my whole life.*

Anyone close to Chloe, anyone who had known her for any length of time, even ten minutes, would know that something was amiss with her, just by looking at her, sitting there alone, in the wide expanse of old wooden bleachers. And if they could have gotten inside her head, not her brain, mind you, but her head, they could have looked past that red tab that Chloe's green eyes were fixated on, and seen that her brain was doing a fast double dribble down the basketball court, pulling up, and shooting an air ball for the basket.

Chloe had an invisible "Out to Lunch" sign tacked to her forehead. Her thoughts bounced and caromed. No one had ever told her that they loved her before. Well, that's not exactly true. Her parents, relatives, a few overly ambitious amorous boys, Marcy, and some still, to this day, anonymous stalker, well, they didn't count. Even old Whatshername from college had told her those three important words. *God, my mind is a blank. Marcy always calls her that. I should try and remember.* Chloe tried and immediately gave up. No one had told her that phrase, "I love you" and had Chloe react that way to it. *This time, it's different. This time, it means the world to me. This time, it means everything to me.* Not that Chloe had never loved before, she was quite sure that she'd loved old Whatshername, but not with the mind-altering, heart-stopping, button-popping, feverish intensity that Chloe now felt pulsing through her veins. *So this is it. I'm madly in love, and she's in love with me. She loves me. This is wonderful, I'm totally in love with—*

Chloe's brain came leaping back into her head, got out a staple gun, and tacked itself in around the corners. *—a screwed up, too-tall, insecure, petty, controlling, moody, lying, monosyllabic, manipulative harpy who just happens to have the best red tab on her butt that I have ever seen.*

Just as Chloe was pondering that thought, the object of Chloe's confusion stopped her speech, and turned, and looked at her and said, "And I'm sure Ms. Donahue has a few things she wants to say to you before we get started." Sara gave her a winning smile, and said, with gusto, "Take it away, Chloe!"

"What happened to her?"

"I don't know, one second I was talking to all the kids, and I turned around, and smiled at her, and the next second, she just kind of slumped to her left, like somebody let all the air out of her."

"Get some water, someone, I thinks she's coming around."

"What's that look she has on her face? She's not going to spew, is she?"

"Justin, go back down on the gym floor and shut up."

"Should we call an ambulance? I could call my mother."

"Paul, what is your mother going to do for Chloe? Knit her a doily?"

"Chloe, Chloe, honey, it's Sara. You're in the gym. We think you fainted."

"Wait, her eyes just rolled back again. Maybe we should call an ambulance."

"Chloe, c'mon, sweetheart, I'm here for you baby. Marcy, quit looking at me like that. Oh, all right. We're all here for you, honey. Me, Paul, Mo, Jeanette, Marcy, Nelson, all of the Justins. C'mon, sweetheart, that's my girl, open your eyes."

Chloe's eyes popped open. There were rounded globes covered with blue cotton very close to them. Nice round, soft, inviting globes with blue cotton, and they were moving, away, then closer, away, then closer.

"Hey, Ms. Donahue is staring at Ms. D'Amico's tits! What's up with that?"

"Justin, get down to the gym floor, now!"

Chloe, whose head was being cradled in Sara's lap, had indeed been staring at her tits. "Wha happened?" said Chloe, feeling a little like she had done one tequila shooter too many.

Sara glared at Marcy, who prudently decided to let her take

charge. She turned her attention to the flickering eyelids of her love. "You fainted, honey. You just fell over like—"

"A hundred pound bag of wet cement. I saw her. Kablam!"

Marcy stood up, and her demeanor meant business. "All right, anyone that isn't over the age of nineteen, all right, twenty, Jason, out of this gym, right now, and into the cafeteria until we get Ms. Donahue squared away." Marcy gave them all a vicious stare. "I mean it, I know where Mrs. Raeburn keeps her extra umbrella, and I know how to use it!" That did it, everyone scurried for the door.

Sara unconsciously rubbed her sore arm again. "Paul, do you think maybe you could go down and babysit them?"

Paul, who had to call his mother anyway (it had been nearly two hours since he last checked in), nodded and headed down the bleacher steps.

Sara was cooing to Chloe, who found the inside of her eyelids, to keep her from looking where she shouldn't be looking.

"C'mon sweetheart, open your eyes, you need to drink some water. We need to see if we need to get you to a doctor." *I need to hold you, just like this, the rest of my life. You scared the ever-living crap out of me.*

Chloe opened her eyes, and drank some water out of a small paper cup that Sara held to her lips. She was slowly coming around.

Sara looked at Marcy. "Does she have low blood sugar? Diabetes? Anything that could explain this?" *I don't know anything about her at all.*

"Not that I know of. Although I know she hasn't been sleeping, or eating right, she's been working like a dog, and completely stressed out, do you suppose that has anything to do with it?" Marcy cocked her head at Sara, knowing Sara wouldn't miss the sarcasm.

Sara bit her lip, and decided to act like a grown-up. "Probably." She held the cup to Chloe again. "Here, drink some more."

Chloe did, and tried to sit up a little out of Sara's lap. With Sara's support she almost made it to a sitting position. She felt a little woozy then, and fell into Sara's shoulder and stayed there, with Sara's arms around her.

"Marcy, we need to get some food into her. It will stabilize her blood sugar, if that's the problem. Especially if she hasn't been eating."

"I'll go down to the cafeteria and see what I can find. Here's the water bottle, see if you can get more into her."

Marcy grabbed her purse and headed out on her mission.

Chloe, who was nestled on Sara's shoulder, her head tucked under Sara's chin, felt like she didn't want to feel better any time soon.

"Sara?"

Sara's arms tightened around her just slightly, just enough to make her more secure. "Hmm?"

"You're an asshole," Chloe murmured, and snuggled in deeper.

"Yes. Yes, I am, sweetheart."

"As soon as I eat something, and feel better, I'm going to kick your ass from here to Niagara Falls." Chloe wrapped a hand around Sara's arm.

"That would be swell, honey, it's been a long time since I've been to the Falls."

"What's that smell? You smell good. Kind of like furniture polish."

"Oh. I was cleaning before I came here today."

"Waxy. It's nice."

"And I don't attract any dust all day."

They sat like that for a while, Chloe held securely in Sara's arms, Sara feeling like finally, finally she was doing something right. Holding the redhead like that, in the quiet gym, reinforced all of the emotions that Sara had been feeling about Chloe. *This is meant to be. I'm going to prove it to her in every way I can. Like I told Nelson, I'm a bad, bad person. Chloe feels awful, and yet I feel like I'm going to explode with happiness just because I get the chance to hold her like this.* Sara was pretty sure her amateur diagnosis was correct, that Chloe had toppled because of lack of sleep, a hellacious work schedule, and no food in the voracious blast furnace better known as Chloe's stomach. *And stress. Stress caused by me. The last thing I said to her was that I loved her.* Sara's happiness at being able to hold Chloe helped her but the joy of being so close to her started slowly waning, and guilt started to overcome her. *I did this to her. I make her so miserable that she doesn't eat, doesn't sleep. And then I go and hammer her sensibilities with a glib, well planned, "I love you." I meant it. I mean it. But I timed it that way, to rock her. To shock her into some kind of response. Well, it worked.*

Marcy entered the gym with a tuna sandwich, some grapes and a pint of white milk. She climbed the bleachers, and found Sara still holding a now dozing Chloe.

Sara kept her voice low. "She fell asleep. I think we should wake her, get her to eat, get her down to the nurse's office. Maybe she can sleep some more there, or maybe you can take her home?" Sara said softly, not wanting to wake Chloe before she and Marcy formed some kind of a plan.

Marcy's eyes narrowed as she carefully surveyed her redheaded friend's features. "I can stay with her, so you can work with the kids. We can't afford to waste any more practice time with them."

Sara grimly nodded; she didn't want to leave the sleeping woman, even for a moment, but knew that Marcy was right. *The frig-*

gin' show must go on. "Chloe, sweetheart, wake up. You have to eat something. And then we're going to get you down to that nice bed in the nurse's office."

Chloe, only half dozing, valiantly perked up at the mention of food. She sat up, slowly, as Sara disengaged from underneath her, and propped her up against the bleacher back. She took the food items from Marcy, and quietly ate, while Sara and Marcy spoke about her like she wasn't even there.

"I think I should get her home right away," Marcy began.

"I think she would be better off in the nurse's office for a while. Get her strength back. Plus, if she goes topsy-turvy again, there will be more of us to help out."

Marcy couldn't, as usual, keep the sarcasm out of her voice. "You just want to be there to save her again, don't you? The more I think about it, the more I think that it's all this crap she's been dealing with from you that made her go belly up in the first place. You know what? More and more, I'm thinking you just aren't good for her. And you know what else? I think, way down deep, she knows it too."

Sara, who was used to being on the receiving end of some nasty zingers from Marcy, and could usually give as good as she got, couldn't think of anything to say to that. She pushed herself into a standing position. "I'll go get Paul. You two can get her home, to the nurse's office, whatever you think is best. I'll give you a few minutes, and then I'll bring the kids back up here so we can get to work. I promised her that I would get these kids ready, and I'm going to do that."

Chloe, still seated up against the bleacher back, had finished her sandwich and most of the milk, too, while she watched the anger flowing from woman to woman. She wanted to say something to settle both women, but her mind just wasn't working right as yet, so she listened in rapt silence.

Sara started down the bleacher stairs.

Chloe finally found some words, small ones, but they came out, and she meant them. "Sara?"

Sara stopped and turned around. "Yes?"

"Thank you." Chloe's face was expressionless.

"You're welcome. I hope you feel better." Sara gave her a tiny smile, and strode out of the gym.

Marcy had taken Chloe directly home, and put her to bed. She had been asleep most of the afternoon now, the light of the day had faded away, and Marcy turned on a small lamp next to the couch she was sitting on. It was after five now, rehearsals were over, and Marcy had intercepted well-meaning calls from Mo Dean, Paul, a parent of a Justin or two, and Doris Raeburn. Paul's mother had even called, and had offered several weird tips on how to speed Chloe along on the path to recovery. Nelson called, and it was pretty apparent he was acting as a go-between for his Aunt Sara, who really didn't try very hard to hide her stage-whispered voice. Marcy didn't have much to report. "She's sleeping," "she's still asleep," "she's been sleeping," and "I'm going to let her sleep," were the only real news items she had to report.

Chloe's small form, rumpled in a worn flannel nightshirt, appeared and waved at Marcy on the couch. "Bathroom," she said sleepily. Marcy nodded, and soon heard the toilet flush, then the sink running. Chloe appeared again, "Sleep," and went back to do so. A few minutes later, the phone rang again, and Marcy, irritated, snagged it.

"Hello?"

"Marcy, it's Nelson again. Just checking on Ms. Donahue," he said, sounding a little stilted and embarrassed.

Marcy had enough of this. "Nelson, put your Aunt Sara on the goddamned phone, and you can quit being her Howdy Doody and go do something else on a Saturday night."

Marcy listened to several moments of muffled voices. "Hello, Marcy."

"Hello Sara. She was sleeping, she got up to pee, and she's sleeping again. What else do you want?"

"That was pretty much it." There was a pause, and a sigh. "It's just that I was going nuts all day, thinking about her."

Sara sounded so surprisingly vulnerable and dejected that, in turn, Marcy's hard heart softened a bit. "I wish I could tell you more. I think she just needs a lot of rest, and some decent food. I'm going to stay here for the duration. Your brother is coming over later to keep me company."

Another pause. "Marcy, you were right. This is all my fault. She's all stressed out because of me. I caused this today."

Marcy was still feeling sympathetic. "I'm sure you are a large part of it, but this play and work have something to do with it, too."

"No, you don't understand," Sara's voice was audibly trembling, "I think I kind of startled her today. I told her that I love her, Marcy."

Marcy was a little surprised, but suppressed it. "That isn't a bad thing, Sara, to tell someone you love them."

"No, I did it to shake it her up. Instead of waiting until a time when it would have some meaning, some romantic setting, I just threw it in her face and walked away from her."

Marcy thought about this for a moment or two. "So you think

you maybe overloaded the poor girl, huh?" She let out a rueful
laugh. "You know what, I probably should be mad at you, but in the
long run, Sara, you know what she's going to remember about this?
It's that you told her. If this all works out, it will be a funny story you
can tell on some kind of anniversary."

Sara was amazed at the kind understanding that Marcy was displaying. She hadn't expected this, she expected harsh words, and
wasn't getting them. "Thank you, Marcy. I'm sorry if I upset you
today, but I realize that we both love her. I want to be good for her, I
really do. I want you to think I'm the best possible woman for her to
be with."

Marcy officially called a truce, although she left it unstated.
"You're getting there. Now, tell your brother to get his butt over here
soon. I'm starving, and if Chloe ever wakes up, she's going to have
the appetite of a sumo wrestler or two. So tell him to stop and get a
bit of everything. Tell him to concentrate on the healthier stuff, but
chocolate couldn't hurt, too."

"All right," She hesitated and then said, " And Marcy, do you
think you could—"

"You know what, Sara? That damned Chloe won't let me smoke
in her house. Me. Her best friend. She makes me go outside to do it.
In all kinds of weather. I suppose, during one of my trips outside, I
could take my cell phone out with me and—"

"I'll be at Dave's house, all night, even over night. On the couch.
Just anything, Marse, let me know, okay?"

"I've got it on speed dial. I'll let you know. You'll be hearing
from me."

"Thank you," Sara paused, "And Marcy, if I haven't told you
this before, I think you're perfect for my idiot brother."

Marcy wasn't sure if this was a backhanded compliment or not,
but she decided to let it pass.

Chloe woke up at 3:00 a.m. Sunday morning, feeling very
rested, refreshed and ravenous. She tiptoed out to her living room
and saw Marcy there, snoring on her couch. She adjusted the afghan
that Marcy had kicked off, and went into the kitchen to find something to eat. After happily finding a virtual plethora of goodies
stuffed in her fridge, she loaded up with as much as she could carry,
and headed back to her bedroom to read, and to get crumbs in her
bed.

At a more reasonable time of the day, midmorning, the D'Amico
household started to stir, and to begin their day. Dave and Sara had
plans to work on the counter for the faux pro shop and Nelson was
going over to Charlie Shemp's to ride Cargo again. Sara was a bit

jealous, she really wanted to go with Nelson, but had already committed her time today to Dave. She would spend a good part of her day reminding Dave to measure twice, cut once. She had heard from Marcy once the night before about Chloe, but the news was the same. Marcy had been unable to come up with new and inventive ways to put a spin on "she's still sleeping." And Dave, who rolled in around one o'clock, found Sara watching an infomercial on his TV, and had no news to report either. He did mention that he made sure that Chloe wouldn't have to go grocery shopping for at least two weeks. He was apparently unfamiliar with Chloe's quite impressive appetite.

Marcy finally awoke around ten o'clock and noticed that Chloe's bedroom door was closed. She used the bathroom, and put on a pot of coffee. She went to Chloe's bedroom door and tapped, and when she got no response, opened the door, and found Chloe sleeping. Marcy was comforted to see that there were numerous empty dirty plates on Chloe's night stand, and she seemed to be cuddling a box of graham crackers. Marcy decided to let her be. She drank two cups of coffee, smoked a cigarette guiltily in the kitchen, and sprayed nearly a half a can of room freshener afterwards. She wrote Chloe a note, and left it taped to the bathroom mirror.

Chloe got up around noon, found the note, and the half pot of coffee. She took a shower, dressed in sweats, and decided to spend the day with the remote control clutched in her hand. She called Marcy, told her she felt much better, but she wasn't up for any company, and to extend her thanks to Dave for the smorgasbord. The phone rang frequently during the rest of the day, mostly concerned messages about her health and well being, but she let the machine pick them up. Doris Raeburn called three times in succession, fuming the second and third times that sixty seconds wasn't long enough for her to get across everything she needed to say. Chloe made a pretty fair dent in the food supply in the fridge.

Sara accompanied Dave to the hardware store in mid-afternoon, and on the short ride back, she had a significant panic attack and made Dave pull over. He waited in the Explorer while she paced up and down the shoulder of the road, waiting for it to subside. When it finally did, she got back into the vehicle, and they went back and finished up the counter. Nothing was said about the attack.

Marcy arrived at the D'Amicos around 5:00, and was treated to the odd splendor of the D'Amicos' idea of a Sunday family dinner. She made a comment or two about eating ice cream while the chicken breasts were being sautéed, but eventually gave in to the weirdness, and embraced it. Dessert consisted of coffee and some beef jerky that Nelson found in his backpack.

Marcy called Chloe a little later, and found that Chloe had done nothing to speak of during her day, and seemed quite happy with that. After relaying that non-news to the D'Amico clan, everyone went into the living room, and spent the rest of the evening in front of the television set, making crude remarks about wanting to be touched by that angel, Roma Downey, and then fought for dominance of the remote control.

All in all, a pretty dull Sunday.

Sara was in Dave's kitchen on Monday morning, pouring herself the last cup of coffee for the morning, when the phone rang. She sipped at the coffee, and added a bit of sugar to ward off the bottom-of-the-pot bitterness, and listened as the machine picked up.

"Uh, hello, this is Chloe, and this message is for Sara."

The coffee cup hit the bottom of the sink as Sara tossed it, and then bolted to pick up the phone.

"Hello, Chloe? It's me, it's Sara." For some reason, she was feeling breathless after sprinting the eight feet to the telephone.

"Oh, hi, I didn't expect anyone to be there. I was just going to leave a message for you."

"How are you feeling? Where are you?"

"I'm at the library, I just opened it up. I'm fine. All rested."

"Good. Good. I was worried." Sara listened, and Chloe said nothing to that.

"Sara, we have to get together and have that meeting, so I can leave the dance details to you, and I can concentrate on other aspects of the play."

"Anytime you want."

Chloe scratched her upper lip with her lower teeth. "I was thinking maybe later this afternoon, around 5:00 or so?"

"Sure, I'll be here. Just come on by."

"Uh, no. I thought we could meet here in the library. I have to be here until close tonight, I've got a monthly shipment coming in, no volunteer today, the county auditor is supposed to stop by, and the Dever twins will be coming in at four. I was hoping you could come here. There's a small room off of the periodical section, we could talk in there."

She considers this enemy territory now, huh? "Well, hopefully Nelson will be home after school, and he can give me a ride. He usually comes home before he takes off anywhere. I could call the school."

"I'll be talking to Marcy around lunchtime. I'll have her hunt Nelson down, and relay the message."

"Okay."

"See you then. If you can't make it, just call here."

"Will do."

Those last two words never made it to Chloe's ears; she had already hung up. Sara looked at the kitchen clock, just past nine. *Great, I have eight hours to work myself up into one hell of a mess.*

Monday, the day dreaded by the work force worldwide, was living up to its bad reputation for Chloe. The shipment of new books, over a hundred of them, didn't arrive until after two o'clock. Normally, the monthly shipment was there right after she opened. She had to get them checked in, checked for faults, jacketed, cataloged and entered into the computer system. Ron Johnson, the weaselly county auditor who was coming by to check the books, called and said he wasn't coming until four o'clock because he had a bad molar that needed to be looked at. And since the library was open until eight o'clock, he would have ample time to complete his job. Chloe did very little in the way of having to do anything with the economic part of the library, the only actual money that came in was from used book sales, and late fines. Chloe dutifully did a deposit on Fridays at the local bank, and it rarely added up to more than $150. Payroll and book purchases were taken care of by the main county library in Erie. Chloe was on salary, so she didn't have to report her time, all she had to do, really, was send in the students' employee time cards, and send them off every other Monday to Erie.

When both the twins and Ron Johnson showed up at four o'clock, Chloe was behind the checkout counter, hip deep in cartons of books. She shot the twins an 'I'm not in any mood' look, and walked Ron back to her office, and handed him a folder with the last three months worth of receipts and paperwork. She wanted to get the last carton of books opened and examined before 5:00, when Sara was to arrive. Chloe had already entered them all into the computer, and decided to let the twins work on the grunt work of jacketing them and placing the bar codes on them. *This is stupid, we don't even have a bar code reader.* The library being so small, the county didn't feel the need. So in this little library, they still put a small pocket in the back cover of the book, with a small card to stamp with the return date. It in turn irritated and comforted Chloe, knowing that the library was so old-fashioned.

Nelson dropped off his clearly anxious aunt in front of the library at 4:30, apologizing again that he was sorry he wouldn't be able to pick her up until eight. He had to pick up Jeanette and go into Erie, to get a few more props and dresses that Ms. Donahue had tracked down at several different high schools there. He wasn't all that familiar with the city, other than how to get to the mall, the Peninsula, and he was a little worried that he wouldn't be able to find his way around without getting lost. Jeanette, a native of Erie until a few

years ago, happily agreed to accompany him. Sara waved off his
apology again, and got out of the truck.

Sara checked her watch. She had time to walk off some of this
nervousness before she had to go in there. Sara had been unsettled
for the last few days, feeling constantly like she was on the verge of
an attack. The fear of having an attack is just as bad as actually having one. It was that constant feeling of the maybe, the might, the it
could happen that kept Sara so close to home. The possibility, or in
her mind, the probability, even the certainty that an attack could
occur at any moment had reinforced Sara's belief that home, and her
family, were the safest, least demanding places she could be. So she
avoided going places, or even the idea of going places, because just
that little tiny nugget of the what if could precipitate an episode of
panicked dread. So although Sara rarely had what could be described
as a textbook panic attack now, the memories of past ones and the
possibility of future ones effectively crippled her former natural ten-
dency to be adventurous. *I may be still into avoidance, but at least
I'm not in deep denial anymore.*

It was now 4:45 p.m., and the retreating of the sun had taken out
any warmth that had been in the air. Sara shivered, and decided to be
a little early. She walked into the library, and blinked, for the first
thing she saw was two young men behind the checkout counter, mirror images of each other. She blinked again, and realized that the
young men were twins. Chloe wasn't in the immediate vicinity, so
Sara walked through the small lobby, and toward the old wooden
bookshelves. She hadn't been here in twenty years, and it still looked
the same. Still smelled the same. An odd, comforting smell of old
books, oaken shelves built in the 1920s, after the town's original
library had burnt down. Even the carpeting looked exactly the same,
worn in spots. The carpeting gave way to lightly varnished hardwood
floors between the stacks. *No wonder Chloe likes it here. It has a feel
to it that's comfortable and inviting.* The high ceilings, with carved
archways, gently sloped to meet the off-white walls that held the
faded prints of writers like Whitman, Austen and Twain. It was not
like the crisp, clean, sterile interiors of modern libraries, which often
looked like they were imitating the atmosphere of a Barnes and
Nobles. Sara sniffed the air again. *Ah, that's why Chloe liked my
Lemon Pledge scent the other day. That's what it smells like in here.*
Sara smiled and walked down the new releases section, and picked
up a few different books and read their jackets.

"Find anything interesting?" a soft voice whispered behind her.
Sara turned to find Chloe, in black slacks and a soft gray sweater,
standing behind her.

Sara took a long look, up and down, and couldn't help herself.
"I'll say."

Chloe quickly looked away. "I have a couple of things I have to do yet. Would you wait in the conference room, over by the periodicals? I shouldn't be long." She waited for an acknowledgment from Sara, and then turned and walked away.

Sara shook off her disappointment at finding Chloe still obviously uncomfortable with her presence. Sara looked around the small library, and decided that the conference room must be that room next to the magazine racks. It was a small room, with an old table and six chairs in it, so there wasn't much room for anything else. There were years worth of initials scratched deeply into the wood grain of the table. The room itself was windowed, it looked out into the library, with the remaining exterior walls being lined with the prints of old philosophers. Clearly, this was a room meant for thinking.

Sara laid the small folder she had brought with her on the table, took off her coat and laid it over the chair. She decided to sit in a chair where she could look out into the library. On the table was a copy of the weekly town newspaper, *The Stonecreek Courier.* Sara picked it up, and idly started reading through it. It was a small publication, mostly ads, news stories of weddings and baby arrivals, news of the town council meetings, PTA announcements, high school sports results and other local happenings. Sara found a small headline that captured her interest, and she was just finishing the story when Chloe walked into the room.

Sara looked up from the paper, and said irritated, to Chloe, "This is idiotic, this guy actually reviewed a junior high school play, and gave them a bad review. You don't do that to junior high kids, God, who does he think he is, Roger Ebert or something?"

Chloe, curious, moved behind Sara's chair to read aloud over her shoulder, "Heather Buetikofer displayed a distinct lack of understanding of her character, she was harsh and strident, when the characterization called for a more demure and feminine portrayal." Chloe shook her head. "What character was she playing?"

"I dunno, one of the witches in *The Wizard of Oz,* for God's sake! Since when do seventh graders merit critical review?" Sara shook her head angrily.

"He's just a local jerk with delusions of grandeur. You should have seen what he wrote about us last year. When we did the opera."

Sara winced. "You guys did an opera? In high school?" She shook her head at Chloe. "What were you thinking?"

Chloe felt an odd sense of déjà vu. "Never mind, let's just say it went over like a part-time drama teacher in the middle of some gymnasium bleachers." Chloe managed a small smile. "Splat."

Sara smiled back at that. "Well, that was a sight to see." She turned her attention to the article again. "Who is this guy anyways, who picks on little kids?"

Chloe grimaced. "Jay Caesar. He owns the pizza shop up the street."

Sara closed the paper in disgust. "Well, he'd better watch himself around me. I won't stand for Mr. Caesar crucifying us."

"You already thinking we're going to stink up the joint? Having a premonition, a vision or something?" Chloe had to smile at Sara's heated vehemence.

"Well, no, but well, I just won't let it happen," Sara said grumpily. "Remind me never to get pizzas from that place."

Chloe sat on the same side of the table as Sara, but she left the seat between them vacant. She laid her canvas bag on the empty seat, and pulled out her script and notebook of all her notes and sketches. Just as she was going to ask Sara if she was ready to start, she glanced out the plate glass window separating them from the periodicals section. "Oh, no. I forgot," she said, wide-eyed.

Sara looked out the window, and saw an older woman, settling into a chair around a large round table just on the other side of the conference room they were in. "What?" she said, not seeing what the problem was.

"It's Book Club night," Chloe's voice quavered. "I'm never here for Book Club night. I avoid it. Like I've avoided sex with men."

"What's so bad about the book club?" Sara asked, curious at Chloe's apprehension.

"Too late. Here they come. I was hoping we could make a dash for it."

Sara looked out the glass again, and saw four more women approach the round table, and begin to take their coats off. She didn't recognize any of them, wait, yes, yes it was. "Doris Raeburn," she breathed. She instinctively looked to see if Doris had an umbrella with her.

"The skinny tall one is Mrs. Cellone, my senior volunteer, and the one with the poodles on her blouse, that's Paul's mother, Mrs. Hoderman. The one with the cane is the town council president's wife, Bella Stavros. She's Jeanette's grandmother. And the one with the big bosom, that's Pastor Fuller's wife, Naomi. We have the complete set of the town's biggest gossips, right outside that window, and here come two of them now."

Sara saw Doris Raeburn wave through the window, with Paul's mother in tow, they both came in and stood just inside the doorway. "Well, look at who we have here, Helen, it's our intrepid librarian and play director, and her mysterious friend the Big Movie Star. Chloe, you already know Helen. Helen, this is Sara D'Amico, an esteemed alumna of Fort Lafayette High School, and one of the premiere attendees of my detention hall during her time there."

Sara stood up to shake Mrs. Hoderman's hand. Mrs. Hoderman

made no bones about pulling Sara close, and examining Sara's face in detail. "Nice to meet you, Sara." She let the startled Sara's hand drop, and took a step back. "You were right, Doris. No big deal. Can't hardly see it." She turned her attention to Chloe, who was trying to come up with a quick reason for them to escape. "And you, Chloe, how are you feeling? We all heard about you swooning the other day. You aren't eating right. You need to have a few saltines in the morning, that will settle your stomach, and then you can eat other things. Take vitamins. Drink lots of milk. Have you seen your doctor yet? I'm sure he'll tell you the same things I'm telling you."

Chloe just dumbly nodded and felt her mouth forming words. "Yeah, okay. I'll do that. Sounds good. See my doctor. Well, Sara and I were just finishing up here, we have to get to..." Chloe hadn't gotten that far in her planning yet. She looked desperately into Sara's eyes.

"The Embers. We're meeting my brother Dave there for dinner." Sara checked her watch, and then looked at Helen and Doris. "It's a shame we don't have more time to chat, but we're running late now." She tried to look as disappointed as possible.

Chloe took her cue, and started gathering her things. "Yes, well, I don't want to keep Dave waiting. I just need to grab my coat from the office, talk to the twins and we're on our way."

Sara was already moving, and she grabbed Chloe's arm to make sure they didn't get ambushed and separated during their escape. They made it out the door, and Sara, still pulling Chloe behind her, smiled a movie star smile at the rest of the group at the round table, said, "Hi, we're running late," and kept on going.

Chloe broke away from Sara just long enough to grab her coat from the closet. She glared at the Dever twins, said, "Work, or you're dead," and joined Sara to rush out the front door. They got to the end of the short sidewalk at the front of the library, looked at each other, and started laughing.

Chloe stepped up very close to Sara, and peered up and stared at her face. "No big deal. Can't hardly see it."

Sara stared back down at her. "And she somehow feels the need to tell you to eat? She's never broken bread with you, I can tell."

They both started laughing again. "And Doris, that was great," giggled Chloe. "We never gave her a chance to start on one of her famous monologues."

Sara smiled. "I dunno, I was too busy looking to see if she had her umbrella with her."

Chloe spent some time adjusting her coat and getting it buttoned up. *Now what?* "Well, uh..."

"Guess we'll have to reschedule, huh?" Sara said, suddenly feeling a little less giddy.

Chloe frowned. "Give me a minute here, Sara. I need to think." *I guess it wouldn't hurt.* "Have you eaten yet? We could go to the diner, or really go to the Embers, if you want."

Sara shuffled distractedly. "Nelson was going to stop here at the library to pick me up when he got back. He won't know where I am."

Chloe looked at her Subaru. "I can get you home. It's not a problem. I'll just go back in and tell the twins—on second thought, I'll call the twins from wherever we end up." Chloe's eyes twinkled under the street lamps. "I'm just so relieved we made it out of there. We never would have gotten a thing done." She looked up to see Sara's face. Sara was staring at her, her expression soft and wistful. Chloe got caught up in that gaze for a moment and murmured, "What?"

"You don't want to know."

Chloe broke the moment. "Stop that," she said, exasperated.

"I'm sorry, Chloe. I have to know when we're going to talk about this. This is making me crazy." Sara saw an opportunity to try and get through to Chloe. Her voice dropped low, "You're all I can think about, all I dream about."

Chloe's heart started beating faster. She felt her blood burning through her veins. She turned away from Sara, and then turned right back again. She moved closer to her, so there were mere inches between them. "Sara?" she said a little breathlessly, "Would you like to come home with me?" She looked deeply into Sara's eyes.

Sara hadn't expected this. A smile bloomed slowly on her face. "Yes. I'd love that, Chloe. That would be wonderful."

Chloe backed away from her. "So we could have some big fun?" she snapped, the phrase burning a path to Sara's memory. "Oh, wait, I'm not your type, remember? You were just playing! That's right, I lay it all out on the line with you, tell you I want you, and you tell me you don't want me. I forgot, I was used goods by then, wasn't I, because I slept with Audra. Well, let me tell you, I'd sooner sleep with your brother, because you, you are not my type any longer. Can you get that through your thick skull?"

Sara stepped back, stung by the contempt in Chloe's words. "I gotcha." She was at a complete loss as to what to say, what to do next.

Chloe paced the sidewalk, and then stopped, and hitched her canvas bag over her shoulder. Her emotions clamped down, she began speaking in a monotone. "Now, we have some things to go over. I suggest that we go to the diner, eat, and discuss them." Her lips twitched as she eyed Sara. "Do you think you can manage an hour or two with me, so we can get this done, without pissing me off again?"

Sara rose to her tallest height, and her lips turned down in determination. "I'll do my best."

Chloe turned and headed for the Subaru. "Good. Let's go."

Part XII:
The Odd Couplings

It was 4:30 on Thursday, and Dave had just finished his last day with UPS. Actually, he had finished up around 2:00, but a few of his buddies had insisted on taking him down to Stan's for a few beers. He was in a wonderful mood, relieved that he would finally be devoting all of his time to his dream. Since he had actually started working on the course, some four years ago, he had been working every spare minute on flattening, planning, sloping, running water lines in the old cow pasture, walking miles and miles every day, picking up stones from the earth he had tilled in the old tractor. There were times he would come home from work, and with a canvas sack slipped over his shoulder, walk a small stretch of land, picking up even the smallest stones until the sun had gone from the sky. He was determined to make the ground as pristine as possible, for the second summer he began to plant grass seed, a special blend, that would grow green and sturdy, and hold up through the harsh winters of this region. It took two summers to get the ground cleaned, the grass planted. He and Nelson used the tractor to pull down the smaller of saplings that interfered with the fairways and greens of the course, but he had done this as little as possible, and regretted every plant, every bush and patch of crabgrass that gave its life in the name of his nine-holed vision.

This past summer, Sara had come home, and extended his vision much farther than he could even imagine. The grass was growing strong and lithe by then, but she had a special touch of some sort with everything growing on the land. She seemed to know just how much water each individual green needed, how much fertilizer to lay down without scorching the tender grass. She framed holes with flowering shrubs, and lined fairway fringes with sparkling wildflowers.

The ninth hole was her particular favorite. It was her oasis. It lay near a small pond, with lily pads, leaping bullfrogs, cat-o'-nine tails and reeds. One day late last summer when Dave came home, tired from work, she and Nelson led him over to the pond, and not without a little fanfare, pressed a control knob hidden in some tall grass. Dave stood, enthralled, as a pulsating tower of water shot out of the pond, almost twenty feet into the air, its falling looking like multicolored streamers in the sunset of the day. It was then, and only then, as Dave stood grinning at this beautiful sight, that he knew, with an absolute confidence, that his pipe dream was going to be a success. It was his sister's considerable effort that was going to set his little cow pasture apart from all the other converted cow pastures in the area. He knew he could never thank her for it, never be able to adequately voice his gratitude to her. So he did what a brother could do. He loved her with all of his heart, and silently vowed that whatever he could do for her, whatever she needed, he would try his best to make sure she got.

Dave grinned, and climbed the three stairs that led to the small entrance on the side of Fort Lafayette High. He knew all of his most treasured ones were in this building, and he wanted to share his exuberance of the day with them. He made his way down to the theater entrance, and opened the door. There he saw Chloe, in jeans and hooded sweatshirt, standing off to one side of the stage, watching a gawky redheaded teenage girl singing to an equally ungainly teenage boy, somewhat oddly dressed in baggy chinos and a Dr. Dre T-shirt, his head topped off with a cowboy hat. Chloe saw the light enter the theater when the door opened and saw Dave peering at her. She smiled and waved at him, wordlessly, to come join her on the stage. As Dave strolled down the aisle to the stage, he recognized the song that the teenaged pair were rehearsing. *Ah, "I Cain't Say No." These two must be Will and Ado Annie.* He climbed the small steps to the stage. Dave slipped his arm around Chloe's waist in greeting and stood quietly leaning against her as the pair finished their song, Will twirling Ado Annie, then sweeping her down for a passionate kiss.

That is how it was supposed to play. Chloe's bossy nature, cleverly disguised under a director's mantle, asserted itself.

"Justin, she doesn't have cooties. Wait a minute, you don't even know what cooties are, do you? Okay. You're supposed to be half crazy for the girl, you look like you're afraid she's going to, I don't know, nip you or something during the whole song. She's not a crocodile. And Mo, this girl is lust-driven. You're playing her like you're a singing Mother Theresa. This is not *The Sound of Music*. It's "I Cain't Say No," not *I'd Really Rather Not, Thank You, Anyways*. There has to be some spark, all the way through the song, too, you both have to be wildly flirting, touching, eyeballing each other, not acting like you'd rather be anywhere else. Get a gleam in your eye."

Chloe rolled her eyes at the still-grinning Dave. "Ben," called Chloe to the pianist, "Start it right before the last verse." She turned to Mo and Justin again. "Okay, I want to see it like you have the hots for each other. Do it. Impress me."

Marcy, Doris and Sara were coming up the hall from the gymnasium. Sara had given the kids fifteen minutes; she wanted a few of them to put on their costumes so she could see how they moved around in them. Marcy had suggested they come up and see how Chloe was doing with the reticent lovers, Mo and Justin. Sara had no complaints about going to see Chloe, she had a few questions to ask her that had come up since their meeting on Monday. She hadn't seen her yet today, she'd gone directly to the gym, and started practice. Marcy had shown up in the gym to ask about some props needed for some dance sequences. Doris showed up because, well, she was Doris, and it was her job to be everywhere.

The threesome moved quickly down the hall. Marcy grabbed the theater door and they entered. They all halted, as one unit, staring. On stage, in the spotlight, was Dave D'Amico, singing to Chloe in a rich baritone voice, while the pianist played. He gently twirled her left, then switched hands, and twirled her in front of him again. As he finished the lyric, he put his arms around her, and as he sang the last words, he bent her back farther, then farther, his head ever closer to hers. He drew the last note out, and as soon as it was finished, he kissed her, long and hard. He then swooped her back up into a standing position. Chloe looked positively dazed. Dave smiled a toothy, satisfied grin, and boasted to Mo and Justin, who were watching just out of the spotlight. "See? Now that's how you kiss the girl!"

Marcy squinted at her boyfriend and her best friend. *Do straight people get toaster ovens for turning gay people straight?*

Sara glared at her brother and her almost-girlfriend. *Is it matricide? Patricide? Fratricide? I can never remember.*

Doris Raeburn looked at the blushing Chloe Donahue and that dazzling hunk, David D'Amico. *Yep. Uh-huh.*

Dave put his arm around Chloe's waist, and finally noticed the little audience in the aisle by the theater entrance. "Hey," he called up to them, "C'mon down here. I was just giving a little demonstration," and he puffed his chest out in exaggeration, "on how to knock the socks off of a girl."

Chloe, who limply had her arm around Dave's waist, mostly for support, indeed felt like she was sockless, shoeless even. When she had given in to Dave's playful demand that the two of them show Mo and Justin how it was done, she hadn't expected to be twirled like that, much less crooned to by a very enthusiastic Dave, and last but not least, she had not expected that bent-back, full-on, open-mouthed, molar-cleaning, long, long, kiss Dave had laid on her. So her eyes were still trying to focus, and her lungs were still gasping for oxygen when the threesome of Doris, Sara and Marcy made their way to the stage.

Chloe was running her tongue along her lips to make sure they were still attached when Doris Raeburn announced their arrival. "Chloe, dear, no wonder you like directing these things. I love your choice in an assistant!"

Marcy and Sara, standing away from the group, turned and looked at the wolfishly grinning Dave, and the clearly befuddled Chloe, who gave both of them a weak, blushing smile.

Marcy crossed her arms in front of her. "Hey, Mo, Justin, Ben? Take a break. All this learning has to be a tiring experience for all of you. Be back in ten."

Dave, still in his ebullient mood, said, "Hey, if I can help out in any other way, Chloe, just ask, okay?" He gave her a broad wink and smiled.

"Uh, thanks, Dave. I'll keep that in mind."

Doris and Dave seemed to be the only cheery people in the group. Everyone else seemed to be carefully eying each other: Marcy glanced at Sara; Sara stared at Chloe; Marcy tried to meet Chloe's eyes, then turned to Sara, looking at Dave. Doris examined everyone, one at a time. Dave, his cheerfulness aided by the four or five beers he had, wasn't really focusing on anyone, but he was giving it a manful try. The only one not looking at anyone was Chloe. She was having somewhat of a religious experience. *I didn't do anything wrong, but I feel like I'm guilty for some reason. And I'm not even Catholic.*

A voice called from the front of the theater. "Mrs. Raeburn? Phone for you, in your office."

Damn damn damn. Just when it was getting good. "On my way, dear." Doris took one last look at the group on the stage, and sighed. She headed out the side exit to go to her office.

Marcy, ever the reactionist, shot Chloe a piercing look, and then shot her smart remark at Dave. "Well, I never knew you could be so entertaining. Three stars in the family." She turned on her heel, and marched off the stage, and started up the aisle.

Dave, seeing that his sweet pea seemed to be a little perturbed about something, ambled off the stage after her.

Sara was standing quietly, a few feet from Chloe. Chloe lifted her head to explain the prior awkward event to her, then dropped it again. *I don't need to explain anything to her. Why is she looking at me like I should?*

Sara cleared her throat; it didn't help, her voice still sounded a bit hoarse. "You want me to send Heather, Nelson and Jeanette up here today? They have their routines pretty much set for "Surrey with the Fringe on Top." You said you wanted to see it, singing, acting and dancing, today. I think they can do it. If you want."

"Sure. Send them all up. I'll send Mo and Justin down to you."

"All right then." Sara hopped off the edge of the stage, and began walking up the aisle.

"Sara?"

Sara stopped and gazed up at Chloe, on the stage, hair aglow in the light. "Yes, Chloe?"

Chloe looked at her, and then looked away and waved her off. "Never mind. It'll keep."

Sara looked at her again, and then walked the rest of the way up the aisle, and out of the theater.

Sara passed her somewhat confused brother in the hallway. He was standing in front of Marcy, who looked like she was going to explode from trying to hold it all in.

"Just go home Dave, and sleep it off," Marcy hissed.

"But honey, I was going to get a ride from you, one of the guys dropped me off here."

Sara stopped in her tracks when she heard this exchange. She ignored her brother, and whispered in Marcy's ear. "We could, between the two of us, probably get him to fit in the trunk of your Miata." She looked to Marcy for her reaction to this idea.

"Only if we cut him in half first. Can we get him down to the wood shop?"

Sara tossed her uncomprehending brother a wasted sneer. "I've got to get back to rehearsals. Good luck with Mr. Love Machine, Marse." She patted Marcy on the back, and strode up the hall.

Dave, propped against the wall with one hand, suddenly didn't feel so good. "I think I gotta sit down." And he decided that right there was as good a place as any.

Marcy caught his slide down, and hooked his arm around her shoulder. "Hang on, I thought you said you had four or five beers." She hoisted him into a better position, and looked around. The closest place to take him would be back into the theater. "We're going back into the theater. You can sit down in there."

"Well, and then a shot for every five years at UPS."

Marcy groaned and moved the tall man along. She freed a hand, and yanked open the theater door, and half-carried, half-stumbled with the increasingly heavier man down to the front row. Chloe, coming out of the wings, saw Marcy depositing Dave in a seat.

Marcy propped up Dave as best she could, and then left him sitting there with his head propped in one hand, elbow on the armrest. He moaned once, then immediately dozed off. She walked over to the stage, and Chloe stepped up to the edge to meet her. Marcy looked up, and fixed her friend with a withering stare. "Listen, Miss Lips, you get to babysit him until 6:00. I have to get back down there and fool with some costumes." She took another look at Dave and started up the aisle.

"Marcy?"

Marcy turned a fierce look on her friend. "Yes, Chloe?"

Chloe looked at her, and then looked away and waved her off. "Never mind. It'll keep."

Marcy looked at her again, and then walked the rest of the way up the aisle, and out of the theater.

Doris Raeburn, finally off of the phone, decided to go play catch-up on what she had missed in the theater.

She slowly opened the theater door, and snuck a peek in there, and she saw Chloe, standing alone on the stage, whirling a bit, singing lowly, as an apparently enchanted Dave D'Amico looked on from the front row, head propped on his arm. Doris was just about to enter the rest of the way, when a voice called down the hall.

"Mrs. Raeburn? Mrs. Hoderman's on the phone. In your office."

Damn. Damn. Damn.

Nelson, Jeanette and Heather passed a strangely smirking Mrs. Raeburn in the hallway on their way to the theater.

When they entered, Nelson was startled to see his father sitting in the front row. The threesome went down the aisle, and Nelson stopped and looked at his peacefully slumbering dad.

"Nelson, up here. We need to get started," Chloe called softly. Nelson went up on the stage, and nodded his head in the direction of the front row.

Chloe came up to him, and whispered, "Passed out."

Nelson nodded his understanding. "Oh, Ms. Donahue. Marcy told me to tell you, uh, she said you were in charge of getting Dad home tonight. She has something she has to do. I wish I could do it, but I'm already full up with Aunt Sara and Jeanette." He looked at her quizzically as he continued, "She said, 'Tell Miss Lips to haul Mr. Kisses' sweet butt home.' I didn't know what she meant, but she repeated it, she said you'd know what it means."

Chloe rubbed her face in her hands. She was about to say something, but thought better of it.

He looked at her. "Yes, Ms. Donahue?"

She looked at him, and then looked away and waved him off. "Never mind. It'll keep."

When Heather, Justin, Justin, and Jason were leaving the school for the evening, there, on the far side of the dim parking lot was Ms. Donahue, with a tall man's arms tight around her, leaned up against her Subaru. It looked like she was getting into the back seat with him.

Justin enthused, "Woo hoo! Would ya look at that! Right here, in the school parking lot!"

Justin replied, "Yeah, I wish we were closer."

Heather squinted. "Isn't that Nelson's dad?"

Jason queried, "I thought he and the art teacher had something going?"

Justin smirked. "Not anymore, apparently. Or maybe she doesn't know."

Heather shuddered. "Let's get out of here. This isn't right."

Justin, Justin, and Jason groaned. "Girls."

Sara came out of the house when she heard Chloe's car come into the drive. She came out of the house and stood by Chloe's door as she got out.

"Chloe, I didn't even know about any of this until after Nelson had dropped off Jeanette, and by then, we figured it was too late to get back to the school to help out."

Chloe slammed her car door shut. She opened the back seat door, and both Chloe and Sara peered into see a still-sleeping Dave curled up like a large child on the back seat. Sara reached in, and took hold of his arm, and with a mighty pull, she maneuvered him into an upright position. Nelson appeared to offer his help, and ducked his head under his dad's arm, and pulled him into a standing position. Sara got under Dave's other arm, and they both adjusted until they had a good grip on him.

"Thanks, Chloe." Sara smiled sadly at her.

"Yeah, t'anks, Choey," a suddenly awake Dave slurred.

Chloe sighed, and slammed the back door.

As soon as Nelson, Dave and Sara were safely away from the car, Chloe started the engine. In her headlights she saw the three faces of the Family D'Amico. Each one sheepishly smiling at her, waving goodbye. She sighed again, and returned their wave as she pulled out into the night.

Marcy called around noon on Friday.

"Hey, Sara."

"Hey, Marcy. Dave's out in the garage. I'll go get him."

"I don't want to talk to him. I called for you."

"Huh?"

"Good comeback. Listen. I know this is out of left field, but I need you to do something for me."

"Uh, sure, if I can. What is it?"

"I need you to go out with me tonight. I want to get shitfaced. You can get shit-faced, too, the more the merrier, as far as I'm concerned."

"Uh, Marse? Isn't that something you should be doing with Chloe, or with Dave? You know, people that are friends of yours?"

"Whatever gave you the impression you aren't a friend of mine?"

"Well, maybe that you treat me like dirt, you constantly put me down, and we do nothing but argue."

"Exactly."

"Huh?"

"Get with the program, girlfriend. That's how I treat my favorite people! Are we on, or not?"

"What did you have in mind?"

"Dinner. Lots of cocktails. Then, whatever."

"Should I tell Dave?"

"Nah. It's girls' night out!"

"Oh. I guess so. All right."

"And Sara? Dress up a little. I don't get seen with just anybody, you know. Leave the orange coveralls at home."

Sara smiled. "You too, Marcy. Let's knock 'em dead."

"That's more like it! See you at seven. I'll pick you up at your house."

"See you then." Sara hung up the phone. *Well, this is different. What could it hurt?*

Dave spent his first UPS-free Friday nursing a headache and upset stomach, and vainly trying to remember what he had done, given that his sister wasn't speaking to him. He tried to call Marcy several times during the day, but she quite effectively blew him off by hanging up on him. Not being a deep thinker, Dave attributed their behavior to the fact that they were women, as if that little fact in itself explained everything.

When Nelson got home from school, he avoided talking to Dave, too. No one at school had said anything concrete to Nelson on the subject, but he got the feeling that his friends were looking at him with a mixture of sympathy and amusement, and Nelson didn't like that feeling one bit. *They must know that Dad was trashed and passed out in the theater.*

Chloe spent a good five hours looking for a receipt that Ron Johnson had called about and said was missing from the paperwork she had given him on Monday. It totaled a whopping $18.62, but he acted as if Chloe was somehow being extremely derelict in her duties. By the time five o'clock rolled around, the missing receipt was still missing, and Chloe was royally pissed off. She gave up and went home. She thought it strange that she hadn't heard from Marcy, but quite accurately attributed it to the thought that Marcy was probably ticked off at her. *I'll explain all of this at rehearsals tomorrow. It's dance day, so we should have plenty of time to get this straightened out.*

Dave was sitting in the kitchen, fixing himself a sandwich, when Nelson came in and announced he was leaving for his date with Jeanette. He grabbed his coat, went out the door, and Dave looked at the clock. *Hmm, almost 8:00, I should try calling Marcy again.* He called her house, no answer, then called her cell phone and got the same result. He decided to take a spin past her house. No little Miata was parked in the drive. *Maybe she went out with Chloe.*

Audra Simmons called Chloe that evening, and after some awkward moments, settled in to having a little girl talk, lesbian style. Chloe described some of the more interesting events of the last week, but left out the more damaging details of her problems with Sara. *I guess I still feel protective of her.* Chloe also told a bemused Audra about the ninety-proof kiss she had undergone with Dave the day before. Audra described the hijinx that occurred during her trips to teacher union activities. She announced that teachers, as a lot, weren't great partiers because they were too concerned with their status as role models. Chloe dryly replied that surely wasn't the case at Fort Lafayette. When Chloe got off the phone with Audra, it was nearly 10:30. She decided to take an over-the-counter sleeping aid, to get a good night's sleep. She spent the remainder of the evening in bed, reading until the sleeping pills kicked in, and she zonked. Around 12:30 a.m. she got a phone call from a flustered-sounding Dave.

"Chloe, it's Dave. Get dressed. We have to go on a rescue mission. I'm getting into my Explorer now, and I'll come get you."

Chloe, who had been sleeping deeply, was dimly alarmed at Dave's words. "Is anyone hurt? Is it Sara? Is it Nelson? Marcy?"

"Nobody's hurt. Nelson's not home yet. I just got a call from my best friend Stan, and he asked if I would come down to his bar and pick up Marcy. Seems he thinks she's too drunk to drive."

Chloe shook her head, trying to clear it. "This may be a stupid question, Dave, but isn't this something you could handle by yourself?"

"Well, normally, yeah. But she's got Sara with her, who also is apparently three sheets to the wind, and I sure as hell can't handle the both of them. See you in ten."

Chloe was too sleepy to even ponder the absurdity of the situation. Dave picked her up, and he spent most of the drive to Stan's Bar and Grill describing his surprise at finding out that Marcy and

Sara were together. He kept saying, over and over, "I didn't even think they liked each other."

Stan's was packed because it was the popular karaoke night, so Dave had to find a parking place quite a ways up the road. He said to the small redhead, still being pretty quiet, on their walk to the entrance, "We'll just go in, grab them, and be out in five minutes. I'll have you back in bed in a half hour."

Chloe smiled, and rubbed her eyes as Dave opened the door for her.

The recorded strains of the beginnings of an old Carpenters' tune played through the speaker system. Dave first looked behind the bar for his friend Stan, who waved at him and pointed at the small stage area, lit with neon and a small spot, across the barroom floor. The bar was standing room only, and Dave put his arm around Chloe and moved her quickly through the crowded tables and the standing, hooting patrons. Dave, being much taller than Chloe, saw their quarry before Chloe did. He stopped for a moment, and then gripped Chloe's arm tighter as he moved them closer to the little stage. Chloe may not have seen them as soon as Dave did, but she soon heard them, and moments after that, Dave had maneuvered them to within view of the stage.

Sara, looking very much like a glamorous Vegas lounge singer in a deep cut black cocktail dress, was on the small stage, sitting on a high bar stool. Marcy, in a multi-patterned, tight slinky number of her own, was sitting comfortably in Sara's lap, her arm around her waist. They were both holding onto the microphone, fingers entwined.

Sara was singing in her low smoky voice, and staring meaningfully into Marcy's eyes as she sang the sappy lyrics. Marcy pulled the microphone toward her, and returned Sara's longing gaze as she sang directly to her. And then they both turned their heads to the crowd and sang together, Sara harmonizing with Marcy and their eyes turned back to each other, their foreheads touching as they finished "For All We Know" in unison.

The crowd's whistling and stomping started before the last strains of the song faded away. Sara grinned at Marcy, who hugged her, laid a fat smooch on Sara's cheek, and waved regally at the cheering crowd. "More! More! More!"

Stan had worked his way over to Dave and Chloe, who both were standing there, staring, eyes wide, mouths hung open in some kind of mutual paralysis. Stan clapped his hand on Dave's shoulder, and pulled him down low, so Chloe could hear what he was shouting. "They've been up there for almost two hours now. Crowd loves them, I tried to shut them off but the crowd keeps buying them drinks, and throwing out requests."

He shook his head and he stopped to laugh. He continued, loudly, "That was pretty tame. You should have been here when they did "I Touch Myself"—that was something to see!"

Sara stumbled, in her high heels, on the long walk to the car. Chloe, who was keeping a light hand on Sara's higher-than-normal back to steady her, reached and tried to keep her from falling all the way, and grabbed Sara's ass in the process. Sara, glassy eyed and grinning, looked down at Chloe, said, "Fresh!" and continued her unsteady pace along the uneven sidewalk to the Explorer. Dave had given up trying to walk Marcy after about ten steps of her wandering off; he just leaned over, picked her up and slung her over his shoulder. She was bouncing up and down, grinning like a wild-eyed drunk and waving at her new bestest friend Sara, who was trailing along behind them with Chloe.

"You and me, baby. You and me! We killed 'em all!" she joyfully crowed. Her eyeballs were bouncing in perfect syncopation with her long curls.

Sara stumbled again as she tried to dip low enough to find Chloe's ear to confide, "I really love her. She's the best!" She blew a kiss to Marcy, who caught it, and smacked it onto her cheek.

Dave stopped at the front passenger side of the Explorer, got his keys out, unlocked it, opened the door, and being mindful of Marcy's head, still managed to plop her down ungracefully into the front seat. He belted her in, and then turned and helped Chloe get Sara into the back seat. He then headed back around, and got into the driver's side. Chloe, pushing Sara over to the other side of the vehicle, searched around, and found her own seat belt and buckled it.

The ride to Marcy's was blissfully uneventful, although Chloe thought she might suffocate from the heat pouring through the SUV. They had been unable to find any coats for either Sara or Marcy, and Dave said that maybe they had left them in Marcy's car, wherever that might be. So Dave, being considerate of the flimsily dressed women's welfare, cranked up the heat. Chloe stole a few glances over Sara's way, and saw that although Sara's eyes were closed, she had a tiny smile on her face and seemed to be singing small snatches of songs to herself.

Chloe couldn't help but be awed by the way Sara looked.

Chloe had seen Sara in T-shirts, sweatshirts, the occasional work shirt and jeans, but she had never seen her look anything like this before. She had make-up on, with lipstick, and her already long eyelashes seemed impossibly longer. Her hair, lustrous and free flowing, fell down over the thin straps of material that held up the extremely low-cut black dress she was barely wearing. The top cut below Sara's breasts, and Chloe valiantly struggled to keep her eyes off the rounded, soft exposed flesh there. The dress stopped mid-thigh, and had a very nice cut up the hip that accentuated Sara's long strong legs. Chloe didn't know if it was the elevated heat in the vehicle that was making her squirm, or the thought that kept invading her mind about how nice it would be to slip her hand under one of those small pieces of shimmering black fabric just barely covering that curved softness and—

"We're here." Dave grinned into the rearview mirror. Chloe sat upright and stared straight ahead. "I'll get her in the house. You keep doing such a good job watching my baby sister, I'll just get Marcy settled in, and be right back."

Chloe watched as Dave crossed in front of the vehicle, opened the door, and started gently extracting Marcy from her seat belt. He cooed soft words to her as she softly moaned her protests at having to be moved. He got her out, and carefully walked her up her front sidewalk to the front door. He unlocked the door, and they disappeared inside.

"Alone at last," murmured Sara, who had opened an eye and was looking Chloe's way, one side of her mouth curled up into a sexy grin.

Chloe sucked her teeth and tried to keep her face a mask. "It would appear that way. Have fun tonight, did we?"

Sara let her head roll back against the headrest. "Oh, yeah, big fun." She laughed at her own small joke. She turned to Chloe again. "What are you doing here? Hmm? Why aren't you home, all snuggled up and warm in bed?"

Chloe was feeling way too tired to be spiteful. Plus, a major amount of her energy was being used to fight off the very erotic sensations she was feeling every time she looked at Sara. She focused on Sara's upturned lips. "Well, Dave called and asked me to come help. He thought you would be too much of a handful," her eyes just naturally tracked to Sara's exposed cleavage again, and then she forcefully willed them back up to meet Sara's grinning countenance, "for him to handle the both of you. So here I am."

"S'nice. Thank you." Sara closed her eyes again, and let out a small sigh that left her lips softy parted. Chloe's thoughts turned to a whole new area, as she imagined those lips, that mouth, that tongue.

The front door opened, and Dave got into the car, seeing Chloe exactly the same way he had left her, sitting very upright, and staring straight ahead. The overhead light lit the smile on his face, and he looked at Sara, and then at Chloe. "Well, I got the Captain in bed, now we'll get you home, and I can get Tennille here back to the shack, too."

Chloe just nodded, and closed her eyes, too. The ride back to her house was quiet, the car warm and soon Chloe was dozing, inhabiting a wonderfully hot and steamy dreamscape. Erotic images of Sara, in that inviting dress, invaded her dream. There was Sara, gently kissing and sucking down the length of her neck, and Chloe responded by using her hands to urge the unresisting Sara to straddle her. Chloe slid her hands down from the center of Sara's long neck, down into that warm cleavage, then her hands parted and traveled outward, under the material covering what Chloe what so desperately wanted to possess. She heard Sara moan as her palms lightly traced a pattern on warm, pliant flesh. Chloe felt herself give her own moan in response, and her hands tightened around those giving mounds, gently increasing the pressure with each fluid squeeze. Chloe felt Sara's tongue trying to gain access to her mouth, and she opened it willingly, and felt that tongue dart deeply in and meet with her own. Sara's moans were increasing in frequency and duration as the kiss deepened.

"Ahem. You two want to get a room?" asked Dave, trying as hard as he could not to look in the rearview mirror.

Chloe's eyes flew open to see what she suddenly knew was a reality, that Sara was straddling her, and looking down at her with such undisguised lust in her eyes that it drove all the breath out of her. Chloe's hands tightened in an involuntary reflex, and her palms felt the nipples beneath them harden anew.

"Oh, God!" Chloe yelped, and she shoved Sara off her, into a satin heap onto the far side of the bench seat.

Sara gave her an amazed look of bewilderment. "I thought you wanted..." she moaned in disappointment.

Chloe's hands were desperately searching for the seat belt release, and finally found it. She focused on Sara in embarrassed shock. "I'm so sorry, I was asleep. I thought I was dreaming it." She looked up front and caught Dave's eyes glancing in the rearview mirror. Her embarrassment grew tenfold. "And Sara, your brother is in the damned car!"

Sara, still way beyond the boundaries of any semblance of sobriety, said "Oh, yeah, well, I forgot all about him when you—"

Chloe's hand was on the door, pushing it open. "Don't say it. Just don't say it." Chloe opened the door, hopped out, eased it shut, and trotted up the path to her front door.

Dave watched as soon as Chloe safely entered her house, then pulled the car out and headed for home. He caught Sara's bleary scowl in his rearview mirror. She narrowed her eyes at him. He heard her, although she never spoke it aloud. *Don't say it, just don't say it.*

Saturday dawned with the promise of a beautiful, warm spring day, the kind of day that makes people think they may commit hara-kiri if they are forced to remain indoors. By ten o'clock, people were opening windows that had not been moved since October. The stifled presence of winter quickly escaped out screened windows to be replaced by the breeze carrying in the freshness of the lake, the meanderings of birds and sounds of CD players blaring rap music, as teenagers, dressed in hastily found shorts, washed their cars.

Sara D'Amico, in her little house by the eighth hole, was unaware of the ambiance that the day carried. She was too busy scrubbing her tongue with a toothbrush, trying to rid her mouth of the remains of Jim Beam and cigarettes. She gagged several times, and washed her mouth out liberally with mouthwash, and repeated it again with another capful, just for good measure. Her head ached a little, her throat felt vaguely sore, and her eyes looked like she'd watched a *Little House On the Prairie* marathon including the episodes when Mary Ingalls goes blind.

She trudged the worn path from her house up to Dave and Nelson's and for the first time noticed the change in the air. *I should have opened my windows before I left.* Since she was nearly there, she shrugged and promptly forgot about it. She entered the kitchen door to find both Nelson and Dave seated at the kitchen table, reading the newspaper. They both looked at her and grunted. *Rough night for everyone.* She grunted in reply and poured herself a cup of coffee.

Over on the east side of town, Chloe had all her windows open wide. She had been up since seven o'clock, infused with a new energy that seemed to wake her and pull her from her bed. Her sleep had been deep, and filled with images, emotions and desires that stole her mind and warmed her loins. She awoke just before dawn, and, feeling somewhat unsatisfied by the abrupt end of the dreams but not the feelings they had evoked in her, found herself in desperate need of relief, which, with a skilled hand, she provided. By her second cup of coffee, her romantic notions had turned to musings of a purely scientific, rational nature. *Oh, this is just great. I'm in trouble now. I cop the greatest feel ever, get a mind blower of a kiss, and now I'm not going to be able to think or dream of anything else. I may as well give up, I'm useless.*

At 11:45 a.m., newly washed cars were arriving in the parking lot at Lafayette High. Teenagers in shorts, too excited by the warm weather to want to enter the gymnasium yet, gathered around their cars in small groups and watched as others arrived. A small murmur of interest went through the small groups, as they saw the Subaru of their director arrive, followed in by a red Miata, and bringing up the rear a green Ford pickup truck. Although all three vehicles arrived together, it seemed that the drivers took great pains in not parking anywhere near each other. All the occupants of these vehicles got out, and the teenagers all watched covertly as all three adult women steered clear of each other in their trek to the building. Sara stayed at Nelson's arm, Chloe stopped and spoke to Mo Dean, and Marcy just trudged straight ahead, looking at no one, and up the stairs into the building.

Paul was already in the gymnasium when Marcy came in. She walked up to him, and he noticed her rather unkempt appearance, and the black circles surrounding her eyes. She said two words to him, "Nurse's office." And then turned and headed in that direction, never to be seen again that afternoon.

Paul, whistling while he worked, used a long pole to open the high gymnasium windows. Sara walked in, followed by Nelson and Jeanette, and they headed over to the table with the CD player on it. Sara put down her stack of CDs, and strolled over to Paul. "Good afternoon, Paul," she smiled. He smiled back, and resumed his whistling. "Paul! Can the whistling. Now." She gave him another smile and walked away. The whistling ceased.

Paul was opening the last window when Chloe entered, in yellow V-neck T-shirt and khaki shorts and sneakers. She walked over to greet him, and stood and watched as he propped the window open. He looked at her and smiled. "You look chipper today." Then he frowned, curious. "What's that on your neck?"

Chloe, confused, immediately went to the girls' room, and returned a mere minute later, murderous eyes glued to the back of a long-legged, blue-jeaned, white T-shirted dance monkey. Nearly everyone had arrived in the gym by then, and watched, with major interest, as their beloved little director stormed across the gym to stop behind their choreographer, and tap her very insistently on the shoulder.

Sara, chatting with one of the Justins, turned and saw a red-faced, red-haired woman glaring at her. "Hey Chloe, is there—"

Chloe didn't wait for her to finish. She grabbed Sara by the wrist, and hauled her in the direction of the gym doors leading out into the hallway. Sara got the idea, and followed her without being dragged.

Chloe continued up the hallway, until she found an empty classroom that was open. She stopped and waited for Sara to stop her momentum, and then entered, and after Sara came in, she closed the door, none too softly, behind them.

"What's up, Chloe?"

"This is what's up. This!" Chloe was pointing to her neck, just below her right ear.

The classroom was unlit, and sort of on the dim side, so Sara stepped up closer, and peered at the area Chloe was pointing to. "I don't see anything."

Chloe's hand shot out and flipped the nearby light switch on. "This!"

Sara stepped up and looked again. She wore a very big, sly smile on her face. "It's a hickey."

Chloe looked like she could strangle her with just her pinky fingers. "Thank you, Dr. D'Amico, for the diagnosis," she snarled.

Sara just smiled back at her. "What're you complaining about, you're the one who started it."

"I am not."

"Are too."

"I did not start anything. You did. I was sleeping, and the next thing I know—"

"You're running your hand up my thigh, and pulling me on top of you."

"How would you know, Sara, you were drunk."

"Not that drunk that I don't remember what happened."

"Wait a minute, I remember what happened, you were kissing my neck. See! I have proof! And then everything else started."

"Chloe, that was after you snuck your hand across the seat, and up my thigh. Oh, right about here."

"I did not."

"Did too."

"I wouldn't do such a thing. I was asleep."

"I think you were acting out on some deep-seated desires."

"I was not!"

"I had no idea you were asleep. From what I could tell, you knew exactly what you were doing." Sara grinned at the memory. "It sure felt that way to me."

Chloe couldn't argue with that logic. She leaned up against the blackboard in defeat. "But what about this?" she asked wearily. She pointed at her neck again.

Sara took a step closer. She could feel the heat coming off Chloe's body. Sara placed her hands on the blackboard, on either sides of Chloe's shoulders, and leaned in, so she was almost nose to nose with Chloe. Chloe trembled, but did not move away.

Sara's eyes bored into the unblinking green of Chloe's. Her voice was husky. "I promise that next time, I'll be more careful. I won't leave any marks, at least ones that anyone can see. As long as you promise me," she backed away a mere breath, "that next time, you'll put your mouth where your hands were last night. I can still feel them on me, now."

Chloe was only human, after all. There was only so much she could take, and she had never heard a sweeter, sillier, or sexier promise. She wrapped her arms around Sara's neck, and hesitated only briefly before stating, "I promise."

Sara smiled, for at last her heart was free. She leaned in the remaining space, and lightly ran her tongue across Chloe's lips, moistening them before she placed hers there, and the kiss began at last. It began slowly, tenderly, both with the good intentions of not wanting to rush the other. But time and desire had effectively muted their ability to hold back. They surged forward, unstoppable, each new thrust of tongue escalating their desire, multiplying it. Chloe's hand reached boldly for the breast it desired, and finding it brought the kiss a deeper urgency, a moan and another thrust of tongue, biting of lip, clashing of teeth. What had started slowly was stoked to a fever pitch in the merest flicker of time. So long had they held back, it seemed impossible to slow down now. Gasping for breath, Sara dropped her head and began kissing Chloe below her hairline, and she dropped her hands and placed them on Chloe's butt and lifted. Chloe's legs rose and wrapped themselves around Sara. Sara stopped kissing her neck, and pushed Chloe up against the blackboard, so they were eye to fevered eye. Sara dove her tongue into Chloe's mouth again and swirled it, and was rewarded with a return thrust and a tightening of legs around Sara's waist. Chloe's hand was just about to slide up Sara's T-shirt when there was a noise in the hallway. Sara almost dropped her, but then slowly let Chloe slide her legs down to the floor. Their eyes locked, and they nervously watched the door for a moment, quietly catching their breath, and then when nothing happened, they returned their gaze to each other.

Small smiles grew larger on both faces as they recognized and accepted the love and desire reflecting back and forth between their eyes.

"Wow!" blinked Chloe. "That was the greatest two minutes of my life. I wonder what we could do with, say, hours? Days?"

"Yeah." Sara panted, and her hand reached out and stroked Chloe's warm cheek. She ran her thumb across Chloe's nose, and down across her parted lips. "The way my heart's pounding now, five minutes may be the death of me," she said, her voice dropping, and looking a bit shy.

Chloe laughed softly. "You're feeling shy after what just happened here?" Her lips kissed Sara's lingering thumb, and then she took it playfully in between her teeth and bit it. Sara's heart, which had just settled down, began to beat a little faster, and then faster yet, as she watched Chloe pull her thumb into her mouth and began to softly suck on it, never taking her eyes off Sara's. Sara felt a renewed jolt pass through her. And then she laughed, and pulled her warm and wet digit from Chloe's mouth. Chloe gave her a mock frown, then grinned. "Soon, Sara. Soon."

They stepped away from each other, knowing that soon was not going to happen soon enough. There was dancing to be done. Both women sighed and smiled. Sara leaned and placed a soft kiss on Chloe's lips. "Let's have some fun today, Chloe, it's springtime, and I'm in love." She watched a wonderful sparkle explode in Chloe's eyes. Chloe nodded, and after sneaking a giggling look up and down the hallway, they headed back up to the gym.

Part XIII:
Wrap Your Lips Around This One

Chloe was sitting on the folded-down rear gate of Nelson's pickup truck, next to Paul. She had her sleeves rolled up past her shoulders, enjoying the sun here on this early Spring day. It was nearly seventy degrees, definitely not a typical March day here in the Northeast. There was little to no breeze, which kept the temperature higher; if there had been a wind, it would pick up the coldness of the nearby lake water, and spread that cool temperature over the land. She was glad she'd decided to wear shorts today, even if her legs were an embarrassing shade of eggshell white. Chloe's pale strawberry blonde hair and fair complexion did not lend to tanning easily, more of a golden glow would overtake her, and she would erupt with freckles on her nose, shoulders and knees over the course of the summer. When she was younger, and put a premium on achieving a tan, she would spend hours in the sun, on the rough sand beach, wasting away many hours. Now that she was older, she thought more about preserving her skin, staying out of the sun unless it was incidental time, such as today.

She was thoroughly enjoying herself. She hadn't done much in the last two hours, other than sit back on the tailgate and watch the show. Sara had decided that it was too nice a day to spend rehearsing indoors, so she suggested that the whole cast move out to the parking lot; they could practice just as easily out there, with the assistance of a couple of PA speakers hooked up to someone's car CD player. This suggestion was greeted, not surprisingly, with a roar of approval from the ensemble. Normally, they were an enthusiastic bunch, but even the most dedicated of souls could lose their zeal when faced with having to be in a smelly old gymnasium on a day like today. They had moved a few cars, and had ample space to practice their moves.

Today they were rehearsing the box social scene. Every member of the cast was involved, and the scene included square dancing, singing, waltzing, a fight between farmers and cowboys, and running dialogue between different leads. Everything was to be a mass of motion, unending for nearly ten minutes. It had taken a lot of planning, and some of Sara's ideas did not translate well to the small stage. There was a need for the audience not to be distracted by too much background clutter during the dialogue and lead singing parts. She kept adjusting dancers and their movements as the day wore on, but she was still not happy with the results. Some of the kids were getting restless, and although she had told them a half hour ago that they would be breaking soon, she had forgotten that promise and kept them working at it, over and over. Chloe could see the frustration showing on the kids' faces.

Time to exercise my power as director of this thing. They need a break. She waited for an opportune moment to interrupt the proceedings. It came pretty quickly, when two couples plowed into each other during the umpteenth do-si-do of the afternoon. When it looked to Chloe that the farmers, cowboys and their significant others were going to start a real life range war right there on school property, she stood up on the tailgate, inserted two fingers in her mouth and let out a piercing whistle. All eyes turned toward her, including those of her love, who raised an eyebrow when Chloe caught her eye.

"Ms. D'Amico, could I interrupt you for a moment and talk to you?"

"Why certainly, Ms. Donahue." Sara turned to her hot and tired troupe. "Why don't you all take ten minutes, make that fifteen, and relax?" Some of the group gave her a grateful look, but the majority of them knew that their true benefactor was Ms. Donahue. Ms. D'Amico was a slave driver, pure and simple.

The group dispersed, some into the school, some on the on the brick ledge on the side of the building.

Sara walked across the parking lot, eyes never leaving those of her heart's desire as she approached. She waited as Chloe and Paul moved to make room for her on the tailgate, and she hopped up.

How can we get rid of Paul? He doesn't look like he's going to budge. "You had something you wanted to discuss with me?" Sara asked.

"Well, Ms. De Mille, as a matter of fact I did. Are you trying to kill these kids? They looked like they were planning a coup out there, a mutiny. I was worried for your safety," Chloe said half seriously.

"You think I'm working them too hard? This is a long involved scene, and we need big chunks of time to practice it. We need to get all the way through it without any hitches. The other scenes are all pretty easy compared to this one."

"Yeah, I know, but I think you need to let up a bit on it. We have plenty of time before May to nail it. It's just a suggestion, but why don't you do something that the kids will have some fun with after the break? Then go back to it." *I don't like to butt in, but I'm getting tired just watching them.*

Sara thought that over. *Everyone's a critic.* "All right, you're right. I'm being a killjoy, aren't I?"

"Maybe just a little bit."

The three of them sat there for a while, just enjoying the day, and then Paul, who had been silent, said, "Hey, Sara, my mom said she met you the other day at the library."

"Yes, I did, Paul. She seems like a lovely woman." *Crazy as a loon.*

Chloe had an idea. "Paul, have you called and checked in with her lately?" *Five. Four.*

Paul looked a little disconcerted. "I don't have to check in with her. I'm a grown man. What gave you that idea?"

"Oh, I thought you did, never mind, sorry." Chloe gave him an apologetic look. *Three. Two. One.*

Paul fidgeted, and checked his watch. "Uh, well, I guess I'll go to the men's room, if you ladies will excuse me."

He hopped off the back of the truck, and casually walked toward the school.

We have blast-off! Chloe gleefully smirked, "Ten bucks says..."

"That's a sucker bet," Sara replied, chuckling at the ease with which Chloe had pulled that little maneuver off.

They gave each other the real smiles, intimate smiles, that they had wanted to share all afternoon.

Sara looked around the parking lot, and then at the pinked face of the small director. "Think anyone will notice if I toss you into the pick up bed and ravish you?"

"You seemed to perform pretty well last night in front of a crowd." *I like flirting so much more than fighting.*

"Well, yeah, but they were buying me drinks. What's in it for me today?" Sara challenged, and quite purposely raised a single brow.

"You have no imagination. Plus, I'm sure I could come up with a couple of requests." *Damn that eyebrow, what it does to me.*

Marcy's little red Miata caught Sara's eye. "Hey, by the way, where is my little Cher today? I haven't seen her since we pulled in. And how'd she get her car back?"

"Cher?"

"Oh, that's right, you weren't there when we did "I Got You Babe."" Sara smirked, and did that eyebrow thing again.

Chloe laughed, and slapped Sara lightly on the shoulder. "Seems like I missed a lot last night. You'll have to tell me about it."

"What I can remember I'll tell you." Sara looked around. "Anyway, where is she?"

"Paul said she went straight to the nurse's office. I figured she's sacked out in there. She doesn't have good recuperative abilities like you apparently do."

"I have many, many, you know, talents." *Am I overdoing this eyebrow thing?*

"I look forward to learning what exactly those might be," Chloe said, a flirtatious gleam in her eyes.

"You, madam director, are going to witness them," Sara tapped the tip of Chloe's nose, "one at a time, little by little. I wouldn't want to overwhelm you. Your brain would explode." Sara raised both eyebrows, and crossed her eyes in demonstration.

"I'm pretty sure it has several times, and was put back together wrong." *If we put the tailgate up, and crawled back, I'm sure no one would find us for a least five minutes. I think that's all it would take.*

"So that explains it," nodded Sara.

"I have an explanation for everything. It might be wrong, of course, but it makes my life simpler knowing that I know everything," Chloe said, with an absolute air of confidence. "Oh, boy, here comes Paul again. We don't have much time." Chloe hesitated for a moment, and then said, "I was wondering if I could offer you a ride home tonight?"

"Are you going to do that old 'oh, look, here we are out on a deserted road, and I just ran out of gas trick' with me? Hmm?"

"Maybe." *Definitely.*

"Sounds perfect to me," Sara said, quickly running her fingertip along Chloe's arm.

Paul was a few steps away. "Good. Because I think we need to have a little talk." *And I know how you love doing that.*

It was Sara's turn to say it. "Oh boy."

"I can't think when you're doing that," Chloe gasped. Sara's lips were softly working their way up Chloe's neck, getting dangerously close to her ear.

"Thinking is so overrated," murmured Sara, as her tongue found a delightful little divot of skin to stop and memorize.

Chloe fought the overwhelming urge to just let Sara have her way with her. Several times. In several different positions. She grasped Sara by the shoulders, and reluctantly pushed her away. "God, you are worse than a teenage boy. All hands, all lips."

"All total frustration," growled Sara, and sat back on the blanket, propping herself up by her elbows. She stretched her long legs out, and growled again, just to emphasize her point. She looked around at their surroundings. They were about forty-five yards, a wedge shot, from the sixth hole. It had been Chloe's suggestion that they continue their day outdoors after rehearsals finished for the day. *Huh. She just didn't want to be caught indoors with me, where one thing would naturally lead to another. And another.* Sara sighed, and looked at Chloe sitting cross-legged, who had worked her way up from the semi-prone position that Sara had worked so hard to get her into. *A few more inches down, and I would have had her. Damn.*

Chloe was rubbing her knees, trying to regain her composure. "Listen, sweetheart, may I remind you that this ground is still awfully cold, and this blanket is feeling a little damp." She saw Sara's expression soften. "Not my idea of an ideal place for our first time. Now, if it was June or July, you would be getting no argument from me. I like the thought of getting mosquito bites in the oddest of places as much as the next girl." Chloe cracked a wide grin.

Sara relaxed. "I'd be happy to scratch any of those hard to reach places for you. You just let me know."

"I'll keep that in mind." Chloe picked some grass off of her sneaker. "Meanwhile, we need to talk." She studied Sara's face. "You think we need to talk too, right?"

"Of course I do. We need to talk." *God, I am such a lousy liar. All right, enough of this, time to get the talking over with, so we can move on to other things. Get a grip. Talk.* Sara gave Chloe an encouraging smile. "Where do you want to start?"

Oh God, that's a tough one. Okay, let's just get to the big stuff, right off the bat. "I need to know why you felt the need to blow me off like that. That really hurt." Chloe's stomach lurched a little at the thought.

Sara was equally dismayed by the quick way Chloe had gotten to the point, and the miserable expression on the smaller woman's face. "I-I'm sorry about that. It just seemed like the only way I could handle things, the way I was feeling at the time." Sara looked for Chloe's reaction to that. *Apparently that wasn't a good enough answer.* "And, well, there was that mix-up about me thinking that, you know, that you and Audra had..." It was Sara's stomach that felt the roiling sensation now. *Way, way in the back of my mind, I still feel like it might have happened. Like she did, even though she says she didn't.*

Chloe heard the uncertainty in Sara's voice. "We didn't." *But if that tea kettle hadn't started whistling and interrupted when it did, I'm not sure that I would be able to say that to her right now. The moment may have carried over into something else. I know Audra wanted to continue. I can't say with a certainty that I, at that time, didn't want it to continue. But I put a stop to it, and that's what counts.*

Sara wasn't quite sure how to put it, but she tried anyway. "It's not that I haven't slept with women that were currently sleeping with other women, it never bothered me then, as long as I knew they were being safe, you know." Sara's face colored a little at her admission. "But for some reason, with you, well, it seemed different, more important to me. That you hadn't." *I wanted you to be mine and mine alone.* "And I've never felt that way about anyone, and that kind of scared me."

"You don't want to feel that way about someone?" Chloe steeled herself for Sara's response.

Sara thought about this for a moment. "It's not that. It's just that it's never happened to me, so I was surprised when it did."

Chloe leaned over and placed a soft kiss on Sara's lips, and then leaned back.

Sara's eyebrows lifted in surprise. "What was that for?"

"For feeling that way about someone now." Chloe's voice was light.

Sara felt a blush appear. "I told you before, the night we first kissed, that I don't necessarily think that me feeling that way is good for either one of us. Look at how much trouble that's already caused you."

"Do you think we have any kind of a future?" *This is tough, I feel like the ball's about to drop. On me.*

Sara looked at her doubtfully. "We're not talking about someone renting an orange moving van tomorrow, right?"

"Gimme a break. No. I was thinking next weekend, so I could get packed first," Chloe said sarcastically. She tempered that with a small grin, then her face got serious. "You said I was a small town girl, and you're right." She looked down at her knees. "I don't want to be just another in a long list for you. I'm not built that way. I'm not affair material."

Sara reached out a hand, and put it on Chloe's knee. "I knew that when I first met you," Sara said softly, and gave the knee a squeeze, and then sighed, and looked across the green span in front of her. "My brother, Mr. Kisses? That's what Marcy was calling him last night. Anyway, he told me that all I ever do is say 'no' first, and then wait to be convinced otherwise." She pursed her lips at that thought. "I know he's right, it's just easier for me to say 'no' and then not have to deal with anything beyond that." She scooted a little closer to Chloe, and gently grasped her hand. She brought it up to her face, and drew Chloe's fingertip down the length of her scar. "This scar, Chloe, is the easiest 'no' I've ever had." She dropped her hand back into her lap, but didn't let go of Chloe's hand. "It gave me permission to say 'no' with more ease than I could ever imagine."

Chloe looked at her, clearly confused.

Sara drew her lips into a small rueful smile. "People probably think that I quit the movie business, became some kind of a hermit, because of this scar." She shook her head. "It just gave me permission to quit, and hide myself away. I wanted to do that before the accident happened. I had no clue what was going on. Every day on the set for *Star Gazers* and probably even before that, I was a wreck. I would sit in a trailer, waiting to get called, and from out of nowhere, bang, it would happen. The attacks. And the more I worried about getting them, the worse I got. There were days I couldn't even leave my apartment to get to the set. Rumors started, you've probably heard them, that I was doing drugs, right?" She looked to Chloe quickly for confirmation. When she got it, she stared again, unfocused, across the greenery. "I never did, although I came close. Jennie, in all of her misguided concern, suggested I might consider trying a little to help me get through my day." Sara grabbed some blades of grass with her free hand, and tossed them, hard. "You haven't heard about Jennie yet, have you? That would take a week in itself to explain. For right now, let's just keep her description short. Agent, manager, sometime lover."

Sara stopped talking, and continued to pull, and then toss, grass tufts. Chloe pulled up closer to her, and added a second hand to brush across the hand she was already holding. "Is this upsetting you? We can stop. We don't have to talk about this anymore if you're uncomfortable."

Sara yanked her hand free, and stood up so quickly that Chloe was startled. "No! Don't you see that's exactly what got me into trouble in the first place? Avoiding things?" Sara looked at Chloe, and saw that she had upset her. She sat back down, this time, cross legged from Chloe, so that their knees were touching. "If there's anything I've learned, it's that I can't avoid talking about it, or fighting against it. No matter how much I want to."

Chloe ran the back of her hand across Sara's thigh. "I just meant, you don't have to go into the whole story now, if you didn't want to, I don't know. It's hard seeing that you are getting agitated. I just don't know, what to say, or do." Chloe was at a loss.

"I just want you to know what you might be getting yourself into. You deserve that. Knowing what kind of woman you seem to want to get involved with."

"It sounds like in some ways, you're trying to talk yourself out of getting involved with me." Chloe sighed. "Okay, forget I said that. Take our relationship out of the equation. Talk to me on some other level."

"It's hard for me to talk about it because it's all so personal to me, and so embarrassing. I'm embarrassed about all of this. The scared, panicky person, I don't see her as me. I just see her as someone who's life I'm being forced to live for the time being. I keep waking up, hoping she'll be gone, and I'll be back. The tough assed, devil-may-care, could handle anything with a sneer on my face, me,"

Sara scowled, and her face showed her frustration.

"But look at how much you've done. I mean, you came home to your family, you've met other people now, you seem to get out on a more regular basis. And all those kids you have to deal with now. And you went out last night, and got trashed with the person you love to hate the most, our dear Marcy. Don't you see any of that as progress? Can't you be happy with smaller victories?" *She's so hard on herself.*

"You have no idea what it takes me to get psyched up on these days that I spend with the kids. I almost had Nelson take me home this morning, several times." Sara shook her head, and her brow creased.

"But you don't seem the least bit, I don't know, rattled around them. You're always smiling, laughing."

"Working them like dogs? Yeah, I don't mean to say I don't enjoy them. I just wish I could enjoy them with some peace of mind attached. And Marcy, last night, she's pretty good around me, and I had several drinks in me before I had time to think about being someplace strange, with someone strange, and then had several more drinks to the point where I believe I was singing "Sexual Healing" to her in front of a bar full of grape growers and cherry pickers." Sara glanced to see what Chloe's reaction to that was, and she saw Chloe's eyes dancing with mirth. "I shouldn't be drinking like that either, with the meds I take. I don't take anything powerful or strong. Just maintenance meds, I don't think that last night put me in harm's way, I just don't think I should be doing that on a regular basis."

"Singing "Sexual Healing" to your brother's girlfriend, or drinking to excess?" Chloe teased.

"Probably both." Sara laughed, and pushed her hair behind her shoulders. "Drinking is a horrible thing. It gets me to where I can remember what I used to feel like, without the aid of alcohol. You know, fearless, brazen, maybe a bit of a flirt. I don't believe in any way, shape or form that I am, or ever have been close to being an alcoholic. But the capacity is in me, and I know it. If I had, as Jennie suggested to me at one point, taken the kind of drugs she was offering me, I've no doubt that I would have been spending some major time doing rehab for drugs."

Sara paused, and studied Chloe. "You talk about your small town mentality like it's something you shouldn't be proud of. Well, my being brought up here, in this small town, is exactly what saved me from abusing drugs and alcohol. Don't ever think that I think it's a fault in you, Chloe, not being as worldly as I am. I admire it about you. I came back here to try and get it back."

"So you want to be just like me, huh?" said Chloe, glad to see some of the worry easing out of Sara's face.

Sara reached across and fluffed Chloe's hair. "Just like."

"So, still keeping me out of the big picture here, what is it you want to accomplish, or do, with the rest of your time here on this planet, big girl?" Chloe was trying to keep Sara comfortable, asking the hard questions but phrasing it so Sara could relax into her answer.

"Well, I guess it changes. Has changed. I used to be happy just getting by, you know, getting through the day. Dave pretty much told me that's a pretty lame goal, just getting through the day. I know that he's right. Damn, I hate it when he's right. He's a lot smarter than he comes across, you know? So, I've come up with some new ones and I'm working on them."

"Care to share?"

"Well, this play is one. Not only being involved in it, but enjoying it, too, as much as I can. And, trying to get comfortable with a new set of people, letting them become part of my comfort zone. And see how things go with you, of course. And I want to get my license back. I know that seems like a small thing to most folks, but I let it lapse, using it as yet another reason why I couldn't go anywhere." Sara squinted at Chloe. "There's absolutely no medical reason for why I haven't been driving."

"I didn't want to ask."

"Well, to tell the truth, I feel better when I'm the driver. Back when I used to drive, and got the attacks, well, I knew I was in control, in command. I wouldn't have to put myself in the situation where I had to tell someone to pull over, to do my little walkabout."

Sara looked to Chloe, who had her arms wrapped about herself. The sun was quietly disappearing, and a chill was coming into the air. "Hey, you're looking a little chilled there. You want to go up to the house? Dave's house. We can get you warmed up. And you can feel safe from worrying I'm some wolfish predator waiting for the right moment to drop my fangs into you."

"Who's to say you're safe from me?" Chloe replied. She put her hands onto the cold blanket and pushed herself into a standing position. She held out a hand to help Sara up. "You think you have me all figured out, don't you, Miss Complicated? I have a few skeletons in my own closet."

Sara accepted the hand up, and she closed the short distance between them, wrapping her arms around Chloe and pulling her into tight hug. She smelled the sunshine of the spring day clinging to Chloe's hair. "I have the distinct feeling that I'll never figure out all there is to you, Chloe."

"Oh my God.! A girl takes a four hour power nap in the nurse's office, and the next thing she knows, all hell breaks loose."

Chloe and Sara, engaged in a pretty intense kiss on the front porch, both started laughing into each other's mouths.

"You two look like blowfish. Are you poisonous, too?" Marcy said dryly, as she stood inside the screen door, watching her two friends blush and steal shy looks at each other. "Why do I feel like I need to ground one or both of you?" She opened up the door for them to come in. "You're just in time. Dave just went to pick up a couple of pizzas." She gave Chloe a quick hug. "Are you on some kind of quest to get caught kissing all the D'Amicos this week?"

Nelson, sitting at the kitchen table, had caught all of the conversation, but not the actual act. "Uh, excuse me? I'm in the room, well, I was." He quickly scooted out to the living room to rid himself of his blush.

Sara, with her arm draped casually over Chloe's shoulders, winked at Marcy and yelled, "Hey, Nelson! Come back! I'll protect you from Chloe!"

"That's Miss Lips, to the both of you, if you don't mind." Chloe gave Sara a quick smooch on the chin. "And leave the poor guy alone. Things are strange enough around here as it is without you two stirring up more trouble." She turned to Marcy, who seemed to have benefited from her beauty nap. "Marse, or should I call you 'Cher,' how many pizzas did you say Dave was getting?"

"Two, extra large." She looked at Chloe, then thought about Nelson out in the living room. "Looks like I'd better call and order a couple more. Dave can wait for them." She turned and picked up the kitchen phone.

Sara took this opportunity to try and kiss Chloe again. She leaned in, and just as lips were about to meet lips, lips met cheek instead. "Huh? What's with the cheek, Grandma?" said Sara disappointedly. She pulled Chloe in tighter and gave her a puzzled look.

"I'm not much for audiences," Chloe shyly said, and laid her cheek onto Sara's chest.

"That's not what I hear. I hear I missed quite the show after my chauffeur dropped me off last night. He said it was like watching one of those really bad girl-on-girl tapes you can rent down at Bob's," Marcy chided.

Sara, not relinquishing her hold on Chloe, turned them both to face Marcy. "And exactly how does my brother know about those kind of tapes? Hmm? And I don't even need to ask you, you were displaying some mighty stereotypical moves on me last night, so I know you're familiar with them."

Nelson yelled from the living room "You know, I can still hear you out here! I am going to be so warped by the time I get out of my teens!"

Sara yelled right back, "So turn the TV up! And you were born warped, all of this can't do anything but unwarp you!" She took a look down at Chloe, who seemed perfectly content to be wrapped loosely in Sara's arms. She noticed that Marcy and Chloe were shooting little grins at each other.

Sara felt a small warm feeling creep over her. *What's that? I couldn't possibly be feeling happy? Yeah, that's it. I'm happy.* She gave Chloe another squeeze, and kissed her forehead.

"So, Chloe, I was wondering, are you in need of a cigarette or anything?" Marcy squinted at her. "A beer? Need to relieve some guilt with me?"

Chloe blushed, and shoved her face deeper into Sara's chest. She spoke directly into Sara's shirt, "Not yet. Thanks for thinking of me, though." She could feel her warm breath seep into the fabric of the shirt, and knew that Sara could feel it too, because she got yet another squeeze.

Sara didn't have a clue as to what they were talking about, but she figured it had something to do with that universal subject, sex. "She really is shy, huh?" Sara said, directing her question to Marcy.

"Sara, Chloe and I have been friends since the third grade, and I've never, ever seen her in anything less than her underwear. Not in gym classes, not at sleepovers, camping trips, not when we used to visit each other at college. I can't say with a certainty she is a true redhead, other than the fact that I've known her for so long." Marcy laughed, still amazed at the modesty her best friend displayed.

"That did it, I'll be in my bedroom. Call me when the pizzas get here!" Nelson's voice came ringing from the living room. *God, a guy can only take so much.*

The three women burst out laughing. Chloe turned and grabbed Sara's shirt, and buried her face deeply in Sara's chest. "Oh God!"

"Hon, you're going to suffocate yourself in there." Sara laid her arms across Chloe's shoulders, and put her chin on the top of her head.

"Mfrpp, die happy," said Chloe, hugging Sara even harder.

Marcy, extremely pleased that her brain was going to be freed from any more plotting, sat down at the kitchen table. A weird thought hit her. "You know, looking at you two, I can't help but be reminded of, you know, those two women on TV. Don't tell me, it will come to me. Really good friends, one short, one tall, a red-blonde and a brunette, do everything together, always getting into trouble."

Sara's eyebrow rose, and she quirked a grin at Marcy. Chloe, totally relaxed, feeling right at home snuggled against Sara's chest, peacefully asked, "Who?"

"Oh, yeah, I got it now. Do the words schlemeel, schlimazel, hasenfeffer incorporated mean anything to you?" Marcy did a few head bobs as she chanted the words.

Sara looked around to see if there was anything she could throw that she wouldn't have to sweep up later. All she could find was a dishtowel, so she tossed it at Marcy's head. Marcy ducked. "Sara, you could start wearing an 'S' on the front of everything you wear." Marcy giggled.

"Marcy, I liked you better when I hated you. And you'd better hush up, or I'll tell Dave you were singing "I Kissed A Girl" to me at karaoke last night."

"But I didn't!" *At least I think I didn't.*

"Yeah, well, he wasn't there, so how would he know?" Sara reached out, and pulled out a kitchen chair, and maneuvered Chloe to sit on her knee.

"Are you two going to be glued together like that all the time now? And I thought Dave and I were bad."

Chloe happily put her arm around Sara's shoulder. "Shaddup you, we're in love. We're allowed."

Sara sat up straight, and pulled a little away from Chloe, so she could look at her. "We are, huh? First time I've heard it from you." She grinned.

Chloe realized what she had said, and got a little tongue-tied. "Well, sure, yes, I mean, I wouldn't have put up with, you know, you acting like such an asshole and all, if I wasn't in love with you, right?" she finished brightly.

Sara gave her a quick kiss, smiled with everything she had in her, and then winked at Marcy. "She has quite the romantic way with words, doesn't she?"

"Quite the little wordsmith. Remind me to ask her to write my wedding vows for me when I get married."

Two figures in one chair straightened up in unison and stared at Marcy.

Marcy fidgeted. "Let me amend that to if I get married."

The same two figures looked at each other skeptically, then returned to staring at Marcy.

Marcy, whose body language was speaking in foreign tongues now, squirmed and complained, "God, can't a girl mention the *M* word without getting hassled?"

Chloe, who considered herself an A1, top drawer, hassler extraordinaire, spoke up. "Well for God's sake, Marcy, everyone in town knows that Herb Harris financed that new sun porch on his house by using all the nonrefundable deposits on the reception hall from your weddings that never took place." She turned to Sara. "Do you know how many altered, nonreturnable maid of honor gowns I have in my closet? Because she," and she cast a disapproving eye toward Marcy, "thought it would be bad luck to use the same dress for a different wedding, to a different guy? So, yeah, when you say the *M* word, I get a little nervous."

"Apparently, not as nervous as she does," Sara said glibly.

Chloe was doing a little mental addition. "Five. With matching shoes."

Marcy was quiet. *Here it comes.*

Sara was thrilled that Marcy was on the receiving end of some needling for a change. "So I shouldn't be putting any money on Marcy becoming a bona fide D'Amico that you get your lips on, huh, Chloe?" A thought struck her. "Marcy, what is your last name, anyway? I don't think I've ever heard anyone ever use it. Dave, Nelson, the kids, Mrs. Raeburn, Chloe here, they all just call you Marcy."

Marcy cleared her throat and said, "Wojciechlowski. Not a soul can say it, everybody avoids trying to pronounce it so they won't look stupid screwing it up. So as far back as I can remember, I've always been just Marcy. Like Madonna, Sting, or Cher." She smiled at that last name.

Chloe rolled her eyes. "Tell her the best one, Marse. When I thought the wedding was never going to take place because I was plotting to kill the bride before her big day."

"Huh? Oh, yeah, you mean the first squelched wedding. Yeah, come to think of it, you did give me quite the hard time about that." She gave a sideways grin to Sara. "Seems that Chloe here was a little upset with me because I was insisting that I was going to go with a hyphenated name after marriage." She pursed her lips several times, in order to stretch them out for the upcoming effort. "Marcy Wojciechlowski-Krkoska." She grinned at how big Sara's eyes got at that. "Has a nice, post-Berlin Wall, gold medal gymnast sound to it, don't you think?"

Chloe reached out and smacked her on the shoulder. "And this idiot wanted me to get that on matchbooks. You know, the kind that's at the table at the reception? I talked to three different bridal supply outlets, and they all hung up on me, thought I was playing a joke. And the ones that didn't hang up, they had to listen to me try to pronounce it, slaughter it really, and then I would spell it for them. The last guy said, 'Lady, my pen doesn't have enough ink to write down all those letters, how in the world am I going to get them all on a matchbook?'"

Dave came through the door, laden with a hernia-inducing load of pizzas. He gave a stilted grin when he saw the laughing occupants of the kitchen.

"Hey, all, looks like we have the whole gang here." He dropped the pizzas into the center of the table, and then gave Marcy a token peck on the cheek. He took off his coat, laid it on the back of a chair, and then settled down into it. "Having a little girl talk, huh? Sorry I missed it." He toyed with a corner of one of the boxes, looking a little ill at ease.

Sara kicked him with her sneaker. "Seems you have a little side job now, delivering pizzas? Marcy here, I'm sure, will want to tip you."

Chloe jumped off Sara's lap, and smoothed her hands on her shorts. "I'm going to go wash up, and get Nelson." She smiled at Dave, who didn't return the eye contact, and continued fidgeting with the pizza boxes.

"Uh, Chloe, you may want to hold on to that thought a minute," said Dave, picking nervously at the cardboard.

All three women looked at him curiously, as he kept his eyes down and wrinkled his forehead in thought.

Chloe bumped his chair with her hip. "Why the gloomy look, Mr. Kisses?"

That remark brought a real frown to Dave's face. He turned in his chair and looked deeply and apologetically into Chloe's green eyes.

"Well, Miss Lips," he replied softly, "it seems that everyone in town knows that we've been secretly having an affair."

Part XIV:
People Will Say We're in Love

Hearing the hush that had fallen over the room at his statement, Dave thought perhaps he hadn't been understood the first time he said it, so he felt the need to say it again. He couldn't quite remember how he said it the first time but tried to approximate its message.

"Seems that everyone in town has found out about my affair with Chloe," he repeated.

Nelson, who had heard his dad pull in the driveway with dinner, had wandered down from his room and heard his father's statement the second time around. He couldn't quite figure out what he meant, so he looked around the room for further illumination.

Chloe was the first to speak, and she looked to Dave when she said it. "What?"

Dave frowned and said, "You really want me to say it again?"

Marcy looked to Dave and Chloe, trying to gauge their reactions. Seeing blank faces, she said, "No, we want you to explain it. What are you talking about?"

"That would be nice," intoned Sara, her body reflexively assuming a defensive posture.

Dave cleared his throat and began, "Well, I was down at Buddy's, waiting for the extra pizzas to get done, and in came Mark Benson, you know, the guy that works for the county license board?" He looked around for acknowledgment, and continued, "and after a few 'how's it going' stuff, he said he saw Marcy," and Dave pointed at her, "and Sara out last night at Stan's Bar. I was going to make a comment about it, but he just said something weird like 'she looked good, but didn't look good,' kind of implying that you were upset about something. He went on to say that maybe Marcy wasn't doing too good with our 'break-up,' especially considering the circumstances of the reason being, you know, 'her best friend since grade school.'"

"Wait a minute. Let me get this straight, straight being the operative word here," said Sara. "Some guy thinks you're having an affair with Chloe, and broke up with Marcy because of it?"

Marcy answered for Dave. "No, he means that he and Chloe were having a secret affair behind my back, and somehow I found out about it, and then we broke up."

Dave looked at Sara, then Marcy. "I'm not sure what the difference is between what you said," pointing to Sara, "and what she just said," pointing to Marcy.

Nelson, following along from the doorway, clarified things for his confused dad. "Dad, Aunt Sara thinks you were sleeping with Chloe, then maybe decided to do the right thing, and came clean and you broke up with Marcy. Marcy, on the other hand, thinks you were sleeping with Chloe, and got caught, and Marcy broke up with you."

Dave wasn't grasping what the gist of the question was. "I'm not sure what I did." He thought a moment. "I do know this, I've been sleeping with Chloe."

"Wait a minute, sweet cheeks, are you telling us that this is true?" snapped Marcy. Sara and Marcy's eyes bored into Dave.

"Of course not! I can't believe you would even think such a thing! I would never sleep with Chloe," said Dave defensively.

Chloe finally piped up. "And why not? What's the matter with me?"

Dave got all flustered, and replied to Chloe, "Well, for one thing, you're gay, and seeing my sister."

Marcy interjected, "That's two things. Oh sure, you'd sleep with her behind my back if Sara wasn't in the picture, wouldn't you?" She turned to Chloe, "Some friend you turned out to be!"

Sara rolled her eyes at Marcy, and squinted at Chloe, "Are you trying to tell me you're bi?"

"Where the hell did you get that idea?" said Chloe, incredulous. "I simply want to know why Dave thinks it would be so terrible to sleep with me—"

"Chloe, Chloe," Dave interrupted, "I don't think it would be terrible, I'd love to sleep with you."

"Well, okay, then," Chloe blushed and mumbled, "that's more like it."

"Well, listen, buster, let's just let it be known, right here and now, that I broke up with you when I found out about you two sneaking around behind my back," insisted Marcy.

Dave said, "What's the difference?"

Sara, Chloe and Marcy all stared at Dave like he was from some alien civilization. "It's an ego thing, Dave," Sara drawled. All three women nodded at each other, being from the same planet and all.

Nelson, eyeing the pizza boxes on the table, and thinking he might get some dinner around breakfast time tomorrow, decided to inject a voice of reason. "Isn't the real question here, how did this rumor get started, and what should we do to get the truth out?"

All four sets of eyes looked at Nelson.

Sara just waved him off. "He's young. He doesn't understand how these things work."

Chloe went over and patted the tall young man on the back. "Yeah, but you can't fault him for trying."

Nelson was truly puzzled. "I don't get it, why don't you just find out the source, and then go to them, and explain things?"

Sara, proud of her nephew, but sympathetic of his ignorance in the matter, said, "Let's all sit down, eat some pizza, and maybe we can explain to Nelson how this works."

With plates, napkins and drinks in hand, everyone sat down at the table. Sara, who had appointed herself his mentor in this matter, began. "Nelson, as a few wise people have said, 'The truth is out there.' That being said, the rumor already exists, probably in a great many people's minds, as the truth." Seeing the doubtful look in Nelson's eyes, she continued, "We could knock on every door, call everyone in this town, and try and find out the source. But you have to realize that the source already believes that whatever he or she said is the truth. And will be entirely unconvinced by anyone who is directly related to the matter as being schemers and liars trying to cover up their own poop in their litter box of life, so to speak."

Nelson, finishing his second piece of pizza, said, "I still don't get it."

Chloe wiped her mouth and rephrased Sara's rather obtuse explanation. "Anyone who has heard this about us, won't believe whatever we say about it, because we're directly involved, and it'll appear like we want to save our own asses."

Nelson reached for pieces three and four. "Oh, I get it. So what do you do?"

Marcy winked at Sara and said, "We could put a spin on it."

Sara, picking off mushrooms from her pizza, and watching as Chloe nabbed them, smiled. "Yep. We could take what we know of the rumors, and turn it, add to the rumor, so it all comes out to our advantage, where none of the principals, Dave, Chloe, or Marcy, end up looking bad."

Dave opened up another box. "Your Aunt Sara knows what she's talking about, I mean, she had to deal with Hollyweird and all."

Sara smirked. "Hollywood isn't anything compared to living in a small town. In this town, once someone hears the rumor, the whole populace knows of it within days, probably hours. And who's to know how much it has changed from the original rumor? It may have started out as innocuous as 'Chloe gave Dave a ride home,' and then mushroomed," she picked some more off her slice and popped them directly into Chloe's waiting mouth, "from there. So, we have to figure what we know, and then take it from there."

Chloe reached and picked the last few remaining mushrooms off Sara's pizza and with mouth half full, summarized, "Okay, what we know. We know that Dave was seen, ahem, tickling my tonsils last week. And that neither Sara or Marcy appeared to be happy about it." She noticed the disapproving glances she was getting from them both. "Go ahead, get all defensive, it won't help our cause here." She saw them sheepishly look away. "All righty then. Dave smooched me, I gave Dave a ride home." She looked around the table. "Anyone else have anything to add?"

Nelson shifted and waved his hand. Everyone waited for him to stop his chewing, and the swallow afterwards. "Dad was tanked on Thursday. I thought some of the kids were acting a little strangely toward me on Friday and today. Everyone seemed very interested in what Marcy and Chloe were doing today, they kept asking me where Marcy was."

Marcy ran a fingernail along a gap between her teeth. "So people may be thinking there's bad blood between Chloe and me. And Sara and I went out last night, and who shows up to rescue little old poor suffering me? Dave, with Chloe tagging along behind."

Chloe laughed. "I did you wrong, baby, and I'm trying to get you to forgive me for it. Penance, maybe?"

Dave thought for a moment. "Well, it's hard for me to believe that one isolated, even two, incidents equals an affair. When I was talking to Mark, it seemed to me, now that I think about it, that he was under the impression that this had been going on for a while. So, I'm thinking, that something must have happened before all of this that got someone thinking in the first place."

Sara wadded up her napkin and pelted him with it. "See, Chloe, I told you that he's a lot smarter than he comes across."

Dave shot the napkin back at her. "Thanks, sis." He thought about that a second. "I think."

Nelson poured himself some pop, and gave the bottle to Marcy to pass around. "So, we figure out the damages, and then decide on a plan of action?"

Everyone at the table beamed at Nelson. "By George, I think he's got it," said Dave. "Meanwhile, we just go on about our lives. Sometimes, although rarely, rumors die out on their own. And if they do die away, they have a nasty way of resurfacing later to bite you in the butt."

"Or," said Chloe, her eyes brightening, "We have two other courses of action. We get pro-active, like, we make a big deal of Dave and Marcy being seen happy together in public, that being the most boring scenario, or we have some fun with it, and try and boggle some people's minds by playing along with the rumor. It all depends on the extent of the rumor in the first place."

"Aha, the revenge is sweet plan of action," nodded Marcy. "I only want to do that if the rumors are downright nasty in the first place. I think we need to wait and see."

Nelson was finally understanding the warped rationale concerning all of this. But somehow, it still was bothering him that it couldn't simply be handled by telling the truth. "Are you sure all of this is necessary? It seems kind of like we're fighting evil with evil here, like there's really no good guys involved. Why can't we be the good guys? Aren't we the ones in the right?"

Chloe sighed. "You know, he's right. We certainly can claim that we have the moral high ground here. I wish there was another way to go about this. But time in this town has shown me that it just doesn't work that way. Of course, we could just call a press conference and deny everything."

"There's an idea." Sara laughed, and tapped her sweetie's nose. "I do have an idea though, that if and when we decide to do anything, there is one perfect place for us to start."

Chloe puzzled on this for a moment, and then said, "Doris Raeburn."

Sara nodded, her eyes shining in admiration of her astute little girlfriend.

Marcy said, "Talk about the horse's...mouth."

Dave grumbled. "More like the horse's mouth talking."

"Well, now that this is all sorted out, and we all know that I'm sleeping with Dave, and everyone is okay with that, the big question would be..." Chloe paused dramatically and looked at her empty plate. "Is there any pizza left?"

Nelson stood and waited for Jeanette to slide in to the booth first because he knew she liked to play with the little jukebox when they came here. Once she had her jacket off, he hung it on the hook on the supporting post at his end of the booth, and sat down. He smiled up at the waitress, Katie, as she handed out menus to all of them. Heather and Justin slid into the bench across from them, the girls across from each other, so they could carry on a decent conversation when the boys started to lag behind. Katie flipped the cups, and poured coffee for all of them.

"Damn, I can't believe it's raining like that, after what a nice day it's been," griped Justin, glancing through the menu although he knew it by heart.

Heather flipped her straight brown hair back, and tore open three sugar packets to add to her coffee. "We saw those movies at the theaters in town anyway."

"Who said I wanted to watch the movies, I wanted to go to the drive-in. I know Mr. Grettler was planning on opening it up this weekend. And they have those little car heaters," Justin said, passing her the cream.

"Yeah, well, I've had enough of the great outdoors for one day," Jeanette said, grabbing the cream from Justin before Heather could get it. "Look at me, I think I got a sunburn today."

Nelson looked at the face tipped his way for inspection. "I think you're right, your cheeks are pink," and he quickly pinched Jeanette's nose, "and your nose is a nice shade of Rudolph red."

Jeanette giggled, and gave him the creamer container, ignoring Heather's impatient "Hey!" "It felt good to be outside today, even if your aunt was trying to kill us today. I swear, I threw her so many dirty looks when she wouldn't let us get a break, I know she saw some of them. Good thing Ms. Donahue took pity on us."

Heather snatched the coffee creamer from a grinning Nelson. "Yeah, Ms. Donahue rocks! I can't believe she's as old as she is, I look at her and think she's Allison's age." Allison was Heather's older sister, a junior at a college in Ohio. "I wish we could have seen her on Thursday, Nelson. Justin here said he thought she was going to faint again, she was so embarrassed when your Dad kissed her on the stage."

Nelson saw Heather's body do an odd shake, it was obviously from a nudge, under the table, from Justin. Nelson just grinned and raised an eyebrow, displaying a family trait. "Yeah, me too. Dad wasn't feeling any pain that day, he'd just come from a little celebration at Stan's for his last day at UPS."

"Well, he certainly wasn't feeling any pain when we saw him later in the parking lot." Heather leered. This time the whole table shook, because Justin missed his frantic nudge toward Heather and hit the center table support instead.

"What?" said a clearly impatient Heather to Justin. "I'm sure Nelson knows what's going on between them better than we do."

"What?" echoed a visibly interested Jeanette. "I didn't hear about the parking lot, just the kissing part." She looked toward Nelson, trying to make sure that this conversation wasn't bothering him. He was smiling, and even looked a bit interested himself. "What about the parking lot?"

Justin, seeing that his buddy seemed to be doing just fine, although it was his Dad that was the topic of conversation, stretched an arm across the bench back, and got a cocky smile on his face. "Ms. Donahue was all over his dad out there. We saw them," nodding toward Heather, "when we were coming out of play practice. Plain as day. And he was pushing her into the back seat of her car." Justin laughed, letting his devilish grin finish his sentence for him.

Nelson raised another eyebrow. Jeanette, although her curiosity was killing her, rubbed his shoulder. "Nelson, are you sure this isn't bothering you? We can talk about something else. I mean, this is your dad and all." She was reassured when he smiled at her and shook his head at her. She looked him in his amazingly blue eyes and said, "Well, we all here know and like your dad a lot. It's not like we're trying to put him down or anything."

Heather laughed. "Yeah, it's just fun to talk about somebody else's love life for once. And Ms. Donahue, you know we love her."

Justin cracked, "Yeah, and she's such little hottie! I wouldn't mind if—"

This time, Justin was on the receiving end of a well placed kick under the table. "Ow, well, c'mon, even Nelson has eyes."

Jeanette punched Nelson in the arm. "You'd better not be looking at her like that," she said with a mock frown.

Nelson picked up his spoon, and flicked some droplets of coffee at her. "Me? Think about Chloe like that? Not me."

"Chloe, huh?" said Heather, looking around for the waitress, "Now we know something's going on." She looked at her other two friends and said, mischievously, "Well, if Chloe is going to end up being his new stepmom, he would tell us first, right?"

Nelson straightened up, and mimicked zipping his lip. *Stepmom?*

"Doesn't he drive you nuts, Jeanette, I mean, the boy hardly talks!" said Heather, confounded with the mute, grinning Nelson.

"I like that about him. What he does say to me, it seems more important then," said Jeanette, a soft smile coming to her lips.

Katie showed up with a pot of coffee, refilled their cups, and took their orders.

"Well, where were we?" said Heather as she scarfed the coffee creamer first this time. "Oh, yeah, Nelson and his new mom Chloe. I mean, Nelson, come on, quit sitting there like a big grinning lump, and tell us what's going on! You think they'll get married? My grandma said that she knows your dad would want to make an honest woman out of her."

This time, two feet from different directions aimed for Heather's legs under the table. "Ow! What was that for?" She looked under the table and whined, "I'm gonna have huge bruises!"

Nelson, unzipping his lip, got a serious expression on his face. "What, exactly, Heather, does 'make an honest woman out of her' mean, huh?"

Heather was getting some pretty nasty stares from both Jeanette and Justin. She stared into her coffee cup. "Nothing. Never mind."

Nelson leaned over the table and pulled her coffee cup away from her. "Tell me. I want to know." Nelson gave the other two ominous glares, they sat back, both knowing what was coming next.

Heather avoided looking at Nelson, she dragged her cup back to her side of the table again, and stared down into it. "You know, Ms. Donahue being pregnant."

Nelson repeated the two syllable word, "Pregnant?"

Heather, forgetting she had already added sugar to her coffee, nervously opened three more packets and added them while she answered him. "Well, yeah. She's pregnant. You remember when she fainted last week? That's why. My grandmother said that she and her book club friends saw Ms. Donahue at the library the other night, and Mrs. Hoderman asked her about it, asked her if she'd been to the doctor yet. Ms. Donahue said she was going soon. Mrs. Hoderman says that Ms. Donahue was having, you know, morning sickness troubles, not eating right, that sort of thing." Heather finally got up the nerve to look at Nelson, who was frowning at her. "Nelson, don't look at me like that. My grandmother said that Ms. Donahue admitted it. Mrs. Raeburn was there, too. Both of them talked to her."

The implications of all of this suddenly hit Nelson. "And you guys are thinking that my dad is the father?"

"Well, yeah, nobody could figure that part out until, you know, we saw them together on Thursday. Before that, I think everyone was just guessing. I mean, we all thought your dad was dating Marcy." Heather looked at the silent, strained faces of her friends. "I feel bad for Marcy. I mean, did she even know what was going on?"

Do I even know what's going on? Nelson stood up, and took his jacket off the hook, and then pulled his wallet out of his back pocket. He dropped a ten dollar bill on the table, and looked at his friends' chagrined faces. "Here, this should take care of mine and Jeanette's. I'm not feeling very well." He looked at Jeanette. "Would you mind if Justin took you home?" She silently shook her head and looked at him, pained sympathy showing in her eyes. He turned and headed out of the diner, and walked to his truck in the cold pouring rain, jacket slung over his arm.

Dave leaned back in the kitchen chair, and put his hands on the back of his head and stretched. "Damn, Chloe, a one-armed man could shuffle those cards faster than you."

Everyone watched with amusement as Chloe struggled to get the cards shuffled. They just wouldn't shift and slide for her the way they did for everyone else. And when she split the deck, laid them down, and tried to curl them back, they ended up spraying half way across the table. Marcy sighed, and scooped the cards in front of her to shuffle them herself. Chloe, too tired to get miffed, just let her do it for her.

"I've never, ever been able to get the hang of that. It's embarrassing." Chloe pouted. "I feel like such a spaz." She glanced up at the kitchen clock. Nearly 2:00 a.m., and she yawned wide and long, showing the assembled clan at the table that she had no fillings in even the remotest of molars. She put a hand over her gaping mouth. "'Scuse me. When I get this tired, I lose my manners." She tossed her head in a little grin.

Sara sighed, and watched as Marcy slid the cards back to Chloe, so she could deal. "Let's make this last hand, okay? Marcy, what's the score?"

Marcy pretended to look at the sheet in front of her. "Pretty much as it has been all night long, Chloe kicking our asses all over tarnation, us, totally screwed. I probably should've warned you two that although she can't shuffle, she's a terror at playing cards. Any kind. *Hearts, Spades, Uno, Poker, Pinochle, Hand and Foot, Go Fish and War.*" She cast a small smirk at Chloe, who was trying to hide the smug grin on her face. "And not only that, she's a damned poor winner. Likes to lord it over you for days. I think that inept shuffling thing of hers is an act so she can bamboozle us so we won't notice her sticking cards up her sleeves and stacking the deck." She grinned as Chloe stopped dealing long enough to display her short-sleeved arms. "Dave, check behind her ears. Better yet, I think she stuffed a few cards in her mouth when she yawned a minute ago."

Chloe stuck her tongue out at Marcy. "Sthee? Uthin ere, stho sthut ut, arthy."

Sara smiled as she picked up her cards and sorted them. "Who dealt this mess?" she said, as she had after every hand dealt that night. It was traditional with her. *As much as I'd have liked to have spent this evening alone with her, I'm having a really good time.* She watched as Marcy played a card to start the game, and she picked one from her hand, and tossed it on the table. *I think the best part is how much I feel I'm learning about her. Marcy keeps telling little stories about her, from when she was young, or college, or from a year or two ago.* The play went around the table a few more times. It was her turn again, and she pulled a card, and then pushed it back in, and played another card instead. *I never knew that her parents are gone. That must be hard, her an only child.* She glanced up from her hand, and watched as Chloe intently studied the cards already played on the table. *I'll bet she can count cards or something. That's the only explanation I can figure for her so completely annihilating us tonight. She gets that really determined look in her eyes. She's really competitive. I like that.*

Chloe looked up from her cards, and blushed when she saw Sara was watching her. Her mouth twisted into a tiny grin, and she shrugged her shoulders. "Sorry, guys," as she played her last card. "Out!"

Everyone groaned. Dave tossed his remaining cards on the pile. "I'm taking her to Atlantic City, and we're going to play blackjack. I may mortgage the property to finance it. I could probably buy Pebble Beach with the winnings."

Sara threw her cards in too. "Maybe we should play *Monopoly* or something next time."

Marcy's eyes widened at that comment. "Oh, no, no. You don't want to put us through that. She gets all wheeler-dealerish, making a pest of herself trying to buy up property from everyone all night long, with this really scary look on her face. And she keeps counting her money over and over and over, she's an absolute maniac."

Dave said, "*Chutes and Ladders? Scrabble? Risk?* Oh, never mind, I bet she's a fiend at all of them." He smiled at her fondly. "Oh, wait, how about outdoor stuff? Badminton, croquet?" He laughed softly as Marcy slowly shook her head back and forth at everything he mentioned. "Tennis? Bocce? Horseshoes?" His chuckles got louder as Marcy continued to shake her head. "Oh, c'mon, she can't be good at everything! Hopscotch? Jacks? Oh, wait! Golf?"

Marcy sucked her front teeth long and hard. "She's gonna roar through your little course when it opens up."

Chloe sat, head propped on one hand, while she tried to appear humble and shy. But her dancing eyes gave her away.

Sara pursed her lips. "Yeah, it figures. She looks so harmless, and yet underneath, she's nothing but dangerous."

"You don't know the half of it," purred Chloe, her eyes slitted with feline menace.

Dave and Sara both raised a mutual eyebrow over that comment. Dave harrumphed and said, "On that note, Marcy, sweet pea, I think I should escort you home. If it clears up tomorrow, I'm going to be mowing all day. And Sara is going over to see her other girlfriend with Nelson after noontime." He scratched his chin. "I hope he feels up to it. He didn't look too good when he came in tonight."

"Just a long day in the sun, getting his ass danced around by his pushy aunt, and then running around in the rain. He should be okay." *I hope so, not only for his sake, but I would really like to take a ride if the weather is decent.* Sara looked across the table to see that Chloe still had her head propped up in her hand, but her eyes were lightly shut. "Looks like I'd better see to Chloe here, she looks like she's going to take a header off the table and onto the floor."

Dave and Marcy stood up from the table, and Dave went to get their coats. Marcy looked at her dozing friend, and then at Sara. "What're you going to do with her?" she whispered.

"I think I might just tuck her in on the couch out there. No sense in sending her home, she's half comatose, by the looks of it," Sara said, keeping her voice low.

Marcy stood closer to Sara, and they both looked down at the redhead looking so peaceful and angelic in sleep. Marcy leaned and said into Sara's ear, "I'd better warn ya, she's hell to wake up."

Sara bumped her shoulder on Marcy's. "Yeah, I know."

Marcy's eyes questioned a quietly grinning Sara, but Marcy was too tired to pursue the matter. Dave came up, stood behind her, and helped her on with her coat. "See ya tomorrow, Sara. Say goodnight to Chloe for us," he said quietly. They slipped out the kitchen door and Sara closed it behind them.

She looked again at the sleeping redhead, who was slowly dropping toward the tabletop. She crossed over to her, and knelt beside her. "Chloe, hon, let's get you out to the couch." She put her hand on Chloe's wrist to support her arm. Chloe stirred a little. "Chloe, c'mon, bedtime. Out to the couch with you." She tugged on Chloe's arm, and Chloe's eyes opened a bit. "C'mon, here we go, out to the big comfy couch." Chloe allowed herself to be pulled into standing, and Sara moved behind her, putting her hands on Chloe's hips. "Chloe, walk. Forward out to the couch." She gave a little push, and Chloe, on automatic, started toward the living room, and made it to the couch with Sara guiding her. She sank down into it, and Sara untied her shoes and placed them underneath the coffee table. She got the afghan off the recliner and carefully covered her with it. She bent over and placed a soft, long kiss on Chloe's cheek. She grabbed her coat, and flipped off the remaining lights in the house. She was taking one last look when she heard a soft moan.

"Sara?" came Chloe's voice, barely audible to Sara's ears.

Sara knelt next to Chloe's head, and brushed her hair off her cheek. "Yes, Chloe?"

"This is a really big couch."

Sara smiled, and tossed her coat onto the recliner, and pushed off her sneakers. She lifted up the afghan, and slipped in next to her love. Chloe let out a soft sigh, and moved into the waiting arms of Sara, who was silently thanking her brother Dave for his great taste in furniture.

Part XV:
Three's Twisted Company

Nelson woke up on Sunday morning with oddest itchy feeling in his ears. He stuck a pinkie finger in his ear, burrowed around a bit and tried to alleviate the feeling. It wasn't working, with either ear, the itchiness continued and he decided to get up, hit the can, and try a couple of cotton swabs. He threw on a pair of sweats and a T-shirt, and went into the bathroom. He opened up the medicine cabinet, found the swabs, and dug around in his ears. It helped a little, but not a lot. He yawned, scratched and looked at himself in the mirror. *I could use a couple more hours of sleep, I still feel really tired. Dad or Aunt Sara will be around, they can get me up later.* He went back into his bedroom, shut the door, and within minutes, he fell back to sleep.

Out on the couch, Sara began to wake up. *Something's different. I've been on this couch dozens of times overnight, but this morning, it feels smaller. And I'm practically falling off the edge. The couch used to be so much wider. And not this warm.* "Ssnrrkk." She smiled. *And not nearly this noisy.* She felt the small form of Chloe spooned perfectly behind her, with her nose buried between Sara's shoulder blades. "Ssnrrkk." *Funny, I don't remember that snore from the last time we slept on this couch.* Sara carefully lifted the arm that was wrapped around her waist, and turned by inches until she was lying on her back. She eased an arm under Chloe's head, and Chloe stirred, made a couple of awkward movements toward Sara until she found a comfortable niche on Sara's shoulder, snnrked her contentment, and rewrapped herself around her, this time finding a handy breast to clutch. Chloe was definitely a breast woman, she always seemed to gravitate toward them.

Sara's mind turned to the other night when, quite lustily, Chloe's hands had been occupied with them, and she felt a lovely bit of arousal as she remembered that, and looked down at the small hand that was covering its prize now. *She's going to make me crazy if she keeps doing that. Of course, she makes me crazy just walking across a room, or shuffling cards like a three-year-old.*

Chloe made another small snoring sound, and Sara looked at the redhead on her chest. *Look at that wasps' nest of hair, what a mess. Definite bed head.* Chloe's red-blonde hair was shaggier-looking than usual, as if she had been picked up by a small tornado and then deposited on Sara's shoulder. She reached with her free hand, and brushed some of the hair out of Chloe's eyes. *She's so warm, so very warm.* Sara frowned. *Too warm.* Sara put her hand on Chloe's forehead, then on her neck behind her jaw line.

"Chloe? Honey, wake up." Sara shook her a bit, and then put her lips to her forehead in a lingering kiss, half affection, half checking for temperature. Really hot. "Chloe, wake up, I think something's not right." Chloe stirred a little, and her hand did that lovely reflexive squeezing action to Sara's breast. *I like the way this woman wakes up. If she wakes up this slowly every day, and does the same thing each time, I could really look forward to mornings.* "Chloe, sweetheart, you need to wake up." Chloe's eyes slowly opened, and Sara could see a flicker of awareness come to her. She smiled a little, looked at Sara. "Good morning, Chloe. Did you sleep well?" Chloe's eyes closed again, the smile remained, and just when Sara thought that Chloe had dropped off again, there was another, more deliberate squeeze to Sara's breast, and her index finger lightly traced a circle around the center of it. *Oh yeah, she's awake, all right.* Eyes still closed, Chloe's hand traveled spiderlike down to the bottom of Sara's T-shirt, and slowly began to tug it upwards. Sara watched its progress without moving. She glanced out of the corner of her eye, saw that Chloe now had her eyes open, and was looking at each inch of the exposed flesh. Just as Chloe's hand, easing up the material so deliberately, so tortuously, was about to unveil an area of vital importance to them both, her hand stopped, lifted and put it over her own face instead.

"Atchoo!" Chloe's hand remained in front of her nose, and she tilted it out just a bit to take a peek. "Eww."

Sara's free arm quickly reached behind her to the end table to find the tissue box that was sitting there. She plucked a few out and handed them to Chloe. "God bless you." She smiled, and watched as Chloe sheepishly wiped her nose, and then her hand. "Need a couple more?"

Chloe nodded her assent, and gratefully accepted more tissues, and then cleared her throat. "Whoa, I think I lost a couple hundred brain cells on that one." Her voice sounded a little high and deep at the same time. She lifted away from Sara's shoulder, and blew a mighty honk into another tissue.

Now that Chloe was a little farther away, Sara could take a good look at her, and didn't like what she saw. "Uh-huh. I thought you felt a little too warm, and your eyes are all red and watery. And your voice sounds a lot like Debra Winger's did at the end of *Terms of Endearment.* You know, her dying scenes." She watched as Chloe felt her own forehead, and then the glands at the front of her neck, and then saw the tell-tale frown of discovery. "Not feeling your best, are you?"

Although tangled up in Sara's limbs, Chloe tried to sit the rest of the way up. Sara disengaged, sat up, and helped Chloe to do the same. She handed Chloe the tissue box and watched her as she did a little stretching and shaking out of her limbs.

Chloe, looking as bad as she felt, croaked, "Do I look as bad as I feel?" She saw the look of sympathy on Sara's face. "I must look really terrible, because, whoa, that's how I'm feeling." She took a few more tissues out and blew her nose again. She watched as Sara stood up from the couch. "And here I was, feeling all frisky, what with waking up with such a beautiful, wicked woman whose butt I kicked at cards last night." Chloe smiled up at her, and then winced at the pain that sentence brought to her throat. "Damn it all to hell, anyway," she rasped miserably.

Sara laid a cool palm on her cheek. "Yeah, just my luck, I finally get you where I want you, and then you get all terminal on me." She saw that her little joke didn't appear to make Chloe feel better. "Listen, you just lay yourself back down on the couch. I'm going to get you a cup of tea or something."

"I think I have to make a pit stop first. Thanks, tea sounds good." *It feels like somebody sandpapered my throat last night.*

She tottered off to the bathroom, while Sara went into the kitchen to rustle up something for her little patient. *I'm so lousy at this. I hate it when I'm sick, and I know I'm supposed to be helpful and caring when someone else is sick. But all I know to do is make tea and, I dunno, pet her or something?*

"Hey," a gravely voice said from the kitchen doorway. Nelson was standing there, looking pale and red-eyed himself. "Is that Chloe in the bathroom?"

"Oh, not you, too. Let me guess, you're sick, right? So is Chloe," Sara said, a little impatiently. When she saw the defeated expression on Nelson's face, she regretted her tone of voice. "Aw, Nels, I'm sorry. Listen, I'll make you a cup of tea. I don't know what else to do." She walked over, and felt his forehead; it was hot. "Yup, we've got to get some fluids into you. And toast or something. Feed a something, starve a something. Sorry, I can never remember which is which."

"Not hungry. Just got up to get something to drink and go to the bathroom. I want to go back to bed." He leaned up against the archway, looking like he would be satisfied to sleep right there.

"Bathroom's free." Chloe appeared in the kitchen doorway, and looked up and recognized a kindred soul. "Two sick puppies are we, huh, Nelson?"

Nelson rubbed the back of his hand across his eyes. "Guess they should just put us down. Euthanasia sounds good right about now. Maybe Aunt Sara would."

Sara sighed. "Give me a few hours to get to that point first. Normally, sick people make me want to kill myself, not the other way around."

Chloe's eyes seemed to look even more watery at that comment. "I need to get home and into my own bed. I don't want to be any trouble."

Sara immediately went to her and took her into her arms. "Aw, Chloe, I'm sorry. I just am not very good at dealing with illness. You stay here, we'll put you on the couch for a while." *Jeez, can I be more of a jerk?* "C'mon, what're you going to do at your house all alone? Let me take care of you, huh?" She felt Chloe relax a little in her arms, and Chloe wiped her nose a little on Sara's sleeve.

"Sorry, it'll wash out," Chloe said feeling like a whiny little kid. "I just hate being alone when I'm sick, I guess I'm just high maintenance."

Sara pulled away a little, and grinned down at the weepy wet eyes of the adorable librarian. "I love high-maintenance women; I thought I told you that?" She watched as Chloe pulled another tissue out of her shorts pocket and gave a huge blow. "I wish I could take you home and take care of you there, maybe when Dave gets back, so he can look after Nelson."

Nelson was dumbly staring into space. When he heard his name, he looked at the two women hugging and got a little tired grin. "Bathroom for me. Bed. Yeah, fluids." He was just turning to walk off when he stopped, and said to Sara, pleadingly, "Do you think you could call Charlie Shemp and tell him I, well, we won't be over today?"

Sara nodded over Chloe's head. "Yeah, I'll call. You go get back to bed. I'll bring in some tea to you in your bedroom. I'm," she looked down at Chloe, still dressed in yesterday's clothes, "gonna get your Aunt Chloe here some different, warmer clothes to throw on." She smiled at Nelson, and went in search of the promised clothes.

Nelson and Chloe's bloodshot eyes slowly met, and they both mouthed to each other in silent unison, "Aunt Chloe?"

Dave looked at the peacefully sleeping form of Marcy, buried underneath the covers. *Finally, maybe now she can get some rest.* He quietly got out of the bed and in his boxers and T-shirt, walked out to the kitchen and dialed home.

"Hello."

"Hey, Sara. How's it going?" He didn't wait for her to answer. "Marcy's down for the count. She was sicker than a dog this morning. I'm going to stay here and—"

Sara moaned and interrupted him, "Sounds like we need to open up an infirmary. Both Chloe and Nelson have fevers and sore throats, you know, the works. Nelson went back to bed, and Chloe's asleep on the couch. I was hoping that you would be able to make a run for us." *Stupid me with no driver's license.*

"Sounds like I'll have to buy two of everything. I was heading for the store for supplies anyway, I'll go there first, and then home. I don't want to leave Marcy alone for too long. Let's see, food, chicken soup, Kleenex, cough syrup, cold pills, juice, ginger ale, and cough drops, anything else?"

"Chocolate. Chocolate always helps," Sara added. *It'll keep me sane.*

"Well, she just got to sleep, so I'm out of here. See you soon, and Sara?" Dave knew his sister's little inadequacies all too well. "I know that you're not exactly the Florence Nightingale type. So buck up, babe."

"Let's see, we have, for your enjoyment, a wide variety of soup products of the chicken persuasion." Sara was standing in the kitchen archway, looking at the multitude of items that Dave had picked up, and then dropped off with barely a greeting in his haste to get back to an ill Marcy. He promised to call later. Sara had unloaded the bags, and happily, found some chocolate, which was going to make her stint as primary caregiver a little easier on her psyche.

She called out to the fevered, but awake form of Chloe on the couch, now dressed in a T-shirt and baggy sweats. "We've got chicken and stars, chicken noodle, chunky chicken noodle, chicken with kluski noodles, um chicken and rice, chicken vegetable, cream of chicken, eww, that always seems to gag me, I think of chicken in a blender?" She noted the smile that brought to her sick friend. "Well, does any of that sound appealing to you?" She watched as Chloe wiped a hand across her brow, and wiped her nose again with the tissue that she clutched in her hand.

Chloe cleared her throat a little, and said huskily, "I don't know, how about something with chicken. Surprise me." She wiped her eyes with a new tissue, and tossed the old one in a wastebasket that Sara provided her next to the couch. "You sound like that guy from

Forrest Gump, you know, the shrimp guy, except with chicken this time." *I hate being sick. I have too much to do. I think I'm dying. I should go home. I don't want to be there by myself. I gotta call off work for tomorrow. What if I have strep?* "Sara?" She saw Sara come back into the archway. "I probably should just go home while I still have the strength. I think I'm going to get worse before I get better," she said, her voice craggy and worn.

Sara gave her what must have been her one hundredth sympathetic look of the afternoon. "Listen, sicky, let me shove some soup down you, and then we can talk about your last will and testament. You just lay there and relax, and try not to miss the wastebasket anymore."

Chloe looked down to see she had missed it quite a bit, and quickly scooped them off the floor and into the can. "Oops," she croaked, and saw Sara just smile and shake her head as she headed back into the kitchen. *She's being so good. I wish I could talk better, or felt better. I just feel like a lump here, she could be doing things, instead of fussing over me. Although it's been a long time since anyone has fussed over me. It feels good.* She closed her eyes. The next time she opened them, Sara was depositing a tray on the coffee table with a large mug of soup and crackers.

"I brought you some juice too. Gotta keep your fluids up. That's the extent of my medical knowledge. Fluids, rest, and chicken soup." Chloe sat up a little, grabbed the mug off the tray, and stirred it around to cool it. Sara lifted Chloe's feet, sat down, and settled her feet onto her lap. "And maybe a foot rub?"

Chloe blew on her soup, which was still too hot to eat. "Oh, just sell my clothes, I'm going to heaven," she sighed, as Sara pushed her thumbs into the arch of her foot and started a luxurious massage.

Sara grinned. "You enjoy. I'm going to talk; you eat. Here's what I'm thinking." She smiled as she watched Chloe's eyes close, and head waver back and forth in pleasure to the pressure that Sara was applying to her foot. "I'm thinking you are going to stay here again tonight." She saw Chloe's eyes open at that, and look at her curiously. "You can either stay on the couch, or I can make up Dave's bed for you, and you can sack out there. I'd take you over to my place, but I'm pretty sure that he's planning on staying over at Marcy's tonight, and I'd like to stick around here for Nelson. He's been in and out of that bathroom at least five times in the last three hours. So he must be having some sort of intestinal upset." Sara's nose crinkled, and then she continued. "Maybe he ate a pizza box. Anyway," she grabbed a toe and gently twisted it, "you're not planning on going to work tomorrow, right?" Chloe, caught up in the foot massage, the warm soup and the soothing tones of Sara's voice, simply shook her head no. "I didn't think so. So what do you think, you think you can maybe hang out with me here for a couple of days?"

Chloe crumbled a handful of saltines and dropped them into her soup. She opened her mouth to pop her stuffed ears, then said worriedly, "Well, that sounds nice, but I'm afraid I'll just get you sick. I mean, we can't afford to have the whole team down."

Sara sat up straighter, and switched her attention to Chloe's other foot. She winked at her, and said, "I never get sick. Well, very rarely, and then it's for ten minutes or so, and then, voila! Perfecto again." When she saw Chloe's doubtful gaze, she said, "Really, you can ask my mom. It must be in my genes. I never missed school, for sickness, that is. Just, you know, skipping."

Chloe finished off her last spoonful and set her cup down. She swished some juice around to clear the food out of her teeth, and blew her nose several times in succession. She made a deliberate display of hitting the wastebasket this time with the dirty tissues. She sighed, then sighed again, as Sara waited for her decision. She sniffed a little, and said, hesitantly, "Well, if you're sure I wouldn't be too much trouble." Sara grinned, rewarding her answer with a delighted smile and renewed vigorous attention to her foot.

"You are trouble, but I like trouble." Sara chuckled.

Nelson was dreaming the twisted dreams of a fevered, flu-battered, mentally conflicted young man. Familiar figures in unfamiliar situations were flitting in his subconscious mind, and his synapses were sputtering like an old lawn mower in tall grass.

In his dream, he was standing at an altar in a small church, next to his dad. They were both in suits, and looking down an aisle. His dad kept nervously smiling at him, and straightening his tie. An organist, unseen, was playing "Poor Jud is Daid." Nelson was so fascinated with the surroundings, he nearly didn't notice his Aunt Sara coming out and standing on the other side of the raised platform. She was nearly upon them when he saw her, but when he did, his mouth dropped open in confusion.

She was dressed in blue jeans and cowboy boots, with ornate leather chaps over her long legs. A six-gun and holster were at her waist. As Nelson's eyes traveled upwards, he saw she was wearing a light blue silk cowboy shirt replete with white fringe, and her long dark hair was loose. He met her smiling eyes, which were shadowed by the brim of a white Stetson she was wearing low over her forehead. She winked at him and took a place at the other side of the altar. Her gaze broke from him and she turned, with the rest of the assembled folk at the altar, to look toward the back of the church once again.

Doris Raeburn, dressed in what looked like a graduation gown, appeared from the side of the church, and came and stood, waiting, between Sara and Dave. She smiled at both Dave and Nelson, and turned her attention to the back of the church. The pews of the church, Nelson noted, were filled with faces, some he recognized, most he did not. As he tried to ascertain who some of the pew dwellers were, all the heads in the pews turned and looked toward the back of the church. There at the end of the long aisle was Jeanette, in her cheerleader outfit, and she began a slow, cadenced walk up the aisle toward them, to the organist's somewhat jazzy rendering of "Oh, What A Beautiful Mornin." She smiled a nervous smile at Nelson, who returned the smile, but his eyes were drawn to her bouquet as she neared them. It seemed to be made of an assortment of Kleenex, pompom tassels, and odd white flowers the shape and size of golf balls. She stopped and stood just to the left of Sara, who tapped her hat brim in greeting.

Officious organ chords struck, and then a sexily swaggering version of "I'm Just a Girl Who Cain't Say No" began intoning through the building. The church was packed with people Nelson couldn't quite recognize, and they all stood up as the bride began her solo waltz up the aisle. It seemed to Nelson that waltzing was exactly what the bride, Chloe Donahue, was doing. She had on a lacy white gown with veil, and instead of a bouquet, there was some sort of book in her hands. As she sashayed slowly up the aisle, the words to the song came into Nelson's head, and he found himself singing them aloud, and then he saw his grinning Aunt Sara join in, and their voices lifted into a strong, clear duet as a beaming Chloe made her way up the aisle toward them.

Just as Chloe was beginning to ascend the three short steps up to the altar, Nelson noticed the large telltale bulge extending from Chloe's satin-covered abdomen, and when his mind comprehended her condition, he abruptly stopped his singing, leaving his Aunt Sara to finish the song all alone.

Chloe did a quick little twirl, and stood between his dad and Aunt Sara, giving a small, sparkling grin to both of them, as they did the same in return. Nelson stood closer to the right of his dad, and heard the congregation settle into their seats behind them.

Doris Raeburn opened the thin white booklet in her hands, and began speaking, sounding oddly like her voice was coming out over a PA system.

"Dearly beloved, we are gathered here today to join these people in holy matrimony. As is befitting a solemn and sacred ceremony such as this, we will begin with a reading in unison. Will everyone please open their scripts to page thirty-seven, Act Two, Scene One? And please, no accents. Not a one of you, I know, was born in the

South, so any budding Blanche DuBois out there, just suppress your south of the Mason-Dixon line tendencies for the duration of these proceedings. And Chloe, quit slouching. May we begin?"

As Doris and the throng behind Nelson began a toneless incantation of some bit of unrecognizable dialogue, he shifted uneasily on his feet, trying to catch the expressions on first his dad, then his Aunt Sara, and finally, Chloe. He noticed the three of them sneaking grins at each other.

The reading stopped, and Doris Raeburn began addressing them anew.

"Since the early time of women and men on this earth, it has been traditional for... couples to make a public declaration of their love and commitment to each other. That's why we are gathered here today. But I digress." She cast a stern eye toward Sara. "Funny, you coming out in public. Coming out! Well, you've always been a troublemaker, and still seem to be that way. But if Chloe here wants to put up with that, who am I to say different? I mean, was this really necessary? Couldn't you have maybe carried on with her in private? This is a small town."

Nelson heard both his father and Chloe give a spontaneous harrumph to break into Doris' little diatribe. Doris blinked, and huffily smoothed out the front of the blue graduation gown she was wearing. She recovered, and went on.

"We are gathered here today to join this man," and she nodded toward Dave, "and this woman," and she looked at Chloe, "and," she settled her eyes on the resolutely unflinching Sara again, "this woman in matrimony. Before we go any further, is there anyone, *anyone* out there who objects to this union?"

Nelson's eyes followed the motion of his aunt, dad, Chloe, and Doris' heads as they turned toward the alcove where the organ was. He noticed a top of a head just barely visible, with auburn curls on it, raise a little. Marcy.

Mrs. Raeburn's voice then was pitched ominously in that direction, too. "Anyone?"

Marcy stood up just a little and hesitantly gave a little embarrassed wave. "S'okay by me!" she chirped, and then, as an afterthought, she said, "I broke up with him!" and sat back down on the organ bench.

Doris cleared her throat and turned her attention back to the couple, or couples, before her. "All right, then. Where was I?" She fumbled with her white book, and found her place. "We are gathered here, oh wait, I said that already, let's see. Nobody objects, although I guess I can't ask me that, now can I? Nobody objects, so then we go on to the vows." She sniffed her nose, and began with Sara.

"Do you, Sara, take this woman, Chloe, to be your—can't say

'lawfully wedded,' this is Pennsylvania, not Vermont, for God's sake, although really, is it legal there yet? Unions maybe, I'm not sure about marriages. I'm no lawyer. Do you, Sara, take this woman, Chloe, to be your bride?"

Sara saw Doris' mouth had stopped moving, so she went for it. "Yeah," she drawled. She and Chloe exchanged sincere, loving glances.

Doris then looked to Dave. "Do you, David, take this woman, Chloe, as your lawfully wedded—and I think that I can say that, lawfully, here, in this instance, because, really, you're marrying Chloe, not your sister, which I am pretty sure isn't legal in any state, anywhere, not that there aren't a lot of West Virginia jokes in circulation regarding that very subject—bride?"

Dave appeared to be nearly as astute as his sister was; he seemed to be watching for the cessation of Doris' mouth movement. "Yes," he rumbled.

The slightly blushing bride became the center of Doris' attention. "And now, you, Chloe, our little pregnant town librarian. Never again will anyone in this town associate the term librarian with the words shy and retiring. Hmm? Still waters do run deep in you, don't they, dear? You're positively a whirlpool of wild inconsistencies," Doris quipped, once again not waiting for an answer to her question. "Do you take this man, and his sister, as your husband and wife, respectively? Relatively? I want you to think about this, we all know how addlebrained you can be. Stubborn, even. I mean, what are you thinking? Do you know what you're getting yourself into here? Have you talked to a reputable therapist? Don't slouch, this is your wedding for God's sake, try to stand up straight. It's better for the baby, good posture starts in the womb. Never can start too soon, can we?"

Doris sniffed her nose again, and before Chloe could get an answer out, she said, "And while I think of it, what about Nelson here, Chloe? My mind reels, you would be his stepmom, and his semi-aunt, sort of an uncle at the same time, wouldn't you? And the baby would be his niece or nephew. Do you know the sex yet? Will it be a stepbrother or maybe sister? And although I heard from a reliable source that you denied being bi, couldn't you, can't you make up your mind or something? Couldn't flip a coin?" Doris finally took notice of the small frown that was forming on Chloe's face, and her voice softened. "Do you, uh, Chloe," Doris fumbled with the page in front of her, for she had completely lost her place. "Uh, do you, Chloe, remember the question?"

Chloe sighed. "I'll say," she smiled.

Doris raised her shoulders in a gesture of conciliation and defeat. "All right then. I pronounce the three of you hitched." She crinkled her brow on her softly lined face. "I guess you can take turns kissing the bride."

"What?" questioned Chloe, who had just gotten off the phone, having made arrangements for someone to fill in at the library for her for the next few days. "Is Nelson all right?"

"I just checked on him. He's still sleeping. But it was the weirdest thing; he was singing in his sleep; sounded a lot like "I Cain't Say No."" Sara rolled her eyes and flopped down in the recliner.

"Figures, he's rehearsing the wrong parts in his dreams." Chloe was sucking on another honey-lemon throat lozenge. "You should probably wake him up and make him eat something."

"Next time he makes a trip to the bathroom I'll intercept him and make him take on some fluids and food." Sara turned in the recliner, and draped her legs over the arm of it, so she had a better view of Chloe on the couch. "Did you talk to Dave, too?"

"Actually, I talked to Marcy. Dave is staying there tonight. She sounds pretty good, other than her stomach is revolting like crazy. She says she feels queasy, otherwise, no sign of a cold or anything. Sounds like the three of us have all different combinations of this thing." She scrunched her face up. "I'm glad I don't have the stomach gurgles part. This is bad enough." She blew her nose again in demonstration.

"So, you called off for the next couple of days?" asked Sara, a little hopefully.

"Yeah. No problem. The county has a floater librarian for situations like this. So it looks like I can suffer in peace." *You don't know what you're getting yourself into, Sara.*

Sara quirked a little grin at her. "I'm sorry, Chloe, I may sound like a sadist here, but I'm just a little glad that you're sick." She saw the uncertain look on Chloe's face. "I get to spend time with you. I'd prefer that you were feeling good, and didn't have a ton of snot in you, but I like having you around." She saw that Chloe's already red and watery eyes seemed to get even more so at that statement, and a pleased, shy smile appeared. "I made up the bed in Dave's room. He won't mind if you, we, sack out in there tonight." She watched Chloe for her reaction.

Chloe coughed into a tissue. "Are you sure I won't infect you? You really want to hear me hacking all night?"

Sara looked directly into her red-rimmed eyes. "No, I don't want to hear you hacking all night." She paused. "I want to hold you all night." *Even with that red nose, seeping eyes, and rat's-nest hair, you are the sexiest woman on the planet.*

Chloe's heart beat double-time, and she grinned, then put on a false air of defeat. "Well, if you insist, I mean, if it would make you feel better." *It's gotta be good medicine for me.*

"Oh, I see, you're concerned with my well-being. Well, yes, I'm sure it would make me feel so much better." Sara cocked her head. "It sounds like Nelson is up and around. I'm going to go check on him before he sneaks back to bed." She got up from her chair, stood over Chloe, and gently ran her fingers through her bangs. "Why don't you try and get some rest? I'm going to heat up some more chicken soup, I'll wake you and force you to eat it in a while. Gotta get some into that growing boy, too."

Chloe's eyes closed at the soothing feel of Sara's fingertips. "Okay. I can do that."

Sara bent and replaced her fingertips with a small kiss. "See you in a bit."

Nelson was still feeling a bit woozy as he made room on his nightstand for the tray that had held his first food of the day. He had dutifully downed the soup that his aunt had provided, and sucked up a large glass of juice. He was staring moodily at the Cleveland Browns poster over his chest of drawers when Sara stuck her head into his room, and grinned at him.

"Eat it all up, like a good boy?" she asked, crossing into the room and pulling out the desk chair to sit down. "Want any more? How're you feeling?"

Nelson knew exactly how what the cat dragged in felt like. "Rotten. No, no more." He rubbed his eyes and gave her a weak smile. "I can't believe I slept all day." It was after 7:00 now, Sunday night, and except for his digestive system waking him and insisting on making hurried journeys to the bathroom, he had slept the day away.

Sara propped her feet up on the edge of his bed smiled sympathetically. "Well, you're a good, non-bothersome patient. You and Chloe, both. She's out there now, snoozing, chest rattling, nose running, eyes watering. Pretty damned cute for a sick girl." She watched as Nelson nodded, closed his eyes and sighed, pulling his blankets up tighter around his chin. "Your dad is over at Marcy's, she's been sick all day, too. Mostly potty stops for her. If you all didn't have different variations on this thing, I'd be calling up a shyster lawyer and blaming it all on Buddy's Pizza Place."

Nelson was content to keep his eyes closed. He didn't feel like sleeping anymore, besides, some of those dreams he had been experiencing were nagging at the back of his mind. Nagging him so much that he felt compelled to find some answers.

"Aunt Sara, um, have you ever had a bi girlfriend?" Nelson coughed, he couldn't believe that sentence actually made it to his mouth.

Sara blinked at a question that seemed to have come far out of left field. She looked at Nelson, his eyes still shut, and decided to give him a straightforward answer to his weirdly timed question. "Nels, I haven't had what you would call too many girlfriends of any length of time in my lifetime as yet." *That's going to change, with Chloe.* "But, yes, I've dated, here and there, women who have identified themselves as bisexual." She pursed her lips. "Something in particular you want to know about them, or is it the bisexuality thing that you're curious about?"

Nelson sighed. He couldn't tell her what Justin, Heather and Jeanette were saying about Chloe and his dad. He had to find another way to understand this, and when he opened his eyes to sneak a peek at his aunt, he saw that she was looking at him, waiting for his answer, a patient look on her face.

He decided to deflect attention away from what he was really trying to ask, and center it on himself instead. "Well, I've been thinking, you know, I've got a girlfriend now, and..." Nelson shut his eyes again, so he could hide from his aunt's all-too-inquisitive stare. *Where do I go from here? Okay, I'll lie.* "But one of the guys at school, in the play, he's been..." Nelson took a deep breath and opened his eyes again, and his hand came out from under the covers, and began tracing the pattern on his comforter. He glanced at his still patiently waiting aunt, and looked away again. "Well, you just hear things, people say things, you know, and it gets you to thinking." He closed his eyes again, pissed that he had even brought the subject up.

Sara could see that something was troubling Nelson, but he couldn't, as usual, get to the point. *I'll try to ease into this, give him the broad picture.* "Well, I don't know what exactly you're getting at, Nels, but," Sara stretched out farther in the desk chair, and touched her feet to Nelson's under the blanket. "I've always heard, or known, or read that there's a line of thought that sexuality is a very fluid thing. Not something that necessarily has to be a sure thing, screwed down tight." She waggled her feet to have a connection with Nelson. "I've always, pretty much—no, not pretty much, *been* a lesbian. I've never slept with any men. I've never had the desire to do that." She stopped a moment, considering. "When I was younger, I didn't like or accept people who identified themselves as bisexual. It was against my politics, you know, I felt that someone should stick to the party line. Be a Democrat or Republican, but don't confuse me with your Independent party." She laughed, and continued. "But I've gotten older, and a lot wiser, and realize that there are a lot of nice Independents out there who really don't deserve to have me judging them. I don't think it's a matter of them not being able to make up their minds. In my mind, now, it's more of a matter of them having the, I don't know, ability to see the best of both worlds, and to be able to enjoy the best of both worlds."

She stopped there, waiting to see if what she said would garner any response from Nelson.

Nelson fidgeted under the covers, and brought his knees up under them. He looked at Sara, carefully controlling any signs his face might be giving away. "So, you don't think it's a bad thing, then?"

Sara was still confused, but answered him truthfully. "No, I don't think it's a bad thing." She studied his face, finding only sincere thoughtfulness in his eyes. "Why would you ask that?"

Nelson shifted yet again under the covers, and pushed the comforter off him. "Well, it's not like I've thought about it much, but how could you ever trust anyone who was like that?"

Sara pondered the question for a moment before replying. "Oh, you mean, if someone, say me, had a girlfriend who was bisexual, how could I trust her not to be wanting to hook up with some guy?" She waited a moment, and saw the affirming nod Nelson gave to her statement. "Nelson, I think that there's a big misconception out there about bisexuals being promiscuous. I don't see that as true, not in my experience. To tell ya the truth, Nelson, I think I've been more promiscuous than any bisexuals I've been involved with, or met. No, I think they have every capacity to be monogamous, no matter which sex they're involved with at the time."

She saw Nelson nodding along in seeming understanding to what she was saying. "I think that everyone has the opportunity to love and be loved. I don't doubt there might be a lot of people out there who would disagree with me, for whatever reasons. I think we all, gays, straights, and whomever in-between, have issues about feeling insecure with who we are, and the ability of our loved ones to remain faithful."

Nelson played with his fingers a bit, interlacing them, and rubbing a thumb along a palm. He was trying to decide if he wanted to ask her, point blank, about his recently acquired doubts about Chloe. What with all the rumors flying, and the confidence of his friends when they relayed their absolute certainty about her pregnancy, he was just too apprehensive to want to upset his aunt with all of his confusion. He decided to do what he always did, sit back and watch and listen, and watch the adults around him deal with whatever the future held. He would keep his mouth shut, and hope everything turned out all right.

"Okay," he said, his tone signifying that he seemed to be satisfied with what Sara had told him. He smiled and stretched. "Thanks. I think I need some more juice, and to take some pills." He rubbed his throat. "I'm probably not doing school tomorrow."

Sara got up from her chair, and although the curiosity she felt about Nelson's sudden peculiar interest in bisexuality was killing her, she decided to be prudent and let it go for now. She knew that he'd ask her if there was more to it at some point.

She straightened her sweatshirt, and lifted a half smile. "Yeah, I figured you weren't going to school. That's okay. Chloe is spending the night, and taking tomorrow off, too." She headed to the doorway, and turned. "What a fun threesome we'll make." She walked out of the room.

Threesome? Nelson buried his head in his hands, trying to dispel the images from his earlier dream, and the images that his aunt had just innocently planted in his fevered brain. *Oh my God. I'm such a pervert. I'm never going to be able to look Chloe in the eye again.*

Part XVI:
Ladies and Germs

Chloe was in the interior waiting area of her doctor's office, writing a check for her co-payment to the doctor. From her vantage point, she could see the waiting room, and was amused to see that Sara was leaned, legs sprawled out, and head tilted back, rather unglamorously snoring in a chair with an open magazine in her lap. There was a two-year-old little girl standing in the chair next to Sara, her head just inches from Sara's face, intently studying the inside of the slumbering woman's nose. The little girl's mother, familiar with her daughter's usually benign curiosity, was unaware of the depth it was now achieving. She was sitting on the other side of the little munchkin, perusing a magazine with one hand, with her other hand placed firmly on her daughter's behind to steady and insure her safety during her unnoticed exploration of the snoring woman's nasal cavities.

Chloe stood, fascinated, and watched as the little girl dipped her head lower, presumably to peer farther up Sara's nostrils. The receptionist, taking Chloe's check, noticed Chloe's attention was fixed elsewhere, and she followed Chloe's grinning gaze out to the waiting room. The receptionist giggled when she saw what was happening, and shared a grin with her. Marcy appeared at Chloe's right elbow, having finished her own checkup with the doctor, and joined the two women in their rapt fascination of what was happening in the other room. Marcy smiled, too, when she saw the little girl looking deeply into Sara's open, snoring mouth, apparently trying to find out where that awful growling racket was coming from within Sara's body. Sara's mouth closed in her sleep, and the little girl, fixing on a plan, cautiously and carefully began to stretch her hand to Sara's nose. Marcy silently elbowed Chloe, and the receptionist put a hand over her own mouth in an effort to muffle the giggles that were threatening to erupt full force.

All three women watched, transfixed, as the little girl carefully inserted a tiny finger into Sara's nostril, and held it there, delighted to see that it was a perfect fit. The mother of the little one, diligent in her daughter's safety, finally looked up from her magazine, and a horrified look covered her face.

"Debra!" she hissed, and pulled her daughter toward her. Unfortunately, the little girl's small finger was still lodged within Sara's nose, so when the little girl was being hauled into her mother's lap, she, by extension, brought Sara's head along with her. Sara woke up to a very odd sensation of falling to her left, with a strange object up her nose. Sara reflexively pulled back the other way, and the foreign object was removed, but by then she was teetering on the edge of her chair; she lost her balance, and slid with a thud onto her rump to the carpeted floor. She blinked, and heard riotous laughing coming from the receptionist's area, but from where she was sitting, she didn't know who the source of the laughter was. The startled woman looked at the little girl held in her mother's arms, and figured them as the culprits responsible for her current situation. She raised a single eyebrow, and gave them a scary, feral look. The two-year-old immediately burst out in a terrified wail, and buried her head into her mother's shoulder. The mother quite prudently and efficiently lifted her daughter and purse, and found empty seats as far from the dark-haired glowering woman as the small waiting room would allow.

Sara was just pushing herself off the floor and back into her seat, when the door to the waiting room opened, and two madly grinning women appeared and walked toward her. *Perfect. They saw everything. My life is complete.* She settled into the chair and reached to grab Chloe and Marcy's coats, and thrust them at her silent, but wildly amused, friends. Sara, still groggy from her nap in the chair, and her rather unpleasant awakening, frowned her most terrorizing glare at both of them, and stood up to put on her own coat. Chloe and Marcy gave each other little knowing smiles; it clearly wasn't smart to tease Sara about this. Yet.

The path to leave the office crossed directly in front of the mother and her terrorized, still whimpering little girl. Sara, leading the group to the door, paused in front of the little girl, and, feeling badly about scaring her, stopped a moment and gave the little one her best and gentlest smiles. As Chloe, Marcy and the mother watched, the little girl took a long look at Sara's smiling face, and then proceeded to wail anew. Chloe and Marcy burst out in renewed fits of laughter, and Sara just threw up her hands in defeat and pushed the door open so they could all exit. Just as the door was closing behind them, they could hear a final comment from the toddler, speaking in a rather loud voice. "Growly. She's growly."

Sara slumped her shoulders and walked to the Subaru ahead of the two women who sounded like they wouldn't be able to stop laughing anytime soon.

* * *

Chloe slid into the booth, and immediately began fiddling with the knob on the side of the little jukebox so she could look at the song titles flipping by. Marcy settled into the bench across from her, and Sara sat down next to Chloe, smiling at her utter enthusiasm for the old-fashioned music player.

"Ooh!" Chloe said, her voice still shredded and coarse. She looked at Sara and demanded, "Gimme some quarters. I want to play something."

Sara put a hand in her jeans pocket, and pulled out a handful of change. Chloe dug around, and took several quarters. Sara, curious, asked, "What're ya going to play?"

Chloe sighed happily and said, as she inserted the coins into the slot, "Patsy Cline! I love Patsy! It should be a law that every jukebox in America should have Patsy on it." She pushed a few buttons and completely missed the looks of surprise, pleasure and chagrin that passed over Sara's face. "I Fall to Pieces" began to play softly through the diner, and Chloe happily settled back into her seat.

"So," began a sarcastic Marcy, "I assume we're allowed to talk now? Is that all right with you, Princess?" She dropped her eyelids at Sara, and patiently waited for her to answer.

"Humph," said a still growly Sara in reply. "Okay, what's the prognosis? Everyone going to live?" She took the menu that Chloe handed her, and began to study it.

Marcy looked to Chloe, and grinned. "I'm fine, the doc thinks it's some stomach virus. He did some tests, and I'm supposed to call back on Thursday. I get to take one more day off, though. Back to the grind on Thursday. How about you, Chloe?"

Chloe, noticing that Sara was staring at the menu, winked a conspiratorial grin at Marcy, who winked back in understanding. "Well, he did a throat culture on me, and it seems that I have mono."

"Really?" gasped a perfectly playing along Marcy. "Oh shit! That sucks!"

Sara, feeling like she had missed something while she was looking at the day's specials, and hearing the surprise in Marcy's voice, looked up and said, "Huh? Excuse me, what did you say, Chloe?"

Chloe looked her in the eye and said ominously, "Mono."

Sara dropped her menu onto the table, immediately forgotten. "Mono? As in mononucleosis? The kissing disease?" That's what Sara recalled it being called when she was a teenager.

Chloe nodded and replied, deadpan, "Yup. Mono. The doctor said it was contagious, and well, I'm afraid, well, you know...I have to cut back on certain activities, to make sure I don't overdo it."

Sara's eyes were getting wider with every word that was coming from the little librarian's mouth. "What activities, and for how long?"

Marcy settled back further into her seat to enjoy the show that was playing out across from her. "Crazy" began playing on the jukebox.

Chloe, looking troubled, stared down at her folded hands on top of the table, and crooked her mouth into a frown. "Well, I can still work, and work with the play, once the sore throat and cold settles down. I'm going back to work on Thursday, too." She glanced up at the disbelieving Sara, and continued, working her face into an even more pronounced frown. "As for other things, I'm not allowed. I can't, you know..." She saw the look of comprehension and its resultant unhappiness show up on Sara's face. "I'm highly contagious. I'll tire easily. I can't get into situations where I may be—" She stopped there, and shrugged at Sara.

Sara exclaimed, her voice seemingly erupting from the depth of her bowels. "Situations?"

Marcy helpfully answered that question for Chloe. "Swapping spit. Right, Chloe?"

Sara shot Marcy a murderous look, and then looked to Chloe for confirmation. Chloe shrugged again, and hoarsely affirmed Marcy's answer. "Yeah. That, and any other situations that would logically follow the swapping spit scenario." She pursed her lips and gave Sara an apologetic look.

Sara, whose hormones were screaming madly in denial of this new information, breathed out another phrase. "For how long?"

Chloe took a sip of her water, and tonelessly replied, "Six weeks." She paused a heartbeat, and then continued, "At least."

Marcy was thinking she should duck out to the ladies' room so she could release the laughter she was desperately trying to hold back. She looked back and forth at the two women across from her, admiring the way Chloe was so downright convincing in her little lie, and at the total air of despair and desperation, that was encompassing Sara. *Oh, Chloe, you are good. Now how long are you going to torture the poor woman?*

Sara was unable to form complete sentences at this point, so she said the word that was foremost in her brain. "Nothing?"

Chloe clenched her jaw, and repeated Sara's meaningful word. "Nothing." She sighed, and then looked up at the approaching waitress. Chloe knew if she looked at Marcy right now, they were both going to lose it.

Sara's attention was captured by the numerous furious little voices in her head, demanding that she go down and strangle the doctor who had given Chloe this horrible news, effectively ruining all the naked-Chloe scenarios that had been fermenting in Sara's sexually charged brain. She was killing the doctor for the third time, in a new and more imaginative way, when Chloe's voice cut through to her vision, stopping it without a satisfactorily grisly ending.

"Um, Sara, she's waiting for your order," nudged Chloe, whose eyes were tearing at the effort she was applying to keep a serious countenance.

Sara looked up dumbly at the not-too-patient-looking face of the waitress. "Chicken, I'll have the chicken."

As Sara numbly was finishing giving the rest of her order to the waitress, Chloe finally felt strong enough to look at Marcy across the table. Marcy rolled her eyes and tapped Chloe's leg with her toe under the table. She couldn't help herself; she just had to contribute to this bit of fun. "Jeez, Chloe, six weeks. Or longer? Wow, how are you guys going to manage that?" She looked quickly out the window to maintain her composure.

Chloe took her cue, sighed, and then said confidently, "Oh, we can wait. I mean, we've waited this long, right?" She looked at the very frazzled Sara. "We're both grown-ups, we can manage to control ourselves for that long." She mentally berated herself for doing it, but she plunged ahead anyway. "Or longer, if need be, right, honey?" She gave a sweet smile to Sara, full of expectant trust that her sweetie would agree with her confidence in her.

Sara took a quick glance around to make sure no one was in the way of the power of the answer she knew was going to come tumbling, forcefully, out of her mouth. "Hell, no!" she roared. "No way, no how, no, no, not going to happen. No. I don't care if you are contagious, I don't care. You got me, Chloe? Six weeks? Get real. Not possible. Nope. I won't be able to survive that long. I'll die first, and I'd rather die of mono. Got it?"

Marcy blew a mouthful of her iced tea clear across the table and right onto Chloe's sweater. She started laughing, a good cleansing laugh ridding her of all the tension she felt from holding it back. Chloe, momentarily stunned by both Sara and Marcy's reactions, wiped her sleeve, and finally began laughing herself. Chloe then turned her giggling gaze to her glowering girlfriend, who still wasn't aware that she had been the victim of a well-played-out prank. Chloe was laughing so hard, and her throat was still rough, that the waves of mirth coming from her sounded much like that of a braying donkey. Those sounds made Marcy laugh even harder, and she finally broke down, and quickly excused herself to the ladies' room.

Sara watched and listened, and slowly the truth began dawning on her. She took a breath, and carefully measured her tone and words. "What is it, really?"

Chloe wiped a paper napkin across her eyes, grabbed another and blew her nose into it, taking that time to settle herself before she answered, her face softly glowing, her eyes not being able to disguise the twinkle within, "Strep. Just like I thought. I have to take antibiotics for a week."

Sara propped her elbows on the table, and steepled her hands, and squinted at the vacated bench across from her, before carefully turning her head to meet Chloe's eyes again. "You, you little shit, are in deep doo-doo here, you know that, right?" She watched Chloe blink, and then smugly grin at her. "I just might make you wait those six weeks," Sara said in measured, serious tones, and internally enjoyed the wide-eyed response that statement elicited from Chloe. "Yeah. I'll have to think about it." She gave Chloe one more meaningful look, and finished, "I'm a grown-up. I can wait."

Chloe had to physically stop herself from leaping into Sara's lap right there in the tiny diner, and kissing that serious look off her girlfriend's face, strep germs or no strep germs. "Sara," she said plaintively, begging to be absolved from Sara's threat, "I don't want to be a grown-up."

Sara started laughing, freed from the bleak future of a false diagnosis, and took pity on the now contrite Chloe. She slid a hand onto Chloe's thigh under the table, high, then higher, reaching for the interior of her thigh, and then gave a measured and deliberate stroke there. Chloe jumped a little and heard Sara say, "Nah, Chloe, I don't want to be a grown-up, either."

Sara put the remains of her chicken dinner in the styrofoam container provided by the waitress. She looked sheepishly at Chloe, who gave her a small wink before she chided the tall woman next to her. "I thought it was a little weird, you ordering chicken, since that's pretty much all we've eating for the last three days." She turned her attention to her friend across the table, and cocked her head at her. "How's the stomach doing, Marse?"

Since Marcy had been subjected to Dave's limited variety of chicken soup products over the same time span, she had the presence of mind to order a beef vegetable soup, with some homemade rolls on the side. Marcy groaned but her face held a wan smile. "If I eat soup again after all this clears up, it'll be too soon. Stomach is fine, so far. It doesn't feel like it wants to make a return trip out the same way it went in." Marcy saw the *ews* that appeared on both her friends' faces. "It's been hell. What goes in wants to come out." Marcy felt much worse than she was letting on, she still felt very tired, and was glad that they would be heading home soon. She wanted nothing more than to crawl into bed and close her eyes for many comforting hours.

Chloe stretched her hand across the table and gave Marcy a reassuring pat. "Well, old girl, we'll have you home shortly. Can you handle it a little longer, so I can get a piece of pie, or do you want me to get it to go?"

Marcy sighed. "No, have it here. It's nice to be out of the house," she lied, knowing that Chloe and Sara wanted to spend some more time together before they dropped off Sara at the school to direct the Tuesday play practice. It was after 3:00 now, and Sara had to be there at 4:00.

Chloe could tell that her friend felt bad, and was putting up a good front. She smiled at Marcy in knowing appreciation, and waved down the waitress and ordered a piece of pecan pie for herself, and a piece of cherry for Sara.

Sara thanked the waitress for the pie, and then began speaking, "Well, since I'm fill-in director for the rest of the week, and you two are merely my useless lackeys, is there anything I should know, or get done for you, Marcy, while I'm there?"

"Yeah, just make sure a tree looks like a tree, will ya? I don't want any comments from Doris this year, or I'm blaming the whole thing on you."

Chloe, who was resting her voice, and enjoying her pie too much to join into the conversation, grinned and let the two women who liked each other very much treat each other as if they didn't.

"Marse, I know what a tree looks like. I'm just not sure you do."

"Yeah, I believe that. I'm sure you've been mistaken many times for a redwood yourself, oh tall and wooden one."

Sara stuck her tongue out at Marcy, showed her the mostly chewed piece of cherry pie residing there before swallowing, and countered with, "Listen, Miss Bohemian With Name No One Can Pronounce, just be cooperative for five minutes so your damned corn stalks don't end up looking like a field of marijuana plants."

Marcy and Chloe both let out guffaws at that thought. "Actually, Sara," said Marcy mischievously, "I kind of like that idea." Marcy was glad she'd decided to stay a little longer.

Sara directed a rare and affectionate grin at the curly-haired art teacher. "You would. Have any samples growing behind your house we could use as a model?"

"Too early in the season yet. Try me in August or so."

Chloe finished her pie, and was eyeing the remainder of Sara's. Sara noticed, and placed a small guarding hand over the rest of it. "Nuh-uh, Miss Lips. Mine, mine, mine!"

Chloe pouted and pulled her straw out of her soda glass, and shot some diet Coke drops at Sara. Sara rolled her eyes, and shrugged, then shoved her plate over to the now clearly delighted librarian.

Marcy noticed this little surrender, and smirked at Sara.

"Whipped."

"Guilty as charged," admitted Sara, and gave Chloe a very mushy, adoring look. Chloe was surprised, Sara's truly mushy moments were not as frequent as she would like them to be, but she knew that Sara just wasn't built that way. So, when Sara gave Chloe the last of her pie, and cheerfully at that, she was really sharing quite a tender moment with Chloe, in her own manner. To the untrained eye, Sara had just given in to Chloe; to their hearts, it was a gesture as intimate as a stolen kiss.

Marcy had a trained eye. "God, will you two knock it off? I can feel my lunch coming back up, and it doesn't have a thing to do with my flu."

Sara grimaced, and blushed just a little. "Okay. Well, you two are off loafing this week, and we only have two days' rehearsal next week before Easter vacation starts. I think the dancing parts are well in hand, the sets are coming along fine, and the kids will be ready for some full-act rehearsals on the stage after vacation. Right?" She knew she was, so she continued. "You two know that the weekend after Easter, good weather willing, the golf course is going to open up. At least I talked Dave into having the pre-grand opening party on Saturday evening, instead of Friday. If it was on Friday, I'm not sure either Nelson or I could make it to Saturday dance rehearsal."

Sara turned on her commander persona, and began making a list, verbally, and repeating it to her ailing troops at the table with her. "Right! This week taken care of. Next week, next Thursday morning, Dave, Nelson and I will be traveling, gaily, down to visit the parental units in Florida for the Easter holiday. You two, helpless as I know you will be without the Family D'Amico here to guide you, will just have to color Easter eggs all by your lonesome." Sara noticed sly little grins exchanged between her two tablemates, but chose to ignore them so she wouldn't lose her train of thought. "We'll get back the Tuesday after Easter, hauling a U-Haul's worth of chocolate from my mom and dad. Hopefully, we'll get back before rehearsal that day, if not, you'll just have to manage without us. Then, it's all golf course and rehearsals and more golf course right until Sunday's golfing grand opening. Dave's going to put on his chef's hat and burn a truckload of hotdogs for this thing, and he's arranged for some kind of musical entertainment. Then a Sunday's worth of golfers playing at half price. Should be a swingin' time!" Sara's face frowned at the thought of having to mingle with the public that much, but she had agreed long ago to do it, so she was going to do it.

Chloe had watched the frown form on Sara's face, and knew the reason for it; they had discussed it, along with many other things, over their time together during the past few days. Chloe knew that

Sara was not looking forward to it, but had a certain resignation to performing her duties for her brother.

Chloe decided to interject a thought to keep the itinerary ball rolling. "WQEL the next week after that."

Marcy let out a huge sigh at the mention of WQEL. "Sara, you haven't lived through a WQEL auction and Fort Lafayette Musical Showcase yet, have you?"

"No, but Chloe gave me a general rundown. It's from 5:00 'til 10:00, kids from the play answering phones, three or four musical acts from the show interspersed with auctioning bits with you and Chloe in front of the camera, hucstering off donated merchandise and services from local businesses. What's so tough about that?"

"You try talking about six non-related, dull-as-day-old-toast, crap items for ten minutes, in front of two TV cameras, that's what's tough about that. Three for me, three for Chloe to yammer about, ten minutes total, then a new set of six useless items to blather enthusiastically about. All night long. With just the kids' music acts to break the monotony." Marcy gave Sara a condescending smirk. "I've never heard you talk about anything for longer than two minutes, and then I start considering what a drain it must be on your gray matter."

Marcy cleared her voice, and went into mock auctioneer mode. "Hey, listen, people, only five minutes more to bid on that family day pass to Wally's Fun World, it's only up to eight dollars, which is quite a steal, if you ask me. And the five cases of Hires root beer, graciously provided to us from Sam's Warehouse, is currently at sixteen dollars. And there are still no bids on the Wayne Newton in Hawaii video tape, with signed photograph of Mr. Entertainment himself, Wayne Newton. Let's get those phones ringing, folks. What's happening on your side of the board, Chloe?"

Chloe had done this for the last five years, and wasn't going to let a little thing like a sore throat ruin her fun now. She knew the routine in her sleep.

"Well, Marcy, with only four minutes left, there's a fifteen dollar bid on three nine-hole rounds of golf donated by Stonecreek Golf Course, and we're a little low on bids for twelve movie rentals from Bob's Video Shack. That's a thirty-six dollar retail value, and we only have a bid for ten, no, we just got a higher one, that's up to fourteen dollars now. And the seasonal fur storage at Hammond's Dry Cleaners, right in downtown Stonecreek, has a very low bid at five dollars. We've got twelve kids out there from Lafayette High School answering your calls, and a few of them look pretty bored right now, don't they, Marcy? Let's get those phones ringing in support of the fine entertainment here at WQEL Public Television, and remember, your winning bid over retail value is tax deductible. WQEL accepts cash, checks and all major credit cards. How's that Wayne Newton tape doing there, Marcy, what with only three minutes left for folks to get to their phones and start dialing?"

Sara let out a tremendous roar of laughter, and was soon joined in by both Marcy and Chloe.

Marcy raised her eyebrows at Sara. "Five, count'em, five hours of that, just me and Chloe. And since it is Stonecreek night at WQEL, most of our time will be spent shilling items donated by local retailers and businesses, which, when you think of it, consists of oil changes from the Amoco station, dry cleaning, pizzas, and oh, yeah, rounds of golf at D'Amico's Stonecreek Golf Course. Dave said he's going to donate golf lessons, too, just for the auction bidders only."

Sara puzzled over this. "I don't get it. Neither Dave nor I can golf all that well to begin with, certainly not well enough for either one of us to teach anyone else. Where's he going to get a teacher?"

Marcy's eyes tracked slowly to a clearly confused and unsuspecting Chloe. "Miss Lips here. I volunteered her to help out the cause."

Chloe started coughing, and Sara had to smack her several times on the back, and handed her a glass of water to sip. When the coughing abated, Chloe, sounding a little bit like Scooby Doo after a long night of howling, rasped out, "Me? No way. Not me. I can't teach strangers." She stopped when she saw the grin forming on Sara's face. "Oh, wait, you think I owe you guys because of you helping with the dance stuff. Well let me tell you, right here, right now, that," she paused and saw the grin on Sara's face starting to fade, mentally kicked herself and immediately finished with, "I would certainly be delighted to help out the D'Amicos in any way I can." She gave Sara an apologetic grin, and saw by Sara's return smile that she had been forgiven.

"Paybacks," stated Sara, and grabbed the check. Chloe threw some dollar bills on the table, and as Sara paused after standing up, to retrieve her coat off the nearby hook, Chloe took advantage of her perfect positioning, scooted across the bench seat, and pinched Sara soundly on the rear.

Sara squawked, and said, "Hey, whaddya do that for?"

Chloe grinned as her best friend Marcy answered for her. "'Cause she can."

Sara and Chloe watched a very tired Marcy trudge up her back door steps, turning and waving to them before she entered her house. Next stop was to drop Sara off at the school, and then Chloe was finally heading home after her stay at the D'Amico Family Hospice. They both knew that this was going to be their last chance to share a few intimacies until they saw each other again.

Chloe turned off the engine, and glanced at her watch. Sara was sadly frowning from the passenger seat of the Subaru. Her hand already placed on Chloe's knee, she reached and took Chloe's hand into hers. They both looked at their joined hands, then their eyes raised to meet and consider each other quietly.

"We haven't had much kissing time in the past few days, you know," Sara finally said, her eyes memorizing all that was Chloe.

"I know. It's not much fun kissing a snot-nosed librarian who can barely breathe, is it?" Chloe sighed regretfully, and softly ran her other hand across Sara's knuckles.

"I can barely breathe when I kiss you, Chloe, and I'm not even sick."

Chloe's heart pounded at such a sweet message, she leaned closer to Sara, and saw that Sara was leaning in, too. Chloe took a deep breath, and their lips met, so achingly soft and gentle, filled with a tenderness that spoke of their reluctance to be parting from one another. The kiss continued, with Sara bringing both hands up to cradle Chloe's face, and she left the red lips, and began placing small kisses over cheek, nose and forehead before returning to Chloe's waiting lips again. Even these small, lingering kisses evoked a moan from Chloe, and an answering rumble from Sara.

They broke apart, but kept the proximity, Sara sighing her words to Chloe. "I want you so badly. Can you feel it?"

Chloe whispered back, her voice husky from equal parts passion and sore throat. "Oh, yeah! I can feel it." She rubbed her cold red-dened nose across Sara's. "It was nice sleeping with you, even if we didn't get to..."

Sara kissed Chloe's nose and answered, "Well, you're going to need all your strength when we finally do. That's a promise."

Chloe leaned back in her seat, and reached for Sara's hand again. "Oh, I do like your promises. Now if we could just get you to follow through on one of them."

Sara sat back too, and smiled a sly grin. "Go get those antibiotics, Miss Lips, and some vitamins, too. And get some rest; you're going to need it."

Chloe sighed, and shook her head. "I'm starting to think we're jinxed or something." She took a quick look at her watch. "Damn, it's nearly 4:00 already. I have to get the dance monkey to work." She disengaged her hand from Sara's, who let it drop comfortably back onto Chloe's knee. She started the engine again, and before putting the car into gear, took one last look at Sara, who was now sitting back in her seat, a dejected sad smile on her face.

"Hey, Sara?" Chloe said, as she started the car, and began to fol-low the turnaround of Marcy's driveway back out to Route 20.

Sara rubbed Chloe's knee. "Hmm?" she said as the car halted, Chloe looking both ways, waiting for a break in the traffic so she could pull out.

"I love you," Chloe said simply, and accelerated the car onto the road.

It was more than a few moments before Chloe could turn her head and catch the reaction to her first-time declaration. When she did, Chloe was very surprised. Not by the gentle smile gracing Sara's face, but by the tears she saw softly welling in her eyes.

Part XVII:
I've Got a Secret

"How about I take you home, or better yet, how about you come home with me?" asked Chloe, her voice betraying the real meaning behind those words.

Sara, seeing that Nelson and Jeanette were patiently waiting for her in Nelson's truck on the far side of the parking lot, waved two fingers at them, a sign that she would be a few minutes. She and Chloe were leaning up against Chloe's car, play practice for the day finally over. Sara carefully studied Chloe's face once again.

"Sounds really good, honey, but I think you should get some rest tonight. You just got back to work today, and you don't need me hanging around getting you more tired," Sara said sincerely.

Chloe plucked at the elbow of Sara's jacket. "I feel much better. I've told you that a dozen times today. I don't think it would hurt—"

Sara interrupted her. "Now, listen, someone has to look out for your welfare, and I've elected myself to that position." She let her voice drop to a lower tone. "I want you fully recovered and good as new."

Chloe's bit of tiredness showed when she replied, irritated, "My throat's fine, the aches are gone, I've been pretty much sleeping non-stop for the last four days, I did nothing today but sit around at work and here." She heard the crankiness in her voice, and tried to lighten it. "I miss you, Sara. I just want to spend a little time alone with you. I haven't seen you since Tuesday, and I need some alone time with you."

Sara pushed back her natural inclination to want to lean in and kiss Chloe for her words. She gathered her wits, and said in a commanding, no arguments tone, "Not tonight, Chloe. I want you to get more rest, Dr. Sara's orders." She reached and quickly stroked Chloe's arm, and gave her an apologetic smile. "I miss you too." She looked over at Nelson's truck again, and then turned back to Chloe. "Gotta go. Now go home and get better, I'll call you later." She pinched the end of Chloe's nose, and giving her one last smile, strode off across the parking lot.

Chloe was feeling very testy now because Sara hadn't let her get her way and Chloe wasn't one to accept defeat easily. She had lied to Sara, her body did ache, but not from the lingering effects of her illness. When Chloe had been feeling her worst, earlier this week, her sickness had effectively muted any physical longings she was harboring. Now that she was feeling better, and wasn't concentrating on all of the symptoms that had plagued her, her body was taking Chloe's mental longings for Sara, and multiplying them into physical urges that were becoming more and more distracting with every minute that passed. Even though Chloe was working in the theater this afternoon, and Sara was down the long hallway in the gymnasium, Chloe swore she could feel her physical presence from that distance. She felt as if their bodies were calling to each other. It appeared to Chloe that she was the only one feeling these stirrings. She felt rejected by Sara's cautious refusal to spend the evening together. Chloe got into her car, and started it up. *She apparently doesn't miss me the way I miss her. I couldn't make it any plainer, I was practically rubbing myself on her at some points today, and she didn't react at all.* Chloe watched the pickup truck leave the parking lot. *Maybe we had too much time together already this week. Maybe this is her way of telling me she needs her space.* Chloe growled aloud, and then let out a small laugh when she realized it sounded very much like the growl Sara made when she was frustrated about something. *I'm growly now. Great!* She put the car into gear, and headed home.

Chloe changed into a comfortable pair of sweatpants, doffed her bra, and pulled a T-shirt over her head. She ate a small dinner of leftovers, did her dishes, and walked through each room of her already clean, neat house, straightening things that really didn't need straightening. She thought several times that she wanted to call Sara, but it was only over an hour since they had parted, and Chloe was getting increasingly irritated with herself for obsessing about her. The more she tried to stop thinking about her, the more she did think about her. *Christ, I'm turning into a needy bitch.* She thought briefly about releasing some of her pent-up frustration by taking matters into her own hands, but for some reason, that idea didn't appeal to her. She was idly plumping the throw pillows on her couch when she began to laugh again. *I'm feeling up the pillows, for God's sake. I've lost it.* Her giggle was interrupted by a knock on the front door.

Chloe jumped up from the couch, and looked out her peephole onto her front porch, expecting to see Marcy standing there. Instead, she saw a distorted view of a blue-eyed, dark-haired woman grinning right at the location of the peephole. Chloe's heart leapt; she threw open the door, grabbed Sara, who had already opened the screen door and was standing inside of it, and hauled her inside her home. Sara was grinning slyly, but the look was lost on Chloe, who was simultaneously pulling Sara's head down to hers, and shutting the door behind her. Chloe's lips were seeking Sara's even before the door clicked shut. The momentum of Chloe's attack pushed Sara up against the door, and Chloe took this opportunity to start climbing all over her like a jungle gym. Chloe had eight hands, three mouths, four legs, fifty fingers, and they were all over Sara, all at once.

Whatever clever greeting Sara had in mind when she had decided to surprise the small librarian was immediately forgotten in the fury of the redhead's assault. Chloe began an endless moan, which called to Sara's senses, and the moaning became a duet. Chloe's hands found their rounded targets and latched on. Then her lips stopped their wandering and centered and locked onto Sara's mouth, forcing an insistent tongue deep within, so hard and so strong that Sara felt her ears ringing from the sheer forcefulness of it. Sara's hand, still clutching onto keys, somehow found her jacket pocket, and dropped them in. Both hands were now freed and Chloe was sucking mightily and rhythmically on her tongue, driving her half crazy. Sara popped one eye open, and quickly tried to survey the room. Her hands went to Chloe's rounded butt, swiftly lifted her, and started walking them haltingly toward the sofa. Once there, never breaking their kiss, Sara bent her knees and deposited Chloe onto her back, following down with her until—

The phone rang. And rang. And rang. Chloe's erotic moans continued, feeling the weight of Sara's body settling down on top of her. The answering machine picked up as Sara was nudging a knee between Chloe's thighs and settling her hip high into the apex between them.

The machine in the kitchen, set on loud volume so it could be heard throughout the house, boomed with the sound of Marcy's voice. "Chloe? Pick up. It's Marcy. I need to talk to you."

Sara could feel the heat emanating onto her hip from where it settled between Chloe's legs. Chloe had taken a breather from the kiss, and was running her tongue up Sara's neck, and reveling in the position of Sara's hipbone. Sara's hand was under the bottom of her T-shirt, stroking a path ever higher over the smooth skin of Chloe's stomach.

"Chloe, dammit, pick up. It's important. I mean it. I know you're there." The answering machine clicked off.

Sara's hand had just made contact with a newly peaked portion of Chloe's body, and her fingertips lightly caressed it. Chloe arched up into Sara's hand, her moans increasing in volume when she heard the heated growl that slid from Sara's throat when she made that heavenly contact. A shot of heat traveled down both their bodies and settled, warming them below their waists. Chloe's hands settled in Sara's dark hair, pulling her in for another kiss, and Sara's other hand began tugging at Chloe's T-shirt, pulling it up higher so her hand could join its mate in fully exploring Chloe's breasts.

Ring. Pant! Ring. Groan! Ring.

"Dammit, Chloe, I don't have time for this. Pick up. It's an emergency!"

Chloe gasped for air, placed her hands on Sara's shoulders, and pushed a little as Sara simultaneously lifted. Chloe whined, "I don't believe this!" She disentangled regretfully from Sara, and stood up, rather shakily, straightened her T-shirt and gave Sara a disbelieving look, which Sara returned. Sara sat up on the couch, and watched as Chloe made her way into the kitchen and picked up the phone.

"Marcy," she said breathlessly, "What's wrong?"

Marcy, irritated but thankful Chloe had finally answered, huffed, "You name it. Listen, I need to talk to you. Now!"

Chloe could hear the deflated tone of Marcy's voice, and did her best to concentrate on it, rather than the feeling between her legs, and the cause of that feeling, who was waiting for her on the couch.

Chloe hesitated, and then her better self took over. "Sure. You want to come by? Sara's here, you could—"

"I want to talk to you, not Sara. No offense, but just you. You think you could come to my house? I'm not feeling my best."

"Give me a half hour. Can't you tell me?"

"No. See you soon. And, Chloe? Thanks." Marcy hung up.

Chloe dropped the phone into place, and sighed, staring at it. *She's my best friend and she needs me.* She turned and saw that Sara's eyes were watching her from the couch. Chloe ran a hand through her hair, and gave Sara a small smile as she walked back into the living room, and dropped back onto the couch. She propped her head onto Sara's shoulder, and let out a heavy, frustrated sigh. Sara dropped an arm around Chloe, and pulled her close. They stared, straight ahead, not focusing on anything but trying to get past their own disappointment.

Sara finally broke the silence. "Well?"

Chloe rubbed her head on Sara's shoulder. "Jinxed."

Sara let out a growl.

Chloe smiled ruefully, and took Sara's hand into her own. "Yeah, growly. Me too. I have to go over there. She needs to talk to me about something. She sounds really upset."

Sara lifted a concerned eyebrow, and then drooped her shoulders. *I'm going to die, and my obituary is going to say, "She died of unnatural causes. Terminal frustration."*

Chloe ran her hand across Sara's cheek. "Look, I'm sorry. I'll run you home, and then..."

Sara said, with a chuckle, "No need. Here." She reached in her jacket pocket, and pulled out a plastic card. "Got it this afternoon before play practice. Dave took me."

Chloe took the card in her hand and examined it. Then she surprised Sara by lifting her head off her shoulder, and placing a good-sized punch there instead. "Bitch. Nobody has a good driver's license picture. Nobody. This is great!" She laughed. "Look at that wonderful smile on your face! Can we get an 8 X 10 of this made? What made you smile like that?" Chloe asked wonderingly.

"The girl who was taking the pictures looked exactly like Drew Barrymore." Sara laughed when that statement brought another light punch from Chloe.

"Bitch!" Chloe's mind turned over and grasped the reality of another situation. "So, this afternoon, when you were being so nonchalant after play practice, when I was throwing my lustful self at you, and you were all calm."

"Yeah. That was sneaky, huh? I wanted to surprise you, and get you back for that mono scare on Tuesday."

Chloe handed the card back to Sara, and placed a soft kiss on her cheek. "I'm the Pope. I forgive you, my child." Chloe sighed, yet again, put her feet more firmly onto the floor, and stood up. She looked down at Sara. "I'm really glad you're driving again. Now there won't be any more excuses."

"Yeah," agreed Sara, looking into those green eyes that made her feel boneless. "Except for our family, our friends, high school students, town gossips, broken down cars and natural disasters."

"Don't remind me. How'd you get here?"

Sara stood up; she knew that Chloe had to get over to Marcy's house. "Nelson's truck. But I think Dave and I are going car shopping tomorrow. I want one of my own."

Chloe grabbed her coat off the hook, put it on, and grabbed her car keys from the small table by the door. She looked up into Sara's softly shining eyes, and got lost for a moment. "Get something sturdy. A Volvo, a Subaru or even a Honda."

Sara returned her gaze. "Hell, no! I'm gonna get me a babe magnet of a car. I do have a rep to preserve." Her eyes twinkled, and she dropped her head to give Chloe another breath-stealing kiss.

Chloe murmured, "Listen you, you have yet to magnetize this babe. Try and keep your priorities straight, okay?"

One more kiss, and Sara said, "Yeah. I'll try and keep that in mind."

"Trust me." Marcy called from her kitchen. "You're going to want a beer."

"All right, bring me a beer," Chloe called from the couch in Marcy's living room. She let her eyes travel around the room again, always amazed and amused at the number of colors and patterns the room held. There were paintings, drawings and photographs seemingly covering every square inch of wall space, mostly works of Marcy's own doing. There were mobiles and hanging knotted things coming down from the ceiling. Shelves and tables held smaller objets d'art, sculptures and works in clay, recognizable forms and abstracts. The room, as was the whole house, was a conglomeration of light and dark, swirls and straight lines, and so many harmonious colors that it was eclectic, not garish. This was the house of a romantic, an eccentric, an independent soul, an artist.

Marcy gave Chloe her bottle of beer, and sank down in her usual place at the other end of the couch. She grabbed her pack of cigarettes from her coffee table, lifted a brow, and said to Chloe, "I'm smokin', and don't give me any shit about it tonight."

Chloe knew that Marcy was always very gracious about not smoking when Chloe came over, so she knew something was very wrong. "Okay." She watched Marcy draw one out of her pack, and light it. She sat, patiently, waiting for Marcy to begin.

Marcy sighed, and let out a long stream of satisfying smoke. She tossed her lighter onto the coffee table, and then looked Chloe straight on.

"I called the doctor for my flu results after play practice," she began, her voice atonal. "Then I drove around. And around. Then I came here and called you."

Chloe's stomach and heart both did a little turning. She kept her gaze fixed on Marcy, who took a few more puffs and ran a hand through her hair before continuing.

"I'm pregnant." She looked at Chloe's expression of surprise. "Yeah, me, too. I'm about six weeks. I don't have the flu, he said I may be a little run down, but mostly it's been morning sickness that's been mowing me down for the last week or so." She watched as Chloe silently reached over, and extracted a cigarette for herself from Marcy's pack. "Help yourself. I plan on chain-smoking every last one I have, which is, I think, around a pack and a half. I have to quit. For me, and the baby."

Chloe blew out her own smoke, and looked at her best friend. "So, what are you thinking, about this?"

"Well, considering the initial shock of it, which I'm still dealing with, and the thought that there is something growing down here," Marcy's hand traveled down and rubbed her belly. "I'd say I'm doing pretty shitty, considering." She let out a rueful laugh, and shook her head at Chloe. "Sorry you weren't here to do the blue stick test with me this time. That way we both could be sharing the shock and the joy." She spoke sarcastically, and then looked away from Chloe.

Chloe remembered that time. Marcy restlessly pacing, swearing up and down she didn't want children. Raising her voice to the ceiling promising to give up sex if she wasn't with child. Marcy's relief at the negative results of that test was so joyous and intense, Chloe had thought her longtime friend might actually be seducing her, what with the way she was holding on to Chloe, rubbing her in relief and abandon, kissing her friend's face. Chloe had finally settled her friend down, and had a small laugh at the thought that all of the physical contact with Marcy was actually turning her on a little bit.

Chloe took a long drink of her beer and asked, "Does Dave know?" Then she stopped, and before she could stop herself, she asked, seriously, "It is Dave's, right?" She swore at herself for even saying something like that, but as well as she thought she knew Marcy, there was always that certain unpredictability about her.

Marcy was insulted for just a mere moment, and then blew it off. "Yeah, it's Dave's. I may like men, Chloe, but I usually stick to one at a time. And no, he doesn't know. I haven't made up my mind yet as to what I'm going to do." Marcy looked at Chloe. "Funny thing is, I should be talking to him right now, not you. But when I found out, you're the first person that I thought of, not Dave. There's something intrinsically wrong with that line of thinking. I think. Who knows?"

Chloe stubbed out her cigarette in the ashtray, knowing it wasn't the first, nor last one she'd be smoking tonight. Marcy looked at her, and asked, "What do you think? About me being pregnant?"

Chloe didn't know what Marcy was fishing for here, what kind of statement Marcy wanted from Chloe. "Well," she began slowly, and searched in Marcy's brown eyes, "I'm not going to be happy about this unless you are, Marse. That baby," she said as she pointed at Marcy's abdomen, "will be either equally as loved or equally as not desired by me, in support of what you want. I'm not going to talk you into my agenda. I've tried that before with smaller, inconsequential matters, and it's never worked. So, I support you and any of the decisions you have to make. You come first, Marse. I'm not going to judge you. I may try and stick my two cents in, but no, you always come first with me." She smiled at her little speech of solidarity, and was pleased to see the relieved smile Marcy directed her way.

Marcy lit another cigarette, and picked up her bottle of water. "I know this won't come as any surprise to you. I'm not sure that I want to have it." She took a sip of her water, and then looked at Chloe. "Actually, my first reaction is to not have it, and do whatever is necessary just to stop it now." Marcy frowned, and pursed her lips. "What a great thing for me to say, huh? No joy in Marcy about this bit of good news. I must sound like an absolute asshole creep."

Chloe leaned over toward her friend sitting so dejectedly on her end of the couch, and stroked her arm. "No, Marse, I understand. I've known you since the third grade, and not one time, never once, did you ever mention the desire to have mother listed in your resumé. All you've ever said is how you had no desire to have children. So, no, your reaction to this doesn't surprise me in the slightest. Don't beat yourself up about it."

Marcy had so many alien emotions swirling in her brain at this moment; she didn't have the first clue as to what she thought. "I know this, I'm going to call and make an appointment for counseling about my options. I want you to go with me."

"What about Dave?"

Marcy knew that this was going to come up, and knew that Chloe was going to hate what she was about to say. "I'm not telling Dave. Not until I have to."

"And when is 'until you have to,' Marse?"

"I'm going to tell Dave, if, and only if, I decide to actually have the baby." *Here it comes.*

"You mean, you won't tell him before, you won't tell him if you want to abort? You aren't going to make these decisions together?" Chloe's voice was becoming louder and more annoyed with each word that came out of her mouth. When she saw Marcy silently agreeing with Chloe's statements, she got pissed. "This is something entirely different than me supporting you as to whether you want to have a child or not, Marcy. This is someone who should be involved in the process, I mean, he was there to help start this chain of events, right?"

Marcy took on a patient air. "He'll want me to have the baby. He'll want me to marry him."

"Well, that's where you two are headed, isn't it? Engagement number six for you?"

"I don't want to marry him."

Chloe blinked, and couldn't find anything to say.

"I like him too much to marry him. Or should I say, put myself in the position of promising to marry him. I don't want him to be Mr. Dumped at the Altar number six."

"Do you love him? Are you in love with him?"

"I think so. I know he's in love with me. He's said so, many times. Frankly, I've been getting a little worried lately that he might be thinking of popping the question. And now this." She threw her hands in the air. "I like him, I love him, and dammit, I even love his family. I think the world of Nelson, I can't tell you how glad I am that he's nearly a grown-up, and not a child that I would have deal with. I couldn't do that. Hell, I even love Sara." Marcy squinted her eyes at Chloe. "Don't you ever tell her that either. I have the upper hand with that woman, and I don't ever want to lose it."

Chloe had to smile at that. But the smile soon disappeared. "Marcy, it's just not fair of you not to allow Dave into the decision-making process. It's not right."

"I know it; you're right. But I look at it this way. If I decide to have an abortion, he never has to know that a baby existed. We can just go on from there. If I decide to have the baby, well, I know he'll be pleased, and want to do the right thing by me. That part is negotiable. Either way, I get to keep Dave, no matter what my decision is." Marcy, for the first time, looked like she was going to start crying. "If I decide to have an abortion, and he knows, he'll fight me about it, and we'll end up not together. He'll leave me if I have an abortion. I don't know if I could deal with that."

"So if you have an abortion, without him ever knowing you were pregnant, you two can just go on your merry way? There's something wrong with that, Marcy, it involves lies. Big, big, bad lies. And if you ever do grow up, and really want a real relationship with him, and that lie ever became known, you'd lose him anyway."

"At this point, I'm not decided on anything. I want to go get some counseling, I want to talk to you, and I just want to think." Marcy sighed, and reached for her cigarettes again. "Stupid. This is my last night of smoking, just in case, just in case I decide to have it. I have to torture myself even more, giving up my beloved smoking, on an if."

Chloe decided to help Marcy on her way. "Gimme another one. I'm going to sound like Kathleen Turner tomorrow anyway, at this rate." She watched, and smiled, as Marcy lit two cigarettes, as in old movies, and handed her one.

Marcy stood up. "You want another beer, too? You may as well ruin your recovery all in one night."

You don't know the half of it. I was just on my way to having an exhausting evening with Sara when you called me, friend. Oh my God. Sara. "Marcy!" yelled Chloe needlessly, as Marcy was already stepping back into the living room.

"What?"

"Sara."

"What about her?"

"We—you, I—somebody has got to tell her about this!"

"Um, Chloe, I told you it's Dave's, not Sara's."

"She's his sister."

"I noticed the resemblance."

"No, I mean, we're this big extended family group. I mean, if she doesn't know, and finds out that I knew without letting her know, then I don't know, I just don't know how she'd react."

"You're my best friend. You're keeping your word to me to keep it in confidence. What's not to understand?" Marcy couldn't hide the impatience in her voice.

"She's my lover, or, let me amend that, we have big plans so she will be my lover. She's my prelover. She hates any kind of manipulation. She likes everything out on the table. She'd never forgive me for that."

"I don't want her to know. I'm sorry, Chlo, but I'm afraid I don't trust her not to speak to Dave about it."

"You don't appreciate the kind of position that puts me in?"

"I understand that you want her to be Mrs. Donahue some day, or you want to be her Mrs. D'Amico. Chloe, calm down. I haven't made any decisions just yet. When I have, I'll talk to you about it, and we can decide how you can deal with Sara. I'm sorry, but she just isn't my biggest concern right now. She's a bystander."

Chloe regretfully decided to quit thinking about Sara for the moment, and direct her attention to where it was needed most. They talked long into the evening, until Chloe finally had to extricate herself, and go home and get some rest. They hugged a long time, both smelling like an ashtray full of cigarette butts.

Dave looked up from his newspaper, very surprised to see Sara shrugging out of her coat. She tossed Nelson's truck keys onto the table to the left of him.

"Didn't expect to be seeing you so soon, Sis," Dave said, seeing the tired look on her face. She crossed the kitchen, and opened the fridge and pulled out a bottle of beer. She held it up to him, and he nodded. She retrieved a second, and sat down in the chair across from him, and he folded close the paper while she opened both bottles, and then handed him one.

She sighed, took a very long swig, and sighed again. "I'm not meant to have sex, dear brother. I am doomed to eternally be a frustrated, nearly half-crazed lesbian, never to achieve the release I'm seeking." She had to grin a little bit at the look of discomfort that passed her brother's face. "Oh, sure, Dave, we can talk about your sex life as easy as talking about the weather, but, let me bring up my lack of a sex life, and you get all uncomfortable." She laughed. "What exactly is your problem? Can't picture two women doing anything together, or is it just because I'm your sister?"

Dave harrumphed, and even blushed a little, which for him, was rare. "Male or female, a guy isn't supposed to think about his sister having sex with anyone. I prefer to think that you and Chloe just kiss a lot."

"Well, Dave, that's not far from the truth," Sara snorted. "That's about all we have done. And I think I'm going to explode from repressed desires that should be pressing forward with abandon."

Dave deflected the conversation into another direction, without being rude and totally dismissing the topic. "So, why aren't you over there now, pressing your advantage?"

Sara had thought about Marcy's call on her short ride home, and had decided to see how much Dave knew before revealing anything that had transpired earlier at Chloe's house. "Chloe got sort of an emergency call, had to go see about something."

Dave rubbed his chin. "Is everything all right, what's the emergency?"

Sara knew right then that Dave was unaware of any problems concerning Marcy, and if he and the artist had been fighting, his demeanor would be much different than it was now. Sara had just assumed that Marcy's demanding call had something to do with a lovers' quarrel between Dave and Marcy. But that wasn't how it was playing out now, in Sara's head. *I wonder what the problem is. I shouldn't mention it to Dave; it's not my business. Marcy would have called him if she wanted him to know, or help out. This is something she wanted to share only with Chloe. I hope Chloe calls me later and fills me in.* Caught up in her thoughts, she didn't notice that Dave was still waiting for a reply to his question until he tapped his beer bottle against hers.

"Earth to Sara. Is everything all right in Chloeland?"

"Hmm? Oh, yeah, just some library stuff she needed to go take care of."

Dave was sure there was more to it than Sara was letting on, but let it go. He wasn't a particularly inquisitive man; he preferred to deal with things as they came along. Except for the one thing that had being weighing on his mind lately, and he wanted to talk to his sister about it.

"How's it feel to be driving again? Find anyone to drag race down Route 5 with you?"

Sara laughed, relieved that Dave had dropped any further inquiries about Chloe. "No, not tonight, but in Nelson's pickup truck, I doubt I could outrun Doris Raeburn's mouth at full speed." She and Dave both shared a grin over the mental image that placed in their heads. "Hey Dave, you got some time you can free up for me tomorrow morning, or afternoon? Thought I could get you to go car hunting with me in Erie."

Dave clicked his beer bottle on hers again. "Sure! And while we're shopping for you, you can help me with a little something that I want to do."

"What?"

"You'll see. A guy has to have some secrets, doesn't he? You women can't possibly be the keepers of them all."

Part XVIII:
Of Mice and Magnets

"Uh-huh," Chloe mused, as she walked around the large vehicle parked in her driveway. Sara was standing away from the car, gazing lovingly up and down the exterior. The car was an old but lovingly cared for classic, with a highly buffed cherry-red exterior and an extravagant abundance of shiny chrome. "Uh-huh," said Chloe again, not knowing quite what to say.

"Isn't she a beaut?" Sara sighed, as she ran her hand sensually down the tail fin on the back end of the car.

"Uh-huh," repeated Chloe, as she leaned in the open driver's side window and her eyes took in the old dashboard, replete with oversize buttons, dials and gauges. She noticed that the steering wheel had a manual shift connected to it. The bench seats in front and back were covered with a blood red material and over that were semitransparent plastic seat covers that almost resembled bubble wrap. Chloe pulled her head out, and turned to face Sara, who was intently rubbing away an invisible mar on the top of the car. "What, exactly, is it?"

Sara turned, folded her arms, and leaned against the car, albeit it very gently. "It's a 1963 Mercury Comet Cruiser. Completely restored! Only 63,000 miles on her." Sara, obviously very proud, leaned and looked pointedly at the tires, and waited for Chloe to do the same before she continued, proudly, "Look! Whitewalls!"

"Uh-huh. Pretty sharp." Chloe was trying to put some enthusiasm into her voice. *I think my grandmother had one of these.*

Sara finally caught on to the decidedly unexcited tone of Chloe's remarks. "You don't like her?" Sara blinked, dismayed and feeling a little hurt.

Chloe thought about it for a moment before she replied. Hesitating, she began, "She's really pretty. And really old. I was kind of expecting you to pull in here with, oh, I don't know, something that actually runs on unleaded gas?" Her lips turned up in an amused smile.

"Well, I was looking at Jeeps, Blazers and some Acuras, but I wasn't getting, you know, that feeling," Sara uttered defensively. *How can Chloe not love this car?* "And frankly, I was pretty bored with the whole process. Then this Ford salesman said he had a small collection of classic cars out in a building behind the dealership, and well, we just ended up out there and—"

"And you got your babe magnet." Chloe chuckled, as her disbelief slowly was replaced by cheerful resignation.

Sara's body assumed a more rigid posture. "No, I bought a classic." She noticed the large grin on Chloe's face, and she finished up, grinning right back at her, "Babe magnet!"

"Uh-huh." Chloe peeked in the window once more. "Well, I gotta admit, I do like the bench seat. Has great potential." She smiled, and wiggled her eyebrows suggestively at Sara.

"You want to try it out after dance practice today?" Sara purred, somewhat relieved that the ever-practical Chloe was being accepting of her purchase. "I'll let you play with the knobs." She ducked away from a jab that Chloe threw her way.

"C'mon inside and have a cup of coffee before we go spend our day do-si-do-ing, you hedonist." Chloe just loved it when Sara's voice took on that luscious low quality.

"I am not a hedonist," Sara protested, as she happily followed Chloe into her house, her eyes lovingly glued to Chloe's posterior.

Once inside, both women turned and faced each other, their glances unmistakably exhibiting the pleasure they shared at being alone. Chloe gratefully leaned into Sara's arms, and they shared a kiss that demonstrated their dismay at being apart since Thursday. Sara tightened her hold around Chloe, and deepened the kiss. Chloe responded with a moan, and let her hands drop to Sara's firm backside, sliding her hands into her jeans pockets. They continued, and then Chloe abruptly pulled away when she felt the deliberate path that Sara's hands were taking on her body.

"Whoa. We only have a half hour before we have to leave for the school, tiger." Chloe's heart was pounding like she had just finished a 1000-meter sprint, and took the medal.

"I can accomplish a lot in a half hour," huffed Sara, searching Chloe's eyes.

"Well, I'd rather not go there until we have real time to explore." Chloe sighed, and laid her head on Sara's chest.

"Yeah, you're right. But keep the thought, okay?" Sara echoed Chloe's sigh.

Chloe disengaged from Sara's arms, and gave her a shy bat of her eyelashes. "Like I can think of anything else." She grabbed Sara's hand and tugged her into the kitchen. She poured them coffee, doctored it up the way they liked it, and sat down at the kitchen table. Sara pulled another chair, close to Chloe, so she could keep within reach of her. They held hands while they conversed.

"Not exactly a practical car for around here, Sara." Chloe blew on her coffee. "I mean, I know it hasn't snowed in a few weeks, but you never know." She ran a fingertip delicately up Sara's arm while she took a sip from the cup. "Let's see, hmm, no front-wheel drive, no air conditioning."

Sara responded, up to the task of defending her purchase. "260 V-8 engine, no rust, two owners, original AM radio."

Chloe smiled into her cup. "Can't wait to see you try and navigate it around the potholes in Dave's driveway."

Sara continued, unfazed, "Two door, shift on wheel, cherry red." She scooted her chair even closer to Chloe's.

Chloe, noticing the move, shifted her chair until she and Sara were shoulder to shoulder. "Leaded gas, right? Can you even buy leaded gas anymore?" Her voice took on a decidedly smoky tone.

Sara leaned, maximizing their contact, and dropped her voice in tandem with Chloe's, "Be glad it's not a convertible." Her eyes met the swirling green of Chloe's. "Cherry red bench seats."

Chloe, caught up in Sara's intense blue eyes, repeated, "Cherry red bench seats."

They shoved their coffee cups out of the way, and heads leaned down and upturned, respectively, so they could share another long and heated kiss.

Sara pulled away, eyes alive. "Who would think that bench seats could sound so erotic?" She smiled.

Chloe licked her lips, and pushed against Sara's shoulder. "We could be talking brake linings, and I think I'd be getting hot and bothered."

Sara nodded, and playfully ran her finger down the bridge of Chloe's nose. "Don't worry, hon, I plan on taking good care of her. No winter driving for my magnet. I'll probably get something more—"

"Practical?" nudged Chloe.

"Well, I was going to say boring, but yeah, more practical in the fall."

"You equate practical with boring, do you?" challenged the red-head.

Sara knew that Chloe was definitely not talking about cars now, and didn't fall into her trap. "Practical can be exciting, too. I was looking at a Toyota 4-Runner, that had some very appealing characteristics, too."

"Nice lines?" Chloe's voice practically drew an hourglass figure in Sara's imaginative mind.

"Wonderful form for such a practical vehicle." Sara moved in, and her lips met Chloe's again.

When that kiss finally ended, they joined hands again. Sara sighed happily. "Well, enough car talk. There's only so much I can take." She smiled, and nipped Chloe's nose. "So, let's see. What's up with Marcy?"

Chloe was expecting this eventual line of questioning with Sara, and she had prepared an answer for it. "She's okay. She was panicking about something the other night, needed to sound me out about it. That's all." *I hate this. Misleading her.*

Sara heard the 'that's all' at the end of Chloe's sentence, and recognized it as a stop sign for other questions she might have. *Something's going on with Marcy, and Chloe isn't going to tell me. I'm not sure I like this.* Sara bit her bottom lip, and tried to decide whether to push Chloe for other information. *No. I might not like it but, no. But it hurts to know I can't be trusted or included.* Sara, not able to come up with anything better, just nodded, and moved a little away from Chloe, her unconscious reaction to the rejection she was feeling.

Chloe noticed the almost imperceptible way that Sara drew away from her, but she knew if she said anything at all, it would draw them into further conversation about Marcy. She hated not being able to share this with Sara. *I know it must hurt, I just can't...dammit all, Marcy, you and your secrets.* Chloe straightened up in her seat, and changed the subject, further emphasizing the end to any talk about Marcy. "So, you and Dave had brother and sister day out, huh? What did you guys end up doing, besides buying the Comet?"

It was Sara's turn to do a little maneuvering to avoid relaying information that she had promised to keep in confidence. "Well, after driving around Erie and looking at every blasted late-model gas-hog SUV in existence, and then buying the Comet, getting the registration at a notary, getting insurance," Sara finished the rest of her coffee, giving her time to think. *And Dave surprising me by dragging me into jewelry stores, so I could help him pick out an engagement ring for Marcy.* "Well, then we drove around, and ended up going out to dinner. We then made a stop at Stan's Bar pretty late last night."

Chloe's eyes widened. "Karaoke night again?"

"We didn't stay long, but..." Sara blushed and looked away.

"But?" Chloe grinned.

"Well, the crowd did kind of encourage Dave and me into singing Prince's "Little Red Corvette."" Sara laughed, remembering the crowd's enthusiastic reception. She glanced at the still-grinning Chloe. "Seemed kind of appropriate, given the circumstances of the day."

Chloe pushed her chair back, and grabbed their empty coffee cups and put them into the sink. "Dammit. I miss all the good stuff. And Dave sang? With you?" she said, surprised.

"Well, yeah, Miss Lips, as you may recall, Mr. Kisses has quite a pleasant voice." *I could still strangle him.*

Chloe reddened at the memory of Dave crooning to her. "Well, yeah, that he does." She smirked, and moved over to the now-standing Sara. She wrapped her arms around Sara's neck. "Now, I wonder if I can convince you to give a command performance for me later today." She raised her brow, and waited for Sara's reaction to her shrouded invitation.

Sara pulled Chloe in, taking careful aim for those enticing lips again. "Oh, yeah." Just before their lips met, Sara softly growled her intentions while looking into Chloe's eyes. "I'm gonna try and tame your little red love machine."

Marcy couldn't help but get the feeling that Sara was giving her the once-over through her dark tinted sunglasses while Marcy was examining the flashy red Comet out in the parking lot of the school. Sara's cool eyes behind the darkened lenses were surely sizing her up, scrutinizing her, and Marcy was doing her best to ignore the uncomfortable feeling that seemed to permeate her skin. Marcy pushed the feeling down, and wryly commented, "Why do I hear "Greased Lightning" in my head when I look at this thing?" She caught the amused expression on Sara's face, and then looked away. "Won't they allow you to drive something from this century, Sara?" She snuck a peek at the softly giggling Chloe, who was witnessing the teasing interaction. "Chloe, it looks like you're going to spend your Sundays at classic car shows and tooling up and down Route 5 at fifteen miles per hour. And going to sock hops?" Marcy danced a sober, and thus terrible, version of the Twist.

Chloe winced and smiled. "More like eight-five miles per hour." She laughed in Sara's direction, giving her a wink. Sara had just driven them from Chloe's house to the school in what felt like less than two minutes. "I think my bladder and other vital organs are still back at my house."

Sara, sticking out her tongue, drolly replied, "It's not the final destination that matters, it's how fast you can get there."

Marcy shot back, "And how many senior citizens you can mow down along the way?"

Chloe leaned in to her friend, and whispered in Marcy's ear, "Please, oh, please, don't mention the words fuzzy dice."

Marcy clapped a hand over her mouth, and spoke through it, just loud enough for Chloe to hear. "Oh, it's such a temptation. I wanna, I wanna."

More students were arriving at the school, and making their way over to check out the red automobile. While Sara proudly engaged them in conversation, Chloe and Marcy began walking toward the entrance of the school. Chloe laid a hand lightly on Marcy's shoulder. "So, how are you doing today? What did you end up doing last night?"

Marcy walked them over to a small bench near the doors, and sat down. Chloe sat down beside her, subtly watching as Sara opened car doors and demonstrated gadgets while the appreciative students looked on.

Marcy elbowed Chloe in acknowledgment of where Chloe's eyes were fixed. "She's a fine looking woman, Chloe. Even I can see that." She grinned at the embarrassed pinking of Chloe's cheeks. "I stayed home, did some art work, told Dave I had a headache. End of Friday's story." Chloe turned and looked cautiously at her. Marcy set her face. "No, nothing new, and no, I don't want to think about it, or talk about it today. Got it?"

"Got it," Chloe answered.

There was still ten minutes or so before everyone would go into the school to begin rehearsals. Marcy surreptitiously looked around, and pulled out her pack of cigarettes from her purse.

Chloe raised a disapproving eyebrow at her as Marcy lit one. "I thought you were through with that. Plus, geez, Marcy, this is school property!" *How Doris Raeburn of me!*

"You gonna tell on me, Miss Prissy? Today, I don't give a rat's." Marcy blew out a satisfied plume of smoke. "And I'm going to go get a box of those patchy things right after rehearsal today. I can only wear them for two weeks, God help me. The doctor said it would jump start me to be a, oh my lord, a former smoker!"

Chloe just shrugged, and pointedly turned her gaze to Sara again. "She asked me what was up with you, and I didn't give her a straight answer. I think she felt hurt that I was so evasive." Chloe watched as Sara laughed at the six students who had somehow squeezed themselves into her new purchase. Although Chloe couldn't see her eyes because of the sunglasses Sara wore, the tilt of her head and the flash of white teeth in her direction let Chloe know that the smile was just for her. Chloe tittered. "Look at her, six feet of adolescent joy. You'd think she was sixteen again with her first car."

"Yeah, we sure got us a nice pair of D'Amicos, didn't we, Chloe? Sara's tall, gorgeous, mysterious, and cranky. And Dave, well, he's..." Marcy choked off a laugh, and rolled her eyes at the bemused face of her friend. "Tall, gorgeous, funny. And as simple as an unbuttered pancake."

Both friends began laughing at Marcy's dead-on assessment of the D'Amico siblings. "Uh-oh," warned Chloe, between snorts. "Here comes Miss Cranky now. Straighten up!" Both Marcy and

Chloe immediately sat up, and tried mightily to wipe their guilty grins off their faces.

Sara slowly flipped up her sunglasses, squinting at the two friends in turn. She began interrogating them. "Uh-huh? Are you planning to overthrow the government over here? Or thinking of devious ways to talk me into buying a Taurus? I got it, you're trying to remember who's a Justin and who isn't? I have trouble with that myself sometimes." She grinned and looked back toward her car, which was still surrounded by inquisitive students. She gestured for Chloe to move down and make room for her on the small bench.

Marcy leaned across Chloe, who had to sit back, and flippantly said to Sara, "No, Chloe was just telling me what she has planned for you later today."

Sara leaned across Chloe, too, effectively sandwiching her awkwardly between the actress and the artist. "Do tell! Did she mention anything about Little Debbie's and Vicks Vapo-Rub?"

Marcy brought her head even closer to Sara's, squeezing Chloe even farther back. "Nope. Sorry to disappoint you. It was more along the lines of her dressing up like Evita Peron. And then you—"

Marcy didn't get a chance to finish her sentence, because a quite flustered Chloe pried her friends apart. "Oh, c'mon, Marcy, that was five years ago!" They all laughed, and Sara lightly squeezed Chloe's thigh. The students were starting to file into the building past them, so all three stood up, and Chloe walked up the steps first. Chloe heard both women behind her snigger, then a soft rendition from her two friends wafted up the hallway from behind her. Her shoulders cringed in an embarrassed reflex.

"Don't cry for me, Ar-gen-tin-a, the truth is, I nev-er left you."

Chloe threw her jacket on the hook by her front door, and smiled as Sara did the same with hers. They stood there a moment, just looking at one another.

Sara, never wavering from her gaze, said, "Turn off your answering machine, Chloe."

Just the edges of Chloe's mouth rose upward. She walked into the kitchen and completed her mission, then returned and leaned in the doorway, looking at Sara, who was standing, waiting, just to the side of Chloe's coffee table. The tall woman hitched her thumbs in her jeans pockets, and looked expectantly at Chloe.

Looks like it's up to me. Chloe leaned a little farther into the archway, and folded her arms. Her smile was inviting and coy. "Answering machine is off. I even turned off the ringer on the phone. Front door is locked, so is the back."

Sara's eyebrows rose, and then dropped, a smile playing across

her lips. "No storms coming. Marcy and Dave, and, I think, Nelson,
are out for the evening." She raised her eyebrows again, just for
emphasis. "Have any late fees you need to go collect?"

"Not tonight," said Chloe, not moving from her spot. "Have any
greens that need watered?"

"Not tonight," echoed Sara, admiring the pink glow gracing
Chloe's features.

"Any ideas about what you'd like to do this evening?" Chloe's
voice was low, and teasing.

"More than a few," Sara replied, head tilting to one side. She
looked Chloe up and down very slowly, and then stopped to catch
Chloe's eyes again. "How about you? Any ideas? I'm open to sugges-
tions."

"Well, I thought maybe..." grinned Chloe, whose body was getting quite warm from the purposeful examination Sara had just given
it. Her eyes never leaving Sara's, she walked over to her near the coffee table, carefully extracted a hand from Sara's pocket, and held it
lightly in hers. Chloe flipped it over, and lightly ran her thumb down
it, and then tracing the arced lines across the soft palm. She raised
the hand, palm toward her, and softly kissed it. She looked up at
Sara, whose eyes were showing a mixture of emotions that Chloe
quite easily understood. Sara ran her palm across Chloe's cheek, and
stepped closer to her, their bodies not quite touching, and she cupped
her cheek, waiting for Chloe to finish her thought. Chloe, still lightly
holding Sara's hand at her face, blinked and nearly trembled at the
light caress. She gazed intently into those darkening blue eyes.
"Maybe I should take you on a tour of the rest of the house?"

"I'd like that," Sara's voice was so low, she barely heard herself
speak. "Where do we start?"

Chloe softly pulled Sara's hand down from her cheek, and intertwined their fingers. Pulling slightly on her arm, Chloe started moving toward the short hallway past the bookcases. Her voice was
serious, ripe with a single-minded purpose. "I thought the bedroom."

Sara felt no need to reply to that as she let Chloe pull her down
the hallway and into the small but cozy bedroom. Even given the
importance of the moment, Sara couldn't help but be staggered when
she saw the bed, with the carved mahogany headboard that climbed
nearly halfway up the wall. Chloe never stopped her gentle pull on
Sara's arm until they were both standing next to the behemoth. Sara
was fascinated with the bed, whose mattress surface seemed to be
even with Chloe's waist. Sara, amused, looked at the bed, and then
met Chloe's eyes. "I thought you were afraid of heights."

Chloe ran her hands up Sara's sides, and then placed them
lightly on Sara's shoulders. "I'll have you to hold on to," she said
firmly, and then smiled. Sara's arms wrapped around her waist, and

pulled Chloe closer to her. Chloe let her arms entwine around Sara's neck, and began to pull the tall woman's head to her for a kiss.

But just as their lips were to meet, Sara spoke. "Uh-uh. First things first." Chloe, just a breath away from the lips she wanted to kiss, felt Sara's hands tug on her shirttail and slowly pulled upwards, trailing her fingers along newly exposed skin as she went along. Chloe's heartbeat increased in proportion to the height that Sara's fingers achieved. Chloe loosened her grasp around Sara's neck, and for a quick moment, their gaze was broken by the necessity of pulling the garment over Chloe's head. After a quick glance, Sara tossed the sweatshirt onto a nearby chair, and with an ever-broadening smile, she bit her bottom lip as she appreciatively pondered the new expanse of skin, of softly delineated cleavage that lay before her. Her breath hitched, and knees usually strong and purposeful now felt slightly weak and unsure. Sara caught the shyness in Chloe's eyes, and ran a hand lightly through the red shagginess of Chloe's hair. "You've got bed head already." She smiled, and took a moment to revel in the softness of Chloe's hair between her fingers.

Chloe closed her eyes at the soft gesture, and then slowly opened them, again locking onto those features of darkening blue that she felt so helpless to escape. Her hands traveled down, and pulled Sara's T-shirt from the waistband of her jeans. Chloe's fingers wafted lightly over Sara's navel, then just as quickly, she tucked two fingers down into the edge of the denim, lightly stroking the skin of Sara's abdomen, then pulling them out again, and taking her time, she deliberately began to roll the T-shirt material upwards. Sara's arms dropped loosely to her sides, and she watched as Chloe carefully rolled and lightly stroked Sara's belly, across her ribcage and then Chloe paused, took a breath, and deftly lifted the rolled cotton just high enough to expose Sara's breasts.

Chloe's eyes lingered over each breast in turn, and she could feel the heat of Sara's gaze as she watched her. Chloe's thumbs, hooked under the T-shirt and holding at heart level, could feel the pronounced thrumming of Sara's heart. Chloe leaned in, and almost, but not quite, let the skin of her cheek graze across a hardening nipple. She repeated this again, and smiled as Sara unconsciously arched toward her, wanting the real contact. Chloe smiled in her denial of this, and turning her head away, she looked up again at Sara, who was now visibly shivering. Chloe pulled even higher on the T-shirt, and the taller woman had to step slightly away from her so she could bend to help in the removal of the clothing. Chloe flipped the shirt to join her sweatshirt on the chair.

"We've got to even things out, don't you think?" said Sara, her voice smoking a path to Chloe's ears. She noticed the slight blush that began to deepen, ever darker, on Chloe's cheeks, eliciting a low chuckle from Sara. Her arms encircled Chloe as she brought her hands to the clasps that held Chloe's bra, and began to unfasten it. "I forgot. You're very shy," Sara whispered, and task efficiently completed, she pulled the loosened straps over Chloe's shoulders, and both women stopped breathing for a moment as defined cleavage gave way to the now fully exposed fullness of breasts. Sara did not tease them, as Chloe had done to her, her desire belaying any notion of restraint. She quickly cupped them with warm hands, and let out a small moan of appreciation at the feel of them. She felt the quick intake of breath that her touch brought from Chloe. Her need spiraled higher, and both women discarded previous ideas of constraint simultaneously.

Hands now traveled and sampled each other's skin, lips following their own course, tongues expressing the desire to taste and pleasure the other. Exchanging moans in realization of caresses both given and received. Fingers kept brushing the boundaries set by their remaining clothing, and as Chloe aimed for the button on Sara's jeans, Sara's mind grasped the intent, and directed her to accomplish the same task that Chloe was pursuing. With zippers sounding out at their lowering, both women, caught up in the exchange of kisses and licks elsewhere, blindly and instinctively succeeded in ridding themselves of the rest of their clothing. Only socks remained, and deep in the recesses of their minds, they knew that these last vestiges of clothing would be shed, too, at some opportune moment, but not this opportune moment.

Chloe, her skin demanding more intimate and prolonged contact, wavered slightly, lifting onto the edge of the bed. With eyes calling her desire, she leaned back, and pushed her way almost to the large headboard, prone, speaking a silent invitation for the still standing Sara to join her. Chloe watched as Sara carefully placed a knee on the end of the bed, and then sinuously prowled her way up Chloe's body, straddling her, raven hair trailing an erotic path on Chloe's skin, and finally arriving, hands propped at either side of Chloe's shoulders. Blue eyes looked down into summoning green, and she waited there, asking for yet one more invitation. Chloe's arms did her bidding for her, pulling Sara down for their first kiss, mouth to mouth, all shared with a delicious feeling of body on body. Sara's lips met with Chloe's and as their mouths opened, and tongues met, she lowered herself down, legs between legs, then a meeting of abdomens, and finally, breasts first softly grazed, then melded together.

Complete contact established, Sara wrapped her arms about Chloe, and quickly rolled them over, so Chloe was now on top, and Sara could experience the wondrous weight of Chloe on her. She kissed up a groaning Chloe's neck, pausing at her ear to murmur,

"I'll remember my promise if you remember yours."

Chloe's mind, usually stymied by recalling past events, snapped to, and latched onto the memory of the promises shared in that dim classroom on a Saturday not long ago. That remembrance ignited an even more intense fire in Chloe's core, and as Sara made good on her promise of marking her where no one could see, Chloe slid down, and without hesitation, exuberantly delivered on her end of the bargain, by replacing her hand on Sara's breast with her mouth. Sara arched into her, lifting them both off the bed, but Chloe merely rose to the occasion, her tongue enjoying the different textures beneath it. When Chloe switched her attentions to Sara's other breast, Sara growled in pleasure, and rose again, this time rolling them over so Chloe was on her back. Chloe, engrossed in what she was doing, almost didn't realize the turning had happened, until she felt the tickling of the ends of Sara's hair brush across her cheeks as she pushed into Chloe's mouth.

Sara's brain and body were spinning in near-frenzied tandem, there were too many things she wanted to do, too many emotions she wanted to experience, and she was floating and falling at the same time. She opened her eyes to enjoy Chloe's heated administrations to her aching breast, and the sight made her cry out in pleasure. Sara lifted off a complaining Chloe, and straddled her hips, resting her hands on her thighs while she took a moment to consider how she wanted to proceed. Chloe, opening her eyes and seeing that Sara was lustily planning her next move, stilled and enjoyed the sensations of Sara's center touching and warming her abdomen. Sara sat back and looked down over her new lover, taking in the milky white skin, lightly covered with freckles, with a decorously placed mole here and there. She could feel Chloe's hipbone beneath her, a sharp and hard contrast to the softness of the rest of her.

"I love you, Chloe," Sara said simply, but never meaning anything more in her life. She leaned back down toward her, expecting to seal that utterance with a kiss.

Chloe rose up to meet her, and pulled her back down as their lips met again. Chloe tangled her fingers into Sara's thick hair, gently holding her, yet pulling her in deeper as their kiss became more burning and demanding. Sara broke for a breath, then nipped at Chloe's bottom lip; her hands found Chloe's breasts and the kiss began anew.

There was a new urgency now, as Sara felt Chloe begin to writhe in response below her, and Sara's mouth wanted to explore the territory that her hands found so enjoyable. Her mouth was just closing over the surface of Chloe's breast when she heard Chloe gasp out a fevered "Yes. Sara."

Replacing words with moans, the two women continued their explorations of each other. The room, cool when they had entered, now was warming in response to the heat rising from the women. Skimming fingers followed impatient tongues in the hollows of necks, light fondles became deliberate squeezes when urged on by an encouraging sigh. The cotton sheets beneath them cooled skin heated by their caresses. Eyes closed and then opened, adjusting to the light, and to the sight of the new lover before them.

Their loving was almost a battle, for neither woman was the most passive or submissive of souls. It became apparent to them that positions did not matter, the top holding no power, the bottom ceding no surrender. Control, or the lack of it, passed back and forth between hands, mouths, legs, bodies and minds. Strategies for the aggressor of the moment were waylaid by clever counterattack strokes. Both women wrestled their thoughts and notions of their perceived roles, and mutually tossed preconceived notions about the other out the window.

"You're not going to give in, are you?" panted Chloe before she began nipping Sara's shoulder. She was again straddling Sara, whose hands were kneading the muscles along Chloe's spine, trying to pull her closer, before she dropped her hands even lower, to scrape her nails across Chloe's rounded buttocks.

"No. You aren't either, are you?" Sara growled, and put her hands on Chloe's shoulders, tugging the fiery redhead above her down, and then bending her leg and raising it firmly to maximize the contact with Chloe's center.

Chloe closed her eyes and, for a long moment, indulged herself in the feel of Sara's firm thigh pressing onto her very energized flesh. She was enjoying this contact too much to want it to end, but needed more. She dropped a hand on Sara's other thigh, and her fingers teased their way higher, adding more pressure to her circling strokes until those fingers reached their goal. Those fingers stopped there, and then began a maddening dance, ever deeper past dark, slick curls.

Sara, who moments earlier had been very sure that Chloe would succumb to her desires, now blinked back her surprise at being ambushed by a very crafty and determined redhead.

"Oh God, Chloe," she said through gritted teeth, enjoying each stroke of Chloe's fingers, and lifting and moving into them. Her desire stoked higher; wanting to feel Chloe the same way she reached her hand and deftly infiltrated the space between her thigh and Chloe's center. Sara's discovery of the hot wetness she felt there made her shiver with breath-stealing need. Her attention was alternately and dizzyingly split between the pleasures she was giving and receiving. "Chloe, you feel so good."

"Oh God, Sara," echoed a heated Chloe, who paused only a moment in her ministrations when she felt Sara's fingers grazing, then massaging her very core. The pressure was intoxicating, and she shifted only slightly to give Sara total access. Sara grunted her approval, and renewed her massage. Each woman's heartbeat now became an incessant drumming, echoed in the throbbing that would now only cease in the moment of release. Chloe felt gravity and desire pulling her down from her sitting position high on Sara's thigh, and she slowly dropped her head into the space between Sara's breasts. Sara sensed the change in Chloe's breathing and the growing turgidity beneath her strokes. Her fingers slowly began a descent deeper into Chloe. Pausing just a moment, she entered her, and began deliberately stroking, outside and in again.

Chloe, breathless for a moment at the feeling of Sara inside of her, cried out her name, and began rocking to the motion of Sara's fingers. Her own fingers, envious of the intimate contact, took their cue from Sara's actions, and gently urged the dark-haired woman open. Sliding ever deeper inside, Chloe's fingers were greeted by the warm, wet muscles that contracted around them.

"Chloe, oh Chloe. Yeah, that's it," Sara rumbled, her demanding tone betraying the desire and pleasure she felt.

The lovers had similar thoughts. They both wanted to sustain these pleasures, to bask in the heady pulsing coursing along all of their nerve endings. But this was their first time, and the need to feel the sweet and heated release was too great to prolong this any longer. Their breathing labored as strokes continued. Grunts, moans and sighs intermingled, passions flared, and blazing determination set in. They inspired each other, their utterances urging and encouraging the other to let go, to succumb to their need for the other's release.

Sara felt Chloe's impending surrender, and, needing to see her lover's face, she reached her other hand and gently lifted Chloe's head from her chest, just far enough so she could look into her lover's eyes. Green eyes darkened with desire blinked as Sara delivered the touch and the words that sent Chloe up and over the edge to a powerful climax. "Chloe, I need it. Please. I want you."

With those words echoing in her ears, Chloe felt herself begin to give way, delicious sensations and tremors coursing through her body. Sara watched with hooded eyes as Chloe's body tensed and stiffened, and felt the circle of muscles quaver tightly around her now-stilled fingers. Chloe's eyes hopelessly tried to remain in contact with her lover's, but the emotions were too great, and her eyes fluttered shut. Chloe released a mighty and soulful cry of unbridled carnal celebration. The combination of the excitement of Chloe's loud, lusty cry, and the torrent of emotions flowing over her face, stormed Sara's senses, and her own powerful climax began just as Chloe's reached its peak. Sara's own guttural cries mingled with that of her lover's, and she closed her eyes to ride it out, still seeing the flush of the redhead's face in her mind, intensifying an already fierce and overpowering orgasm. Arms reached out blindly and they shuddered into each other.

The sound of pounding heartbeats in their ears slowly gave way to awareness of the other's labored breaths. Chloe had collapsed fully on top of Sara's body, and Sara's bent leg slowly descended onto the mattress, bringing the rest of Chloe down in the process. Little hums of contentment vibrated in their throats as they languidly shifted into each other, Chloe breathing softly into her lover's ear. They lay prone, spent and peaceful, each silently giving thanks for the other, each conveying in small touches their profound reverence for the moment.

Chloe stirred herself first, lazily draping both a leg and arm across Sara, and after blowing a satisfied sigh into Sara's ear, she murmured, "I love you, Sara. I really do."

Sara shook herself out of her reverie, and tightened her arms around the smaller woman. Not opening her eyes, but having to clear her dry throat, just to make sure she could speak, she quietly agreed. "I can tell." She squeezed her arms tighter, and smiled at the squeak that Chloe emitted. "I love you, too."

The two women lay quietly a little longer, then Chloe moved and propped her head onto her elbow, examining the dark features of the woman before her. Sara's eyes were still closed, but as Chloe reached out to tenderly move some tendrils of hair from Sara's forehead, Sara's lips curled into a sexy grin, and she blinked her eyes open to meet the eyes of her new lover. They regarded each other seriously, trading small touches, allowing their eyes to speak for them for a short while. Sara ran a thumb across Chloe's lips, remembering the feel of them on her body, on her mouth. Quietly, deliberately, she pulled the redheaded woman to her, to share a slow and reaffirming kiss. Chloe's lips lingered on Sara's, softly moving her kisses over her chin, nose, cheeks and hair before again settling her head next to Sara's ear. Chloe sighed, a long and heartfelt one, and Sara let out a startled chuckle.

"What are you giggling about?" Chloe smiled.

"That sigh into my ear." She lifted an arm into Chloe's view. "Look, goosebumps." She chuckled again, and then added, "And I don't giggle. I haven't giggled since I was ten."

"Oh my God, I still have my socks on! And it sure sounded like a giggle to me."

"Was not. I chuckle, maybe. Laugh, yes. Giggle, no." Sara's glittering eyes betrayed her false attempt at sounding annoyed.

"That was too high to be a chuckle. Chuckles are deeper. That had a certain Minnie Mouse quality to it. Minnie doesn't chuckle," Chloe challenged.

"There's nothing Minnie Mouse about me," Sara defended herself, and then chuckled, making sure it came out as deeply as possible. "Maybe Mighty Mouse, yeah."

Chloe slid more of her body onto Sara's, and looked with dancing green eyes into her lover's laughing blue. "Okay, it was a chiggle, how's that?" Before Sara could answer, she darted her tongue between Sara's lips, who got the hint, and parted them to allow Chloe access. Their tongues mingled, Sara's arms pulled Chloe's body more fully on top of her, and the kiss deepened, and the two new lovers began a new and heated embrace, effectively ending the debate over chuckles, giggles, and the subtle nuances of mice's laughter.

Part XIX:
I See Trees of Green, Red Roses, Too

Sara was never a good sleeper in strange surroundings, and sleeping at Chloe's was no exception. She woke several times during the night, to survey the clock on the nightstand table. The red numbers flashed 3:30, 4:15, 5:28, and 6:40, deep into midmorning for the exhausted but quite happy dark-haired woman. As the hours passed, and Sara woke and checked the clock, she pondered getting up, and quickly discarded that idea when she discovered the redheaded comfort that lay within her arms. Although she woke too frequently, she found the satisfaction and contentment of the warmth of Chloe so soothing, she fell asleep again without delay. Chloe was spooned against Sara, or maybe she was spooned around Chloe. Chloe's body against hers seemed a custom fit, her butt laying perfectly against the flat of Sara's stomach and pelvis, her back lined upwards to where her shoulders stopped in conjunction with Sara's breasts. Sara found that the smaller woman's position still gave her plenty of space for her to move her arms, shoulders and head, although Sara discovered she didn't want to move away. During the night, she merely adjusted herself to Chloe; gently holding a breast, tucking a hand into generous warm cleavage, or lightly grasping a hand. She was also delighted to find that during her short awakenings that Chloe seemed to be quite aware of the tall woman, even in her sleep. When Sara would adjust, Chloe usually responded with a tiny scoot backwards, ensuring a tight fit, with maximum touching of skin surfaces, and letting out an almost childlike moan of contentment. Sara would hear this moan and find herself answering back with a deep sigh of her own, the ardent call of two lovers in the night.

As the morning wore on, and the red numbers flashed 8:15, 9:13 and then 10:20, Sara woke yet again, and as she glanced at the clock, and was just settling her nose into the tickling presence of red-blonde hair, her senses detected something was different. There was a new smell in the room, a familiar smell that the sleepy woman couldn't quite pinpoint. As her mind tried to put a name to the aroma, Sara's sense of hearing piqued. There were small, but infrequent dull noises emanating from somewhere else in the house. Sara blinked her eyes open, and found that Chloe was just where she had been most of the night, still nestled in Sara's light embrace. The room was quite light, the sunshine of midmorning illuminating it, unfettered by any heavy materials on the three windows of the small bedroom. Then there was the unmistakable sound of a toilet flushing, and water running.

Sara, still not fully awake, but getting there, pulled away from Chloe, and lay on her back, deciding what to do. *I should go investigate. What's going on?*

"Chloe. Chloe," nudged Sara. *Coffee, that's what it is, coffee.* "Chloe, wake up, I think someone is here."

Chloe, true to form, merely grunted and, missing the warmth of her partner, scooted her butt back to where it was again touching Sara's abdomen. "Hmm," she replied.

"Chloe." Sara tapped on her shoulder. "Chloe, wake up. I think—"

She never got to finish her sentence, because she felt, and then saw, a familiar presence leaning against the door jamb, smiling, bemused, at her.

Sara blinked, and although never much of a modest woman, pulled the quilt up over her bare breasts before she spoke. "Mornin', Marcy." Her hand kept up its insistent light poking of Chloe's shoulder.

"Well, good morning to you, Sara! Sleep well?" Marcy's grin was getting wider and wider, noticing the combination of sleepiness and annoyance that showed plainly on the tall woman's face. "Nice hair there, Sara. Do you always let badgers nest in it overnight?" Marcy let out a laugh as she saw Sara interrupt her nudging of Chloe long enough to reach up and try to smooth down her disheveled hair. It didn't help a bit, but Sara didn't know that, and Marcy did. Marcy laughed, just as Sara gave her a decidedly unamused stare, and combined that with a not-too-gentle shove to Chloe's shoulder. This finally seemed to roust the redhead. Sara and Marcy continued their staring, Sara's eyes narrowing with hurtful intent, and with that, Marcy started giggling with unhidden glee.

"Wha?" slurred a slowly waking Chloe. She noticed that her tall warm comforter was no longer wrapped around her. "Whatsa matter?"

Sara kept her eyes glued in a staring contest with the art teacher. Chloe was just turning over to find out what happened to Sara when Marcy made her move, surprising even the quite alert Sara.

Marcy threw her arms outwards, and then took a running leap for the bed, shouting, "Group hug!" as she landed, butt first, between her best friend and her startled, glowering lover. Marcy scooted up the bed just a little, and grabbed a pillow from under Sara's head so she could prop her own auburn curls up against the headboard. She crossed her legs at the ankles, and laid a hand on a bare shoulder of each of the women beside her. "Rise and shine! Rise and shine, my friends!"

Sara adjusted the covers once again; the heavy landing on the bed had displaced them to where she was displaying her charms again. "Chloe?" Sara grumpily called across to an awakening, but aware and grinning Chloe. "Do you own a gun?" She ignored the snickering Marcy, who was helpfully tugging on the comforters in an insincere effort to help Sara maintain her modesty.

Marcy, satisfied that Sara's dignity was now intact, turned her attentions to her redheaded friend, who was eying her, amused. "Well, Chloe, good morning! Interesting hairdo you've got there. Very fetching, especially to other roosters. Very '70s. Rod Stewartish." Marcy reached over and picked an invisible nothing out of Chloe's hair. "And what's this? Were you two doing kinky things with trail mix?"

Chloe slapped a none-too-gentle forearm across Marcy's stomach, and left it there. "That's a gerbil pellet. Gerbils, Marcy, gerbils," she said with an air of impatience. She rolled her eyes.

Sara raised an eyebrow. Marcy furrowed hers.

Sara snaked her arm across Marcy's belly, and took the hand of her lover in a soft grasp. She lifted her head to look across Marcy, and into the eyes of the small librarian. "Mornin, Chloe," she drawled, allowing the first smile of the morning to cross her face.

"Mornin, Sara." Chloe's eyes got wider when she got her first good look at Sara. "Did I do that?" Her gaze fixed on the chaotic tangle on Sara's head.

Sara distractedly tried to smooth her hair with her free hand. "I guess that egg beater wasn't such a good idea."

The clasped hands of the lovers vibrated with the movement of Marcy's belly as she chuckled.

Chloe yawned, and squeezed Sara's hand. "It seems that maybe we'd better get up, huh? Is that coffee I smell?"

"Yup," teased a cheery Marcy. "And there are bagels, muffins, and other surprise goodies, too."

Chloe brightened at those words, and caught Sara's eye again. "Can we shoot her after we eat? Please?"

Sara nodded, a conspiratorial grin on her face. "Sounds like a plan. I guess we should get up." She winked at Chloe, and slowly, very slowly, started counting aloud, so her lover would have time to figure out the plan. "One."

Chloe cocked her eyebrow at Sara, silently questioning her. Sara waggled her eyebrows in reply.

"Two." Sara droned purposefully, then saw the comprehension

appear in Chloe's eyes, and the grin that turned up the corners of her mouth.

"Three!" Chloe and Sara shouted in unison, and whipped back the covers onto a usually unflappable Marcy. She was now treated to the rare sight of two completely naked, nicely bare bottomed women as they dashed across the bedroom and out the doorway toward the bathroom.

Marcy smoothed out the covers on the bed on either side of her, and grinned, then laughed. She shook her head, and announced, quite loudly, "Damn! I still don't know if she's a true redhead!"

"I forgot she had a key!" Chloe apologized again to a still slightly surly Sara, who was sipping her coffee and picking at a blueberry muffin. Freshly showered and hastily dressed, they sat at the kitchen table. Marcy was at the counter, pouring herself another cup of coffee.

"You said that already," sniped Sara, throwing the smirking Marcy another sneer. Marcy lazily leaned against the counter, then picked her keys out of her jumper pocket, and waved them, jangling, at Sara. She jumped back when Sara whipped out a hand in order to grab them from her. She just barely missed, and Marcy dumped them, victoriously, back into her pocket.

"Uh-uh. Mine. And it will come in so handy in the future, I'm sure," gloated Marcy. "I'll bet I could sneak a film crew in here some morning."

Chloe, two bagels down, and happily working on a poppy seed muffin, decided to quit feeling guilty. "We go fifty-fifty, Marcy. Try and get *Inside Edition*, I hear they pay better."

Marcy was just about to answer that when there were loud raps on the front door. She glanced at the startled faces of her two friends seated at the table. She started moving out of the kitchen toward the front door, calling over her shoulder as she walked. "Oh, yeah, did I forget to mention that Dave and Nelson were stopping by after going to Charlie Shemp's?"

Chloe buried her face in her hands just in time to block the light impact of the blueberry that came sailing across the table at her.

All three D'Amicos had cheerfully agreed to make a run to the grocery store to pick up the makings for Sunday dinner. After Chloe had confusedly insisted that she had plenty of ingredients around to make up an adequate meal for the five of them, Marcy finally took pity on her, and nudged her as Chloe continued to study the blank, expectant faces of the three patiently waiting family members.

"Chloe, buy a clue," said a quietly exasperated Marcy. "They want to go grocery shopping. With Sara's car."

Chloe blinked, and then, with some slowly awakening comprehension, said, "Oh." She saw the three smiling faces of the D'Amicos nodding in happy, yet silent, agreement, to Marcy's explanation. "Oh!" She returned their happy nod, saving her best smile for Sara. "Got it."

Sara wanted to reach over, take Chloe into her arms and kiss the woman senseless, just because she was so cute and so astute, even if Marcy had to nudge her into a little reality. Dave and Nelson stood up from the table, not hiding their eagerness to get rolling.

Dave looked thoughtfully at Nelson. "You've never driven a manual, clutch on the wheel, have you?"

Sara stood up, too, and gave a grin in response to the disappointed look on Nelson's face. She winked at Dave, and scratched at the nape of her neck. Hesitating just long enough to tease the young man just a little longer, she finally sighed and pursed her lips into a tight grin. "'Bout time you did."

Three pairs of blue eyes lit up, and matching grins and deep chuckles followed. Dave leaned over Marcy, and gave her a soft, lingering kiss. Nelson noted that Chloe's ceiling was painted white, *how unique*. Sara bent over Chloe to do the same, as Nelson contemplated that no, the ceiling really didn't need a fresh coat, it was still pretty much a pristine white.

Sara, upon straightening up from the kiss, noticed a small, pronounced red mark just below Chloe's left earlobe, just at the point where hairline gave way to the white skin of the side of her throat. She leaned back down quickly and whispered into her ear. "I'm so sorry. Honey, don't tuck your hair behind this ear for a few days, all right?"

She straightened up, and Chloe ran her fingertips to the area where Sara had indicated, then a small frown of awareness hit her lips. She looked up at Sara, who guiltily gave her an apologetic grin, and narrowed her green eyes at her. Sara shrugged, giving Chloe her best pitiful pout, and Chloe melted. "I'll live. But you, on the other hand, I'm worried about your life expectancy."

Dave couldn't help himself, watching the cute interaction between his sister and her new love. "Marked your woman, huh, Sara? I noticed that first thing as we came in today." There followed three chuckles, with two very silent abstentions. Chloe's hand shot back up to the area, and covered it. "Great, I'm really the town harlot now," she remarked, rather angrily. Her features darkened, and she glared at each person in the kitchen. She then broke out into a laugh of her own, and said, cheekily, "It's kinda cool. I like it. This time."

Four tense people let out a silent sigh of relief. All four had been privy to the volatile outbursts of the small redhead in front of them, and three of those people were quietly thanking their higher power that her anger hadn't segued into a pacing, cranky diatribe. Sara, the most relieved of their little group, had to lean down and lay a grateful kiss on her lover's forgiving lips. Nelson regarded the ceiling again, murmuring to himself that it wouldn't need a new coat of paint for a year, or maybe two.

Chloe watched as her lover rose again, and she couldn't help but think some racy thoughts as she regarded those cool blue eyes. *God, all the places those lips were last night. Never mind those lips, it's that tongue, yeah, that tongue. Who knew I could respond like that, and so many times? I lost count.*

Chloe woke from her daydream to see that Dave and Nelson had already exited the kitchen.

Marcy tapped her coffee cup to snap the women out of it. "Sara, the boys are waiting. Nelson is dying to ruin your clutch. Do you have a grocery list?" Chloe began gazing at Sara again, wanting to see her lips move.

"List?" murmured Sara, whose mind inexplicably was comparing how much the word list sounded like lust. Just change one letter. The "i" into "u." That thought happily morphed into "I into you," and her eyes unconsciously began traveling over Chloe's blushing flesh. Her mind then grasped that Marcy was again tapping on her coffee cup again, this time with more gusto. "What'd you say, Marcy?"

Marcy gave an impatient sigh. *We aren't going to see these two for weeks, only when they decide to come up for air. Good thing I have my key.* That thought brought an evil grin to her face as she repeated, "List, Sara. List."

Sara broke her gaze when she suddenly noticed that Chloe's face was rosy red, and that she had shyly turned away from Sara's blistering hot gaze. Sara grinned, delighted and warm, and finally looked at Marcy. "Uh, No. D'Amicos don't do lists. We live in the moment at grocery stores."

Marcy and Chloe both laughed at the absurdity of the statement, and the absolute truth that shone through it. Sara was pleased that the women understood; she didn't know why they so easily understood, but accepted it without further comment. She reached and ran a hand to feel the softness of Chloe's reddened cheek. "We'll be back later." She broke the touch, and finally started moving her feet to the front door, where Dave and Nelson were discussing the idea that Chloe really should consider opening her book-filled home as a library annex.

Marcy and Chloe, still seated at the kitchen table, smiled and waved, and watched the D'Amicos depart out the front door. Dave was pulling it closed behind him when he stopped and blew a kiss to Marcy.

Marcy caught it, grinned and then said, "Hey, you, where are you guys going grocery shopping?"

Dave's eyebrows did a little mambo before he answered, looking her directly in the eye. "Mayville," he cheerfully replied, as he disappeared behind the closing door.

Marcy and Chloe just looked at each other, and then burst into laughter. Mayville, New York, was fifty miles away.

Sara had called shotgun; after all, it was her car, and that brought its privileges. Dave had grumbled, and then acquiesced, struggling to find a comfortable position for his long body in the backseat of the two-door car. He finally leaned his back into the side of the seat behind Sara, and stretched his legs across the seat onto the floor behind the driving Nelson. Sara was fiddling with the radio dials, trying to find an acceptable AM station. This wasn't an easy task, and she traveled up and down the dial several times before she settled on a station that was touting itself as the "Music of Your Life."

Nelson, who had quickly caught on to the mechanics of driving a manual shift on the steering wheel, was happily transporting them at close to sixty-five m.p.h. up the lakeside highway. "This sure isn't the music of my life."

"Would you rather listen to Polka Party? That should still be on a few more hours," teased Sara, and then pinched her nephew on the arm.

With Tony Bennett softly crooning in the background, all three D'Amicos, the quiet family sat back to relax into the joyride. Each mind was busy twisting around in its own thoughts.

I wonder if I can convince Aunt Sara to let me take Jeanette to the drive-in in this car? It'd be so cool, and I'll bet everyone there would be coming by to look at it. I'll have to ask her more about it, so I don't look like a jerk when people ask me questions about it. This bench seat has definite possibilities with Jeanette, too.

Great. Just look at those buds coming out on those trees. Soon there'll be leaves, and flowers. Flowers. I should get some red roses for Marcy. She's seemed so different lately, kind of distracted. The golf course will be opening soon; I should make some time and take her somewhere romantic before we get busy. Maybe Sara would lend me the car.

She sure is flexible. She was so far gone, I had to catch her from falling off the bed. And those sounds she makes when she is...

Maybe Aunt Sara would let me take Jeanette to the prom in this car, too. It'd be so much cooler than some dumb limousine. Justin and Heather could fit in the back. We'll go to Erie for dinner, then back in time for the dance. I wonder if Jeanette wants us to pose for prom pictures. Those are so cheesy. Not if we were standing in front of this car.

Patti Page began singing about "Old Cape Cod."

I suppose I should try to make it a romantic setting for the proposal. Maybe even down on bended knee. She'd probably slug me.

What was it, eight, nine hours, without taking many breaks in between? The woman is insatiable. And who knew she loved Little Debbies like I do? The perfect energy pick-me-up. I wonder if she wants me to spend the night again. I don't want it to be too much, too soon. I bet I could convince her. I really love how aggressive she can be. She pushed me right to the edge of sanity. I still can't figure out how we got into that one position.

I've got to make a decision soon about college. Why does this have to be so hard? Dad's not going to like me going so far away. I think he expects me to stay closer to home, but...

Funny thing is, even if she does say yes, there's no guarantee that she'll actually go through with it. I don't want to be Richard Gere, chasing Julia Roberts down the street. God, that movie stunk. Chick flick. Maybe I can get her all liquored up and haul her butt to a justice of the peace. Would she want to live in my house? I don't know about some of those works of art. I'm just a simple guy. What's she going to say about my Arnold Palmer autographed picture? Would she want to move it? I think it looks nice there in the bathroom.

Peggy Lee now had a "Fever."

Oh, yeah, Peggy, sing it, baby! Fever? I thought we were both going to combust a few times. She is loud. It was a shock, at first, but it makes me so crazy! Good thing she doesn't live in an apartment. As it is, I think her screaming shocked a few cows into sterility. And they're at least a half mile up the road.

Stan, no, Nelson will be my best man. Of course, Nelson. I keep thinking of him as some kid. Look at him, he looks just like Sara. Mary will be coming in from Arizona for Nelson's graduation. It's going to be awkward enough to deal with her, and then there's the fact that the woman who helped break up my marriage is now my girlfriend, soon to be fiancée. Maybe I should wait until after graduation to ask her.

I could live at Chloe's, I think. It's small, but my little bungalow is even smaller. What am I thinking? I'm such a cliché. No need for anyone to think about moving anywhere. I do need to pick up a toothbrush at the store.

At least I can dance better now. Not like we'll be high-steppin' at the prom, but at least I can keep a beat now. Jeanette's going to go to the University of Arizona. I can visit her there when I go visit Mom. Tempe, I wonder how far that is from Phoenix? At least my being in this play didn't shock Mom. I wish she'd come to see me in it. Really, if I got any singing talent, it's from her. I wonder if Rick will come with her for graduation. She seems happy with him. She's always fought with Aunt Sara, well, from the times I can actually remember them being together. She never approved of her being gay. I don't get it, it embarrasses me, sure, but Chloe seems to make Aunt Sara so happy. I don't even like seeing Dad kiss Marcy, so maybe it's just a shy thing on my part. And California is loaded with gays. That's what that idiot Jason says, anyway. It's a wonder that he is even graduating with us. He's such a loser. No, he's okay.

And in August, maybe I could pick up two more used golf carts. I hope Marcy doesn't want a big wedding.

I have an extra key I could give her. Wonder if Chloe will offer to give one to me?

Jeanette has the greatest eyes. She gets all quiet, and just stares at me, and I get all...

Chloe is so emotional. Before, during and. afterwards. I wish I could be like that, but she does seem to bring something out of me that I didn't know was there before. I feel all...

That woman has my number, all right. I don't know what I'll do if she says no. Just be patient, and keep trying, I guess. She's something, one look from her and, bang, I'm all...

Sara's hand shot out, and turned up the volume on the radio. She and Nelson exchanged knowing grins as the beginning bars of a very familiar song began playing through the small and tinny sounding single speaker of the old Comet. Dave, in the back seat, nodded in pleased agreement when he recognized the song, too. It was Patsy Cline. All three voices joined in, singing along.

The miles stretched out behind them as they traveled along in the warmth of the sun of early spring, and pondered the endless possibilities that lay directly ahead.

"You, my dear Marcy, have a filthy, dirty mind. I like that in a person." Chloe was on her second beer.

Marcy, who had just recently discovered that she had an oral fixation, was centering her thoughts about sex so she could forget, even shortly, about her all-consuming desire to run to the store to buy a pack of cigarettes. She rubbed the patch on her shoulder hoping to release more nicotine into her deprived system. She was drinking bottled water, jealously eying Chloe's beer bottle. "Tell me again how it's the right thing to give up smoking. Tell me again how I should not be drinking right now, even before I come to any conclusions."

Chloe, ever predictable in some of her habits, was picking on the label of her beer bottle. "How about that appointment? Did you make one?"

Marcy was thinking about asking Chloe if she could have her beer bottle, so she could pick the label, and keep her nervous hands occupied. "Oh, yeah, it's Friday. Good Friday, of all things. A counselor, uh, a Ms. Cardinger. I'll, uh, we'll be talking with her." She looked to Chloe's face, and saw a bit of surprise reflected there.

"We'll be talking with her? I thought I was just the chauffeur with this."

"Well, I was thinking, I'll just have to repeat everything she says to me to you, anyway, so you might as well be in the room while we discuss it. I mean, if you don't mind. And I was thinking we should just leave from there for our—"

Chloe finished, "Spin the Car. Are you sure you still want to do that, Marse? I mean, you'll have a lot on your mind after that appointment."

Marcy sighed, and unsuccessfully tried to pick at the label on her bottle of water. "All the more reason to play Spin the Car, Chloe, and besides, it's traditional for us to do this every Easter."

Chloe smiled at those words. They had taken short trips over Easter vacation, and other school breaks ever since they had begun college. They had never done the warm-climate sojourns that their college cohorts had, they found that they preferred to renew their very important friendship over the breaks from school, and returned home instead, to reunite in taking little adventures to cities in the surrounding area. Pittsburgh, Cleveland, Buffalo, even to Wheeling, West Virginia at one point. Why should this year be any different?

Marcy was reading her mind. "I don't know how you feel about this, Chloe, but I'm sort of glad the D'Amicos will be leaving for Florida on Thursday. I don't think I could be around Dave right now, I mean, it's hard now, with all this deep thinking that I've got to get done."

"Well, of course, I'll miss her." *I'll do more than miss her, God, we just start this new aspect of our relationship, and she'll be leaving for five, six days.* Chloe plastered a smile on her face again. "I think it'll be good for all of us," she lied. But she was very truthful when she continued, "I like our trips together, Marcy. I always have." Chloe was suddenly swept up in the emotions she had been pummeled with the last few weeks or so. The news about Marcy's pregnancy. The explosion of sexual desires. The depth of the love that she felt for Sara. For Marcy. For Dave. For Nelson. For that old busybody, Doris. For homeless people. For the guy at the Amoco station who looked twenty years older when he didn't wear his teeth. For all of friggin' mankind. Chloe started sniffling, her eyes wet with emotion. "I love you, Marcy." She leaned over to hug her oldest, dearest friend.

Marcy, who had been wondering if there was maybe a smokable cigarette butt under the front seat of her car, and how she could sneak out there to check, was a bit thrown by the sudden emotionality of her friend. She leaned into the hug, and held her tightly for a while. "I love you, too, Chloe."

Chloe finally leaned back into the couch, and blushingly said, "Sorry, I know you don't normally like that kind of stuff, but I just felt all, you know, "What A Wonderful World" there for a minute."

Marcy grinned at the reference to the optimistic Louis Armstrong song. She narrowed her eyes at Chloe, and then said, with certainty in her statement, "PMSing, aren't you?"

Chloe blinked, and then laughed. "That must be it." *Oh, please, Lord, not until Thursday. Let it stay away until Sara leaves for Florida.*

"That, and being totally sexually satisfied, and in love, I would think." Marcy cracked knowingly.

"Well, there is that," said a blushing, giggling and very satisfied Chloe.

Marcy looked at the clock on the wall. "It's nearly five, they've been gone for almost three hours, so they should be coming back soon."

Chloe put her beer bottle down on the table, and stretched to crack her back. "Yeah. I suppose I should—"

"Go brush your teeth, Chloe. I need to go get something out of my car, anyway."

Chloe got up from the couch, and gave her friend a skeptical look, and was going to say something, but decided to stay quiet. *I'm not her mother.*

When Chloe returned from the bathroom, satisfied that her breath was more palatable, and her hair looking respectable, her front door opened, and Marcy came in, trailed by Dave, Sara, Nelson, and, to Chloe's surprise, a bashfully beaming Jeanette. Sara caught Chloe's eye, smiled broadly, and shrugged her shoulders.

Dave, juggling bags of groceries in his arms, gave Marcy an unembarrassed long smooch, and then looked to Chloe, who was smiling at the family and friends before her. He shifted the groceries and put an arm around Jeanette, and gave her a quick squeeze. "Look what we found, all alone on a D'Amico Sunday Dinner night. Nelson here was afraid she would waste away, and, well, Sara and I figured that she's irreplaceable," he said as he punched his blushing son in the arm, "to the play and all. So, we picked her up, threw her in the trunk, and here we are." He looked at Chloe for acceptance, and was pleased to see that she was smiling back him.

Jeanette looked shyly at Chloe, and held out a covered dish to her. "I hope it's all right, Ms. Donahue. And, here, I brought a cherry pie."

Chloe graciously took the pie from Jeanette, and clucked her tongue at her before she bestowed a shining and welcoming smile at the nervous girl. "Jeanette, in my own home, you may call me Chloe. And it looks like, from what I've heard, you and I will soon be initiated into the singular, spectacular experience of the D'Amico Sunday Family Dinner."

Nelson both groaned and grinned at this, and then, suddenly brave, he took Jeanette's hand, and led her toward Chloe's kitchen, as four smiling adults trailed behind.

"See, it's like this, Jeanette," said Nelson, his voice holding a teaching tone, "first, we'll start with the pie, and then..."

Part XX:
In the Family Way

Chloe was on her back, enjoying the white fireworks that were bursting on the inside of her eyelids. She was freefalling, and her control of her musculature had caught an express bus to Mars several minutes ago. She was panting hard enough to extinguish the candles on God's birthday cake. There was a noise vaguely echoing in her ears, and as she was slowly coming back to reality, she realized that faint joyous echoing was from some rather lusty howls that had emanated from her own throat and lungs. She giggled, and soon found that her arm actually worked, she could move something now, so she reached out on the bed beside her in the darkened room, and felt nothing. She fanned both arms out, and found nothing.

"Sara?" Chloe called, finally opening her eyes, and looking about. Sara was nowhere to be found. "Sara? Where are you?"

A muffled voice lifted up from the side of the bed where Chloe's legs hung over the edge. "Down here."

Chloe rolled up into a sitting position, and then laid down on her stomach to look down to where Sara's voice had resonated. Chloe peered down over the edge of the bed to see, in the single candlelit glow of the room, Sara, on her back, hands locked behind her head for a pillow, an ankle crossed at her knee. She looked quite comfortable on the carpeted floor.

Chloe assumed a Kilroy position, with just her eyes, forehead, nose and fingertips showing over the edge of the bed. "Hey, yer nekkid!" she drawled.

Sara smiled, and wiggled her foot at her. "So are you. Very much so."

Chloe opened her eyes wide, and then reached behind her, and gave her own butt a loud smack. "Hey, yer right! Whatcha doin' down there?"

Sara waved her bent elbows up at her. "I was wondering when you were going to notice I never quite made it up there."

Chloe's eyes blinked behind shaggy bangs. "Sorry. I took the last train to Clarksville there. You know, up, up and away in my beautiful balloon. Left on a jet plane."

"Flew you to the moon?" Another foot wiggle from a smiling Sara.

Chloe's eyes became smaller because of the way her cheeks rose when she smiled. "Yep. Hey, you are good with that thing, ya know?"

Even in the candlelight, Sara could see the sparkle in Chloe's eyes. She pursed her lips, and looked up at the redheaded nymphet squinting down from the high mattress. "What thing would that be, huh?" she teased, knowing full well what Chloe was talking about.

Chloe's eyes squinted shut before she replied, "You know, that long pink thing sitting between your teeth and gums."

"Oh, that thing. Yeah, I like it. It seems to work well. It really loves you." Sara stuck out that thing at Chloe. "You seemed to like it too."

Chloe giggled and brought her whole beaming face into Sara's view. "And then some! Want to come join me up here? You've been down there a long, long time. Not that I'm complaining."

Sara sat up into a cross-legged position, and cocked her head, running her hand through her dark hair, trying to arrange it into some sort of order. "I just want to say one thing, well maybe two or three, for the record. I am extremely thankful, as are my knees, that you have extra padding under the carpeting in this room. And if I complained about that mattress being too high off the floor, I take it back. It's the perfect height!" She jumped up, and tackled a giggling Chloe on the bed. They rolled around, tickling and kissing, until they got themselves positioned near the headboard, and Chloe snuggled into Sara's shoulder and sighed. Sara wrapped her arm around her, and pulled the covers up around them.

"I'm going to miss you," said Chloe, enjoying the light fluffing and scratches Sara was applying to the top of her head.

"Yeah, me too." She ran her hand through Chloe's hair, lifting it, and letting it drop softly, then repeating it again. Even though they had just made love, Sara was feeling anxious and sad.

"How long is it since you've seen your parents?" Chloe said carefully, hoping she wasn't spoiling the sweet afterglow.

Sara stopped her fluffing for a moment while she thought about it. Finally, she began playing with Chloe's mop again. "Eight, maybe nine years."

Chloe lifted her head off its comfortable spot, and looked at Sara. "That long?" She searched Sara's eyes, and saw the frown that had set in on the dark-haired woman's lips. "Really?"

Sara lightly pushed Chloe's head back into its previous position. "Yeah. That long. It's going to be interesting to see them again."

"How so?" *Why do these questions keep coming out of my mouth? I can feel her tensing up under me.* Chloe stroked Sara's shoulder in an effort to reduce the tension building in the muscled form beneath her.

"Well, let's see, I went to L.A., got my career started, and sent cards and presents for holidays and birthdays. I called less and less. And then, after the accident, I dropped off the face of the earth, and well, I still sent cards, presents, but no phone calls." *God, Chloe, I'm a schmuck.*

Chloe tried to soothe the obviously uncomfortable woman by rubbing her hand in small circles on her abdomen. "I was kind of wondering, how did you manage to do that, without them finding out where you were? I mean, return addresses, postmarks?" *This is lousy pillow talk. But I have to know.*

Sara sighed, and gave a rueful laugh. "Same way I ran my whole life then, from the Internet. I sent cards, presents and stuff that way. I just got online with my credit card, and had everything delivered securely, without it being able to be traced back to me. I lived that way, too, Chloe."

"How can you live off the Internet?" Chloe asked. She didn't even own a computer, and her Internet experience was limited to what pertained to her job.

Sara laughed, and gave Chloe a quick tight hug. "I forgot. You're still living in the '70s, aren't you? Let's see, most places deliver UPS, or Fed Ex. For food, I found a place that would deliver. I asked that it be dropped off without me signing for it. Medicines, I got my prescriptions three months worth at a time, through the mail."

Chloe burrowed deeper into Sara's shoulder, troubled by the loneliness of Sara's missing years. She pulled herself in tighter, wanting to maximize contact.

Sara felt the compassion in Chloe's embrace. *Thank God, I can talk to her about this now. Thank God for her.* "So I've talked to Mom since I've been back, but it's strained. Always was, really. And Dad, well, he just acts like no time has passed at all, that none of it ever happened." Sara began her massage of Chloe's head again, she knew that the redhead loved it, and it was pleasing for her to do it. "Mom's mad. That might be an understatement. She never put up with any crap from us, of any kind. She worked thirty-five years as a legal secretary, and she saw the worst dregs of society pass through the office's doors. And Dad, he retired after forty years at Dammermill Paper. He's blue collar all the way, a very simple guy. He just went to work, came home, and did his thing. Mom, on the other hand, she knew everything about us, like she had eyes in the back of her head, plus I think she had surveillance teams on me and Dave." Sara snorted. "It seemed like she knew about things before we even did them. She's smart, all right. Too smart."

Chloe heard the seriousness that had crept into Sara's voice as she had relayed those facts about her parents. *This isn't going to be a good Easter holiday for her.* She paused a moment before she said, "This, you're really not looking forward to this, are you? This is going to be tough."

"I have to do it. It's going to be hard, because Mom just isn't going to let things go. She's going to ask me tough questions, and she's not going to stand for any bullshit answers from me. She won't let me escape into myself when I'm there. I'm going to have to tell her stuff that I'm not even ready to tell you, Chloe." Sara sighed, regretting that what she said was the absolute truth. "I'm sorry."

Chloe again lifted from Sara's shoulder, and propped her head up into her hands. She looked deeply into Sara's eyes, and said, firmly, "You don't have to apologize to me for anything, Sara, not for your past. Not a thing." She saw the deep blue eyes regarding her, and she decided to lighten the moment, so they could relax with each other on their last night together before Sara left tomorrow morning. "Now, your future, that's another thing. I expect you will be spending a lot of time apologizing to me, I am high maintenance, and well, there's no way you can consistently deal with that on a satisfactory basis for any length of time without screwing up." She grinned, and dropped down, and kissed Sara's now smiling lips. She tucked her head back down onto Sara's warm shoulder again, and felt the vibrations of Sara's soundless mirth. "What?"

"Groveling." Sara drew out the words, growling the first few letters.

"Groveling?"

"Yeah, Marcy said I would be groveling every day of the rest of my life just to keep you." Sara's silent laugh turned into a light, but audible, chuckle.

"That Marcy. She's got our numbers, doesn't she?"

"That she does, Chloe. She sure does."

As the women settled in to each other, and lapsed into quiet breathing in preparation for sleep, Chloe's thoughts turned to Marcy. *Yeah, she might have our numbers but she hasn't got a clue about herself.* Chloe placed a small kiss on Sara's shoulder, and soon fell asleep. Sara, on the other hand, spent a good part of the darkest hours of the night idly fluffing Chloe's hair, and dreading the coming of the new day.

Dave was bending in front of the dryer door, stuffing white underwear, socks and undershirts into an opened suitcase. "Nelson!" he bellowed, irritated, "Come help me with the packing!"

Nelson stood grinning, not three feet from his grumpy father, watching quietly as Dave packed. "I'm right here, Dad. What do you need?"

Dave nearly clutched his chest when Nelson's voice answered him from such close quarters. Feeling his face turn red, Dave refused to look at him, pissed that Nelson had embarrassed and scared him to death. "Did you find our shorts? And T-shirts?" he grumped.

Unlike Dave, Nelson was aware of the concept of folding prior to packing. "I did that last night, Pop. I just finished packing all the bathroom stuff. Our dress clothes are in a garment bag, and I've closed all the windows, locked them, and checked all the appliances. Aunt Sara's stuff is already in the Explorer, she put it in there before she left for Chloe's last night." Nelson had given up any pretense when it came to Chloe's name anymore. She didn't seem to mind him calling her Chloe, even when he screwed up and called her that in front of the other students. He grinned at the memory of Jeanette's hesitating stutter when Chloe insisted that Jeanette call her by her first name last Sunday. By the end of that Sunday dinner, Jeanette and Chloe were howling about the peculiarly paced meal, and Jeanette was sing-songing the redheaded director's name. "Oh, Chlo-o-o-Wee! That's s-o-o fun-ny!"

Dave had no idea why Nelson's quiet competence was disturbing him, it just was. "Jeans? Jackets? Camera? Film?" Dave ticked off items, hoping Nelson would say no to at least one of them. It didn't happen.

"Got 'em all. I gassed up the Explorer last night, like you asked. The oil and tires are fine. I have my Walkman and a bunch of CDs. Aunt Sara checked on all the golf course last night, and the barn is locked. We have an hour before we pick up Aunt Sara at the library at 9:30." Nelson knew he was supplying more information than Dave wanted, he just felt like tweaking his dad.

Dave finished shoveling clothing into the small suitcase, and zipped it closed. "Well, here, take this out to the Explorer. I'm going to get my shower and get dressed." He stopped a moment, unzipped the bag, and picked through it until he found two socks, a T-shirt and a pair of white boxers. He zipped it shut again, stood up, and handed the bag to his softly smiling son. He gave Nelson a sheepish smile. "Sorry, bud. I don't know where you get it from, all these organizational skills, must be your mother, it's sure not me, is it?"

Nelson had nearly twelve years of experience dealing with his father's pre-vacation jitters, ever since they had started taking their yearly Easter trek to Florida. "It's okay. I still can't figure why you always get upset right before we go to Florida. I mean, it's just Grandma and Grandpa."

Dave's smile faded and a frown crossed his face. "I'll tell you why, Nelson. They may be your grandparents, but they're my parents, and well, they're weird, that's why!"

Nelson nodded, completely understanding.

Sara felt the tip of Chloe's nose run up the bare skin of her back along her spine, and she nearly dropped the cereal bowl she was washing right into the sink. She began to turn around, but the smaller woman pushed up against her, keeping her abdomen pinned to the counter. Small hands began a light fondle along her bare sides, making her tremble at the erotic quality of the touch, and the ticklish sensations that it elicited.

"Uh, Chloe, just what do you think you're doing?" murmured Sara, who paused in her washing to close her eyes, enjoying the light caresses of Chloe's hands. Lips touched her back, and softly kissed a line between her shoulder blades. Sara leaned back into them, and felt the addition of Chloe's tongue in between her kisses.

Chloe stopped her mouth, but not her hands. She rested her nose on a vertebra, then said into the skin of her lover's back, "Well, you're leaving today, and the hot water in the shower gave out." Chloe paused to gently bite a nearby shoulder blade, and smiled at the twitches rolling through the muscles in Sara's back. "And I didn't get a chance to reciprocate." She slid a hand under Sara's arm, and reached and found a breast, trailing a finger across the tip of it. She felt Sara's quick intake of breath, and continued tantalizing her prize.

Sara again tried to push away from the counter, to turn and face Chloe. Chloe held her firmly in place with the weight of her body, and to add emphasis, she pushed a khaki-covered knee between Sara's legs, separating them. She began massaging the breast she had in her left hand, and with her right hand, she moved Sara's long hair forward, over her shoulder. With more skin exposed, she slowly slid her free hand down and around to feel the soft, silky skin of Sara's abdomen, tickling her navel.

"Um, Chloe?" hummed Sara, not really meaning anything at all, just letting words tumble from her mouth. Chloe was placing harder nips along her back, and Sara was awash with the pleasurable sensations, getting lost in the delightful mixture. She felt some very definite warm clenching sensations beginning well below the height of the countertop, the edge of which Sara was now gently clutching.

Chloe stopped the bites along Sara's back so she could speak. By nature, Chloe was a talker. She delighted in talking during these special times, and was pleased to find that the content of her words and the tone of her voice seemed to spur Sara on. "That's what you get. I told you those white cotton Fruit of the Looms briefs do it for me." She pinched and rolled Sara's hard nipple in her fingers, and felt the tall woman's body shiver. "So don't you dare blame me for this, you standing nearly naked at my kitchen sink," she brought her right hand up to Sara's right breast, and mimicked her other hand's movements there, "in nothing but white cotton undies." Her left hand dropped down and snapped the elastic band on Sara's underwear before traveling back up to its former position. "And sexy white crew socks, washing up our breakfast dishes, with me having to leave for work in twenty-five minutes?" She laid her cheek on Sara's firm back, and began attending to Sara's breasts.

Sara could feel her knees weakening at what Chloe was doing, and her heightened sensitivity prompted her to open her legs wider. She tried to gain balance against the unsteadiness she was feeling. The incessant rising of her desire began to unhinge her thinking. She could feel the light brush of Chloe's silk shirt on her back, and then the full contact of the shirt, with ripe breasts beneath it, as Chloe pushed her legs even farther apart. Sara clutched at the counter and moaned.

Chloe's heart was pounding along with the one she could hear under her ear, pressed to Sara's back. She noticed the widening of Sara's stance and smiled. "Good girl. You're going to give me what I need, aren't you?" Her voice was breathy and low, laced with carnal intent. Chloe's right hand snaked down Sara's abdomen, to the elastic band, slipping her fingers down, stopping only when she could feel the beginning of the dark curls that lay there. She grasped Sara's breast tighter with her other hand, and punctuated each of her next words with a harder squeeze. "Tell me. Tell me you're going to give me anything I want," letting her strong words reverberate into her lover's back.

Sara couldn't believe her easily won compliance to the smaller woman's words and forceful manner. She was quivering to the words and the touches. "Yes," she gasped, and felt her footing falter, and the determined redhead behind her immediately held her tightly in place.

"Yes, what, Sara?" Chloe coaxed, moving her hand further into the dark curls, pulling on them, entwining them in her fingers.

"Yes," Sara hissed through her clenched teeth, just as Chloe's hand and fingers made contact with Sara's very heated center. "Anything you need." Sara clamped her mouth shut at the touch, unable to speak any more coherent words.

"Oh, that's nice," murmured Chloe, with her eyes shut, concentrating completely in what her hands were doing. She moved her fingers lower. "And that's even nicer," she finished as her fingers began a purposeful assault, massaging Sara with teasing, hypnotic touches. Chloe was a fast learner. She'd learned what Sara craved, what she needed in their short time together, and was putting her newfound knowledge to sensual use.

Chloe, her name repeated in Sara's head. The tall woman's knuckles were turning white from her grip on the counter edge, and she dropped her head down, unmindful that her long hair was almost touching the surface of the water in the sink. She felt Chloe everywhere and yet wanted more. She pushed down into Chloe's hand, and felt the redhead using a magical, relentless combination with her fingers, slow then speeding, soft then harder, sliding and pushing through her moisture, pulling and plunging until Sara was gasping. Her socked feet sliding on the linoleum floor, only to be caught and held steady, until the merciless pressure brought Sara to where her breath hitched, and then hitched again. She stopped breathing altogether as her body tightened, and she heard, as if in a distance, Chloe's persistent words possessing her with constant urgings, "Yes. Sara. Yes. C'mon, baby. C'mon, Sara. Yes."

Sara's breath faltered, and then she rose taller, and arched sharply into Chloe behind her, moaning through her intense release. She threw her head back, somehow trusting in the redheaded woman to keep her from falling, boneless, to the floor. She shuddered, and with heaving chest, she leaned into the counter again. Both stood there many moments, memorizing this feeling, letting their heartbeats resume a normal pace. Sara sighed as she felt Chloe's hand lift from her center, only to skim a damp trail across her abdomen, then wrapping her securely in her embrace. They stood straighter, Chloe rubbing her cheek against Sara's back, Sara shifting her feet to gain a firmer stance. Sara lifted a hand off the counter, and put her arm across Chloe's on her belly, her fingers finding, and then entwining with hers. Chloe placed soft kisses across her back until Sara pushed away from the counter, and keeping hold of Chloe's hand, she turned at last to meet the eyes of her love. Wordlessly, she kissed Chloe's forehead, and then leaned down and met Chloe in a sweetly searing kiss. She pulled away, and saw the emotions swirling in Chloe's misted eyes.

The dark woman sighed, and pulled the redhead into her arms, tightening the hug to convey the love that she felt. She tucked some strands of hair behind Chloe's ear, before whispering, softly and without deceit, "Anything. Anything you want, anything you need, Chloe."

Nelson walked into the library, noticing his lanky aunt right away. She was casually leaning on the counter, head propped in one hand, grinning at the animated, scowling face of Chloe, who was still spouting off about the twins' inability to get any work done, and how she should just fire them. She was just starting to repeat herself when Chloe noticed Nelson strolling up to the counter.

"Hey, Nels," Chloe beamed, now in the habit referring to Nelson in the same manner that Sara did.

"Hey, Chloe. Aunt Sara." He couldn't understand how, with all the time he was spending around Chloe, she still could make him feel very bashful. He liked how she called him Nels now. He turned to address Sara, who was idly playing with the date stamp on the counter. "Dad's double parked out front, everyone in town is at the liquor store and dry cleaners. There's no spaces out there. He said to tell you 'to quit playing footsie with Chloe, and get your ass out there.'" Nelson liked to be a good messenger, and relay messages the way he got them, no matter how much it made him blush.

Sara laughed. "Well, go tell your Dad that you and I plan on sleeping all the way to Orlando, and he's doing all the driving. That'll fix the bum." She winked at her snickering nephew. "I'll be right out. There's something in Chloe's office she needs to show me."

Nelson blushed again, and turned his shy gaze at Chloe. "See you next week, Chloe. You and Marcy have a nice Easter."

Chloe just adored this young man. "Thank you, Nelson, and please, make sure you and your Aunt Sara have a good time. Your dad is on his own."

Nelson nodded, and made his way out the front doors, leaving the two women to look at each other. Chloe looked needlessly around the quiet library; no one had come in besides Nelson since she had opened the front doors at nine o'clock. "C'mon, I want to show you a very fine first edition that I have locked in my office."

Sara followed her down the short corridor, and into Chloe's office, and shut the door quietly behind her. "Now where's this first edition you need to show me?" she whispered.

Chloe let out a guffaw. "Why are you whispering?"

Sara blinked, and then continued, grinning, in her muted tone. "It's a library, silly. I may get hit by lightning or something if I raise my voice above a certain decibel level." She took the small redhead into her arms, and held her lightly, surveying her face, memorizing every eyelash.

"Decibel level? You've certainly never been around here on delivery day, when I'm just about to skewer the twins, have you? Decibel level, my ass!" Chloe laughed, and wrapped her arms around Sara's neck.

"Your ass? What about it?" She reached down and gave both cheeks a firm squeeze. "Seems in pretty good shape to me. I wouldn't worry."

Chloe's eyes twinkled as she leaned in for a quick kiss. Her smile faded a little, and she looked a bit sad. "Jeez, we just get started, and you decide to blow town. Talk about love 'em and leave 'em."

Sara quirked an eyebrow. "I'll be back. You stay out of trouble with your friend the wacky artist. Those bohemian types are trouble." Before Chloe could answer, she leaned in for a deeper, sweeter kiss. "Now, what were we talking about?"

Chloe opened her eyes slowly, savoring the kiss. "I think, your late fees, and what you're going to do to work them off when you get back."

Sara laughed, and pulled Chloe in for a warm hug. She lifted the smaller woman into the air, and twirled her around. "How's that for starters?"

"Well, for starters, it's damned good," gasped a giggling Chloe as Sara slowly deposited her back to earth level. Chloe's keen hearing picked up the jingling sound of the bell hanging on the entrance door to the library. "Duty calls," she said disappointedly, although she knew that Sara had already dawdled too long with her, and that Dave was probably getting pretty antsy out there. "I love you, Sara. Be good."

Sara briefly considered feigning illness, and blowing off the whole trip. *Nobody would ever believe it. Damn this never getting sick thing.* "I love you, too, Chloe. I'll call Marcy's cell phone when we get there, okay?" Sara was vaguely uncomfortable with the knowledge that she wouldn't know where Chloe was going to be over this long weekend.

"Okay." Before Sara could pull away, Chloe pulled her in for one more long, languid kiss. Chloe disengaged to find Sara dreamily staring at her. "Hey, tall, dark and double-parked, get your ass in gear."

"I'm going." Sara opened up the door, and headed out, Chloe not far behind. Chloe went behind her counter, and watched as Sara stopped at the doorway, looked left, then right, and then blew her a kiss. She grinned as Chloe stood wide-eyed and frozen at this decidedly mushy, un-Sara-like gesture. Sara waved, and walked out the door. Chloe looked left, and then right, and then blew a kiss at the empty doorway.

Marcy reached into her open jacket collar, moving her hand into her knitted sweater, across her shoulder blade and down. Chloe could hear a sound. *Something being removed?*

"What're you doing?" Chloe asked, but Marcy's actions were already answering her question. Marcy's hand reappeared from out of her jacket, and a half-dollar sized tan patch waved briefly in Chloe's face before Marcy smacked it on the dashboard in front of her, where the adhesive held it in place.

"I'm smoking, goddammit." She pulled a pack of cigarettes out of her jacket pocket, looked silently at Chloe, who sighed and quickly nodded. Marcy pulled another one out of the pack and lit both, handing one to Chloe. "I bought them last night. And before you yell at me, I only smoked two. Mostly I sucked on unlit ones most of the night. Christ, I hate being good."

Chloe rolled down her driver's window a few inches, and waved out some of the smoke. They were only fifteen minutes from their destination, Harmercreek, and both women were in foul moods this Good Friday morning. Chloe had picked up Marcy fifteen minutes late; she'd overslept, and a nearly ranting Marcy had stomped out of her house, gotten into the Subaru, and slammed the door closed, quite intent on showing her anger with Chloe at being late on such an important day. They were now just leaving the outskirts of Stonecreek, and were headed east on Route 20, toward the outlying suburb of Hammercreek, where Marcy had her appointment at 11:00 a.m.

The remarks about smoking were the first words the women had exchanged.

Marcy sucked hard on her cigarette. "You know, if you'd gotten to my house on time, you could have talked to Sara. She was disappointed that you weren't there," Marcy said, agitation clearly showing on her face and in her voice.

Chloe took a quick glance at Marcy, and turned her eyes back to the road. "Shit," she replied, her tone matching her friend's.

"Yeah, shit."

"Well, are you going to tell me anything, or do I have to pull the car over and—"

"Why the hell are you in a bad mood, Chloe? You're the one that was late, you're not the one who's in need of this appointment, you know. I am."

"I have monster-sized cramps. So shut the hell up and tell me what Sara said."

"She didn't say anything."

"You just said..."

"Well, Sara was right there. I talked to Dave. They were at some truck stop, about three hours out of Orlando, in some southern state, I don't know."

"Why didn't you just say that?"

"Because I don't have to, you were late!" Marcy stubbed her cigarette out in Chloe's pristine ashtray, and dumped the butt into it.

Chloe glared at Marcy, took a final pull off her own cigarette, and tossed it out the window.

"Litterbug," huffed Marcy. "And another thing, I've had the trots all morning. I've taken enough Immodium and Pepto-Bismol, I may never take a dump again. I goddamn wish I had my period, you know? Then we wouldn't be taking this little hike up the road, I wouldn't be caffeine-deprived, nicotine-shorted or any of this crap.

We could be in this car taking a much more pleasurable trip, like, off the end of a dock. So, I don't care if it feels like your cramps are equivalent to giving birth to a baby elephant, or the fact that you didn't get to talk with your movie star girlfriend. Too goddamned bad for you, Chloe."

"Fuck you."

"Well, fuck you too."

Both women smiled.

"Wow," marveled a now grinning Chloe. "Period or no period, are we bitchy, or what?"

"You are. I'm just being me, just more so." Marcy replied.

The familiar buildings of the outskirts of Harmercreek were now coming into view. Marcy pulled out another cigarette. "This is stupid," said Marcy, trying to talk and light her cigarette at the same time. "I'm already not used to smoking. I feel lightheaded." She drew on her cigarette a few times. Chloe kept her remarks to herself. Marcy pointed up the road to a small plaza on the right hand side. "It's right up there, in that little plaza. Right across from the nursery."

Chloe flipped on her turn signal, and pulled into the small parking lot. She navigated between two cars, and put the Subaru in park. She leaned forward, and gazed up at the row of three businesses. There was a pizza parlor at the end, then a taxidermist, and then an office front, with a stenciled window reading "Harmercreek Family Planning." She turned to her friend, who was staring ahead, intent on hoovering as much nicotine into her system as she could in as short a time as possible. "This must be the place," Chloe said rather pointlessly. "Unless you were planning on having a skunk stuffed."

Marcy turned a glaring eye upon her, and silently threatened her redheaded friend. Chloe took the hint, and kept her mouth shut while Marcy finished her cigarette. Marcy butted it out, and again, tossed it into the car's ashtray. She checked her watch. "At least we're not late. We have a whole friggin' three minutes to spare. Let's go."

Chloe followed her friend in the front doors, and took off her coat while Marcy walked over to a small receptionist's window. A smiling blonde woman handed Marcy a clipboard with sheets attached, and Marcy took it, turned and then motioned Chloe to sit down in the small, stereotypical waiting room. There was one other woman in there, but she appeared to be dozing in her seat. She was quite obviously in the late stages of pregnancy, by the looks of the size of her belly. Blue chairs, blue carpeting, cheery but boring pictures, and magazines strewn on tables splitting chair groupings. Chloe grabbed a magazine and sat down, settling in while Marcy filled out the forms, bitching under her breath the whole time. She returned the completed forms to the receptionist, and sat down, grabbing a magazine for herself. She was just paging through it when both women heard a voice calling a name.

"Ms. Wojciechlowski?"

Chloe glanced toward the pregnant woman on the other side of the room, who was still sleeping in her chair, and then went back to her reading.

"Ms. Wojciechlowski?"

Both women started at the familiarity of the name, and the unfamiliarity of it, too. Marcy, who never blushed, did so now, as she quickly stood up and smiled at the dishwater blonde smiling at her from the doorway. She poked at an uncomprehending Chloe, who was still trying to figure out where she'd heard that name before.

"C'mon, Chloe." Marcy started toward the smiling woman, who was standing, waiting for them in the open doorway. Chloe took a quick mental scan of her as she followed both women up the hallway and into a small office with blue carpeting, a blue couch, mild and uninteresting pictures on the wall, and two blue armchairs facing the couch. There was a coffee table between the couch and chairs, and in the corner of the room was a small, unobtrusive desk.

The blonde woman motioned for Chloe and Marcy to sit down on the couch, which they did, staring up expectantly, waiting.

"Hi, I'm Julia Cardinger, I'm the counselor here. I'm sorry, we usually like to make our introductions in the privacy of the offices here." She stuck out her hand, and both Chloe and Marcy stood up again to shake the woman's hand.

"I'm Marcy, and this is Chloe." All three women sat down, the counselor in a chair across from both of them. She tried to put the two nervous women at ease.

"Oh, dear, I forgot to get your information from the receptionist. I'll be right back in two scoots." She went out the office door, shutting it quietly behind her.

Chloe and Marcy looked at each other.

"She's gotta be our age," said Chloe in her library-quiet voice.

"Yeah," whispered Marcy in reply, "I was expecting someone like Doris."

The office door opened again, and Julia Cardinger reappeared, clipboard in hand. She smiled, showing white even teeth set in a round and open face. She had oval glasses perched on the end of her nose, and was dressed, as Chloe would dress for a day at work, in dark khaki pants and button down shirt with a cardigan sweater. Her dark blonde hair was streaked, and cut in a short, boxy style. She glanced at the clipboard again as she sat down in her chair.

"Feel free to call me Julia. And I will call you Marcy? And Chloe? Okay?" she said sincerely, waiting for agreement to her statement. Both Chloe and Marcy mutely nodded. "I'm going to tell you both about some of the services we offer here at Harmercreek Family Planning, and then we can get to your questions." She looked at Marcy, and then, pointedly, at Chloe. "Don't be bashful to ask questions, Chloe. Just butt in at any time."

"Oh, she will," said Marcy flatly, and felt the nudge of her red-headed friend's elbow in her ribs. Inexplicably, they had both sat close together in the center of the couch, hip to hip, shoulder to shoulder, facing the counselor. Perhaps it was their years of friendship that made them both feel better, stronger, more united with this close proximity.

Forty-five minutes later, after many explanations from the counselor of services offered and details of the procedures rendered, Marcy had finally gotten the answers to all of her questions, and sat back into the couch, visibly shaken and emotional. Chloe had been helpfully handing tissues to a friend she rarely had seen cry. Chloe was feeling the gravity of the situation too, so she wrapped her arm around Marcy, and with lack of anything better to do, she gave her a small kiss on the cheek in encouragement and solidarity.

Julia Cardinger gave a small sigh. "I know it must be a hard decision. But you've some time to think about it, don't try to make a decision right now, right in this office. You have plenty of time to think before you come to any conclusions. You can call me with more questions. Talk to Chloe about it. You've come in early enough in your pregnancy that you have a wider window than a lot of the clients I see."

Marcy had heard the phrases, "your pregnancy" and "your baby" one too many times from the lips of this blonde stranger. She stood up from the couch, and said to the still-seated counselor, "ladies' room?"

"Right up the hall, to your left," she said, smiling a small smile of sympathy.

"I'll be right back." Marcy disappeared out the office door, leaving a softly sniffing Chloe behind, alone with the still smiling counselor.

"You okay?" she said softly to the upset little librarian, who had been trying to hold her teetering emotions in check for the benefit of her long-time friend.

"Yeah. It's just so hard." Chloe blew her nose into a Kleenex, and smiled sadly.

"Well, Chloe, it's wonderful you came with her today."

Chloe nodded, and sniffed. "I had to be here. She means the world to me."

Julia leaned across, snatched up a tissue, and handed it to Chloe, who was starting to cry a little more freely. "I'm sorry, where did you say you lived?"

Chloe took the tissue, and gave the woman a grateful look. "We live in Stonecreek." She blew her nose again.

"How long have you two known each other?"

"Seems like forever," said a weepy-voiced Chloe. She wanted to pull herself together before Marcy came back, so she took a couple of deep, cleansing breaths.

Julia sat back in her chair, and shook her head. "I have to tell you this. It is just so lovely, so refreshing to see the kind of unconditional love and support that you're showing her, Chloe."

Chloe sniffed and smiled grimly.

The blonde counselor looked down, adjusted her glasses, and then returned her gaze to Chloe, a small smile on her lips. She took a deep breath of her own, before she leaned forward to address Chloe, meeting her eyes. "Most of the couples that I counsel, the ones like you and Marcy, are here to find out about alternative ways to conceive a child. I think it's very brave of you, under the circumstances, to help Marcy along in her time of indecision. I don't know the exact circumstances of how Marcy got pregnant, but the fact that you've stayed with her when this must be so difficult for you, well, I just think that's inspiring."

Chloe's brain was having difficulty doing the math that would allow her to put two and two together about what the counselor was saying. She blinked, and then blinked again, trying to shake loose a few brain cells into activity.

Encouraged by Chloe's blank smile, the counselor went on. "That you two have worked out your problems, and are still together. Well it just does my heart so good. If only my ex- lover could witness this kind of devotion I'm seeing right now, I'm sure she would—"

Marcy interrupted the counselor's heartfelt tribute by returning at that very awkward moment in time. She looked much better, and smiled a more controlled and relaxed smile at them both.

Chloe's mouth began to sag open and she struggled to speak. Too bad nothing remotely intelligent wanted to come out. "Uh. Um. Marcy?" She saw that Marcy was looking at her strangely.

"You ready, hon?" Marcy smiled a very grateful smile at her best friend, and saw Chloe stiffly nod. She turned her attention to the counselor, who was now standing. She put out her hand, and gave the counselor a tight and vigorous handshake. "Thanks, Julia, for your time and your wisdom, and your insight. You'll be hearing from me."

Julia waited for the somewhat conflicted librarian to stand up, and Chloe just gave her a small smile but a big handshake. "Uh. Yeah. Thanks, Julia."

When the two women stepped out onto the sidewalk, into the refreshing breeze, both paused a moment, closed their eyes, and took in twin deep breaths. Marcy reached into her jacket pocket, and pulled out her cigarettes. She pulled one out, and stated, "I promise this is the first of the next five last ones I'll smoke today." She lit it, and noticed the smile playing across Chloe's lips. "What?"

Chloe cleared her throat, and tried to downplay her grin. "Did you notice anything odd about Julia?"

Marcy ran a hand through her thick curls, and looked at her friend curiously. "You mean, something besides the bad haircut?"

Chloe willed her lips into a straight line. "Yeah. The way she treated us."

"I'm not floating in the same current here as you, Chloe. What do ya mean?"

Chloe wanted to play this out, it was too good. "Did you notice how she kind of skirted around the father issue?"

Marcy took another puff, totally bewildered at what her friend was getting at. She scratched her head, then reached over and scratched Chloe's for good measure. "Well, we really didn't discuss Dave." She looked at Chloe for further enlightenment.

Enlightening, Chloe wasn't. "Exactly."

Marcy, so confused it was actually making her smile, caught some of the sparkle in Chloe's eyes. "What are you getting at, huh?"

"Well," started Chloe, now unable to keep the smile off her face, "I think she did that in deference to me." When Marcy just shook her head, not getting it, Chloe continued, a little giggle threading through her voice. "Marcy, I think, no, I know, that Julia thinks that if you have the baby, it will have a father. Me." Chloe stopped there, waiting for Marcy's reaction.

The art teacher's eyes widened, and she gasped out, "You mean?"

Chloe slapped her arm around the shoulders of her shocked friend, and began walking them to the car. "Yeah, Marse, I'm your daddy."

The tension broken, both women had difficulty getting into the car because every time they would catch the other's eye, they would start their incredulous, hysterical laughter again.

Paul was loading a flat of petunias into the trunk of his mother's gaudy luxury sedan. She was standing by the passenger side, compact in hand, putting on a touch up of lipstick. She was just closing her compact when she noticed two women exiting an office building in the small plaza across the street. Putting her lipstick and compact back in her purse, she pulled out her bifocals and put them on, focusing on those now-familiar figures. She saw them talking, and then begin laughing, as they walked to a brown station wagon. Her interest in the two women faded as they got into the vehicle, and was diverted to the sign office window they had exited. *Harmercreek Family Planning.*

"Paul?" said Mrs. Hoderman, her eyebrows twitching.

Paul slammed the trunk shut. "Yes, Mother?"

"Hurry up. I don't want to be late for my lunch with Doris."

Part XXI:
The Bitter and the Sweet

Sara woke up, feeling vaguely chilled. She reached a hand out from under the pile of light blankets she was under, and touched the tip of her nose. It was cold, like a puppy's. She stretched her long legs out and felt the cool metal bars of the end of the daybed with her toes. She rubbed her eyes open, and saw the stripes of daylight peeking through the slats of the mini-blind on the single window here in the small room. It was more of an all-purpose room, outfitted with the daybed, but without any other furnishings that would identify it as a bedroom. She rubbed her eyes again, dislodging some of the small sleepers that had formed there overnight. The sun of midmorning was lighting the room, even with the nearly shut blinds, and Sara rolled on her side to look around. Her suitcase was propped near her father's exercise bike in the center of the room, and the opposite wall held a sewing table and machine. There were scraps of material lying over the ironing board in front of the modern machine, her mother's hobby ever since Sara could remember. On the white walls were photographs and pictures that Sara recognized from her parents' house in Stonecreek, set almost in the same patterns as when they had been displayed there. Sara smiled at the comfortable familiarity of it.

Even the pictures in the bathrooms, the colors of the towels, the fish on the shower curtains, the soaps on the back of the toilet, were pretty much the same as in their old house. The couches and the chairs in the living room were new, but set in the same pattern as when she'd been growing up. She could go into the kitchen, find things, and just know that the water glasses will be in the cupboard to the right of the sink. The teddy bear cookie jar was on the counter, and when she opened it, there were cookies in it. Sara grinned. *Not like Mom ever made any, but she always had it full with the ones she bought.* She used to think that the jar was magical, and cookies just appeared in there. *Everything is the same here, just a different house, but I could probably close my eyes and navigate through it, find things, touch paintings on the walls, and know exactly what they* were. *Everything is different, everything is the same.*

Except for Mom and Ernie. Sara had seen photographs of them in recent years, but was not emotionally prepared for the reality when they arrived here yesterday afternoon. Her dad, never a large man, seemed even smaller now to her, thinner than she remembered, slower in speech and mannerisms. *What is he now, seventy-three? Seventy-four?* The skin on his arms felt soft to her as she hugged him, the hair on the top of his head was thinner, sparser than she recalled. He was not as tall as his sturdy children, he was a good four inches shorter than his amazonian daughter, and when she held him, her cheek lay half on his forehead, half on the pepper gray of the slicked backed strands of hair on the top of his head. He smelled of equal parts of Old Spice and cheap cherry cigars, with maybe a hint of WD-40 thrown in for good measure. When she pulled back from him, he shyly smiled at her, his delight clearly showing in his hazel eyes, and she smiled back, glad to see there was no recrimination staring back at her. Ernie was a simple man, not simple minded, and not judgmental. That trait he left to his wife.

Sara thanked God her mother wasn't there when they arrived, although she felt it was just postponing the inevitable. Her mother had shown up an hour later, to find them all sitting on the back patio, talking and having a beer. The tall woman appeared behind the screen of the sliding glass door, and Sara, facing the house, was the first to see her there. They exchanged measured glances and smiles of acknowledgment, eyes blue on blue, both women taking a moment or two to emotionally gird themselves for their reunion. Marjorie slid the door open and stepped through it, and her son and grandson were immediately on their feet to greet her, to hug the tall woman, their voices animated and joking. Sara remained seated in her lounge chair, her nerves a quiet jumble, steeling herself, unsure of the reception her mother would give her after all these years.

Mom looks good. She looks older, that's natural. Her hair doesn't give away her age, it's the same color I always remembered. It's been that deep chestnut color, never varying in shade or tint, forever. Since I used to sit at the beauty shop, fascinated, as—what was her name? Oh, yeah, Betty—would touch up her roots for her, every six weeks or so.

The low heels that Marjorie wore brought her eye-to-eye with her daughter, and both women averted their eyes when they finally did hug, a hug of informal greeting that did not last long, did not carry an extra squeeze of affection in it. Sara was surprised to find that she desired to hug her mother with meaning, but her wariness made her hold back from displaying the relief and joy. She felt it in her heart but did not extend it to her arms when they went around the older woman.

The rest of the afternoon, into evening, was spent in conversation on the patio, at the dinner table, and finally in the living room. Dave held court most of the time, his good humor and easiness around his family infectious. Sara sat back, smiled and even laughed at her father's bad jokes. Dave spoke about his golf course and the working histories of it. He spoke proudly about his shyly blushing son, the football star on a terrible team and musical theater neophyte. He bragged affectionately about his irreplaceable sister and all of her contributions to his nine-hole dream. He even, blushing and hesitant, told them about the art teacher he was dating, and with a quick wink to his quiet and smiling sister, told them about his hopes to marry her. Sara had looked to Nelson for his reaction to this statement. Nelson blinked, turned his gaze to his aunt, and looked at her questioningly. Sara rolled her eyes at him and gave him a toothy smile, which after a moment, he returned in full force. Nelson then looked at his dad and gave him a smile of enthusiastic acceptance.

As the evening wore on, and more beers were opened, more coffee was made and the family group shifted into the living room, Nelson was gently prodded into talking about his involvement in the school play. Nelson, usually very reticent to speak, warmed to his subject, his enthusiasm overcoming his natural shyness. He spoke long and excitedly about every aspect of the play, from his aunt's gentle tutoring of his singing in the cold garage, the rehearsal catastrophes of the colliding Mo Dean and Charlie Shemp, the pure joy he felt when he discovered he had gotten the role of Curly. He spoke affectionately of Marcy, Paul, and finally of his small red-blonde director, Chloe, and at the mention of her name, the nephew and aunt exchanged a meaningful glance of acknowledgment. Chloe's name brought such a smile, a gentle balm that eased his aunt's tense features, that Nelson went on and on about the librarian, and his father cheerfully joined in with tales about her verve, her spirit, her gentle good humor, her tendencies to get a bit crazy. Dave and Nelson enthusiastically took up the task of informing their parents about Sara's new love, and through their stories, indirectly introduced Chloe as integral part in Sara's new life. They vocalized for the quietly appreciative long-haired woman what she could not. Both father and son took the time and care to imply that this Chloe Donahue was a person of great importance to them, and their loving words for her slowly clued Marjorie and Ernie into the status that she held in all their lives. Quite touched by their words, Sara found herself nearly on the verge of tears during their accolades for her younger lover. They thought of Chloe as family, and they wanted Mom and Ernie to know that. Ernie, just as quiet as his daughter, sat watching and listening, and got up to get more coffee from the kitchen. He passed by the armchair in which Sara was sitting, and stopped and laid a hand on his daughter's shoulder. "She sounds like a pistol, Sara. I hope we get to meet her," he said with a delicate smile, and then went on his way.

Sara stretched her arms over her head, and propped a lazy hand under her chin as she turned on her side. Her thoughts, as they did every morning now, turned to and were totally encompassed by Chloe. Each of her senses took stock of the memory of her. Her eyes filled with a vision of Chloe's trademark thoughtful chin scratching, something the librarian did to grab a moment to collect her thoughts before reacting to something. Sara's nostrils momentarily ignored the artificial spring freshness of the sheets of the daybed, and conjured up the mixture of deodorant soap, herbal shampoo, and Vaseline Intensive Care lotion that mixed into a surprisingly pheromone-inspiring reaction in Sara. Sara laughed and rubbed her belly. *And her feet, well, frankly, they stink.* Sara laughed out loud again at that thought. Sara's mind heard the enigma of Chloe's laugh, a sound that burst forth with all the power of a snort and then changed into some-thing almost childlike and lilting by its conclusion. Sara's ears heard the high tones of Chloe's voice when she was anxiously angry and spoke with rambling unchecked train of thought. The echoes of the lows and breathiness those tones took on when whispering, hesitat-ing and stammering, trying to convey the depth of feeling she felt for the dark woman she held so tightly in her arms.

I wonder where they ended up? Spin The Car. As if those two weren't spinning enough as it is, they want to go and get even dizzier. Sara looked at the window of the small room almost expecting to be able to look out it, and picture Marcy's red Mazda speeding down a four-lane highway.

Nothing like falling in love to make you think about reevaluating your future, is there? Things are going to change, they always do. As much as I like how things are right now, there's a certain progression to everything in life that I can't ignore, even if I want to. Sara had recently begun to think beyond her day-to-day existence, and to think in terms of weeks, months, and when she was feeling especially opti-mistic, even years into the future. The shared strength of new friends, the support of family, and the satisfaction of work worthwhile and rewarding was quietly fortifying Sara's soul, surely rebuilding it into a steely facsimile of her former self. *I forgot what, who I was. I really had no sense of self for so long. I didn't recognize myself. I can feel myself coming back into being. The problem with that is, how much of it do I want to bring back?* Sara's thoughts again turned to Chloe. *I know I love her, I want us to be together. For how long?* An uneasy nagging feeling stole over Sara, not an anxious reaction, but an awakening sense of the inevitability of decisions that would have to be made between them, individually and together. Sara had to ascertain within herself what her own decisions were, what they would have to discuss and ponder mutually, and which questions Chloe had to decide on her own. *I'm just finding myself again, and now I don't know how much of that to harness in deference to a lover.* Sara rubbed the remainders of the sleepers out of her eyes. *I've never made decisions in my life considering the feelings of a lover. I made choices; they lived with them, or they went on their way. Who am I kidding? I drove them all away.*

Sara scratched her chin, the long-buried actress in her not realizing she was perfectly mimicking the mannerisms of a small redhead who was now somewhere, spun out, north of the Mason-Dixon line.

Chloe decided it was too good an opportunity to miss, even if Sara wasn't there to share the moment of revenge in person. *I've been waiting to get Marcy back for her interruption of our first night together, and using her key to sneak up on us that next morning.* Chloe quietly exited the bathroom of the motel room she and Marcy shared, and crossed over to the double bed that Marcy was sprawled out in the middle of, snoring with a precise and measured cadence that a drum major would envy. *I don't really need to be quiet, this woman is just like me, and could sleep through a stampeding herd of cats in heat.* Chloe threw the towel from her damp head onto the other double bed, and dressed only in her matching light blue panties and bra, quickly slipped into bed with Marcy. She inched closer and closer to the body of her slumbering curly-haired friend, knowing that her patience in approaching her would help in the ultimate success of her sneaky little plan. *Oh Sara, I wish you were here to see this.* Chloe spooned her body slowly into Marcy, and watched for any wakefulness that action might bring. *Nope, still out for the count.* Chloe pulled a pillow into position under her cheek, and brought her head and then her lips close to Marcy's ear. *Almost there.* Chloe slowly draped an arm around Marcy's T-shirted waist, and slowly tightened her grip. Chloe nearly lost it then, and had to take a moment to regroup when Marcy, scooting her butt tighter into the spoon, startled her. Chloe bit the inside of her cheek to keep from laughing, and then once she was sure Marcy was settled and content, she began her stealthy assault.

Chloe's pink tongue danced a delicate line around the perimeter of Marcy's ear, and Chloe, drawing on all her inner strength to keep from giggling, breathed a deep and drawn out "Mmmmmm" while continuing her wet path around the artist's ear. Marcy stirred, but did not wake. Chloe kept up a steady bass moan, and then combined soft nips to Marcy's earlobe combined with soft flicks of her tongue. Chloe was surprised to find that these attentions to her friend's ear caused some vague stirrings to her own core, but she swallowed them back, determined to see her vengeful plan through to completion. Chloe added a new variation on her attack. She began slowly rubbing Marcy's belly in light circles. Marcy's shoulders gave a small jerk in reaction, and when she did this, Chloe gave her earlobe an especially meaningful sucking, along with the deepest "Mmmmmm" she could manage. Marcy twitched, and the next thing Chloe was aware of was that she was flat on her back, being lustily kissed by her best friend, who in of twenty-three years of friendship had rarely even hugged her.

"Marfph," choked Chloe, who was unable to form words around Marcy's diving tongue.

Marcy's sleepy brain was barely cognizant but happy to find that Dave had taken the time to shave before his seduction of her this morning. Although his voice was sounding somewhat strange. *He must have a pillow across his chest, it's too soft and his hands on my shoulders are smaller and seem to be pushing me away for some reason.*

Chloe's frantic pushing helped Marcy's slippery brain to achieve some traction. Marcy flew straight up before unceremoniously taking a right turn in mid-air, her destination the floor between the two beds.

Chloe flipped onto her side to make sure her friend was all right after her quick flight, and looked wide eyed at her.

Marcy, on her butt, propped herself up on her elbows, and after a quick inventory of her important parts and finding them all in working condition, leveled a bleary and red-faced glare at the redhead staring down at her from the edge of the bed.

"Jesus H. Christ, Chloe! What the ever-livin' fuck was that all about?"

Chloe's cheeks rose impossibly high in conjunction with the huge grin on her lips, and she threw herself into the pillows in the middle of the bed and started roaring with laughter, knowing she would be unable to verbalize any acceptable explanations to her livid friend. Chloe pulled the two pillows tighter around her head for protection when she felt the beginning blows of another pillow raining down on her from above. Each hit was punctuated with a bohemian and artistic-sounding string of curses. Finally, Marcy's anger abated and the calls of her desperate bladder won out, so Chloe was able to peek out from under her pillowed fortress and catch her breath as the bathroom door slammed closed.

Chloe gulped a grateful lungful of air. "Vengeance!" she half yelled, half giggled sweetly toward the closed door.

"I hate you!" rang the muffled, bitter reply.

Marjorie D'Amico arrived home from her errands and having her hair done to find the house empty. She put a few grocery items away, and headed into her bedroom to change into something more casual now that she was home. She never went out without looking groomed and stylish. She rarely ever went to pick up a prescription in less than a perfectly matching outfit and heels. She was a woman who radiated style and substance, and she hadn't succumbed to the casual breeziness of Florida in the twelve years they had lived here. One of Marjorie's friends had gently teased her once by saying that Marjorie always dressed, seven days a week, as if she might be called to a funeral, a garden party, or to be sworn in as a supreme court judge at a moment's notice. Marjorie took it with quiet good nature, it was just another variation on the comments she'd heard when she had still lived in the small town on the shores of Lake Erie.

She walked by the open door of her sewing room, and noticed with a quick glance that it was empty, the daybed was lightly made, and Sara's suitcase lay open on the floor. *Maybe she's out back taking a swim.* Marjorie entered her own comfortable bedroom, and carefully removed the clothes she had on for a few hours, and considered putting on her own bathing suit. *It's not like Sara and I will do laps together. More like we'll have one long arm wrestling match, using strong words instead of strong arms.* She put on a pressed pair of shorts and a sleeveless top, and pushed a pair of sandals on her feet. She paused in front of the full-length mirror to ponder her image. *Not bad for a sixty-two-year-old broad.* Then her vision changed, and she tilted her head to one side, using her recent memory of the image of her long-missing daughter as a comparison to what she saw in the mirror. Sara took after her, as did Dave, and not after her diminutive husband. Sara's hair was much longer, much darker, and it appeared to Marjorie that Sara wasn't using any products to hide gray as of yet. Marjorie began doing that when she was just a few years older than Sara was now. *What is she, thirty-five, thirty-six? I'm terrible, I don't know how old my own kids are.* She did the quick mental addition, and since Dave had turned forty this year, she concluded that her daughter, five years younger, was thirty-five. *It's not as if I'd sent her birthday cards for years, considering I didn't know where to send them.* She studied the reflection of her blue eyes, her sculpted cheeks, her lips, her tall thin frame, and concluded with a wry smile that there was no way she could deny she was the mother of a movie star.

She appeared, coffee cup in hand, on the open patio and settled into a chair at the small round table there. She'd been right, her daughter was swimming leisurely laps in the small in-ground pool. It only took her five strokes to reach the end of the pool, where she flipped, and began her trek back to the other end to repeat the process. Marjorie drank her coffee, and casually perused the front page of the morning paper, waiting for her daughter to notice her arrival.

The rhythm of Sara's measured strokes finally stopped, and Marjorie looked up from her article to find her daughter treading water in the middle of the pool, black hair slicked back off her face, looking at her, grinning.

"Hey," said Sara.

"Hey," replied Marjorie, not exactly returning the grin.

Sara, never one to take the easy way out, ignored the steps on the end of the pool, and instead pushed her way up and onto the patio stones from the edge. Marjorie had a chance to further study her daughter, now standing, dripping, in a one-piece black bathing suit, wiping the excess water off of her tall, lithe form before padding over to her mother and settling into a chair across from her. Eye contact, at this point, was not an option for either woman so Sara turned her attention toward the pool, while Marjorie went back to her paper.

"What time is it?" Sara began, angling her body to make more of it available to the warm sunlight.

Marjorie intoned, never looking up, "Nearly noon." She turned a page. "They'll be back probably around one, or two, depending on how many idiots Ernie has to introduce them to down at the golf course." She paused and checked out an editorial cartoon before continuing, "Or unless they play another eighteen. It's certainly cool enough today and they're using a cart."

Sara got a mental image of Dave, Ernie and Nelson racing around the parking lot in golf carts and chortled to herself, before allowing herself a small internal sigh. She took a small sip of her own now-cold coffee, and looked at the unmarred blue skies and silently cursed the absence of rain clouds. "That's good," she said, not meaning anything, just letting words fill the air between them. She was going to let her mother begin this conversation.

Another page was flipped. "There are sweet rolls in there, or you could make yourself a sandwich. I'm not much of a hostess."

"I'll get one after I dry off a bit."

Her mother went back to her reading, and Sara concentrated on dripping dry.

Her mom broke the silence by giving a small derisive snort. "Brainless morons."

"Hmm?"

"School board here. They're living in the '50s. There seems to be to two major issues about this year's prom. The first being whether they should allow same-sex couples to attend. The second is whether to hire security for the proms to pat down the attendees for weapons. Guess which one they're fighting over?"

"Let me guess, the same-sex couples, right? I would think that would be old news by now. I mean, haven't kids been doing that more and more over the years?"

"Yes, but unsanctioned by the holy and mighty school board. Seems this year someone pushed the point and wants the school board to officially bless what they've successfully avoided recognizing for years now." Marjorie shook her head.

Sara laughed, and decided to push the envelope a little. "I'd have liked to have gone with Roberta Bockman, you know."

Marjorie's mind left local politics, and searched for the meaning of Roberta Bockman. "Ah. The Central High forward from Erie, huh?" When Sara slightly smiled, Marjorie went on. "No, bad idea. That girl had absolutely no sense of style. You looked great in your gown, I remember. But her! Did they make gowns in plaid flannel back then?" She gave her daughter her first eye contact, a daring straight-on stare, tinged with just a hint of a smile.

Sara smiled, pleased with the flash of sparkling blue in her mother's eyes. "I'm not sure, Maude." Sara waited for her mother's reaction to her old nickname; one that Sara had given her after noting too many similarities between her dryly witty and abrasive tall mother and Bea Arthur. Her mother had outwardly disapproved of the nickname, but Sara had always thought that it secretly pleased her mother to be compared favorably to the actress and character that they both liked so much.

"Not that you didn't cause a big enough scandal without Roberta Bockman at your side. And don't call me Maude." Her mother scowled, unconsciously imitating a Maude mannerism. "You leave the house in a gown, and you come back to the house in a gown and a black eye. Most girls get corsages."

"Well, most girls get taken to the prom. John Bentzel took me directly to the Ramada Inn. I didn't like his sense of direction."

Marjorie's eyebrows rose. "Well, that little bum. But how did you get the black eye? You never said." *And I knew better than to ask.*

Sara stole a quick glance at her mother before she answered. "It was purely self-defense on his part. His elbow was stuck in my eye when he tried to cover up from the second punch I threw at him. We were in a Toyota Corolla, I didn't have the proper amount of room for a good punch the first time, so I went back for a second one." Sara bent her elbow, and demonstrated the shortened, awkward swing. "Bang, I get the black eye. He got us to the prom, Doris Raeburn took one look at my eye, and promptly sent him home. But I think she got my revenge for me, I think she was in charge of the prom queen's scepter that night, and she put it to good use before he ran out of there."

"Ah. Doris." Marjorie grinned, remembering with affection the verbose high school principal, who frequently called Marjorie during Sara's high school years, the long winded one-sided conversations always beginning with complaints about the tall beauty, then ending with a combination of praise and frustration for her behavior.

Sara rubbed her left elbow. "Yeah, Doris. I was on the receiving end of a well placed umbrella thwack from her just recently."

"You probably deserved it. She's just making up for lost opportunities. With the crap you pulled in high school, it's a wonder you didn't spend your senior year in detention hall."

"And my later years in a state prison."

Marjorie turned her attention back to the paper, but decided to get to business at last. "Well, at least we would have known where to send your birthday cards," she said, her voice dry with undisguised bitterness.

I could get up right now, and take an hour showering, and another hour getting dressed. But this has to happen. "Yeah." She looked at her mother again, and then looked away. *Now or never, or we'll never get this resolved. Not like I have any hopes for really resolving this.* "What do you want to know, Mom? I know Dave has filled you in to a lot that was happening to me over the years, you know all about the accident, you know about my panic attacks, my disappearing, you know about my face. You can see my face, it's good, and it's not a problem now. What is it exactly that you want to know?" Sara queried, trying to keep her voice even and without defensive overtones.

Marjorie closed the paper and carefully folded it before she replied, sitting back in her chair to look full on to her silently waiting daughter. "I want to know if you're going to let this happen again. This," she paused, trying to come up with something concise, "forgetting that you have a family that cares about you, whatever happens to you. Because I am telling you right now, Sara," Marjorie steeled herself for the coming words, "If you do it again, I am not going to stand for it. You won't have a mother to come visit. I had a hard enough time dealing with it the first time around, and I can't, I won't do it again." The serious blue eyes of her mother settled on the sad blue eyes of her daughter. "I mean it. It may take me the rest of my life just to reconcile these past ten years of your unjustified and undeserved behavior toward your dad and me. He'll forgive you for anything, past, present or future. So will David. I won't. I'll try for the past and present, but if the future holds any chance of this bullshit lack of consideration of your family again, well, consider yourself motherless." Marjorie's face settled into expressionless tightness, but she was suddenly feeling very emotional. "We all deserved much better than this bullshit of yours." *I wish I could come up with a better word to describe it, but actually, bullshit is exactly the right word.*

Sara, feeling a wave of guilt pass through her, couldn't immediately come up with a response. *No sense in arguing with her, or getting defensive. Bullshit is what I did to them.* "It's not going to happen again, Mom. I won't let it." Sara took a shaky breath, and said it out loud. "I'm sorry. I'm really, really sorry." She looked out to the pool again, her eyes blurring, her heart softly pounding, her hands twisting the towel in her lap.

"Well, your words hold a lot of conviction, Sara. Just live them." Marjorie's unfocused gaze joined her daughter's out to the gold white glints of sunlight on the pool. She sighed and said the words again. "Just live them."

Chloe was still too much of an unrepentant adolescent not to revel in her victory. Marcy finally came out of the bathroom, freshly showered, and studiously ignored the grinning redhead sitting propped up against the headboard of her bed.

Chloe patted the space next to her loudly. "Hey, Marse. I never realized what a good kisser you are. How about you bring some of that sweet stuff over here and—"

Marcy was pulling on her jeans. "How about you stuff the room service menu right up your sweet—" Marcy had to stop tugging on her zipper to duck the pillow that flew her way.

Chloe's voice became even more teasing. "You know you liked it. Admit it. We don't have to go anywhere today, Marcy. We can entertain ourselves, right here." Chloe tried to inject a sultry tone into her voice but failed; it came out more like an old man's lechery. "If I'd only have known years ago. Just look at all the time we've wasted when we could have been so much more!" She successfully ducked another flying pillow. "Now we just have to find a way to break the news to Dave and Sara."

Marcy pulled a loose shirt out of her bag, slipped it over her head, and adjusted her damp curls before replying testily, "Well, Miss Lips, seems you are living up to your rather tarty reputation. Dave, Sara, me; who's left? Nelson?" She enjoyed the look of horror that crossed the face of the librarian at that name. "And then, who else is there to conquer? Paul? Doris? Audra?"

"Been there, kissed that," said Chloe, glad that the mention of different names wiped out the Nelson reference.

"And is she a good kisser? As hot as me?"

Chloe's mind returned to the memory for a moment, and

allowed herself to enjoy the pleasure of it. "Oh, yeah, she's a great kisser," she said, honestly and a bit too dreamily.

Marcy dug out some socks, slipped one over her toes, and said measuredly, "Humph. Well, imagine that." She grabbed her other sock. "Doris Raeburn is a great kisser. Huh."

Marcy couldn't dodge the pillow that came hurtling her way. She laughed, and finished pulling on her other sock. "Point for me."

Chloe swung her feet off the bed, and reached for her sneakers. "Ew. Ew. Ew. Thanks a friggin' lot, Marse, for putting that visual into my head. Ew."

"My pleasure. Just as, apparently, that smooch this morning was your pleasure." Marcy was saved from heavier, more dangerous objects being lobbed at her head by the muted sound of her cell phone ringing in her overnight bag. She quickly scooped it out and hit the on button. "Hello, Donahue's Brothel. Where you get so much more than just laid." A low chuckle sounded into Marcy's ear, she recognized it as a D'Amico, but she wasn't sure which one. "How may we help you today?" She shifted her laughing eyes to Chloe, to signal that the call was from someone they actually wanted to hear from.

"I was wondering if you still running that Saturday Two For One Special?" drawled a clearly delighted Sara.

Marcy nodded at Chloe, indicating that it was Sara on the line. Chloe smiled.

Marcy paused only a moment, and answered Sara's question. "Well, no, ma'am, actually, this being Easter weekend, we have a Hestian virgin special right now. Would you like to talk to one of our specialists and set up a reservation?"

"That would be fine. Thank you," replied Sara, her mind immediately putting the little librarian into a very specialized scenario.

Marcy hit the mute button on the phone, and handed it to Chloe, who sat laid back onto the bed again, and propped herself up onto some pillows.

"I'm going down to the lobby and get us some coffee and a continental breakfast. Raisin Bran or Fruit Loops for you?"

"Lots of rank coffee, a dried-out bagel and some warm orange juice, please," Chloe said, and released the mute button.

Marcy smiled and grabbed the room card on her way out.

"Hello, Sara," Chloe murmured into the phone.

"Hey, Chloe." The hairs on Sara's neck danced just at the low tones of Chloe's greeting.

On the other end, Chloe felt a distinct wave of pleasure wash over her at the sound of Sara's voice. "How's Florida? Have you stolen a pink flamingo from someone's lawn for me yet?"

"Not yet. Although I saw a house with those plastic Easter eggs hanging on it. Very festive."

"Sounds so very pastel." Chloe hugged a pillow to her. "How's the famdamily? Alienate anyone yet? How's the parental units?"

"They're good. They're still feeding me, so I figure that's a positive thing."

Chloe's voice turned serious. "Really, how did it go with them?" She hesitated. "Or maybe you can't or don't want to talk about it now?"

Sara sighed, pulled a throw pillow from the end of the couch, and clutched it to her with her free hand. "Nah, it's okay. Mom is out having a swim and a nap, and the guys are all at some local golf course shanking balls at unsuspecting senior citizens. I can talk for a little while."

"Good. Well, I miss you."

Sara strengthened her hold on the pillow. "Miss you too. Mom and I are getting things straightened out. She's telling me what's what, and I'm agreeing with her."

"That's what you expected, right?"

"Pretty much. She just wants to make sure that she'll know exactly where to send my birthday cards the rest of my life. I told her she would."

Chloe still had a few unanswered questions of her own about Sara's mindset when she disappeared from her family those years, but now was not the time to pursue them. She did understand that Sara's parents would have some very big issues about it. "So, are you having any fun? Are you glad to be there?"

"I am having some fun, and yes, I'm infinitely glad I came down here to see them. I'm really glad I got brave. Mom can be a terror, but she's been very civil considering what I put them through," Sara said regretfully.

"Well, yeah." Sara sounded so sad, Chloe decided to lighten up the conversation. "Want me to fly down there and hide some Easter eggs in strategic places on my body, and let you hunt for them?"

Sara's dark eyebrow crooked at that remark. "Well, that would be a fine idea. I'm almost afraid to ask where you two ended up when you spun the car."

"We're in Pittsburgh. Home of the Pixberg Stillers, and Heinz Ketchup." Chloe affected the unique Pittsburghese way of speaking. "'N' later, we're goin' dawn to East Carson Street, 'n' at, and pick us up some lezbeen literature at a gay bookstore down 'nair, and maybe a pride bumper sticker for the Miata. Marcy needs to broaden her horizons." Chloe was going to save her story about just how broadened Marcy's horizons had recently gotten to when she could tell the story in front of a more appreciative and chagrined audience. That being in front of Sara and Dave and Marcy. *Life can be sweet.* "An' continuin' our 'Lezbeen Saturday' theme, we're hitting a dyke bar that I know of up on West Liberty." Chloe giggled. "I love to watch Marcy fending off amorous lesbians. She gets pissed when I don't step in and protect her."

Sara smirked, and then with a marked feeling of possessiveness coming over her, she asked. "So, the big question is, will she protect you from them?"

Chloe grinned at the undisguised jealousy Sara was displaying. "Well, calm down there, tall, dark and green eyed." Chloe snorted. "Funny thing is, whenever Marcy and I go to gay bars, everyone assumes she's the dyke, and I'm her straight friend. Go figger."

"Well, if I was in that bar, I would definitely go for her straight friend," Sara declared, knowing it was very true.

Chloe blushed, quite touched at Sara's sentiments. "And I'd help you get a toaster oven for converting me." She brought her knees up, hugging the pillow in her arms with a determined fervor. Both women were quiet a moment, relishing the feelings between them.

Sara spoke first, wishing she had it in her to be a sappier woman. "Well, here, we're doing steaks and playing cards tonight, then church tomorrow, and we have reservations somewhere for Easter dinner. Then, I don't know, I may actually go play golf with them on Monday, if Mom doesn't have something else planned."

"Well," Chloe started, then saw her friend come through the room door laden with two coffee cups, and assorted foods stuffed in the crooks of her bent arms. She got up from the bed to help her friend unload her burdens, but continued, "Marcy just got back with brunch. We're going to get cultured tomorrow, and go to the Warhol Museum so Marcy can commune with her muse. Dave's not there, huh?" When Sara responded in the negative, Chloe shook her head at Marcy, who was peeling back the lids from the styrofoam containers.

"He'll probably call later, but I guess it's not a good idea for him to call too late, just in case you two are involved in a little lezbeen action, huh?" Sara teased.

It was a good thing that Sara was not there to witness the raspberry-colored blush that covered Chloe's face at that idea. "Uh, I would guess, uh, before ten o'clock. Definitely have him call before ten." Chloe took her cup and sipped the strong brew with a grimace.

Sara sighed, and patted her pillow for comfort. "All right, I guess it's time we all got started with our day." She stroked the telephone receiver with her finger, and then said, "I love you, Chloe. I'll try and call tomorrow. You have fun. But not too much, okay?"

"You too." Chloe averted her eyes from Marcy, to avoid the teasing grins she knew were going to be coming. "Uh. I love you too."

Sara smiled at Chloe's shyness, caused by the appearance of her best friend. "Alrighty then. Hey, Chloe, let me speak to Marcy a minute, okay?"

"If you insist. Well, bye." Chloe stopped herself from making a further fool of herself in front of Marcy, who was making mock gagging sounds in her direction at her words of love to Sara.

"Bye Chloe. Be good." Sara waited, as she heard the two women exchange the phone.

"Hey, Sara. How's Ef-L-Aye?"

"Hey, it's a family paradise, what can I say? I've already put a deposit on my retirement condo."

Marcy guffawed, and then waited for Sara to get to her point. She heard Sara clear her throat several times, and then the dark haired woman spoke, a bit of embarrassment coloring her request.

"Uh, Marse. Do me a favor tonight, will ya?"

"Sure."

"Take a butch pill before you guys hit that bar, will ya? It's not that I don't want you two to have a good time tonight."

Expecting to be teased soundly about this morning's kissfest with Chloe, Marcy was relieved to think that perhaps Chloe hadn't told her lover that story yet. "Uh-huh, okay."

"I mean it. I don't want any other woman's lips within ten feet of Chloe, and I'm counting on you to make sure it stays that way."

Marcy's coffee almost ended up in her lap. "Uh, gotcha, Sara. Will do. That's a big ten four." Chloe was quizzically giving her flustered friend a careful eyeballing.

"Well, good. Thanks. And I'm trusting you not to say anything about this directive from me. And, just so you know, Dave has been pretty much talking about your charms non-stop since we got here."

Marcy laughed, and felt her own blush start. "Tell him I love him." Marcy looked up to see Chloe with mouth hanging open, sticking a finger down her throat.

Sara was surprised at the moody artist's admission, but a smile of appreciation spread on her face. "I'll do that. I may wait until the whole family is gathered around to do it, but I'll tell him. You two have a good time, and Happy Easter, Marse."

"The same to you and your family, Sara. Now, we'd better get going here, Chloe is eager to continue, er, I mean, start my lesbian indoctrination." Marcy's blush turned full-fledged after her little verbal miscue, and Chloe quickly buried her face into a pillow to muffle the sounds of her hysterical giggles.

"Bye, Marse." Sara wasn't sure, but it sounded to her like Marcy was sounding a little choked.

Marcy desperately hit the end button on the phone, and just barely got her styrofoam cup to a safe level surface before she threw her body down next to Chloe's on the bed, and they laughed until their coffee was nearly cold.

* * *

"Why does it take three grown men to watch a grill heat? A gas grill, at that?" Marjorie posed an eternal unanswerable question to her daughter, who was carefully hacking mushrooms into pieces and tossing them into a frying pan.

"It's a male thing. I do it, too, when I can. But I'm in here with ya, Mom. It's a solidarity thing." Sara grinned, not looking up from her task.

"I guess I shouldn't complain about small favors, huh? We could have them in here, underfoot, trying to put marshmallows and chocolate chips into the salad." Marjorie laughed. *It feels good to joke around with her again.*

"And guaranteed, the three of them will be arguing over whether to cook the steaks with the lid up or down, or when to flip them." Sara nicked a finger with the blade, but was relieved it only took a small piece of fingernail, not flesh.

Marjorie saw her daughter wince, and hipped her out of the way. "Put that knife down, OJ, and let me finish. You have no patience for small details."

Sara sighed in agreement. "I guess I can rip the hell out of the lettuce then. That should work off some of my nervous energy." She grabbed a head of the just-washed lettuce, and started ripping chunks off it and putting it in a large wooden salad bowl. "I still can't cook, you know. I never learned. It's lucky I can open a box of Bugles for dinner."

"Cooking is a learned art. You just never learned." Marjorie looked to see how Sara was progressing with the lettuce. "And I see that you still think people are billy goats. You think you could tear that a little smaller?"

Sara shrugged her shoulders and grinned. "I haven't mastered many arts, I guess. Not the important ones, at least. I can rip apart a carburetor. Into smaller pieces than this." Sara stuck her hands in the bowl and started tearing her completed work into bite-size portions. "Great wife I'm gonna be," she said, quietly frustrated.

"Wife, huh?" Marjorie tossed the remaining mushroom slices into the pan, and looked around for the butter.

"Did I say that out loud?" Sara smiled, and dipped her head low enough so that her long hair covered the embarrassed smile on her face.

"Either that, or I have my hearing aid turned up too loud." Marjorie added the butter, turned on the heat, then turned and faced her daughter. Her expression was buried beneath her dark hair. "Tell me about her, Sara. Is this the real thing this time?" she prodded gently.

Sara disappeared even further behind her long tresses. *This just had to be next.* "I was kind of hoping so. I just don't know."

"Don't know what?"

"How to have a relationship, I guess." Sara looked up quickly to see the interested look on her mother's face. "I'm afraid I'm going to screw it up." Her face disappeared again, and she continued with the lettuce. "She's too good for me. I have no track record with relationships. I have no idea what I'm doing."

Marjorie grabbed a paper towel, and wiped her hands on it. She paused a moment, choosing her words carefully before continuing her gentle interrogation. "Why is she different, Sara? Chloe, right?"

Sara finished the head of lettuce, and grabbed for the second one before she answered. "Because I care if I hurt her, Mom. I never did before. The way my life was going...the way my life might go in the future."

"You think you're going to hurt her with the way your life might go, Sara?"

All of a sudden, Sara desperately needed to get some air. She dropped the head of lettuce into the bowl, and wiped her hands onto her shorts. She took several rapid, shallow breaths in succession, and tried to still her beating heart. She opened her eyes, and gave her mother an apologetic look as she headed for the sliding glass door toward the porch. "I gotta go for a few minutes, Mom."

Marjorie watched her daughter close the sliding glass door behind her, and then turned and began finishing the salad. Marjorie shook her head, in silent sympathy for the small librarian that her daughter seemed to care very much about. She pursed her lips, and then said aloud to the empty kitchen. "Yeah, Chloe, if I know my daughter, yeah, you're going to get hurt."

Marcy looked at the small, bookish college-age woman with whom she was partnered with in this losing effort at playing pool. *Damn, Chloe is trashed off her ass, and the drunker she gets, the better she gets.* Marcy eyed the brown-haired woman in the Slippery Rock college sweatshirt that was Chloe's partner. She was enjoying giving Chloe tips on her shots. *I wonder if I should...* She watched as Chloe giggled in reaction to the brunette's remark, and saw Chloe lay a lazy hand on the woman's shoulder. *This can't be anything but trouble. Ol' Slippery Rock there is this close to putting her hand on Chloe's butt.* Much to Marcy's surprise, her prediction came true just seconds later. Slippery laid a proprietary hand on Chloe's rear and left it there. *C'mon Chloe, cut that out. Ms. College Senior is just looking for a good time.*

The hand was removed only long enough for Chloe to miss her next shot. The hand returned, but this time, it wrapped itself around

Chloe's waist while the two of them waited for Marcy's partner to make her shot. *I don't think Chloe has bought a drink all evening. Slippery there has kept her in, what, four beers, and I've lost count of how many shots they've done. This being sober is no fun.* Marcy's partner, the bookish one, made two shots in a row, and then missed her next one. Chloe's partner now was up, and Chloe gave her a giggling word of encouragement before looking up and meeting Marcy's eyes. She winked broadly, propped her cue against the wall, and then made her way over to Marcy.

"Hey. I gotta do the ladies' room." Even though the dance floor and DJ were in the next room, Chloe had to shout to make herself be heard above the din. She grinned again at Marcy, took a deep breath, and got her bearings.

Slippery Rock Senior missed her next shot, and shrugged at Ms. Bookish, who was now standing next to her. They had a short conversation, and then Marcy grabbed Chloe's abandoned cue to take her next shot. She made two lucky shots in a row, and when she looked up again, Chloe had still not returned and Slippery Rock was MIA, too. *Hmmm.* Marcy purposely missed her next shot, and caught Bookish's eye, and nodded her intentions toward the ladies' room door. Bookish took a seat, to sip her beer until her pool partners returned.

To say that Marcy was surprised at what she saw when she walked into the tiny ladies' room would be an overstatement. She was perfectly prepared for the scene she found there. It was one of the few times she had witnessed it sober. Chloe was backed up against the wall next to the hand drier; her hands tucked behind her back, and was being soundly and thoroughly kissed by Slippery Rock, who was starting to move her hands from Chloe's shoulders to parts lower on her anatomy. Chloe looked as if she was fully involved, and completely enjoying the college student's attentions. Marcy let out a small growl of exasperation, swiftly hooked a finger into a belt loop on the back of Slippery's jeans, and pulled hard, hard enough to break the kiss.

Slippery Rock turned to see who had the gall to interrupt her. Marcy was prepared with a wolfish and very butch scowl, and said exactly five words to the startled student. "Take a hike. Game's over." Slippery Rock frowned at her, and then looked to Chloe, who was studying the scuffs on her sneakers.

Slippery apparently knew when to retreat, because she made a hasty exit from the room. Marcy took another step, and leaned up against the wall next to Chloe. Staring straight ahead, and not at her tipsy friend, she said, "Ah, the Kissing Bandit strikes again, huh, Chloe? Can't you keep your lips to yourself just once on Lesbian Weekend?"

Chloe squinted her eyes against the harshness of the fluorescent lights in the small ladies' room. "It's, ya know, traditional, you know, Marse. I gotta kiss somebody when we go out, it's the bet."

Marcy watched as a very inebriated woman made her way out of a stall and over to the sink in front of them. "Don't you think things are a little different this time, Chloe?" she asked quietly.

Chloe just nodded, and then laid her head on Marcy's shoulder. "I'd rather be kissing her, you know. Much rather."

Marcy tilted her head down to meet the top of her dear friend's. "Then why are you..."

Chloe straightened up, and made a few faltering steps to the exit door, and as she opened it, she focused on Marcy for as long as it took her to get her sentence out. "Because, Marse, I know I won't be kissing her much longer." With those words, Chloe disappeared out the door.

Marcy, not knowing how to reply to that, decided to make use of the empty stall before she went back out into the crowded bar again to search for her very confusing friend.

Part XXII:
The Truth Will Set You Free (and Then Bite You in the Ass)

The week following Easter was a torrent of non-stop activity. When Chloe wasn't at the library, or at rehearsals, she was over at the D'Amicos with Marcy, helping to get ready for the grand opening that had been rescheduled for the following Sunday. Saturday night was to be the Open House party, and Dave and Sara were busy putting the final touches on the converted barn/pro shop/clubhouse. Workmen were busily adding a lavatory to the old building, and in the latter part of the week, the driveway's nearly crater-sized potholes were finally plugged, and a fine layer of gravel laid down from the road to the parking area near the barn. If the weather was decent, Sara was out on the course itself, walking it, making notes, fixing holes, mowing and fertilizing with a frenzy. Nelson brought assorted friends home with him each day to help with whatever chores needed done, and Jeanette even showed up, looking like Sharon Stone in overalls. But she pitched in, too, and as the week wore down, everything fell into place, the exhausted crew looking forward to relaxing on Saturday night. The whole town was invited, from town council members, to schoolteachers, to library patrons, to Doris Raeburn and her posse of gossips, to Chloe's friend Audra, who had left several worried messages on Chloe's answering machine, complaining that she hadn't heard from Chloe in a long while. Chloe and Sara passed each other in the hallways at rehearsals, and waved to each other from the barn to wherever Sara was out on the course. At night, they fell quickly asleep holding tight to each other, either at Chloe's house or at Sara's small bungalow, and although conversation was limited, the comfort of each other's arms had not diminished.

Sara settled into the golf cart, parked next to the beer keg, and handed Chloe a hot dog wrapped in a paper towel. "How's beer patrol going?"

Chloe accepted the hot dog, and unwrapped it. She grinned at it, and then at Sara. "Um, is there anything you didn't put on this? Is there a hot dog under all of this stuff somewhere?"

Sara elbowed her, then sat back farther in the small seat and folded her arms. "I wasn't sure what you liked on them, so I put everything I could think of on it." She watched as Chloe took a wide-mouthed, cautious bite, and then saw the happy expression on the redhead's face as she began to chew. "I did good, huh?"

Chloe, mouth full, just nodded, a little bit of mustard sticking to the corner of her lips. Sara held out Chloe's cup of beer to her. Chloe finished chewing, and swallowed, and took the cup from Sara to wash it down. Finally, she wiped the corner of her mouth and gave the smallest of satisfied burps. "I'll take three more just like this. I'm starved." She promptly bit off another huge bite, her cheeks bulging. She smiled sheepishly.

Sara teased, "Nelson's over there burning a whole new batch of them. I'll get you some more to fuel that stomach of yours in a few minutes." An approaching figure caught her eye. "Hello, Jason. How are you tonight? The pop is over by where Nelson is burnin' the dogs."

Jason eyed the beer keg, and then put on his best begging face. "Aw, c'mon, Ms. D'Amico. I'm nearly twenty, and I'm graduating soon, and c'mon, no one will see."

"Jason, no. This is my brother's golf course, and though it doesn't officially open until tomorrow, he doesn't have a permit to have this beer here on an official basis. And we have a few town big wheels here. So, that's why Ms. Donahue and I are so zealously guarding this keg. You don't want Nelson and his father getting into trouble just for the likes of you, do you?" Sara's voice sounded like a combination of patient mother and no-nonsense state cop. She stared Jason down until he just gave a sigh and grinned in defeat. As he walked away, she yelled after him, "And tell all your little friends that it's a lost cause here, bucko!"

Chloe was just washing down the last of her hot dog. "Bucko? Bucko? What bad TV shows have you been watching?"

Sara gave her an imperious grin. "Hey, I don't have to watch bad TV shows. I was in them."

"Yeah, I was going to ask if I could borrow some tapes. I really want to see the one where you played the Beverly Hills madam slash undercover cop who had to seduce half of the city council."

"Oh, yeah, "Sins of the Skin Trade," a true classic. I spent two weeks on the set parading around in not much more than a thong." Sara blinked back bad memories of that time in her life, and then blew a raspberry through her lips. She and Chloe shared a quiet smile, and then their attention was diverted to Dave, who hopped up on the plywood-covered platform that was serving as a stage area for the karaoke set up. The multicolored lights hung around the 8 x 8 area gave a festive glow to his face, which already seemed to be shining from within. He waited a moment, and then Marcy joined him there, standing a little behind him. He pulled her up next to him, and settled his arm around her tightly.

Sara and Chloe exchanged quizzical glances, and then watched what happened next.

"Is this thing on?" Dave tapped the microphone in front of him. The feedback assured him it was, and he moved it away from him just a little. "Hello? Hello! Good evening one and all, and welcome to the pre-opening blast off for the Stonecreek Golf Course, which will be officially opening tomorrow morning, so don't drink too much!" He waited for the clapping and whistling to die down, and continued. "Thank you all for coming on this beautiful Saturday night. Karaoke will be starting up in a few minutes. I'd like to thank my man Stan, over there, for letting me use his equipment tonight. We were supposed to have a band, but my son Nelson apparently doesn't know the difference between live and elevator muzak! He's over there, by the barn—well, I guess it's the Clubhouse now—burnin' the bejesus out of a ton of hot dogs, so eat up!" He gave Marcy another mighty squeeze, and she looked rather like a kitten being smooshed by an overenthusiastic five year old.

He paused a moment, gave Marcy a dazzling smile, which she returned, although rather weakly. He began speaking into the microphone again. "I have quite a few blessings to give thanks for tonight. First and foremost, I want to thank my family, Nelson and Sara, for putting up with me these last few years, and helping me get my dream here off the ground. I have to say this: it wouldn't, no, it couldn't have happened without them." He waved at Nelson over by the grill, and then searched the small crowd for his sister, who he finally found in her perch next to Chloe in the golf cart. "To both of you. My sincerest thanks, and I love you both!" The group offered more clapping and whistling. Marcy knew what was coming next, there was no way to stop it, and there had been no time to discuss it with Dave.

Dave was starting to tear up, so he cleared his throat, and gave Marcy another hug for strength. He leaned into the mike one more time. "And last, but certainly not least, not only does my dream of opening a golf course seem to be coming true, but another dream of mine looks like it's going to happen." Dave sniffed. "Marcy here, just tonight, has agreed to become my wife. Or should I say, she has agreed to allow me to become her husband! I asked, and she said yes!" He threw both arms around her, and hugged her for all he was worth. She hugged him back, her nervousness allayed, and gave in to the joyous moment. He pulled back a little and then with his friends, family and all attendees watching, gave her a long, deep kiss while everyone cheered.

Sara and Chloe blinked at each other, matching huge smiles on their faces. They gave each other a quick hug.

Just as Dave and Marcy were breaking their kiss, someone yelled up from the throng. "Hey, Dave! When's the happy day?"

Dave, red-faced and teary-eyed, looked quickly at Marcy before he answered. "Um, we haven't gotten that far yet! I just asked her ten minutes ago." He wiped at his eyes. "I suppose next year sometime!"

Stan, standing behind them, yelled, "You'd better make it sooner than that, she's a slippery one!"

Marcy gave Stan a withering glare, and then tugged at Dave's shoulder, and whispered in his ear.

"November?" Dave said into the microphone, repeating the word that Marcy had just whispered to him. "Okay, looks like November of next year!"

Another tug, another whisper. "This year?" Dave couldn't hide the look of surprise on his face, but he was so happy, he just accepted it. "November of this year! All right!"

Sara leaned over and made a comment to Chloe, who was raptly watching the expression on her best friend's face. "November, why so soon?"

Someone in the crowd had the same question, and yelled, "Why so soon? You afraid she's gonna run off on ya?" The whole crowd chuckled; there were a few of Marcy's formerly disappointed castoffs in attendance.

Chloe shrugged it off, she was trying to catch Marcy's eye. Then the curly-haired woman seemed to have the same thought, and she gazed around and found Chloe staring at her, a large grin on her face. Marcy lifted up crossed fingers to Chloe, tilted her head in a smile, and nodded slowly and very deliberately at her. Marcy tugged at Dave one last time, and whispered a few words in his ear. He backed up and looked blankly at her, and then she pulled him down for a few last words. He stepped back, holding her at arms' length, while she looked up at him, a wary look upon her face, scanning his handsome features for a reaction to the words she had just spoken. Slowly, an unbelieving smile broke across his face, and he pulled her into his arms, and lifted her up twirling her around, before letting her down, giggling and flushed. He leaned into the microphone with a cocky smile, and boomed, "November? November? Because that's when Marcy and I are going to have our baby!" He picked her up again, and kissed her while he spun her around.

Sara could do nothing more than sit there, her mouth hanging open in surprise. "Holy shit. Holy shit in a hand basket. Holy shit!"

Chloe once again caught Marcy's eye, just as people were heading for the stage to give the couple their congratulations. Both Marcy and Chloe saw the tears glistening in each other's eyes. Chloe began softly crying in earnest, tears of happiness, and of relief that such a difficult decision in her best friend's life had come to such a happy conclusion. Sara saw Chloe's tears, and softly grasped her hand and squeezed it.

"Chloe?"

Chloe's eyes were on the small stage, and she watched as Nelson approached both Marcy and his dad, and they both looked at him. Both father and son looked a little shell-shocked by the news, but after a moment of uneasiness, the three of them embraced the news, they slowly moved into a hug, Nelson beginning with his dad, then, hesitantly, one with Marcy, which then turned into a more vibrant and excited one. Chloe's tears began falling more swiftly now.

"Chloe? Do you think we should get up there?" Sara asked, watching the scene on the stage with her own tumult of emotions.

Chloe finally turned to see the softly smiling face of her love. "In a minute. I want it to settle down. Let the other folks go first."

"Okay." Agreed Sara, wiping her eyes with the edge of a mustard stained paper towel. "Hey. Chloe."

"Hmm?" Chloe was looking around for something to wipe her own eyes with.

"I'm going to be an aunt again," Sara said, her voice reflecting the giddiness she felt.

Chloe laughed, and said, "Well, me too, Sara. This is the closest I'll ever come to being an aunt."

"Hey, yeah, that's right! You don't have any brothers or sisters."

"No," sighed Chloe. "I have something better than a sister." She smiled at Marcy's bobbing head up on the stage, where she was being bombarded by a seemingly endless flow of congratulations from Doris Raeburn. "I have Marcy."

Sara looked with affection at the quiet redhead next to her, and squeezed her hand tighter, and then handed her the paper towel she was clutching in her other hand. She chuckled as Chloe took it, and tried to find a clean dry spot on it to wipe her tears. A thought interrupted her gazing. "Hey, Chloe? You don't seem surprised at any of this." It was true, Chloe had shown no outward expressions of surprise, no gasps, none of the usual verbosity that someone as reactionary as Chloe would tend to display.

Chloe found one inch of clean area on the paper towel, and wiped her eyes with it. Then she folded the whole thing, and blew her nose into it several times, then wadded it, and softly chucked it into a nearby garbage can. She glanced quickly at Sara, who was looking at her, waiting for an answer. Chloe looked at, and then wiped her hands on the knees of her jeans, and left them there, gripping them softly.

"I'm not surprised," she said, her voice barely above a whisper.

Sara lifted an eyebrow. "You knew? I thought Dave just told me, Nelson and my family about asking Marcy."

Chloe wiped her hands on her knees again. "I kind of figured that he was going to ask her sometime, I just didn't know when."

Sara puzzled on that a moment, then, the real meaning to Chloe's answer became apparent to her. "You knew that she was pregnant? Right?"

Chloe cleared her throat, and shrugged. "Yeah. I knew." She shifted uncomfortably in the vinyl seat, and directed her stare at the colored lights above the stage area.

Sara was momentarily distracted by a Justin making stealthy movements toward the keg. "Not in this lifetime, buddy." She threw him a murderous gaze, and he backed off. She paused a moment, then asked, still confused by Chloe's reply. "How long? How long have you known?"

Chloe pursed her lips, and watched Justin rejoin his fellow plotters on the other side of the large driveway. "I don't know. Three weeks, maybe a month now?"

Sara did some mental math, and tried to match events into a time frame. "When she was sick? When you were sick?"

Chloe chuckled, not really amused. "She wasn't sick, really. It was morning sickness. That trip to the doctor, that's when she found out."

Sara pondered this, an uneasy feeling creeping over her. "And you knew, and kept it a secret? Why? I mean I'm not exactly untrustworthy, I mean, I can keep a secret."

Chloe was very reluctant to continue, but was resigned to the fact that she had to tell her the entire truth. "It wasn't that, Sara. She just didn't know what she wanted to do yet and as far as I knew, I mean, this announcement tonight was just as big a surprise to me. But in a different way." Chloe turned her head and stared directly out in front of the cart, her eyes unfocused.

Chloe's words slowly made an impact on Sara, and she realized the import of the meaning of what Chloe was saying. *This can't be true.* Sara put her hands on Chloe's shoulders, turning her to face her, and left them there, so the redhead couldn't turn away from her next question. "What do you mean, she didn't know what to do yet?" Sara's hands tightened their grip. "Wait a minute, wait a minute here. She was, what? Thinking of not having it?" Sara saw the pain of omission on Chloe's face, and her sense of disbelief was being replaced by something else. Anger? Hurt? "Why didn't you tell me?"

"Because she asked me not to." Chloe sighed and frowned, seeing the tightness of Sara's face, and feeling it in the grip on her shoulders. She couldn't help but see the confusion in Sara's face, and it made her stomach churn around that hastily-eaten hot dog.

Sara continued soaking in the truth, and it was overwhelming her. Her grip on Chloe's shoulders tightened measurably, and then she gave Chloe a little shove, and released her hold on her. She turned, and gripped the steering wheel instead, letting out a long breath of air. *Something's not right here.*

Chloe kept facing her, knowing she had to explain it so Sara would understand. Word after word spilled out of her mouth. "I wanted to tell you. I wanted her to tell Dave, to discuss it with him before she did anything, anything at all. But you know Marcy, she made it entirely her decision. All I could do was support her in it, be there for her while she found out about it, weighed her options. I was trying my damnedest to be her best friend, to be there for her, until she decided what she wanted to do. I even argued with her about my wanting, needing to tell you. I told her it put me in a very awkward position, but everything was so tightly interwoven." Sara's blank expression fueled Chloe's desperation to get the whole story out in the open. "I mean, look at this, look at us. My best friend is Marcy, my lover is her boyfriend's sister, who is also the aunt of the child, and Dave, who I dearly love, is the father of the child. She asked me to keep it a secret, I hated that she asked me, but I did. I hadn't a clue as to how this would turn out; just last week we went to family planning, and she still hadn't made her mind up what to do." Chloe was rambling now, her words a tidal wave that was pounding on Sara's sensibilities.

Sara abruptly interrupted her, irritation ripe in her voice. "Family Planning? Last week? The both of you?" *She was thinking of not having it, and didn't discuss it with Dave at all?*

Chloe regrouped, and tried to focus on Sara's words. It was plain Chloe was on the defensive now. "Uh, yeah. You know that woman with Audra here tonight? Her friend that went to college with her? Julia? That was our, her, Marcy's counselor at Family Planning. That's how she knew me. I went with her to find out about—"

"When?" Sara demanded.

"Uh. Last Friday. Good Friday." Chloe reached out her hand and laid it softly on Sara's arm, trying to make a physical contact that she hoped would dispel some of the tension between them. She felt no reaction there, no pulling away, no moving toward her. "I am so sorry," she said sincerely, her voice heavy with frustration and more than a bit of worry, too. "I wanted so much to tell you. I didn't think it was fair. I was hoping that it would all turn out this way. But—"

Sara's hands ran back and forth around the steering wheel. "Anything else?" Her words were completely toneless.

Chloe's hand on Sara's arm stopped its light stroking. "Anything else what?"

Sara's eyes did not meet hers, but her voice was serious and verging on nasty. "Anything else you haven't told me?"

Chloe's heart picked up its pace. *What does she mean?* "About Marcy? No, I think I've said everything."

Sara's eyes narrowed. "About anything. Anything at all that you've been keeping a secret from me." Sara's eyes briefly flashed at Chloe, before she returned to staring straight-ahead out into the night. "Now's the time, Chloe."

Aw, fuck. She wants true confessions. Aw, shit. What am I supposed to do here? Chloe watched people as they were milling around the stage area. Dave and Marcy were no longer there. Chloe shook her head, to try and clear it, and then to think about her next words. "Secrets, huh? You want secrets?" *She obviously isn't interested in any explanations. She just wants to find reasons, any reasons to convict me.* Chloe suddenly felt very tired and a wave of resentment shook her being. Her words were machine-gun staccato. "All right. You want my dirty little secrets? Sure. Let me see."

Chloe's face turned into a mask, her emotions flat. She looked at the dark hair of the woman beside her, and she reached out and softly touched it before she began.

Her voice very controlled and low, she started divulging things that maybe, maybe not would be of some consequence to Sara. "Let's see. How about last Saturday? Marcy kissed me last Saturday in our motel room. I didn't tell you about that yet, so you might consider that a secret. And also last Saturday, I made out with some college girl in the ladies' room at that bar. If Marcy hadn't come in and hauled her bodily off me, I'd be wearing turtlenecks until June." Chloe caught sight of two figures walking nearby. "Oh yeah. There's more. I kissed Audra that night of our date, and if my teakettle hadn't started whistling when it did, I maybe, might have, could have slept with her. Who knows? Saved by the bell, or whistle, I guess." Chloe's anger took over. "You want more? Ms. Julia Cardinger, probably right up until Dave and Marcy's announcement tonight, thought Marcy and I were a couple. You know, lovers." Chloe stopped and took several breaths. She looked at Sara, who had ducked her head down, and had her fists balled in her lap. "Is that enough for you now? Have I disappointed you enough?" Chloe choked on those last words, and found her own hands were in fists too.

Sara opened her hands, and flexed out her fingers. *That's enough.* She let out a totally inappropriate snort of laughter, and finally looked at Chloe, who was looking at her, trying to figure out the meaning behind Sara's amusement. Sara looked away, her lips curling into a frown. She could still feel Chloe's eyes upon her when she said, cold words icing the crisp spring air, "Just last week, I told my mother you were 'too good' for me. And at the time, I believed it. Now, I don't know what to believe." Sara got up out of the golf cart, and walked toward the crowd in front of the stage area, leaving Chloe behind.

Dave had Marcy behind the barn, almost in the same spot where he had proposed to her less than an hour ago. Her back was snuggled warmly into his chest, his arms around her, her hands on his. He let out a contented sigh, and propped his head on top of her mass of auburn curls.

"Well, hit me over the head and call me Mr. Roofing Nail." He sighed, giving her another embrace.

"Huh?" Marcy laughed, and returned the squeeze on his arms. "That one really sucked, Dave. Mr. Roofing Nail. Okay." She rolled her eyes, knowing he couldn't see her do it, but she did it anyway.

"Funny how things work out, huh?" Dave said, looking up at the stars and contemplating the deeper subjects of fate and destiny and other stuff.

"Yeah, I was afraid I'd have to ask you to marry me. Now that'd be different, huh?" Marcy sighed, a weird feeling of contentment settling over her. *Wow, I think way too much. This feels so right. First time for everything.*

"Well, it certainly was a surprise. I mean, I surprise you with a proposal, and you surprise me by—"

"Saying yes?" teased Marcy.

Dave chuckled, and kissed the top of her head. "Well, yeah, that and that other minor surprise."

Marcy turned in his arms, and looked up at him. "I should've waited longer to tell you, in private, but you dragged me up on that stage after your proposal, and I suppose I wasn't thinking straight when they started yelling. I just wanted to tell you, and I was so excited, I just had to..."

"Scare the livin' shit out of the poor man?" A familiar voice came from around the side of the barn. Sara arrived to stand in front of them. "Sorry, I heard you as I was coming around the side of the building. I swear I wasn't eavesdropping much." She wrapped her arms around a startled Marcy, and gave her an extremely warm and welcoming hug. "I'm glad you told him that way. That look on his face was priceless." She felt Marcy return her hug with gusto. "I haven't seen that kind of look on his face since the time he was teaching me how to do a chip shot, and I didn't realize he was standing right behind me during my backswing." She released her arms from around Marcy, and smiled down into her eyes. "It's a wonder that the guy could have children after that. He was icing his family jewels for weeks."

Dave grimaced at the memory, and then took his sister into his arms, and lifted her off the ground, and the grimace turned into a grin. "Can you imagine, Sis? She said yes! To me!" Dave shook his head at the wonder of it all.

Sara, still in her brother's bear hug, reached out and tapped Marcy on the head with her knuckles. "You in there? You sure this is what you really want, to marry into this family? Hel-lo!" She tapped a few more times and cocked her head to listen for echoes.

Marcy popped her in the stomach with a quick jab. "Not only marry into the family, but, good lord, what am I doing to the world by bringing another D'Amico into it?"

Dave finally let his sister back down to earth. Sara blanched a little at the thought that Marcy might have come close to deciding not to do exactly that thing, but dropped the idea. *She did the right thing, that's all that matters. Thank God.* "What, no hyphen? No Larry Moe Curly Whatchacallit-D'Amico?"

Dave guffawed, and gave his sister a brotherly poke in the shoulder. "Hey, I was thinking. How about Salvador? Salvador Dali D'Amico. Has a nice artsy-fartsy ring to it."

Marcy cringed and Sara's faced pursed into a mock distressed look. "Oh lord, the poor child. It's going to turn fourteen, and we'll all end up on Springer, and he'll be throwing plastic chairs at us."

"Or she," said Dave and Marcy, almost in unison. They grinned at each other again.

Dave groaned. "Damn, I hate to break up this happy little party, but I need to go pee in our new lavatory, and then be sociable. All of this lovey-dovey stuff aside, I have my golf empire to think about. I have to keep the wife and kiddies in the lap of luxury. I have to go take some man-sized ribbing." He leaned down and tenderly kissed his wife-to-be. "You two come around and sing some karaoke, will ya? I know that's why half of the male population showed up here tonight, you two have become local legends." He kissed Marcy one more time on the tip of her nose, and then impetuously leaned and placed a big sloppy kiss on his startled sister's cheek. "No, I don't want to hear "Havin' My Baby."" He grinned at them both, and walked off around the side of the barn.

Marcy and Sara smiled at one another again, shyly, both recognizing the change in status of their relationship. Sara turned and leaned up against the barn next to Marcy.

"Hey, where's the Chloester? Is she still doing keg duty?"

Sara shuffled her feet uncomfortably in the grass and dirt beneath them. "Probably. I suppose so."

Marcy picked up Sara's subtle change in mood almost immediately. "She told you, huh? About family planning? Our trip there?"

"Yeah, Marse, she told me."

Marcy could hear the difference in Sara's tone. It was sad, and a little brittle. "Listen, it wasn't her fault. I wouldn't let her tell you. It was my fault, my selfish need to figure this out on my own, before anyone else knew."

Sara cleared her throat. "So you tell her, and not Dave?"

Marcy turned and leaned against the building on her shoulder, so she could look directly up at Sara's stony face. "I had to figure out how I felt about him. And the baby. By myself. Before I could make any decisions. I really was leaning one way, but I needed some time. Chloe was there for me, and she gave me that time, with no pressures at all. She's been my best friend, before this, and during this. Your brother isn't exactly the most devious man on the planet, Sara. I had a feeling he was going to ask me to marry him, even before I found out I was pregnant. I wasn't sure how I felt about it. I really wanted this to be different this time. I wanted to be able to say yes, and make it stick. I don't exactly have a great track record on following through with engagements, you know. But this time, Sara, baby or no baby, I realize this is exactly where I'm supposed to be. With your brother." Maybe it was the events of the evening, but Marcy was feeling very calm, and very sure. She took a chance, and reached out and grasped Sara's hand. "And the baby. I never figured on being a mother. But Dave will help me out. So will Nelson. So will you, and Chloe. I don't have to be alone in this. I was thinking about it wrong. It's not all on me, it's on all of us."

Sara swallowed hard, and the hard lines in her face softened, and she gave Marcy's hand a light squeeze. "You figured that all out by yourself, huh?" *If there's hope for independent Marcy, maybe there's hope for me.*

"Not by myself. With Chloe and a crazy confused counselor, Julia Cardinger, who somehow got it into her head that Chloe is going to be the father of this child. How she ever thought that, well, it's a mystery to me." Marcy trailed off with a light giggle.

"That woman with Audra? I was wondering why she was giving me and Chloe strange looks before."

Marcy smirked delightedly. "Oh, man. I'd have loved to see that. She probably thinks Chloe is this womanizing slut." Marcy was laughing so hard, she didn't feel it when Sara let go of her hand.

Sara let out a laugh that had no amusement behind it. *Might as well get it all now, while Marcy is in such a good mood. Any other time, she would be cursing my head off.* "Speaking of womanizing."

Marcy's interest piqued. "Yes?"

"Chloe also mentioned something about a kiss, a kiss between two certain best friends at a Pittsburgh motel."

The moonlight and the floodlights of the barn combined to help Sara see the blush that formed on her future sister-in-law's face. "Oh my God. She told you? I thought she was going to wait and use that as a bargaining chip at some future date. That was really sneaky of the little twerp."

Sara kept the blank smile on her face. "Sneaky?"

"Well, yeah, the whole revenge thing for me busting in on your first morning together. I'm snoozing away, dead to the world, when I feel teeth nipping at my ear, and a hand rubbing my stomach. I must have been in the twilight zone, because I thought it was Dave, and the next thing Chloe knows, I'm sucking her tonsils out before I realized it was her. When I did realize it, I flew clear to the ceiling before I landed on my ass on the floor. I can't believe Chloe didn't tell you before this! I'm still so embarrassed!"

Sara was slowly nodding her head, and to her distinct amazement, found herself truly tickled by the story, and imagining the little redhead sneaking up on her sleeping friend with mischief on her mind. Sara grinned in spite of herself, until she thought of the last part of the tale that Chloe wove.

"And, Marse, I thought I left you in charge of Chloe's lips that night you went out. And you find her in the ladies' room?"

Marcy froze at that part, and didn't laugh. She sighed instead. "Wow. She really came clean with you with everything, didn't she? Wow." Marcy paused a moment to try and gauge the look on Sara's face. Sara was impassive and waiting. "Sara, I was pissed at her beyond belief for that. 'The Kissing Bandit' strikes again. Sure, she was about as drunk as I had ever seen her, and she didn't even remember doing it until the next day when I reminded her of it, but at the time, I think she was just really missing you, and feeling terribly insecure. You know, insecure about her feelings for you. No, strike that. Insecure about how you feel about her. That and the tradition thing."

"Tradition?"

"Well, yeah, every Easter holiday since college, say, ten years now, we've 'gone gay' for our Easter Spin the Car. I think we did it on a few other holidays, too, but always Easter. We always end up in a gay bar in Erie, or Pittsburgh, or Cleveland, Buffalo; one time even in Toronto." Marcy stopped again, and ran a hand through her hair. "We did it originally, the first time, because Chloe was lonely in college before she met old Whatshername, and she wasn't out, you know, all four years of college. She had to sneak around, just to sleep with her girlfriend. So when we first started doing these little gay trips, it was just so Chloe could feel normal for one night, and be a lesbian, out and out, so to speak. First year we went, she was so shy, I made her a bet she couldn't get kissed by the end of the evening.

She seemed to gain more self-confidence, what with me razzing her on, so, yeah, that night she became this little flirtish Super Gay Chloe, the Kissing Bandit, and she got a woman to kiss her. Nothing else, just kiss her. And every year, the bet has gone on, even when she was with Whatshername. We figured it was harmless, which I still think it is. She wasn't feeling particularly confident about things, you, I guess, in Pittsburgh, so I think she just reverted to the Kissing Bandit for a night. No big deal. Really kinda dumb, and she felt terrible about it the next day. But that's just Chloe, she does silly stuff, and you forgive her for it."

Sara's anger had disappeared somewhere in the middle of Marcy's story. *She was lonely all through college. She never was out, and she had to sneak around? I can just imagine Chloe trying to get up the nerve to get some stranger kiss her. She doesn't even like to kiss me in front of anyone.* Sara mentally slapped herself upside the head. *Jeez, Sara, not like you do anything to give that girl any confidence about our relationship. No, you just judge her and write her off, even for the silliest of reasons, and for the big ones, too, without giving her a chance to explain. You expect her to hurt you, and you find ways for her to do it, even if her intentions were pure and noble, like when she's just trying to be a best friend to her best friend.*

"Sara?" Marcy was watching Sara's face with trepidation. Sara's mouth was contorting into a scowl, then a frown, then a smile, then returning to a frown. "Sara? Ground control to Sara."

Sara snapped to, and then looked around quickly. "Sorry, Marse. I gotta go," Sara said, sounding a little anxious. She was just about to bolt when Marcy grabbed her elbow. "Sara, are you okay? You look a little panicky."

Sara stopped, and gave Marcy a quick hug. "Nope, not panicking. I just need to find the Kissing Bandit."

Audra had dragged Chloe to a picnic table as far away from the karaoke stage as she could find. Nelson, Justin and Jason were doing a credible job whooping their way through some Beastie Boys' songs, but other than the high school kids that were obviously enjoying the performance, most of the adults had moved themselves into the large barn/pro shop for warmth against the cool air. Some still-sober adult had moved the keg of beer in there, too, so Chloe's stint as keg patroller was over. Julia Cardinger had disappeared somewhere, too, so it was just Chloe and Audra, and Audra had pulled a good bit of the story of Chloe's misery out of her already. Chloe was getting more morose with each detail she was imparting to Audra, and Audra was in turn getting angrier on behalf of the woman she had a long-time crush on.

"Well, Marcy's your best friend, and if a best friend tells you not to tell anyone something, that's that. No apologies, no arguments," said the blonde schoolteacher, defending Chloe's actions. "If she doesn't understand that, then tough shit. The woman probably doesn't have the first concept about what best friends do for each other."

"I guess. I don't get it. Thank God everything turned out for the best. I don't know how she would have reacted if it hadn't turned out so picture perfect, if Marcy had made some kind of other decision. I don't want to think about it. I mean, I spent a month thinking about poor Marcy, and trying to support her, and then on top of it all, I'm worrying about how Sara's going to react to it, and when she found out, I knew all along, how she was going to react to me knowing and not telling her. It turned out just fine, and Sara still gets mad at me. Jesus, I can't win."

"Well, you certainly were right to worry. Look at how she reacted. All she could do was blame you, right? Blame you for being a friend, blame you for not breaking a confidence, and blame you for Marcy needing some time to make a decision on her own. That's not fair to you, Chloe, and you had her figured out way before this even came out. Thing is, if you knew she was like this, why..."

"Do I bother? Because I love her. And most days, I think she loves me." Chloe snorted, and took another sip of her beer. "Today not being one of those days, of course." Chloe threw her hands in the air in frustration. "Should be one of the happier days of my life, my best friend is getting married and having a baby with one of my favorite guys in the whole world, it's a party, and here I am bending your ear with the tales of my stinking love life."

"Hey, you just need to talk to someone. You would think that would be her, wouldn't you? But don't feel bad, Mel was the same way. I would want to talk to her, and she would just turn a deaf ear. She was just waiting for me to screw up, so she could say 'I told you so,' but I didn't have her to lend a sympathetic ear, so I felt lost most of the time. And I screwed up."

Chloe nodded in agreement. "And this whole kissing thing, in Pittsburgh."

Audra snorted in derision. "Shit, Chloe, when I was a student teacher at your school, I remember you and Marcy coming back from Buffalo; the Kissing Bandit of Stonecreek had struck again. I was howling when you two told me the story. It's no biggie, Chloe, you just got looped in Pittsburgh, and well, used some bad judgment. Really bad judgment. But it's not like you cheated on her. Well, I guess a kiss is bad, but, c'mon! She should be able to see it for what it was. But hell, if I were you, I wouldn't waste my time trying to explain that to Sara, apparently the woman can't empathize with anyone but herself. If I were you, I'd—"

Neither woman heard Sara's approach, and were both surprised when Sara slid onto the picnic table bench next to Chloe, and set her beer down. She raised an eyebrow at Audra, who was not hiding her displeasure at Sara's arrival.

"Hey." Sara said to Chloe, not looking at her, but sitting close enough that their hips and legs were touching. She looked directly at Audra, and drawled, "Do go on, the last thing I believe you said was, 'if I were you, I'd—' I'm curious, what would you do, Audra?"

Chloe moved just slightly away from Sara, so they were no longer touching, but Sara moved her leg so it was again touching Chloe's.

Audra was not intimidated by this tall, imposing woman. "If I were Chloe, I'd dump you, and find someone that appreciated me."

Sara gritted her teeth, and kept her voice even and low. "And are you volunteering for that position, Audra? My replacement? Because I don't appreciate her?"

"Chloe could have anyone she chooses, just as long as it's someone who loves her, someone who sees how wonderful she is. Yeah, it would be nice if that could be me. I have no problems in saying it," Audra countered.

Chloe interrupted, she had heard enough. She was in no mood to be fought over, and it showed in her condescending tone. "Okay, first up, the pissing contest. Let's see which one of you can pee the most accurately while standing up." She scowled at the both of them.

Sara had to grin at that one, and she knocked her knee in appreciation against Chloe's.

Chloe wasn't about to be placated by that, though. She took another long sip of beer and looked, in turn, at both women. "Friggin' dykes," she spat with derision. "Neither one of you fools me for a second. Audra, you're being all sympathetic to my troubles, and I appreciate your listening ear, but don't think I don't know that you have an agenda here." Audra frowned, looked into her beer cup, and said nothing. Chloe then turned her attention to Sara, who was grinning at Chloe's caustic remarks to Audra. "And you, you obviously either are sorry for the way you treated me before, or maybe you're not, maybe you're just over here making sure that Audra doesn't encroach on your property. Well, you know what? Fuck you both. I don't need either one of you. Audra, you're right. I can do better. I just lack confidence once in a while. But if my lack of confidence is what sticks me with either one of you, then, well, I am gonna get a whole shitload of it in a hurry, so I don't have to mess around anymore with the likes of you."

Chloe drained her cup, and then continued on her rant, looking at the surprised and troubled face of her lover. "And you. At least I know where Audra stands. You, it changes every day, depending on the day of the week. If you love me, act like it. Act like you have some trust in me. I know I screwed up, but the last thing I want to do is hurt you, but you act like that's very thing you expect me to do. I love you, Sara, but if you love me, you'd better quit playing around with my heart, and love me the whole goddamned way." Chloe grabbed her cup, stood up from the table, and headed off toward the barn and the keg that was waiting for her there.

Audra and Sara stared into their beer cups for a moment, and then warily eyed each other.

Audra spoke first. "I suppose I should go find Julia, I think she's in line for karaoke."

Sara nodded and stood up. She blew a long breath. "I just want to apologize, I guess. She's right, you're right. I should treat her better, and I don't. I'm gonna go fix that right now."

Audra gave her a hesitant nod. "Good luck. And, if you screw up...I'm just warning you."

Sara shook her head. "I'm not going to give you another chance with her. Count on it."

Chloe had managed to bum nearly a whole pack of cigarettes off Jay Caesar, the pizza shop owner cum local drama critic extraordinaire. She took advantage of the situation, and chatted him up amiably in the crowded barn, hoping that a little harmless jawing with him would in some small way influence a favorable review of their presentation of *Oklahoma!*.

Once she felt she had him sufficiently charmed, a very insistent Doris Raeburn ambushed her. Not feeling particularly charitable with either her manners or kindness, she abruptly interrupted Doris with a very impatient air. "Listen, Doris, I've had about four beers now, and only one hot dog, and I just spent ten minutes trying to charm that asshole Jay Caesar into giving us a decent review. If you want to talk to me, come outside, and don't complain about second hand smoke, 'cause that's what I plan on doing. Drinking, smoking, and hopefully finding something else to eat. So, c'mon, if you want to chat."

Doris Raeburn, perhaps for only the second time in her entire life, was speechless, and found herself obediently following the determined little play director outside into the cool night air. Doris had to trot after her to keep up. Chloe found a semi-warm hot dog on the side of the grill, threw it in a bun, and wolfed it down in about four bites, washing it down with the large beer she had gripped in her hand.

Doris' amazement at Chloe's behavior quickly turned to curiosity, and Doris reverted to her normal self. Chloe was apparently in a bad humor, and Doris was sure she knew why. They settled into a small table between the karaoke platform and the barn, and Chloe unapologetically lit up a cigarette.

Doris widened her eyes, but soon her words were flowing like hot gravy over a Thanksgiving dinner. "Who the hell is that up there singing?" commented Doris, irritated. "She's been up there for twenty minutes now, and I think a few people in front of the stage have committed suicide, not that I can blame them."

Chloe blew out a lungful of smoke, and snorted. "That's a friend of Audra Simmons, Paul's old student teacher from a few years back. Her name is Julia Cardinger." Chloe snorted again. "Not great, is she? I think that's "You Light Up My Life" but I'm only guessing by the melody from the karaoke machine." Chloe was pleased, not only in the fact that she realized that there actually was a singer out there worse than she was, but because she had actually been able to get a word in edgewise with the usually impenetrable Doris Raeburn.

"Well, it's been awhile since we've actually had a chance to talk, hasn't it, Chloe? I do miss talking with you. I know you've been terribly busy with the play and work and, well, you've been helping out here with the D'Amicos, haven't you? I know, because I'm good friends with Jeanette's grandmother, and Jeanette mentioned that you were out here the nights she came out to help. She and Nelson make a handsome couple, don't they? One so dark, one so light. Like yin and yang, like dots on dice. Nelson came in to speak to me the other day, he's decided to go to school in California. USC. You could have knocked me over with a dead cow when he told me that. He wanted some kind of letter of recommendation from me, to help him secure a partial scholarship. I know he could have had a full scholarship to play football somewhere in the East, but he wants to go out there for acting, and play football, too. I guess he's an unknown commodity out there, I don't know, but whoever gets him will be lucky to have him. Of course, if Sara goes back out to Hollywood, well, he'll have someone he knows out there. Is she going back? She should, she looks wonderful. She's positively been glowing the past month or so."

Chloe lit a new cigarette off the butt of her old one. No sense in wasting a perfectly good match.

"Good lord. Just when I thought it couldn't get any worse." Doris directed her attention toward the stage, where Paul Hoderman had joined Julia, and they were mutually mauling "You Don't Bring Me Flowers Anymore." "Poor Paul, saddled with that gossip of a mother. I can't imagine. I mean, she is one of my closest friends, but the woman absolutely drives me bonkers. To the moon, Alice. I mean, the woman almost had me convinced that there was something

going on between you and David D'Amico, can you imagine? I told
her that he was Marcy's boyfriend, and that you would never come
between the two of them, you being best friends forever with Marcy.
I told her a million times not to believe the gossip. Just because
David kisses you in public, I think that was just him fooling around, I
mean, not with you dear, I mean in the joking sense. That Hoderman
woman, though, she just would not take my word for it. She was
absolutely convinced that you were sneaking around with him behind
poor Marcy's back, and you're not going to believe this one, dear, but
she thought you were with child!"

That one was a new one on Chloe, and she choked a couple of
times on her cigarette smoke.

"I know, I know. Ridiculous, right? Well, funny thing is she saw
you and Marcy coming out of that Family Planning clinic in Harmercreek last week, so she had proof positive! But the joke was on her,
huh, Chloe, because with Marcy's little announcement tonight, we
know who really is in the family way, don't we? The old goat. She
nearly choked on her partial plate when Dave gave the news about
the engagement, and then Marcy surprised us all, including Dave, I
think, with her bit of good news. Funny how these stupid rumors get
started, isn't it? These old biddies in town have nothing better to do,
and I have to spend a great amount of my own personal time defending people's good reputations. It's enough that...well, would you
look at that? Isn't that Sara up on the stage? I heard she sang at
Stan's one night, with Marcy, and they practically brought down the
house. I'm going to get closer, dear, and see what all the fuss is
about. Are you coming?"

Chloe just shook her head. "You go ahead. I think I'm going to
go get another beer."

Doris sighed, and smiled at her. "You look tired, dear. This is a
party, try and have a good time, all right?" Doris got up from the
table, and moved down toward the stage area. Chloe got up, and took
a few steps toward the barn and then halted mid-stride. Smoky alto
tones wafting from the stage area seemed to paralyze her feet. She
recognized Sara's voice, seemingly channeling Patsy Cline as she
sang "Crazy."

Patsy. Chloe turned and took a few steps toward the stage.
Sara's face came into focus, with her blue eyes centered on the red-
haired woman who was slowly approaching the stage. The mesmerized librarian was oblivious to the people streaming past her from
the barn. Chloe's eyes never left those of the dark-haired woman who
was so obviously singing this song just for her, even if it wasn't
apparent to the throng surrounding the stage. Marcy and Dave and
Nelson were up front, but they knew where the song was directed.

With every verse caressing her ears like that of a longing lover,

Chloe forgot about cigarettes, beer, food and the need for air and stood unmoving. Sara finished up on a low, long held note and searched Chloe's eyes expectantly.

The crowd went wild. Sara graciously took a quick grinning bow, but ignored the demands for encores and requests. She handed the microphone to Marcy, and whispered a few words in her ear. Marcy hopped up onstage, dragging Dave with her, as Sara made her way past complaining members of the audience, and made her way back to Chloe.

She stopped in front of her, and gave her a small smile, projecting her love through her gaze, and waited for Chloe to answer her in some way. Chloe turned away and took a step toward the house, and then stopped, and looked back at Sara, and nodded. The two of them walked their way across the green grass, heading toward the warmth that lay ahead, leaving the cold night behind them.

Part XXIII:
And on the Seventh Day, God Created Golf

Chloe's hand slammed down erratically on the flat space next to her, trying to find a way to stop the buzzing of the unfamiliar alarm clock. The room was dark, and she pounded around on the night-stand fruitlessly, even when her fuzzy mind settled on an object that she thought was the clock radio. The buzzing continued unabated, her hand moved and found the small bedside lamp, and she switched it on.

"Goddamnsonofabitchfriggin!" Her eyes adjusted to the light, and she found the button, at last, to shut off the infernal racket of the alarm. The clock, in red numbers, flashed 7:00 at her bloodshot eyes, and her weary mind figured out she had been haplessly smacking a box of Little Debbie Swiss Cake Rolls in her attempt to silence the alarm. She pushed out an arm to the other side of the bed, not sur-prised to find it was empty. Sara had said she was going to get up early, and get things rolling for today's grand opening of the course. Chloe's eyes shut again, and she imagined the tall woman out in an electric golf cart, in the dark, riding from hole to hole, placing a numbered flagpole in each hole. Chloe listened for any sounds that might indicate inclement weather, a drumming of rain on the bunga-low's roof, a gust of wind. Her sense of hearing picked up neither of these sounds, and she sighed, a bit disappointedly, that she had no excuse now to rebury herself under the covers. Damned weather peo-ple. They forecasted a beautiful day, in the low 70s. *Why, for once, do they have to be right?*

If Chloe's eyes could be described as bloodshot, then one would have to describe Dave D'Amico's as devil red, with a definite tinge of 'my whole family was just wiped out in a flash flood, and I'm the only survivor' glaze to them. He was sitting in the barn/garage/pro shop, on the low stool, staring at a display rack of golf towels, gloves and tees. No matter how much he blinked, the items were still merely a colorful blur. In Dave's exuberant celebrating of all the happy events of last night, he had, with numerous friends, decided the best way to keep underage teenagers from snitching any beer from the keg was for them to drink it all themselves. It'd seemed the perfect and smart solution at the time. Now Dave was perfectly sure that smart was a word that really didn't apply to him.

He glanced at his watch, and then again, because the numbers and the placement of hands had no meaning to him the first time around. *Big hand on the quarter hour, little hand on seven. Sara should be back soon. Chloe, I wonder where she is? I think, yeah, she stayed with Sara last night. Marcy's still in bed, I should go wake her up. People will be arriving shortly, for the first tee-off at 8:30.* Dave felt no embarrassment when he groaned loudly, and rubbed his pounding temple with his hands. *I absolutely deserve this hangover. Oh God. I have to be one of the first official foursome.* Dave wracked his fermented brain. *Me, Mark Benson from the zoning board, Chuck Fugate from the Chamber of Commerce, and,* Dave rubbed his eyes, *Uh, oh yeah, Stan.* All three of them had been present last night, and the same three had happily helped Dave as official keg killers. *And Paul, he's going to follow us around from hole to hole, taking pictures for the Stonecreek Courier. Somewhere around the third hole, Paul's going to get some monster shots of four grown men puking in the lilac bushes.*

Dave's stomach turned over at that thought, and he immediately got up to use the newly installed lavatory facilities conveniently located in the barn. Five minutes later he emerged, a scowl covering his face.

"Goodgoddamnedfreakin."

"What's the matter, Pop?" said Nelson, a little bleary-eyed himself, but none the worse for wear. He was freshly showered, casually dressed up in his new golf shirt, and was standing just inside the opened barn doors.

Dave was loudly rooting around on the other side of the barn, where the tools were kept, still cursing dementedly under his breath.

"Nelson! Do you know if we have a toilet plunger?"

"Hey, Marcy. How's it going?" asked Sara cheerfully as she entered the kitchen at Dave's house. It was only 7:30, the course looked good to her even in the dim light of early morning. She'd been fondly reminiscing about last night, which had ended up with an energetic and imaginative Chloe in her bed, and she was experiencing some very satisfying afterglow flashbacks. She walked over to the coffee pot, poured herself a cup, and then turned to face Marcy.

Marcy was sitting at the kitchen table, completely enveloped in Dave's terrycloth bathrobe, looking small, forlorn, and, yes, lethally grumpy.

"Marse?" grinned Sara, not knowing what to expect, but expecting something not friendly. *Poor woman, first no cigarettes, now no caffeine.*

"Uh-huh." Marcy turned a jealous eye to the cup of coffee in Sara's hand. "What?"

"You all ready for today?" Sara tried to keep the beatific smile on her face toned down to a minimum. "Did you get a chance, over the last few days, to read that cash register manual?" Marcy and Chloe had volunteered to run the clubhouse for the day, taking green fees, selling golf accessories and pushing pop and snacks on people. Dave had bought a secondhand cash register to tally and hold his new earnings. Marcy had been elected to become the expert on its use.

"How hard can running a cash register be?" snapped Marcy, her tone letting Sara know for certain that Marcy never got around to reading the manual.

"Well, those dorks down at the Quickie Mart seem to have a hard time running theirs."

Marcy pushed a hand through her amber curls, skewing them in rather odd patterns, and pulled Dave's huge bathrobe up in wadded bunches around her. She squinted meanly at Sara. "Do I look like a Quickie Mart dork to you?"

Before Sara could come back with a retort to that, the kitchen door opened, and Chloe stepped inside, wearing off-white khakis and a green "Stonecreek Golf Course" polo shirt that Dave had supplied his family and friends. Even though she was sleepy, her red-blonde hair still damp and awry, Sara lit up at the sight of her, and felt a warm sensation she couldn't attribute to the coffee she had just sipped. They exchanged lovers' smiles, and Sara grabbed another cup from the cupboard, filled it, and wordlessly handed it to Chloe. She knew from experience not to speak to Chloe before she had at least a half a cup of caffeine in her bloodstream.

Chloe smiled gratefully at her, and settled down at the table, across from Marcy. Marcy practically sneered at her in greeting. No one wanted to speak to break the church-like stillness of the kitchen, but then Dave briskly entered, with Nelson trailing behind. Dave said nothing to disrupt the silence; he just walked straight to the coffee pot, and saw that it contained perhaps half a cup. His blood red eyes narrowed. Sara grabbed the pot, and poured the remainder into her own lukewarm half-full cup, and then handed it to Dave, who nodded a reluctant thanks at her. He took a sip, testing it for warmth, then without further hesitation, lifted it to his lips again, and drained the whole cup. He handed it back to Sara, who cleared her throat and said, "I guess I'd better make some more, huh?"

Dave looked at his rumpled, pregnant fiancée, and held out a hand. "Shower?"

Marcy grabbed his hand and stood up, the hem of the robe pooled at her feet. "Uh-huh." The newly engaged couple dragged themselves out of the kitchen. Before they had made it a few steps into the living room, Dave stopped, and spoke in Nelson's direction. "Uh, tell your aunt about the clogged toilet in the barn, wouldja?" before they continued on their way.

Three eyebrows in the kitchen rose, obscenely high on each one of the D'Amicos standing there and one moderately high on a seated Donahue.

Nelson looked at his Aunt Sara, her formerly cheery demeanor now flown. He nodded and shook his head at her.

Sara sighed, and brushed Chloe softly on the back as she headed for the kitchen door. "Goodlordalmighty."

"Sara?" Chloe was standing in the open barn doors, staring wide-eyed across the gravel-covered parking lot and to the driveway leading from the road beyond. "Sara?" She called a little louder, hoping her voice would carry without her having to turn her head from the bewildering spectacle that had her mesmerized. A steady stream of cars was turning into the long driveway that led from the road, and Chloe had lost count at thirty. She watched as an increasingly desperate Nelson, also in a smart green polo shirt with a logo, directed cars to park in a lot meant to hold perhaps twenty at the maximum. People were departing their cars, dressed in various states of golf attire, and were opening their trunks, taking out golf bags and greeting each other. A few leaned against their cars, taking off street shoes and were hopping around one leg, trying to put on their spiked golf shoes without getting their socked feet wet on the dew-covered gravel.

"Sara!" Chloe yelled, knowing that her lover was in the lavatory, trying to get the toilet to flush without large masses of water gushing onto the floor.

"What?" growled Sara, now in a hellacious mood. She was getting nowhere with the damned toilet, and the overflow of the toilet was nowhere near the overflow of impatience that showed in her voice.

Chloe glanced around quickly, and waved at her to join her in the doorway. Sara grabbed a towel to dry her hands, and strode quickly over to the door.

"Jesus Christ," whispered Sara in reverent awe, on this day of our Lord, Sunday, 8:00 a.m.

"Amen to that," murmured Chloe, a large dose of wonder and amazement in her voice, as they stood and watched even as more cars made a mini traffic jam in the driveway. Nelson was now walking around, nervously asking people to move their cars, so even more vehicles could be jammed into the already maxed-out available spaces. Even if he succeeded, there wasn't a prayer that all the cars now parked in driveway would find a niche in the lot.

Sara laid a hand on the small of Chloe's back. "It looks like Frank Sinatra's funeral procession out there. Holy shit!"

Chloe moved closer to Sara. "Does Dave know? Good God, somebody had better go get him, so he can figure out what the hell we're going to do."

Sara nodded, shook her head, and strode off toward the house, keeping an eye on the poor figure of Nelson, who had apparently come across a person who wasn't being cooperative with Nelson's polite plea to reposition his car.

Just as Sara's feet hit the steps of the porch, the door swung open, and Marcy stepped out, took one look at the Armageddon in the parking lot, and saved Sara the effort.

"Dave?" Marcy shouted over her shoulder, as Sara stepped up and stood beside her. "Dave!" she shouted one more time. She looked up at the stunned visage of Sara, and then she whistled, low and long. "Goddamnsonof..."

The inaugural tee-off time was pushed back until 9:00 a.m. The overflow of cars had been diverted to the land behind Sara's house because it had a driveway leading to it just up the main road, and just the grass in front of Sara's house had been manicured for the eighth hole. The land behind it was still cow pasture, and no one gave a second thought to its demise. A Justin from school had shown up, hoping to golf nine holes, but he was soon converted into being a helper. He was now blocking the entrance to the main driveway, and waving cars down to the next driveway, leading to a less-frustrated Nelson, who was pointing the way to park behind Sara's house. The morning was cool and fresh, the sun beginning its climb in the sky, and even with the convoluted and unexpected parking situation, most of the arriving golfers seemed cheerful and content to wait to begin their round on the new course.

Cheerful and content could not be used to describe some of the people in the barn/clubhouse, who were gathered behind the John Deere tractor, as another unsuspecting volunteer, Jeanette, bobbed and wove behind the counter, signing people in for their rounds. To simplify things, she was chucking coupons into a nearby trash can, and was charging a flat three dollars per person per round, tossing the money into a hastily crowbar-pried-open cash register drawer.

"Good lord, Dave, what do you mean, you don't know how half-off coupons work? And did you have to blanket a three-county area with them? There's people from Dunkirk out there, for Christ's sake, and that's sixty miles from here," sniped a very pissed off Marcy.

"How the hell did I know they'd all show up on the same day? I mean, come on!"

Even Chloe was showing Dave no mercy. "Good Lord, Dave. Didn't you know to put something on the coupons that said 'not good with any other offer?' I mean, you're giving them half off, and then they're using the two dollar off coupon on top of that. Do you know how many people I had bitching me out, all smug and explaining the 'rules of couponing' to me, like I was some kind of friggin' idiot? And to top it off, there's no expiration date on them." Chloe threw up her hands in exasperation, wishing she was tall enough to get a good grip around Dave's throat.

Dave looked persecuted, to say the least. "I know, I know, I know! Now, can we get rolling here, to get these people out of the barn and the parking lot, and out onto the course? The last time I looked, there were eighty people waiting to play. Eighty." He said the number twice, hoping to shock these bitching women into action, and away from reaming him multiple new assholes.

He was gratified to see his sermon had some effect on them, and they stilled their tongues, and just stared accusingly at him instead. "I have to go grab Paul, and have a quick, really quick ribbon cutting ceremony at the first tee." He noticed two of his starting foursome standing not far away from them, waiting impatiently, a little Kermit-greenish, just like him. "Damn." He called over to Mark Benson. "Where's Stan?"

Mark coughed and answered him. "Worshiping the old porcelain god at home. He's not coming."

Dave let out yet another irritated breath. "Great. I have to have some kind of representative from the town do this. I can't ask some-one to break up their group out of all these folks." His brain then worked for a millisecond, and he grinned. "C'mon, Chloe," and he firmly grabbed her by the elbow and started pulling her through the crowded barn toward the exit. "Let's see how good a golfer you really are!"

Marcy looked around, looking for Sara. She had an epiphany, and realized she and Jeanette were being left in charge of the disaster in the clubhouse, while her fiancé and best friend got to go out and play a pleasant nine holes of golf. She was not in a forgiving mood.

"Goddamit, Dave!" Marcy shouted as loudly as she could over the milling throng, "I want a divorce!"

At precisely 10:30, Sara finally had the mess in the lavatory cleaned up, and she exited it to find a few grinning, if desperate-looking, people congregating near the door, blissful now that she had fixed the problem. The crowd in the clubhouse had diminished; more people were coming in, but at a more reasonable rate.

She didn't even have time to go over to speak to a glowering Marcy, whose face was a stark contrast to Jeanette's beside her at the cash register. Jeanette was blondely bouncing and angelically gracious, talking up the waiting golfers in the barn as if she was a first cousin to them all. Sara smiled at the girl's natural ability to charm, and was going to go praise her when Jason raced into the barn, and stopped breathlessly in front of Sara.

"Ms. D'Amico?" Jason panted, and took a moment to catch his breath.

"What's up, Jase?" Sara asked with concern.

"Um, Nelson sent me." He gulped and looked at her with a sympathetic half-smile. "Your brother just hit a five-iron shot right through the front window of your house."

Chloe was enjoying a heavenly swig of cold water outside the barn. It was nearly noon, and she had arranged with a very vicious Marcy to relieve her behind the cash register at midday. Dave was busily glad-handing every person that crossed his path. Paul was standing beside her, snapping odd pictures here and there of golfers both arriving to play and those finishing their rounds. Church would be out soon, and everyone expected a new influx of golfers wanting to try out the new course. Chloe just finished tallying the scorecard from her round, and didn't disguise her grin at the results. *I kicked those guys' asses. Big time. And except for that problem on the eighth hole, with Sara's window.* Chloe looked around again to see if she could locate her missing lover. *She's probably at her house, putting up some kind of barrier.* The foursome had felt bad about the window, well, after Chloe stopped laughing at the look of horror that had covered Dave's face after he had teed off, and the four of them stood and watched the flight of the ball take its left-leaning arc, and the resounding crash that followed when it hit glass instead of green. They had regretfully decided, once Chloe had regained her composure, that there was nothing they could do about the unfortunate incident and decided to play on, not wanting to hold up any golfers behind them. They however, took a moment to argue about how many strokes to penalize Dave.

Jason came sprinting across the parking lot, and stopped in front of Paul, gasping for a breath.

"Mr. Hoderman." Jason was no track star, and his lungs knew it. "Mrs. Raeburn sent me to get you. Come quick, it's your mother." Jason took on another lungful of air.

Paul, frightened, simply stared at the young man before him.

Chloe jumped in, and quickly questioned Jason, who was bent over, hands on his knees. "Jason, should I call 911?"

Jason looked up looked at her, confused, and then grinned. "Oh, no, Ms. Donahue. It's a miracle. Mrs. Hoderman just got a hole-in-one out on seven."

Sara's back was screaming in protest. She and Nelson had spent a good part of the afternoon pushing cars out the soft, mud-covered ruts that now covered what used to be her back yard. The light was fading from the sky, and the dribble of golfers was lessening, and soon it would stop, not because of lack of devotion on their part, but because of the fading of available sunlight on this Sunday in April. They had pushed the last car out, and the only remaining cars were parked in relative safety up at the main parking lot up by the barn. Sara was filthy and tired, and said little other than giving departing drivers grunting commands as she and Nelson heaved cars, spinning tires baptizing her with mud. She hadn't seen Chloe since eight o'clock this morning, it was nearly 5:00 now, and she was eager to see her, filth or no filth.

She and Nelson settled in, side by side, in the electric golf cart she had parked near the front of her house, its window boarded up with an old plywood sign that had "Cherries, You Pick" painted onto it. She sighed, and wiped her hands off onto her blue jeans now brown with dirt. They sat, taking a breather, and looked across the nine-hole paradise shining green and lush in front of them.

Nelson returned his aunt's sigh. "We did a good job, huh, Aunt Sara?" He smiled, knowing he was right, and feeling very proud.

Sara knew he wasn't simply talking about the day that had passed. No, he was describing the whole golf course adventure, the hours they had spent together fussing and fertilizing, picking and grooming the expanse that lay ahead of him. She smiled, and did something very atypical for her: she reached across, and grabbed his hand, squeezing it and not letting go. Nelson, a little surprised, then feeling very blessed and content, returned the squeeze and lightly held on. Their eyes traveled over green again.

"So," began Sara softly, "gonna be a big brother, are ya?"

Nelson chuckled. "Yeah, isn't that something? I mean, it's great how that all turned out. I was so surprised when Marcy did that."

"You and me both, nephew, you and me both."

"And here I was thinking that maybe Chloe was the one." Nelson stopped, suddenly guilty over his previous perceptions, and not wanting to tell his Aunt about them.

"Chloe was the one what?" Sara's voice was encouraging, and

curious.

Nelson shook his head, and laughed, embarrassed. "I heard things. I was thinking that the rumors about Chloe were true, ya know? That maybe she was really sleeping with Dad, and was pregnant, that she was sleeping with you both." Nelson really laughed now. "I wasn't sure what was going on, I didn't want to get her in trouble with you, or Dad, or Marcy by saying anything." Nelson felt another tight squeeze on his hand, and a light chuckle from the aunt he couldn't quite bring himself to look at just yet. "I am such an ass. I thought she was bisexual." Another squeeze, more chuckles.

"Jeez, Nelson, I was worried about you for a minute or two there. I mean, I thought maybe Jason had been hitting on you."

Nelson snorted, laughed a hearty laugh, and finally met his aunt's eyes. "Oh, yeah, like Jason would hit on me."

Sara just grinned, opened her eyes wider, and kept looking at him.

Nelson blinked. "Jason?"

Sara's grin grew into a smile, and said nothing, but then she gave Nelson a quick nod.

Nelson sat back, and pondered this a moment. He looked at her again for confirmation, and there it was. His face split into a very wide grin. "Well, I'll be damned."

Sara gave his hand one more squeeze before she let it go, and pushed the start button on the cart. She pushed on the accelerator, and aunt and nephew rolled in silence, with a glorious sunset behind them, to join their family across the yards of grass and gravel ahead.

Dave was out in the parking lot, still chatting with a few stragglers who were in no hurry to get home. Sara watched as Nelson hopped off the cart, waved at his dad, and then walked up to the porch and into the house. She pulled the golf cart into the barn, relieved to see that there was no one left inside. She slid out of the cart, pulled a large electrical line over, and plugged it in to recharge it overnight. She took a quick glance around, and saw that the register was now firmly taped shut. She smiled to see that the revolving golf accessory rack was now more than half empty. *I've been so busy all day playing Handy Dyke, I have no idea just how many people actually came through here.* The glass on the display case of the front counter was a mass of fingerprints and smears. She walked over to the small stand-up pop cooler, grabbed a Diet Coke out of it, and sucked down nearly half before she stopped and had to take a breath. *I think I got a sunburn.* She'd never had the chance to put on her official polo shirt today. *Good thing, it would be covered in mud right now.* She wandered the barn a few minutes, glad for the few minutes alone to relax and collect her thoughts.

Let's see, I still have to take the cart around and collect the flags. I probably can get Chloe to ride with me. Or I could just leave them there tonight. Sara liked that idea so much she decided to just go with it, not to question the decision, or berate herself for her irresponsibility. She finished off the rest of the pop, and tossed the empty can into a recycling bin near the wall. She stretched, pushing her elbows far behind her, and heard a few satisfying creaks and she groaned. *Wow, I'm tired. Poor Dave, he looks like the walking dead. And Marcy, I wonder if she actually killed anyone today?*

She grabbed a ruler from under the counter, and started scraping dried mud off her sneakers. *Everyone was great today, from the family and friends down to the kids. Jeanette. Jason. Justin.* She shook her head and chuckled. *Those kids aren't just kids, they're friends.* She laughed again. *They're all going to be college students very soon, there's no reason I can't think of them as friends. I think that's the way they look at me. Damn.*

Sara started pushing dried lumps of crusted dirt off her other sneaker. *And someone said Mrs. Hoderman had a hole-in-one. That's friggin' amazing. I bet it took twenty years off her life. Maybe she'll let loose of Paul a little? Nah, that's not going to happen. He'll be with her until she dies, or until he does. That's okay, he seems happy.* Sara sighed. *Happy, wow, what a word. For years I never considered myself happy, never dreamed of being happy. Now I am. I can say it, in my head, and out loud. I'm happy. Just since the night since Nelson came to me, telling me he wanted to be in his senior class play, and the whole thing just started snowballing on me. Nelson, Marcy, Dave, Doris and Chloe. Chloe.*

Sara walked across the barn, and stopped in front of her beloved John Deere tractor, rolling the name that she adored through her head, and even whispered it a few times just for the sheer joy that it brought to her. *Chloe. Chloe.* She patted the old leather seat of the tractor. *I've got to make some decisions, Chloe hasn't asked, and I haven't been very open, mostly because I don't know what to do. I didn't think she could be happy with someone like me. Panicky. Scarred. Scared. Just a mechanic on a tiny golf course. But I was wrong. I was the one who didn't think I could be happy doing this, but I am. I feel needed and productive. And I feel very, very loved.* Sara's smile grew with that word, love. She stroked the steering wheel of the old green John Deere, and whispered softly to it, a little embarrassed that she was speaking to a tractor. *Ah, hell, it's not like the first time I've done it.* She leaned in, and softly said, "Goodnight, old girl. Tomorrow, or the next day, I'll take you out for a good long ride, all right? And I'll wash some of that dirt off you, and make you look real nice." One more pat, a gentle kick to a tire, and Sara turned and left the barn, turning the lights off and shutting the doors behind her, and headed toward the house.

Nelson, Marcy and Chloe were seated at the kitchen table when Sara strolled in. Dave was perched on the sink counter. Sara was pleased to see a whole stack of pizza boxes stacked in the middle of the table, as she grinned her hellos to everyone, she walked purposely around the table directly to Chloe, and leaned in and gave her a resounding long smooch that she realized midway through that Chloe was pulling away from. Sara released her from the kiss, and still leaning over her, teased, "Oh, c'mon Chloe, still shy?"

"She's always been shy, Sara. I've known her longer than you have. You're embarrassing the poor girl."

Still bent over Chloe, Sara didn't straighten up when she recognized that voice coming from the archway leading into the living room. Her eyes met Chloe's and they stared at each other, amazed at how wide the other's eyes were getting. Sara froze in place. She heard a few chairs being pulled away from the table, and a couple of bodies settling into them.

Sara straightened up, her heart pounding, although she wasn't frightened, wasn't panicking. *All right, okay, maybe a little panicky.* "Hiya, Doris," she said genially, looking away from Chloe, who was displaying a full body blush. Sara turned her head a little more, and then said, "I didn't realize that you and Jeanette were still here."

Doris sniffed, her face unreadable, and usually a woman of excess words, spoke one of the shortest sentences anyone in the kitchen had ever heard her say. "Obviously."

Jeanette, the undervalued and always underestimated young woman that she was, broke the silence in the roomful of mortified adults. "Well, Mrs. Raeburn, if you didn't know about them, you must be living on another planet. I mean, just look at them. They belong together." This blonde girl was brave, much braver than the silent, stunned adults around her were. Everyone looked at Jeanette with a quick look of surprise and respect, and then their eyes turned back to the gray-haired school principal.

Dave slid off the counter and silently stood just to the side of his sister, who had placed a comforting and protective hand on Chloe's shoulder. Everyone was waiting for Doris to say something. Normally, they were waiting for her to shut up. They didn't have to wait long.

"Well, Jeanette," Doris turned her eyes to the blonde cheerleader who was wondering if she had done the right thing, "I'm not sure about that. I certainly have to admit that I don't like," and her gaze turned to Sara and Chloe again, and her mouth slowly formed a smile, "being the last to know about such a lovely couple."

Marcy, whose pregnancy hormones were running amok and screwing up her emotional stability, simply broke down in tears at that moment. She started sobbing in Doris' direction, a grateful and relieved smile on her face. "Oh, God. Oh, God. God, Doris," she snuffled.

This unexpected turn of events and Marcy's very uncharacteristic outburst made everyone start laughing nervously. Dave moved over and stood behind the bawling Marcy, wrapping his hands around her neck and cooing at her in between disbelieving chuckles. Sara's mouth was hanging open, an uncontrolled strangled braying sound emitting from deep within her as she moved her gaze from Doris to Marcy back to Doris again. She felt Chloe stir beneath her hand, and watched as Chloe got out of her seat, moved around the table, and over to the side of her long-time friend, Doris Raeburn, and simply put her arms around her in a wordless and long hug. Doris blushed at the sentiment; that spurred Sara into movement, and she too, made the trip around the table and waited quietly until Chloe released her hug on Doris. Chloe looked up expectantly at Sara, a small smile gracing her face. Sara grinned and shook her head, first at Chloe, and then did the same to Doris, before she swooped down and gave Doris a hug of her own. Doris snorted as Sara let go, and wiped at her eyes. Sara and Chloe joined hands, and moved around the table until they were both standing next to Jeanette, who had decided, happily, that she'd said the right thing after all. Chloe leaned over, placed a soft kiss on Jeanette's cheek, and gave her a gentle smile of appreciation. Sara merely reached out, and patted the red-faced and pleased cheerleader on the back.

Doris shifted in her seat, and looked around at each of them in turn, clearing her throat a few times. She watched as Chloe settled in her seat and Sara pulled a chair up next to her, comfortably taking Chloe's hand into her own, settling their clasped hands unapologetically on the tabletop in front of them. Dave handed his suddenly emotional fiancée a few paper towels. They all listened to the melodious sounds of a softly sobbing Marcy, the usually pessimistic and smart-ass art teacher, who was now reduced to blowing her nose like an overwhelmed six-year-old who just got a pony for her birthday.

Doris took a full breath. "Well, as I was saying before someone rudely interrupted me—I'm sure that's what happened, one of you interrupted me, and I forgot what I was going to say. That damnable Helen Hoderman is going to be an insufferable presence on this earth for the rest of her days. You would think she saw the Virgin Mary on that seventh hole, she was so incredibly smug after that hole-in-one. And let me tell you, the woman three-putted every other hole on the course. Sara, since I'm bringing my summer golf league out here to play, we'll be here most every day, perhaps you and your girlfriend can find a way to drown her somewhere out by that beautiful ninth hole? What a fountain! Where was I? Oh, yes, everyone, save your money for bail, I may need it if she keeps acting like she walks on water. Chloe, stop slouching."

Part XXIV:
The Reluctant Replacement

The D'Amicos would have busy lives now, busier than ever before, and the golf course, on its second day open, was inundated with retirees armed with coupons and curiosity about the new course. Dave, Nelson and Sara had agreed upon a schedule, a routine, to work the place. On rotating mornings, they would switch off the responsibility of rising at 5:30 a.m., and making a circuit around the fairways, putting flags in holes, watering greens, stocking the ball washers, filling water canteens. As summer got closer, the time to rise to complete these chores would get earlier, to accommodate golfers who preferred to golf during the cooler hours of morning. But for now, 5:30 a.m. was certainly early enough for any of them.

Dave and Sara agreed that Nelson should have the least responsibility over the care and handling of the course right now, since he was occupied with the last month of school, and all of the activities of a soon-graduating senior were plenty enough to keep the young man busy. Dave would be running things from the barn/club house, while Sara spent her day tinkering with patching divots, mowing grass and greens, and generally working the land she knew so well. Although she agreed to do it when needed, she wasn't entirely comfortable with the thought of working behind the counter, having to have casual conversations about new putters and golf shoes. She was out in the public eye again, but never had been, even pre-anxiety attacks, the most sociable of beings. She preferred one-on-one contact with people she knew, or small groups of people with whom she was familiar. Even on Sunday and at the party the night before, she felt many curious stares directed her way, and it made her uncomfortable.

Saturday night, a few hesitant town people had even approached her, and shyly asked her for her autograph. She acquiesced, saying little, and not chatting them up. And Sunday, while she and Nelson were pushing cars out of the muddied soft ground behind her house, she had been aware, out of her peripheral vision, a handsome thirty-something man standing off to the side, watching her. She and Nelson pushed, they heaved, they grunted and finally the car gained some traction, and went bumpily along its way. She and Nelson gave quick nods of victory to each other. The handsome stranger welcomed the interruption of their physical labors, and with a confident look on his face, he strode over the short distance to Sara, and stood in front of her.

"Hello. You're Sara D'Amico, aren't you? From *Star Gazers*, right?" he asked, giving her his best smile.

"Yup, that would be me," Sara replied, giving her standard reply. Nelson was a few yards away, watching curiously.

The man's eyes dwelled briefly on her scar, and then traveled to meet her eyes. He wanted to make the eye contact, make a connection. "I'm a big fan. And you're lovelier in person, if that's possible, than you are on screen. Even covered in mud." He grinned, turning on as much charm as he could.

Sara didn't want to be rude, and didn't want to encourage further conversation, either. She dropped her gaze, and distractedly glanced at the man's hands, expecting to see a piece of paper, a pen there, so she could scrawl her name and she could be on her way. She saw that the man's hands were hitched in his shorts pockets. *Hmm. Okay. Not a signature hound, he's a Romeo.*

Her eyes came up and met his again. "Thanks. I appreciate that. Now, I have some things I have to do."

"Kevin. Kevin Shipman." He put out his hand, and she sighed internally, quickly shaking it, noticing that he tried to prolong the contact.

I'm not in the mood for this. "Hello, Kevin, and thank you again. Now, I really have to be on my way." She turned, and found the man moving with her, staying in front of her, blocking her way.

He flashed another smile. "I was thinking that, well, that if under different circumstances, you might like to..."

Sara found that Nelson was now at her elbow, and had placed a quick arm around her waist. Her mind tumbled around when she felt Nelson pull her close.

"Sara, honey, is this man bothering you?" Nelson said, narrowing his eyes at the man, and sounding like John Wayne. He leaned toward the man, all 6' 2", 210 lb. of him speaking of unfriendly menace.

"Uh, no, I was just leaving. And so, I think, was he," she said purposely, narrowing her own eyes in collusion with Nelson.

The man, so full of confidence and bravado just a moment before, now felt cool, nearly cold blue eyes staring him down. He had the sensation that he was a kitten, cornered by two very threatening Dobermans.

"Uh-huh, well, gotta go. Good luck," the man said as he back-pedaled, suddenly searching for his car. He gave a quick smile that turned just as quickly into a frown as he strode quickly to his vehicle.

Both Nelson and Sara noticed that his car was parked very near a torn-up area, potentially dangerous for getting stuck. They stood back and watched as the man backed right into the mess, and then stood a little longer, watching as the man spun his tires, putting the car in reverse, gunning it, and then in drive, hammering the accelerator, digging himself in deeper. They just stood there, arms folded, watching and waiting. Finally, the man got out of his car, refusing to look at them, and went up and looked at his buried tires. He sighed, and then turned to the D'Amicos, his eyes asking for help.

Sara and Nelson walked over, and Nelson took command. "Put her in drive. Slow. We'll push." They got behind the vehicle, and a couple of mighty heaves later, the man was on his way, and he beeped his thanks as his car hit the driveway leading to the road.

Nelson looked at his tired aunt, and patted her on the back. "It's funny, Aunt Sara, I've never seen a guy hit on you before. You were pretty nice, even when he was being obnoxious. How did you handle that out in Los Angeles, when you must have run across that kind of guy, what, every five minutes?"

Sara just shook her head. "You know what, Nelson, I don't even remember any more. I was a flat out, scary bitch, and probably just told them to fuck off." She saw Nelson's eyes widen slightly. "Yeah, I wasn't very nice. I didn't like myself, and I didn't give anyone a chance to like me, either." She stretched her back a little, and rubbed his arm quickly. "I don't know if it was the place, or the time, or me. All I know is, thank God, I don't have to deal with assholes so much anymore. I have no patience for it. I'm not good at it." She saw the frown on his face, and she laughed. "Hey, c'mon Nels, lighten up. It's not like anyone is gonna swoop in here and try and talk me into going back to that kind of life." She started walking back toward the golf cart, and after a moment, he started after her.

She had no idea how wrong she was.

"All right, wow, give me a minute, would you?" Chloe laughed. "I don't have supernatural recovery powers, ya know."

Sara grumbled into Chloe's belly, putting her lips to it, and blowing hard. A noise like a strangled tuba sounded, and she enjoyed the rolling of Chloe's vibrating belly when she giggled. Sara turned her head, and laid her cheek on the soft skin near Chloe's ribs. Her hand, on Chloe's thigh, snuck up higher.

"Hey, cut that out, you. I just told you." Chloe reached down, and softly thwapped Sara's head. "Behave." Chloe was feeling very warm but tired, and it was just her luck, her lover was still feeling very frisky.

"That's not what you said a while ago," teased Sara. "A while ago, I believe you were begging me not to stop," she declared smugly and settled her arm contentedly across her lover's hips. She felt Chloe's hand drop into her hair, and the gentle scratching that began. "Oh, yeah, that's so nice, don't stop," she sighed, loving the feeling.

Chloe didn't stop. "Are you begging me now?" she purred, and pulled a long length of Sara's hair through her fingers, and letting it drop. "I like playing with your hair."

"I like you playing with my hair, too. Sell my clothes, I'm going to heaven."

"Sara, it is like heaven to me. I love you." Chloe was slowly drifting off, enjoying the peace and loving haze that enveloped her. "Don't forget, WQEL tomorrow." She made an effort to keep up the soothing stroking of Sara's head, but she was losing the battle. Just as she surrendered into sleep, she heard Sara murmur into the soft pillow of her belly, "I love you too."

Early Thursday afternoon the small redheaded librarian, already anxious about the upcoming evening, answered the telephone in her office.

"Hello, Stonecreek Public Library, how may I help you?"

"Hi. You got a minute?"

"Sure, Mrs. Cellone is manning the front desk. I'm in here hiding from all the people who are pissed off because both copies of Stephen King's latest book haven't been returned yet. These people can get mean, let me tell you."

Oh, yeah, mean, thought Marcy, laying sprawled on her couch, *we'll see about mean.* "Uh, Chloe, don't kill me." *I've lived thirty years, I suppose that's long enough.*

"What?" Chloe glanced at the clock on her desk. "Hey, don't you have a class right now? Why're you calling me?"

"I'm not at school. I took the day off." Marcy squinted in preparation for the pain she knew was going to come.

Chloe drew out the word, her voice rising as if she were climbing the scale. "W-h-y?"

"I-I'm okay but..." Marcy was glad she lived as far as she did from the Stonecreek library as she did. Otherwise, she would have to duck the flying objects that would certainly be lobbed her way. "I'm really tired, have a bit of a sore throat, and, well..."

Chloe finished for her. "You're not going, are you?" Chloe picked up the rounded glass paperweight, shaped like a grape, from the corner of her desk and gripped it.

"Uh, no, I'm really tired and my throat's sore and..." *I'm going to die single. There is justice in this world.*

Chloe tossed the grape paperweight in the air and caught it. "Marcy," she said, desperation and aggravation mixing in her tone. "What the hell am I going to do tonight on WQEL? I can't talk for five hours by myself."

Marcy tried her best not to make a smart remark. "Well, I figured maybe Doris could help tonight, I mean really, she'd certainly hold up her end of the conversation."

The glass grape went flying even higher. "Oh yeah, sure, she'd be great. She'd talk about her three items on her side of the board for the whole ten minutes we have to sell the stuff off, and I'd just be standing there on camera, doing a Vanna, pointing silently at my side of the board like some demented nitwit. Plus, I'm pretty sure Doris' bowling banquet is tonight, Mrs. Cellone mentioned it earlier to me."

"Oh." *There goes that perfect solution.*

"Yeah, oh."

Marcy furrowed her brows. "How about Dave?" As soon as the name came out of her mouth, she knew it was a bad idea.

"Okay, that would leave me with the reverse situation. I'd be talking for ten minutes at a time, while he stands there pointing at his side of the auction board. He's not exactly Monty Hall."

Marcy sighed. "You got me there." Another thought. "Paul?"

"Oh my God, don't you remember the first year we did this? Paul completely went into a coma in front of that red blinking camera. Not an intelligible word came out of his mouth. He forgot how to read. He pronounced pizza like piazza for ten minutes, and the callers thought they were bidding on a twelve dollar trip to Italy. No, way, not Paul."

"Well, there is the perfect solution, we both know it, and we both aren't saying it," Marcy finally offered, reluctance marking every word.

Chloe remained quiet, she wanted Marcy to be the first to say the name they were both thinking. Marcy proceeded exactly as Chloe expected. "A woman who has tons of experience in front a camera. Who we're pretty sure knows how to read, and enunciate, and turn on the charm, and she could probably wing it quite well." *If she only has to speak in two-word sentences.*

Chloe hated saying it, but it had to be said. "A woman who loathes making chatty small talk, knows jack shit about public television, hates to be the center of attention, and is prone to having really terrible panic attacks without warning."

Marcy cleared her throat. "Yup, sounds perfect. Chloe, you know she'll do it if you ask her." *And I'm guaranteed roadkill if I ask her.*

"No, I don't know that. Don't say that, she may go ballistic if I ask her."

"Well, get Nelson to ask her for you. She's absolutely a sap for that kid, and you know it. Just get him to ask her for ya."

"I can't do that, Marcy. You remember the last time I didn't approach her directly about something? The choreographer thing. Nope, I have to ask her straight out, and then get shot down." Chloe blinked. "Wait a minute. Wait a minute. You're the one bailing on me here. It's your responsibility to find a replacement, and you need to ask Sara. You do." Chloe suddenly felt a little lighter, and the paperweight stopped flying so high out of her grasp.

"Me? Why would she do it for me?" Marcy's voice got progressively hoarser.

"Well, she's practically your sister-in-law, which, in my book, makes you family, and family can screw each other over asking lousy favors."

Marcy rubbed her face and sighed. *She owes me, sort of, I think.* "Okay. I'll do it. Let me call her, and I'll call you back."

Chloe grinned, and put the paperweight safely back onto the corner of her desk. "Good luck."

"Yeah, yeah. It's been nice knowing you."

Chloe didn't get much done during the last two hours at work. Marcy called back, and told Chloe the good news. Sara called, and complained for twenty minutes about the good news. Dave called, and wanted to know why his sister flipped him the bird, twice, when he mentioned to her in passing something about tonight's WQEL auction. Nelson called from school and told Chloe he had tried to call Marcy at home to see why she wasn't in school today. Marcy's line was busy, and so was his father's, so he called Chloe. Marcy called back and told Chloe of her plans to leave the country for a few months, until Sara calmed down, and it was safe to come back to town again. Sara called, and calmly asked Chloe what she should wear for this fucking goddamned idiotic waste of her time, and casually mentioned that she knew a few shady types back in L.A. that could "take care" of the "Marcy problem." Chloe finally stopped answering the phone around four o'clock, and made a bewildered Mrs. Cellone field calls for her, so she could leave to go home and get dressed for tonight.

As Chloe was heading home in her beat up but finely tuned Subaru, she thanked her higher powers for two very disparate things. One, she was thankful to God that she had decided never to purchase a cell phone. Two, she was grateful to the Commonwealth of Pennsylvania for the outdated and arcane laws that wouldn't allow her to actually marry into, and thus become a full fledged member of, the looned-out D'Amico family.

* * *

"Are you going to bitch the whole way to Erie?" Chloe was tired of it already, and they had another thirty-five miles to go to get to the tiny public television studio just south of Erie. She glanced in her rearview mirror, and saw the two grim faces of Nelson and Jeanette sitting in the back seat of her Subaru. She glanced over to the passenger seat, where a stunningly dressed and completely unhappy Sara D'Amico was sitting. "You could have just told Marcy no, ya know."

Sara scratched at her elbow, and then at the shoulder of the dress she was wearing. "Damned itchy material." She adjusted the clothing again. "And no, I couldn't say no, I owed her, as the artiste herself not so graciously pointed out to me."

Chloe glanced in her side view mirror, to make sure the two vans full of cast members were keeping up with her. One was being driven by Paul, and the other by a parent volunteer. "What do you owe her for, anyway?"

Sara looked out her window, and gave the tiniest of gulps. *Oops.* "Just some family stuff, that's all. Anyway, that's not the point."

"What's the point?"

"Nothing. Never mind. It's only five hours of talking about oil changes and buckets of chicken wings."

Chloe looked to Nelson and Jeanette again, and caught the look in Nelson's eyes. "Uh, Sara, not that I'm not sympathetic, but I have to do the same goddamned thing. And there are other things to consider, like the fact that your nephew and his girlfriend have to sing and dance in front of a TV camera tonight, in between fielding bidders' phone calls. So, shut up, grow up and bite the bullet, babe. We've all got a job to do."

Sara blinked. "Oh." *Oh, shit.* She turned in her bucket seat, and said to both Nelson and Jeanette, "Oh, I'm sorry, I'm really sorry. I just get all rattled and I don't think of anyone but myself. You two are going to be great, I know. And the rest of the kids, too. I'm sorry I'm being such an asshole." Sara's bitchiness segued into a quickly pounding heart, and she turned in her seat, and quickly closed her eyes. *Nope, here it comes. Here it comes. Goddammit, I don't need to have an attack right now.*

A minute or two later, there were three vehicles pulled over to the edge of the highway, and a beautiful woman was standing in the grass, fighting alone in a world of her own, oblivious to the passing cars and trucks that zipped by. Seven minutes later, the three vehicles were pulling back onto the road, and proceeding along to their destination.

"Sacre Merde," the buxom brunette whistled through her teeth, "no wonder you volunteered us to work Stonecreek Night." Her eyes widened, and she stared through the control room window at the sight before her. "Mother of God, she's a stunner, holy hell."

Her partner in the control booth laughed. "See, I told ya, and wow, her friend is something, too, huh? Wonder where she came from? Last year, she had some artsy fartsy type working the auction boards with her. She wasn't bad, either." She adjusted her headset and looked at the clock. 5:35. Twenty-five minutes and they were underway. "The tall one looks familiar. I can't quite place her though."

"Wait, I was talking about the tall one before, although, come to think of it, the redhead is a babe, too. You were talking about the redhead? She's the one that's done this before?"

"Geez, Fran, yeah." Her companion laughed, and adjusted her own headset. She swiveled in her chair, and gave the brunette a tsk through her teeth. "You're letting your fantasies loose again, aren't you? You like the brunettes, don't you?"

Angie laughed back. "Well, yeah, I do. You're the only exception to my rule," she said affectionately. She grabbed a few sheets of paper off the soundboard. "Oh, great, the school is doing *Oklahoma!*, I guess I can suffer through that. Five songs. Did someone give us the music yet?"

"I imagine Nancy will bring them in with her after she gets done talking with the both of them. That tall one, does it say who she is?"

"Uh, it says here, Chloe Donahue and Marcy, Marcy something I can't pronounce. I think Chloe is the redhead. And the Marcy name sounds familiar too, I think it's the woman that was here with her last year. And whoever that tall drink of water is out there, I don't think she's Marcy."

Both women watched as Chloe and the mysterious tall woman were fitted for their lapel microphones.

Angie sighed and chuckled. "Boy, what I wouldn't give to be Tony right now." She felt a smack on her shoulder, and laughed again. She adjusted her headset microphone down, and in front of her mouth, and reached and flipped a switch on the console. "Hey, folks, we need to do a sound check. How about we start with Chloe first? Just say anything, we need to make some adjustments in here."

Chloe's head bobbed up when she heard the voice of the woman wafting out over the studio's speakers. She looked at Sara, who in turn was glaring at the man who was having difficulty attaching the microphone to the V-neck of Chloe's green silk dress.

"Hey buddy, watch where you're putting your hands," Sara said, squinting her eyes.

Chloe licked her lips, and tried to ignore the now-nervous man who was fumbling in her cleavage area. He moved away, taking a quick look at the glowering brunette. He said into his own headset, "Okay, Angie, she's ready to roll."

Chloe began speaking, in normal tones. "Peter Piper picked a peck of pickled peppers. You talkin' to me? You talkin' to me? On our shoe tonight, right here on our stage, we've got Arvid Angolese and His Magic Spinning Plates. One moment please, and our opera-tors will direct your call."

A laugh came over the speakers. "That's great, Chloe. Now for your friend."

Sara's eyes directed themselves up to the small control window glass, where she knew the woman was sitting. "Sara."

"Hi Sara, now, it's your turn. Just a few words, in normal tones. We need to get some highs and lows. Start anytime."

Sara cleared her throat. "Captain's Log, star date 11032.244. The first officer..." she trailed off, and continued to stare past the cameras.

"Uh, Sara? I'm Angie. Do you think you could give us a little more? Your voice is a little low."

Sara frowned, and thought a moment. A slow, feral grin graced her face. "A mighty princess, forged in the heat of battle. The power. The passion. The danger. Her courage will change the world."

The two women in the control booth looked at each other with startled eyes. They shrugged their shoulders, and shook their heads.

"Uh, Sara, that's great, that'll work."

Chloe saw the camera was now fixed on her wary partner, who, even after three boards, hadn't relaxed very much into auctioneer mode. *She's stiffer than Al Gore. Poor thing. I'm glad I didn't get her items.*

Sara was doing her damnedest to sound interested and cheerful. "And on item number six, two one-hour visits to Piotrowski's House of Electrolysis, we currently have a bid of $35, and it's a $100 value. Surely we can get a higher bid on this? Surely someone out there has some unwanted facial hair or something they need removed?" She faltered for a moment, and twisted the item description sheet in her sweaty palms. She opened it up, and quickly looked at it, and then her face came back up to grin grimly at the camera. "The description says it, well, I guess it doesn't have to be on your face, uh, it could be anywhere, uh, like, on your...back? I guess?" She took a big breath, and looked to the dry erase board, sitting on an easel, between her and Chloe, who had stepped out of camera range, and now had her back to Sara. The redhead's shoulders were shaking.

Sara blinked, and returned to item four. "And with four minutes left, the bid on the furnace twenty-three point clean and check from Cotter's Heating is up to $15, and that's a $29 value. And don't forget, folks, it's almost summer, and I'm sure that you're thinking about getting your furnaces checked for next winter, right?"

Hey, I'm getting the hang of this. No sweat. "And on number five, the hyacinth bush from Barb's Flower Patch is up to $12, that's a $22 retail value. Let's get that up there; it's all for the benefit of WQEL. It's spring, and who wouldn't like to get a little bush?"

Marcy and Dave, who were watching the show from the comfort of Marcy's home, both slid off the couch and onto the floor at the same time.

Nancy, the stage manager, was standing next to Sara, as they both watched as Jason and Moreen perform a very credible job of "It's All or Nuthin" in front of the cameras. A boom mike was out of camera range, above their heads as they sang. She looked at the tall woman sympathetically. "No, really, you're doing a great job. We're going to run the station promo tape after the song, so you have about eight minutes until you have to get out there again. And where's Chloe?"

Sara sipped at her water, and said miserably, "She's getting her mascara fixed. She got it all messed up when I was droning on about the magical aspects of 'getting a little bush.'" She looked at Nancy, and said seriously, "Do you think the cameras picked up the tears that were rolling down her cheeks?"

"I'm sure Fran or Angie in the control booth kept that camera off her. Don't worry."

Meanwhile, in the control booth, Fran was placing a fresh videotape into the Camera Two tape machine. The tape she had just removed, of Chloe reacting to Sara's bush commentary, was going straight into Fran and Angie's private collection.

Paul, who was supervising the students while they answered the phones, was not really paying attention to what was happening in front of the cameras. He took his job very seriously, making sure that the cast members were filling out the bid cards correctly and fully, and when someone got a new bid, he checked the card carefully before he gave it to the stagehand. The stagehand then went and entered the new bid onto the dry erase board that listed each item's name, its donor, and its current bid. He tried to stay out camera range as much as possible, he especially stayed clear of the tall brunette who had snarled at him earlier.

Paul looked at his watch, it was nearly 7:20 p.m., time to pull Nelson and Justin off the phones, and get them ready to do "Poor Jud is Daid." He motioned to both of them, and tapped his watch face.

Nelson finished getting information from his caller, got up and handed the card to Paul, and stood next to him and waited for Justin to join them. When he did, Paul whispered, "Okay, head for the men's room, get your vests and stuff on. And really, take a minute and warm your voices up while you're in there, okay? I know it sounds silly but you won't sound so rusty. Stretch your voices out, do something with highs and lows in it."

Louie, the Number One camera guy, was feeling a little desperate, and was glad when Angie gave him the okay to fix his camera in a tight shot on Chloe so he could go relieve himself before the next musical number. He strode quickly to the men's room down the hall, and when he entered, there were two large young men in there blocking the path to the two available urinals. The one boy was bent in front of the other, fussing with the front of the dark haired guy's leather pants. They were so involved, they never noticed the camera man enter. Louie did a double take, and exited the room quickly, because it was all too surreal. They were also singing with each other.

"People will say we're in love..."

"Hey, that's guy's a natural," praised Fran, watching how beautifully Nelson's face filled up her screen. "Look at those eyes, that face. And he can sing, I mean really sing, too."

Angie nodded appreciatively. She looked at the sheet in front of her. "Says his name is Nelson D'Amico. Wow, I've seen tons of kids come through here for these auctions, a bazillion every night from every damned high school in town. I've never seen anything even close to him. He has something."

"D'Amico?" said a puzzled Fran. She thought for a moment, and then comprehension struck. "D'Amico. That's who Sara is, Sara D'Amico, the actress! I mean, cable television and that movie, I never saw it, *Star Gazers*."

Understanding dawned on her partner's face then, too. They both looked at the monitor in front of them, filled with a tight close up of Nelson's singing face, and then they looked out into the studio, where the newly rediscovered actress was leaning up against a cool cinderblock wall with the redhead right next to her. Both Chloe and Sara were smiling, proud and happy with how well Nelson and Justin were doing with their song.

Angie whispered into her headset mike. "Hey, Matty, real quick, give me a headshot, tight, on Sara over there by the wall."

Matt, out in the studio, did as requested.

Angie and Fran looked at the side by side monitors, and saw Sara's and Nelson's images there.

"Wow," they both murmured together.

Angie nodded to Fran, and went over to the cabinet on the back wall of the little control room, and pulled out a fresh six pack of videotapes.

Chloe had done the last three hourly "big boards" with Nancy, because she had taken pity on Sara. But Sara seemed settled down now, and had loosened up considerably, so much so that Chloe almost asked her if she had found a bottle to get a nip from somewhere.

But in reality, Sara had just calmed down, and she had done it because of the comforting presence of her lover. Chloe had kept a very careful watch on her, and when Sara seemed halting or unsure, Chloe jumped in, and quite naturally, with no pretense, set the nervous woman at ease, even on camera, with a soft smile, a helpful comment or silly remark. Sara was almost enjoying herself now, almost. So she volunteered to do the next "big board" with Nancy.

Chloe felt compelled to give her a few quick tips while the station's informational tape played for eight minutes. "Okay, all of the items, it looks like art work this time, are valued at over $300 each, and they're donated by some well-known local artists." Chloe squinted her eyes at Sara. "And listen, just because the artists are known locally, doesn't mean they're any good, you know what I mean? Try to avoid the phrase 'will look great over any sofa,' it ticks the artists off, got it?"

"Got it." Sara grinned. "See you in ten. Nancy's waving me over there. I guess I should look at the painting first, huh?" She tossed her water bottle into a trash can. "Hey, who's up after the big board?"

Chloe grinned, "I think Jeanette with her solo."

"Well, if you talk to her, give her my best." Sara smiled, and headed off toward where Nancy was standing next to, what Sara could tell already was a garishly done painting of a sunset over Lake Erie. *Oh my God. I wouldn't hang that thing under my sofa.*

"Dammit Paul, where the hell can she be? She's not in the ladies' room, I looked there. We have four minutes to find her. The song is all queued up in the control booth, and I can't switch songs now, the other songs involve a lot of the kids, and they're all manning the phones. It's 8:30 p.m., it's prime time, everyone and their goddamned mother is calling the station right now, and the donations always go up during the performances. Well, except for last year, but hell. Where can she be?"

Paul glanced again at the three long tables where the cast was busily answering phones. "I'll go look again. Make sure the stage-hand guy knows to grab the cards."

Chloe nodded, and started fretting. Three minutes. She strode over to the control booth's door and lightly tapped, and the door opened to a lovely woman with a great set of...lungs on her. Chloe nodded shyly. "Hi, uh, I'm Chloe, and I have a problem."

The brunette waved her in, and softly shut the door behind her.

"Listen, Heather," Jeanette said impatiently. "We can't stand out here in the bushes in the dark all night. I mean, your song isn't even up for over," she glanced at her watch, "an hour and twenty minutes now. And I have to be in there in ten minutes to get ready for my song, and this really isn't helping me." Jeanette patted her best friend on the back again. "Can't we just go back inside and you can puke there?"

Heather answered that question by heaving her guts up again in the bushes that lined the outskirts of the dark and full parking lot. She moaned.

Jeanette blew out a breath and tried to regain some patience. "I take it that's a no, huh? Okay, I'll stay out here with you for ten more minutes, try and get it together. At least we have some time."

The station's second promotional tape, approximately four minutes in length, began playing immediately after the finish of Nancy and Sara's big board.

Sara came strolling up and grinned at the frowning Chloe, who was nervously perched on the corner of a large table. "Can you believe some idiot paid $1200 for that piece of paint by number crap?" Sara shook her head and laughed, and then noticed the unhappy look on her partner's face. "What's wrong?"

"Sara, you told me once that I need to be straight out with you, no beating around the bush." Chloe's frown disappeared for a moment at the mention of the word bush, and then resettled on her face. "This is prime time, the hour the station gets its most donations, so we save some of the best musical numbers for now."

"I know all of this." Sara said, confused.

"Well, what you don't know is that we can't find Jeanette anywhere. And Heather is missing too. And if she doesn't show up in the next two minutes, well, it's too late to pull anyone else off the phones and get them prepped for their number. Flat out, Sara, I need you to do it if she doesn't show."

"What? No way."

"Sara, I need you to do this. I'm begging you. Please. You know it inside and out, you taught her all the motions to it, I've heard you singing it myself. Angie and Fran have it queued up to the second version, that's your key, I know. So, are you going to do it?" Chloe looked at her as if she expected a yes to fall from Sara's lips, and no other answer. There was all the trust in the world in those green eyes, and Sara couldn't ignore it.

Sara blinked, and grabbed Chloe by the arm. "Tell Nancy to stall for two minutes, and let's get my make-up fixed."

"Dave!" yelled Marcy in disbelief. Dave was in the bathroom. "Dave, get your ass out of the bathroom now! Your idiot sister is going to sing on friggin' WQEL!"

Nelson, still dressed in the leather pants with the stuck zipper, had covertly taken his bid phone off the hook, so it would ring busy, and held the receiver to his ear, so it looked like he was doing his job.

No way he was going to miss this.

Angie, irritated, asked Fran, "Where's that damned phone number list for the local major network affiliates?"

Doris Raeburn was standing in the bar of the Embers restaurant. She had gotten tired of waiting for the poor overworked waitress who was serving their bowling banquet to come around for their next drink order, so Doris decided to enter the bar and get it herself. There was a TV perched on the wall over the bar, and she idly glanced up at it and saw that it was tuned to the WQEL auction. Doris smiled; she had a tape in her VCR taping the whole thing at home. But just as she caught the bartender's attention, and as he was approaching her, Doris heard what the ash-blonde station manager was saying.

"And now, something a little different here on Stonecreek Night at WQEL. One of Stonecreek's most famous residents and the chore-ographer for their presentation of *Oklahoma!*, Sara D'Amico, is going to grace us with a song from *Oklahoma!*, "Many a New Day.""

Sara's face appeared on the screen, and music started. Doris threw a ten on the counter, and settled into a stool. She stared at the screen, and never looked at the bartender who was waiting for her order. "Manhattan. Make it a double."

Chloe had seen Jeanette perform this song so many times that she had every word, every motion, every choreographed movement memorized. It was a song sung with impetuous and defiant innocence, by a young woman jealous of her sweetheart's seeming interest in another. Chloe was aware that Sara was thirty-five years old, and had no resemblance to a young and coquettish seventeen year old.

That's what Chloe thought, that is, until the song began, and Sara transformed herself completely in front of the camera, effortlessly shedding the years with every gesture and word.

In Stonecreek, even Dave and Marcy didn't recognize the raven-haired, blue-eyed creature singing coyly on their screen.

Doris blindly reached for her drink, she found it, sipped it, and saw the same high school girl who had so captivated her so many years ago.

And, witnessing it all from mere yards away in a small public televisions station's tiny control room, Chloe couldn't help but fall in love all over again.

When everyone left the building together that night, tired and excited with the way the evening had gone, they were surprised to find a local ABC affiliate remote van parked nearby, and the form of a very recognizable local news reporter standing near Chloe's Subaru, with a cameraman filming their approach.

"Sara D'Amico? I'm Meg Talarico, from Channel 23 Action News. I was wondering if you would consent to speak to me a few minutes, on camera?"

The students stopped and stared at the reporter. Here was a real live celebrity in front of them, wanting to talk to their Ms. D'Amico. They had, in the course of the months they had spent with her, completely forgotten that Sara was anyone other than their workhorse choreographer, who worked at a golf course, and was the aunt of that sweet, shy guy, Nelson D'Amico, and lastly and most importantly, their neighbor and friend.

Everyone, including Chloe, turned and looked at the stunned golf course mechanic, waiting to see how she would respond to Meg Talarico.

Sara looked around at everyone, and then at Chloe. Chloe's face was unreadable.

Sara closed her eyes, and then slowly opened them. "Sorry. No thanks." She opened the door to the Subaru, got in, and closed it behind her.

Meg Talarico and her cameraman left with no interview, and only some minor footage of Sara exiting the WQEL building.

The kids in the vans chatted excitedly on the way home, and sang a few songs.

Four subdued people, traveling in a late 1980s model Subaru, rode in an uneasy silence all the way back to Stonecreek.

Part XXV:
I Said 'Yes'

It was Friday morning, the day after Stonecreek Day at WQEL.

It began not long after Sara began her trek on her John Deere tractor, crossing fairways in front of waving golfers, who patiently waited for her to pass in front of them so they could tee off.

The metaphoric poop came from somewhere unknown, dropped itself onto some kind of karmic fan blades, and was flung, far and wide, hitting all four corners of the tiny town of Stonecreek, leaving almost no one in town untouched by the stench it left behind.

The day began, like others before it, with a sleepy librarian opening up the old oak doors to the town library, bending to pick up the newspapers on the stoop. She entered the library, dropped off her coat, and made herself a pot of coffee. She began opening up the plastic packaging on the various local and national newspapers, readying them to put out in the periodicals section. The Erie paper was first, and quickly glancing at the folded paper's headlines, she flipped it over to scan the obituaries, as she always did, at the bottom of the page. Instead, her eyes were drawn to a picture, black and white, and by the looks of it, none too recent, of her tall and dark lover. She blinked, and blindly reached for the telephone while she read the accompanying headline.

Out at Stonecreek Golf Course, Dave was chatting about national politics with Ralph Henderson, already a regular at the tiny golf course in the few short days it had been open. Dave realized, the third day that Ralph showed up in the early morning, that Ralph really wasn't here for the golf, he was there for the company and conversation. Dave was just thinking of offering the garrulous and cheerful retiree a part-time job working behind the counter when his cell phone rang. He excused himself from Ralph, and answered it. After a short, terse conversation, Dave hung up, excused himself from Ralph again, and went to the wide barn doors to look out over the golf course to see if he could spot his sister anywhere. Not seeing her, his eyes tracked to the parking lot, where a white van was parked, with the call letters of a local TV station written artfully on its exterior. Not seeing anyone in it, or around it, Dave trotted over to an electric golf cart, unplugged it from the wall, and quickly asked Ralph to watch the front counter, for he had to go find Sara. Ralph happily agreed, and watched as Dave came close to peeling out in the small vehicle.

Over at Stonecreek High School, Doris Raeburn had already finished her morning announcements, and was perusing her schedule pad for the rest of her day. She'd already taken numerous phone calls from different parents who had students involved in the senior class play, and even some from people who didn't even have students at Fort Lafayette High School. Every single call she took was complimentary of all the adult advisors to the play, from Paul and Marcy, to Chloe and Sara, and the talented students who appeared on the PBS station the previous evening. The conversations eventually turned to Sara D'Amico, and the surprise of her not only appearing on screen to auction off items, but her amazingly touching performance of that song. Doris had to cut her conversations with these complimentary callers much shorter than she would have liked, but all three lines to the school were constantly ringing busy, and people were waiting on hold to talk with her. Just as she finished speaking with the last one, and was about to get out of her chair in search of a cup of decaf, the phone rang again, and she answered it.

She recognized the voice of a very frazzled-sounding play director, who seemed to take great pleasure in cursing on the line, not directly aimed at Doris, but about her displeasure at being unable to get through to the school for nearly an hour and a half now. Doris grinned her amusement at the sound of the little librarian's exasperation until she heard the reasons Chloe had been trying to call. Doris listened intently, only interjecting the mildest of disbelieving curse words of her own. After a brief back and forth, she hung up, and hit the buttons on all three lines of the phones, so they would effectively be tied up, and no more calls could come through until she released them. She walked directly over to the microphone of the PA system, flipped it on, twice repeating her request for Paul Hoderman and Marcy to report to her office immediately. Once Paul arrived, she would send him to get Nelson out of whatever class he was in at the time.

The scene out at the golf course was remarkably like that of the one the night before. This time, though, Sara was ambushed while she was down off the tractor, fixing some divots some inconsiderate schmuck had not bothered to stop and replace. She was bitching the bastard out, under her breath, when she heard them approach. She looked up, and found they already were upon her, and the camera was rolling, perched on a burly man's shoulder. This morning, it was a handsome man, carefully groomed in suit and tie, who spoke the words, as he extended his hand in greeting. Numbly, she grasped and shook his hand as he spoke to her.

"Sara D'Amico? I'm Mitchell Parks, from WJMM TV News over in Erie. I wonder if I could ask you a few questions, on camera, for our noon news."

Sara, who was still holding a clump of sod in her hands, eyed the man, and pursed her lips, thinking. She was just about to reply, when her brother rolled up in a golf cart. He got out, stepped in between his sister and the reporter, and spoke before she could.

Dave stuck out his own hand to shake that of the reporter's. "I'm David D'Amico. I own this golf course," and Dave gave him a hearty smile, still gripping his hand. "And you have five minutes to get off this property before I call," he pulled his cell phone out of his shirt pocket, "the State Police, who have jurisdiction over this area." He gave the reporter's hand a very definite squeeze, bordering on painful, before he let go. He stood in front of his sister, and effectively blocked the camera's view of her.

Mitchell Parks was no inexperienced reporter and had successfully cajoled innumerable reluctant interviewees into changing their mind, and these two were not going to be his on his list of failures. "Thank you, Mr. D'Amico. I'm sure we can get out of your hair very quickly. I was just hoping your sister would answer a few questions for the local folks out there, just about her being back in the area, and appearing on the WQEL auction last night." He smiled encouragingly at her. "And she hasn't answered me yet as to whether or not she'd like to speak on camera."

Sara answered him by leaning down, replacing the sod in the ground and firmly tamping it in with her foot. She patted her brother on the back, and said, "What my brother here says, goes." She turned away, heading for the tractor again. The cameraman tried to follow her, but Dave stepped in front of him, and did a little dance of obstruction until he heard the tractor start up and thrown into gear. He continued with his blocking until he tired of it, and simply put a large hand over the lens, and the cameraman dipped the camera down.

He looked at Mitchell Parks again. "Now, Mr. Parks, I believe you've wasted more time than necessary. This is private property, and I've asked you to leave. And while I'm at it, I am going to ask you, and your television station, to not step foot on my property again without calling first and asking for proper permission from me. Although," Dave grinned, "feel free to golf nine holes, without having a camera along, next time you're out this way. But if I see a vehicle with your station logo on my property again, I'll call the police first, and not be so accommodating. And my sister lives on my land, so you can't bother her here."

Mitchell Parks, pissed, but schooled in the idea that one has to remain ever polite, in case circumstances changed, and the opportunity to interview the movie star arose at some future time, merely nodded, and said nothing. He and his cameraman began their long walk back to the van, with Dave, back in the cart, rolling along slowly behind them. He almost offered them a ride back, and then shook his head. *Let 'em walk.*

The wagons were being circled, and the D'Amico Family Anti-Harassment Militia was taking its ready positions, having planned strategy the night before, once they had returned to the house, and Dave and Marcy had shown up. Their defensive strategy was formed with only one goal in mind: keep the press away from Sara until they simply gave up, and got bored with the story. They figured they had a week of battles before their war was won, and their lives would return to normal.

What they hadn't taken under consideration was that in no way, shape or form, should they ever have assumed they had what could be considered normal lives.

The last of the local TV stations, WSEM, had been turned away from the golf course even before anyone could exit from the vehicle. They pulled back out on to Route 20, and proceeded into Stonecreek, at once finding the old library building, tucked between a dry cleaner and a barbershop. The other two local station vans were already parked there. The driver of the WSEM van parked next to an old brown Subaru station wagon, and got out, dinging the Subaru with a hastily thrown open van door. The WSEM reporter got out on the other side, and began walking to the library entrance. She'd only taken a few steps when two cameramen and two disgruntled reporters exited the building in front of her. She recognized them all, and stopped, nodding her greetings.

"Meg, Mitch. How goes it in there?"

Meg blew out a breath. "Hey, Chandra, good luck with that one. She's like a pit bull guarding her puppies. It took Mitch here ten minutes of sparkling ass-kissing wooing for her to even admit she was the same Chloe Donahue that was on WQEL with D'Amico last night." She shot disdainful smirk at the competing station's preening reporter. "She has some mouth on her. Mitchy there was cowering under a table by the time she got through with him. She verbally castrated him, and pretty much treated him like he was three-day-old roadkill. And she did it all in a whisper." Meg shook her head and laughed.

Chandra looked at her cameraman and frowned. "I guess we'll head out to Fort Lafayette and try our luck there." She looked back to the two reporters still standing there. "I'm guessing that's your next stop, too. We got kicked off the golf course without even seeing

D'Amico, but we had a lovely non-productive conversation with her brother, who looks like he's going to be in the running for the next president of the NRA."

The six of them headed back to their respective vans, not noticing the peeking eye of Mrs. Cellone through one curtain to the left of the door. They also couldn't see this same Mrs. Cellone flashing the pit bull librarian a thumbs-up sign as they walked away. Chloe growled, and picked up the telephone again, dialing a number she had memorized.

"But it's public property, officer," argued a very agitated Mitchell Parks, while the two other reporters looked on, waiting for their chance to make their case with the unsmiling, gray-uniformed State Trooper. "We can wait for them to come out, or something, if we're not allowed to go in."

Officer Grafton nodded his stony demeanor at the three of them. "Principal herself called the barracks. Requested that you not disrupt the school day. I have to follow her wishes." He laughed to himself, not letting it show on his steeled features. *Ha. Aunt Doris always said I wouldn't come to any good. Guess I'm proving her wrong.* "You are not to enter the property, with your vans, or personally. And seeing how you're all parked in the driveway of the volunteer firehouse, I'm going to have to ask you to move from here, too."

Meg was quickly losing what was left of her patience. "Listen, you had the driveway to the school blocked when we got here. There's no place else here out in," she stopped herself from saying the word bumfuck, "the area to park, there's nothing out here but this firehouse on this side of the road, and the school over there."

"Can we pull up on the side of the road?" asked a cameraman.

"No, I would consider that a hazard to drivers," said the state police officer, politely but firmly. "And school property stretches from there," and he pointed far up the road, "to there," and he pointed even farther the other direction. "So let's take a moment and consider your options. You can't park on school property, you can't park on the side of the road, and you need to move your vehicles out of the fire department's way. Immediately, please." His voice invited no further comment, and he tapped the corner of his hat. "Have a nice day, folks." He looked both ways, and then quickly strode across Route 20, and got back into his patrol car, and sat, watching them as they had a short conversation, and then got into their vehicles, pulled out, and drove back up the road to Stonecreek, a pathetic small convoy of irate members of the fifth estate.

Reporters from local newspapers met with the same reception, and resorted to writing meaningless, news-lacking blurbs for the weekend editions of their rags.

Nothing much of consequence got onto the six o'clock news that night, and the same nothingness was repeated at eleven, too. A glimpse of a woman getting onto a tractor. A polite and handsome brother who owned Stonecreek Golf Course firmly stating that his sister wished to maintain her privacy. File footage of Sara's interviews of years ago, and a rehashing of unsubstantiated rumors about drug abuse and her vehicular accident.

Each reporter had at least succeeded in finding a local yokel to speak in front of the cameras about the mysterious Sara D'Amico.

Meg Talarico spoke with Stan, owner of Stan's Bar and Grill.

Stan grinned. "Yeah, I don't know how long she's been back. She sang out here one night, I can't remember when. I haven't heard much of anything. She's something, isn't she?"

Mitchell Parks talked with a grizzled senior citizen, who he waved down after seeing his car leave the golf course property.

Ralph Henderson, a new employee of Stonecreek Golf Course, spoke sincerely into the camera. "I just met her. She sure has a great hand with machinery. She has that John Deere running like a top. No, I don't know much of anything about her, she's nice to me, but keeps to herself. She sure is a pretty thing. I didn't even know she acted."

And Chandra Lindstrom had the plummest interview of them all. A freckle-faced, pudgy young man, who she had found coming out of the Quickie Mart, he seemed eager to talk about Sara D'Amico.

"Ms. D'Amico? Yeah, I know her. She comes out once in a while and rides my horse, Cargo. She loves my horse. My horse is going to be in *Oklahoma!*. She teaches the dancing parts. I wish she would bring Ms. Donahue with her. Ms. Donahue is so nice. I guess they're friends. I don't know if Ms. Donahue really likes horses."

Saturday morning rolled around, with all the significant players in the defense of Sara's privacy feeling confident and victorious in the aftermath of yesterday's skirmishes with the press. This Saturday was significant in that it was the last dance Saturday before the play. The following Friday and Saturday was the Senior Prom, with the Prom actually taking place on Friday night, and carrying over into Saturday. No one expected the kids to go all night without sleep, and then to show up at rehearsals on Saturday. The following Friday after that would be a full dress rehearsal, and then the musical's opening night the next evening.

So, along with the tensions of the previous day draping over her head like a tangled parachute, Sara was feeling the pressure of this last opportunity to work with the kids as a whole group, solely concentrating on her responsibility: the dancing in *Oklahoma!*.

The dancing parts were not complicated, she had kept the routines to simple, evocative movements. She tried not to have anything too flashy that would end up looking awkward when performed by students whose dancing skills, until their involvement in the play, had mostly been limited to jumping up and down and bouncing off each other as if they were in a mosh pit at a Nine Inch Nails concert. A few of the kids actually had the abilities of the world's worst "Soul Train" dancers but those skills didn't translate well to the country-inflected or waltz-time ballads of *Oklahoma!*. The mere fact that these kids could now whirl and swirl and stomp with some agility and rhythm should have given Sara some measure of pride and a sense of achievement. But, being the perfectionist that she was and always too hard on herself, and then placing those high expectations on those she was responsible for, she was not a happy dance monkey leading into the last full day of dance rehearsal.

Between her tensions caused by her outing by the press, and her desire to get fifteen hours of dance practice pushed into a four-hour day, there was only one way to describe Sara's emotional state here on this Saturday morning: Sara was a nervous wreck.

Nelson had left early for rehearsals at 11:00 a.m., so he could pick up Jeanette, and they could stop at the Quickie Mart for a brunch of microwaved egg and cheese muffins and chocolate milk. The blonde cheerleader picked up something a little more nutritious, a pint of Orange Juice and a veggie burrito. They drove along in the truck toward the school, eating and chatting on the short trip.

Nelson was more or less surreptitiously picking melted american cheese fragments off his front teeth when they turned into the parking lot at 11:40 a.m.

Finger still jabbing at a stuck morsel on a back molar, Nelson took in the scene in the parking lot, and blurted. "Howy hwit!"

Jeanette's blonde mind had no problem translating that, and even though she was usually too demure to resort to cursing, she automatically repeated Nelson sentiments, only with more clarity. "Holy shit is right!"

The parking lot was full, not only with student's cars, but with vans, too many to count, more than ten, but less than a new car lot. Nelson quickly pulled into a vacant space, and scanned the lot for Paul, Marcy, Chloe's or his aunt's vehicle. Not seeing them, he looked again. Not here yet.

"What do we do?" inquired Jeanette, looking around, bewildered, and spotting most of the cast members over by the wall, stand-

ing in a clump like a small flock of sheep. There were men and
women, strangers, with cameras and microphones, waving them in
their friends' faces. From what Nelson could see one of these students was actually moving his mouth, being interviewed. His anger
built up within him, and he grabbed his door.

"C'mon." He got out, and walked straight over to the group, not
caring if Jeanette was following. He stopped a moment behind the
reporters, to listen to what Jason was saying into the numerous
microphones that were being held in front of the young man's face.

"I think I speak for everyone here, nobody is going to talk to
you. We like Ms. D'Amico, and we think you should just leave her
alone. You guys are such fucking vultures." The assembled group
behind him called out their agreement, and Jason continued. "Go
someplace else. We're not going to help you assholes," he said, a
determined and mean grin on his face.

Nelson smiled in relief. *I wonder if anybody has a cell phone, I
could call...*

A reporter called out in general to the united students. "Sara
D'Amico is a movie star! Don't you kids think it's odd that she's
here in Stonecreek, and hiding out from the public? Maybe she has
something she's hiding from you? There were rumors about her
using drugs in Hollywood, and then getting into that accident?
Doesn't that bother you?"

Those were fighting words to the quarterback of the football
team, and he pushed his way through the reporters to stand next to
Jason, and turned a belligerent eye toward the cameras now pointing
directly at him.

"She's not hiding in Stonecreek, she's living in Stonecreek. She's
not a movie star anymore, she's my aunt and she's everyone here's
friend." Nelson felt Jason clap a supportive hand on his shoulder,
and it bolstered his angry resolve. He turned to the cast assembled
behind him, and said in a loud voice. "Now, I believe there has got to
be somebody that has a cell phone and can call the State Police?
911? Disturbing the peace?" he said meaningfully. He heard a
"yeah" and smiled, and then turned back to glare at the reporters in
newly resolved stony silence. All of the students followed his lead,
and folded their arms, set their faces set in different variations of
determined scowls, and waited. More questions were thrown their
way and they met them with mute defiance.

The reporters gave up their shouted questions when the object of
their inquiries appeared in the lot behind them, getting stiffly out of a
cherry red, polished and babied classic car.

The reporters all tripped over themselves in an effort to get over
to her. The redheaded woman getting out of the other side of the car
was ignored.

"Sara! Sara D'Amico! We're from..." and names of assorted tabloid news shows were called out. Sara walked a few steps, and parked her rear comfortably on the hood of her car, not sitting, not standing. Chloe stopped near the front of the car, just off to the side, and they both waited. Sara folded her arms, and waited for the assembled reporters to get comfortably situated in front of her. She saw Chloe handing the school keys to Nelson, and whispering instructions for him to take the students inside while Sara dealt with the media. Nelson nodded, and shot his aunt a grim smile of encouragement. She smiled back, genuinely, a feeling of warm affection momentarily overshadowing her tension.

She continued to stare down the reporters, who were still shouting questions at her. She cleared her throat a few times, licked her lips and began. "Excuse me. Excuse me. I'll make a short statement, if you want to shut the hell up and quit screaming at me."

This quieted the reporters down, and they all shoved microphones in her direction.

"I understand that you're curious about what you consider my mysterious disappearance from Hollywood. I understand, too, that this curiosity stems from my having once starred in a very popular movie, and that my reappearance here in Stonecreek is somehow big news to those who follow the gossip in the entertainment industry."

She swallowed, focused and continued, trying not to be distracted by all the people, microphones and cameras hanging on to her words. "I no longer consider myself a part of that entertainment industry. I consider myself a private citizen who has returned home to try to lead a quiet and productive life. I have no plans to return to the industry. I appeared on WQEL the other night, not in an effort to revitalize my career, but to help WQEL and to support the students here at Fort Lafayette High. I am working with them as a volunteer advisor to their production of *Oklahoma!*. I'm having fun doing it. I work at my brother's golf course now, and I'm very happy doing so." She blinked, and said firmly, but with a smile, "End of story." She straightened up, knowing exactly what was coming next, a barrage of questions from the media who was certainly not content with her rather bland explanation of her recent life events.

After much jostling and mixture of shouted questions, a reporter finally made himself heard. "There's been talk for years about the producers of *Star Gazers* searching for you in hopes that you would agree to do a sequel. Are you simply holding out for more money?"

"I'm not interested in doing a sequel to *Star Gazers*."

Another reporter shouted. "You must have known that the public's curiosity would be piqued when you appeared, after all this time, on that public television station the other night. Why, if you want your privacy, would you agree to be seen in such a public forum, if not to put yourself in the public's eye again?"

Sara glanced over at Chloe, and saw that a glowing, pregnant art teacher had joined Chloe. Sara grinned quickly at Marcy, and then answered the question.

"Someone very special to me asked me to do it, I was needed, so this time..." Sara paused, and smiled broadly at the deeper meaning of what she was about to say. "I said 'yes.'"

Marcy warmed at the sentiments clearly directed her way. She and Chloe gave each other a quick hug around the waist, and left their arms wrapped there.

"And the singing? You're not known to be a singer. Why did you sing?"

"Same situation. I was needed. I said 'yes.' And," she glanced swiftly at Marcy and Chloe again, "I've been known to sing in front of my family and friends on an irregular basis, whether they like it or not." She couldn't quite stop the grin that appeared on her face at that comment. Cameras flashed, capturing that white and sexy smile. That small bit of relaxed emotion disappeared with the asking of the next question.

"It's been rumored that you were a drug user in Hollywood, and that you were difficult to work with because of your drug abuse. And that your continued drug use led to you having your accident. How do you respond to that?"

Sara's face turned very serious. "I have never, ever abused drugs. Never. My drug of choice was always alcohol, and I never had any kind of problem with it. The day I had my accident, I was not under the influence of alcohol or any drugs. It was a combination of two things that caused my accident: one, a truck in front of me that suddenly came to a complete stop," she paused, and closed her eyes a moment, trying to calm herself, "and two, I was talking on my cell phone at the time, and wasn't paying attention. So," she gritted her teeth and continued, "if you want to make me the poster girl, spokeswoman for something, I guess I'd be happy to speak out against the truly dangerous aspects of talking on a cell phone while operating a moving vehicle."

"And your notorious lateness, your absence, your temper tantrums on the set? If not drugs, then what was it, Sara?"

Sara felt a nudging of blackness wave over her being. She chose her words carefully.

"Although employed as an actress, at that time, I was not emotionally suited to all the tensions that the career can bring. I didn't deal with it well, and I apologize now for that behavior, and the difficulties it may have caused those I was working for, and with." She snorted. "What can I say, I have a lousy, difficult disposition." She glanced at her watch, and then looked up. "I have things I have to do, and that's all I have to say to you folks. I will answer no more questions today, or in the future. I am a private person, and wish to lead a quiet, private life. Thank you." She moved away from the reporters, ignoring the many more questions that were being called her way.

She walked solo to the building, pulled the door, and walked in, hoping to find a quiet place where she could collapse and be by herself to attempt to reclaim her tenuous hold on any kind of serenity.

That moment of needed seclusion would have to wait for a few minutes, for there was a line of people inside that building, young and old alike that were waiting, one by one, for their opportunity to hug their shaken choreographer. She was about to tell them "no," she couldn't handle it, but then she looked at them again. *No more no's.*

She did not deny them.

Sara sighed, and found the strength to give the assembled cast in front of her on the gymnasium floor a very appreciative smile. They had just completed running every dance number in the show, one after the other, with nary a hitch or flaw. Instead of her usual constant hammering of them, she was effusive in her praise, and they were eating it up. They knew, innately, that they were performing with flair, and were taking inordinate pride and care in displaying their hard-earned skills today. They wanted to impress the tall former actress today, by showing her that she had taught them well, and that they had been paying attention. And that they did care. It showed in their performance, it showed in her reactions.

She was darn near feeling choked up, as the cast looked at her, grinning and expectant. They quieted. And waited.

"Uh, that was pretty good. Really good, as a matter of fact." More grins were sent her way. "We may, uh, have to take this thing on the road over the summer." Sara grinned back at them, a sight they had found themselves yearning for an approval from the usually tight-faced and demanding scarred woman. "Why don't you all take a fifteen minute break? I could use one. And we'll, I don't know, do something when you get back." It seems like overkill to have them do it again. She watched as more undisguised, satisfied smiles were directed her way, and she felt a blush coming to her cheeks. *Damn, these kids are getting to me. The little shits know they did good. And they did it for me.* A very foreign feeling came over Sara, an unexpected wash of affection for these students, and the realization that the feeling was mutual, that they were liking her just as much as she was liking them. *My troop. My gang of dancing idiots. My soldiers of the light fantastic.*

Sara turned and looked around the gymnasium, looking for a

familiar adult face, for Marcy, for Chloe, even for Paul. They had disappeared earlier, once that they had seen that the dancing was well in hand. She thought for a moment about going to look for them, when the gym door opened and Marcy walked in, with a police officer in tow behind her. Marcy smiled, and they made their way over to Sara.

The police officer, sharp in his gray starched uniform, had his trooper's hat tucked under his arm. His hair was styled in a severe brush cut, and he looked every bit the imposing law enforcement officer, from his rock-hard, chiseled physicality, to the way he carried himself and stood almost at attention when they pulled up in front of Sara. The only trait that betrayed the perfect stereotypical image of the ideal Pennsylvania State Police Officer was, well, the man was no taller than 5'7", and that made him a tad bit shorter than the lanky dark-haired woman standing in front of him.

Marcy introduced them, a gleam in her eye. "Officer Grafton, this is my friend, and future sister-in-law, Sara D'Amico. Sara, Officer Marshall Grafton."

Sara shook the officer's hand. She was unsure if he was here on official business, or was a friend of Marcy's, but she had a feeling that maybe it was a little of both.

"Officer Grafton. Pleased to meet you." She gave him a little bit of her movie star smile; she wanted to impress the man.

"Ms. D'Amico," he said, officiously, then a small grin cracked his stern features. "Can I just say I've seen *Star Gazers*, oh, probably, over a hundred times?"

Sara blinked, and then laughed. "Oh, God. Why would you want to do that to yourself? I could hardly stand to watch it at the premiere."

He laughed, more friendliness infusing his face. "I'm a sci-fi nut. It's essential to the genre." He couldn't help himself, this was his big chance. "I'd love to talk to you about that one scene." He saw Sara patiently smile at him, so he swallowed, and went for it. "There's been talk for years on the Internet as to the real reason why your character, Officer Calla, put herself in harm's way like that at the end." He looked at her, still not believing he was actually talking to Officer Calla. He quickly went on. "Was it a death wish, suicide? Altruism? Trying to redeem herself?"

Sara laughed. This was not the first conversation she had with an ardent, if over-zealous, fan of the movie. "Officer Grafton, I have no idea. I think she did it..."

The officer leaned forward, hopeful of some inside information.

"Because the director told me to act it that way." She laughed again, this time at his confused reaction. "Yup, he told me to act it as ambiguously as possible. I guess it worked." She frowned for a moment, unhappy memories of that director returning to her. "If you want a tidbit of truth, Officer Grafton, the director was a complete egotistical bastard. He made that movie in hopes that it would make his career. He was praying that it would generate interest in a sequel, and apparently it did. So, I hate to be the bearer of bad news, but he left all those parts as incomprehensible as he did just to play with people's minds. Not because he's deeper than the Grand Canyon." Sara paused again, as this information swirled around in the man's head. "Well, Officer, I hope that enlightens you a little. Now, is there some other reason you stopped by today?"

The sci-fi fanatic in front of her straightened up again, and once again became one of Pennsylvania's finest, but not before he gave her a small smile of thanks for her candor and patience with him. He cleared his throat. "Just wanted to give you a run-down on what's been happening," his voice deepening, and speaking much more formally now. "The media vans made a sweep through Stonecreek, out to your brother's golf course, and then apparently left town. I guess they ran into some townies, and a few of them got interviews. Jim, down at the hardware store, got interviewed. He was thrilled. He gave them all kinds of information about how you had a great eye for a piece of wood, and that you fixed a couple of lawn mowers that he was having trouble fixing himself." Officer Grafton said this last bit without the least bit of amusement in his voice or his face. He was practiced at keeping a stoic visage even in the face of the most idiotic, mundane scenarios. He continued. "Then they blew out of town, some east, some west."

Sara and Marcy both nodded. This was good news.

"But there are a few stragglers. A couple of guys, not together, I think, that were asking questions, at the diner, at the Quickie Mart, about your habits. Where you go, when, with who."

Sara bit her lip and scowled. "Freelance photographers. I figured. They'll probably be skulking around, hiding in bushes, trying to get candids of me."

Officer Grafton nodded. "Not a thing I can do about that, unless they cross onto private property. And then if they do, you can call—"

Sara shook her head. "They're hit and run. They knock off as many shots as they can, and then take off, waiting for their next opportunity."

Marcy cursed under her breath. "Hey, it's not like you ride around on that John Deere topless, and in your skivvies."

Officer Grafton's face reddened at that thought, and he was trying to regain his former composure, when a familiar voice called across the gym.

"Moonie!" The three of them looked over to the gym doors, to see a delighted Chloe Donahue trotting their way, and she jumped right at the startled officer, threw her arms around him, crushing his hat beneath his arm. His face broke into a large grin, and he returned the redhead's hug, one-armed.

"Well, Chloe Donahue," he breathed, as she finally pushed away from him, and smiled into his reddened face. "I haven't seen you in a few years now."

Chloe smacked him hard, right in the chest. "Where have you been?" Smack! Smack!

Sara and Marcy both smiled, bemused at the sight of the little redhead beating on an officer of the law.

He backed off, laughing. "I worked downstate for a few years, I just got transferred back up here a few months ago. I live out closer to the state line, haven't had a chance to come visit yet."

Chloe smacked him one more time, just to emphasize her impatience with him. She turned to Sara, who was watching the whole scene with interested amusement.

"This is Moonie Grafton. We went here together, although," smack! "He was a couple of years younger than me. I dated his brother, Frank, for a short time during my senior year." Smack! "Long enough to get to know his brother, Moonie, here."

This time, Chloe moved her assault from his chest, and gave him a resounding smack right on his rear end.

Sara was thinking she was going to have to come up with some bail money for that maneuver. Her eyes widened.

The officer lost whatever composure he had left, and flat-out laughed at Chloe's smack at his posterior.

Marcy smiled, already knowing the story. "Uh, Chloe, why don't you tell Sara here why you are beating up on a state boy, without fear of him hauling your ass off to jail?"

Chloe giggled, and then stuck her tongue out at Officer Grafton, who was emphatically shaking his head, silently begging her to stay silent.

"Oh, sure." Chloe laughed at him. "You did it, you have to live with it the rest of your life, Moonie." She turned to Sara, and began her story. "Here's me and Frank, in Frank's Camaro, and we're parked out on the land in front of their parent's house. Well, we're making out pretty good, and the windows are rolled down. It's dark, and the radio's on. I'm trying to keep Frank from giving me too big a hickey, Frank's leaned across me, I'm practically underneath him, and, well, you know, the whole thing was almost getting out of hand. And then, I opened my eyes, and see, firmly wedged in the opened window on Frank's side of the car..."

She raised her sparkling eyes to the now furiously blushing officer, who was looking down at the gym floor, "A big, pink bare ass staring me right in the face." She grinned, and let the officer wallow in his embarrassment for a moment. "I screamed holy hell, Frank flew off me and hit his head on the ceiling of the car, and we saw Moonie there, laughing his ass off outside. As he's trying to get his pants pulled up, Frank got out of the car, and spent the rest of the evening trying to chase ol' Marshall here down, I'm guessing to try and kill him."

Everyone, including the very chagrined officer, laughed. Chloe had to wrap up her story. "And that was the day that Marshall Grafton died, and Moonie Grafton was born."

Marcy loved this story. "And you really should be thanking Moonie, anyway, Chloe, things between you and Frank were never the same after that night."

"Yeah, I know. He was such a jerk about the whole thing. I thought it was the funniest thing, and he got all mad at me because I thought it was hilarious. He had no sense of humor. "

The officer interrupted. "He still doesn't. Frank's still an—"

"Asshole?" Chloe cheerfully provided.

"Yup." Moonie grinned. He checked his watch. "Well, this has been one hell of interesting visit, but I have to go take care of some of my duties. I think I'll be bringing the wife and kiddies to see what you've done to *Oklahoma!*. Meanwhile, the parking lot is clear, and I'll cruise by again before I go off duty at 3:30." His tone turned serious. "I'm sorry I won't be around when you leave this afternoon, Marcy said you're done about 4:00 today. But I think they're mostly gone. Just pick up the phone."

Marcy dryly replied, "I've got it on speed dial."

The officer gravely nodded. "Again, I hope this is the last of it. It was my distinct pleasure to meet you, Ms. D'Amico. I wish it was under more pleasant circumstances." Just for a split second, his face split into a grin, "When I could grill you more about *Star Gazers.*" He watched as her face returned his grin. "And Chloe Donahue, I'll be seeing you, too, very soon, and not just for the play."

Chloe tilted her head at her old friend, confused.

He chuckled, and placed his hat back on his head, adjusting the chinstrap. "I was the high bidder on some golf lessons out at Stone Creek golf course. I bid as soon as I heard you were giving the lessons." He laughed and started heading toward the door, once again cutting an impressive figure in his officer gray, and nodding at some returning students that were coming back into the gym. He waved, and departed.

Sara gave a huge snort of laughter, which was echoed by both women standing on either side of her. She looked affectionately at both of them, then said teasingly to Chloe, "You sure do have a very *interesting* set of friends."

Chloe sighed and smiled pointedly at the both of them. "Yeah, I do, don't I?"

* * *

It was four o'clock and all of the students and Paul had left the school a half hour ago. Left in the gymnasium were Nelson, Marcy, Chloe and Sara, and Nelson had volunteered to go scout out the parking lot before they, too, left for the day.

Nelson came back into the gym, and strode over to where the three women were waiting, sitting on the bleachers. They searched his eyes for signs of bad news.

"All clear out there." His blue eyes flashed. "No worries at all. Safe as babes in arms."

Sara turned a skeptical eye on her nephew. "Are you sure? I mean these guys are pretty sneaky."

"Oh yeah. Safe. Very sure." Nelson grinned, waiting to be questioned about his air of confidence.

It came from Chloe. "How can you be so...?"

He didn't let her finish, it was too good to hold back.

"Yeah. You're safe." Nelson delivered his next lines with perfect comedic timing. "Mrs. Raeburn has been sitting in the parking lot, in a lawn chair, for the last hour." He waited a beat. "She has her umbrella with her."

Part XXVI:
Them's Fightin' Words

Sunday arrived again, bringing with it a cold front, icy rain and the opportunity to sleep in. Sara had dutifully set the alarm clock the night before, and it went off at precisely 7:00 a.m., although the clock itself was set twenty minutes ahead of the correct time. This little differentiation between clock time and real time afforded the dark-haired woman several opportunities to smack the snooze button on the alarm. After hitting the snooze, she wouldn't immediately try to return to sleep; it gave her time to listen for rain, and happily, this morning, the sound of chilled water glancing off her bungalow roof brought a relieved sigh to her lips, and she tightened her hold around the slumbering redhead in her arms. Chloe, as per usual, slept through the buzzing alarm. Somewhere in their time together, she had learned to ignore the noise of Sara's alarm, and her subconscious would allow only Sara's gentle whispered urges to break through to bring her out of dreamland. The sound of the rain on the roof saved Sara from performing this job this morning, as there was no need to wake the librarian up.

Sara stretched her body, as well as she could, with the 5'3" red-headed naked python wrapped around her in a death grip. *Should I get up? Dave will be up, and heading out to the garage, simply as a sentry person. No one will show up to play yet today, although if it clears, there's always a few diehards in rain gear who may want to slosh across the course.* She readjusted Chloe's head on her shoulder, so she could rotate her neck and crack her shoulders. *I should get up and work on the number two golf cart, it isn't holding a charge like it should.* Sara opened her eyes, and peered at the clock. *7:05. I could sleep in a little longer, what would it hurt?* She closed her eyes again, and played a game of identify Chloe's body parts. *Let's see, that's her left leg slung over my left leg, and her knee from that leg is bent and across my...thank God it's not a little higher, or it would be right across my bladder, and I wouldn't be having this discussion with myself as to whether I should get up yet.* Sara's body shook with a soundless laugh. *And her arm is across my ribs, with her hand resting on righty. Nose is tucked into my neck, forehead up against the side of my jaw, hair tickling my cheek. This is great, I'm used to waking up like this, so soon. I slept years by myself, and this feels so much better.*

The buzzing of the alarm began again, interrupting Sara's thoughts. She reached over, and pushed the snooze again, then rethought it, and turned the alarm off completely. Her motions brought a squeeze to Chloe's hand on her breast, and a soft sigh, as the smaller woman again snuggled herself deeper into Sara's body. That lingering grasp sent new ideas to Sara's brain, the auxiliary brain that was ensconced below her waist, and those thoughts triggered Sara into action. She was now very conscious of all of Chloe's body, the warmth, the smoothness, the appealing soft curves of it, and Sara's hands did what her auxiliary brain commanded, she began slowly stroking Chloe, a hand traveling up her leg to a rounded buttock, her other hand caressing the skin of her shoulder. Her hand left Chloe's hip behind, snuck up under Chloe's arm laying across her, and found access to her breast. She lightly teased the nipple to attention with light circular touches of a fingertip, and the results brought Sara warmer sensations; her plan was now etched in stone, she had a goal, and she hopefully would not be denied.

Sara's gentle attentions to Chloe's breast yielded a soft moan from the sleeping woman. Sara began mixing in contracting motions around it with her long, strong fingers, eliciting even more positive murmurs from Chloe. Sara, deciding that these reactions were an excellent sign to continue, slowly and resolutely began to extract her arm from under Chloe's head, and pushed her onto her back. Thus freed, Sara turned onto her side, and let her mouth take over where her hands had left off, taking the warm pliant flesh into her mouth, and luxuriating in the hard and the soft that greeted her tongue. Her tongue danced across Chloe's nipple, and she moaned at the sheer sensuality of it. She began sucking, gradually increasing the pressure, and was gratified to find that Chloe was reacting positively to her ministrations, because the woman began moving with the telltale signs of arousal.

Asleep or not asleep, aware or not aware, wonderful things were happening to and around the smaller woman. Chloe's auxiliary brain was also shifting into consciousness; way ahead of the brain seated above her shoulders, and was telling the rest of her body that some pretty nice events were occurring. A warmth oozed through her, and Chloe's lips found words passing through them. "Am I dreaming?" she murmured.

Sara stopped her attentions only long enough to reply, "Does it matter?" She then returned to her pleasant task.

Chloe's body answered Sara for her, she gently arched into Sara, an invitation to continue. "Nuh-uh."

Conversation ended, and their communications continued in the form of moans, touches and kisses.

The day continued as it began; it poured without respite, drenching the green of the golf course, the blossoming vines of the nearby vineyards, the posies in Mrs. Hoderman's flower boxes. Dave's emerging business was the last thing on Mother Nature's mind; she had a job to do, it was her time, time to soak the land so later in summer, grapes and cherries could be picked, lawn mowers could clog up and sputter out, leaves on trees could offer shade to sweaty golfers waiting to tee off. A modicum of fanfare was added to the downpour throughout the day, cracks of thunder, bolts of lightning and gusts of wind helping Mother Nature reassert her dominance, to let everyone who was grumbling in their houses about the lousy weather know who was truly in charge of their Sunday.

Overrun with customers, Bob's Video Shack was renting out even the worst of the latest releases to people desperate for a way to pass this terrible day. In some houses, people turned to the welcoming arms of the Internet or the banalities of cable TV, or discovered a long-forgotten pork roast from the back of their freezer in hopes of a later day feast. At a house on a golf course on Route 20, however, a redheaded librarian had talked her companions into digging out a board game from a hallway closet, and was gleefully counting the stacks of paper money in front of her.

"I told all of you, whenever she's that damned wheelbarrow, she always wins," Marcy griped, noting the high stacks of money in front of her best friend, and comparing it to the rather meager pile in front of her. "And no one has taken a turn in ten minutes either, she's been harassing the both of you to sell your properties."

"It's my turn, and I can do that," Chloe said dismissively, the rules of the game ingrained deeply into her quick, conniving brain. "And Marse, how about," she quickly sized up the situation and continued, "I give you a thousand dollars for Baltic, and you can have Waterworks." She smiled carefully, not wanting to irritate further her already-grumpy friend.

"Oh, I can see this is going to take a while, I'm heading for the bathroom." The tall woman sighed, and stood up out of her chair. She smiled a sympathetic smile at Marcy, and then a genuine, admiring smile at her patiently waiting but clearly plotting girlfriend, who was still waiting for a reply to her offer from the irritated artist. *This game's a done deal, Marcy knows it, Dave knows it, and I knew it before the first throw of the dice.*

Dave was watching a basketball game from his seat while waiting out the machinations between the two long-time friends. He looked up at his sister, and mildly commented, "Sure, sure, walk out right before the bloodbath starts. Just make sure to be back in case one of them needs first aid. Or CPR."

Sara stopped in her path, noticed Marcy's narrowing eyes, and pointed directly at a poker-faced Chloe. "Dave, if any CPR needs done for Chloe, you'd better wait for me. You are no longer Mr. Kisses when it comes to her, got it?" She narrowed her own eyes at him, mimicking the glare that Marcy was endowing upon Miss Lips. She watched as Dave grinned and nodded, and then she continued off to the bathroom.

Marcy ignored everyone, her attention was focused solely on Chloe. "What the hell do you want Baltic for? You already have a monopoly with houses, wait, hotels on Boardwalk and whatchamacallit, Park Place. And all the red ones and the railroads."

"It will complete my set. I hate loose ends," stated Chloe, sizing up her mark, and deciding that Marcy was going to take her usual obstinate route on this deal. "Two thousand, Waterworks, and a get out of jail free card."

"I want to be in jail, it's the only place I'm safe from you."

The basketball game that Dave had been watching was terminally dull, one team was running away with the game, not unlike the determined, scheming redhead seated next to him. The outcome was a foregone conclusion. Dave said aloud, mostly to the furniture around him, because the two bartering women took no notice of his words, "Guess I'll start dinner."

He got up, opened the fridge, and stared within, while increasingly heated negotiations took place at the table behind him. A plan was forming in his own mind for the upcoming meal when his sister returned from the bathroom and stood next to him, also peering into the depths of the refrigerator. "Well, what's the plan?" she inquired.

"I was thinking scrambled eggs, bologna sandwiches and teriyaki Rice-A-Roni."

Sara ran that through her mind, and decided it was an attractive offering. "First course?" she inquired.

Dave closed the refrigerator door, and opened the freezer door above it. A bag of frozen vegetables slid out and promptly fell at his feet. "Brussel sprouts?"

Sara nodded, and picked up the bag from the floor, and they both turned to look at the two women at the table.

"Two thousand, Waterworks, a get out of jail free card, and two of my railroads."

"Your railroads? You have the complete set, why would you want to break up your complete set? And railroads, two of them, I can't do anything with just two."

John Scott was sure he was the only occupant of the eight-room Niagara Bluffs motor lodge. His tiny room, though comfortable and tidy, was giving him claustrophobic feelings. He planned later to eat at the diner, hoping to pick up any town gossip about his quarry. He awoke this morning to the sound of rain pelting down on the shingled roof over his room, and had immediately grown irritated and angry.

Every day without a money shot is money out of my pocket. He had been positive that he would have been able to find his target working somewhere on the golf course that she lived on, sometime during the day. He could have surreptitiously blended in with other golfers, found her, taken his shots, and be gone by now, having caught a plane in Buffalo for his home in New York City.

He glanced at his watch. It was nearly 6:00. The local weather should be on soon. He silently swore at his perceived backwardness of this small town. There was no cable in this crappy excuse for a motel. He flipped the stations until he found one with a six o'clock broadcast, and laid back on his bed to wait for his needed information.

Oh my, I hope she's here to sell me a set of encyclopedias. Chloe's eyes were surveying a blonde woman standing uncertainly in the foyer of the library. *She's certainly not from around here, her suit cost more than all of my summer clothes put together. She's probably a few years older than I am. I shouldn't be looking at her like this, but come on, I'm not blind.* Chloe was so busy continuing to stare, and chastising herself for blatantly ogling the glamorous looking woman, that she was startled when the woman made eye contact with her, and then smiled. *Oh God, she caught me staring.* Chloe shook herself, and then smiled back, and watched as the woman made her way over to her at the front desk. Chloe felt the woman's eyes also sizing her up, and found herself blushing at the woman's unapologetic once-over.

"May I help you?" Chloe asked quietly, as the librarian took command for a moment. *That blonde hair, almost white, is natural. Not a root, not an eyebrow to convince me otherwise.*

"I certainly hope so. I'm lost," said the woman, her vocal tones sliding over Chloe like a warm waterfall. The woman smiled, slowly and quite purposely. "I was told you could help me. I was just down at the Quickie-something, and they, well, they weren't very helpful." *Oh yeah, this one's part of the clan, great strawberry blonde hair. And those eyes! Who said small towns had to be dull?*

Chloe curiously was disappointed that the woman wasn't where she wanted to be. Chloe turned on her best charm. "And where is it you wanted to be? Anywhere but Stonecreek, I presume?"

"No, Stonecreek is where I want to be, but..." the woman answered, taking notice of Chloe's name badge. "I'm afraid that neither the Quickie place nor the library was on my itinerary." She looked directly into Chloe's eyes before she continued, her voice imbued with a bit of flirtatiousness, "Although this library, Ms. Donahue, looks like a very, very interesting place for a girl to spend her time." She followed that line with her patently honed smoldering look.

Chloe nearly jerked at the woman's overt flattery. She felt as if the woman had verbally reached out and pinched the librarian on the rear end. Chloe had to take in oxygen and scramble for her next words. "And where in Stonecreek did you want to be?" *Whoa, she has the flirt thing down to a science.*

The blonde woman, merely for show, extracted a small piece of paper from her ivory-colored suit pocket, unfolded it, glanced at it, and put it back in her pocket. "Stonecreek Golf Course, Ms. Donahue." It was an old trick of hers, she liked to repeat a person's name as often as possible, it helped her remember it, and made strangers feel more at ease with her.

"Chloe." Chloe found herself saying. "And the golf course is just a bit farther east up the main road running directly in front of the library, Ms.?"

"Swanson." The blonde woman replied, noting that Chloe had picked up on her name game. "Jennifer Swanson."

She sounded like a female version of James Bond. *She certainly looks the part.* Chloe had a queer feeling pass through her, but quickly dismissed it. "Ms. Swanson, it's just another five minutes up the road. Although I'm not sure why the folks at the Quickie Mart weren't helpful enough to tell you that."

"Actually, someone there directed me to come speak to you, she said I should talk to you about it," said the blonde woman, still smiling. When she saw the confused look cross Chloe's face, she gave a small laugh. "I'm sorry, actually, I didn't ask them where Stonecreek Golf Course was, I asked them where I might find Sara D'Amico, at the Stonecreek Golf Course, and the woman behind the counter wouldn't tell me. I pressed her about it and all she would say was I should stop in at the library, and she gave me directions here." The woman smiled again, noticing the frown that now covered the librarian's face. "Is there some kind of scavenger hunt I have to perform before I can find Sara?" She said that last sentence hoping to lighten the librarian's soured countenance.

"I, uh, we, uh, we're all just trying to protect Sara's privacy."

Any feelings of friendliness that Chloe had been experiencing dissipated, and she looked at the woman warily. "She's not doing interviews; she won't even talk to you about the possibility of doing an interview. If you're a reporter, you'd be wasting your time."

Jennifer Swanson was already moving away from the desk and toward the front door. Unmindful that she was in a library, she winked at Chloe, and said, "Oh, no, not a reporter, Ms. Donahue. A friend." She stopped at the foyer, and made careful eye contact with the librarian as she said her parting words. "An old, and very dear, close friend. Thank you, Chloe." She pushed through the doors and was gone.

Chloe's mind searched and searched again before she could remember the phone number for Dave's house. When there was no answer, she dialed Sara's number. *This is not good.* She repeated that phrase over and over in her head. She called both numbers repeatedly, but there was no answer at either location. *This is not good.*

Sara was riding on a golf cart through the high grass lining the fairway of the sixth hole when she saw the woman. She was a good fifty yards away, but her blonde hair caught and reflected the past noon's bright rays. The cut of her suit and the motion of her walk, unsteady as it was, in high heels as she trudged up the fairway, elicited familiar memories in the tall woman.

They approached each other, Sara in her trusty cart, not speeding to her old friend, and the blonde woman not quickening her pace. They both needed the time to decide what to say to each other when they met again. Sara had many questions running through her mind, and the blonde had many opening lines running through hers. This was Sara's turf they were meeting on, both aware that Sara would be in control of whatever happened next.

Jennifer Swanson was glad that she had worn her designer sunglasses, because she could study Sara as the golf cart got closer. Her old friend and client looked healthy and buff in a green polo shirt and khaki shorts, her hair pulled back in a braid, and her face set in a rather bland smile of recognition as she pulled up and stopped the cart a short distance from her. She looked wonderful. Confident. *And her face, even without make-up, there's barely a noticeable line there.* Jennifer's mind flashed back, as it always did when she thought of Sara, to the magnificently horrid stitches that she had borne witness to even weeks after the accident. It amazed her that something so awful could have turned out so well. *I never could have imagined it then.*

"Hello, Jennie." Sara pulled out her bandanna from a back pocket, and wiped her neck and brow with it. She fixed her gaze firmly on the overdressed woman.

"Hello to you, Sara." Jennie made the last few steps to the golf cart; Sara had made her come to her.

"What brings you out to my neck of the woods? Felt like playing nine holes in an exotic setting, or did your Beverly Hills Country Club membership expire?" Sara was merely making smart-assed chatter, her defenses already up against someone she used to have few defenses against.

"I was in Toronto, and I'm on my way back to L.A., just thought I would stop by to see an old friend." Jennie smiled at her, and waited to see if Sara would return the favor.

Sara didn't. "Kind of out of your way to just stop by here. Nearest airports are Buffalo or Erie."

"Buffalo. I rented a car and drove here. I have a 7:00 p.m. flight out of Buffalo tonight. I won't be able to stay long." Jennie kept her voice upbeat, and friendly, hoping to break through Sara's barriers.

"Glad to hear it."

Jennie wasn't sure if Sara was glad she had made the trip to see her, or was glad that Jennie wasn't staying long. "You look good. Really good. I never would have thought..."

"Yeah, me neither. Miracles of modern medicine, huh?" Sara said offhandedly. She decided to cut to the chase; this woman evoked too many strong emotions in Sara, and the majority of them were bad. *I don't need this. I know why she's here.* "So, not that I'm not glad to see you, you look great, but you always did." Sara saw Jennie's pleased reaction to that, and decided to temper that gladness. "But to tell you the truth, I'm not glad to see you. I'm sure you're here for only one reason, to try to talk me into something I don't want to do. You always had a gift for that." For the first time, Sara smiled fully; it was not a smile of friendliness, rather a smile of self-awareness and accusation.

Jennie shifted uncomfortably in her heels, and looked away before returning her gaze to Sara. She removed her sunglasses, revealing chocolate-brown eyes with almost an almond shape to them. She then looked down before she replied, "I guess I deserve that. I guess you can think of me like that if you need to."

"I don't need to think about you, Jennie. Most days, I don't." Sara's voice was flat and matter of fact. "Time does wonders for helping to forget old friends. And old lives." Sara felt she had the upper hand, a feat she'd rarely accomplished in her last dealings with the woman in front of her.

Jennie stiffened; she hadn't expected outright rudeness from Sara. "The old life wasn't that bad, Sara. I seem to recall you enjoyed much of it, and much of me, during that time." She straightened up, and assumed her confident agent persona; it was what worked best for her, and it was the only way she knew how to be. She watched as Sara remained mute to her last comment, and the darker woman leaned back into the golf cart seat, apparently waiting to see what Jennie was going to say next. "All right, I can see you aren't interested in reminiscing about old times. Would you mind if I sat down next to you in that cart? My feet are killing me, and that was quite a walk out here to find you." She frowned and waited for Sara's answer, which was a silent nod of agreement.

Jennie rounded the cart sat down gratefully in the vinyl seat, and reached down, and removed her shoes, rubbing a few toes through her pantyhose.

Sara started up the cart, and pushed on the pedal, and they began rolling across the fairway. Sara turned to her. "Well, say whatever it is that you came here to say, because I've lots of work to do today. I'm driving you back to your car; you've got that long to say your peace."

Jennie drew an irritated breath in, and her usually smooth voice came out jumpy and stilted as Sara drove the cart across some bumpy ground. "Fine. Here's the story. Don Summerfield is in London until September, putting the final touches on his latest project. I spoke to him yesterday, asked him if he was still interested in making the sequels to *Star Gazers*. He surprised me, he's already had people working preproduction on it. He asked about you. I said I had seen a recent tape of you, and that you seemed to look really good, very healed." Jennie's words practically were bouncing out of her mouth, and she wondered if Sara was hitting every bump on purpose. She glanced at Sara, who had her eyes forward, and her lips lightly pursed, and Jennie knew she was listening. "He's coming into New York City for a week in mid-June sometime, and then heading back to London, but he asked me to contact you to see if I could set up a meeting between the two of you. I also forwarded a copy of the tape to him." She stopped there, thinking she had relayed enough information already, and waited for a response.

"He wants to see it for himself, huh?" Sara said, giving her head a small shake, but not looking at Jennie.

"Pretty much. He was uncertain about your emotional status. I couldn't give him any firsthand knowledge about that either," Jennie said, honestly. "This movie is going to get made, very soon, with or without you. But it would be better with you, and Don knows it." She was happy to see that the cart was nearing the parking lot where she had parked her car. She didn't know what hurt worse, her feet or her butt.

Sara navigated the cart across the gravel to stop near a luxury vehicle that had New York state license plates. Jennie reached down, and put her shoes back on, moved out of the cart, and stood near her rental car. She smoothed her skirt, and once again tried to coax a smile from Sara. She looked around the gravel parking lot, to the old house and converted barn, the blossoming trees and the green of the grass. "This place has a certain charm to it. I can see why you must like it here. You always did talk about your hometown with real affection."

It worked, Sara did smile at this last remark. She sighed and got out of the cart to stand side next to Jennie, who was now leaning against the trunk of the car. She watched a man extract his golf clubs from the trunk of his car, digging around in the large pockets of the bag. She turned to Jennie, and sighed again. A rueful smile planted itself on her lips. "I'm sorry Jennie, that I was so rude to you. It was just such a surprise, and you know how I am with surprises."

Jennie turned and faced her, returning the smile. "Yeah, you don't do them very well. I remember." She hesitantly put out a hand, and stroked Sara's arm, resting her hand just above Sara's wrist. She was pleased that Sara didn't shy away from her touch. She looked at Sara as gently as possible, and tried to inject that feeling into her next words. "The offer is out there, Sara. There's lots of money involved. You could be fixed for life. You could help your brother open a hundred of these golf courses, with just a year or two out of your life." She saw Sara's small smile fade, but saw a glimmer of something— *Curiosity? Interest?*—in the woman's eyes. "Think about it. We could fly or drive to see Don in June, and you could at least discuss the possibility with him. At least, once and for all, you could put this thing to bed. I wish you would consider this. I could be as involved, or not involved, in the process as you need me to be."

She squeezed Sara's wrist, and took a step closer. Their eyes met, yet Jennie couldn't gauge Sara's reaction to all that she'd said. *No need to browbeat her.* She lightened her tone even further. "So, I'm going to be on my way. I'm looking forward to that drive through Hamburg, New York like you wouldn't believe." She broke into a grin, and watched as Sara put a half grin on her face. "How about a hug before I go? I am, no matter what, really happy to see you, Sara, you really do look wonderful." Jennie's voice caught a little, and she looked down at the white gravel below her $400 shoes.

Sara looked at her, and for a moment, remembered only the good things about Jennie, and she put her arms around her, and pulled her into a light hug. "No promises, Jennie."

Jennie buried her head into Sara's shoulder, momentarily caught up in the past, and held on to her even tighter.

So caught up in the moment were the two old friends that they didn't notice the almost continuous clicking and whirring noises coming from the area where the man had been taking his clubs out of his trunk. Jennie saw him first, the camera busily working in his hands, and she didn't move as he began to circle around them.

When Sara finally noticed, and pushed herself out of Jennie's embrace, he was nearly within touching distance of her. "Hey!" she snarled, trying to push Jennie out of the way, so she could confront the man. Jennie stumbled and nearly fell, Sara reached out and caught her, and the man was already backing away, but continuing to snap pictures in his retreat. By the time Sara had Jennie safely righted, the man was already tossing his clubs into the trunk, slamming it and moving toward the driver's door. He opened it, tossed his camera, and got in, shutting the door and locking it just as Sara got close to him. He grinned at her, and started the car. She pounded her fist on his window, and he backed up, threw the car into drive, and gunned the engine, his tires spitting gravel in his quick escape. The flying gravel barely missed hitting the blonde agent.

Sara swiftly moved to her side, inspecting her for any injury. "Son of a bitch. Fuckin' bastard."

Jennie just chuckled, exasperated. "I'm sure you don't miss that kind of shit, do ya?"

Sara shook her head, and walked Jennie to her car door. She opened it for her. "Not a bit. Not one fuckin' bit."

Jennie got into her car, and looked up at Sara, who stood holding the door. She smiled again, trying to leave Sara with a more positive impression. "Hey, I never appreciated those bloodsuckers, either. We had a mutual hatred for them. Try to remember that. I was always on your side."

Sara nodded, and said nothing more. She shut the door firmly, and watched as the rental car slowly rolled down the long driveway.

Jennie waited until the car was safely onto Route 20 before she pulled out her cell phone. She pressed a preset number, and then waited for an answer. "Marcia? Cut a check for that idiot John Scott. I want first look before he shops them. And then after that, we lose his number."

For the second time in the same lovely Monday, Sara looked up from her patching and trimming to see a familiar female form approaching her from across the grassy fairway of the fifth hole. This time, it was a curly-headed woman, and even from this distance, Sara could see the woman's lips moving, frowning, and muttering what were surely curses and epithets as she strode toward the now curious and grinning Sara.

This time, Sara tossed her weed whacker into the back of the cart, and walked out to meet her halfway. She could see that Marcy was a little out of breath, and was really scowling as they met in the middle of the fairway.

"Frickin' A, Sara, what's the matter with the goddamned second golf cart? I couldn't get the goddamned thing started." Marcy unconsciously patted her jumper pocket and then remembered she had quit smoking. Her hand shot to her shoulder, where she gave the memory of her nicotine patch a futile rub or two. She glared at Sara, who was standing there, just smirking at her, thumbs hooked in her shorts pockets.

"H'llo, Marse. What are you doing out here? Lose your balls in the high grass?" Sara asked.

Marcy huffed at her, and narrowed her eyes almost into slits. "I'm here on a mission, dammit. Chloe has been trying to get in touch with you for hours. Where the hell is Dave?"

Sara was alarmed at Marcy's words about Chloe. "Is she all right? What's the matter?"

"She's fine, just worried. Ralph took about a hundred zillion messages from her, why didn't you call her back? Where's Dave?"

"Worried about what? I haven't checked in with Ralph for..." she checked her watch, and then looked back at Marcy, "About three hours now."

"Well, you dumbass, you should check in with him more often. What if there's an emergency or something?" Marcy threw up her arms in exasperated disgust. "I know you're out here communing with nature, and trying to add to your income by finding lost balls in the woods, but c'mon."

"Are you going to tell me what the commotion is about, or do I have to offer you a cigarette first to get it out of you?" Marcy's almost constant rubbing of her former patch did not go unnoticed by Sara.

"I wish. I'm thinking about smoking cat-o'-nine tails right about now. The commotion? Chloe said she was trying to warn you, some blonde floozy was at the library today, pumping Chloe for information about you. Chloe thinks it may be your old agent."

Sara's frown now matched Marcy's. "Jennie was at the library? I didn't know, she didn't mention it to me."

Marcy stopped a moment, gave Sara a disbelieving look, and then quite deliberately kicked Sara in the ankle. Sara jumped in surprise, and not a little pain, too. "You're an idiot, Sara."

"Jesus, what did you do that for?" Sara leaned down and rubbed her sore ankle, but not before she moved a few steps away from Marcy, just in case there were more blows coming.

"I did it because every single time I start thinking that you have your head screwed on straight in regards to Chloe, you prove me wrong by pulling a Linda Blair in *The Exorcist* on me." Marcy twirled her finger in demonstration.

"How was I to know Jennie saw Chloe?"

"How about friggin' checking in at the clubhouse once in a while? Huh? Or are you out here having some mad affair with a gopher or something?" Marcy was in full-frontal bitch attack now. "And where is your brother?"

Sara stuck her hands deeply into her shorts pockets, and looked away frcm Marcy. "I was thinking. I just came back out here to work and to think after Jennie left." Sara felt both embarrassed and defensive. "Ralph does fine running the clubhouse." She looked up, and saw two figures in the distance, and reached out and grasped Marcy by the elbow. "C'mon, there's a couple of people who want to tee off. Let's walk over to the cart, out of the way." Marcy glanced in the direction of the fifth tee, and both women started walking over to the cart, off the fairway.

Sara took this time to collect her thoughts, but Marcy's nonstop griping interrupted her.

"Chloe's been trying to call you for hours. Ralph keeps taking messages, not knowing where the hell you are. He didn't want to leave the barn, sorry, clubhouse unattended. Chloe said some blonde woman who looked like she ought to be a spokesmodel was in asking about you. This is Monday, Chloe is stuck at the library, and she couldn't leave to come find you and tell you, or whatever." They made it over to the golf cart, stopped and stood in front of it, Sara keeping out of kicking distance of Marcy's lethal foot. "Well, c'mon Sara. What happened?"

Sara looked into Marcy's deeply probing brown eyes. "Jennie was here. Yeah, Chloe was right, she's my old agent." Sara paused a moment, and when Marcy surprisingly didn't interrupt, she continued. "Jennie must have seen the tabloid shows. She rented a car in Buffalo, and came here looking for me."

Now Marcy butted in. "Is she concerned about your health or what?" She gave Sara a 'don't fuck with me' look.

Sara sighed. "Or what." She wrinkled her nose in consternation. *I really wanted more time to think about all of this before I talked with anyone about it.* "The producer of *Star Gazers* wanted her to talk to me. You know the sequel thing. And then there was this photographer."

"She brought a photographer with her?" Marcy slowly inched closer to Sara, strategizing for when she could get her next kick in.

"No, he was pretending to be a golfer. He got us in the parking lot right before she left then he took off."

"Shit. Asshole." Marcy noticed Sara's grimace. "No, I meant he was the asshole, not you. You're an idiot." Marcy moved another inch. "So, wait a minute here, you were in the parking lot, having a meaningful conversation with some Hollywood chippie, and a photographer ambushes you, and you just friggin' nonchalantly return out to divotland and continue your little groundskeeping duties, just like nothing even happened? Without calling your friggin' girlfriend, and saying 'Oh honey, a funny thing happened to me today?'" Marcy's voice was rising higher with every word. She maneuvered herself into almost kicking range. "And where the hell is Dave during all of this?"

Sara looked down at her feet disconsolately. "I just wanted some time to think about it, I was going to drive out to talk to Chloe later at the library, I know this is her late night there. I just wanted to think about it, calm down about the photographer. Hell, that was a hard thing to deal with in itself. I could have pummeled the guy, if he hadn't gotten away." She looked at Marcy apologetically. "I was kind of freaked out by the whole thing. Jennie showing up out of nowhere, then the damned photographer had me shook." Sara looked up and stared at a passing cloud. "Guess it was dumb of me to think all of this would just blow over with a little careful planning." She kept her gaze up at the clouds, and turned one side of her mouth down into a frown.

Marcy now was in kicking distance, but held her attack back, for now. She hummed her disapproval. "So, Miss Former Movie Star? Or is that a misnomer? What's the score? What did you tell this woman? And who the hell is she, anyway?"

Sara looked at Marcy again, and swallowed before speaking in halting tones. "Uh, my former agent. And, I guess you could call her my ex."

That did it. Out flew Marcy's foot, hitting Sara in the shin this time.

"Ow! Shit, Marcy!" Sara took two wide, limping strides away from the livid artist. "Cut that out!"

"Idiot. Moron. Dipshit." Marcy took a step toward Sara, who retreated even farther. "Is our dear librarian aware that this agent is your ex?"

Sara rubbed her new sore spot, keeping a careful distance from Marcy. "Well, yeah, I think I mentioned it to her at some point. I really haven't talked much to Chloe about my old life. Don't you kick me again, dammit! I don't like thinking about all of that."

Marcy wished she was taller, with longer legs, and more athletic. She surely would be chasing Sara around the golf cart by now, aiming for a hip, or better yet, a good swift kick in the ass. "Okay, so not only does your old Hollywood agent come around and hit you up with an offer, I'm guessing, for you to return to the big screen and sweet offers of your old life, but she, what? Does this woman still have some kind of hold over you?" Marcy's body tensed, ready to spring into faux Chuck Norris action if she didn't like what Sara said next.

Sara didn't flinch. "Yes to the first part and a great big old hell, no, to the second part."

Marcy was so angry right now, she had to think a moment about what answer went with which question. She matched them up pretty well, and felt a tiny bit relieved. But not enough to stop ripping into Sara. "So, you don't think that this little event was important enough to go have a little chat with your girlfriend about? This is just some little everyday occurrence? You get movie offers everyday, and meet up with your old girlfriend, who, from what I heard, could be Miss July in the upcoming *Playboy?* You have to mull this over in your thick head before you talk about it to the person you profess is the nearest and dearest thing in your life? I thought you were self-centered before, but this just takes the proverbial cake, you—"

Sara'd had enough of this barrage, threat of kick or no kick. "Hang on there one second, Miss Secret Pregnancy. I didn't give you much of a hard time when I found out you were keeping the biggest secret ever from my brother, now did I?"

Marcy's feet all of a sudden became rooted to the ground. She couldn't argue with Sara's logic, much as she wanted to. She tried anyway. "Well, yeah, but that was different. That was life-altering." Marcy absolutely hated being on the defensive, ever. She wasn't used to it, especially when dealing with Sara, who, in Marcy's critical eyes, was the one always in the wrong.

"Life-altering? Movie making, the process takes a year, sometimes more. That's not life-altering? I was going to talk with Chloe about what happened today, tonight, after work, after a few hours of thought; that's not egocentric, that's prudent, if you ask me. Christ, if I had called Chloe right away, she would be at work wondering what I was thinking, what I was going to do, and hell, I wouldn't be able to give her any answers, would I? Everything that happened was so surreal, I'm still thinking I might have dreamed it, so quit your damned bitching at me." Sara almost grinned at her first-time-ever offensive supremacy over Marcy. *Maybe, finally, I'm in the right, and she'll friggin' have to admit it.*

Marcy wasn't going to lose this battle so easily. "As Chloe's best friend, it's my job to look out for her best interests."

Sara shot right back. "And as Dave's sister, my motivations are the same for him."

Marcy pelted her comeback. "My pregnancy secret is old history now; I hate it when people bring up past wrong-doings."

"Your little happy ending to the story doesn't make what you did right." Sara was losing what was left of her patience, and her voice and defiant attitude showed it.

Marcy didn't duck. "And is your ex and your apparent consideration of her offer going to mean a happy ending for Chloe? I can't see how it will."

"What I do about this movie, and how I handle it with Chloe is between Chloe and me, not between Chloe, me, you, Nelson and the folks waiting to tee off at the ninth tee. It's none of your goddamned business."

"Chloe is my goddamned business. I will not sit back and watch you hurt her, nor will I sit back and watch you take her away from here."

Sara put her hands on her hips, and gave Marcy a disdainful sneer. Right at this moment, she was feeling no love for her future sister-in-law. "That's the real problem, isn't it, Marcy? You don't want Chloe leaving here, leaving you. You've had her all this time, and I'm just a continual threat to your hold on her, aren't I? Admit it, you depend on her more than anyone else in your life. Even more than my brother, who you're going to marry and have a child with. Your life wouldn't be complete without Dave, baby and Chloe, would it? That's not right, Marcy, that's just not right. You're not looking out for Chloe; you're looking out for you." Sara couldn't help herself; she pointed her finger directly into Marcy's outraged face, and gave her an arrogant smirk.

Marcy was just about to reply to Sara's yelling and accusations, but Sara was on a roll. "I'm right, Marse, and you know I'm right, and it's killing you, isn't it? I haven't even said that I was considering this movie offer, I was just considering the damned friggin' weirdness of the events of the day, and you have me blowing off Chloe, running off to Moviestarland, or worse yet, dragging her away from a place I know she loves, from the people she loves."

The word love gave Sara pause, and her voice suddenly softened. "I know you love her, but I do too, and I'm through with being confused about it, Marse. She told me I needed to love her all the way, and dammit, you need to do that too. You need to love her enough to let her love me. Not just you, not just this town, but me, too."

Marcy turned away from Sara to grab a much-needed breath, and to take a few paces away from her to work off some of her angered energy. She turned back around, frowned and shook her head at Sara, looked down, and then back up at her again. She frowned yet again, and then blew out a sigh.

She conceded the battle. She tilted her head, and peered at Sara, who was staring at her, arms folded in front of her. She ran a hand through her long curls and then said, with a quick and rueful laugh, "Shit, Sara, when did you get so goddamned smart, huh?" She gave her a halfhearted, defeated smile.

Sara, unafraid that any more swift kicks might be coming her way, gave her a small grin in return. She stepped up to Marcy, reached out, and gave Marcy's arm a few deliberate circular rubs, and left her hand there.

They walked toward the golf cart to go back to the club house. "I dunno, Marse. Somewhere between panic attacks, I realized I had a fainting librarian, a feisty artist, a goofy brother, an amazing nephew, and a whole slew of Justins that I care way too much about."

Part XXVII:
Communications 101

Sara put the Comet into fourth gear, feeling the responsiveness of the old car as she tooled up Route 20 on her way to the library. For a fleeting moment or two, she thought about just flying by the library, the town, and continuing her trek, solo, up Route 20, perhaps then heading north for a bit, to get on Route 5, and take a joyride, a think ride, a calming ride along the lakeside road. She desperately needed to think. Her stomach had been doing mini-bungee jumps from all of the unsettling events of the day. As she neared the town center, and the little library, her right foot decided for her, and she didn't slow, but just kept on going. *I just need a half hour. I can circle back at the New York state line.* Moments later, she was still heading east, and was now passing Chloe's little house, then the driveway for Charlie Shemp's, and soon she was out of the town completely, and speeding along at a comfortable sixty miles per hour.

Jesus, what a day. And I know it's not going to get any easier. Chloe was pissed, I could tell when I called her, although she was at work, and had to keep her voice down.

Sara recalled the rather stilted conversation.

"Hello, Stonecreek Public Library, how may I help you?"

"Hey, Chloe," Sara said carefully, but with warmth in her voice.

"Hello, Sara."

"Sorry, I didn't know you were looking for me, I would've called sooner."

There was a slight pause before Chloe replied. "I tried calling, Ralph said you were somewhere out on the course, or I thought maybe you'd left."

Sara heard the uncertainty in those last few words, and knew that Chloe had thought perhaps Sara had taken off with Jennie somewhere.

"Nope. Didn't leave, was here all day. I should have checked in with Ralph. Dave was off getting parts for the golf cart that isn't running. I'm really sorry." Somehow, Sara knew that she would be

repeating the words 'I'm sorry' a lot to Chloe in the next few hours. That's okay, I'll do whatever it takes. "Maybe we should come up with some kind of warning system; you could send up flares, bang on a pan or something," she joked lamely.

The silence that followed showed that Chloe wasn't in the mood for any jokes, no matter the quality.

When Chloe didn't comment, Sara continued. "Chloe? You there?"

After another pause. "It was her, wasn't it?" *She could barely hear Chloe, she could hear some rustling in the background, and maybe Chloe didn't have the phone directly in front of her mouth. Or maybe she was just being quiet.*

Sara sighed before she answered. "Yup. You were right, it was her. She wasn't here long."

Yet another silence. "Hang on, Sara. I have some folks to help."

Sara heard the complete silence of being put on hold. She mentally thanked someone, anyone, for not having to sit through phone hold music, and the "your call is important to us" recording that was ever present in every other businesses telephone system. Oh yeah, she's mad, or hurt, or both. *She took this time to mentally spank herself.* Why, oh why, didn't I just call her quickly after Jennie left? I was right there, near the clubhouse, just...oh yeah, that damned photographer. *Sara's skin prickled at the mere thought of him.* I just wanted to go cool down first.

"Hello?"

"Yeah, honey, I'm still here. Busy at the library today?"

Chloe's voice showed some of her frustration, at least in regards to her job. "You could say that. Book shipment, my volunteer's day off, the twins' grandmother died for the sixth or seventh time, so they're not here. I'm stuck here until close, and there's book club tonight."

Sara groaned. "Oh shit, I'm sorry. I'll get there as soon as I can, and help you out. Maybe I can at least keep Doris' posse at bay." *Sara's head turned, and looked at the beginnings of the darkening evening outside the open clubhouse doors.* "I just let Ralph go home, Dave's not back yet, I'm not sure anyone is still out on the course. Marcy's up at the house making dinner for him. She's getting so domestic now that she's pregnant."

There was a decidedly pregnant pause before Chloe answered. "That's okay. It'll keep. I have a thousand things to do. I can handle the posse myself. We can get together later, or tomorrow."

Sara knew for sure that she was in deep manure now. She and Chloe were never apart in the evenings now; they either slept at Sara's bungalow, or at Chloe's house, every night. It was something they had never discussed, it just had come about naturally. "No, I'm *going to come help. It's the least I can do,"* Sara said decisively.

"Whatever." Chloe sounded dejected. "It doesn't matter. If you want to, don't want to. I won't count on you. I have to go, someone needs me out in the reference section. 'Bye, Sara."

The phone clicked off before Sara could return the goodbye. Oh shit, oh shit, oh shit.

Sara was nearly at the New York state line now. She pushed the little button on the side of her watch, and checked the neon glow that lit up the dial. 6:30. *I can go just a little bit farther, and then turn around. I still need some time before I go see the person who doesn't want to count on me.*

Marcy glanced nervously at the telephone on the wall again, and then at Dave across from her, who was apparently oblivious to the tenseness of his future bride. She frowned at him as he chewed on his peanut butter sandwich, took a slow swig of his milk, and then scooped up some of his home fries with his green beans, and piled them into his mouth. He looked up at her, and saw that she was not giving him a loving look.

"Wha?" Dave said with his mouth full.

"I should call her."

Dave finished chewing, and then took another mouthful of milk. "We talked about this already."

Marcy was intent on forgetting that conversation, as if it never happened. "She needs to talk to somebody; I know she's stuck at that library and your sister—"

"My sister is on the way to talk to her. They'll figure it out, Marcy." Dave almost felt a little pang of jealousy toward Chloe, for as slow as he was on the uptake, he knew of the deep feelings Marcy held for the librarian.

"But what if she upsets Chloe? What if..."

Dave gave Marcy a tender and patient smile. "They'll figure it out, Marse. They love each other."

Marcy pushed her own green beans around her plate. "I know, but I should..."

Dave tapped his glass against hers, to bring her head up so he could meet her eyes. He smiled, and said nothing, holding her gaze. She stared back at him, her frown finally turning into a sheepish grin.

"Well, Dave, looks like I have to cut the strings on Chloe, huh?" Marcy said wistfully.

"Nah, hon, don't cut them, just let the line out a little bit longer."

Marcy sighed, took one last look toward the phone, and with a determined nod, smiled at Dave, and went back to her dinner.

Chloe was farther behind in her work than she even wanted to admit to herself. After Jennifer left today, and between phone calls to leave messages with Ralph, Chloe had left the cartons of books unattended, and fired up the library's decrepit Internet connection, typing in the search words 'Jennifer Swanson' and 'agent.' She was surprised to find many photos of her there, and even an old website from years back, when apparently Ms. Swanson made her living as a runway and fashion magazine model. Somewhere along the line, Jennifer had moved over to the other side of the business, and Sara, who'd appeared in several print ads with her, was one of her first clients. She worked as an agent now with one of the larger talent management companies, and she had several notable, if not outright famous, names she represented. There was even a picture of Sara and Ms. Swanson together, at a party following the premiere of *Star Gazers*. They stood together, smiling, holding elegant champagne flutes, and looking glamorous and perfect together. It was a spectrum of dark and light, of casual glamour, of comfortable togetherness. Chloe shut down the Internet after burning this image in her mind, and immediately dug around in a drawer for a roll of antacids she kept buried there. She chewed one, then another, her molars grinding them like a starving coyote chowing down on a fresh kill.

That was two hours ago. It was nearly seven o'clock now, and Chloe was still behind the counter, unloading cartons and comparing them against the shipping label. Her mind was barely registering her task. The members of the book club had sauntered in at 6:00, kept her busy with many friendly hellos, and several eyes kept tabs on the little librarian from their table in the back.

Doris Raeburn was the most concerned about her dear friend, confused mainly by the lack of a smile on Chloe's usually smiling face, and the few words that Chloe had spoken. Doris' curiosity was nagging at her, and although she and her friends were actually trying to talk about books tonight, the conversation, whispered and frowning, turned again to the subdued redhead behind the counter.

"Look at her, Doris, she's practically on the verge of tears."

Doris snuck a peek up at Chloe. Helen Hoderman was right. Chloe's face was set so that only teardrops were missing from the picture. *This is too much, I should do something.*

Mrs. Hoderman spoke again, all the eyes at the table were now fixed on Chloe. "I still think she's upset about that Dave D'Amico and Marcy Artist Person getting engaged. I'm sure that's what it is."

Doris spoke sharply to her old friend, and the others at the table were secretly pleased that Doris was taking charge and straightening out the old busybody. "Helen, for the last time, Chloe never was interested in David D'Amico, nor him in her. That was just a stupid rumor. So knock it off, before I do nasty things to you with my umbrella."

Naomi Fuller nodded quickly, and then stole another glance at Chloe. "Well, Doris, even so, that face up there, that's a face full of heartbreak if ever I've seen one."

The pastor's wife's words hit home with all of them, and they all, in unison, studied the librarian again, and each one agreed with Naomi's assessment.

Doris sighed. "Iris, I need to talk to Chloe alone. Would you mind watching the front desk while I do? I want to take her into her office."

Iris Cellone nodded her agreement. She adored the little librarian, and was going to do whatever she could to help.

Helen Hoderman's chair pushed back, and she looked as though she was determined to accompany Doris and Iris up to the front desk.

Doris noticed Helen's move. "Uh-uh, Helen. You stay parked, or I'll tell everyone about a certain operation you had some years back."

Helen's chair moved back toward the table and she glared at Doris. "I just wanted to help."

Doris was already moving away from the table with Mrs. Cellone, and gave the older woman a grin mixed with a glare. "You can help by staying right where you are, and talking about someone else for a change. Like me. You can say plenty about me. Get to it. We'll be back."

Sara was on Route 5, no longer driving, but standing in the deep underbrush next to the road. She had been pacing in the tall weeds for nearly twenty minutes now, trying to take command of her racing heart. She'd used every calming technique she'd learned in therapy, every soothing scenario and even a few things that she had come up with herself, in an attempt to calm herself down, so she could continue her trip back to Chloe.

Every blue sky she envisioned was interrupted by the sad visage of her lover. A frowning Chloe visited every summer night sky. Each beach with softly lapping waves breaking onto the shore soon had Chloe sitting next to her, questioning her with silent green eyes.

The beach scene was easiest for Sara to conjure up; she was a mere fifty paces from the cold shores of Lake Erie. The sounds of the waves lulled her momentarily, but when Chloe appeared in her scenario, it was always in her arms, head on her shoulder. Then the redhead would pull away, giving her a look as if she didn't know how she had arrived there, with her. Sara would look into those confused eyes, and not being able to explain, would look at her, a slow smile crossing her face, trying somehow to reassure her small lover that everything would be all right as long as they were together.

As long as we're together, everything will be all right. Sara began pacing along the highway again. *As long as we're together, everything will be all right.* She started repeating this phrase in her head, and was surprised to find that her beating heart slowed with every repetition of those words. The blackness began to dissipate, and in Sara's mind, she took the redhead back into her arms, and they held each other again, this time the both of them feeling the truth of Sara's words. *As long as we're together.*

Doris and Chloe were in Chloe's private office, and Chloe hadn't said a word, which wasn't surprising, after all, she was in the company of Doris Raeburn. Chloe hadn't even put up a fight when Doris had suggested that Mrs. Cellone take over the front desk for a while, and they should go have a talk. Doris now had proof positive that the usually battling librarian was out of sorts.

Doris, as usual, couldn't put a cap on her usual brusque manner. She eyed Chloe, who had immediately sat down in her office chair, slumping like a weeping willow.

"What is the matter, dear? You look like someone killed Dumbo, Old Yeller and Thumper off in front of a firing squad. You aren't just PMSing, are you? Are you fighting with Marcy over her ineptness in tree painting? Still missing the cow patties?" Doris was trying to get the small redhead to smile, and it wasn't working. Chloe just kept her eyes wandering off into space, not meeting Doris' inquiring stare. Doris pulled up a chair across from Chloe and tried again. "It's something to do with that Sara, isn't it?" She actually waited for Chloe's numb nod of agreement before she continued. "I kind of figured. She, all those years back, used to give me grief that she'll never make up for. And that bull's head! I still need to hire someone to get her back for that. I've had bad dreams of that ever since. I swear, I should trade my umbrella in for something more damaging, like a big stick or something, put some permanent damage to that girl." That brought a faint smile to Chloe, but it quickly disappeared. "So, are you going to tell me, or do I have to go get Helen Hoderman in here so she can start rumors about you wanting to join a religious cult or something? Talk to me." Doris resolutely clamped her lips together; it was a hard thing for her to do.

Chloe leaned back in her desk swivel chair, and turned a little, back and forth before she met Doris' eyes. She cleared her throat, and gave the older woman a sad grimace. "Yeah, you're right, it's Sara." She looked away again.

Doris steeled herself and gathered oxygen, as was her style. "I knew it. That girl is a heartbreaker. She has a knack for screwing up the simplest things. I could tell you stories and more stories of what a terror she was in high school. Every time I thought she was on the right track, wham, right back into trouble again. I was on the phone with her mother twice a day, and even between the two of us, we couldn't figure her out. She was almost self-destructive; she would turn good into bad without blinking an eye. I was hoping she had grown up, and out of it, but from the looks of you, dear, it looks like she hasn't learned. Now sit up straight, quit slouching, take a few breaths, and tell me what's going on."

Chloe looked at her, and did exactly as she was directed. "I think Sara is going to leave here, go back to Hollywood. Her old agent showed up in town today, and talked to her about I don't know what." Chloe's hands flopped down in her lap in resignation. "She never called me to tell me the agent showed up. The agent came here first, so I knew who she was. She apparently went out to the golf course to talk with Sara. But Sara never even called me. Never even gave me a second thought." Chloe's voice began to tremble a little, and she glanced at the file cabinet to concentrate on anything but Doris' unwavering gaze upon her. "So, I'm thinking, all day, that it must be bad news, I mean, for me. That Sara," Chloe's voice cracked now, and tears formed in her eyes, "will be leaving here soon." Chloe's voice broke all the way, and a sob came out. "Will be leaving me soon."

Doris frowned, and leaned across Chloe's desk, pushing a box of tissues at her. *Best let her cry while I talk to her. She needs to cry, no need to try to stop her, poor girl.* "Go ahead and let it out, dear," Doris said as gently as she could. Chloe's chest was heaving now with sobs, and the librarian plucked a few tissues from the box and cried into them. "So, you said you didn't talk to Sara about this? What if she just told the agent—a woman, right?—'no,' and that's the end of it? Are you sure, you're not letting your imagination run away with you? That would be so typical of you, dear, you are the most imaginative woman that I know. Always had your nose stuck in a book in school, you were always writing those crazy essays that the English teachers couldn't figure out. And now you direct plays, and the occasional musical. And I'll never understand why you attempted that opera, for God's sake. I mean, if that wasn't a home run in the ballpark of imagination, I don't know what was!" Doris stopped for a moment, and watched Chloe blow her nose, and her sobbing settled down a little. "Now, tell me why you haven't just talked to Sara about this, so your mind wouldn't be all twisted up tighter than Helen

Hoderman's pantyhose."

"I don't know." Chloe hiccuped between tears. "I talked to her, briefly, hours ago. She said she was going to come out here to the library, but she never showed up." Chloe's eyes filled with tears again. "All I can figure is she's trying to hold off the bad news to me." Chloe began crying anew.

Doris felt like she had yet another sixteen-year-old girl in front of her, her heart in distress, and seeking relief from the older woman. Doris proceeded accordingly. "All right, dear, you keep crying, I'm going to think this out, for the both of us, logically." Doris drummed her fingers on her armrest. "So, she said she was going to be here a few hours ago. Let's give her the benefit of the doubt, although, with her history, that's a tough one for me to achieve, and let's just say she got held up at the golf course."

Doris paused, and sucked in more air. "Now, let's get to your little problem. That's right, your problem. You think she's going to go back to Hollywood, and just leave you behind, don't you?" Doris knew she had nailed it, Chloe's sobs got louder. "Uh-huh. You love her, don't you?" Chloe's sobs paused long enough for her to nod at Doris. "Well, she loves you. Don't look at me like that; I've been around that woman, that girl, really, more than you have. She's not much different from the seventeen-year-old colt that almost took up permanent residence in my office. I know that girl. She's always on the verge of doing something right, but something in her just stops her from doing it. She's been missing something, all these years. When I finally found out about you two, I thought to myself, 'Doris, these two complete one another.' Chloe, you know I'm right. You bring a sense of purpose and calmness to that woman. And believe it or not, she's a godsend to you."

Chloe blew her nose several times in succession. She narrowed her eyes at Doris' last few words.

Doris sighed. "I know you too, Chloe. You're the perfect, bright and hesitant little librarian. This aggravating woman has brought out in you a long-buried sense of adventure. Finally, after all these years of watching you, you're finally coming out of your shell, actually having some escapades. I know, I know, they're small ones, but for God's sake, dealing with that woman, being in love with her must be an adventure every minute. Now maybe, just maybe, you being with her will get your nose out of your books and scripts, and you can actually live an adventure or two, and quit just reading about them." She squinted at Chloe, whose red eyes were getting a little bigger as she took in Doris' words. "Ever thought of just letting go, maybe just, I don't know, running with the lemmings for a while? I know how that woman feels about you. You can see it in her eyes, the way she talks about you. When you were having your little tiffs, I could almost see her heart bleeding on her sleeve for you. You have a power over her that her family, her friends and especially me, never did. I know she'll do anything for you. But the big question is, are you going to make her do anything for you, just so you can stay safe here in this little town?"

Chloe wiped at her nose, sniffed it, and swiveled a little in her chair, obviously uncomfortable with Doris' pointed question. *I could just lock up now, and head for Marcy's. She wouldn't be asking me these questions that I don't want to answer. I don't want to think about it.*

"Chloe?" Doris wasn't about to let Chloe zone out on her now. There was important stuff on the table, and Doris liked to have things settled. Whether Chloe liked it or not.

"Yeah. Yeah." Chloe said distractedly, her worry over Sara now turning into annoyance at being stuck here with Doris. "I don't know."

"That's not an answer, Chloe. That's avoidance."

Chloe's impatience at her feeling that she was being grilled filled her next words. "I said, I don't know. If Sara just wants to leave, who am I to tell her not to go? I mean, you should have seen that woman, that agent today, like something out of a fashion magazine. Hell, she used to be in magazines. I mean, if that's something Sara wants to go back to, more power to her. I can't compete with that." Chloe looked away from Doris, and stonily stared at the shelves on her wall.

"Chloe, listen to yourself. You're talking yourself into just letting her go, and we don't know, right now, if that's even a possibility. What I don't get, what I can't figure, is why you're convincing yourself that it has to be over even if she does want to go. What makes you think she wouldn't want to take you with her?"

"I wouldn't," Chloe said firmly. "She knows I don't want to leave here."

Doris was getting a little annoyed herself. "Well, isn't that delightful? Aren't you just the...maybe I've been wrong about you, Chloe, all these years. I thought you had more grit. You don't, do you? Maybe I overestimated you, and you just are a simple little librarian. A woman who would rather read about love and all of the trials and tribulations of it than take a chance on living it out for yourself." Doris could see that Chloe didn't like her message one bit. Doris plowed on, though, hoping to get a rise out of Chloe. "What are you going to do here? Put up books all your life, read them? Take Dr. Seuss books over to Marcy's and play the doting aunt? Maybe when you do, maybe when you're holding Marcy's and Dave's little two-year-old on your lap, you'll hear stories about Dave's sister, wherever she is, and you can sit and wonder, and regret your lack of spirit. Regret is a horrible, terrible feeling, Chloe. Regrets, I've had a few, some of them with my own love life. Now, I'm afraid I'm going to be looking at you, and having them for you." Doris shook her head, and waited for Chloe to look at her. "We've all heard about Sara's problems with fear, but I'm afraid you are the one with the big problem with fear. Such a waste."

Chloe's fighting spirit was finally coming to the fore. She slowly rose out of her chair, and stood up, her tears now gone, and a glare starting in her eyes. "I am not like that. Don't think that. I fight, and win, little battles every day. I'm not about to apologize for loving this town, these people here. That's not fair of you. Just because I love Sara, doesn't mean I have to give up everything I've every wanted my job, my friends, including you. I've worked hard for," Chloe's eyes slowly scanned the tiny, unkempt room, and her voice faltered, "all of this." She sat back down in her chair, a small look of comprehension sneaking onto her face. She ran a hand through her shaggy locks, and looked at Doris for some kind of help.

Doris let out a small chuckle. "Yup. All of this. Yup, Chloe, I can see how all of this is more important than the infinite glory of a great love. Now you listen to me. I know I go on and on, and on and on, but that's just my way. I think of you, and I don't care if you like it or not, like the daughter I never had. I never had a girl of my own to browbeat and terrorize; thank God, I had strong tough boys. I might have overpowered a little girl. But I always thought, if I did have one, that I would have loved her to turn out just like you. With a bit of Sara thrown in." Both Chloe and Doris smiled at that thought. "And, well, I was kind of hoping you two would be sort of a package deal, meatloaf and mashed potatoes, peanut butter and jelly. Great separately. Better together."

Chloe slouched back into her seat, and this time, Doris didn't comment. She looked sympathetically on the forlorn look upon her favorite redhead's face. She watched as Chloe sighed, and then repeated, tonelessly, Doris' last words. "Better together." Chloe said it one more time, after a moment's pause, this time with a hint of a smile. "Yeah. Better together."

Sara parked the Comet in front of the library, and puzzled at the number of cars still there, five minutes before closing time. She was relieved to see that Chloe's rusted Subaru was occupying a space. *Oh, geez, I forgot about Book Club.* Sara's heart raced for a moment, she took another deep breath trying to still the rushed beats. *Here goes nothing.* She strode toward the front door, pulled it open, stepped into the foyer, and stopped dead in her tracks.

At the checkout desk, four frowning and glaring older women stood, arms folded, sentry-like and imposing.

Mrs. Hoderman spoke first. "And just where have you been?" She squinted at Sara.

"Uh, I got held up."

Mrs. Cellone, behind the counter, twitched her face. "The poor little thing has been upset all night. You should have been here." There was a decided tone of accusation in her voice.

"I tried."

Naomi Fuller, the pastor's wife, her arms just barely making any kind of a barrier over the expanse of her wide bosom, very unforgivingly said, "Well, 'I tried' just doesn't cut it, does it, Ms. D'Amico?"

"No, I guess not."

Bella Stavros, Jeanette's grandmother, had to have her say, too. "She's in her office with Doris. But if you aren't here to help, you can just turn your butt around right now."

"With Doris?"

Mrs. Hoderman gave her a withering glare. "For almost an hour now. We've been holding down the fort."

Sara dumbly stared at all of them in turn, and felt herself physically and mentally shrinking from the sheer power of their disapproval of her. She lost a good six inches in confidence alone. "I suppose, if you ladies wouldn't mind, I should go try and talk to Chloe now." She hesitated, not wanting to provoke the tense pack of mother wolves in front of her.

The ladies all turned and looked wordlessly at each other. Helen Hoderman, temporarily putting herself in charge, turned back to look at Sara. "Well, all right, but maybe you should wait until..."

There was no wait involved; the alpha wolf was coming down the hallway from the office. She stopped to stand with her cohorts in front of the counter. Doris eyed Sara, and then walked past her, over to the round table where her coat was. She gathered her things, and waited as her friends walked over and retrieved theirs, too. They then walked, single file, past a stock-still Sara, each lowering her eyelids and giving her a distrusting look before they gathered behind her at the front door. Doris was last to cross Sara's path, and she stopped, cocked her gray head, and then very deliberately and slowly thumped her umbrella on the floor several times. Sara's eyes widened, and then Doris thumped it again, this time with a little more meaning attached. The ladies then silently filed out the door, and Mrs. Cellone locked it behind her.

Sara let out a long sigh, and tried to shake out her tensed muscles. *Okay, that had to be the hard part.*

Chloe was still slumped in her swivel chair when she heard a light tap on her door. *Oh God, haven't they left yet?*

The door opened, and a dark-haired woman with an apologetic look on her face peeked in. Their eyes met, and Sara gave Chloe a weak smile.

Chloe just stared as Sara slowly walked over to her. Chloe felt weak, tired, angry and extremely relieved to see her beautiful lover.

Sara knelt before her, and gently took Chloe into her arms. Chloe's arms tightened around Sara in response, and then Sara pulled Chloe into a standing position, strengthening her embrace until she was nearly crushing the little librarian with the flow of her love and her sorrow. Chloe responded by returning the power of the hug, and the sentiments therein.

Sara opened her eyes to look down into Chloe's, and what she found there filled her with renewed hope, and an overpowering sense of completeness. She leaned down, and kissed Chloe for all she was worth, and then once again, and again, wanting it to never stop. Chloe returned each one with an equal fervor, trying to transfer all of her being, all of her feelings into each kiss.

They broke for a moment, still holding each other tightly, and then Sara brushed her lips across Chloe's again. Sara, overcome with emotions and desires too strong to hold back, even though they were in the confines of the public library, looked deeply into Chloe's eyes.

"Chloe?" whispered Sara, "do you want to take your pants off for me?"

Part XXVIII:
Some Day, My Princess Will Come

Spring has sprung, the sun has riz, I wonder where the flowers is? In Stonecreek, the advent of Spring, and the short journey from that season to Summer, brought many a smiling, anticipatory giggle from Fort Lafayette students. Many a young lass was busy scouring the local mall in Erie for just the right prom dress, some even traveling out of state in their search, which wasn't saying much considering Stonecreek was just a few miles from the New York state line. Appointments were made for glamorous hairdos and nylon sculpted false nails. The mothers of these young fillies spent their time nervously trying to come up with explanations to irate husbands as to why their darling daughters needed to spend so much money for a dress they would never wear again. Not all mothers were afflicted with having to deal with these events, they spent their time wondering why their little daughters showed no interest whatsoever in the senior year dance, and seemed to prefer to spend time in their rooms watching tapes of the U.S. Women's World Soccer team with their female friends. Those mothers were probably due for a rude wake-up call, probably around the time their daughters hit sophomore year at college.

The strapping lads of Stonecreek's senior high school were planning, and perhaps plotting, along the same lines. The sharpest of tuxedos were rented and fitted, dinner reservations were made, and unflattering, extremely trendy haircuts were being paid for. Corsages were ordered, after checking with their dates to find out what color scheme their dates' dress, nails and shoes followed. A few daring fellows even dreamed big, and dared to rent a room at the local Ramada Inn. Few of these rooms, every year, were ever actually used, much to the delight of both motel management and cheering maids. Some young men, dateless for most of the year, gathered up their courage, and asked a female buddy on the girl's softball team to accompany them to the spring promenade, no thoughts of renting a room ever crossing either of their minds.

And in a small, artfully decorated old farmhouse west of town, a cross and crabby art teacher was yet again arguing with her best friend.

Chloe, propped up comfortably on Marcy's headboard, was watching her pregnant friend root through her closet.

"Well, it's good to know one of those dresses will be worn for something, if not their original purpose." Chloe clucked her tongue in Marcy's direction.

Marcy was tossing dresses onto the bed, covering most of Chloe like a silk and satin comforter. "Well, yeah, so. I still want to know how I got volunteered for this thing. Lately, with all of the forced volunteering I've been suckered into, I should win some kind of award, don'tcha think?" She pulled another dress from the closet, examined it before shaking her curls in refusal, and pitched it onto the pile covering Chloe. "How did you get out of this chaperone gig? Who'd you pay off?"

Chloe reached and adjusted a hanger that was poking her in her fleshy pillows region, and just shrugged, and grinned. "Ah, but you see, my dear friend, I am not a full-time teacher at the high school. I am but a poor part-timer, not expected to fulfill such duties. Just be glad you have a real date this year, and not Paul. And just think of all the high school studs who will think it's their duty to come help you fill your dance card. Ah, the prom. Ah, Spring. Ah..."

"Shut up," said a none-too-happy Marcy. "You know I can't dance, I suck at it, and I can't get smashed before this thing to improve on my skills. Dave's going to find out what a dufus I am, and we're going to end up having a music-less wedding reception. Maybe we could get married, and then, oh, sit around and play cards afterwards?"

Chloe's mind was filled with visions of Marcy's dancing style, which could be described as Marcy spinning around in place as though her foot was nailed to the floor, and she had to swivel around that pivot point. It was not a pretty thought. Chloe snickered. "Hey, as long as there's booze at your reception, I don't think people would give a rat's ass." Chloe idly ruffled through the clothing on top of her. "And, hey, by the by, you never told me if the wedding is going to be pre-baby or after-baby in November."

Marcy stopped her hunt through her nearly empty closet, and turned to face Chloe. "I was going to ask your opinion about that."

Chloe sat up, acting apparently stunned at her friend's request. A box of shoes promptly sailed her way, and she stuck out a hand and deflected them. "All right, let's see. Hmm. Would I rather see Marcy nine months along, ready to burst at the seams, waddling down the aisle, or would I rather wait, and watch you saunter down the aisle with a wailing papoose in your arms instead of flowers?" She watched Marcy's face grimace at both ideas, and it made Chloe giggle. "Gives a whole new meaning to throwing the bouquet, doesn't it?"

Marcy's mind imagined her maid of honor going out for a long one, and dismissed that thought. "I thought I told you, this kid is going to boarding school. One, maybe two days after it's born. I don't plan on seeing him or her until their prom." Marcy brightened at that thought.

A dark-haired head appeared in the doorway to Marcy's bedroom. Chloe threw her a delighted grin, and Marcy stuck her tongue out at her. Sara grinned and took a running leap onto the bed, scattering clothes everywhere, and almost knocking Chloe onto the floor before she reached out and grabbed her. Marcy scowled, and watched as Sara propped herself up next to her lover, extending her arm so Chloe could lay her head on her shoulder. Sara returned Marcy's favor of the stuck-out tongue.

"Hey, you two," Sara said as Marcy picked clothes off the floor, tossing them onto both Chloe and Sara this time, "playing dress up? Is Chloe going to be Evita Peron again? Can I watch?" Sara raised a suggestive, leering eyebrow, reached under the piled masses of clothing, and tickled Chloe in a particularly sensitive spot.

Marcy paused in her clothes-chucking. She lowered her eyelids and stared at Sara. "No, this time, we were thinking you might like to be Cleopatra, Queen of Denial. We were hoping you'd make a life-long dream come true for us," she commented dryly.

Sara laughed, and poked a giggling Chloe again. "Wow. Prom. What a nightmare, huh? I just got back from the tuxedo rental place with Nelson. He got a great black tux, with a loud, bumblebee-yellow waistee thingee."

"Cummerbund," supplied Chloe.

"God bless you," teased Sara.

All three women winced, and then smiled.

Chloe rubbed a hand across Sara's stomach. "So, we were just discussing the possibilities of a pre- or post-baby wedding for Marcy and Dave. My vote's for a last minute, shotgun affair. Doris could supply the shotgun, I'm sure."

Sara did her eyebrow thing with theatrical flair. "Ooh, baby. My thinking is that Marcy should come down the aisle with Curly, Moe or Larry strapped to her back."

Marcy began picking through the stack of clothing on Chloe and Sara. "Or, we could elope right now, saving me from buying yet another dress, and while I still possess my somewhat girlish figure," she mused.

Sara grinned, and her arm shot out, and pulled a protesting, but laughing, Marcy down on top of them and all of that unused wedding finery. Chloe and Sara held her down, and Sara declared, "Oh no, no way Mrs. Future Unpronounceable Name-D'Amico. You're not depriving us of witnessing the spectacle of the elusive town's art teacher finally getting hitched. I want to be there when you make your last minute dash from the altar to the delivery room."

All three friends laughed again, and then all looked at each other. Marcy spoke, a devious grin lifting the corner of her mouth. "Well, now, that would be something for the town to talk about, now wouldn't it?"

As was the way of their world, the three of them settled matters, just like that.

"Film?"

"Got it. Hurry up, we're losing the light out there." Sara and Chloe had been rummaging around in Sara's little bungalow, searching for disposable cameras, Polaroids, the video camera and Sara's old 35 mm. Chloe had them all piled in her arms, and Sara, typically, was underburdened, holding onto a small box of film. Chloe fumbled with her load, and Sara helped by merely readjusting a few things in her lover's arms. "There. Now don't drop anything. Even the smallest amount of moisture can ruin film," Sara preached, tucking a camera strap under Chloe's arm. "Let's haul ass."

Chloe took a few halting steps for the front door, frowning. "What's wrong with this picture? Why am I the pack mule?"

Sara opened the front door, and held it open for the laden redhead. "Because I am the photographer, and you, my sweet, are my assistant. Lackey. Can you spell it with me? L, A," Sara pointed Chloe out the door, and gave her rear end a loving smack as Chloe grumbled by. They trudged across the path leading from the bungalow up to the main house, Sara carefully watching the pile in Chloe's arms, and giving a smiling appreciation to Chloe's butt, too.

The Comet, in its glorious red-buffed glory, was parked directly in front of the house. Chloe headed toward it, in hopes of setting down her burden on the hood. Sara took a couple of quick strides past her, and held out her arms. "Nuh-uh, don't even think about it. You'll scratch her."

Chloe was thinking that both her nose and her butt were getting very itchy, something that always happens to a person when they're least likely to be able to relieve that irritating feeling. That wasn't the only irritating feeling Chloe was experiencing. "This lackey poop is—well, I'd rather be a sidekick. I bet they get paid better. Listen, you, do me a favor. Scratch my nose, will ya?" Chloe turned up her pert nose, and sighed as Sara grinningly complied.

Sara looked up at the available sunlight, and made a few mental calculations. "Hmm, we'll start with my old 35, and then move onto the Polaroids from there, and then the camcorder, and then we can use some of those throw-away cameras you brought." She finished disdainfully. "Although, technically..."

She stopped her little speech, because a golf course mogul and a noted local artist were making their appearance on the front porch. Sara grinned, and quickly grabbed her camera from Chloe's load, almost dislodging the whole mess in the struggling librarian's arms.

"Ooh," trilled Chloe, making sure she could be heard by the engaged couple, elegantly posing on the porch. "Movie stars. Look, honey, movie stars! Quick, get a pitcher an' maybe we can stalk them for their autographs."

Sara already had the voguing couple in her viewfinder, making a few quick adjustments for the light, and began snapping away. "I know, I know! But who the hell are they? They remind me of someone, no, don't tell me." Snap. Forward. Snap. Forward.

"Yes, yes, I do believe it is, yes, that famous couple." Chloe provided, hoping Sara would be able to come up with a snappy finish.

"Yup, hon." Snap. Forward. Snap. "Yer right! It's Lenny and Squiggy!"

If Chloe could have clapped her hands without dropping everything, she would have. She saw Marcy stop her suggestive posing, and place her hands on her hips, giving Sara her best dour look. Sara caught it for posterity.

Sara, having shot half of her film, finally dropped the camera from her face. She and Chloe grinned at the handsome couple, and then Dave, in a very sharp suit and tie, crossed his eyes and contorted his voice into a high and nasal greeting. "Hull-lo."

Chloe laughed. "I was wondering which one was Squiggy. Guess that answers that question."

Dave and Marcy made their way down the porch stairs, and stood next to the photographer and her lackey. Dave checked his watch. "Hmm. What's holding up Nelson and Jeanette? They should be here by now, they said they would."

Marcy nodded her head up the long driveway. "Here they come now." Nelson's pickup truck was just making the turn into the driveway, and the foursome smiled and waved at the truck as it approached them. Well, Chloe didn't have a free arm and she couldn't wave, so she nodded her head like a dashboard Chihuahua.

The truck pulled up a little distance from them, and a handsome and quite debonair Nelson, even with his radical new haircut, climbed out and made his way around to the other side to help Jeanette get out.

The four adults, as different as they all were, were thinking the same thoughts.

Chloe, in a hushed voice, said, "What's with that haircut?"

Marcy murmured, "I was wondering that myself. What is that? He looks like..."

Sara supplied, "A funky Pee Wee Herman. It's bad, isn't it?"

Dave cleared his throat. "It just won't lie flat. He tried for hours, I think he even got the iron out. It looks sort of..."

"Bumpy," stated Chloe.

"Haphazard," Sara whispered.

"Scary." Marcy shook her head. All of them then pasted on their smiles, because the blonde bombshell and her studly escort, his hair looking vaguely like a bad Moe Howard toupee, were shyly walking toward them. Sara began snapping pictures again, her fingers adjusting the lens, and waving them into position.

A half hour went by, and then forty minutes. The unforced smiles on both couple's faces faded into desperate looks that Sara had to cajole them into losing.

"Aw, c'mon, you all look like I just told you that there's a Republican in the White House." Snap. Flash. Wind. Snap. Flash. Wind.

Marcy, standing uncomfortably posed next to her fiancé, her soon-to-be-stepson, and his who-knew-what, grimaced another smile. "Sara, does the car have to be in the background of every goddamned picture? Although I loved the automotive narration you provided when you were filming us with the camcorder. I really think it's important to know that this car can get us to the prom in less than four minutes, I really do, but is this a little vanity project for you? It's really all about the car, isn't it?"

Sara was dutifully, if not a little reluctantly, snapping flash pictures with Chloe's throw-away camera. "Well, maybe."

Chloe sighed. Her arms were tired, her nose itched again, and it looked to her like Jeanette was actually on the verge of frowning, which Chloe feared might scar the young woman for life. Her arms were still busy holding her expensive cargo, so sticking her fingers in her mouth and whistling loudly to gain Sara's attention was not an option. So she did the next best thing: she stood up close next to her, and gave her the best hip shove she could manage without dropping all the cameras. "Hey, Ansel Adams. Jeanette's corsage is wilting. Give it up."

Sara scowled, and sighed. "I got carried away again, didn't I?"

Five voices cried out in unison, with Jeanette's trained cheerleader lungs topping it all off. "Yes!"

Sara rolled her eyes, and shrugged her shoulders. She looked sheepishly down at the impatient redhead next to her. "Hey, look at all that stuff you've got, let me help you with that."

Chloe just barely kept her foot from flying out and making contact with Sara's shin. "Thanks heaps, Kemosabe."

Neither noticed Marcy dragging Dave over to them. Marcy stuck her hand out to Sara, grabbing for the camera. "Uh, uh, not until we get some of you and Chloe. Hand it over."

Chloe felt a little embarrassed handing over her stuff to a fiercely grinning Dave. "We don't really need..."

Dave just kept taking articles from her, and shook his head. "You might not, but we do."

Sara had given the camera to Marcy, who checked the shot count and smiled. "Now you two, over by Nelson and Jeanette there, and then I want some of just the two of you."

Nelson and Jeanette were now standing by the front porch. Sara smiled, and blushed a little toward her red-haired lover. Then she glanced at her red buffed 1963 classic. "All right, but can we go stand by my—"

It couldn't have been rehearsed better. Again, five voices rang out, but this time in the negative.

"No!"

There are kisses, and then there are kisses. Every time Chloe softly put her hands onto Sara's cheeks, her thumbs lightly stroking from the sides of Sara's nose, back to meet the rest of her fingers near the dark-haired woman's jawline, Sara knew that such a kiss was coming, and it gave her heart a small jolt, like traveling over a small speed bump in a parking lot. Sara would gaze down into those green eyes that never failed to disarm her with their sincerity, their clarity of feeling, their possessiveness and desire. The dark-haired woman's breath would catch during these moments, her resolve would flee, and she happily dissolved into a feeling of helplessness, all commanded by a touch and a look. And then the kiss would start, the lips grazing hers in faint greeting, a pause, and then the full on meeting of Chloe's mouth on hers, making Sara's eyes languidly close in the sheer sensuousness of feeling being transferred one to the other and back again. Not each kiss she shared with Chloe was such a kiss, but those kisses came frequently enough for Sara to become addicted to them. This kiss was that kind of kiss, and Sara's heart was skipping like a stone thrown across a small, intimate pond.

Chloe broke the kiss, but not before purposely sucking on Sara's upper lip, nipping it gently before she let it go. Her hands remained on Sara's face, tracing a random pattern, feeling the heat of the skin below her fingers, the lines of the bones beneath. She watched Sara's eyes flutter open and meet with hers, their faces breaking into smiles at the shared acknowledgment of the wondrousness they felt when they kissed. Chloe's eyes fell to those lips she had just traversed, and she couldn't help herself, she just knew that Sara's lower lip was suffering in a jealous quiver over the attention she had just paid the upper. So she licked, sucked and nipped it, too, feeling charitable and heroic for giving it the satisfaction it craved.

"Sara?" murmured Chloe, as she felt small kisses travel a narrow line up the bridge of her nose, turn east and west to both eyes, then return center to rest on her forehead.

"Hmm?" Sara replied, her throat supplying the conversation, her lips being otherwise occupied.

"You're an asshole."

Sara's lips twisted into a grin, but remained firmly parked on the soft skin above Chloe's eyebrows. "Why, yes, yes I am."

Chloe's head tilted down, just a little, so she could enjoy the view of just how little space there was between them. She sighed. "But you're my asshole, and I love you."

Sara chuckled, and her arms tightened around her smaller lover, knowing exactly how they fit best, and achieving that position. She moved her chin up to rest on the silky red-blonde tresses on the top of Chloe's head. "Nice to know somebody finally appreciates the real me."

Chloe could feel Sara's grin in the light touches of the taller woman's hands on her arms. "This was such a nice surprise. I mean, well, it just is."

Sara shifted her head to one side, so her cheek could enjoy what her chin had just experienced. "All we did was move some furniture in here. Not so much."

"Enough so you could dance me around. Just like that night." Chloe's smile dropped into a small frown, remembering how that night had ended.

Sara closed her eyes, and pulled Chloe even tighter, knowing where the redheaded woman's thoughts were going. "I think this night will end much better than that one, don't you?"

Chloe's smile returned, she wasn't about to argue with that notion. "I know so. No arguing Dave and Marcy and no disappointed Nelson to interrupt us."

"Oh, don't say that, you'll jinx us." Sara laughed, and felt the smaller form in her arms trembling with merriment, too.

Chloe ran her hands up Sara's arms, just to the point where she could lightly tug on the ends of Sara's hair, which was tumbled forward, cocooning Chloe's face in lush darkness. "Oh no, not tonight. Nelson can pick a fight with Jeanette, Dave can get his period, and Marcy can come here confused and without a clue, but I'm not letting you go tonight."

Sara grinned, and let those sentiments wash over her. "Ditto." She sucked in a small breath, the smell and warmth of Chloe infusing her with a courage that she thought she didn't possess, would ever possess. But for some reason, she wasn't scared, she wasn't second-guessing herself when she said, "And what about tomorrow night?"

Chloe snuggled deeper into Sara's arms. "Tomorrow night, too, if you want."

"I want." Sara was filled with the assuredness of a seasoned fortune-teller; she suddenly and surely knew how Chloe would answer her next questions, and it filled her with a joy she'd never experienced before. "And the night after?" She rubbed her hands down Chloe's back and spoke again before Chloe could answer. She wanted the librarian to realize the intent of these queries. "And the one after that and after that? And the week after? The month? The year?"

Chloe stopped tugging on Sara's hair, and loosened her grip around the dark woman just enough so she could lean back out of her arms, and to look questioningly into her sparkling blue eyes. Any questions Chloe had about the real meaning behind Sara's words were answered then, and Chloe took a moment before she replied to Sara's question with not an answer, but with another question.

One more search of the sincerity in those blue orbs, and she asked, with just a hint of a smile, "You want?"

"I want," Sara replied, a burden she never knew she was shouldering was lifted from her, and she felt lighter, higher, taller than she'd ever felt before.

"Ditto." Chloe smiled, and then those hands of hers cradled Sara's face again, and Sara leaned into them, knowing that this next kiss would be the kiss of their kisses, the one assuring them both that they planned on sharing those kisses for a long time to come.

"Um, Ms. Woj—er, Marcy, the band says it doesn't know the 'Hokey Pokey.' I asked." Jason couldn't believe he had shouted that idiotic question into the bandleader's ear, and had actually suffered through the scornful, amused look that he had been on the receiving end of, much to his ego's detriment.

Marcy gave Jason a disbelieving stare, not because she was confounded at the band's ignorance of her song request, but that the young man before her had actually gone up and asked about it on her behalf. She almost wanted to lean in, and smell Jason's breath, thinking that would completely explain his behavior. But for some reason, the uncomfortable look on his face made it plain to her that Jason had not been nipping from some contraband flask hidden somewhere on his skinny body. She eyed him, and said, "Uh, thanks, Jase?" She looked around. "Where's your date gone to, anyway?"

Jason flushed, and pretended to be relaxed, bobbing his head to the caterwauling swing beat the band was providing. "Uh, she's in the, you know, ladies' room. She met up with some other girls from her team. I guess they're, uh, fixing their make-up or something?"

Marcy nodded a few times, unintentionally keeping beat with a song for the first time in her life. She had gotten that funny feeling about Jason, and his latest info about his date clinched it for her. "Well, I appreciate you keeping me company. I'm afraid I'm not much of a dancer."

Jason smiled, and both their gazes turned out to the dance floor, where David D'Amico and Doris Raeburn were burning a hole into the gymnasium floor. Marcy rolled her eyes and shook her head. "God, that man. Who'da thunk?"

Jason just smiled some more, and watched as his principal kept up with the younger man with ease. "I knew she was energetic, I mean I saw her chase Ms. D'Amico that one day with her umbrella, but God, I mean, she's practically doing splits out there!" Jason wasn't the brightest of young minds, but he knew enough to recognize a force of nature when he saw it.

Marcy somehow knew that Dave was going to be grumping and groaning about his sore muscles tomorrow, and that Doris Raeburn would be rolling merrily along, with nary a complaint or worry. *Wait till ol' Dave is chasing a two-year-old around with a golf ball in her mouth. We'll see how sore he gets.* "Jason, that's just plain weird, don'tcha think?"

Jason couldn't disagree with that, especially now that Dave D'Amico was twirling and twirling a delighted Mrs. Raeburn in quick concentric circles.

Marcy's eyes widened. "She'd better quit smiling like that while she's spinning her or upper plates are going to go flying."

Jason couldn't help himself, he leaned over, grabbed his knees, and began laughing his fool head off.

Marcy laughed too, and smacked the red-faced young man on the back. "Hey, Jase, I think you're one hell of a date. We should do this more often."

Twirling was also happening in the D'Amico living room, by two smiling and deeply in love women, both as different as milk and whiskey, as feathers and steel, as midnight and midday. But somehow those differences disappeared, faded away, when some months ago, their worlds collided, and after many a near hit and miss, they had joined, body, spirit, heart and mind and changed into the women they were now.

One last twirl by Sara, and a giggling Chloe brought their bodies to a halt into the middle of the living room floor. "Whoa, I need to catch my breath."

Sara's sappier side finally emerged, just for a moment, before it buried itself again. "I haven't been able to catch my breath since I met you, Chloe."

Overwhelmed by this sentiment from her lover, Chloe did the unexpected because she felt so undone by Sara's words. She reached out and smacked Sara on the shoulder. "Cut that out." She smiled, blushing.

Sara was not expecting that kind of reaction to her romantic words. "Ow. Wife abuse. No wonder I never say mushy stuff, I get punished for it." She grinned, glad to see that her sweet words had the desired effect on the flustered librarian.

Chloe immediately regretted the thwap, and quickly pulled Sara to her, and made up for it by bestowing an apologetic kiss on her lips. Chloe melted into Sara's arms again. With the room softly lit by a dimmed lamp off in a corner, the two women started slowly swaying together, beginning another dance.

Sara dropped her mouth down to Chloe's ear, and softly said as they moved about the living room floor together, "Hey, Chloe?"

Chloe just hummed her answer, and then found the energy to make her lips form a reply. "Yes, Sara?"

"Do you think, well, maybe we could have at least one dance tonight with some music playing?"

Part XXIX:
I'm Too Busy for This to Be the End of the World, We'll Have to Reschedule

Let's see, I have ten bucks, with that I can get three hot dogs, or maybe some bratwurst, some oatmeal pies. A Mountain Dew slushie. Nelson was standing outside the Quickie Mart, checking his funds so he could fuel up before Tuesday's rehearsal, which started in less than a half hour. This was the last week of rehearsals before dress rehearsal on Thursday, and opening night on Friday.

He personally felt that the cast and crew were ready to roll right now, but he knew the cautious and exacting director of the musical wasn't quite satisfied with it. Chloe referred to the pacing and flow needing work. She had, a number of times, asked everyone to quit rushing their lines, to think more along the lines of a slow interaction between a major league pitcher and a .345 hitter. She pointed out that the cast, without audience, would have to be aware of the emotions contained within the play, and allow the audience time to react with laughter, applause, or just to soak in plot changes. It didn't matter to her that most of the adults in this community had probably seen *Oklahoma!* more times than they could count, either the movie which frequently played on cable, or community presentations of it throughout the years. No, this was their *Oklahoma!*, or rather, her *Oklahoma!*, and dammit, they had all worked hard, and they were going to make the audience appreciate their labors. And it didn't matter to her, either, that the community, small as it was, would all probably see their *Oklahoma!* during the first three presentations. The other presentations would most likely be performed in front of a repeat audience. Chloe had such attention to detail, she even directed the cast to speak their lines louder on the Sunday matinees, when a good part of the audience would consist of senior citizens bussed in from local nursing homes. She reminded them that she believed that these good folks were even more of an appreciative audience than one composed of their families and friends. They were knowledgeable about musical theater, having had a lifetime of school plays under their belts, and perhaps even a Broadway show or two, and the cast needed to concentrate on every nuance in the play, and not just repeat their lines, but believe them, too.

Nelson opened the heavy glass door to the Quickie Mart, and strolled in, noticing right away that the hot dog roller on the check-out counter was filled with elongated, tubed items made up of mostly indiscernible meat and meat by-products. He was not discriminating, he'd heard what hot dogs had in them, and he didn't care. They tasted good, and that was good enough for him.

He walked up to the counter, pulled out the drawer that con-tained self-serve warmed buns, and extracted three. He was just reaching for the tongs to grab whatever meat product would end up on his bun, when he heard a voice greet him from the magazine aisle to his left.

He turned and smiled, keeping one eye on the rolling grill, con-tinuing his mission, and said his hellos to the rotund Quickie Mart manager, Cathy, whom he had known for years.

"Hey Cath."

"Hey Nelson." Cathy was pulling magazines and tabloids off the shelf, and replacing them with their newer editions. "God, I was wondering if you were coming in here today, the magazines just showed up a half hour ago, and I was paging through them." There was a note of excitement in Cathy's voice, something of an oddity for the usually laid-back convenience store manager. She grabbed a few she had set aside, got up from her kneeling position, and made her way toward him.

Nelson finished putting on his third rolled meat product, and looked at her curiously as she stopped in front of him. "Wait a sec," she said, paging through one of the lurid weekly tabloids that most people never admitted to reading, but read anyway. She found her page in it, glanced at it again, and then turned it open toward him. There was a half-page picture of a dark-haired woman hugging a smaller platinum blonde. Nelson immediately recognized the dark woman as his aunt; her face was clearly showing, her eyes closed, but she had a graceful smile on her lips. In the inset was a picture of her alone, a threatening frown and narrowed eyes.

Nelson completely forgot about his hot dogs, and grabbed the paper from Cathy, who was making some remarks about it that he paid no attention to. His eyes stared at the picture again, and then traveled to the headline above. "HIDING STAR GAZERS ACTRESS MEETS WITH FORMER AGENT, RETURNS FOR SEQUEL?"

Nelson grumbled. "She's not hiding," he said distractedly.

Cathy was making more remarks; this time, a few he actually caught. "Wait, there's more." Her hands opened up another tabloid, and found her mark, and handed it to him, opened and ready for his inspection. It was similar to the first, but instead, the picture content was reversed, the larger of the two displayed his aunt's scowling face, and the smaller, her hug with Jennie. Nelson let out a small whistle of surprise, because the headline read, "MISSING STAR GAZERS ACTRESS TO RETURN TO HOLLYWOOD?"

Cathy finally poked him, because she was irritated that he wasn't paying attention to her commentary. "Nelson, she's in the *People*, and *Entertainment Weekly*, too, although those are just pictures, not much of a story." She began fumbling through those magazines, and found her pages while he impatiently waited. She wordlessly handed them to him, and let him take a good look. "Who's the blonde woman she's hugging? She doesn't look like she's from around here, but that looks like your father's parking lot behind them." Cathy, too, knew the rules of couponing, and had gone to visit the course for the three dollar special.

"Yeah. It is." Nelson shook his head. *Oh God, this isn't good. Aunt Sara's going to blow a gasket. No, wait, Chloe's going to blow a gasket. Oh God. There's going to be a huge explosion.* And things between them had just seemed to settle down. Nelson took a quick glance at his watch, and saw he had fifteen minutes to get to rehearsal, where he knew that two women who had a vested interest in these pictures would be awaiting his arrival. He then looked to the cover prices, and then at the three filled buns on the counter, and gave Cathy a desperate look.

Cathy sighed, but knew what she had to do on his behalf. "Listen, just take the magazines and stuff. Give me what money you have, you can stop in and pay me later."

Nelson sighed and then his eyes traveled to the stack of magazines still waiting to be put up down the short magazine aisle. "Thanks, Cath. I gotta get to rehearsal and show my aunt these. And could you..."

Cathy chucked Nelson on the shoulder. "Yeah, no problem. I'll put the extra copies in the back room until I hear from you."

Nelson gratefully tucked the copies in his hands under his arm, stacked the hot dogs one on top of the other, and moved toward the pop coolers, to grab himself a Mountain Dew. This was too important for him to be fussing with the slushie machine. Nelson knew his priorities. He dug in his pocket for his ten-dollar bill, and handed it to Cathy. "I'll get more money, and pay later today, I promise. And Cathy, thanks." He saw the manager smile a wan smile at him.

"No problem, Nelson." She watched as Nelson moved quickly toward the front door. She couldn't let him leave without one more remark. "That poor aunt of yours just can't catch a break, can she?"

* * *

Sara was slumped miserably in a back row seat of the small auditorium. Four periodicals were tucked under her chair, and she was itching to take another look at them, especially since Chloe was busy on the small stage, commanding her troops in short, impatient sentences. The orchestra pit was full of students, eight or nine of them, this time being the first time that they would all practice together. The rehearsal was to consist of nothing but the musical numbers today, so that the small orchestra or band could get used to playing with people singing along. The cast, used to performing their numbers with a perfect recorded musical accompaniment or with their accomplished pianist, Ben, were in store for a rude awakening. Chloe knew it, Paul knew it, Marcy knew it, and Doris Raeburn had planned for it by hiding out in her cluttered office. There was only so much wincing her older face could take in the course of two hours.

Chloe was pacing the stage like an expectant father awaiting the arrival of quintuplets. "All right. Okay." She nodded toward the motley crew in the orchestra pit. "These folks here have been practicing this right from the start, just like you. Let's start by giving the orchestra a big round of applause, because without them," *the show would go off without a hitch.* "We wouldn't be able to achieve the," *mediocrity.* "Flavor of a true live stage performance." Her acting crew gave the orchestra pit members a somewhat enthusiastic greeting, tempered by their memories of having to sit through many crushingly bad half-time shows, and holiday recitals. Moreen Dean was especially doubtful, to say the very least; she had heard her younger brother, Aaron, dutifully sawing the score on his violin with the flair of a one-armed lumberjack trying to cut down a redwood with a dull ax. "Okay. Thank you for thanking them. Remember, we're all in this together." *And we'll all go down together.* Chloe turned a nervous eye out to the back of the auditorium, seeing Sara sitting there, and they exchanged weak smiles, although for entirely different reasons.

Nelson, standing not too far from Chloe, had a hard time concentrating on the upcoming rehearsal. He had seen the shock, anger, and then dismay in his aunt's eyes when he had shown her the magazines in a private corner earlier. *Oh man. Something is going to hit the fan later, and Chloe's already all worked up, and Aunt Sara is quietly getting herself into a panic, too, I just know it, she's worried about how Chloe's going to react to those pictures.* He made eye contact with his aunt, and flashed her an encouraging thumbs up, which Sara hesitantly returned before frowning again. Chloe was on the return leg of her long pace across the front of the stage, and she didn't catch the interaction between them.

Chloe noticed Paul and Marcy offstage, and grimaced at them.

Marcy was eternally grateful that most of her art duties were now complete, the backdrops looking like corn fields, not marijuana plants, trees actually resembling a known species of tree, and a barn that uncannily resembled one that now housed a John Deere tractor, two electric golf carts, and a cash register nobody knew how to work.

The only thing missing was the horse she had lobbied for, and it had been decided, after much grumbling and arguing on everyone's parts, that the horse's first appearance would be put off until dress rehearsal day. Chloe was insistent that if the horse couldn't act on that day, there was no reason to believe it could perform other days, either. Chloe was dead certain that the horse was still a bad idea, and that Nelson would be ambling across the stage, horseless, on opening night. Charlie Shemp, accompanied by his dad, would bring the horse on Thursday, prior to the beginning of their last practice.

Charlie Shemp was there today, as he was other days, a helpful and eager shadow to Paul. He was Paul's indispensable boy Friday, jumping at his every request, and at times providing Paul with items and information before Paul even requested them. More than once, Paul got the same eerie feeling about Charlie Shemp that Colonel Potter got about Radar O'Reilly.

But Paul never realized the true reason Charlie Shemp was so devoted to the success of this little play. It was Charlie's abiding and ever-present overpowering crush on the redheaded director that made him so completely immersed in the process. He could hardly wait for school to let out, his summer to be over, and his freshman year to begin, so he could join the drama club, and be in her presence for two hours every Thursday afternoon. Charlie's love was not the mis-guided and cruel love of a stalker, no, his was a pure and blindingly innocent love of the very young. Charlie Shemp was a young man of character, not unlike his idol, Nelson D'Amico.

Chloe stopped mid pace, when she saw a grinning young man standing next to Paul, awaiting his instructions. Chloe caught his grin. "Larry, gimme."

Larry trotted over to her, and gave her what she requested. She put the "Porn Star" cap on her head, facing it forward, and turned to everyone, a large teasing smile on her face. "Okay, everyone, places. Ben, you're in charge. Start the overture whenever you're ready. I'm going in the back rows, and watch from there. If you screw up, just go on. That's what it will be like for every performance. I'll try and not interrupt." *I'll try and not head for the nearest bar until this is all over with.* Chloe turned and headed down the steps on the far side of the stage, walking back to where Sara was sitting. She plopped into the seat next to her, patted the taller woman on the knee, and then turned her attention front and center.

Two mouths in that back row began audibly grinding molars

only seconds after the overture began. Not long afterwards, two more people came back, a curly-haired art teacher and a sexually confused English teacher, and joined the unrehearsed chorus of rhythmically grinding teeth. It was almost symphonic in nature. A gray-haired school principal paused outside the theater's doors and then turned and made the long walk back to her office. Her dental work was too expensive to let it be subjected to that kind of torture.

Marcy sighed in her back seat, watching frowning students filing past them, and out the doors. "It could have been worse."

Chloe raised an eyebrow, wishing it could achieve the height that her lover's did. "Really? How so?"

Marcy glanced at her three compadres, and sighed again. "The horse could have been here, taking a dump on the stage. Although, I think that might distract the audience from noticing the clarinet player. I've never heard a cat being strangled before, but I imagine that's what it sounds like. Except more in tune."

Chloe echoed Marcy's sigh. "I'm going to tell Ben to play very loud, and get the other orchestra members to tone it down. Like, dead silence."

Sara had her hands folded in her lap, her fingers intertwined and her feet propped up on the back of the seat in front of her. "Maybe it would be better if you moved them out of the pit, and out to the parking lot."

"Or maybe we could tell Moreen Dean to sing at full throttle," interjected Marcy.

Paul, as usual, was his optimistic, deluded self. "It wasn't so bad. I mean, Ben's pretty good, and the guy that plays the triangle and stuff, he's not half bad." Paul cringed when he saw the reaction to his remarks, and he decided, prudently, to zip his lips.

Chloe noticed a subdued Larry standing in the aisle, waiting to interrupt. "Oh, yeah." She grinned and took off her cap and tossed it to him. He grinned halfheartedly at her. "I'm going to need that for dress rehearsal. And opening night, too. It might jinx this thing if I don't wear it."

Larry nodded, and said "Sure thing, Ms. Donahue." He, too, headed for the exit.

"Hell, Chloe, you might need that hat for a future job possibility if this thing turns out to be a disaster," Marcy joked, only half meaning her words.

Sara glared at her. "Hey, don't kid about that. This thing isn't going to be a disaster. And for being a porn star, Chloe could do quite well at that, don't let those angelic looks fool ya." Sara grinned and winked at Chloe.

Paul colored, and decided now was as good a time as any to make his own exit. "Well, uh, gotta go, Mom's got dinner waiting." He stood up, moved down the aisle, and strode toward the doors.

The three women grinned at each other; they knew their line of conversation had hurried Paul's hasty retreat.

"I'll never figure that guy out," mused Chloe.

"Do you really want to?" Marcy asked, almost seriously.

Chloe and Sara both answered. "No!"

Marcy shifted in her seat, and then decided to stand up. "Well," as she looked at her two seated friends, "I'm going over to Dave's, see what oddities he has planned for dinner, and cry in my nonalcoholic beer for a while. I'm kind of tired."

Sara looked at her, concerned. "Everything okay? I mean, baby-wise?"

Marcy patted her on the shoulder. "Just fine, I just need some extra rest is all. Junior D'Amico is just dandy. Not so sure about his mom, though. I mean that, um, music can't be good for the baby, right?"

Chloe shrugged her shoulders. "Maybe you could swallow some earplugs for it, Marse."

Marcy patted Chloe's shoulder, too. "I'll make sure they're the first course." Marcy gathered up her things, and then gave a rueful grin to her friends, still seated; slouched, really. "See you guys later."

Sara and Chloe were the only ones left in the dimly lit theater, both staring silently at the stage. The stage was dark and gloomy, matching their spirits. Sara idly scratched at her knee, deciding that it didn't matter, here or at home, Chloe needed to be told about the magazines and the pictures therein. Her heart picked up to an almost imperceptible erratic pace, almost like that of the percussion player that had recently been playing in the orchestra pit. She noticed Chloe's sad and defeated demeanor. *Well, at least this will get her mind off the play.* She cleared her throat, reached under the seat, and pulled out the stack of magazines. Nelson had helpfully placed a post-it note bookmark in all of them. He was just that kind of considerate, thinking young man.

Chloe blinked at the small pile of tabloids and magazines in Sara's hands. Her heart skipped a little, although she didn't know why.

Sara gave her an apologetic nod, and held out the pile to her, which Chloe took. Chloe glanced in Sara's eyes once again, and then opened the top one to the page with the bookmark. Sara watched her anxiously, noticing how Chloe's eyes opened wide, and then narrowed. She didn't look up at Sara. Sara began nervously pulling on the ends of her long, dark hair, and biting the corner of her lip. Chloe carefully read the contents of the short article, and then frowned.

Sara wiped her sweating palms onto her blue jeans. Chloe closed the tabloid, and set it in the seat next to her. She opened the next one, Sara carefully watching her face for any reaction, her stomach clenching. Still no reaction, no words from her red-haired lover. Sara glanced at Chloe's hat-flattened hair, and resisted the temptation to reach out and fluff it, fearing her arm might come back with bite marks on it. Chloe placed the tabloid on top of the discarded one beside her, and opened the *People* magazine. The woman next to her felt the veins in her forehead begin to throb in time with her galloping heart. Chloe quickly perused the picture, then opened the last one, and silently examined it. When she was done, she sighed and finally looked up at the apprehensive face of the woman sitting next to her.

"Well?" blurted Sara, sure that this was going to be the end of the world as she knew it.

"Well," sighed Chloe. She narrowed her eyes at Sara. "You didn't tell me you hugged her," she said, her face unreadable, her voice flat like a pancake.

"When she said goodbye, just when she said goodbye." Sara's tongue nearly tripped over itself, trying to get out an explanation.

"Huh." Chloe looked again at the pile next to her before she spoke again. "Well, looks like we have to expect that kind of stuff, huh?"

Sara almost jumped into the smaller woman's lap when she heard that word, 'we.' She liked the sound of that word so much that she repeated it aloud. "We?"

Chloe reached out a hand, and gently took Sara's into hers. *I am not jealous. I am not jealous. Well, yeah, I'm jealous.* "Yeah. We."

Sara didn't care if there were any stragglers left in the theater or not. She reached over, put both arms around Chloe, and squeezed her, her heart rebounding from its former stampeding pace, and slowing into a more assured, quick rhythm of pure relief.

Outside the theater's doors, Doris Raeburn stood, listening, then smiling, forewarned minutes ago by a departing and concerned Nelson D'Amico. Doris nodded slowly to herself, and she turned and stopped momentarily to adjust her rain bonnet, and headed for the front doors of the building, swinging her umbrella with a carefree air.

Nelson and Dave watched a glum and tired-looking Marcy come through the kitchen doors. Nelson had stopped by the ATM on his way home, after dropping off a troubled Jeanette, who demanded that she accompany him to the Quickie Mart to pay for his purchases. Marcy looked at them, her face almost creased with what could be called a frown, and then played the reassuring girlfriend to her anxious boyfriend, which Nelson gratefully acknowledged by giving her a very warm kiss and a hug at her front doorstep.

As she took her coat off, Marcy noticed that the table was littered with stacks of magazines and periodicals.

"What's that?" she nodded toward the table, as Dave got up and helped her off with her coat. "You need that many copies of *People*?"

Dave gave her a peck on the cheek and grumbled. "Nelson bought Quickie Mart out. We were thinking of heading to Shop 'N' Save, and buying those all out too, but I was thinking, they must have a ton of them; it could get pricey." Indecision lined his face. "What do ya think?"

Nelson had already helpfully opened a copy of each of them, ready for Marcy's perusal. She sank down in her seat, pulled them toward her, and then began moaning, louder, with each one she looked at. "Oh God, oh God. I just left them at the school. Does Sara know about this?"

Nelson leaned, and poked his finger at one of the suggestive headlines over his aunt's picture. "Yeah, I told her at practice. She has her own copies there."

Marcy glanced up at him, then at Dave, then back at the scowling face of Sara in the magazine before her. "What about Chloe?"

Nelson shook his head. "Aunt Sara said she was going to wait after play practice to tell her. You know, save her some stress."

Marcy's vivid imagination took her back to the small theater, where she pictured a fainted Chloe lying on the floor next to where Sara was hanging by her feet from the rafters. "Oh, boy. Chloe's going to go ballistic." She saw the pinched frowns on both father and son. "And Sara. I'm glad I'm not her right now. I mean, this is her former girlfriend! And she's hugging her, for Christ's sake."

Dave was determined to remain hopeful, but he wasn't quite sure how to accomplish that small feat. "Should I take out a loan and head down to the grocery store? Or not?"

Marcy blew a raspberry between her lips. "Nah, Dave, what's the point? The whole town already knows she's here, and the one that's going to react the worst to this, Chloe, will have to see this sooner or later, right?"

Dave sat across from his fiancée, and folded his hands dejectedly on the tabletop. "Yeah, well, I just wish I could do more for her, Sara, I mean. This stuff has got to bother her, and then Chloe, on top of it all."

Marcy leaned across the table and wrapped her hands around his. "You can't protect Sara from this kind of stuff, Dave. She was out there, in the public eye, a TV and movie star for many years. I don't think you're giving Sara enough credit. This won't bother her much. But Chloe, well, that's another story, isn't it?" She watched as both D'Amicos nodded a grim agreement. "And this headline here, about Sara returning to Hollywood? Is it true? Has she said anything like that?" She eyed them both, watching for any sign of collusion, and when they both said "no," she wrinkled her brow. "You know what they say, don't you?" She didn't wait for either of them to answer her. "They say there's always a small grain of truth in these articles."

Both elder and younger D'Amico shook their heads, and mouthed many negatives at her. But in the back of their minds, they were not completely sure.

Chloe and Sara settled into a booth at the diner. Neither had felt like cooking after the long, stressful afternoon, and wanted to relax together over a warm meal and hopefully, a large piece of pie afterwards. The waitress had just taken their order, topped off their coffee cups, and breezed away from the table.

"Chicken again?" teased a grinning Chloe.

Sara gave her a mock frown. "Hey, their chicken is great. It's fried. We D'Amicos haven't perfected our cooking repertoire to the extent of frying a decent chicken dinner."

"I can fry chicken, not bad, either."

"Oh, there's just another reason to keep you, I guess." Sara smiled at her, at first jokingly, and then shifting into sincerity. She leaned forward across the table, wrapping her hands around Chloe's coffee cup. "Seriously, though, Chloe, I would keep you even if you admitted to cooking a lousy fried chicken." Her smile turned mischievous again.

Chloe reached out, and let her hands touch with Sara's on the cup, before Sara regretfully withdrew them. "Keep me in Little Debbies, Sara, and you'll never be able to get rid of me."

"Promise?"

Chloe didn't answer; she motioned an emphatic 'cross my heart' instead.

Sara understood that kind of sign language. She settled back into her seat, and held onto her own cup of coffee. "If I could, I'd get that in writing," she said cryptically.

Chloe tilted her still hat flattened head of hair to one side. "You would, huh?"

"Well, yeah, if this great nation of ours would wake up and let us make it legal." Sara was verging on the romantic, and it made her stomach wobble, but only for a moment, especially when she saw the flash of recognition in Chloe's eyes, and the adorable grin that lit up her face. Sara blushed, embarrassed at her own admission, and glanced out the window. "Quit looking at me like that."

Chloe mightily tried to get a more controlled expression on her face, but it only lasted a millisecond before her face erupted into a wide grin again. She gently kicked Sara's leg under the table. "Like what? Like this?" Chloe puffed out her cheeks, and crossed her eyes. Sara looked at her, and then let out a laugh, and kicked her in return.

They both looked away from each other, trying to dampen the outright gooey looks they were bestowing on each other. Chloe cleared her throat, and sucked on her front teeth. "So."

"Yeah?" Sara wasn't nearly as successful as Chloe in quashing her warm, toothy grin. Her blue eyes danced under dark bangs that clearly needed a trim.

"Well, we haven't talked much about it. I mean, I expected the pictures, I really did, not the hug though." Chloe pursed her lips and then quirked them back into a reassuring smile again, "And that headline? The Hollywood thing." *Why am I saying this now? Couldn't it wait until after dinner? After the pie?*

This time, Sara didn't hide the fact that her hand was traveling across the table to make contact with Chloe's hand. She wrapped long fingers around Chloe's hand, and left them there. "You're right. I was in such a bad mood, I wouldn't even discuss all of this. It's just me just being in denial again. We just never talked about it." Sara sighed, and her eyes met Chloe's. "What do you think?"

Chloe was caught by surprise. "You mean, about the possibility about you going back to acting?" *Oh God.*

Sara shook her head. "No, us going back to acting." She saw Chloe's eyes widen at that thought.

"I enjoy acting, but what I really want to do is direct," Chloe said, half teasing, half serious, hoping this would throw Sara off her line of questioning.

Sara wasn't about to be diverted. She grinned at Chloe's small joke, but then spoke that very important word again. "Us."

"Us?"

"Us," Sara said firmly.

Suddenly, the big booth seat that Chloe was sitting on wasn't nearly big enough for the amount of squirming she wanted to do. "Well, I don't know, Sara." Chloe found something out in the parking lot that seemed to draw her attention away from the penetrating eyes of her lover. "I have my job and..."

"You could take a leave of absence. You've been there long enough."

Chloe avoided that statement of fact, and her eyes left the parking lot, and fixed on those of her love's. "What about you? Do you want to go back?" She tried to keep the quaver out of her voice, and it did come out emotionless and steady, to her surprise.

"Not without you," Sara said, and set her jaw.

"Forget about me, what about—"

Sara cut off anymore words from Chloe's lips by giving her a direct look, and her hand a firm squeeze. "I'll never forget about you, Chloe. What I do, what *we* do, from here on out, we do together. Don't you know that by now?"

Chloe used her free hand to get a sip of water from her glass. She let it roll around in her mouth a little before she swallowed. "I know," she said quietly. She smiled a tiny, hesitant smile at Sara, which brought another toothy smile to the darker woman's face. Chloe blushed, and wished that she could match the older woman's assuredness. "Well, it's an option. We could talk about it. When the time comes, okay?"

Sara saw the waitress approaching with their salads. "Okay, when the time comes."

They spent the rest of their meal discussing final preparations for dress rehearsal on Thursday, the impending trauma of opening night, and the Sunday afternoon matinee. That was as far into the future as the small redheaded director/librarian wanted to think.

And yes, more than one diner patron complained about having to hear Patsy Cline over and over, during the consumption of their repast.

Part XXX:
All Good Things

Marcy was clapping and whistling. Paul was also on his feet, whoo-hooing, and Sara let out a few earsplitting, odd-sounding whoops of her own. The three of them were sitting in the back of the darkened theater, giving the assembled cast on the stage the adulation they deserved. The dress rehearsal had proceeded without a hitch, every song was sung in key, and every spoken line was enunciated and well-paced. The lighting crew had performed perfectly, the stage crew worked with clockwork precision. No one forgot their lines, no one tripped over a prop, and even Cargo, the mysterious missing element to the final production, had proudly carried Nelson on stage, a breathtaking sight for all to see, and stood calmly as Nelson sang his opening song as it was meant to be sung, on horseback.

And Chloe Donahue, in charge of it all. It had eaten up large chunks of her life in the past few months, affected her eating, sleeping, and yes, even her unexpected bonus of now having a sex life; it had affected that, too. Because of this musical, she had lost weight, gained weight, gained a lover, almost lost her, revealed her sexual preferences to people she would never have told under anything resembling normal circumstances. She had become a golf teacher, regained and gratefully lost her "Kissing Bandit" persona, been kissed by her best friend, her best friend's fiancé, a blonde former student teacher, a Slippery Rock senior, and still had the grace to wear a "Porn Star" cap without feeling that moniker really fit. The best kisses, she was still getting from a completely dazzling ex-movie star who had announced, on more than one occasion, that she was madly in love with Chloe, and wanted to make a life with her.

So why was the little librarian looking so miserable?

Sara wondered that too, as she looked down at the quiet Chloe, between raucous whoops at the grinning cast members on the stage.

"Chloe? Um, what's the matter, the kids are all waiting."

Chloe slunk even lower in her seat, if that was possible. Any farther, and she'd have been lying on it. "We're screwed," she half mumbled.

Sara, in the midst of another yowl, didn't quite catch what she said. "Huh?"

Chloe turned the "Porn Star" ball cap face forward, and thunked it back down on her head. "We're screwed!"

Three people clapping and whistling don't really make that much noise, and they really weren't doing it in unison, and, as the fates would have it, the comment that was meant only for Sara's ears somehow cut through the pauses between the joyous adults around her, and carried from the back of the theater all the way to the stage. The room went from loud to morgue silent when her comment immediately put a great big cork in their overflowing bottle of enthusiasm.

The students, formerly very proud of themselves, herded themselves together tighter on the small stage, and peered out to where Chloe was seated. Chloe regretted that her mouth had a tongue. "Wait, wait. That's not what I meant."

Marcy, standing behind her, immediately jumped in to support her. "What Ms. Donahue means, guys, is..."   Marcy was at a loss. "She'll explain what she means, right, Ms. Donahue?"   Marcy then showed her support by giving her best friend a thwap on the back of the head.

Chloe jumped up out of her seat, well, after she struggled up into a position that would give her the balance to do so. Sara was silently standing beside her, hands on hips, totally flabbergasted. She just kept looking at Chloe, and then up at the stage, then back to Chloe again.

Chloe cleared her throat, and then began walking down toward the stage from her aisle seat. She stopped just in front of the orchestra pit, adjusted her cap, and scratched her chin several times, collecting her thoughts. She began by giving the students, who were now clustered at the front of the stage, a rueful but genuine smile.

"First off, let me say right now, that I've never seen a better performance of *Oklahoma!* than the one I just saw on this stage. No, strike that. I've never, ever seen a better performance of *anything* better than what you folks have just done, even in my limited experience as director, as actor. You guys never knew I did that, in college, or when I, myself, attended this school. When Doris Raeburn sees you guys do this, I'm sure she'll feel and say the same thing." Her words were having their intended effect, and the tense looks on the cast and crew diminished, but only slightly. She began a slow pace in front of the orchestra pit, and the students' eyes followed her like a crowd watching a tennis match in slow motion.

Her hands began moving in small flings in the air as she searched for her next words. "It's like this. There's an old superstition in the theater, I'm not sure of the exact words, but it goes something like this," she stopped and looked up at them all. "Dress rehearsal bad, opening night good. Dress rehearsal good, opening night..."

She didn't need to finish, these were all bright kids, and they knew how that sentence needed to end. A collective groan arose from the stage.

"Which made me make that stupid remark before, when I should have been standing and cheering right along with Mr. Hoderman, Ms. D'Amico, and Marcy. I'm sorry I didn't, and that I got carried away with thinking about an old superstition. There's no reason to believe that it applies with you guys, right?"

Another collection of moans and groans sounded, even from the back of the theater.

Chloe stuck her hands in her back pockets, and glared at them. "I said, *right?*"

A halfhearted, rather disjointed "Right," sounded back at her.

Chloe stuck out her lip, and leaned onto the railing, letting her eyes roam and make contact with as many kids as she could before she said it, this time with a demanding finality. "I said, *right?*"

This time, the whole ensemble responded, ready to be led down whatever path of opening night disaster the little determined director wanted them to tread.

"Right!" they roared, confident and sure.

Sara, still in the back row, kept mum. She knew, from personal experience, that a jinx was a jinx was a jinx, no matter how you tried to shout it down.

Chloe was sitting outside, on the small brick ledge that out-cropped from the back of the school building, watching as her lover helped Charlie Shemp and his stepdad load a docile and handsome Cargo back into the trailer. She smiled, for Charlie was sneaking sur-reptitious glances her way, and even in the fading of the day, she could almost see the blush of embarrassment that covered his freck-led face when she caught his eye and gave him a grin. His face imme-diately turned away, and he pushed it into Cargo's flank, perhaps to try and rub away some of the redness. Sara, giving the tall horse a final pat on the rear, helped Charlie close up the rear gates, and to Chloe's amusement, she reached over and gave the small guy a quick hug.

Oh, great, now he'll be in love with both of us. Chloe grinned again, and then took a moment to survey the darkening skies above her, the emerging stars just beginning to twinkle in the twilight of the evening. It was chilly tonight, and she pulled her jacket tighter around her, and watched her lover wave to Charlie and his stepdad as they pulled away in a decrepit truck that she was sure was a good fif-

teen years older than her own rusted vehicle. The red brake lights
cast an eerie glow on her lover, who turned around and noticed the
small librarian huddled near the school. She thrust her hands into
her jeans pockets, and grinning, strolled slowly over to where Chloe
was sitting. She stopped, and stood just to the side of her, and
scanned the heavens, just like Chloe had done moments before.

"His stepdad is such a nice guy," Sara said thoughtfully. "He
mentioned that I could come out and ride Cargo once in a while
whenever I wanted. I bartered him free golf rounds in exchange."

"Sounds like you're getting the better end of the bargain."

"Yeah, that's what I think, too." She glanced down at Chloe,
and gave her a quick smile. "So, some day, huh?"

Chloe nodded. "Yup. Some day." She scooted over, and patted
the cement beside her. "Park it, it's nice out here." Chloe had no particular desire to go anywhere just yet, she wanted to think about
thinking about nothing at all, just to sit back and watch the sky turn
an ever-darkening shade of violet, alone with her lover.

Sara settled down next to her, tight, their shoulders and legs
touching. "Feeling melancholy, baby?" she teased.

Chloe let that bad pun slide. "Yeah, sort of. It's the beginning of
the end, you know? It was halfway through the second act, when I
realized they don't need me anymore." She sighed, and leaned in
closer to the warmth of the woman beside her. "You and I and Marcy
and Paul. Well, we're just going to be audience members from here
on out. I have to admit, it does kind of make me a little sad. I feeling
like I've been eating, drinking and sleeping *Oklahoma!* for the last
couple months of my life, and here I am, reduced to being a
bystander."

"You're the director. You're their director," Sara replied, feeling
some of that same sort of loss that Chloe did, but not expressing it.
She wanted to be there for Chloe right now. "These kids are going to
remember this for the rest of their lives. Chloe, they're going to
remember you the rest of their lives. I don't blame them, I spent five
minutes with you that very first day of rehearsals, and I couldn't forget you, now could I?"

Chloe gave Sara an appreciative quick one-armed hug around
the waist. "Nor I, you, you scary, scary bitch." Chloe laughed.

"I guess I was scary the first time you met me."

"Not scary, really; intriguing, definitely."

"Well, I scared Marcy the first time I met her. That has to be a
good thing, right?"

"Absolutely." Chloe felt Sara's hand reach for hers, and she let
her entwine their fingers, and pull them onto the taller woman's
thigh. Chloe sighed contentedly, and let her head drop onto Sara's
shoulder, and they were quiet for a few minutes, just wading in their

own thoughts, their own feelings, their relaxation feeding the other, supplying each other with a needed sense of peacefulness.

Chloe broke their little reverie by needing to stretch her shoulders. "Well, I suppose we can't just stay here all night."

"Nope, Dave probably has them at the house by now."

"I suppose I can't avoid meeting them, can I?"

"Well, Ernie probably wouldn't mind, but Mom, she's not big on women avoiding her. It makes her cranky. Well, crankier than usual, I guess."

Chloe felt a chill of apprehension creep over her. She asked, bluntly, "You think she'll like me, your mom?"

"Nope," Sara said, rather too firmly, and gave Chloe's hand a squeeze.

Chloe lifted up her head, and looked at her lover quizzically. "Nope?"

Sara turned and looked at the woman next to her, and gave her head a shake. "Nope. She'll love you. Just like all of us do. She's a D'Amico, right?"

Chloe smiled, and laid her head back down on Sara's strong shoulder for a few moments more of shared intimacy. But her head was already spinning with dread. *Yeah, she's a D'Amico, all right, but that's by marriage.*

Dave and Nelson were staring at each other, not sure who this woman was who was puttering around graciously, making pleasant small talk, acting like a crossbreeding of Martha Stewart and Donna Reed. Marcy settled Mr. and Mrs. D'Amico into the large couch in Dave's living room, and was now bringing a tray laden with coffee cups, sugar, creamer, and a coffee carafe that neither Dave nor his son remembered being part of their household inventory. They also settled into chairs, having been ordered there by a sweetly insistent Marcy the moment Dave had arrived from picking up his parents at the airport in Erie. Nelson had arrived from dress rehearsal only moments after Marcy, and only minutes passed before Dave showed up, so there had been no time to figure out who this woman was, and to question her as to the whereabouts of the real Marcy.

Marcy demurely sat down on the couch, and began pouring coffee into cups, with a Stepford Wife smile plastered on her face. "Cream or sugar, Mr. D'Amico?" she trilled sweetly.

"Ernie," Ernie corrected her for the fifth or sixth time, he'd lost count. "Just black, thank you." He accepted his cup from Marcy, and glanced at his wife.

Marcy turned her attention to the tall, older woman who was watching her, a careful mask on her face. "And you, Mrs. D'Amico?"

Marcy was already filling a cup.

Marjorie had already decided that there was something not quite right with this curly-headed woman, but she wasn't quite sure what it was. "How about you call me 'Mom,' I mean, you are going to be a part of this family, right?" she said gently, and sincerely.

Marcy stopped pouring, put the carafe down, blushed, and then leaned over and gave the older woman sitting next to her a hug.

Dave and Nelson were wide-eyed, and Dave resisted the temptation to look under the sofa and Lazy Boy in hopes of finding his Marcy.

"Oh, thank you. Mom."   This incarnation of Marcy looked like she was about to get weepy.

Nelson would have choked on his coffee, had he had any yet. He was thinking of refusing it, not sure what had been snuck into their well water earlier in the day.

Further banal atrocities were averted by the sound of the kitchen door opening, and Sara appearing in the living room archway, grinning at everyone. "Hey, sorry we're late." Her own blue eyes widened. Was that Marcy, wearing an apron?

Ernie put down his coffee cup, stood up, walked over to his daughter, and gave her a crushing hug. She got a whiff of the cherry cigar aroma that hung around him like a blanket. Her stomach stopped churning, momentarily.

Ernie peeked around his daughter, and saw a softly smiling red-headed cherub standing shyly behind her. He winked at her. "And you would be Chloe, am I right?" His eyes twinkled, and Chloe blushed.

"Yup, that would be me," said a clearly shy Chloe, not realizing she was echoing her lover's standard reply. She stood awkwardly, not knowing what to do. Ernie solved that problem by stepping away from his daughter, and giving Chloe a warm hug, which she hesitantly returned. Sara watched the interaction and couldn't help but feel warm and fuzzy all over. She then turned her gaze to her mother, who was still sitting on the couch next to Marcy, or Marcy's evil twin sister, Sara wasn't quite sure which.

"Hey Mom."

"Sara."

Yup, same old lovey-dovey Mom. Sara grinned, smiled at her brother and nephew, and then her eyes were somehow drawn back to Marcy. "Hey Marcy."

Marcy blinked, and then turned on a Laura Petrie smile of her own. "Good evening, Sara, you're just in time for some coffee." Marcy leaned over and picked up the carafe, and held it like it was a prize on *The Price is Right*.

Chloe nudged Sara, equal parts confusion over Marcy, and the fact that Sara hadn't introduced her to her mom yet. Sara started, her mother the last thing on her mind right now. Her manners kicked in.

"Um, Mom, this is Chloe Donahue, Chloe, my mom."

Chloe crossed the floor over to Marjorie, and put out her hand. Marjorie had already put down her cup, and she stood up from the couch, and returned Chloe's warm handshake. Chloe was a little stupefied by the resemblance that mother and daughter shared, Mrs. D'Amico being an older and certainly more dignified version of her lanky daughter. *If this is what Sara will look like when she's her mom's age, I am definitely in the market for a long term relationship.* "Hi, pleased to meet you." Her blush returned from wherever it had flown to earlier.

Marjorie gave her a blinding smile, so much like that of her daughter's that it stole Chloe's breath away. "My pleasure, Chloe. And you can call me 'Mom,' too, just like I told Marcy here a moment ago." Marcy's head bobbed up and down like a buoy in enthusiastic agreement. "We've heard such wonderful things about you, from Nelson and Dave and especially from Sara." She watched as the little woman's face colored even more, which charmed her to the bone. "And by the way, that's quite an interesting hat you have on there."

Chloe's eyes widened, and then her hand whipped up, and the "Porn Star" ball cap disappeared from her head so fast, she could have taken a third job as a magician, and done quite well at it. The hat promptly was stuck under her arm, and she quickly fluffed her hair, which didn't help in the slightest; it was flat with strangely obtuse angles pointing toward both the Atlantic and Pacific. She looked rather like a sheepdog that had just gone through a very bad scare.

"Oh. Oh. That's just a kind of tradition, a joke, from the play," she mumbled, and looked around dazedly. Marcy just gave her a weirdly blank and all-too-toothsome smile. Chloe backed away from them both, and in her haste, almost knocked over the coffee table and its caffeinated contents. Sara was right behind her and luckily caught her in her strong arms, and then just as swiftly, dropped them down and around Chloe's waist, and casually held her there.

Mother and daughter shared an eye-to-eye moment, blue on blue, amusement matching amusement. "You'd better keep a tight hold on that one, Sara."

Sara gave the still red-faced Chloe a tight squeeze, and replied. "Oh, yeah, Mom, I plan on it."

Marcy was pacing back and forth in the kitchen, bouncing off invisible walls, and muttering under her breath. Chloe had snuck in from the living room and stood near the table, carefully staying out of her friend's path.

"Son of a bitch, son of a bitch, I'm going to kill that man. I mean, I'm going to marry him first, and then I'm going to kill him, so I can get widow's benefits." Marcy was vaguely aware that her friend had come into the kitchen, and was watching her warily. She caught Chloe's eye on a return path in her pacing. "I mean," she whispered harshly, "a jury certainly couldn't convict me of his murder, right, I mean this would be considered justifiable homicide, right?" She was having a hell of a time keeping her voice down.

Chloe was pleased to see that Miss Manners had left the building, and Marcy had returned in her stead. "Marse, calm down, I'm thinking Dave was just as surprised as you when Mary and Rick showed up here tonight. I mean, we knew they were coming into town for the play, but showing up here?"

Marcy stopped her pacing, and began opening kitchen drawers. Chloe was hoping that Marcy wasn't intent on committing a Lorena Bobbitt on her fiancé. She sighed in relief when Marcy pulled out an oven mitt instead of a six-inch butcher knife. Marcy put it on her hand, and stood in front of the oven, opened it, and pulled the pan out, and looked at its contents. Her friend, curious, came over to take a look of her own.

"What're they?" whispered Chloe, her voice modulating easily into librarian tones.

"Appetizers," hushed Marcy.

"They look like little wieners in pie crusts, sort of, you know, rolled up though."

"Thank you, Julia Child," snipped Marcy, knowing these wrapped wieners would be snapped up in less than the time it took her to get that sentence out. "Start looking for something else in the cupboards to feed these folks. Dinner reservations aren't for more than an hour yet." She took the pan from the oven, and set it on a trivet on the counter.

Chloe started searching through the cupboards, not feeling hopeful in the slightest. She found saltine crackers, and about six different varieties of chicken soup staring back at her. She shook her head, and decided to try the refrigerator instead.

Marcy, deciding that the tray of wiener things needed to cool a bit, joined her friend, who was looking deep into the bowels of the fridge.

"Well, we could have them spray jalapeno flavored Cheez Whiz directly onto their hands and just lick it off," said Chloe doubtfully.

"Oh, nifty, and then my almost-in-laws would be spending their first night back in Stonecreek fighting over the bathroom at the Niagara Bluffs motel."

The two women stood there peering into the fridge, both desperate for the other to find something edible that the other couldn't see. Marcy grabbed the Cheez Whiz, just in case something occurred to her. Both wore frowns that couldn't possibly be turned upside down.

Marcy shook her head. "Great, just great, not only doesn't Dave take the time to stock the larder for when his parents come, but he neglects to tell me his ex-wife and her new hubby are going to just blow in here, on her broom, tonight. I mean, can the woman be any more of a bitch?"

"Yes, she can. I've seen it, and thank your lucky stars she's on her best behavior tonight."

Chloe and Marcy slowly straightened up. That voice sounded so familiar, yet not, as it had a few more years tacked onto it. They both turned to see a bemused Marjorie D'Amico standing just behind them, at the table, looking with curiosity at both of them, and then around the kitchen.

Marcy nearly dropped the can of Cheez Whiz onto Chloe's foot. "Oh God, I, I mean, we didn't know you were there, uh, did we, Chloe?"

Chloe, not pleased to be handed the conversational baton, answered, "Uh, no, Mrs. D'Amico, we sure didn't."

Both women felt like twelve-year-olds who had just been caught smoking behind the barn.

"I'm afraid that it's my fault that Mary showed up here tonight, not Dave's. I talked to her in Phoenix, earlier in the week, and mentioned we would be here; we haven't seen her in nearly ten years." Marjorie's lips edged up into a devious grin. "Although I could have waited another ten years without complaint. I kind of invited them, not realizing how awkward it must be for you. But she is Nelson's mother."

Chloe and Marcy both gave her a dumb smile, and didn't say anything. Marjorie took a few steps, and joined them in front of the still-opened refrigerator door. She put an arm around both women, turning them so all three of them could look into it. "Hmm, now you two had better cool your jets. All the time that woman was married to Dave, I never once told her to call me 'Mom.'"

Ten minutes later, a tray of rolled up mini wieners and a plate of saltines with Cheez whiz on them, decorated with green olive slices, was delivered to a mostly appreciative crowd of D'Amicos, present and former, by three smiling and relaxed women, one now conspicuously sans apron.

Friday at the library plodded along slowly. Chloe Donahue, a professional whisperer and knowledge disperser, was up to her green eyes in tension, and Mrs. Cellone gave her a wide berth. She even suggested that Chloe leave early that afternoon, and she would stay until the twins arrived at four o'clock. Chloe turned the gracious woman down, knowing that if she would leave early, she would go home and worry her small house into a complete and utter perfection of cleanliness. She was too nervous to go and spend it with Sara, knowing that her lover probably had her hands full just trying to have a conversation with her mother. So she compromised, and spent the afternoon cleaning her small office in a single-minded tizzy.

Sara, out at the golf course, was not having a conversation with her mother, probably to the relief of both of them. They had come to an uneasy truce during their visit in Florida, and neither woman felt any compunction to delve deeper into their somewhat cool relationship.

Sara was pleased to see how her mother had warmed to Chloe the night before, and Marjorie had bestowed upon Sara, at one point during the evening, a reassuring and pleasant nod to her about Chloe. She'd even grabbed Sara by the arm when Sara was passing by her, when Sara had excused herself from the table to use the ladies' room at The Embers. Sara had ducked her head low, for Marjorie was pulling her down for a quick and quiet comment between the two of them.

Her mother again nodded toward an animated Chloe, who was telling the story of Doris Raeburn, Sara, a bull's head and an avenging umbrella.

"Don't you dare screw this one up, Sara. Or you won't hear from me in ten years."

Sara's face split into a grin. "I'll try not to, Maude."

Marjorie pinched Sara's arm sharply before she let her tall daughter continue on her way.

Sara smiled at the memory, and returned to patching the small tears on the fourth green. She had just begun to bend down, to repair another spot, when she heard the unmistakable sound of a golf ball whistling on its approach. She instinctively ducked lower, and it whizzed by her, just over the top of her head. She growled her annoyance.

"Fore!" called a woman's voice, a little too late.

Sara turned and looked toward the tee, and since all of these holes were par threes, it wasn't hard for her to see the figure there, waving a club at her in apology.

Sara waved back, and hurried off the green. *I wonder when Mom took up golf?*

"No, no, no, no!"

Sara trotted from the living room of Chloe's house, and toward the sound of her lover's lamenting in the bedroom. She found Chloe standing there, looking into her full-length wall mirror, dressed in the same green silk dress Chloe had worn the night of the auction. Tonight, the dress looked a little different than the last time she had worn it.

"What's the matter, hon?"

"Look at this, look at this! It doesn't fit! How can a dress not fit, it's been, what, two weeks since I wore it last?" Chloe was looking directly into the mirror, trying to figure out why the dress was fitting her like a skin on a sausage.

Sara came and stood beside her, and they both gazed at Chloe's figure in the mirror. Chloe was right, the dress didn't fit. Or rather, it fit too well. "Well," drawled Sara, trying to hide her grin, "We have been eating out a lot lately. And you've been having pie every time." *And most of mine, too.*

Chloe gave her lover a menacing glare in the mirror. "Then how come you didn't put on a pound? An ounce! You've probably lost weight, haven't you?" she said accusingly.

Sara looked sharp and buff, and she knew it, it was staring back at her in the mirror. "Well, I do walk that course all day long."

"Are you calling me a load? Is that it, you think I'm a couch potato? Go on, tell me the truth." Chloe's voice was rising in frustration, as she unsuccessfully tried to smooth the tight buttons across her abdomen.

Sara laid a comforting hand on the rattled librarian's shoulder. "Oh, no, honey, I like your little belly," she said, truthfully, and reached to pat it with her hand.

Now was not a good time for honesty. Chloe slapped Sara's hand away before it made contact with her stomach. "Great, just great! I'm standing here, it's opening night, dressed in my best dress, and looking like a bloated frog, and you tell me you like my belly?" Chloe started popping the buttons down the front of her dress in order to take it off before a deep inhale popped the buttons for her. "Great, great, great." Sara stood away from her, her hand still smarting. Soon Chloe was just in her slip, the discarded dress pooled at her feet. "Oh, God, look at the time, we have to be there in an hour, and I don't have a thing to wear."

Sara forgot about her stinging hand, and stood behind Chloe, wrapping her arms around her waist and kissing the top of Chloe's head. She gazed at their reflections, and began speaking into Chloe's ear, keeping eye contact with her in the mirror. "I think you look great." She punctuated that remark with a running kiss up the back of Chloe's neck. She could feel Chloe shiver from it, and Sara returned to her ear. "And very, very sexy." Her hand stroked a soft path down the side of Chloe's slip, and then ran it up again, this time across the soft roundness of belly, on its way to an equally soft breast. Sara was purring into Chloe's ear, nipping at it and Chloe forgot about the dress, her belly. She watched Sara's movements across her body in the large mirror in front of them, and all she could feel was the warming below her belly, and the way her knees were turning to jelly.

Sara pulled Chloe closer to her, wrapping a long arm around Chloe's ribcage, and then taking her other hand, she stroked across the surface of the white slip, and their eyes met in the mirror as Sara's hand dipped into the neckline, so deliberately and softly, trailing a roughened thumb and forefinger across a hardening nipple. She pinched it lightly, and then lightly again, as she watched Chloe's reflection in front of her. Chloe moaned, and Sara saw the eyes of the younger woman flutter at her touch, so she repeated it, this time just a little harder. Then all was lost, the mirror and the tight dress were forgotten, and whatever clothes the women had on that fit, or didn't fit, lost their meaning, because they were soon being tossed through the air like confetti on New Year's Eve.

"It's seven o'clock, seven o'clock!" Chloe repeated needlessly as she went hurricaning through her closet, trying to find something appropriate to wear. "We're supposed to be there now, the curtain goes up in an hour! I mean, you pick great times to seduce a girl, you know," Chloe said accusingly, as she pulled out a dress, inspected it, and dismissed it.

Sara was almost completely redressed, all she had to do was slip into her boots, and find that missing earring that had somehow disappeared a half hour earlier. Sara turned, and tossed the sheets on the bed, hoping to see her earring fly upward. No luck. "You looked like you needed relaxing, I thought it would relax you." Sara got on her hands and knees, and began searching around the floor on the side of the bed.

Chloe, in bra and panties, turned and stared at her lover. She pointed at her own face, jabbing herself on the nose. "Does this face look relaxed to you? Does it?"

Sara squinted up from her spot on the floor. "Not really, no."

Chloe turned and began rummaging in her closet again. "I didn't think so." She sighed. She couldn't find anything, anything at all to wear.

Sara spied her earring hanging, caught, on the apron of Chloe's tall bed. "Aha! Found it!" she cried triumphantly, grabbed it, and began fixing it back onto her ear.

Chloe turned from the closet once again, hands on hips. "Found what?"

Sara finished adjusting it, and pulled her hair back so Chloe could see it. "Lost my earring sometime during all the excitement there. Found it!" She smiled at Chloe, expecting her to join her in her victory grin. No such luck.

"An earring? An earring? You were worried about an earring? Maybe you should be worried that your girlfriend is going to show up at opening night in a silk bra and panties. No! You're worried about an earring. Well, how's about this, how about we find me some six inch heels, I toss on the "Porn Star" cap, and I show up, just like this. That would really bring the house down, now wouldn't it?" Chloe's arms were flailing faster than her words.

Sara's mouth hung open, she couldn't reply. In her mind, three letters of the alphabet kept repeating. *PMS. PMS.*

Chloe tore her gaze away from her dumbstruck girlfriend's face to take a glance at the bedside clock. "It's seven oh five. Seven oh five!"

And just like a church bell peeling a reply, the phone in Chloe's kitchen began ringing.

"I'll get that!" Sara said, standing up, grabbing her boots, and hightailing it out the door.

Chloe stuck her head back into her closet, and started her futile search again.

"Uh-huh. Okay. Well, just do like I told you, uh-huh." Sara looked up from the phone, and saw Chloe standing there, dressed in a green blazer, white top, and brown slacks. She smiled at her, and gave her a thumbs up. Sara had one boot on, and she was hopping around the kitchen, trying to get the other boot on one-handed. "Well, just hang tight, we can be there in five minutes. Don't worry, I have this all figured out."

Chloe's lips pursed, her eyebrows furrowed, and her hands just naturally settled themselves on her hips. "What?" she mouthed.

Sara couldn't put on her boot, talk on the phone, and wave Chloe off at the same time, so she shook her head at Chloe, and tried to smile reassuringly. "No, really, it'll be okay, you'll get there, we'll all get there. I know it's important, don't worry. Five minutes."

Sara clicked the phone off, and grabbed her boot again to put it on.

"What?" said a clearly impatient Chloe, readjusting her hands on her hips.

"You look great." Sara grinned. "And we just have to make a quick stop, I promise. No need to worry, I've got it under control." *I hope.* Sara slid her black pant legs over her western boots, and grabbed Chloe's hand and began dragging her toward the door. *Now I just have to keep her distracted long enough.*

Chloe only had time to grab her house keys before she was pulled out her front door.

Chloe took another look at Charlie Shemp's tearful eyes, and sighed. "Look, I'm sorry, Charlie, but with the trailer broken, we'll just have to wait until tomorrow night, I promise, and then Cargo can be in the play."

Charlie's heart felt like it was just about to break. "But Ms. Donahue, she's been practicing, with Nelson and all, and I really wanted her to be up there, I mean, it's important." He ran a hand across his eyes, and his voice was cracking more than it usually did. He sniffed, and looked away from her, not wanting her to see him on the verge of crying. She reached out, put a comforting hand on his shoulder, and patted it.

Charlie snuffled, and cleared his throat, which didn't help at all. "Nelson is going to be so disappointed."

"Nelson will be just fine. Won't he, Chloe?"

Chloe and Charlie looked up, and saw that Sara was sitting astride Cargo, reins light in her hands, her boots firmly ensconced in the stirrups. Sara grinned at them, backlit by the floodlight of the nearby barn.

"Sara, what are you doing?" Chloe's eyes were wide, and she stared at the woman who looked so natural up on that horse's back.

"I'm getting Cargo, Charlie, and Jack, and you to the play on time."

Chloe blinked, and words came tumbling out of her mouth. "You're going to ride her there?"

Sara pulled the reins so Cargo was parallel to the little librarian, and they edged closer to her. "No, we're going to ride her there. Charlie and his stepdad are going to follow in my car. C'mon." Sara held out a hand to Chloe.

Chloe backed away. "What? No way! I haven't been on a horse since I was twelve, and, well, just no way!" She looked toward Charlie, whose tears had disappeared, and he was looking at with all the love and hope that he possessed in his thirteen-year-old body. "Have Charlie ride with you!"

Charlie shook his head. "I'd really like to see you on her, Ms. Donahue. I can ride with my dad." He smiled, blushed and looked at his feet.

Chloe looked at him, and then up at Sara, imploring her not to make her do this.

Sara leaned over, and patted the tall horse's withers. "It'll be fine. You can ride up here behind me. We don't have time to take the trailer off the truck, my car is packed with stuff, and well, the school is only a mile and a half up the road." She looked down at Chloe, who was staring at her like she wanted to take the little director off to an alien civilization. She gave her one more smile, and put out her hand again, holding it there, waiting. "C'mon, Chloe. Just say 'yes.'"

Chloe blinked again, and before her mind registered what she was doing, she was hoisted up behind Sara, who had made room for her on the large saddle, and she wrapped her arms around Sara's waist. The earth looked far below her as she looked down at the ground from her perch behind Sara, and she felt the tall woman urge the horse below them into a trot. She heard encouraging calls behind them as they left the barn's floodlight behind, and soon, nothing but the sounds of the horse's hooves and rhythmic breathing rushed by her ears. It lulled her, and she suddenly felt more comfortable, and settled in, loosened her grip around Sara's waist a little as the horse slowed to make the turn onto the tall grass beside the road running to the high school.

Sara felt Chloe's arms around her loosen a bit, and she grinned, and nudged the horse into picking up its pace. They were coasting along now, Sara smiling at the chill air on her cheeks, and the warmth of the librarian at her back. She wished, just for a moment or two, that the school was just a little bit farther up the road, that they had just a little more time. She didn't urge the horse into a full-fledged gallop, fearing that would rattle Chloe's nerves, and Sara could feel Chloe relaxing into the ride, so she didn't want to push it.

They were steadily eating up the ground, the golden horse with its dark and light riders, when Sara's Comet pulled along side them, Charlie's stepdad slowing just for a moment, so Charlie could wave at them from the packed car. The backseat of the car was full of multicolored helium balloons, and Charlie had a careful hand on the huge sheet cake in his lap, the one that read "Happy Birthday Ado Annie! Happy Birthday Moreen!" Sara and Chloe both smiled at Charlie, and he gave a big "wahoo!" just before his stepdad sped up, and carried them onward toward the school.

Sara couldn't look at her watch, but she knew that time was not on their side, and she wished once again that she could speed the horse on a little more without upsetting her precious cargo, on the back of Cargo.

Incredibly, Chloe felt herself enjoying the ride, surprising herself. She craned her neck so she could shout into Sara's ear. "Can't this thing go any faster?"

With those words, Sara grinned, and spurred the horse into a gallop, and she wasn't sure, but she thought she could feel the small redhead laughing behind her. Maybe it was just the bouncing motion of the horse, but it was the way Sara wanted to remember this moment, so she memorized it, and stored it carefully away.

The parking lot of the school was jammed with vehicles, but people were few, as they had already gone into the school in preparation for the play that would begin shortly. Charlie Shemp, after carefully laying the sheet cake onto the front seat of the Comet, told his smiling stepdad he'd be right back, and sprinted up the short steps of the stage door.

Nelson, already impatient and worried about the play, kept glancing at the clock, and was now fretting full-time about the absence of his aunt and the little director. Many bad scenarios were forming in his mind when he saw his little buddy come busting through the stage door at the back of the school.

"C'mon, everybody, come quick!" gasped Charlie. A number of adults just gaped at him, and didn't move.

Nelson looked at Charlie, and Charlie grinned. "No, it's good. C'mon, you'll miss it!"

Nelson hesitated just a moment, and then moved quickly to the door Charlie was holding open, and down the few steps to the sidewalk. Marcy, Dave, Marjorie, Ernie, Mo Dean, Justin, Heather, Jeanette, another Justin, Paul, his mother, Larry, Jason and even Doris Raeburn all clambered down the steps after him, almost all colliding at once when they saw, making the turn from the road, a pale horse and two riders approaching them with the ghostly glow of the lampposts above them. They stopped, and held on to each other in awe, and in support, because their stop was so abrupt, their surprise so complete.

The horse slowed into a prancing canter, and they made quite an entrance in front of that crowd of family and friends. Sara reined Cargo in, and the beautiful horse stopped, and Sara grinned at the unbelieving but smiling throng. She then turned her head, and grinned at Chloe, who looked red-faced, windblown and achingly beautiful to Sara's adoring eyes. She turned quickly, and lifted her leg out of the stirrup, and she was down on the ground before Chloe knew what was happening. She stood next to her, and suddenly Chloe realized how high up she was, and she froze for a moment. But then Sara held out her arms, and waited, a small smile of expectancy on her face. Chloe took a deep breath, and without another thought, swung her own leg over, and slid out of the saddle into Sara's waiting arms.

Inside the sold-out theater, the audience was settling down, waiting for the beginning of the play. That expectant group inside the theater heard a distant sounding cheer go up, and what sounded like applause and whooping afterwards. The best part of the show had just played out, and the orchestra had yet to play a note.

It was later, much later on opening night. The play had gone smashingly well; Jeanette had gotten four curtain calls, Nelson six, and Moreen Dean, three. Mo was tearful as the whole audience and her fellow thespians and crew sang a screamingly loud version of "Happy Birthday" to her. Jay Caesar had enthused to everyone within earshot. Doris Raeburn finally forgave Chloe for that awful opera, complimented Marcy on her trees, but no, Sara was still not excused for that bull's head incident. There were enthusiastic parents everywhere backstage, including those of a pair of grown up D'Amicos, a teenaged D'Amico, and a D'Amico yet unborn. Cake was eaten, backs were slapped, hugs were shared, and lipstick was smeared across each cast member's face, and their adult advisors, too.

But the finest part was saved for last, when a bashfully grinning Larry stepped forward, and held out his "Porn Star" cap to Chloe. The whole cast and crew quieted, and Larry, a stagehand, not an actor by any means, started his prepared speech.

"Ms. Donahue, on behalf of all the cast and crew of *Oklahoma!*, I'd like to present this hat to you. We were thinking maybe we should get you a new one, but considering how superstitious you are, we thought we'd better stick with the original. So, here you go."

Chloe grinned, and accepted the cap from Larry. She plopped it onto her red head, winked at them all, and then shifted the cap around backwards, just as she had worn it on that day so many months ago.

The whole crew and her lover too, burst out in laughter.

"What?" she put her hands on her hips, and stared at them, woefully unaware that the cast had a small addition embroidered onto the back of the cap.

"Nice hat," gasped Sara, wishing she could make a quick dash for the ladies' room.

Chloe scowled, pulled the hat down from her head, and looked at it. A slow smile crossed her lips, and she laughed slowly, and then more loudly, and then everyone joined in as Chloe put the cap back on her head, decisively backwards, and grinned at them all.

The addition on the back of the cap read, Trainees Accepted.

"You didn't eat much of that cake, and it was your favorite. I know, you ordered it," Sara lazily teased, rubbing a light hand across Chloe's belly.

Chloe gave that hand a gentle but meaningful swat. "Well, I'd like to fit into that dress again. Someday." She smiled ruefully.

Sara gave her a squeeze, and felt the woman she loved burrow deeper into her shoulder. Chloe was being uncharacteristically quiet, but Sara chalked it up to a long and stressful evening, although for once, the stress felt good. She sighed, and felt Chloe return that sigh. Sara pulled the blanket up tighter around them, and she looked up into the black of the sky above her. They were lying on the hood of the Comet, their backs and heads pillowed by a jacket on the windshield. They were parked in the high grass just off the ninth hole. The fountain was streaming high into the night, its multicolored patterns weaving a wet and quiet shower of fireworks before them.

Sara could feel the smaller woman's breathing begin to slow. "I love you, Chloe," she whispered, wanting those to be the last words Chloe heard before she drifted off on Sara's shoulder.

"I love you too," Chloe murmured, and stretched into her taller lover's form, and with that, she was fast asleep.

Sara smiled, and looked again to the moon, and the stars and the sky that stretched out panoramically above her. She closed her eyes, and her mind turned to a time when this was exactly what she'd envisioned she needed for her life to be right, for her heart to beat still and measured, for her soul to be set free and floating. That time had come, she knew now, and she would no longer have to imagine it, for it was right here, right now and she closed her eyes to enjoy a sense of peace she had never known before.

The chirping of crickets and the murmuring of other night creatures were the only things breaking the still of the evening. She opened her eyes to the night sky above, and all of the twinkling stars that it held. She looked again for the moon; it was full, and had small wisps of clouds passing through its brilliance. She traced a path between stars; she still had no idea of the names of the constellations, but she'd memorized certain favorite groupings, and she looked for them there. Her breathing became lower, slower, and she gently pulled Chloe closer to her, and gave a soft kiss to her forehead. She let herself enjoy the calmed moment; she embraced it, and let it fill her. She returned her gaze to the moon, and let it settle there.

LA Tucker is a native Western Pennsylvanian with a bit of a Buckeye and Canadian combination accent. A longtime love and fascination with musicals, movies and eavesdropping led her to attempt writing this, her first book. In her spare time away from her less than mesmerizing retail career, she likes to kayak, watch old screwball comedies and read magazines in the bathroom. She shares her life with two dogs, a darling partner, and the occasional oddball friend. She may be reached at ssurething@aol.com.